Lore Olympus

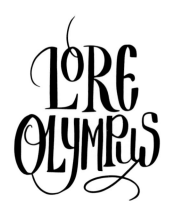

VOLUME FOUR

VOLUME FOUR

RACHEL SMYTHE

LAYOUTS BY
EDWIN VAZQUEZ

DEL REY

NEW YORK

Published in the United States by Del Rey,
an imprint of Random House, a division of
Penguin Random House LLC, New York.

RANDOM HOUSE is a registered trademark, and DEL REY
and colophon are trademarks of Penguin Random House LLC.

LIBRARY OF CONGRESS CATALOGING-IN-PUBLICATION DATA
Names: Smythe, Rachel (Comics artist), author, artist.
Title: Lore Olympus / Rachel Smythe.
Description: First edition. | New York : Del Rey, 2023
Identifiers: LCCN 2021008087 | Hardcover ISBN 9780593599044 (v. 4) |
Trade paperback ISBN 9780593599051 (v. 4) | Barnes & Noble edition ISBN 9780593600078 (v. 4)
Subjects: LCSH: Mythology, Greek—Comic books, strips, etc. | Graphic novels.
Classification: LCC PN6727.S54758 L67 2021 | DDC 741.5/973—dc23
LC record available at https://lccn.loc.gov/2021008087

Printed in China

With thanks to:
Art:
M. Rawlings, Johana R. Ahumada, Jaki Haboon,
Yulia Garibova (Hita), Kristina Ness, Karen Pavon

Editors:
Breanna Boswell, Annie LaHue

Translation:
Anastasia Gkortsila

Penguin Random House team:
Sarah Peed, Ted Allen, Erin Korenko

randomhousebooks.com

2 4 6 8 9 7 5 3 1

First Edition

To Elizabeth Vandiver.
Your lectures are such a gift and
an endless source of inspiration.
Thank you.

CONTENT WARNING
FROM RACHEL SMYTHE

Lore Olympus regularly deals with themes
of physical and mental abuse, sexual trauma,
and toxic relationships.

Some of the interactions in this volume
may be distressing for some readers.
Please exercise discretion, and seek out the support
of others if you require it.

PUSH!
Hey, get a load of this.
UNDERWORLD CORP
Oh my Gods...

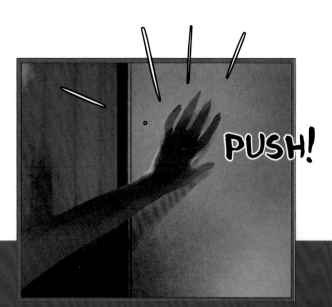

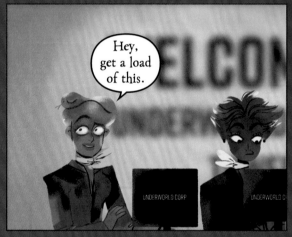

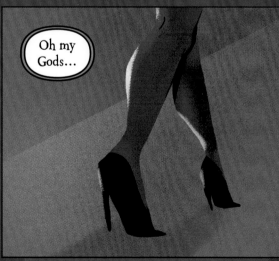

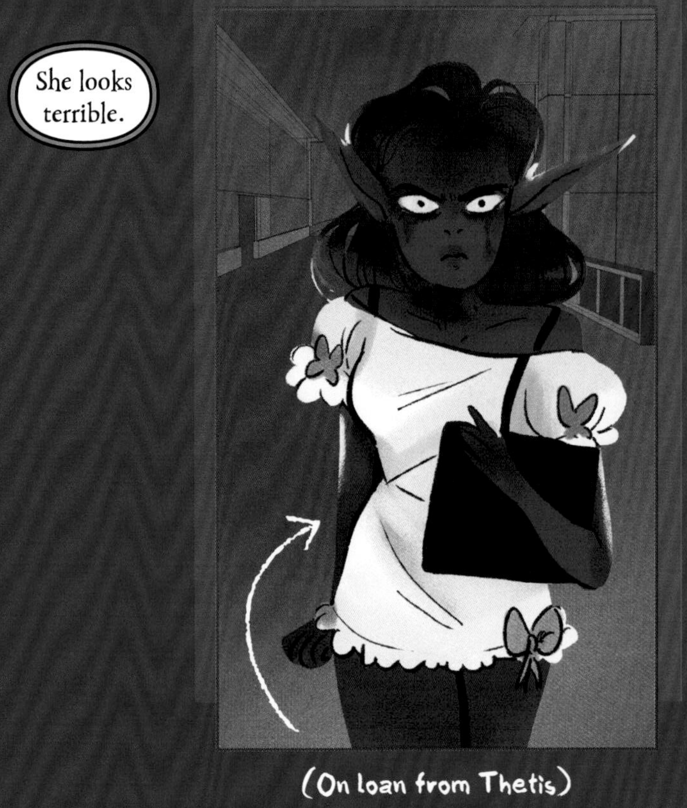
She looks terrible.
(On loan from Thetis)

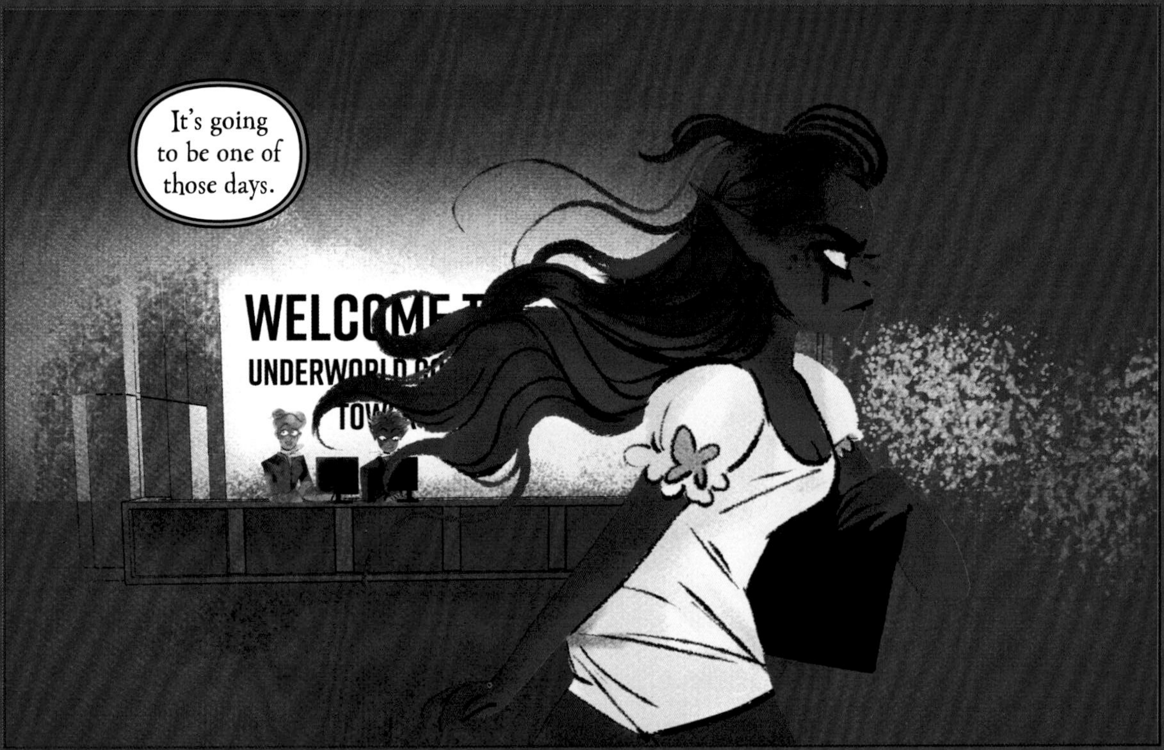
It's going to be one of those days.
WELCOME T
UNDERWORLD C
TOW

EPISODE 76: SPLITTING

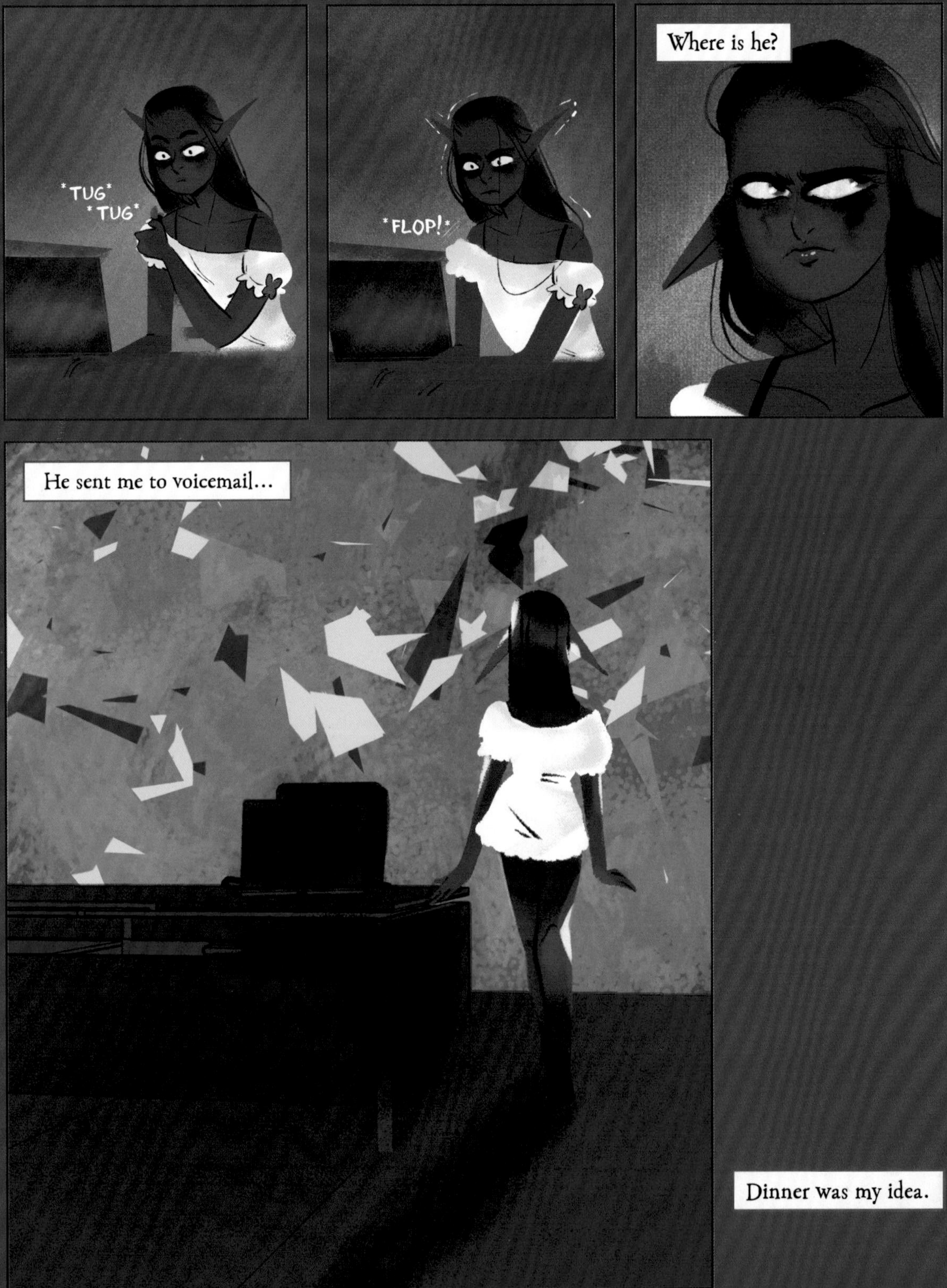
TUG
TUG
FLOP!
Where is he?
He sent me to voicemail...
Dinner was my idea.

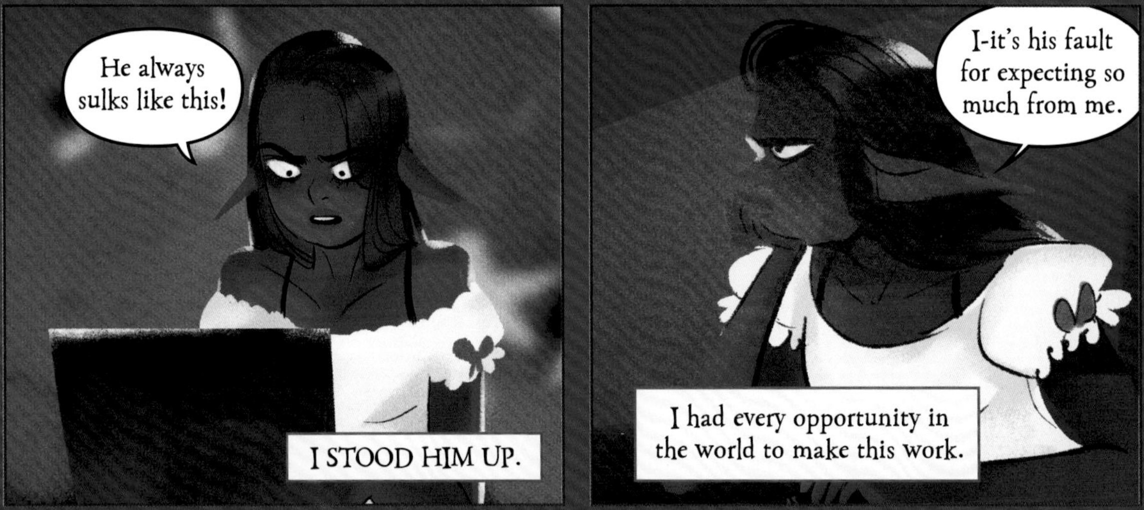
He always sulks like this!
I STOOD HIM UP.
I-it's his fault for expecting so much from me.
I had every opportunity in the world to make this work.

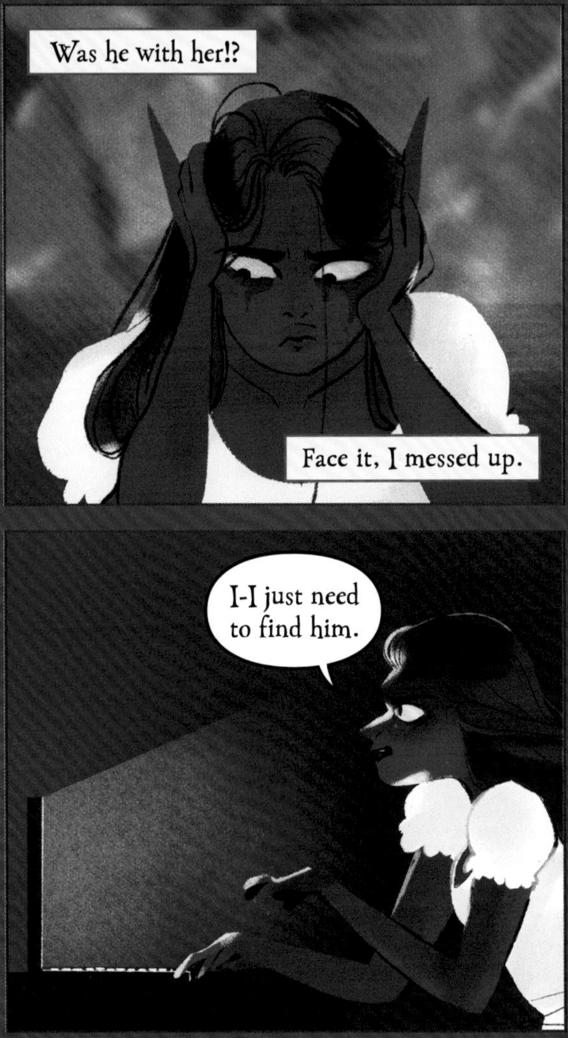
Was he with her!?
Face it, I messed up.
I-I just need to find him.

FRI

9:00 A.M.

MEETING

FATES - AGENDA | N/A

LOCATION | TOWER 3

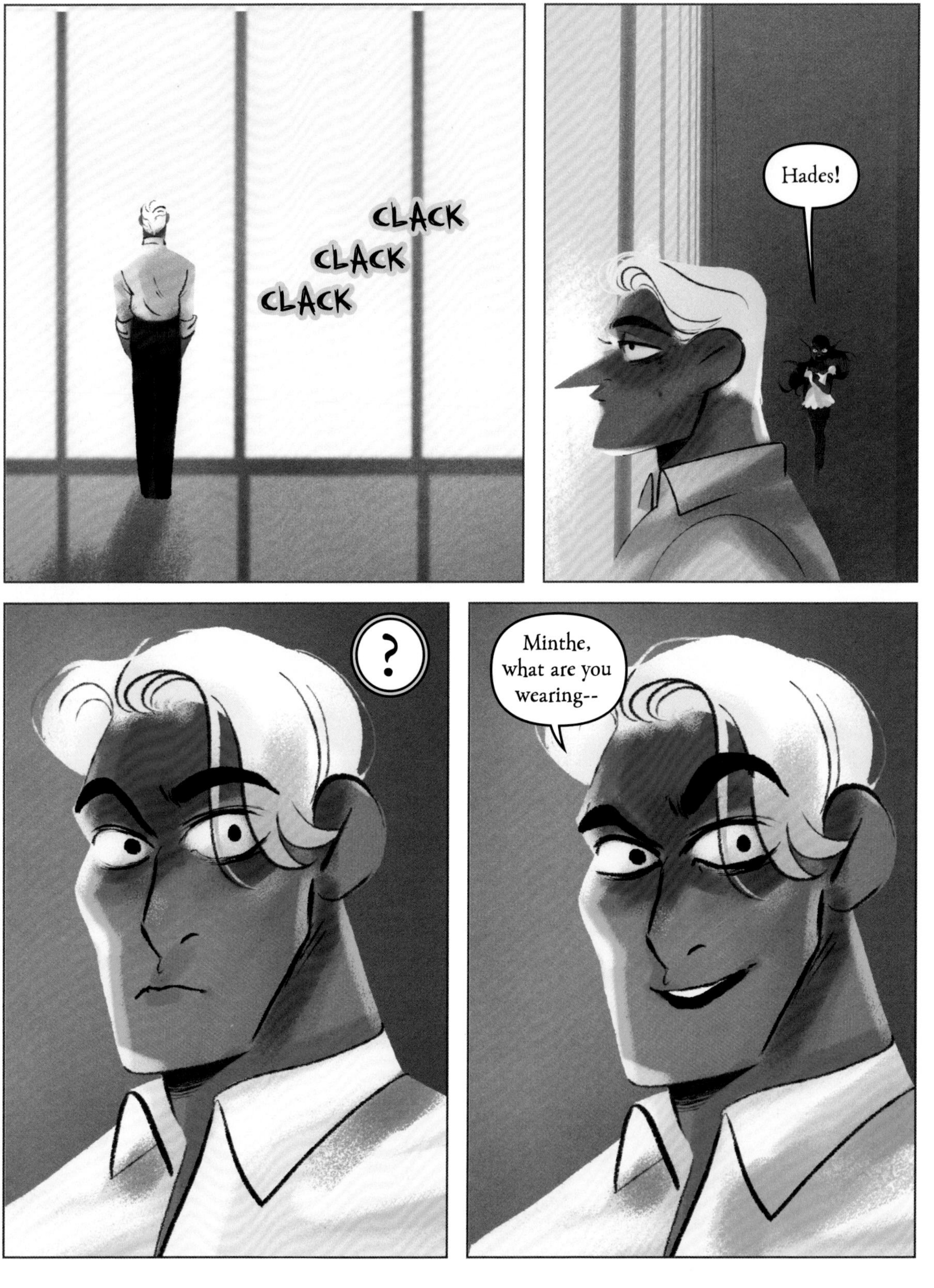
CLACK
CLACK
CLACK
Hades!
?
Minthe, what are you wearing--

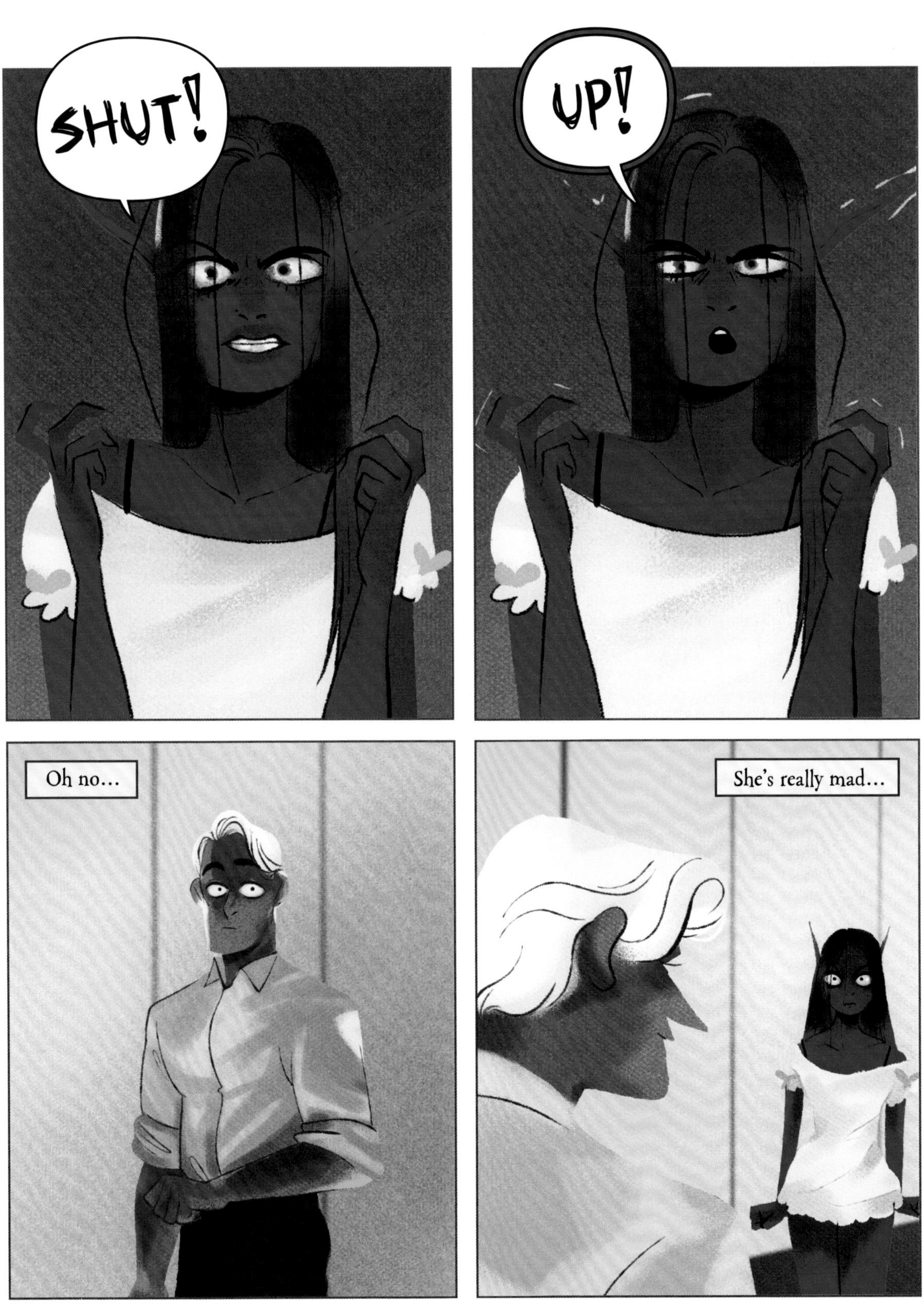
SHUT!
UP!
Oh no...
She's really mad...

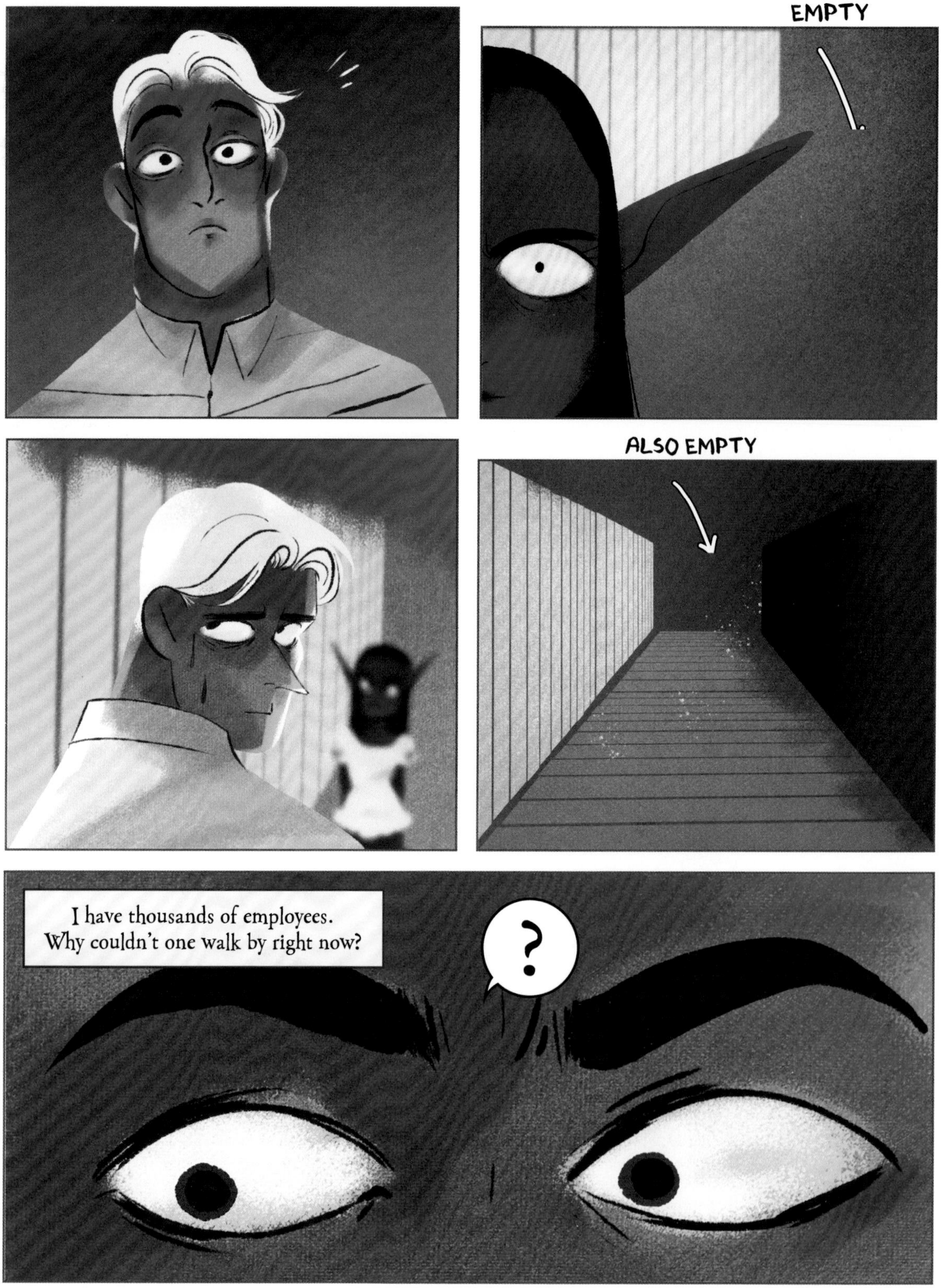
EMPTY
ALSO EMPTY
I have thousands of employees.
Why couldn't one walk by right now?
?

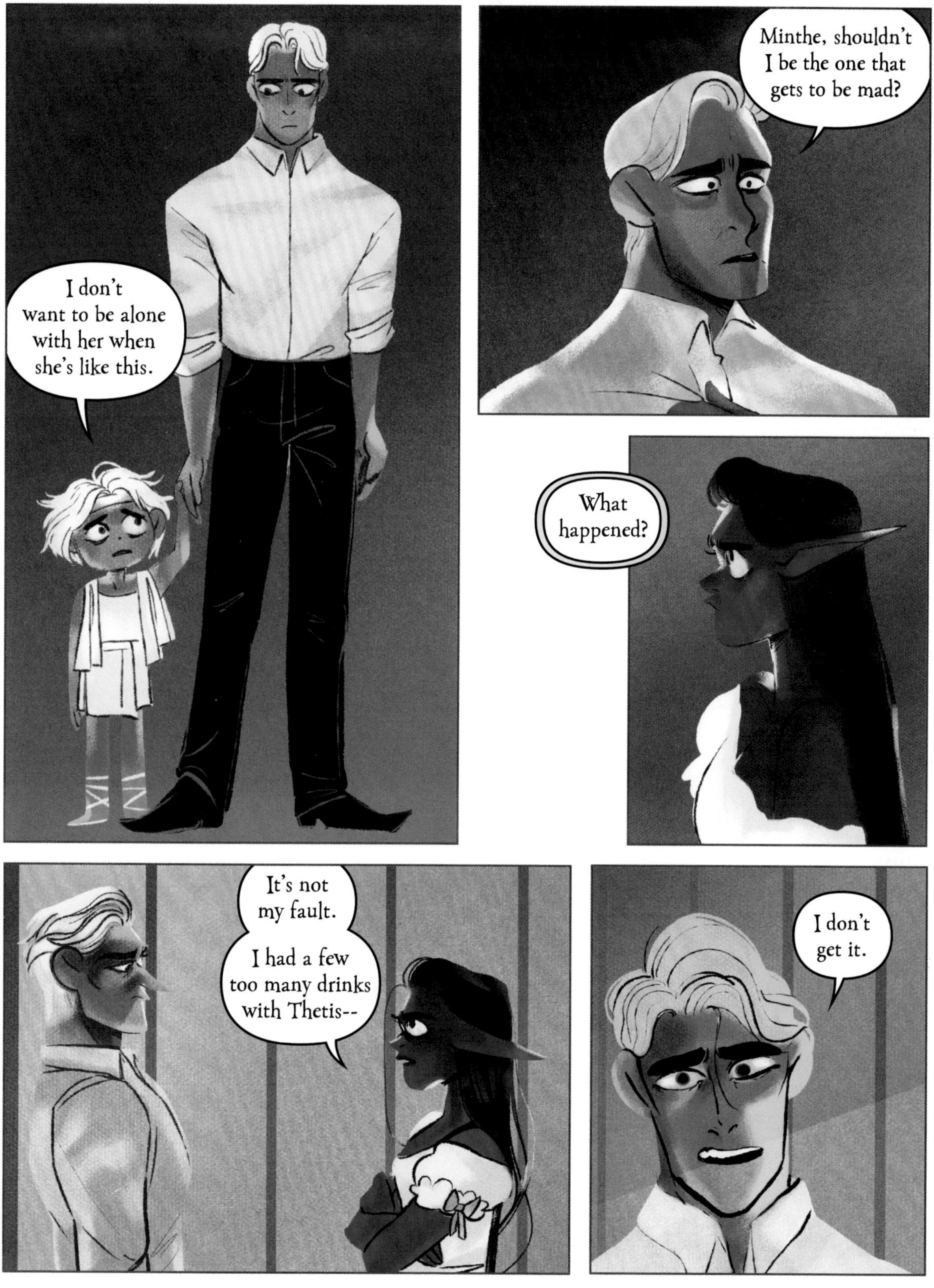
I don't want to be alone with her when she's like this.
Minthe, shouldn't I be the one that gets to be mad?
What happened?
It's not my fault.
I had a few too many drinks with Thetis--
I don't get it.

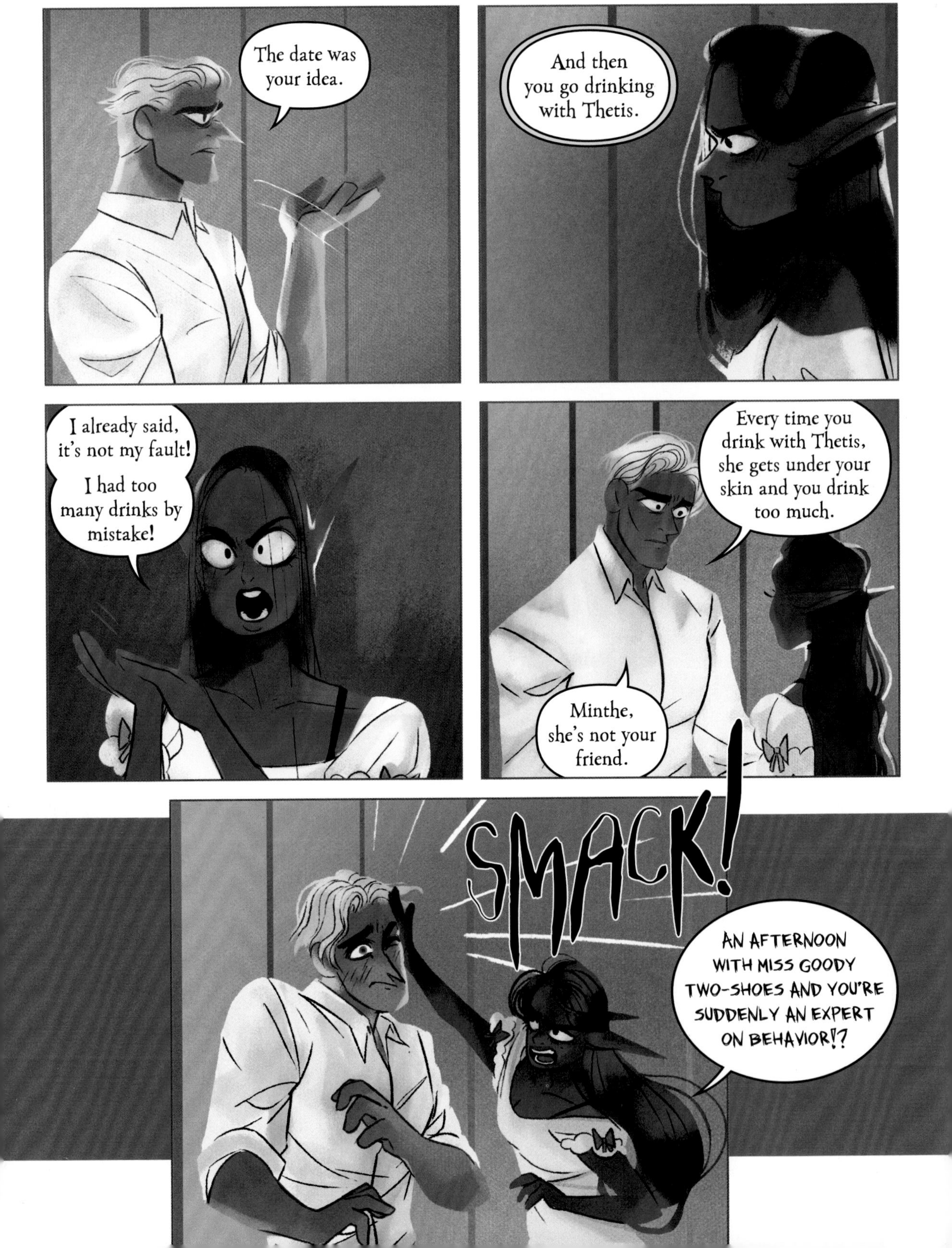

The date was your idea.
And then you go drinking with Thetis.
I already said, it's not my fault!
I had too many drinks by mistake!
Every time you drink with Thetis, she gets under your skin and you drink too much.
Minthe, she's not your friend.
SMACK!
AN AFTERNOON WITH MISS GOODY TWO-SHOES AND YOU'RE SUDDENLY AN EXPERT ON BEHAVIOR!?

Why can't I stop being like this?

YOU'RE LUCKY I EVEN CONSIDER YOU!

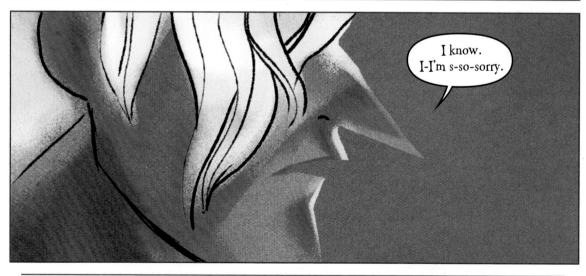

I know.
I-I'm s-so-sorry.

WANNA KNOW WHY!?

I don't know why I'm like this.

YOU'RE THE SPITTING IMAGE OF KRONOS!

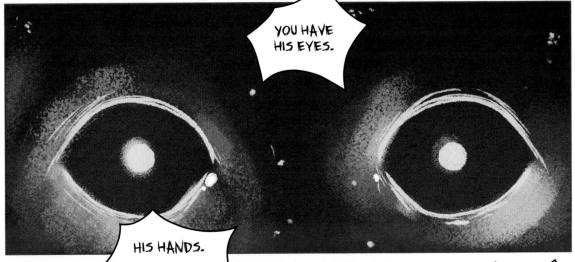

YOU HAVE HIS EYES.

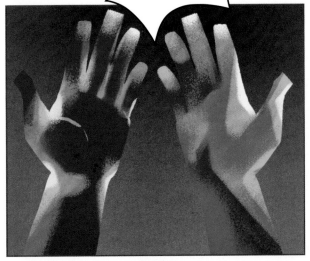

HIS HANDS.

HIS SKIN.

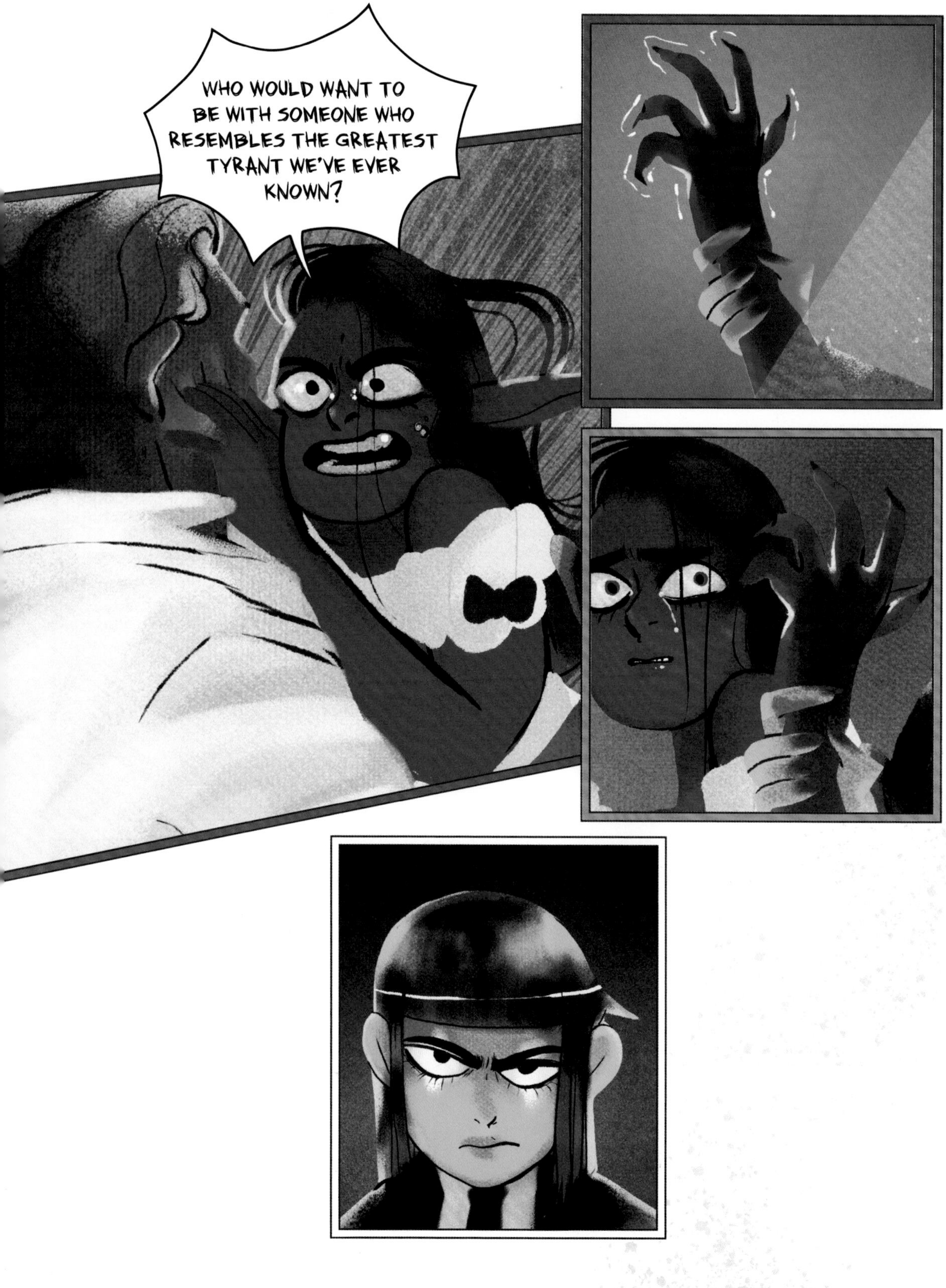
WHO WOULD WANT TO BE WITH SOMEONE WHO RESEMBLES THE GREATEST TYRANT WE'VE EVER KNOWN?

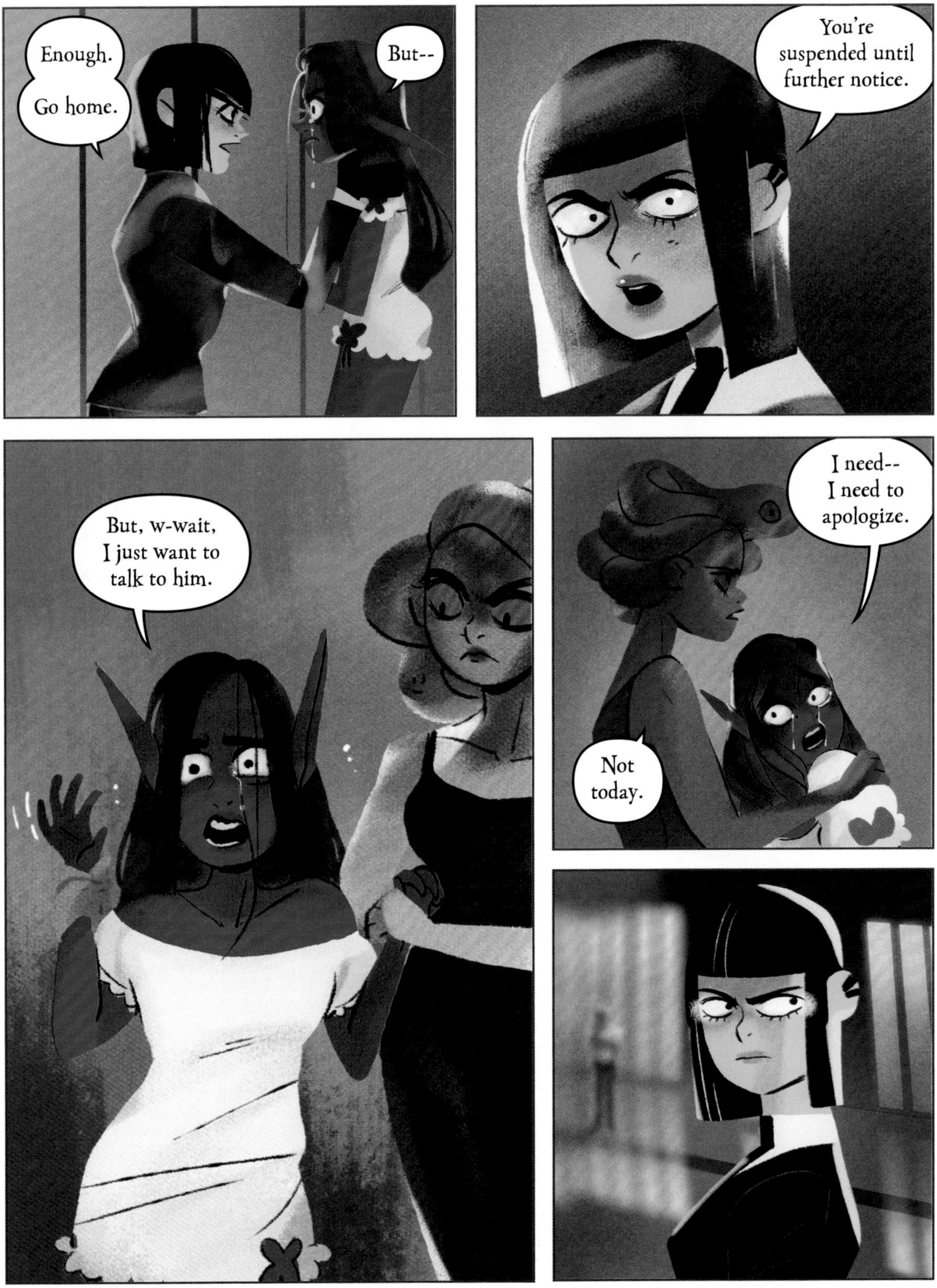
Enough.
Go home.
But--
You're suspended until further notice.
But, w-wait, I just want to talk to him.
I need-- I need to apologize.
Not today.

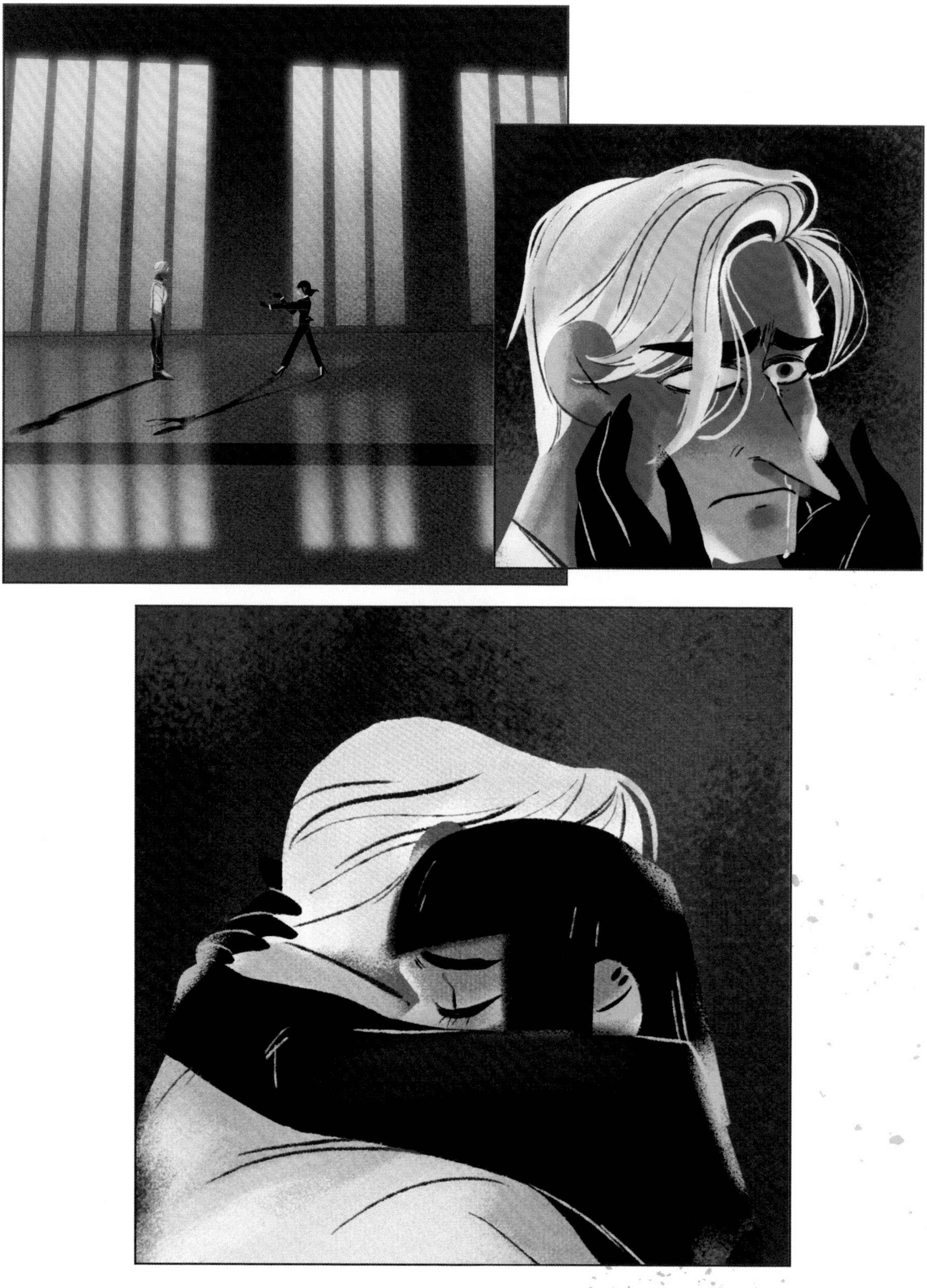

EPISODE 77: DARKNESS

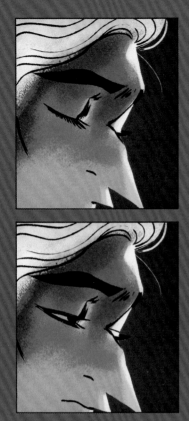

!?

Nyx!?

O-oh,
my apologies!
I'm sorry
for interrupting
you!

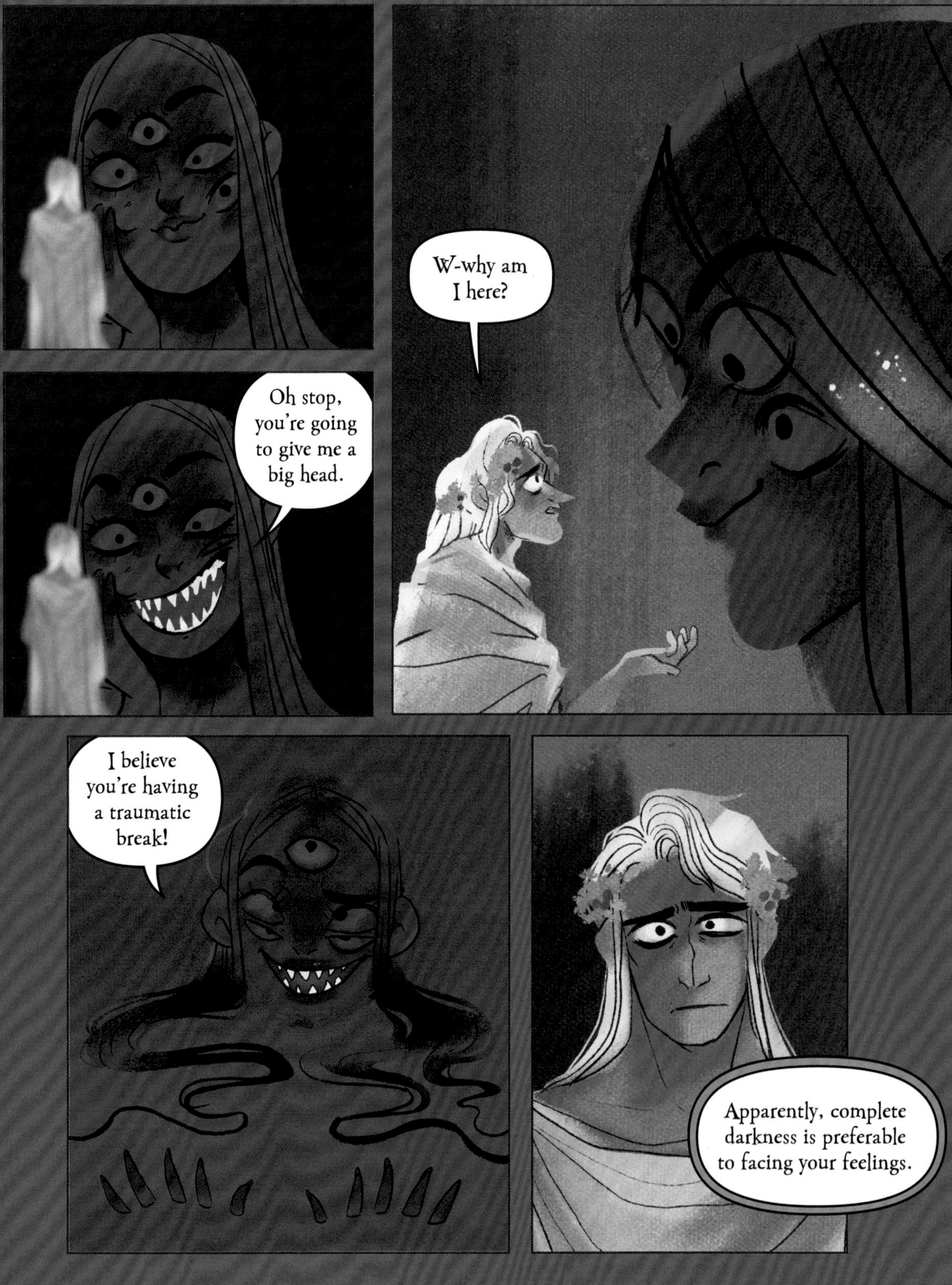
Oh stop, you're going to give me a big head.
W-why am I here?
I believe you're having a traumatic break!
Apparently, complete darkness is preferable to facing your feelings.

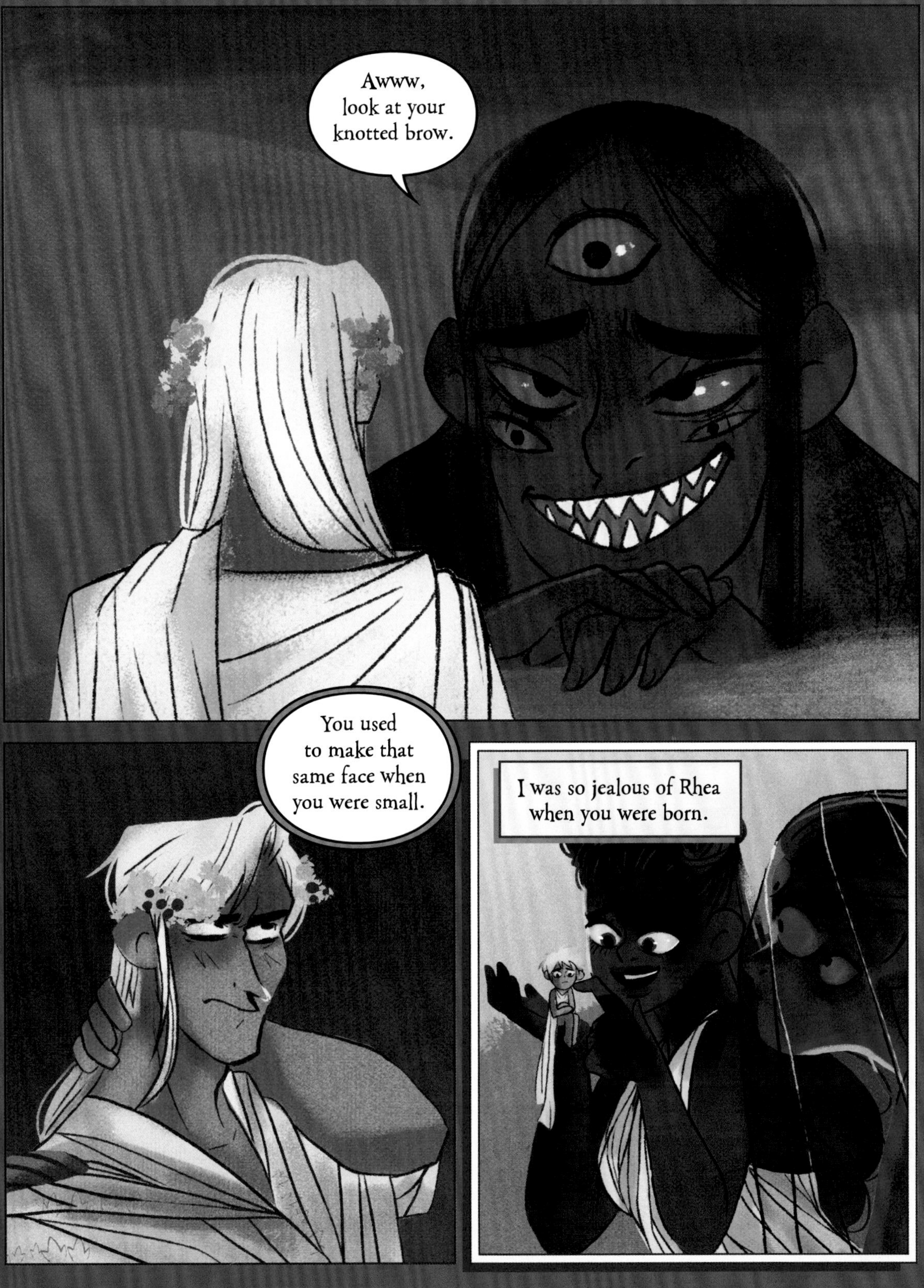
Awww, look at your knotted brow.
You used to make that same face when you were small.
I was so jealous of Rhea when you were born.

I'd never seen a child with so many worries. Adorable.

Thanks...?

I had half a mind to steal you for myself.

Interesting.

You'd better get back. That little golden traitor is here to see you.

SNAP!

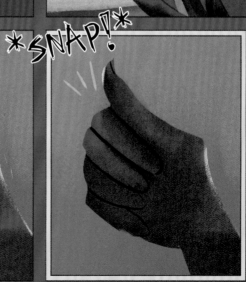

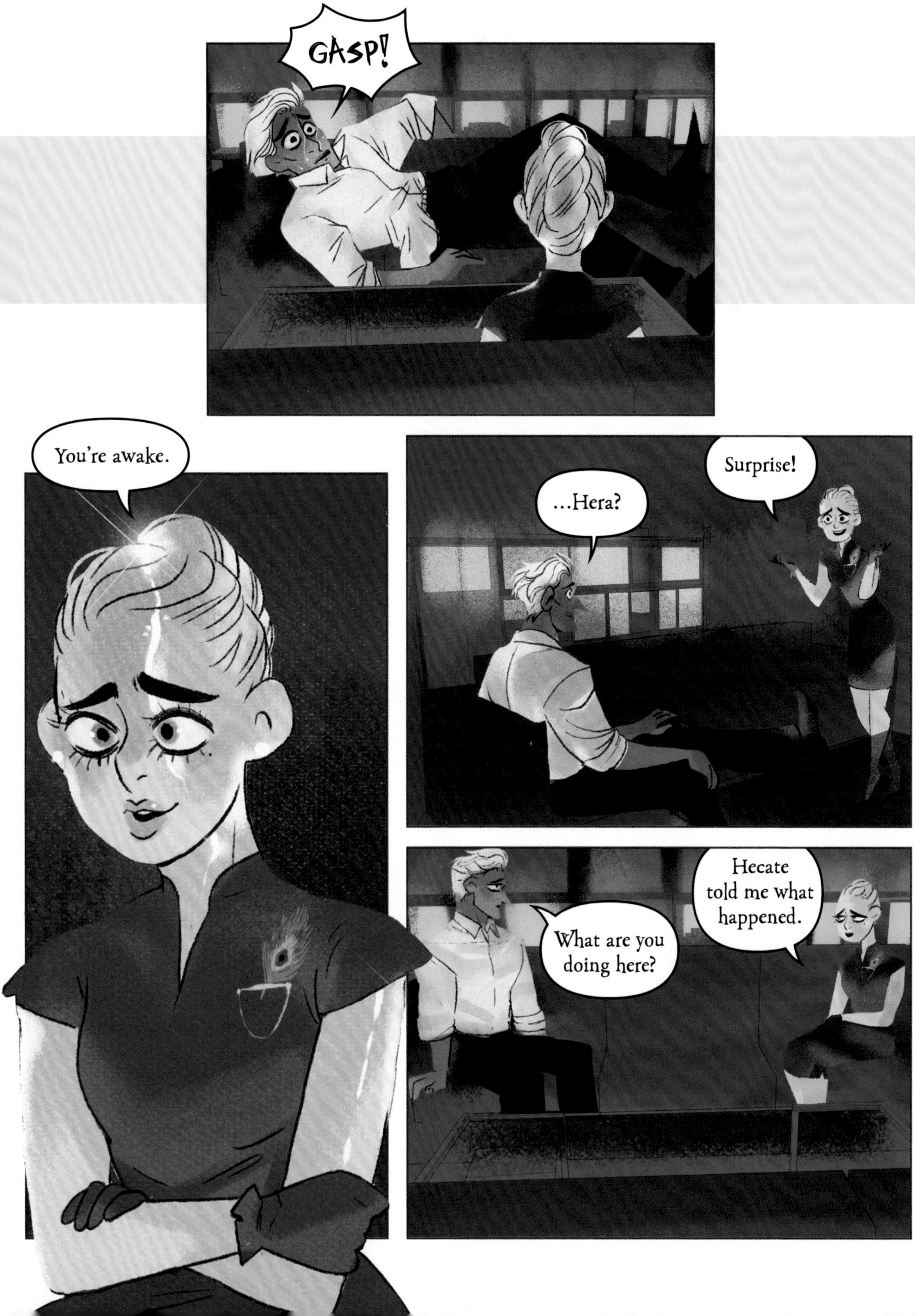
GASP!
You're awake.
...Hera?
Surprise!
What are you doing here?
Hecate told me what happened.

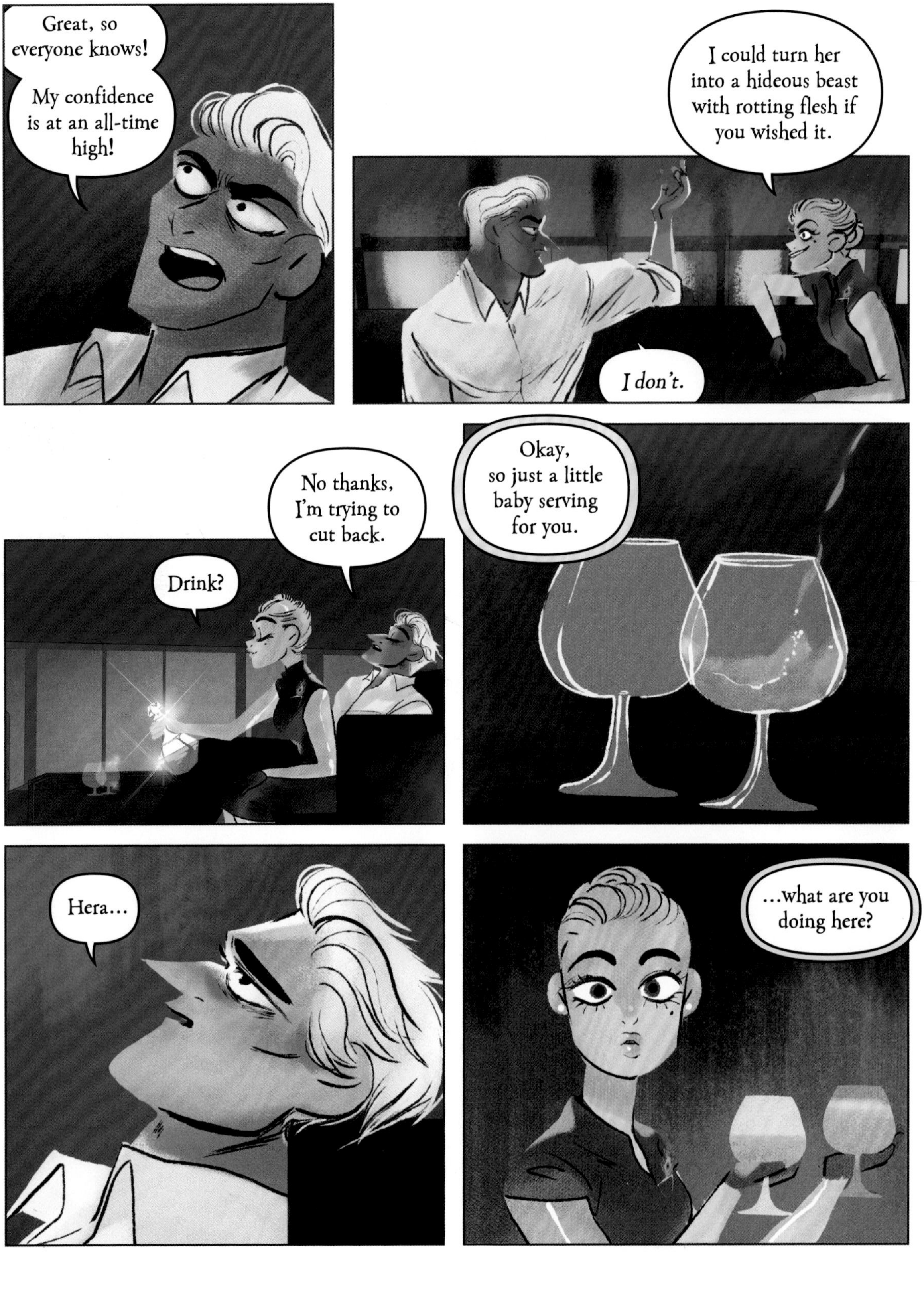

Great, so everyone knows!
My confidence is at an all-time high!
I could turn her into a hideous beast with rotting flesh if you wished it.
I don't.
Drink?
No thanks, I'm trying to cut back.
Okay, so just a little baby serving for you.
Hera...
...what are you doing here?

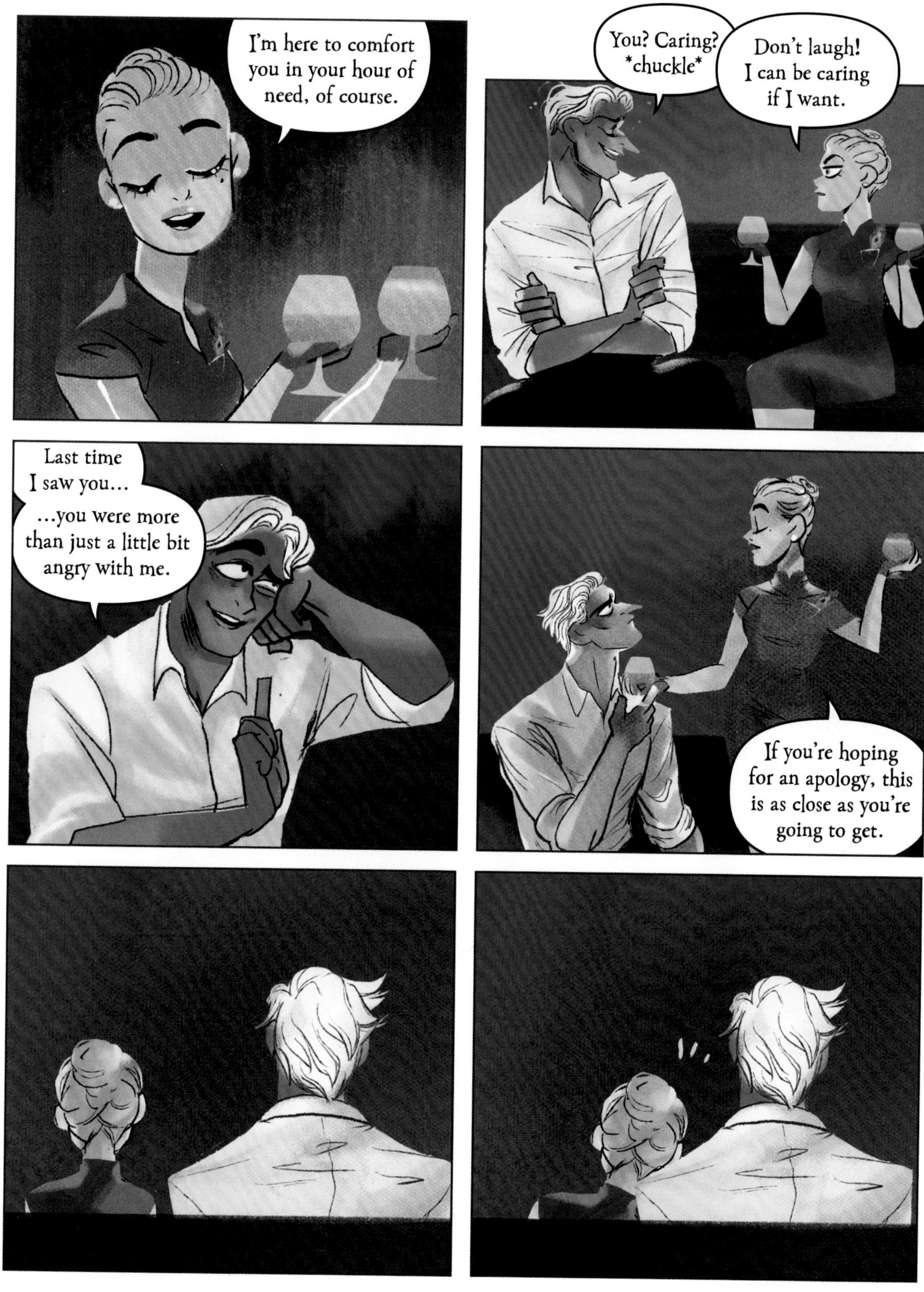
I'm here to comfort you in your hour of need, of course.
You? Caring? *chuckle*
Don't laugh! I can be caring if I want.
Last time I saw you...
...you were more than just a little bit angry with me.
If you're hoping for an apology, this is as close as you're going to get.

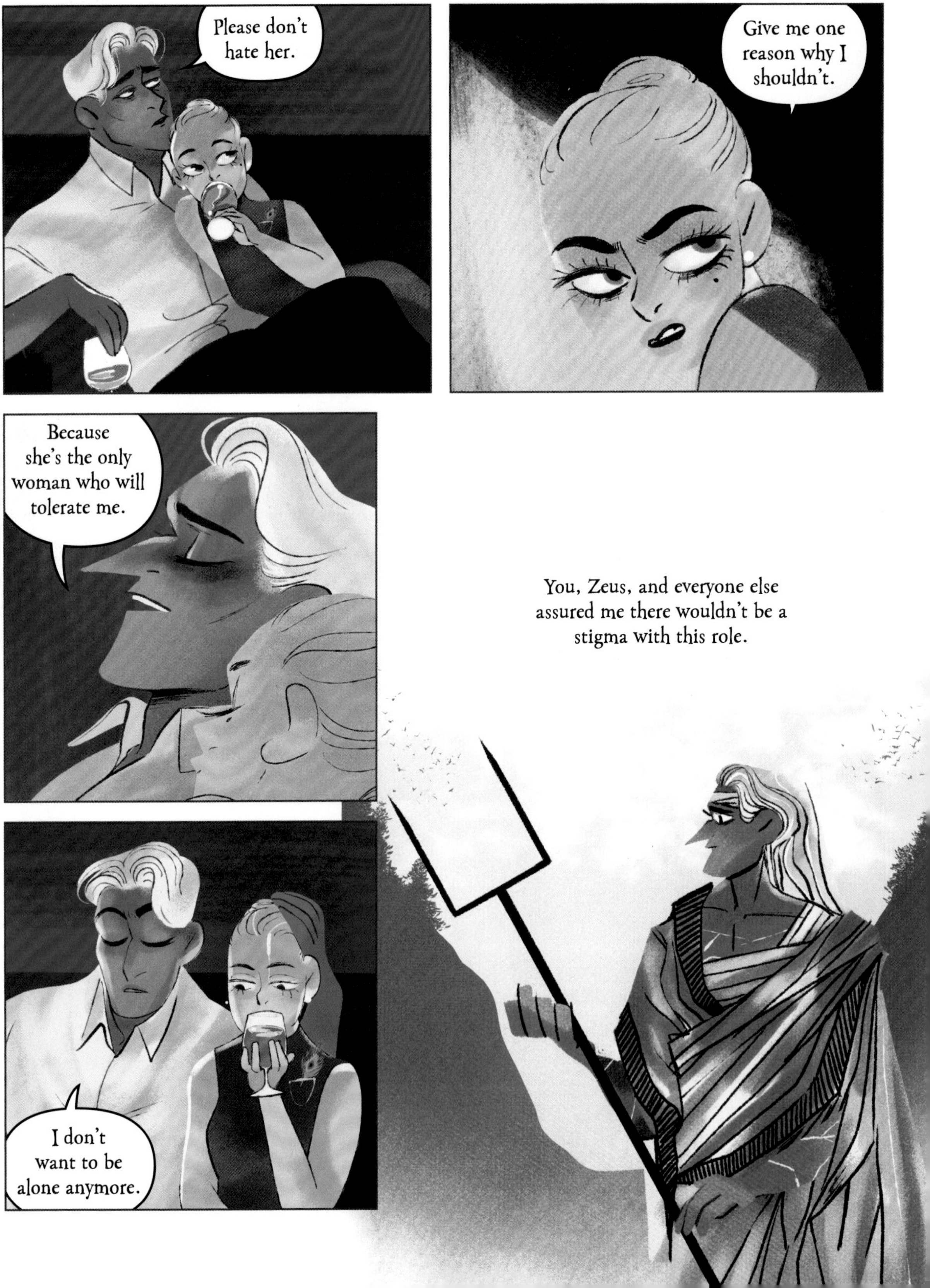
Please don't hate her.
Give me one reason why I shouldn't.
Because she's the only woman who will tolerate me.
I don't want to be alone anymore.
You, Zeus, and everyone else assured me there wouldn't be a stigma with this role.

But there is.

Zeus told me you almost proposed to that nymph.

You didn't come to me first.

I knew you wouldn't go for it.

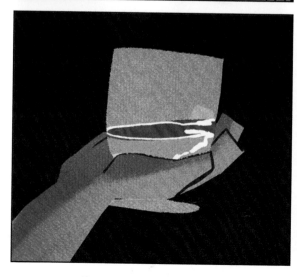

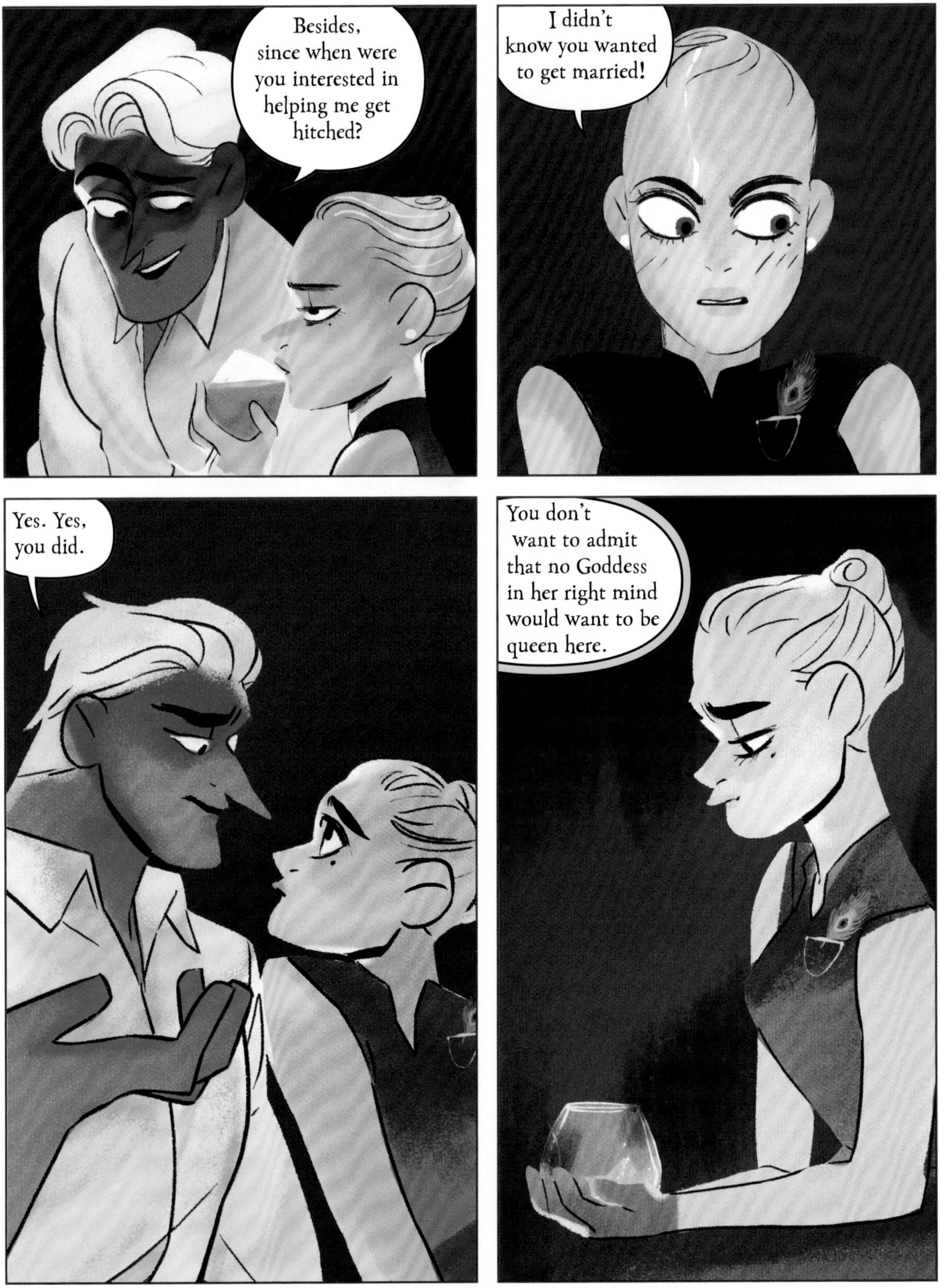
Besides, since when were you interested in helping me get hitched?
I didn't know you wanted to get married!
Yes. Yes, you did.
You don't want to admit that no Goddess in her right mind would want to be queen here.

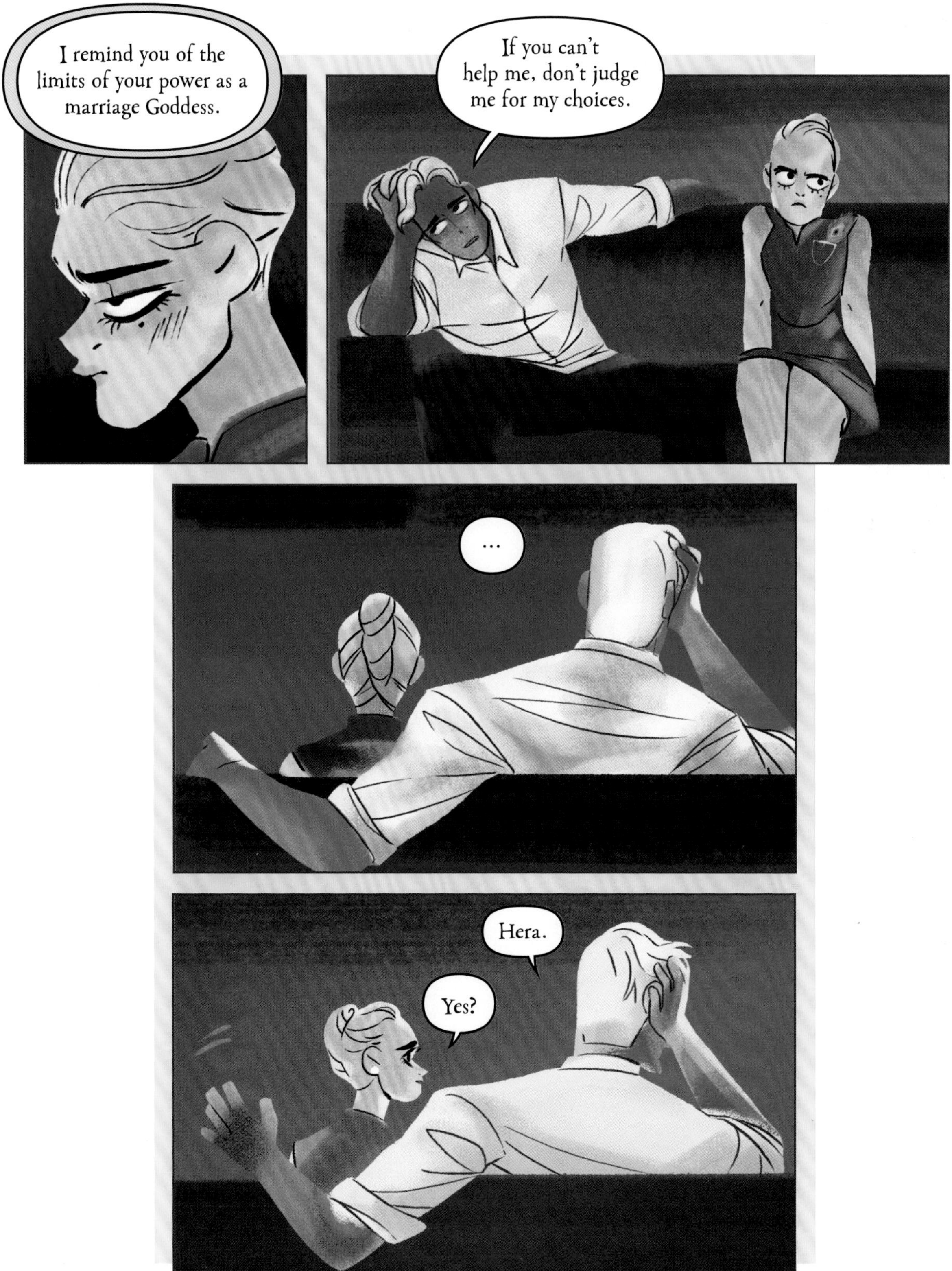
I remind you of the limits of your power as a marriage Goddess.
If you can't help me, don't judge me for my choices.
...
Hera.
Yes?

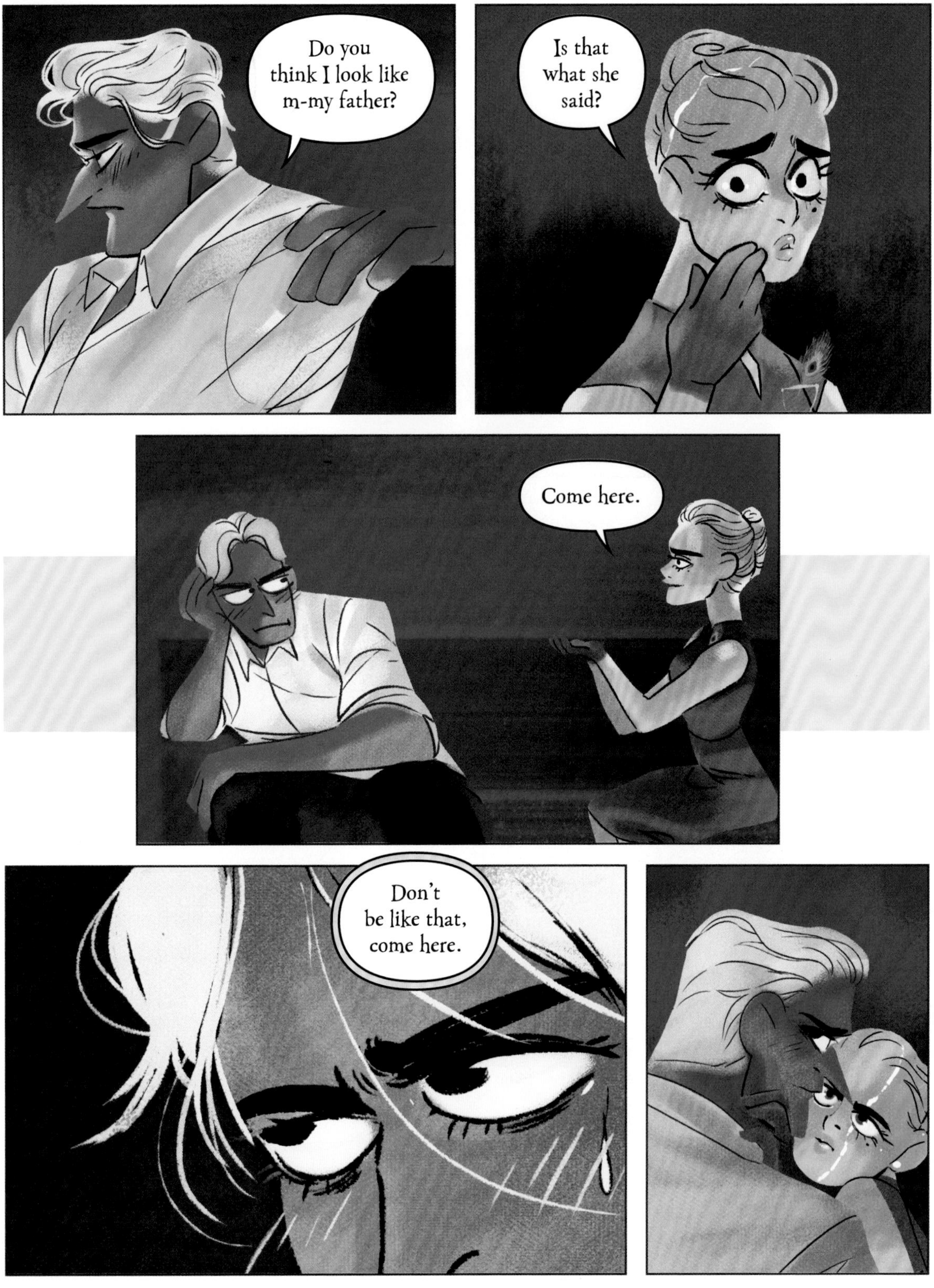
Do you think I look like m-my father?
Is that what she said?
Come here.
Don't be like that, come here.

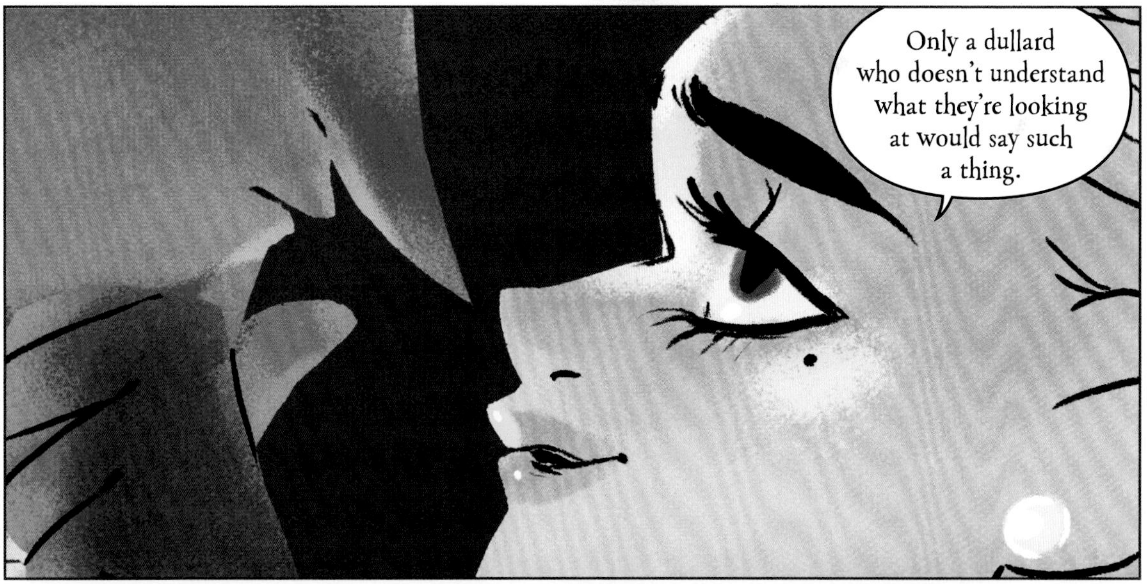
Only a dullard who doesn't understand what they're looking at would say such a thing.

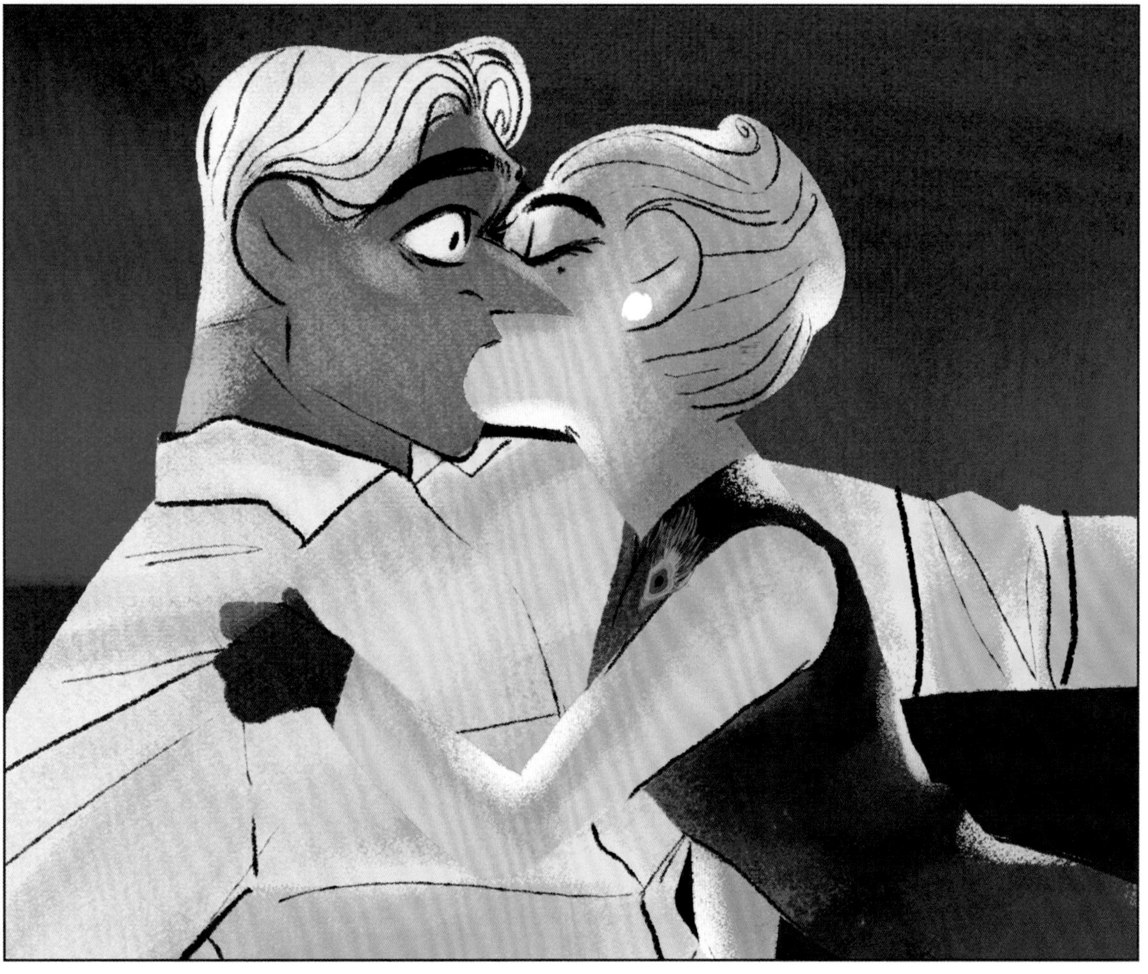

EPISODE 78: HERA

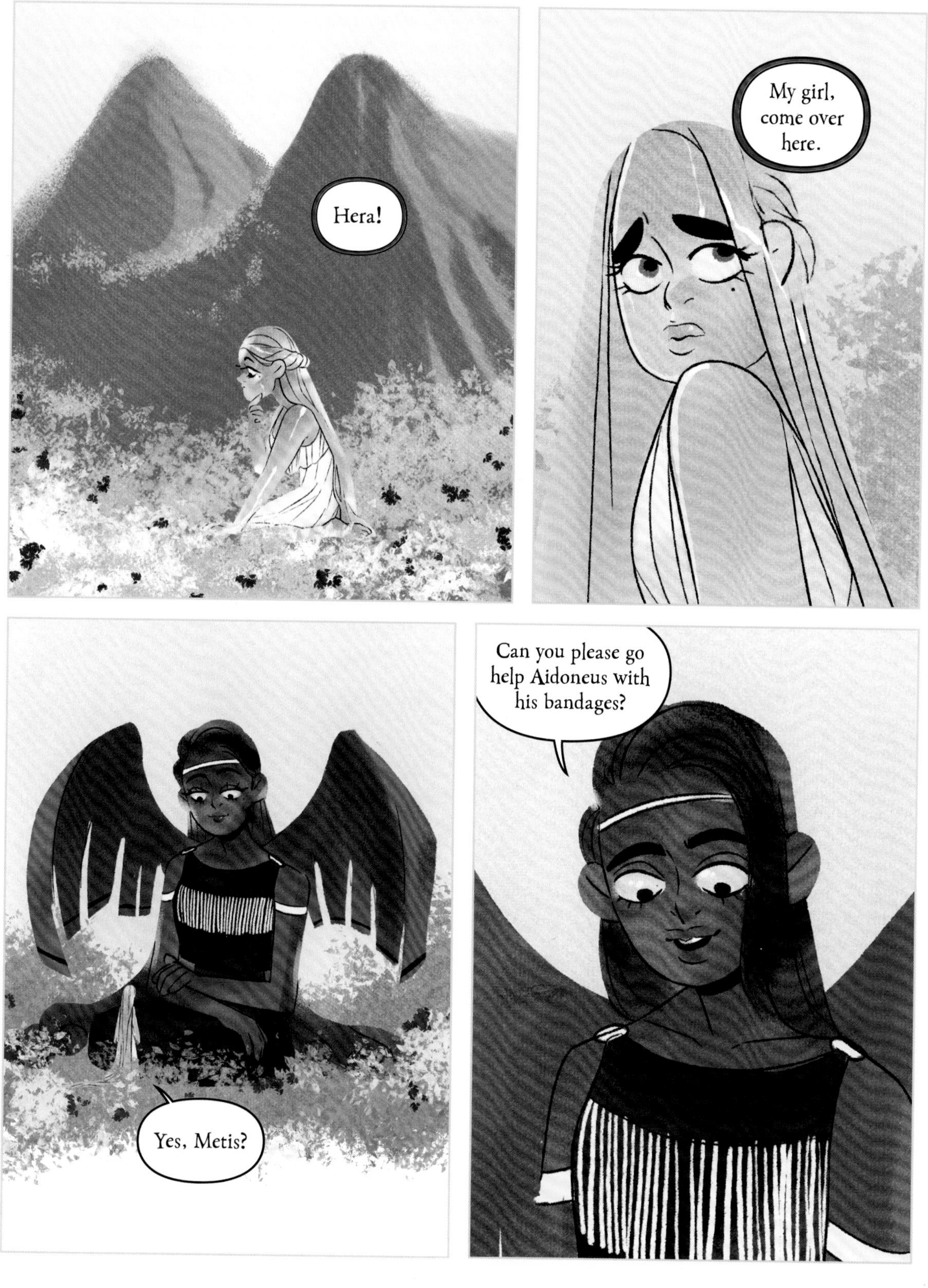
Hera!
My girl, come over here.
Yes, Metis?
Can you please go help Aidoneus with his bandages?

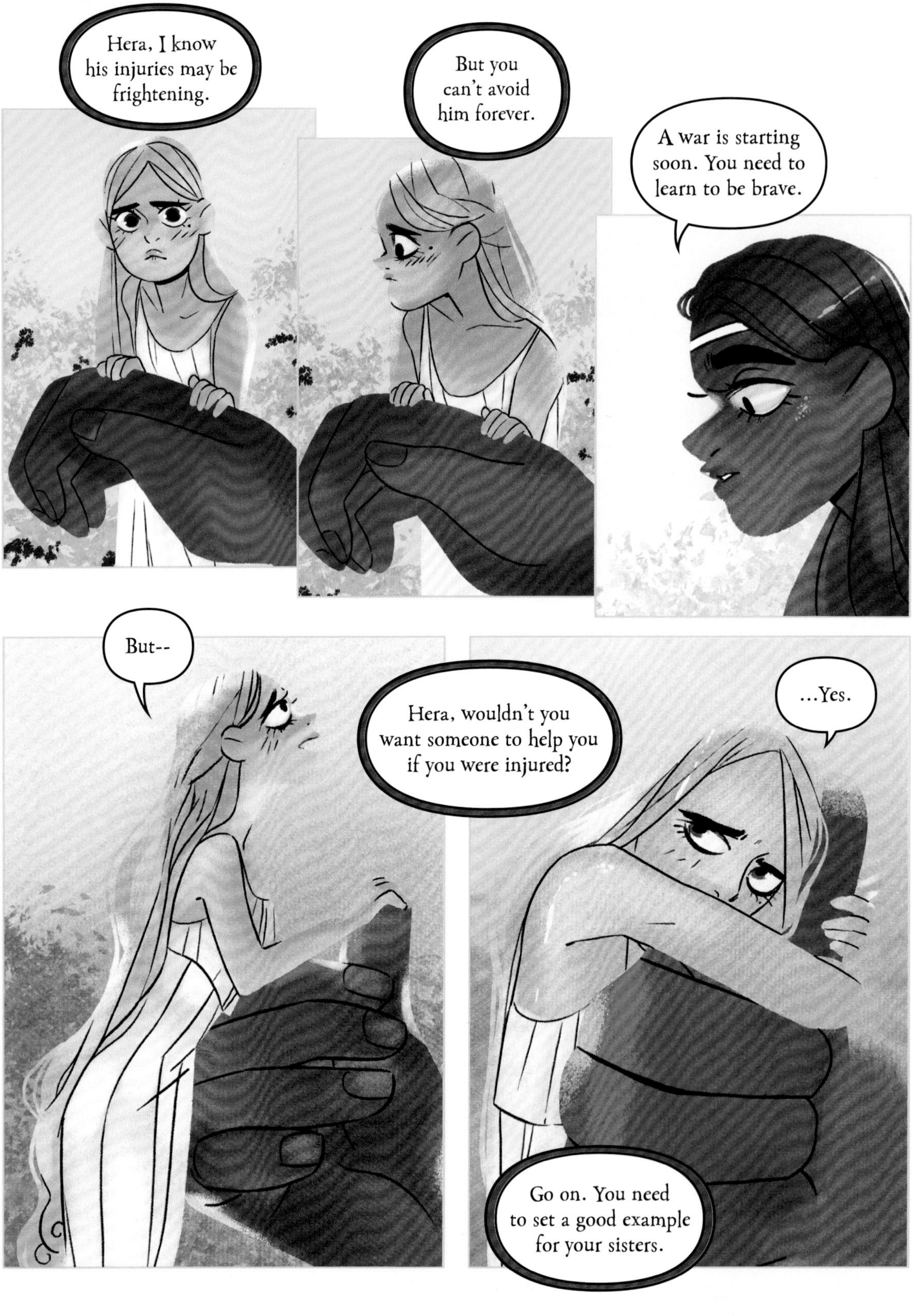
Hera, I know his injuries may be frightening.
But you can't avoid him forever.
A war is starting soon. You need to learn to be brave.
But--
Hera, wouldn't you want someone to help you if you were injured?
...Yes.
Go on. You need to set a good example for your sisters.

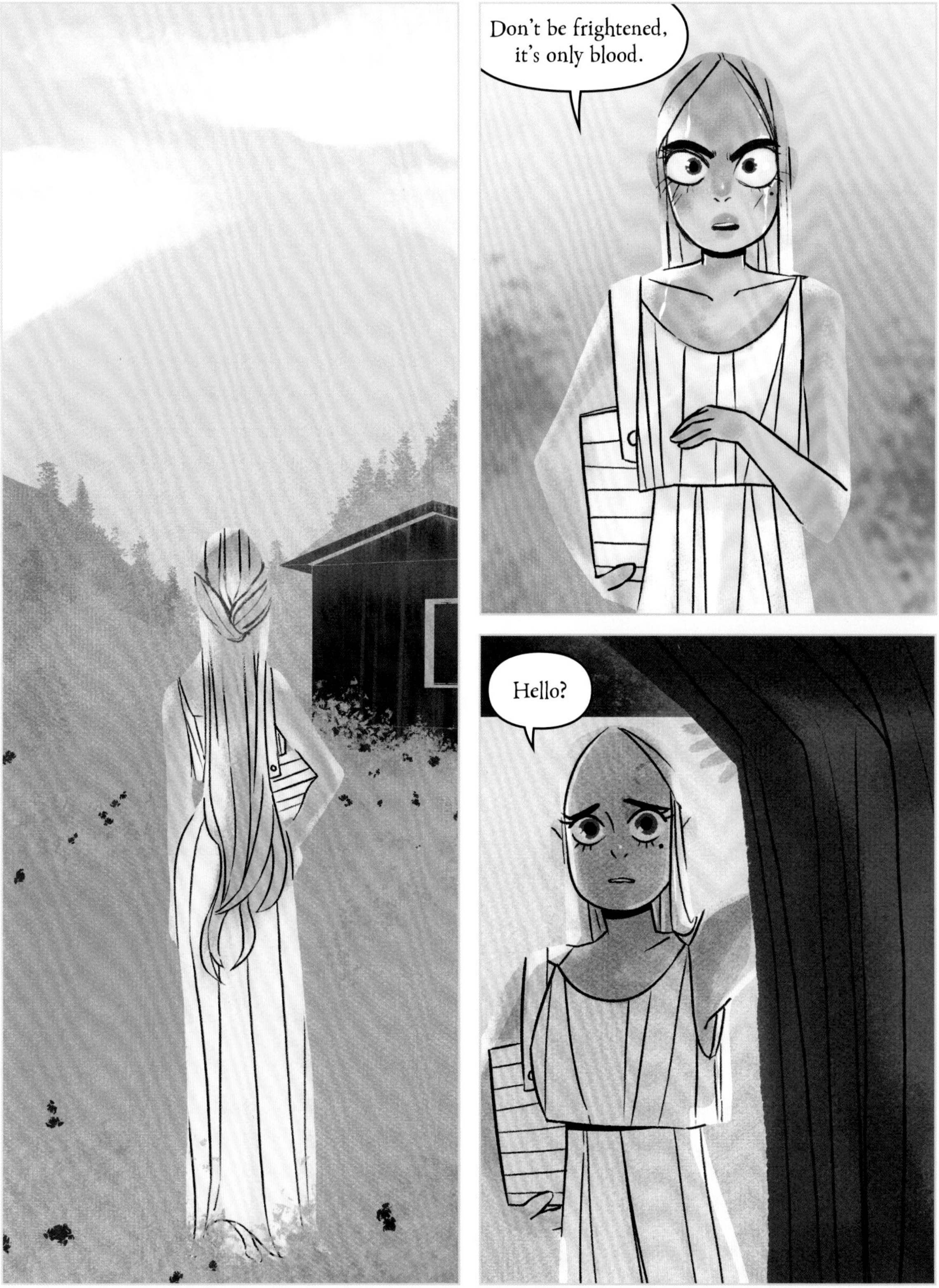
Don't be frightened, it's only blood.
Hello?

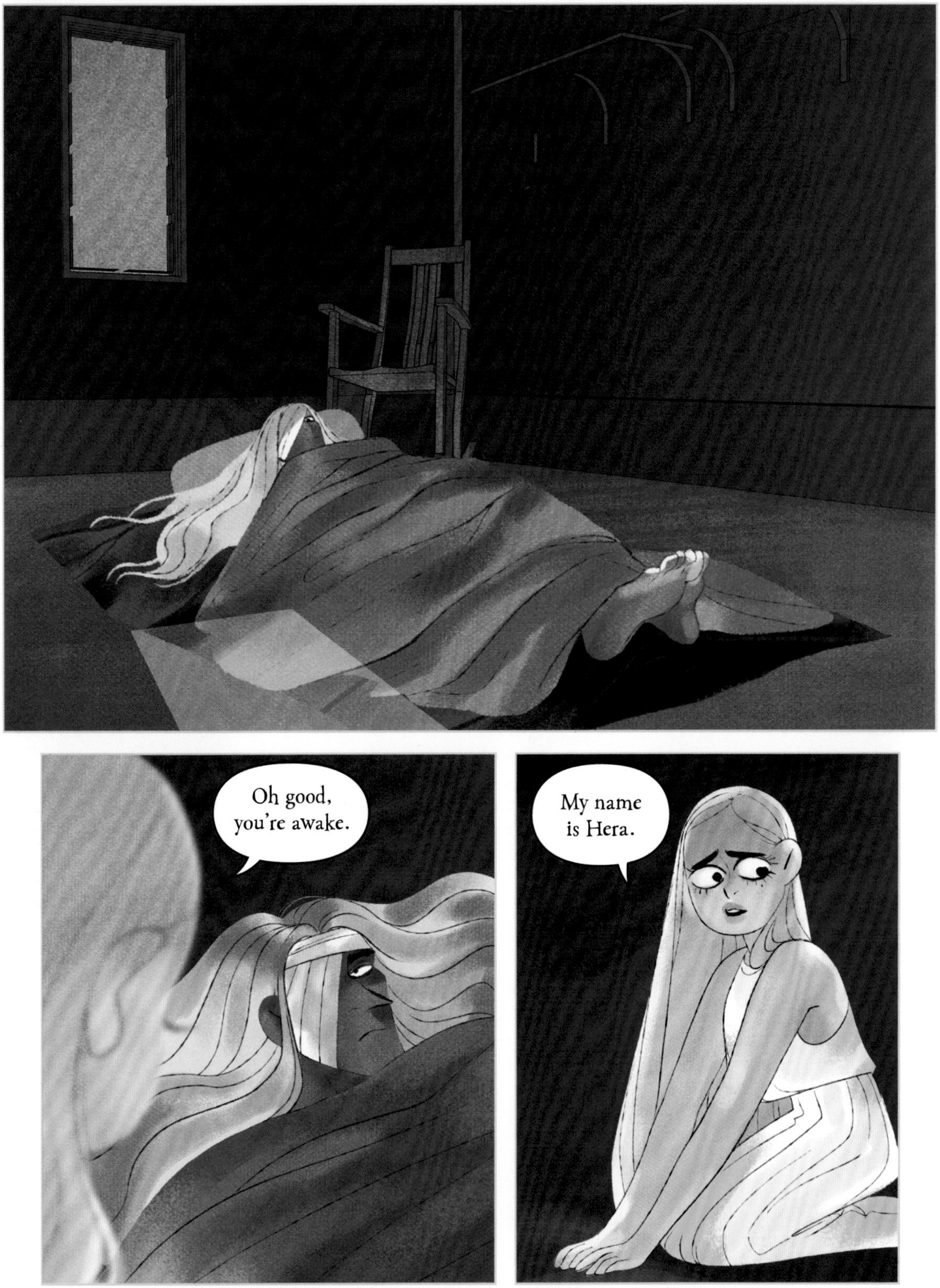
Oh good, you're awake.
My name is Hera.

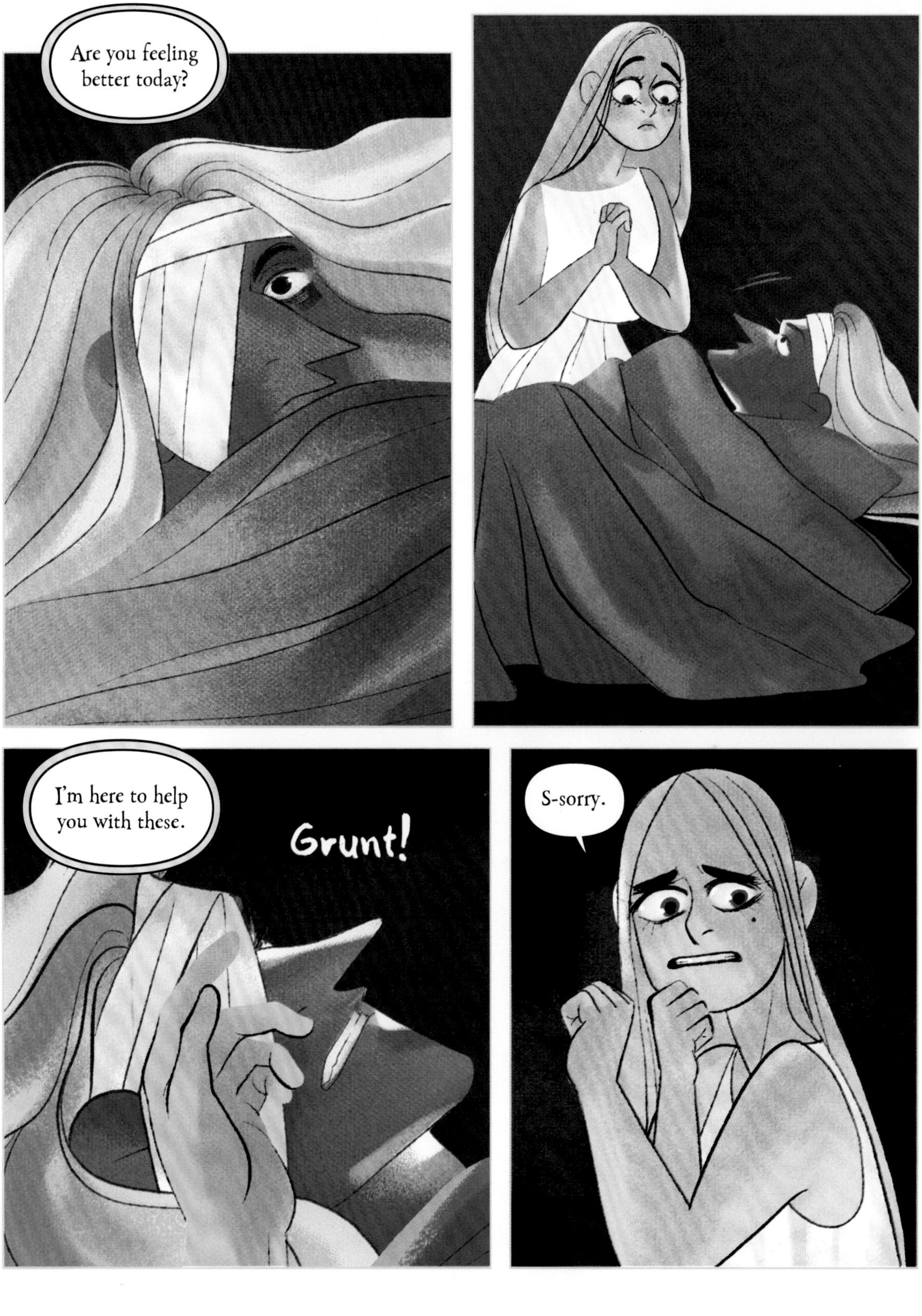
Are you feeling better today?
I'm here to help you with these.
Grunt!
S-sorry.

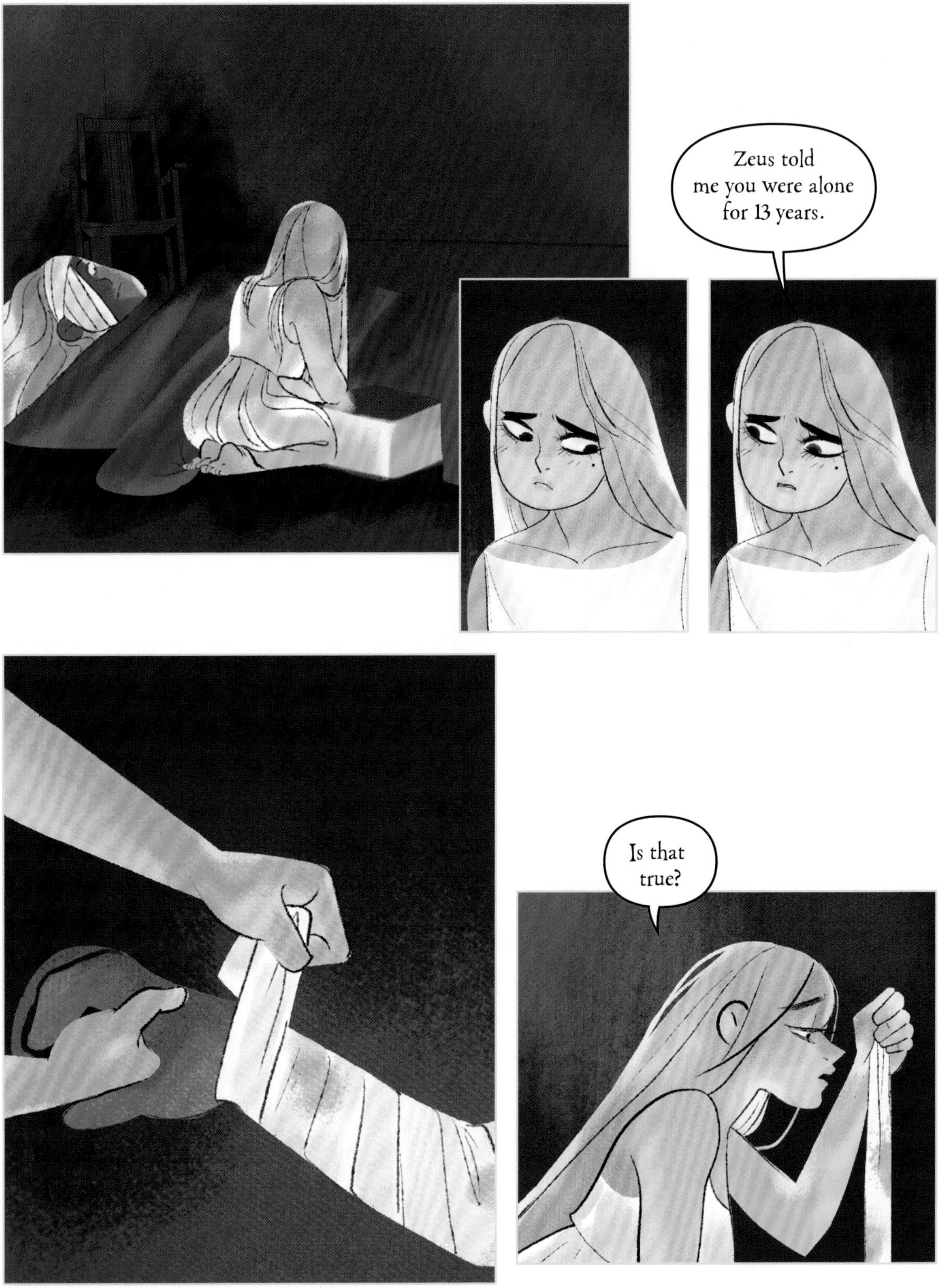
Zeus told me you were alone for 13 years.
Is that true?

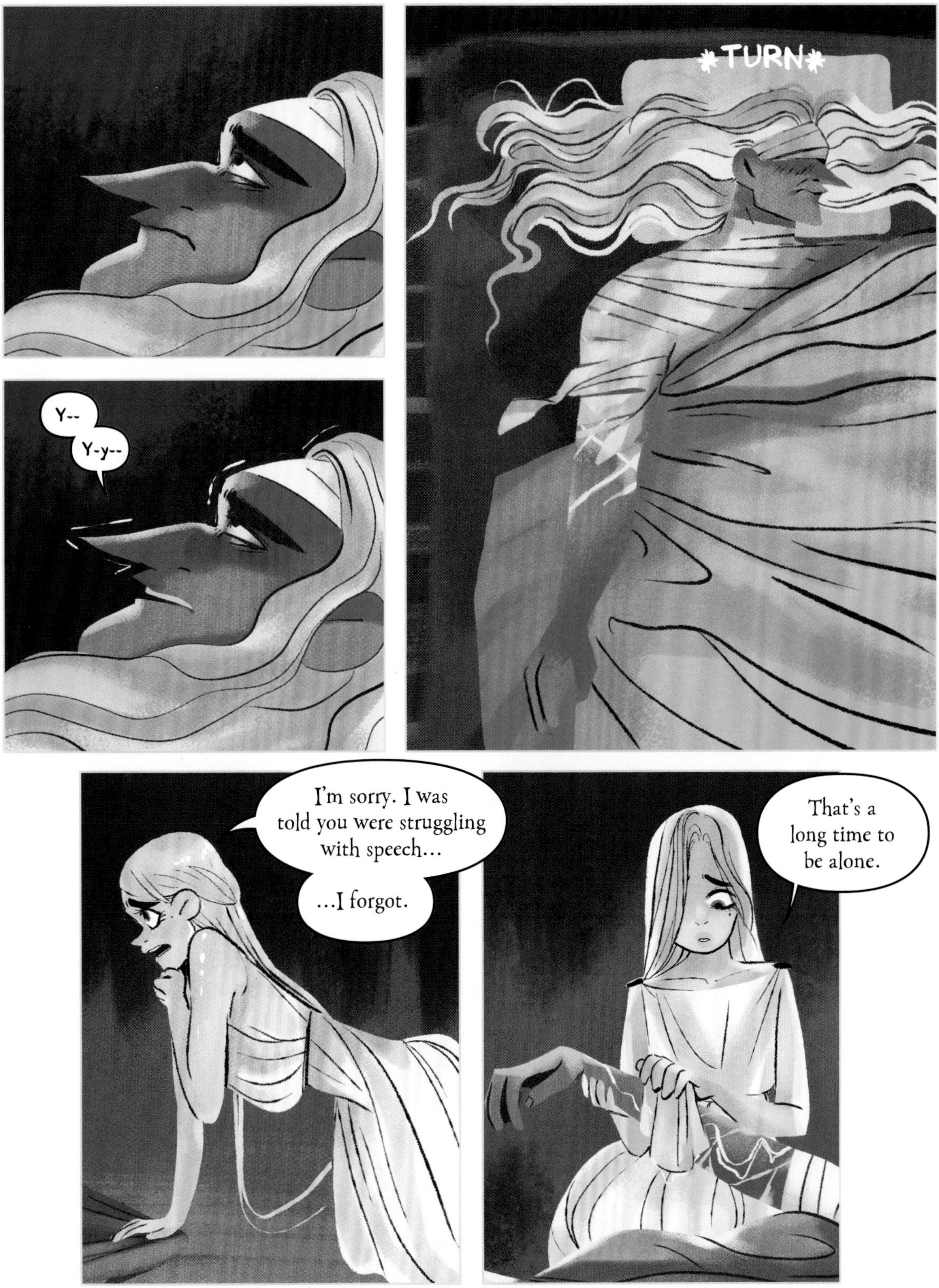
Y--
Y-y--
TURN
I'm sorry. I was told you were struggling with speech...
...I forgot.
That's a long time to be alone.

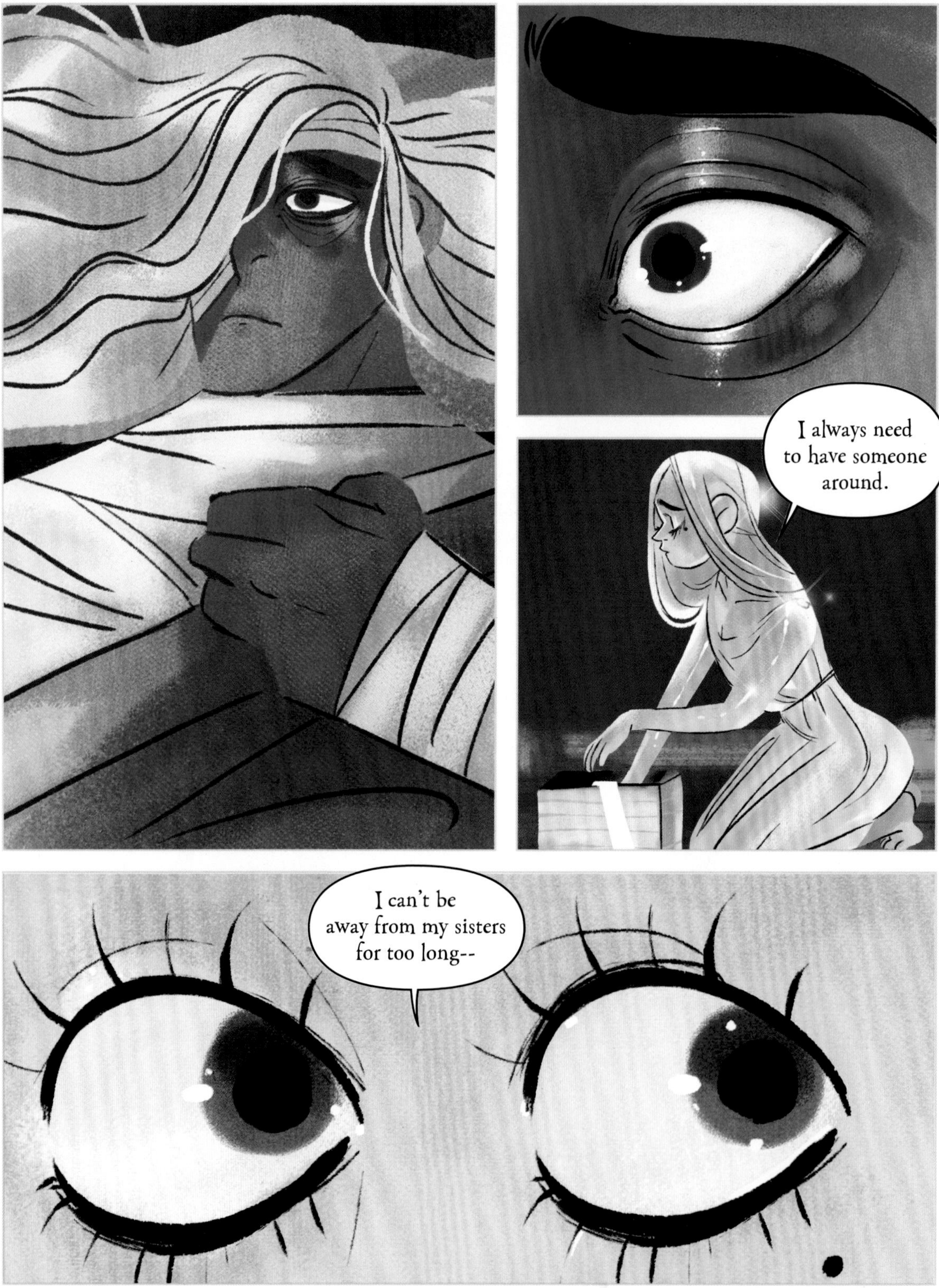
I always need to have someone around.
I can't be away from my sisters for too long--

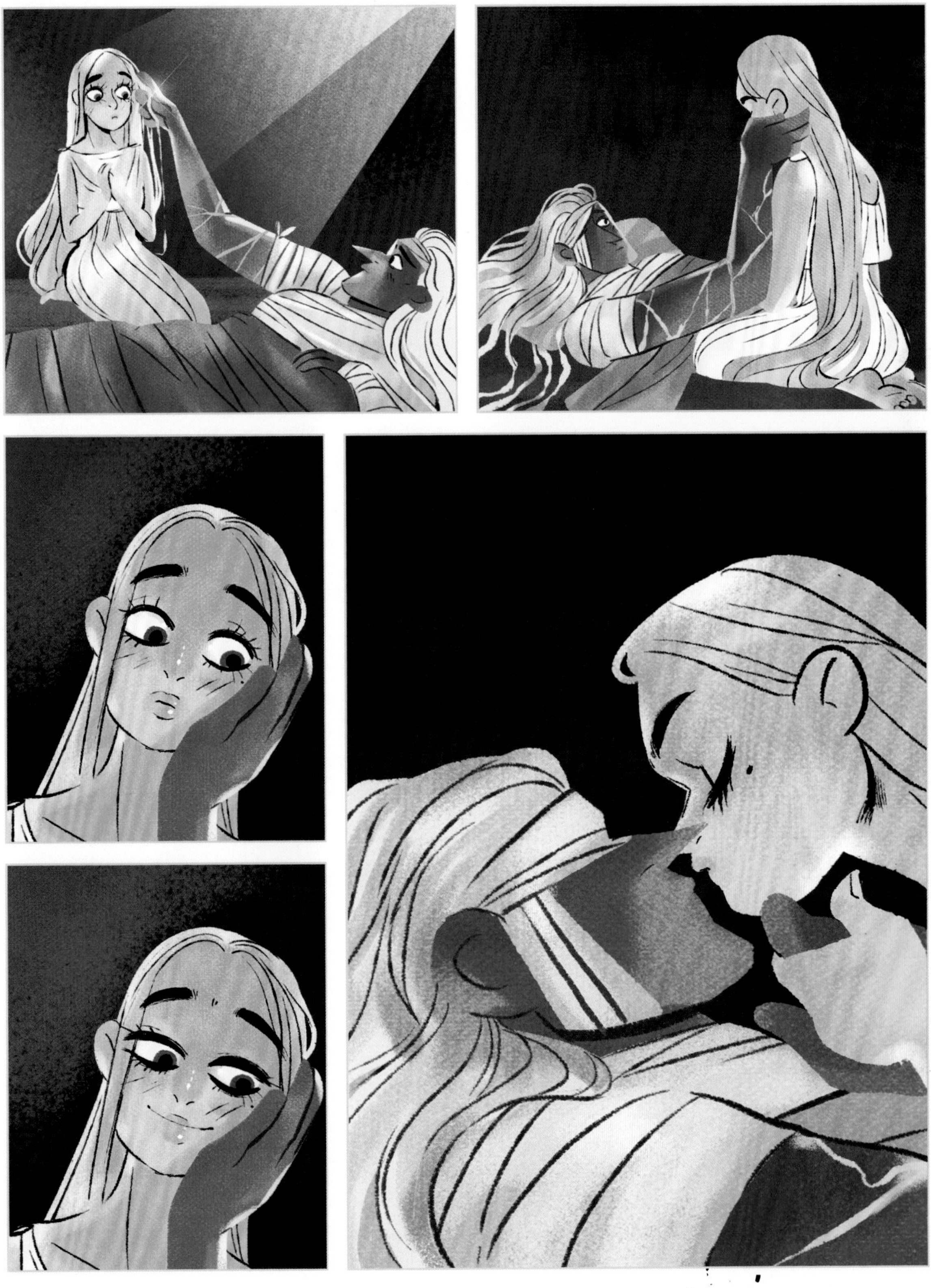

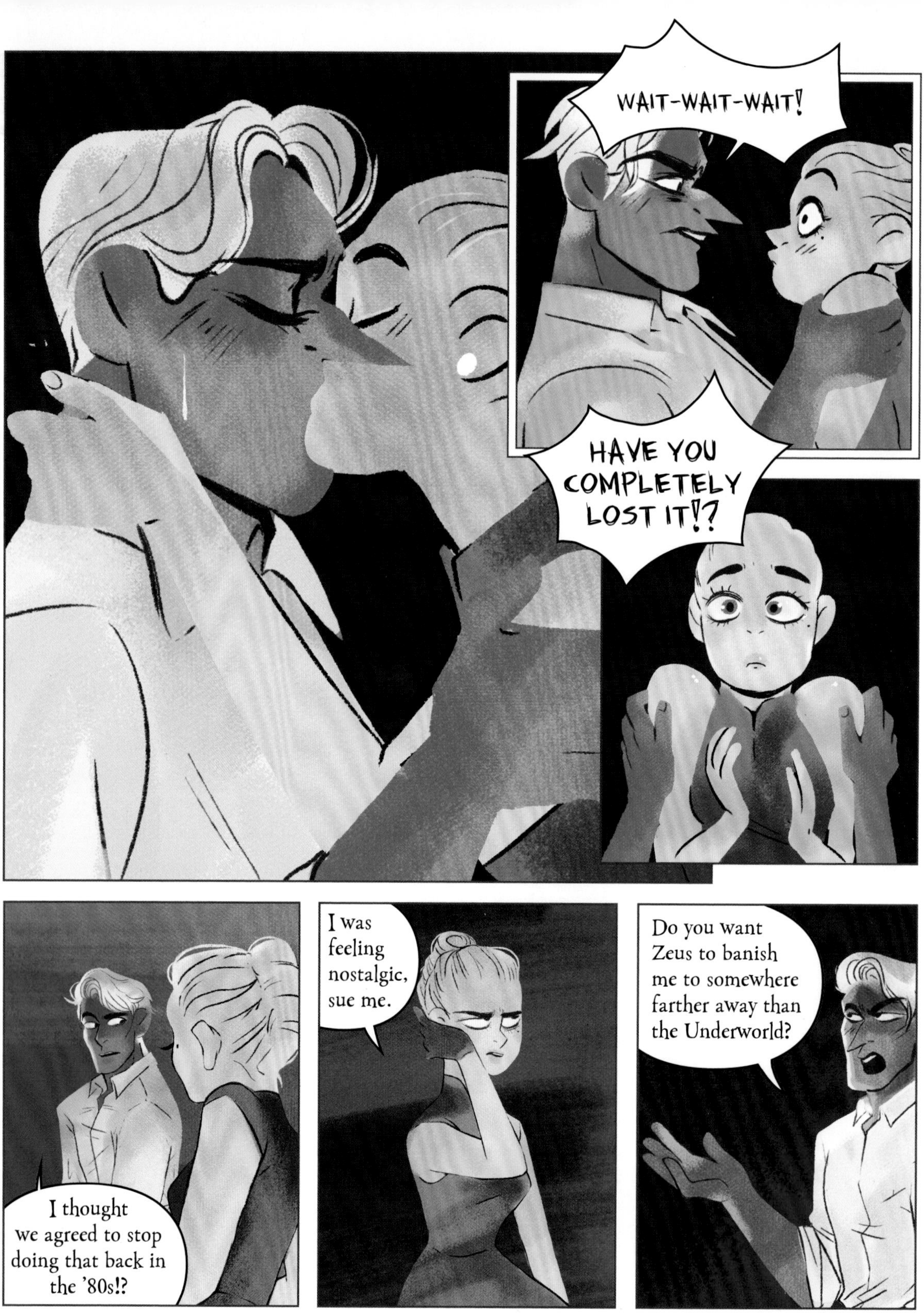
WAIT-WAIT-WAIT!
HAVE YOU COMPLETELY LOST IT!?
I thought we agreed to stop doing that back in the '80s!?
I was feeling nostalgic, sue me.
Do you want Zeus to banish me to somewhere farther away than the Underworld?

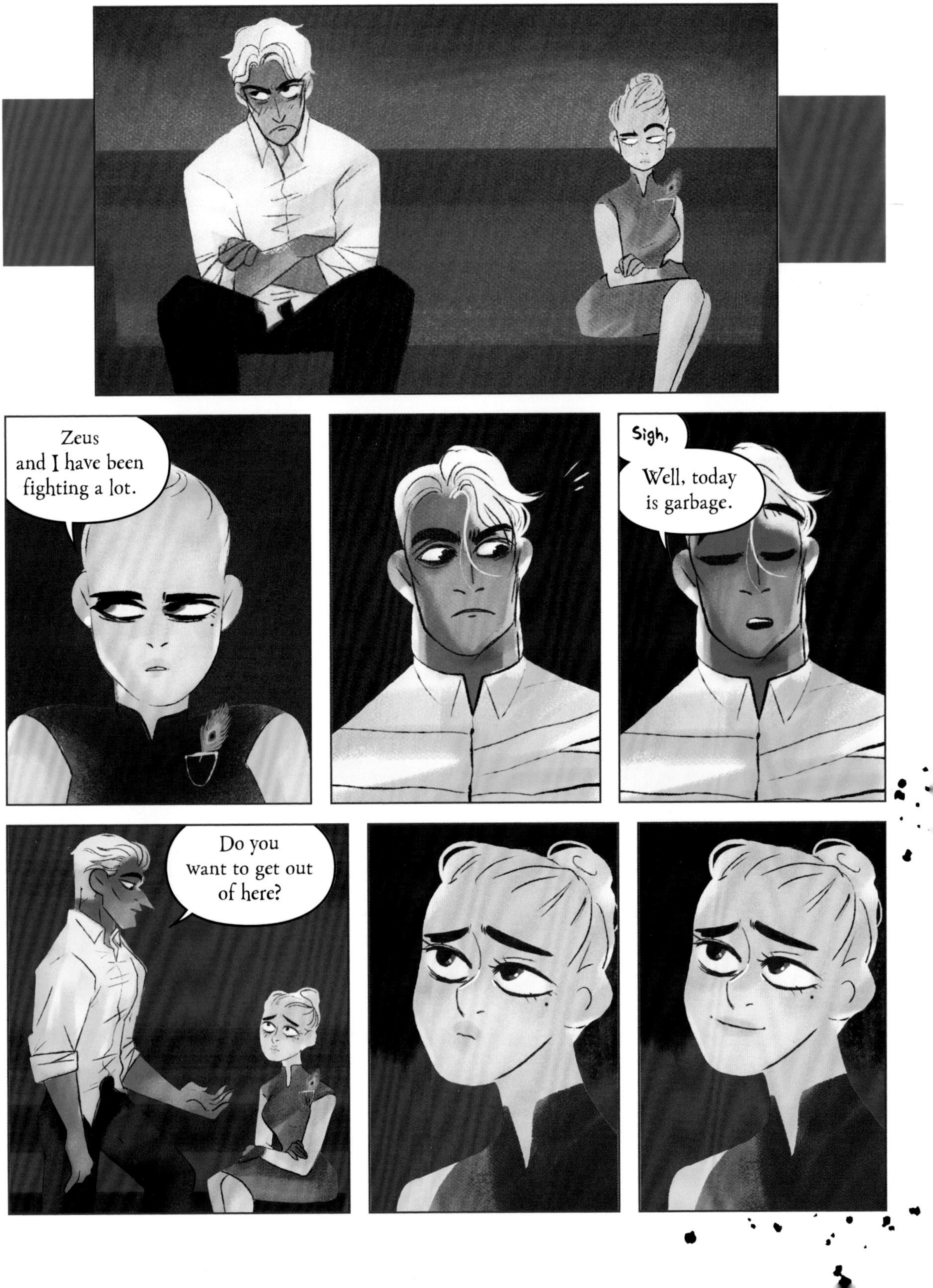
Zeus and I have been fighting a lot.
Sigh,
Well, today is garbage.
Do you want to get out of here?

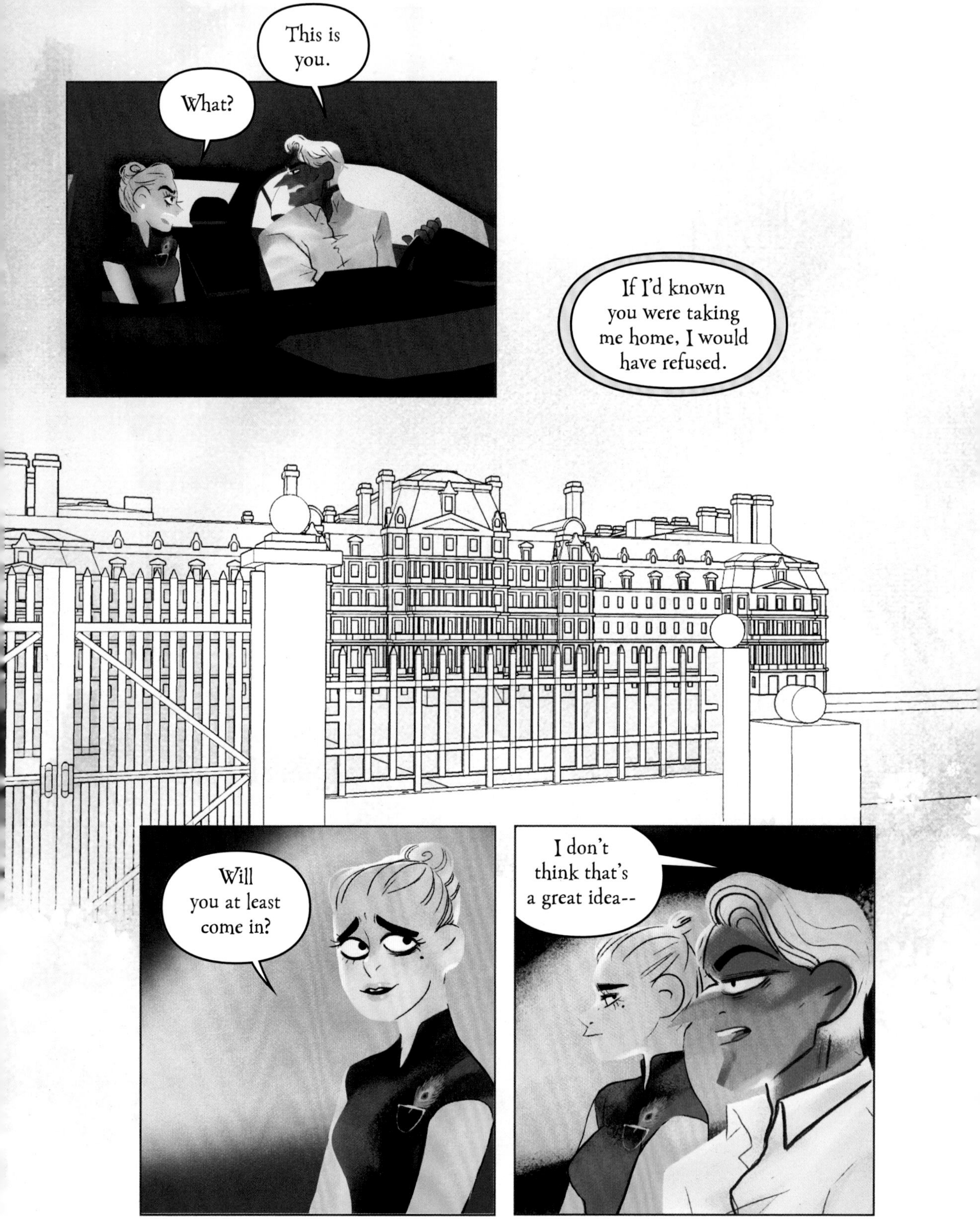
What?
This is you.
If I'd known you were taking me home, I would have refused.
Will you at least come in?
I don't think that's a great idea--

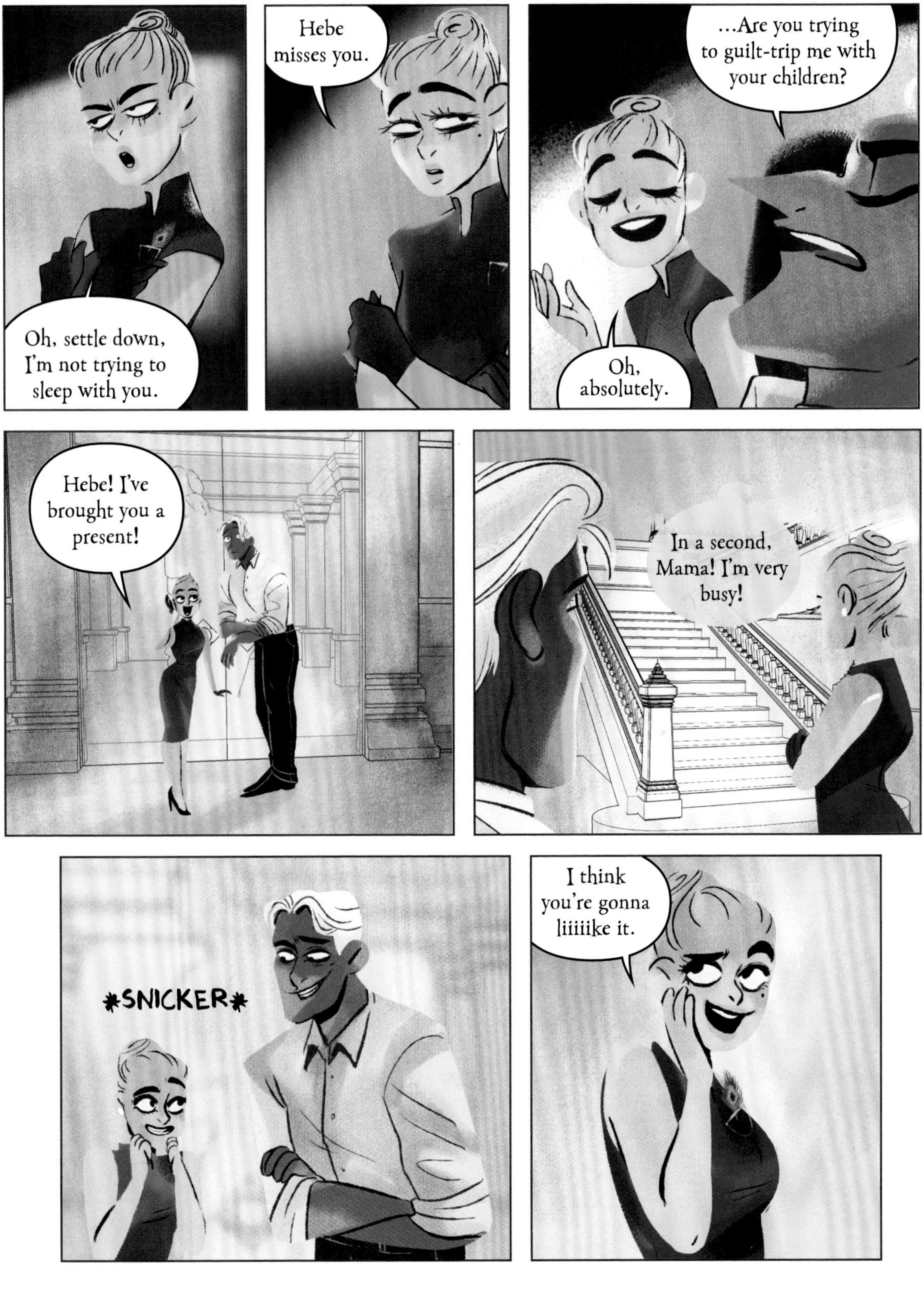
Oh, settle down, I'm not trying to sleep with you.
Hebe misses you.
...Are you trying to guilt-trip me with your children?
Oh, absolutely.
Hebe! I've brought you a present!
In a second, Mama! I'm very busy!
SNICKER
I think you're gonna liiiiike it.

Okay!
I'm coming!

Uncle!

YAAAAAAAAAY!

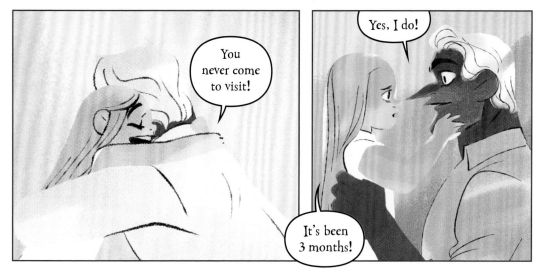

You never come to visit!

Yes, I do!

It's been 3 months!

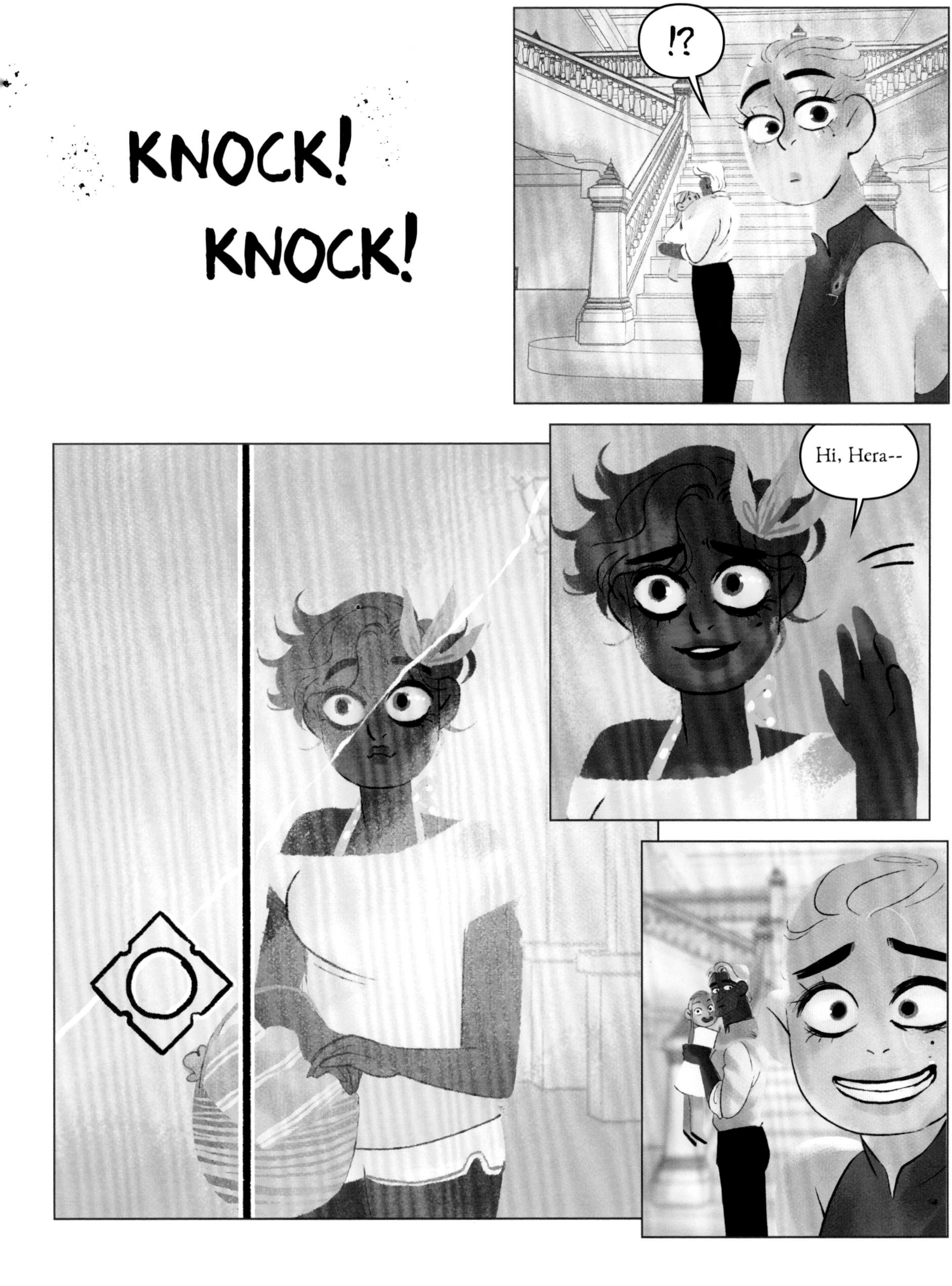
KNOCK!
KNOCK!
!?
Hi, Hera--

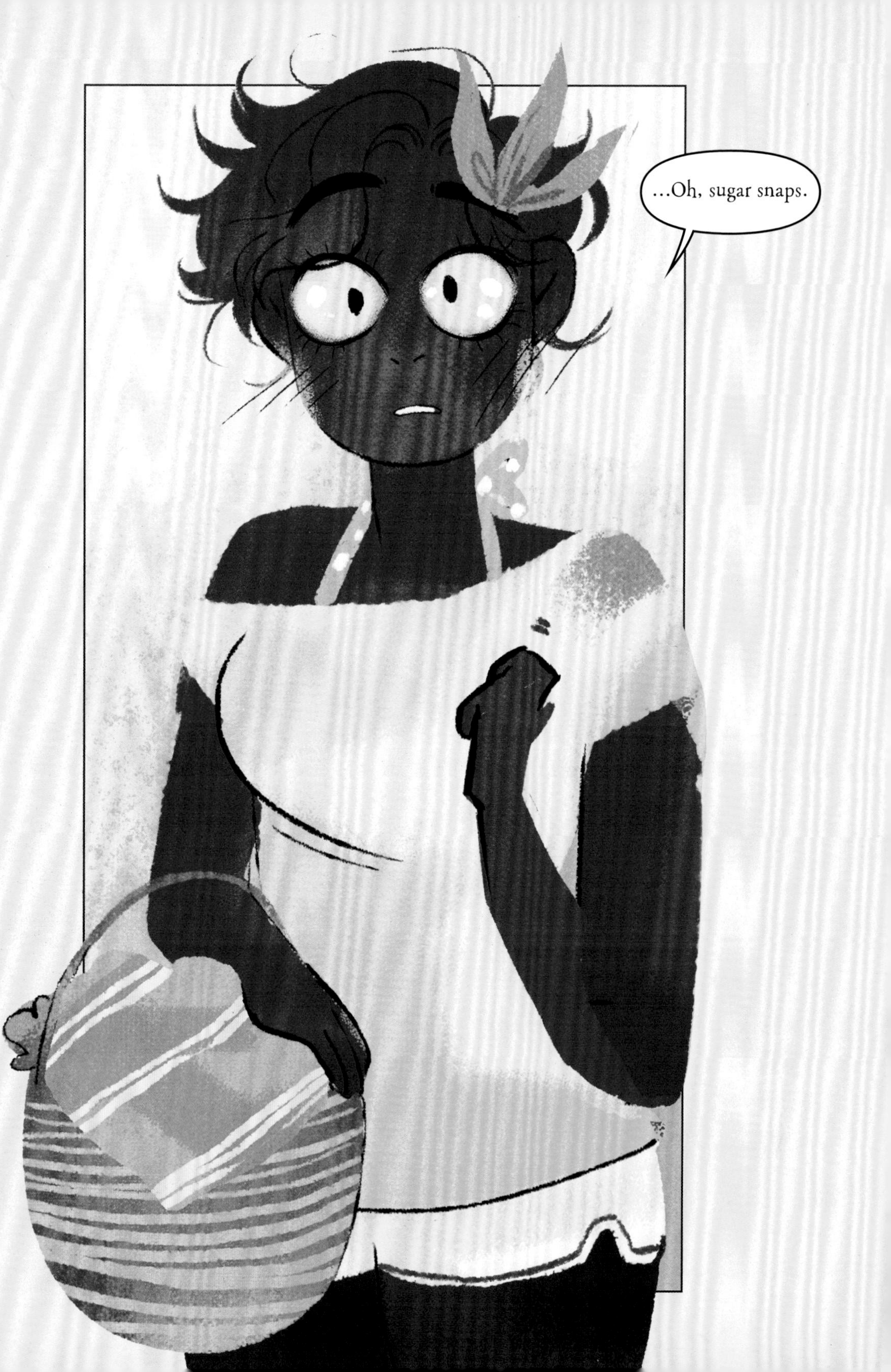
...Oh, sugar snaps.

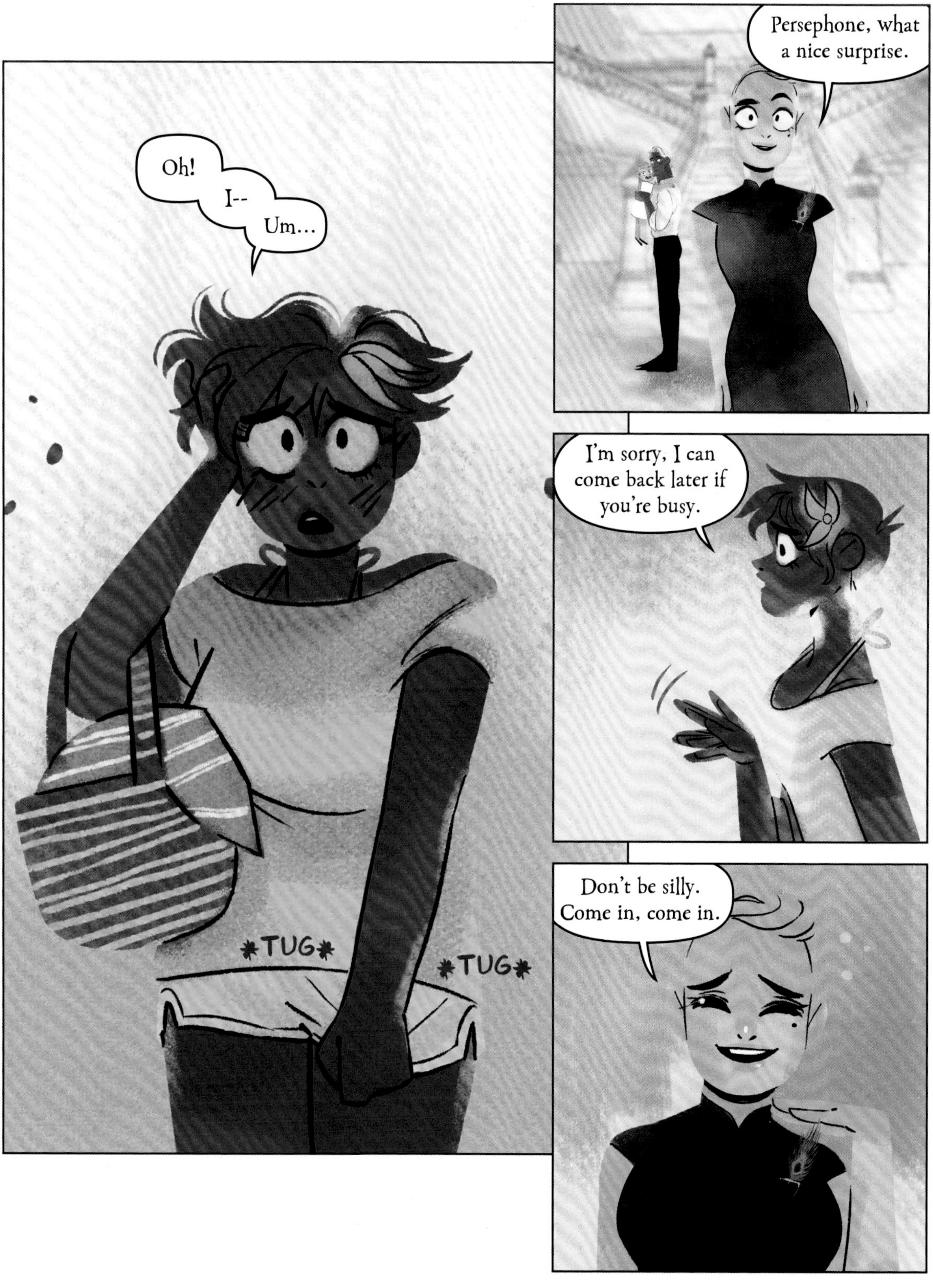
Oh!
I--
Um...
TUG
TUG
Persephone, what a nice surprise.
I'm sorry, I can come back later if you're busy.
Don't be silly. Come in, come in.

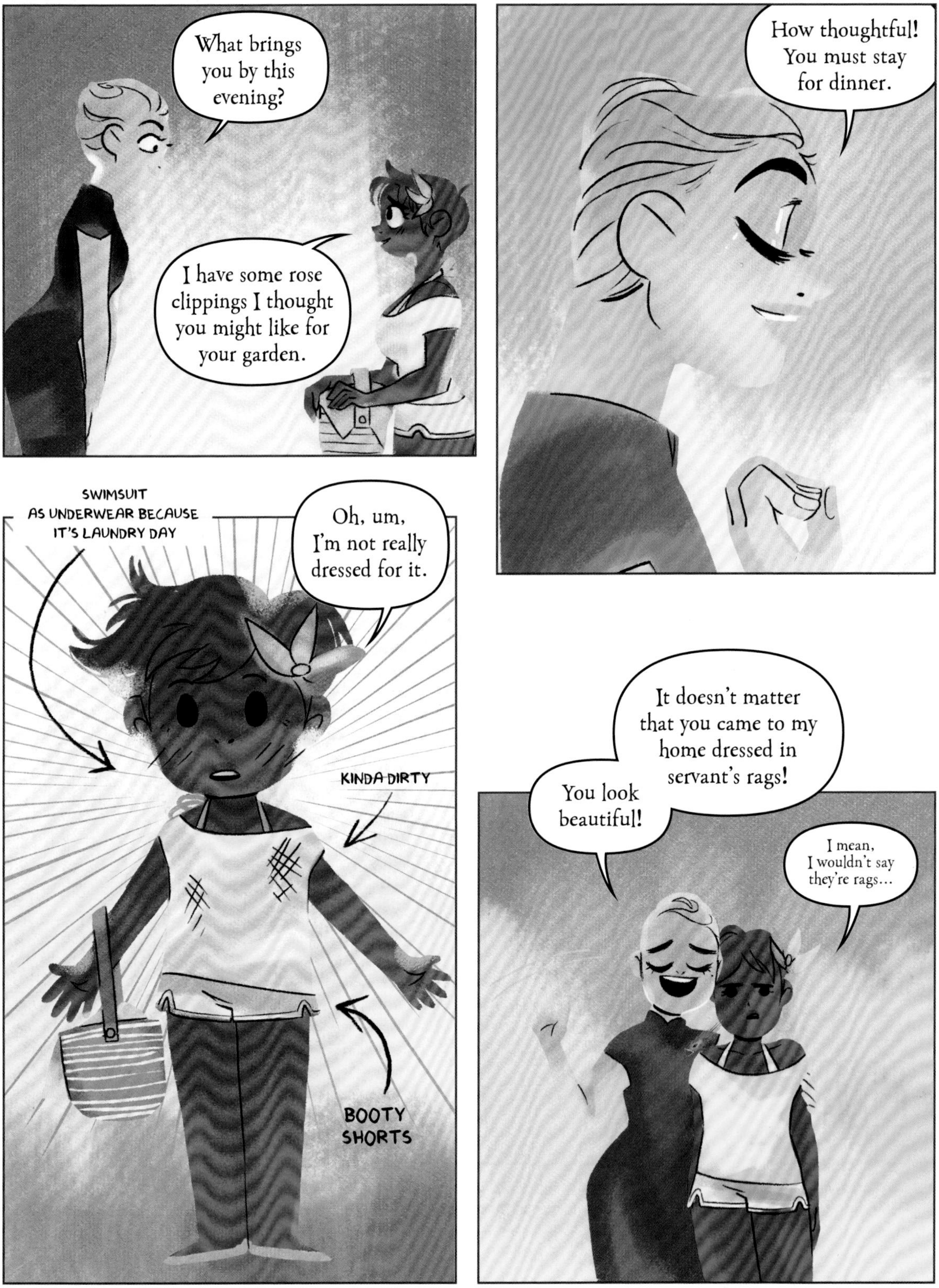
What brings you by this evening?
I have some rose clippings I thought you might like for your garden.
How thoughtful! You must stay for dinner.
SWIMSUIT AS UNDERWEAR BECAUSE IT'S LAUNDRY DAY
Oh, um, I'm not really dressed for it.
KINDA DIRTY
BOOTY SHORTS
It doesn't matter that you came to my home dressed in servant's rags!
You look beautiful!
I mean, I wouldn't say they're rags...

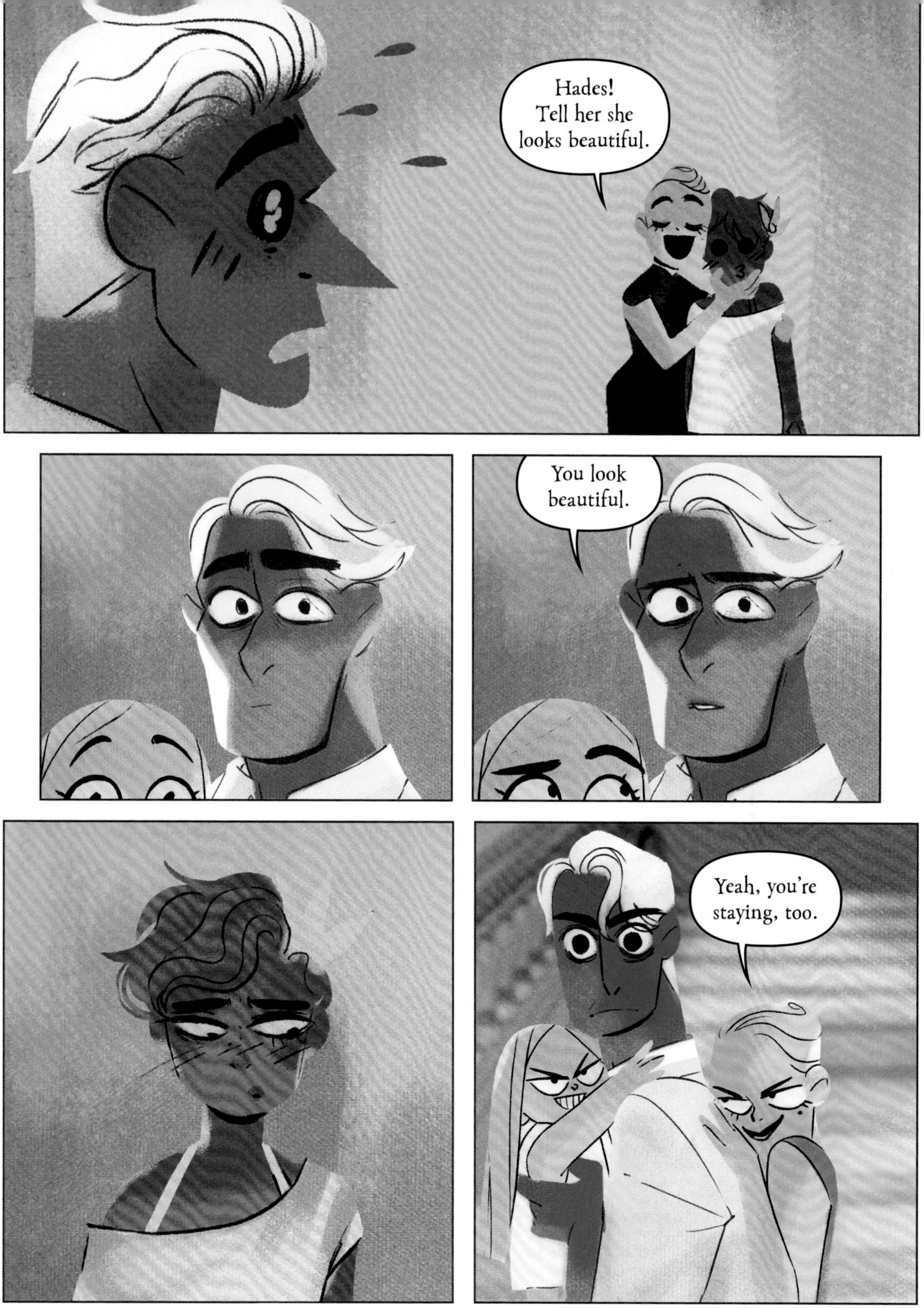
Hades!
Tell her she
looks beautiful.
You look
beautiful.
Yeah, you're
staying, too.

EPISODE 79: SUNSET

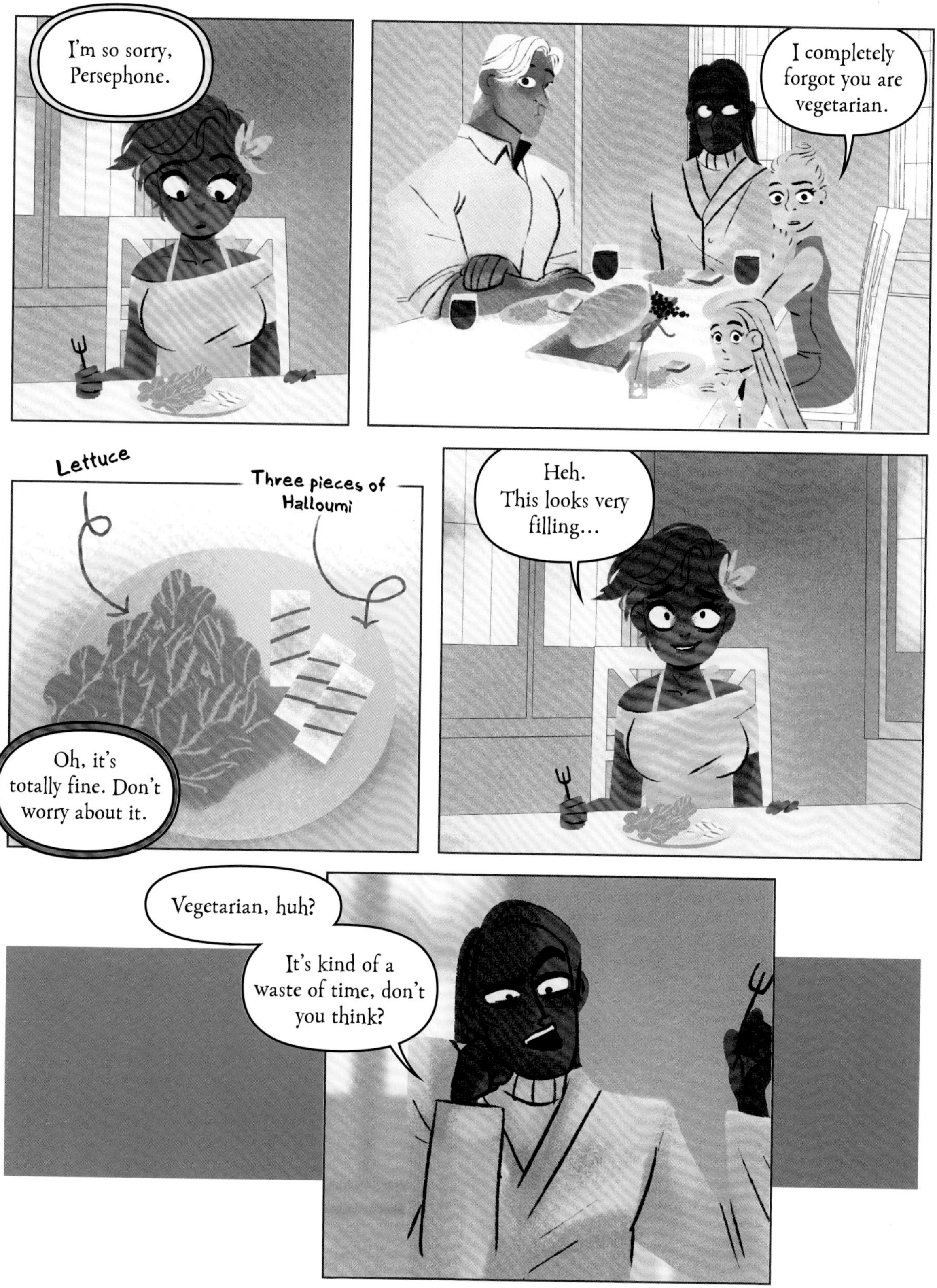
I'm so sorry, Persephone.
I completely forgot you are vegetarian.
Lettuce
Three pieces of Halloumi
Oh, it's totally fine. Don't worry about it.
Heh. This looks very filling...
Vegetarian, huh?
It's kind of a waste of time, don't you think?

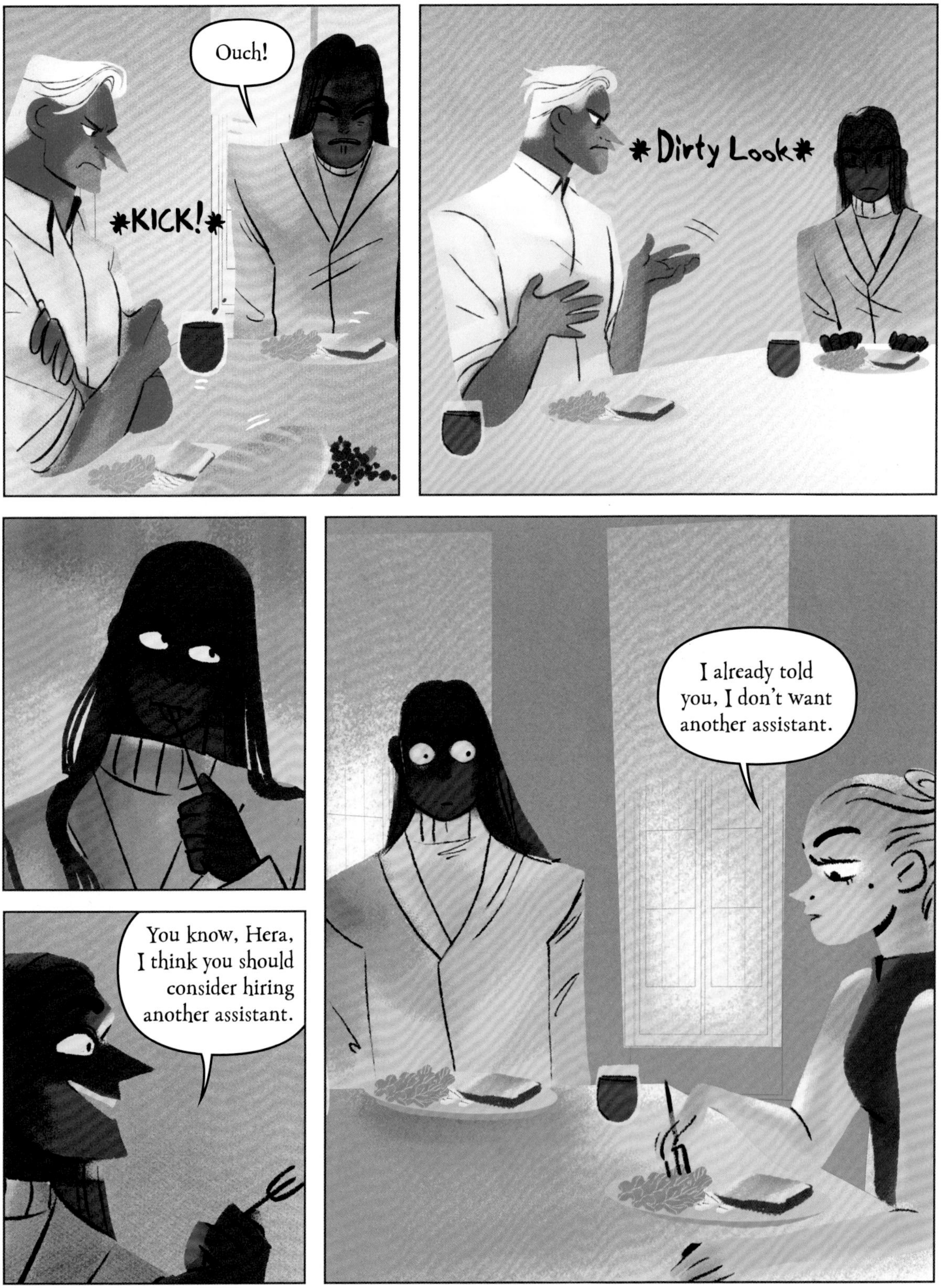
Ouch!
KICK!
Dirty Look
You know, Hera, I think you should consider hiring another assistant.
I already told you, I don't want another assistant.

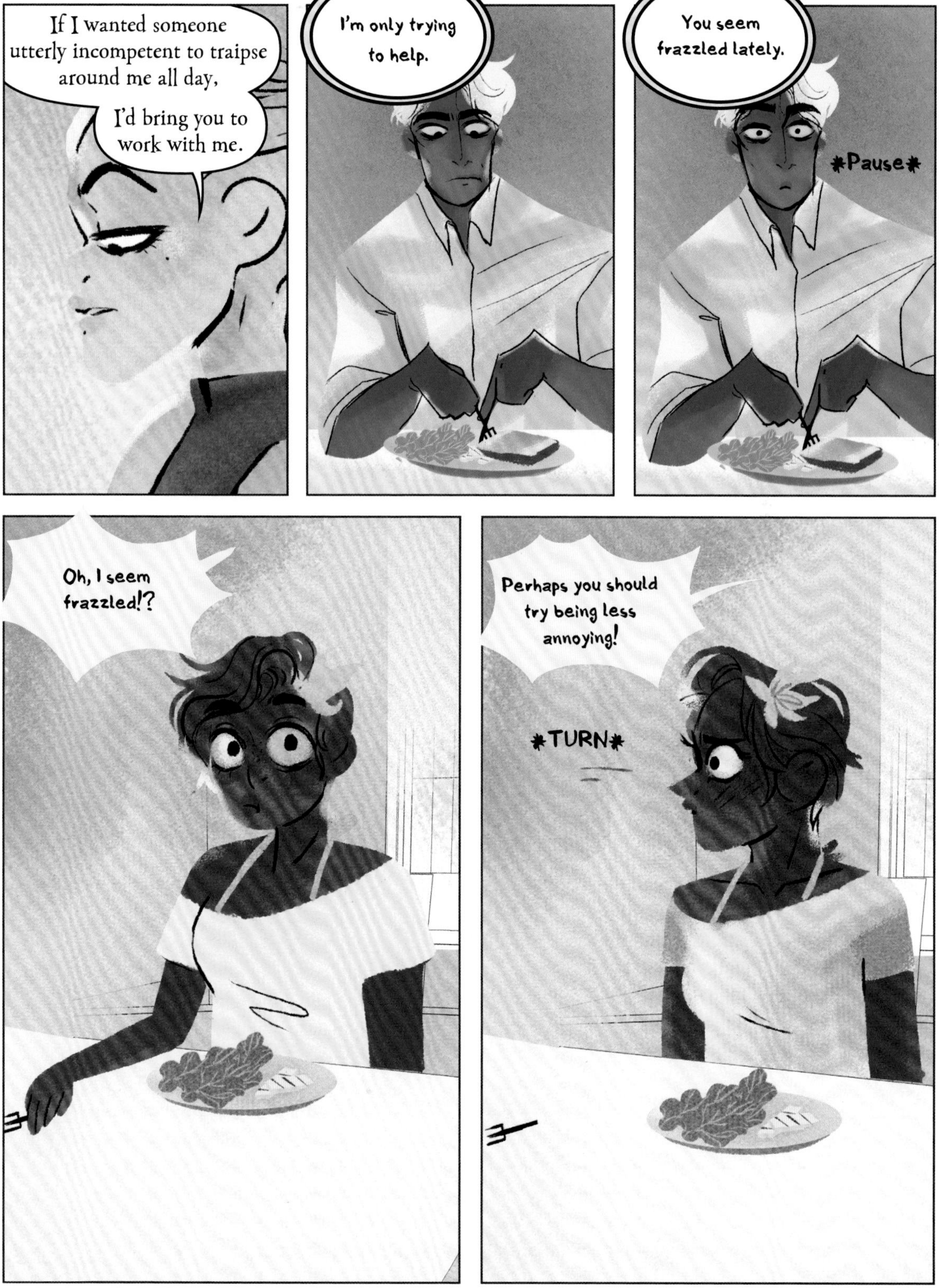
If I wanted someone utterly incompetent to traipse around me all day,
I'd bring you to work with me.
I'm only trying to help.
You seem frazzled lately.
Pause
Oh, I seem frazzled!?
Perhaps you should try being less annoying!
TURN

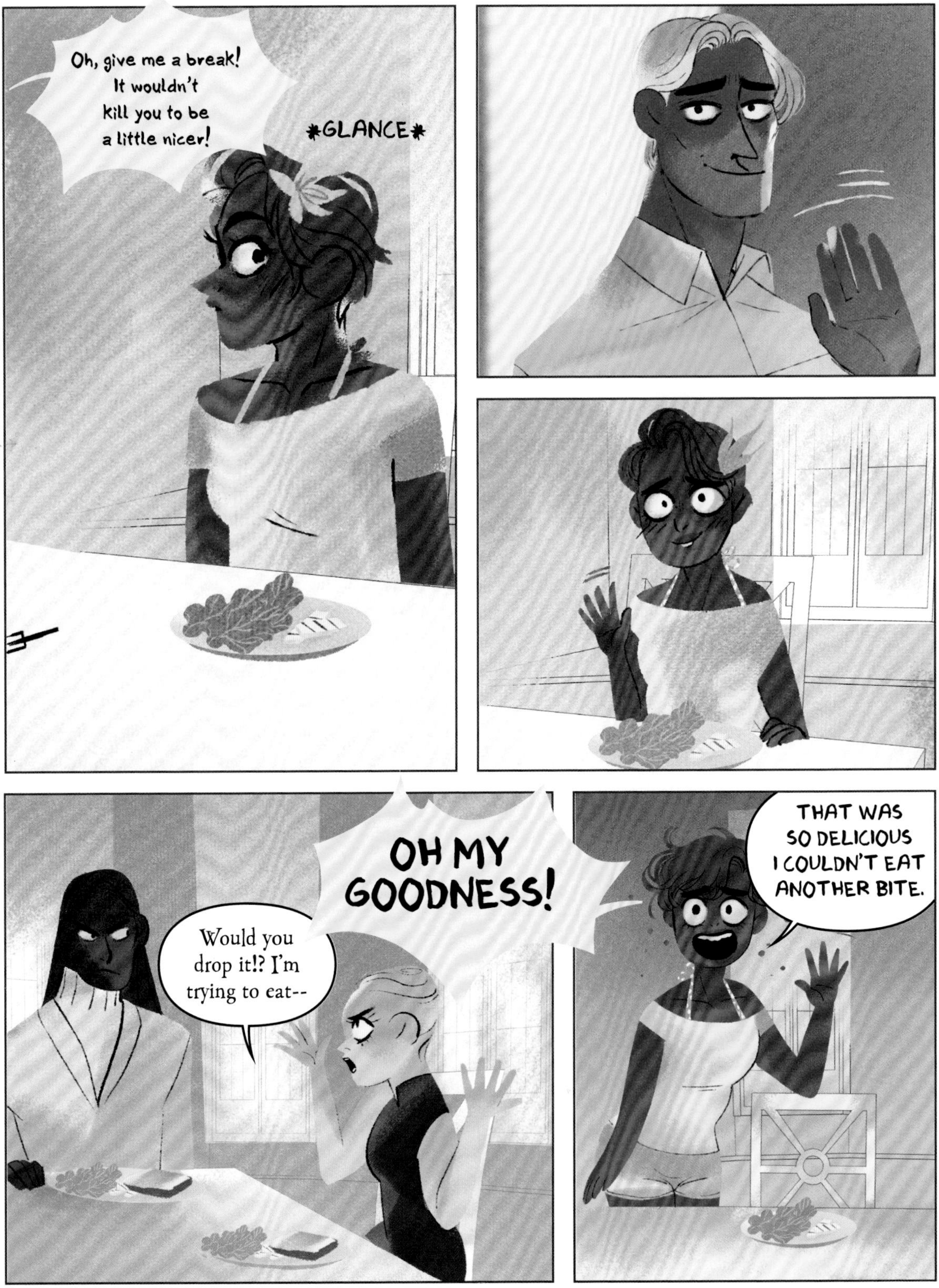
Oh, give me a break! It wouldn't kill you to be a little nicer!
GLANCE
Would you drop it!? I'm trying to eat--
OH MY GOODNESS!
THAT WAS SO DELICIOUS I COULDN'T EAT ANOTHER BITE.

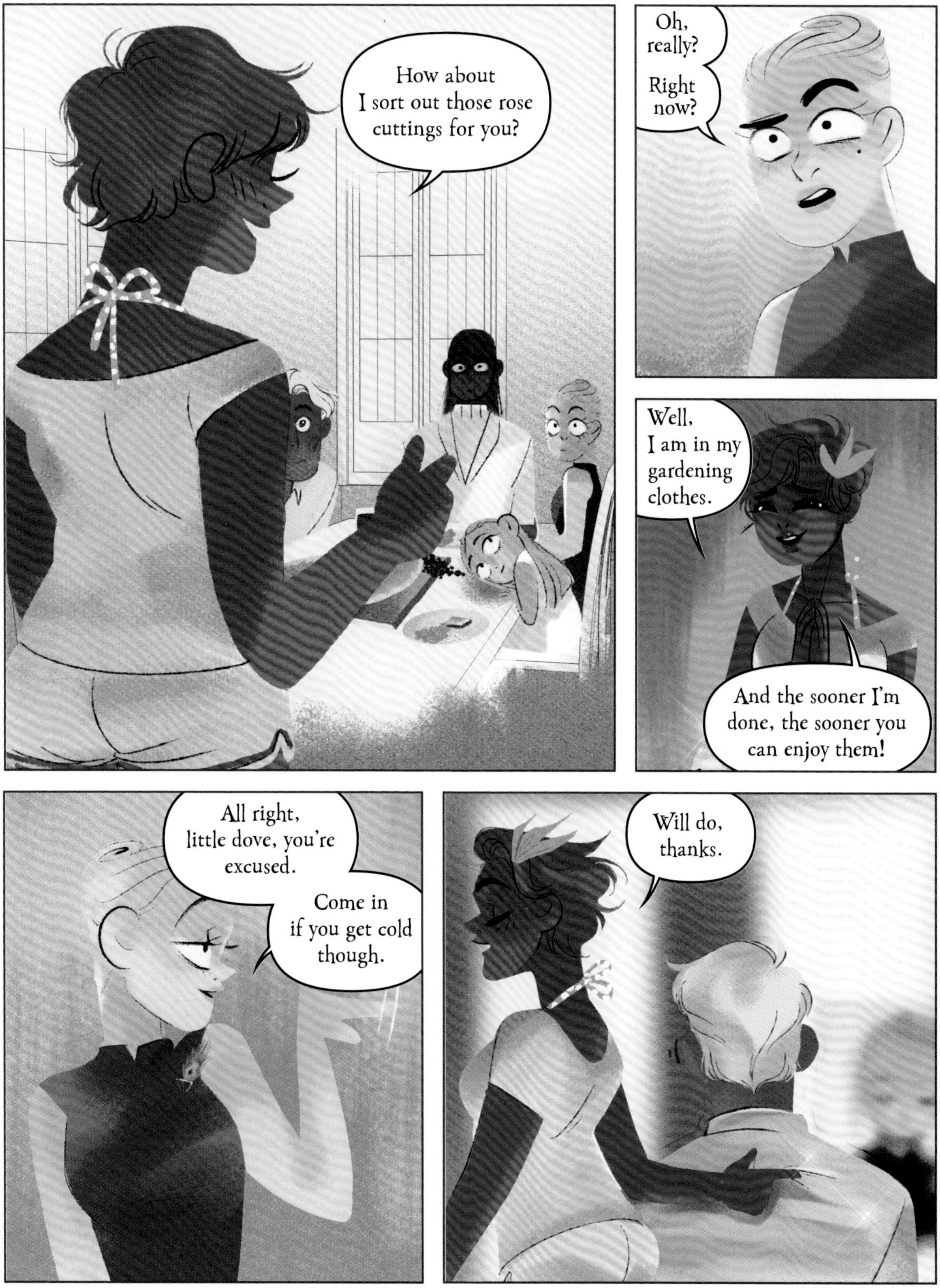
How about I sort out those rose cuttings for you?
Oh, really?
Right now?
Well, I am in my gardening clothes.
And the sooner I'm done, the sooner you can enjoy them!
All right, little dove, you're excused.
Come in if you get cold though.
Will do, thanks.

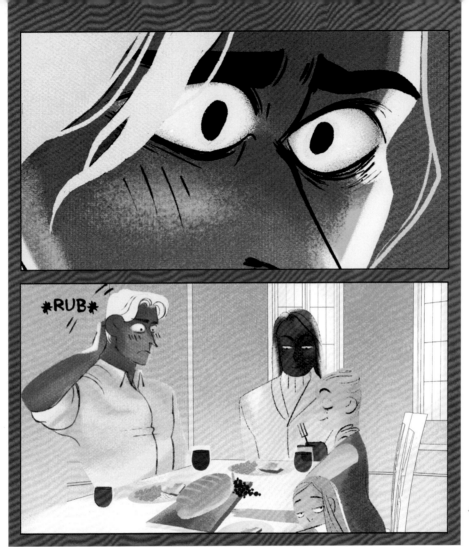

RUB

I-I'm just going to take a call o-outside.

Be careful. Grass stains are a nightmare to remove.

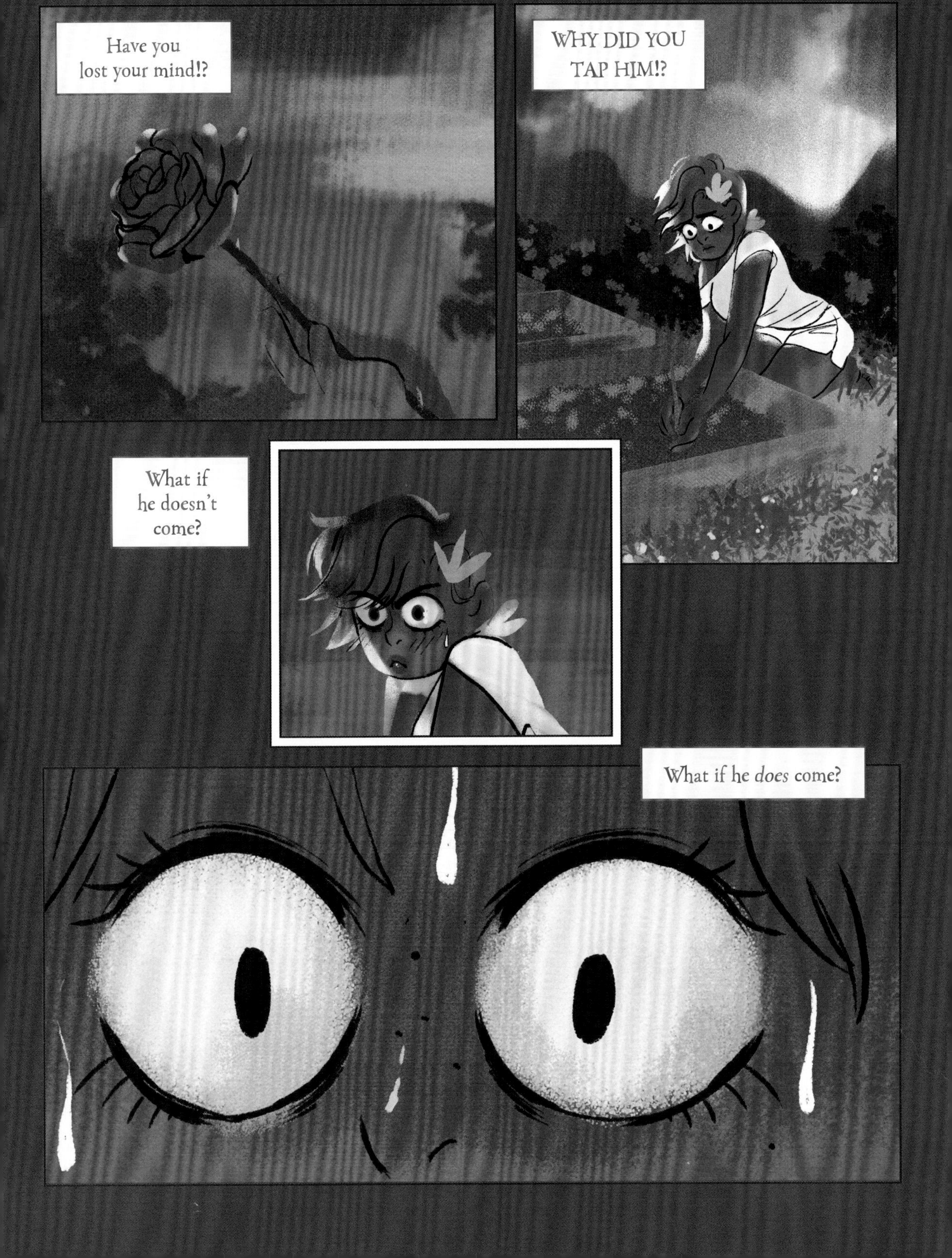

Have you lost your mind!?
WHY DID YOU TAP HIM!?
What if he doesn't come?
What if he *does* come?

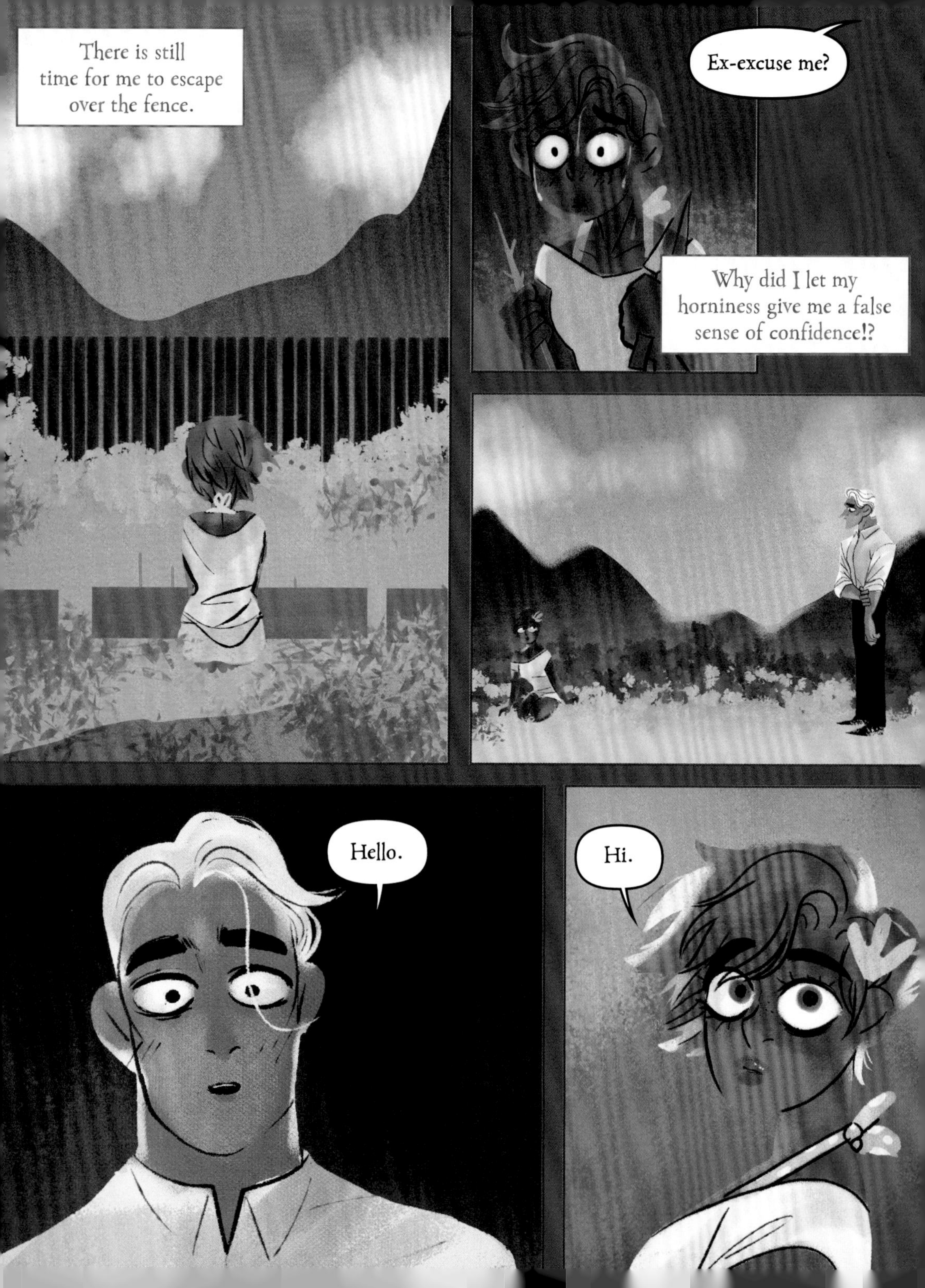
There is still time for me to escape over the fence.
Ex-excuse me?
Why did I let my horniness give me a false sense of confidence!?
Hello.
Hi.

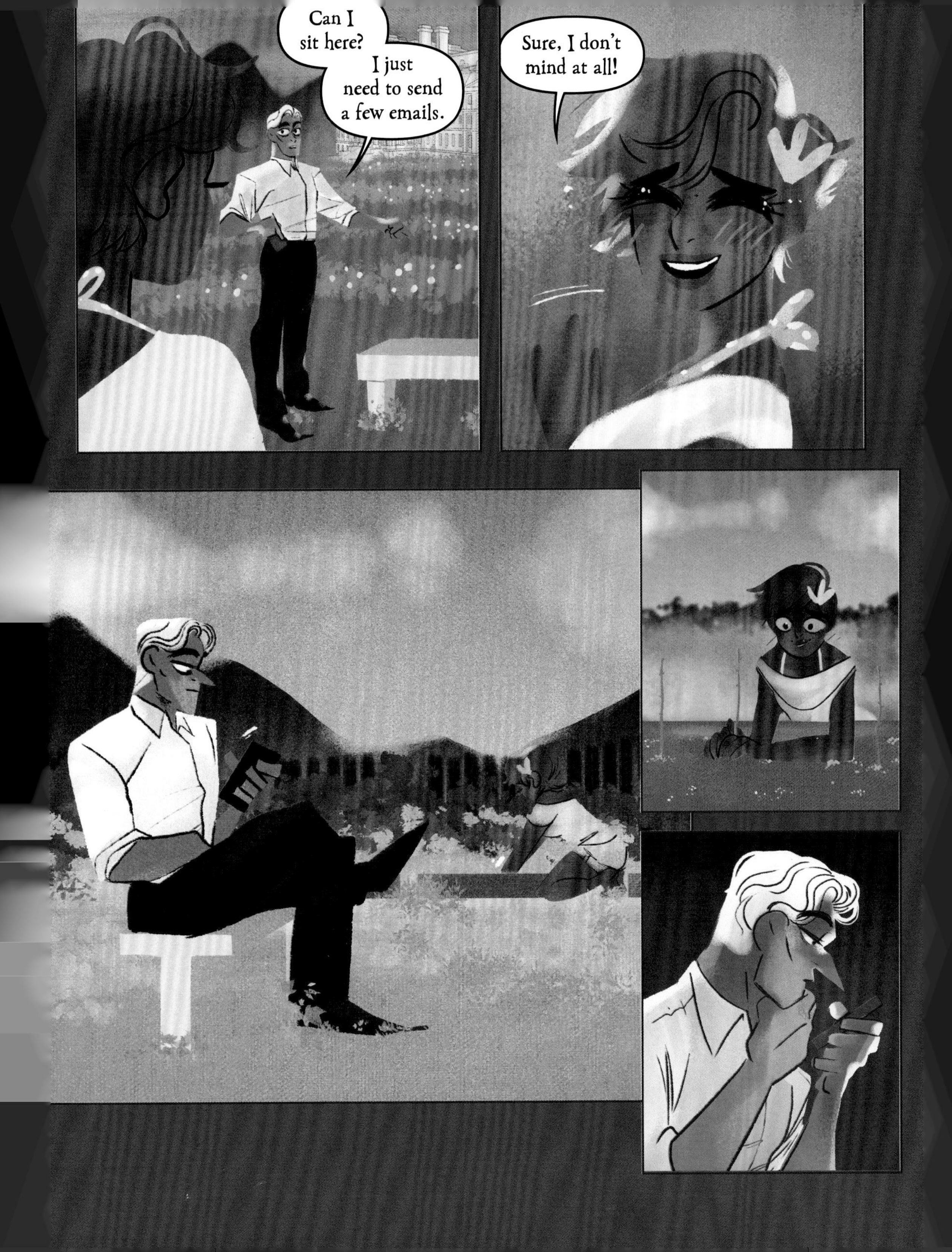
Can I sit here?
I just need to send a few emails.
Sure, I don't mind at all!

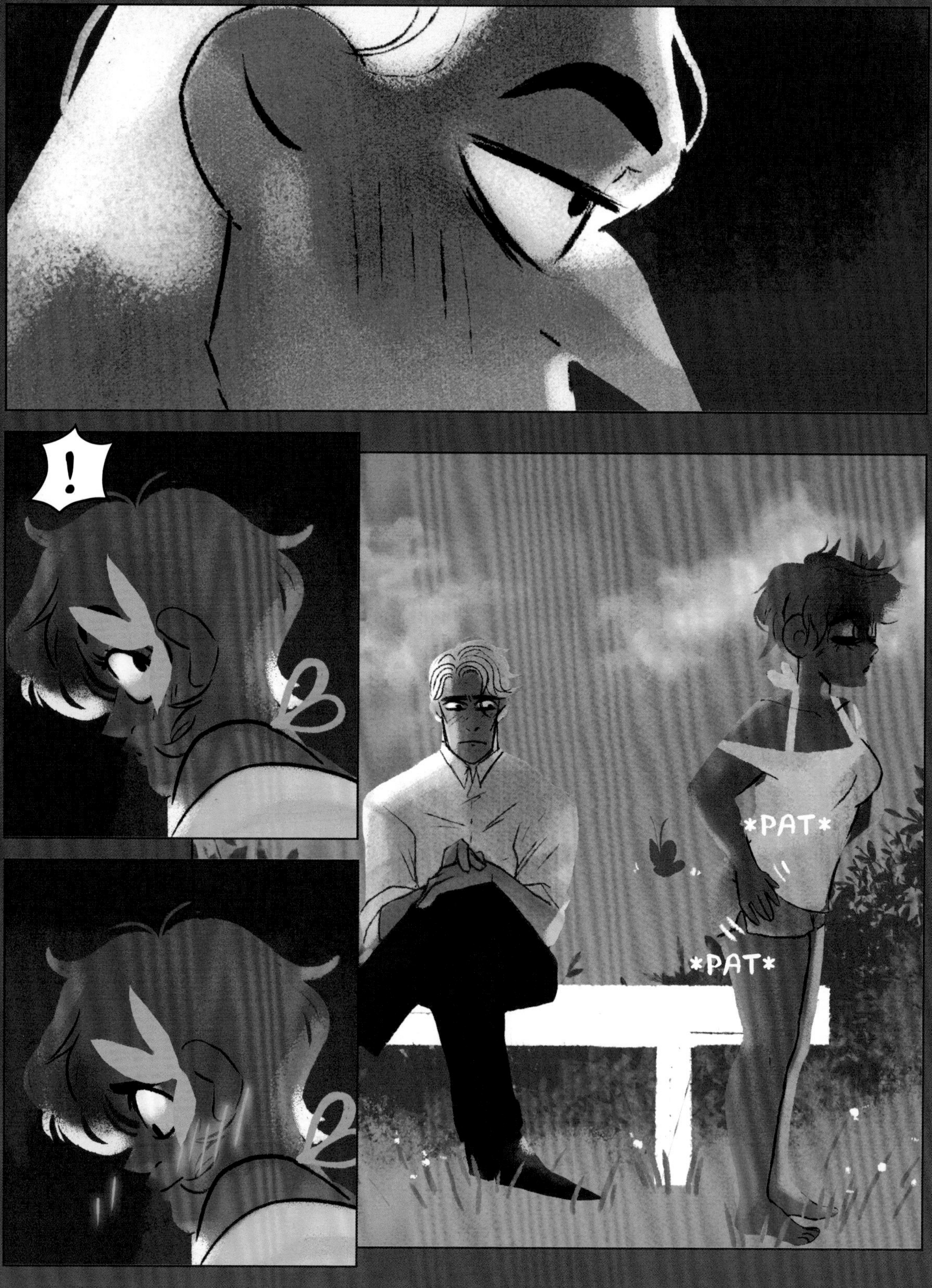
!
PAT
PAT

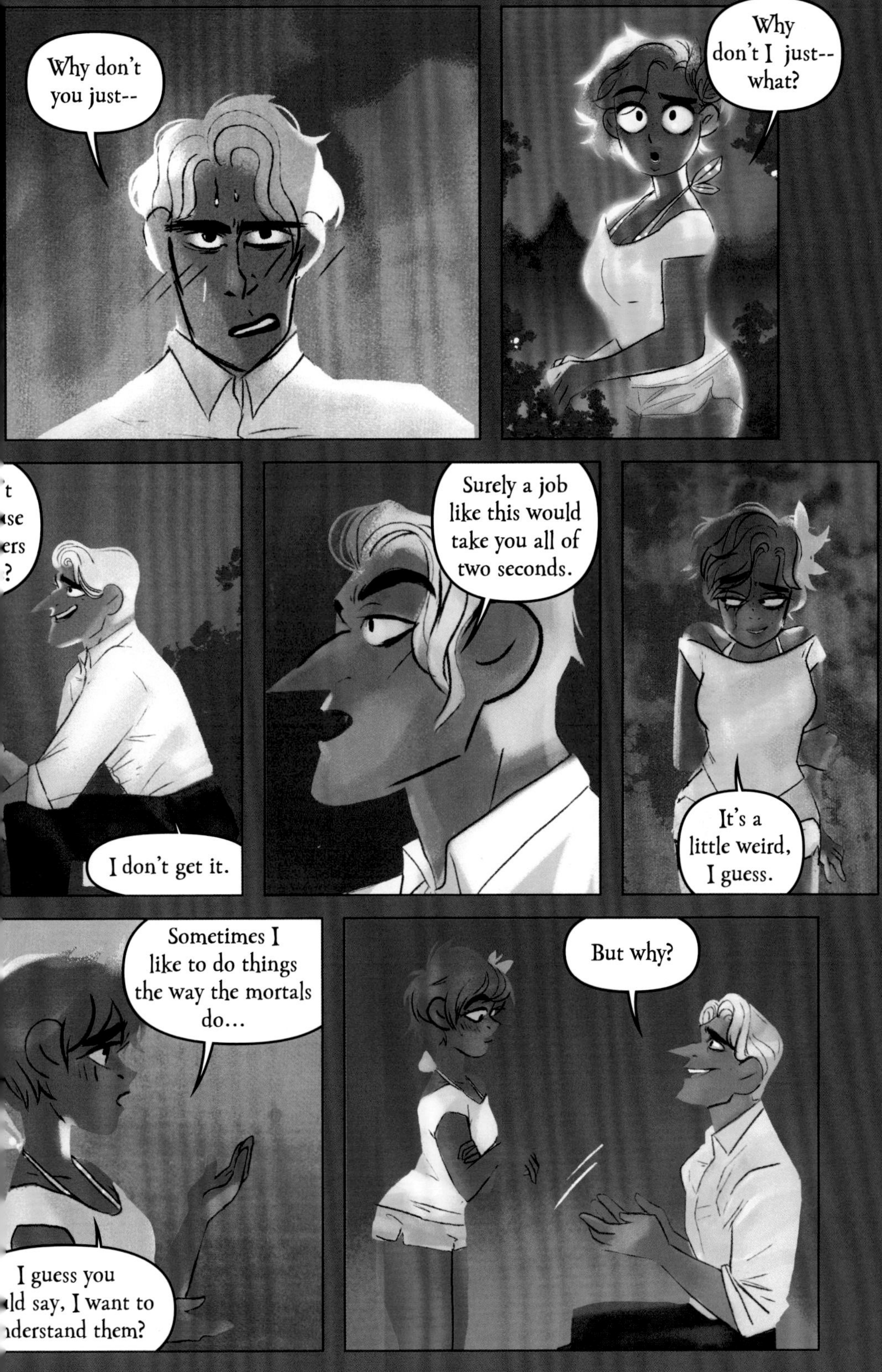
Why don't you just--
Why don't I just-- what?
I don't get it.
Surely a job like this would take you all of two seconds.
It's a little weird, I guess.
Sometimes I like to do things the way the mortals do...
I guess you ld say, I want to nderstand them?
But why?

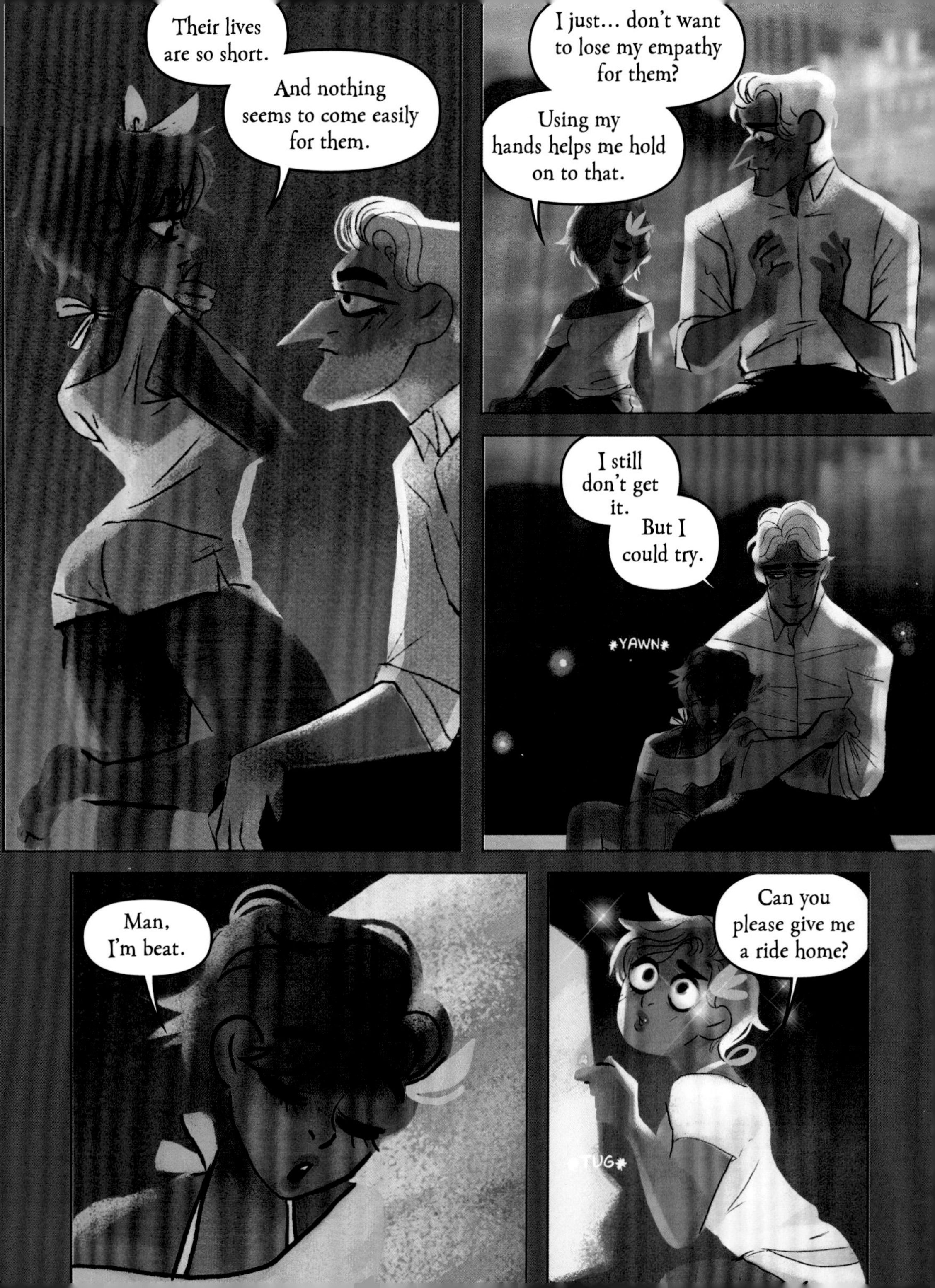
Their lives are so short.
And nothing seems to come easily for them.
I just… don't want to lose my empathy for them?
Using my hands helps me hold on to that.
I still don't get it.
But I could try.
YAWN
Man, I'm beat.
Can you please give me a ride home?
TUG

Can you see them?

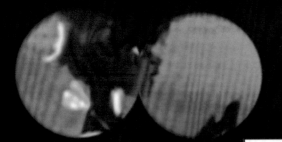

Yeah, almost.
Give me a sec!

What are
they saying?

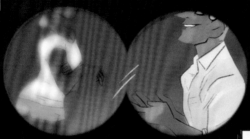

I can't tell.

I thought you
could read lips!

...I never said
I could read lips.

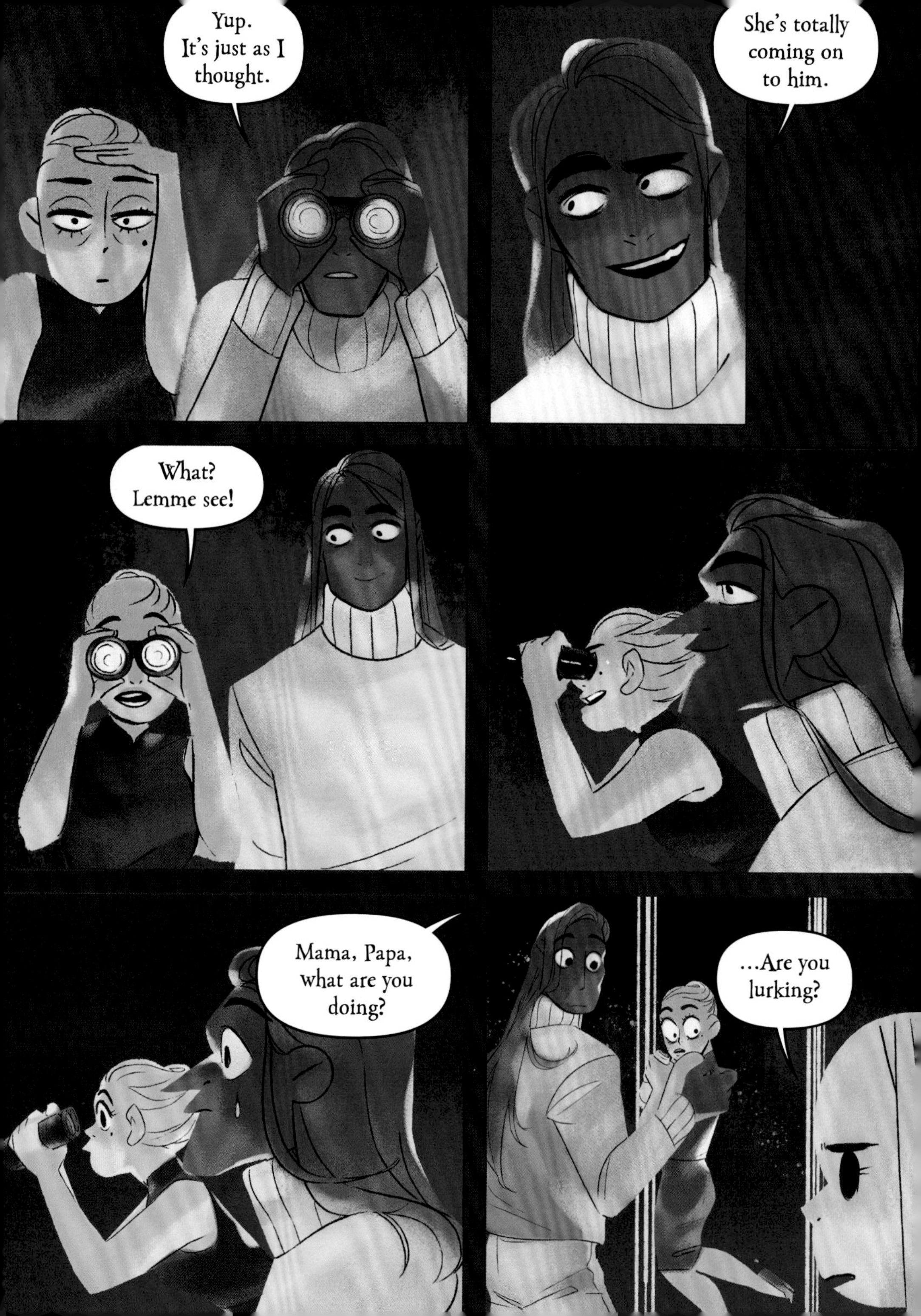
Yup.
It's just as I thought.
She's totally coming on to him.
What?
Lemme see!
Mama, Papa, what are you doing?
...Are you lurking?

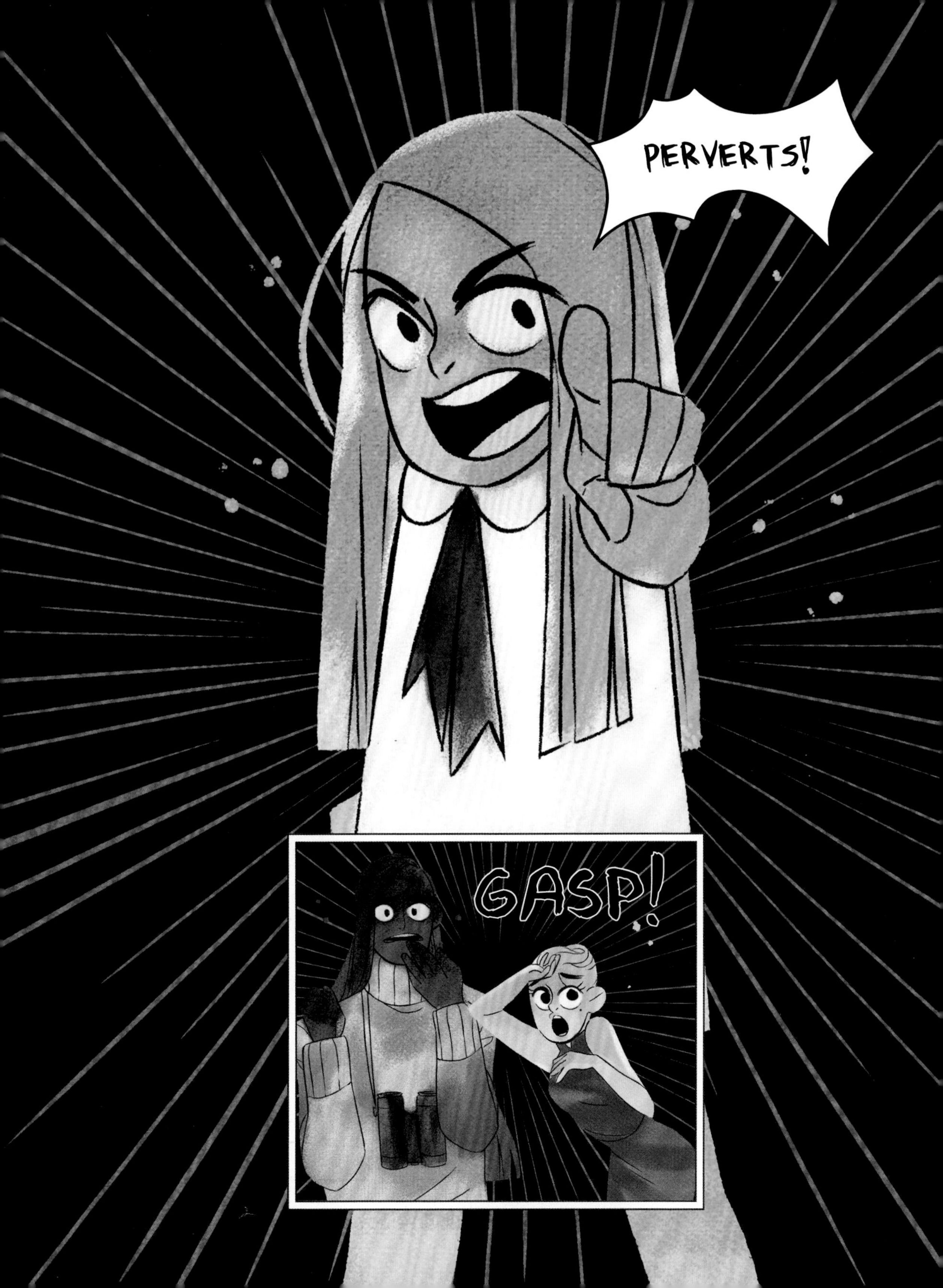
PERVERTS!
GASP!

EPISODE 80: SICILIANA

Are you okay?

Yeah, just tired.

I wasn't expecting the evening to play out like this.

YAWN!

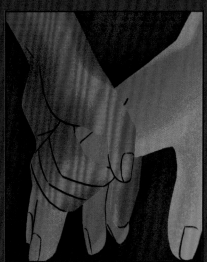

SQUINT

!!

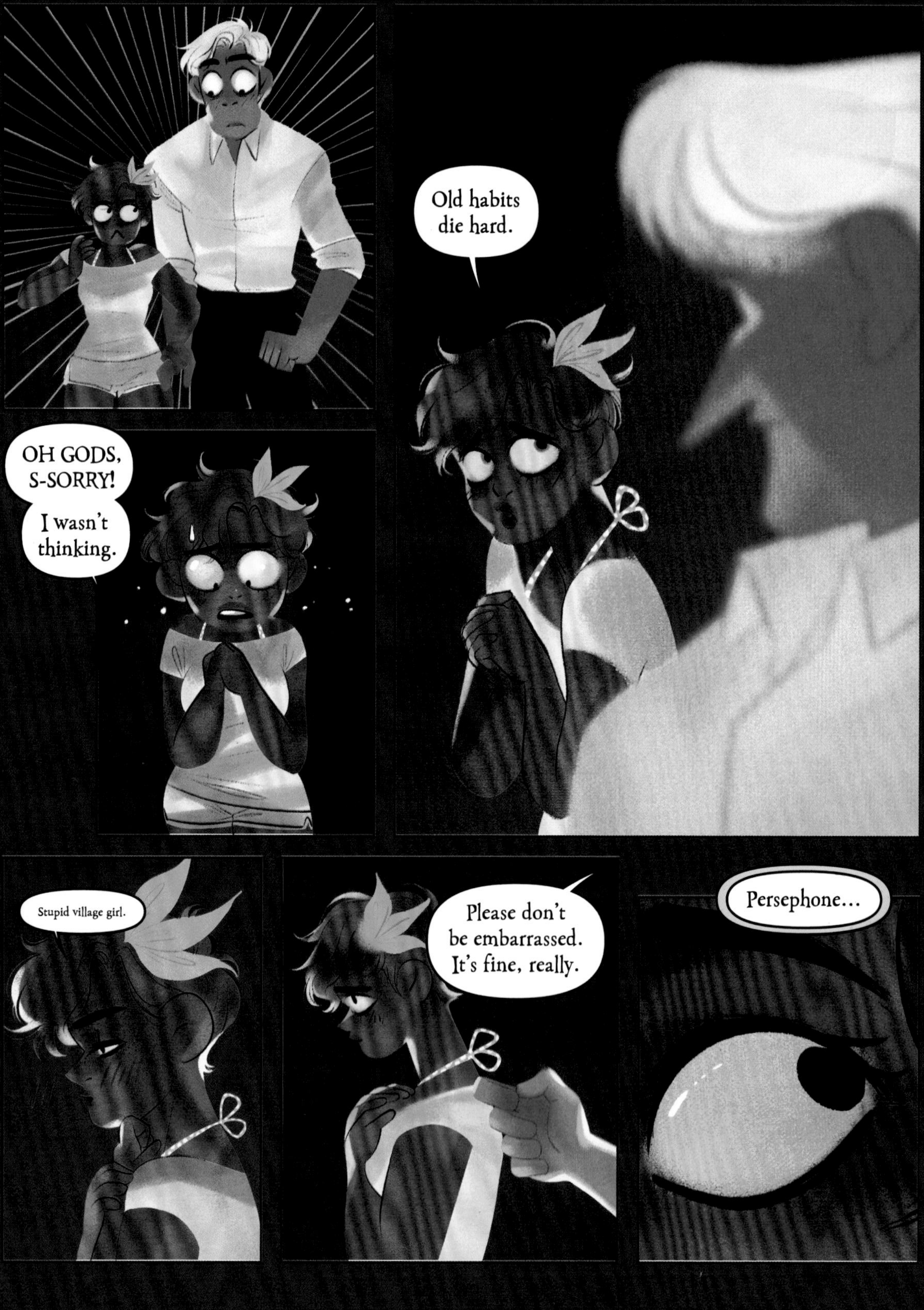
Old habits die hard.
OH GODS, S-SORRY!
I wasn't thinking.
Stupid village girl.
Please don't be embarrassed. It's fine, really.
Persephone...

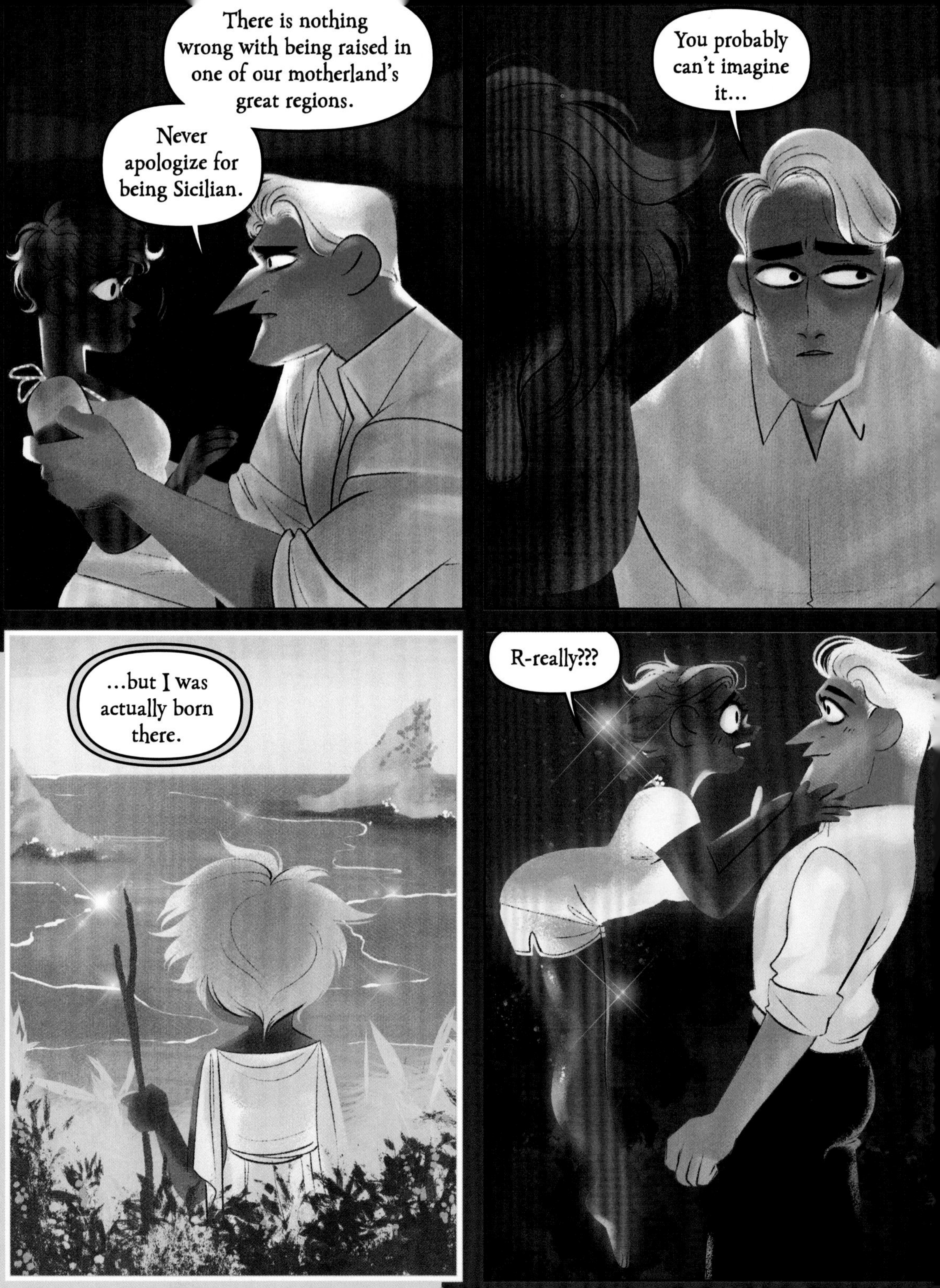
There is nothing wrong with being raised in one of our motherland's great regions.
Never apologize for being Sicilian.
You probably can't imagine it…
…but I was actually born there.
R-really???

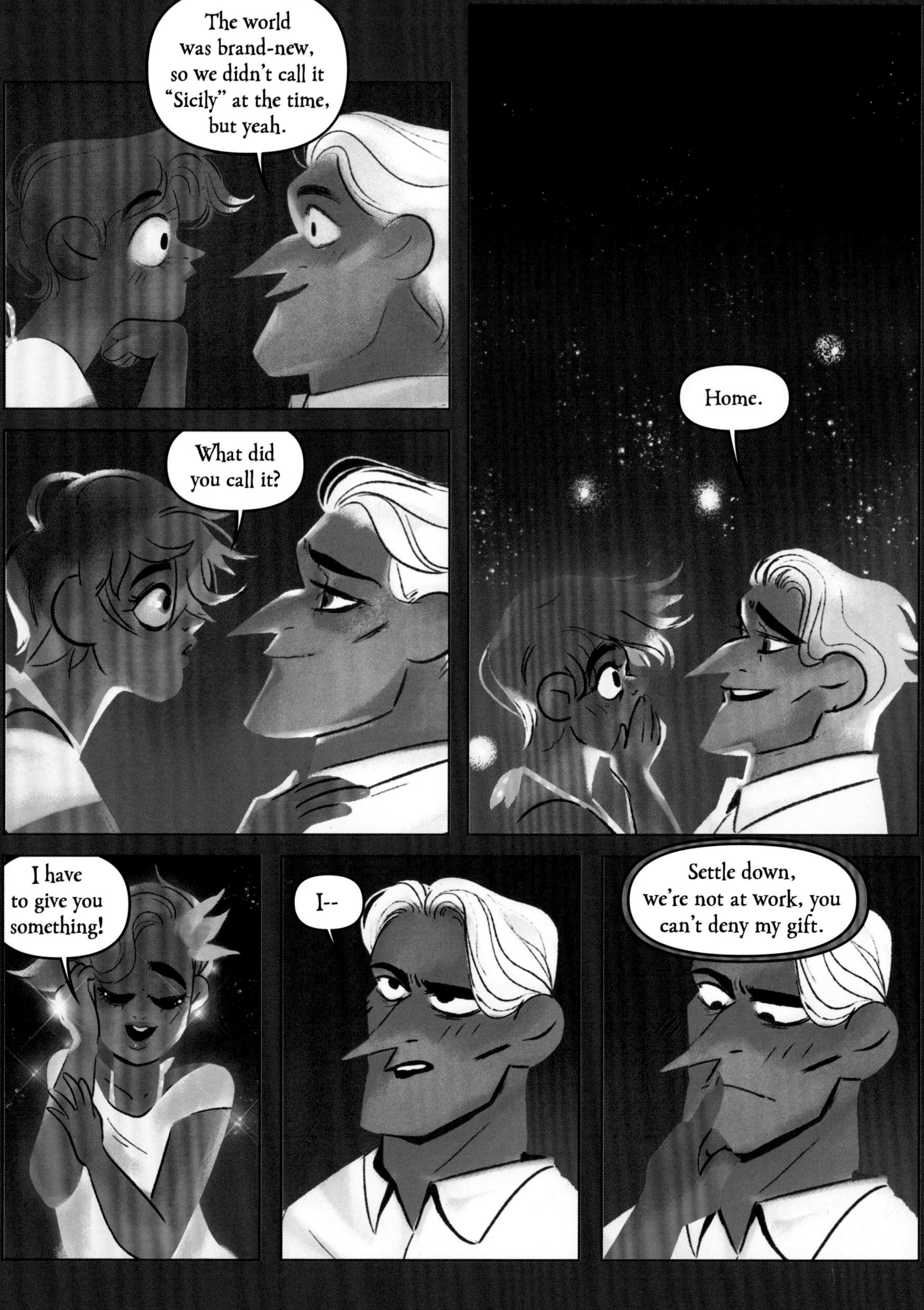
The world was brand-new, so we didn't call it "Sicily" at the time, but yeah.
What did you call it?
Home.
I have to give you something!
I--
Settle down, we're not at work, you can't deny my gift.

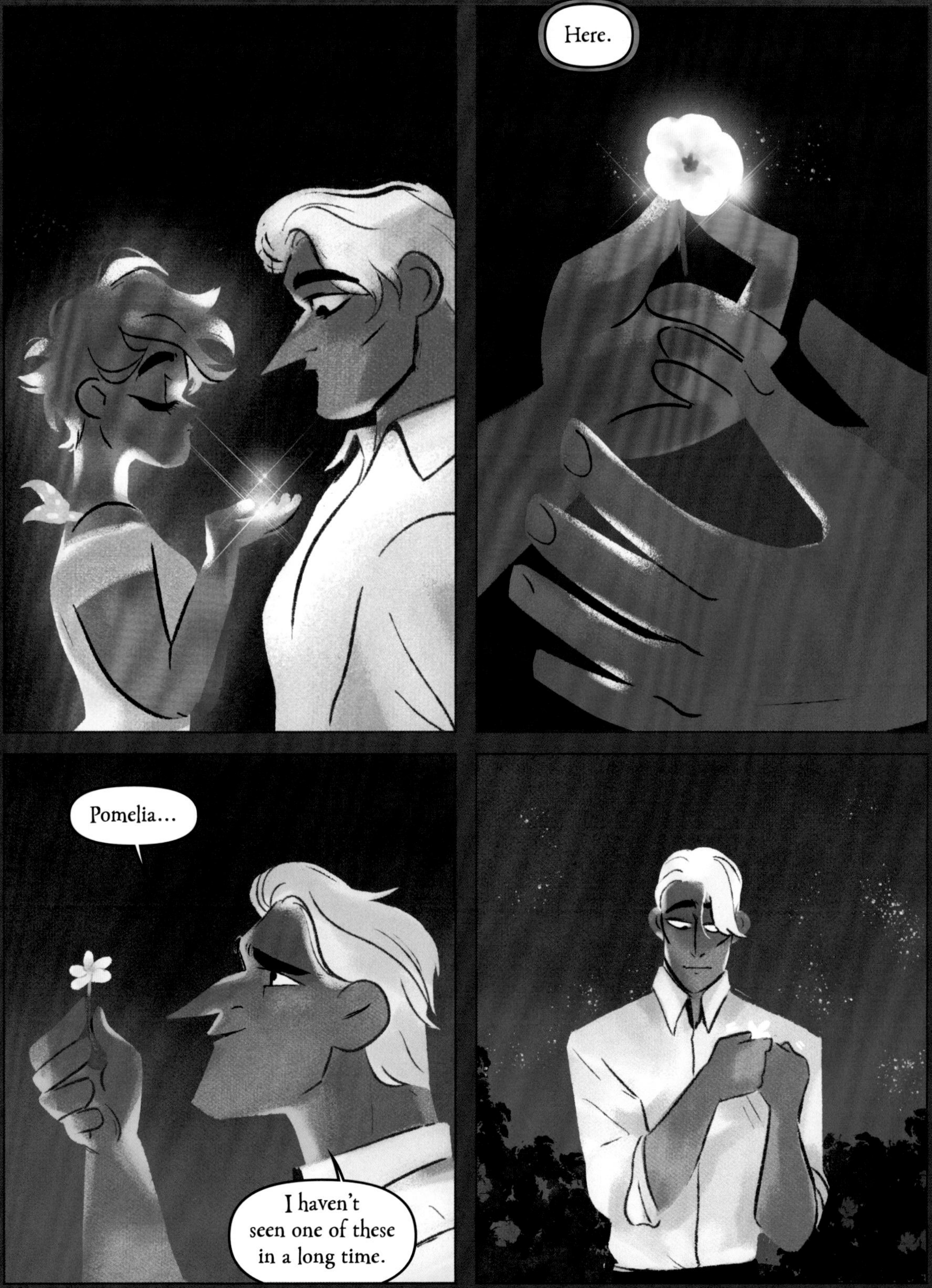
Here.
Pomelia...
I haven't seen one of these in a long time.

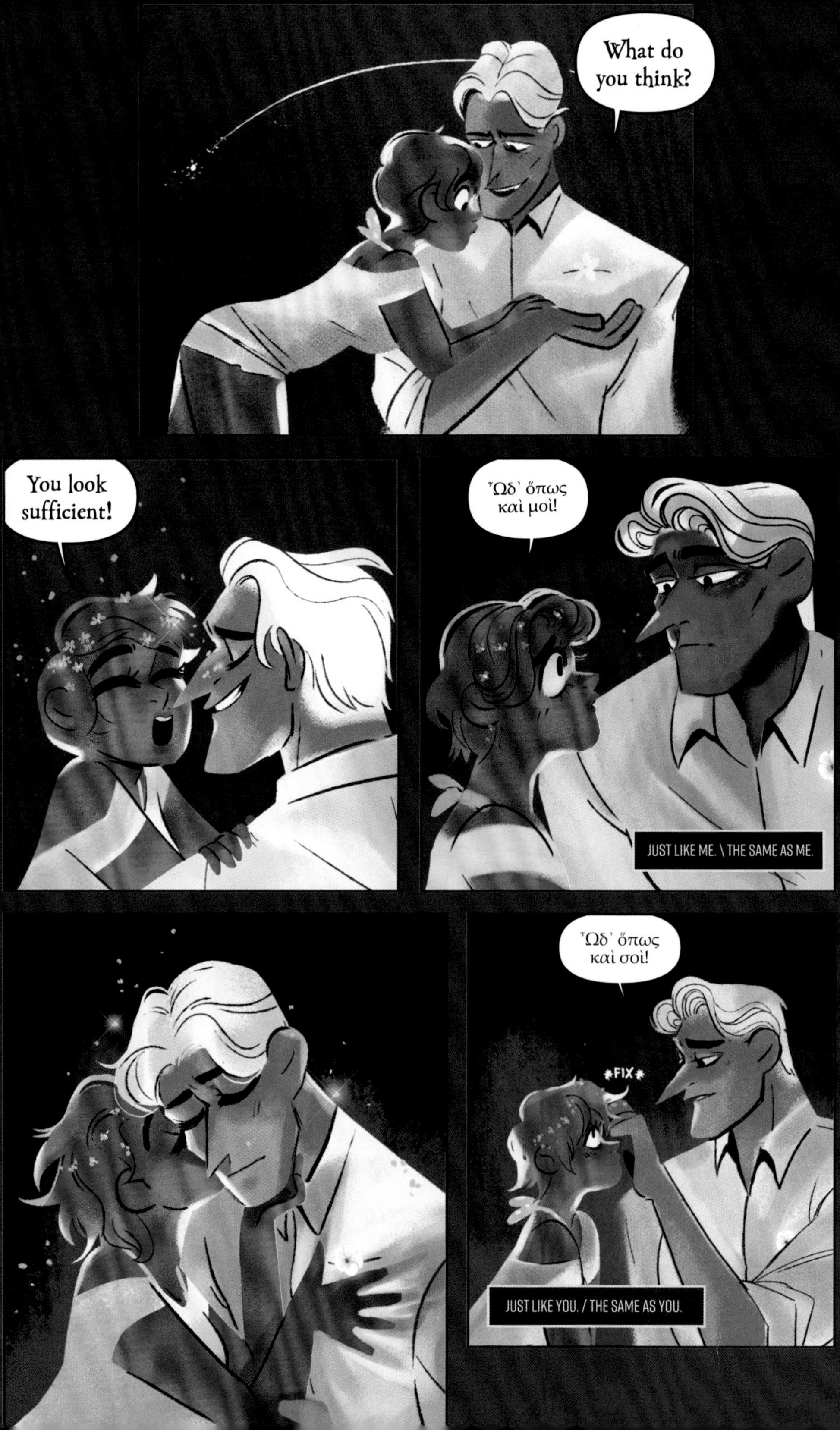
What do you think?
You look sufficient!
Ὧδ᾽ ὅπως καὶ μοί!
JUST LIKE ME. \ THE SAME AS ME.
Ὧδ᾽ ὅπως καὶ σοί!
FIX
JUST LIKE YOU. / THE SAME AS YOU.

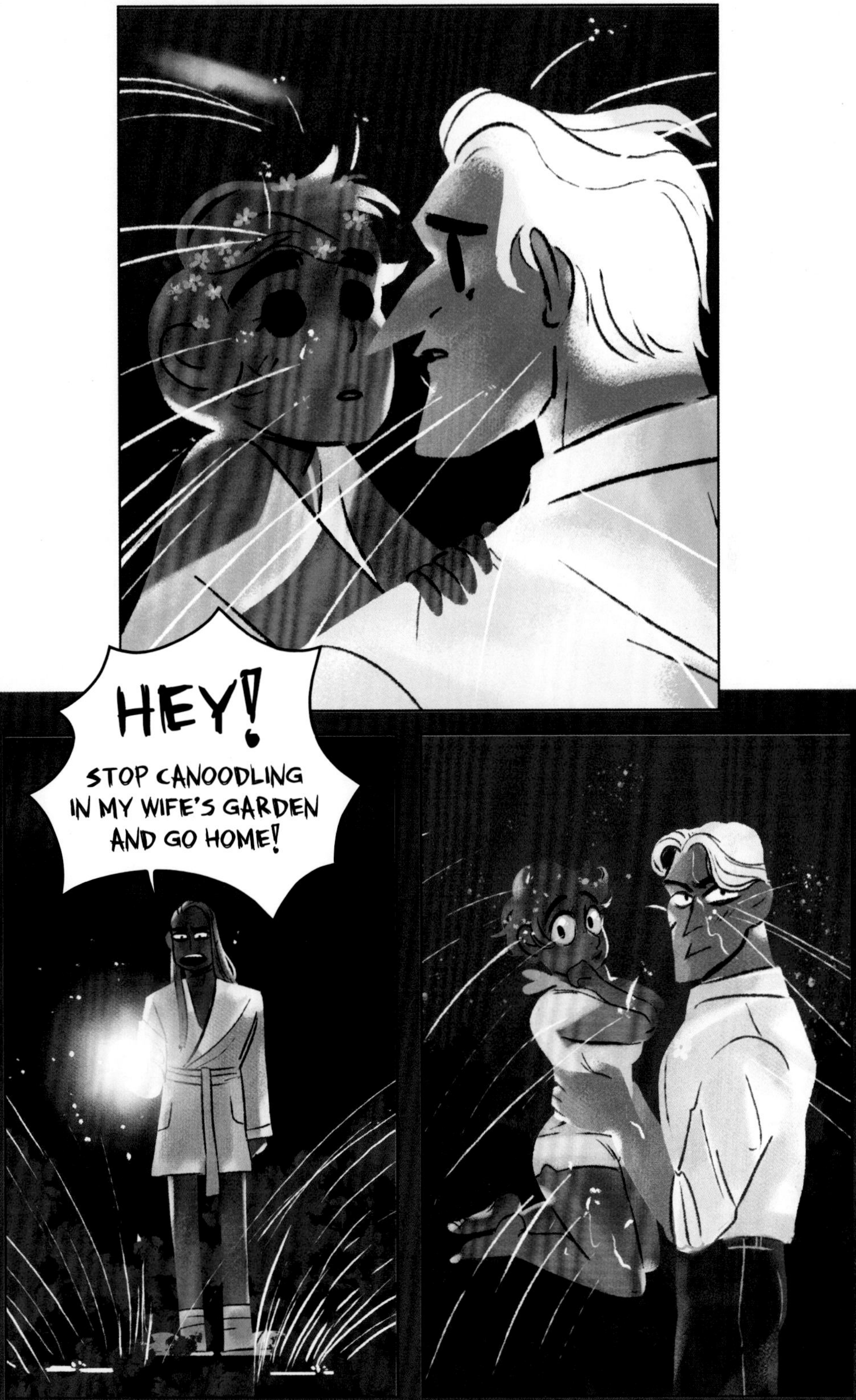
HEY!
STOP CANOODLING IN MY WIFE'S GARDEN AND GO HOME!

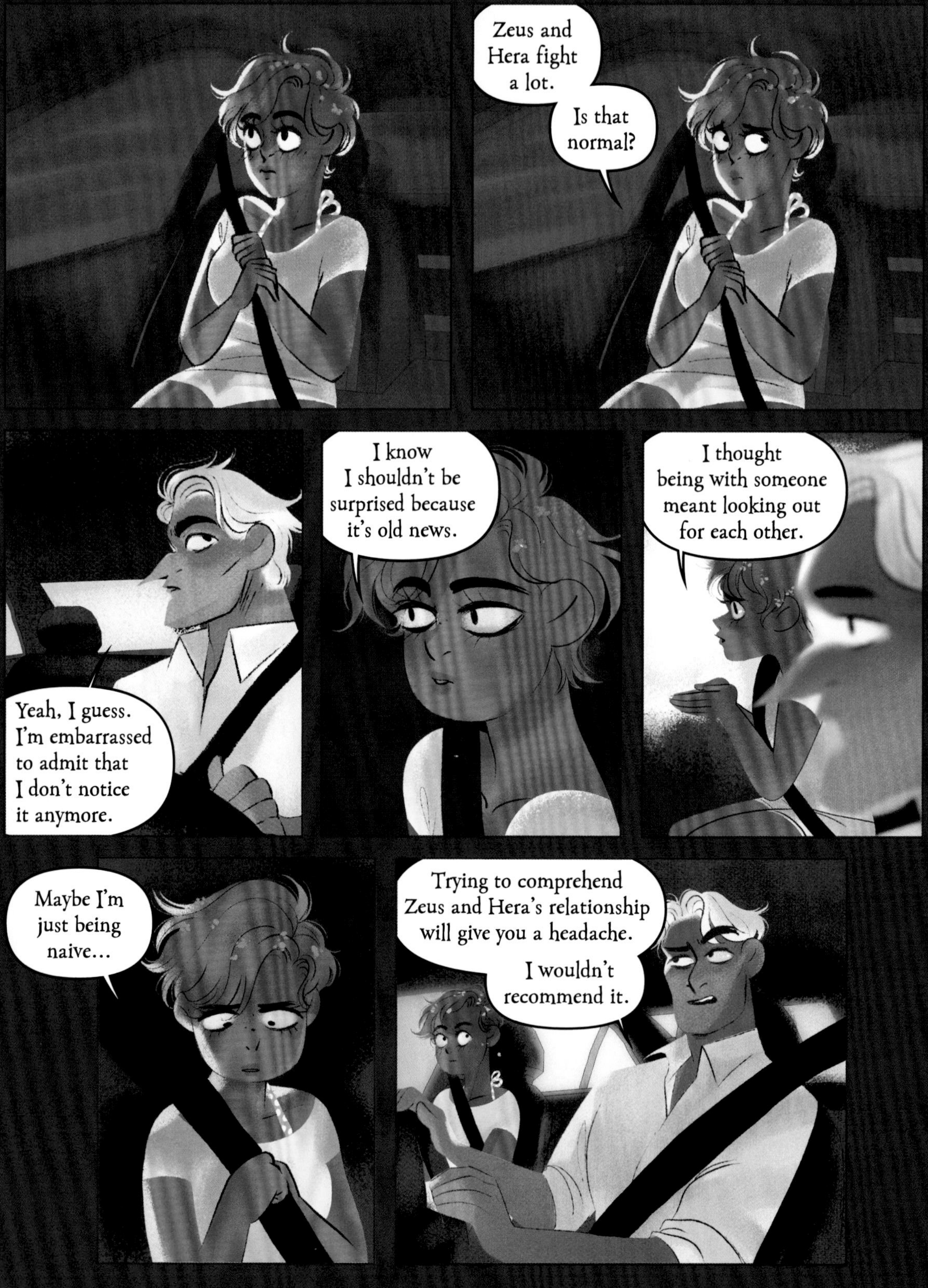
Zeus and Hera fight a lot.
Is that normal?
Yeah, I guess. I'm embarrassed to admit that I don't notice it anymore.
I know I shouldn't be surprised because it's old news.
I thought being with someone meant looking out for each other.
Maybe I'm just being naive...
Trying to comprehend Zeus and Hera's relationship will give you a headache.
I wouldn't recommend it.

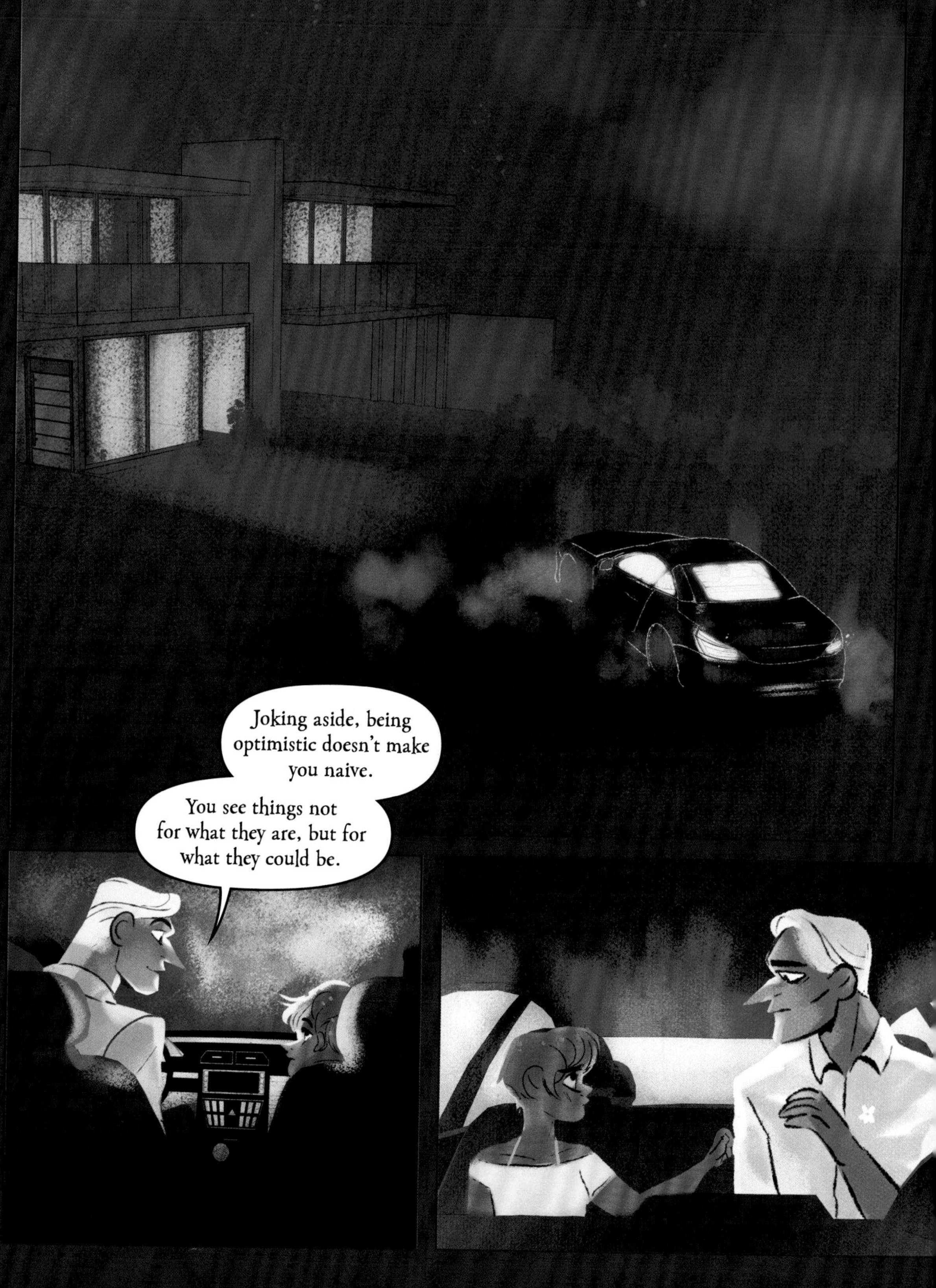
Joking aside, being optimistic doesn't make you naive.
You see things not for what they are, but for what they could be.

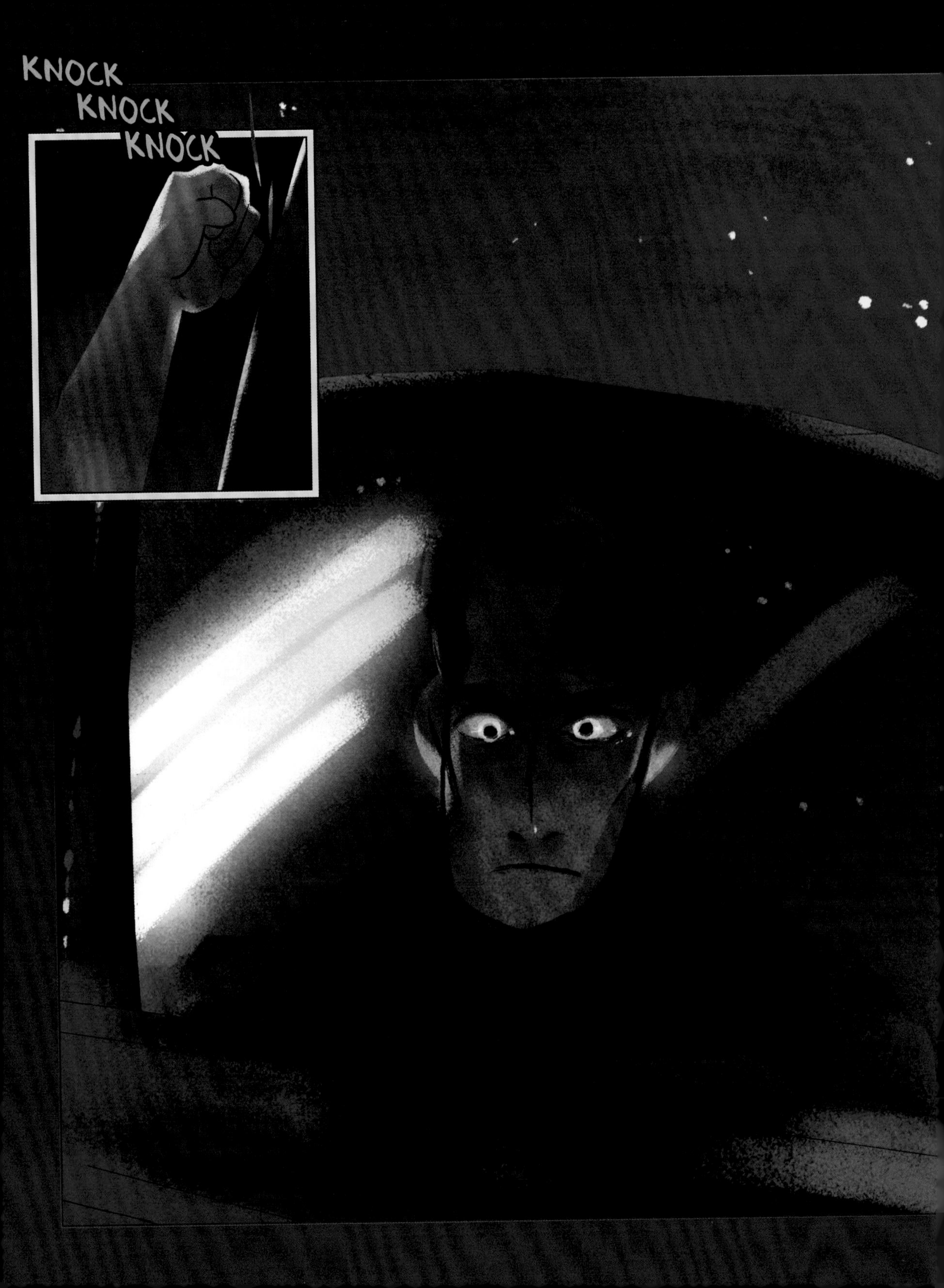
KNOCK
KNOCK
KNOCK

EPISODE 81: TAKE

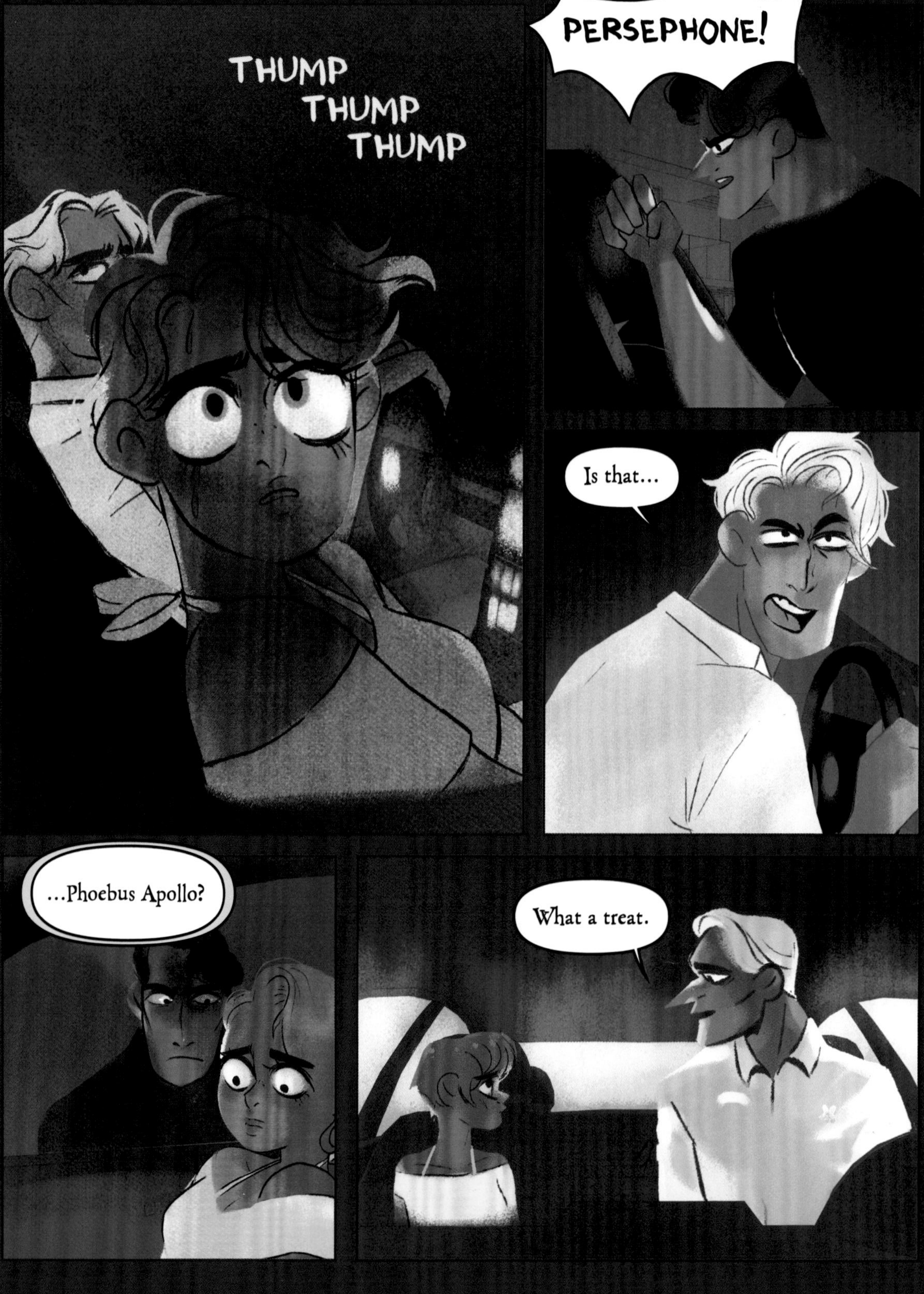
THUMP
THUMP
THUMP
PERSEPHONE!
Is that...
...Phoebus Apollo?
What a treat.

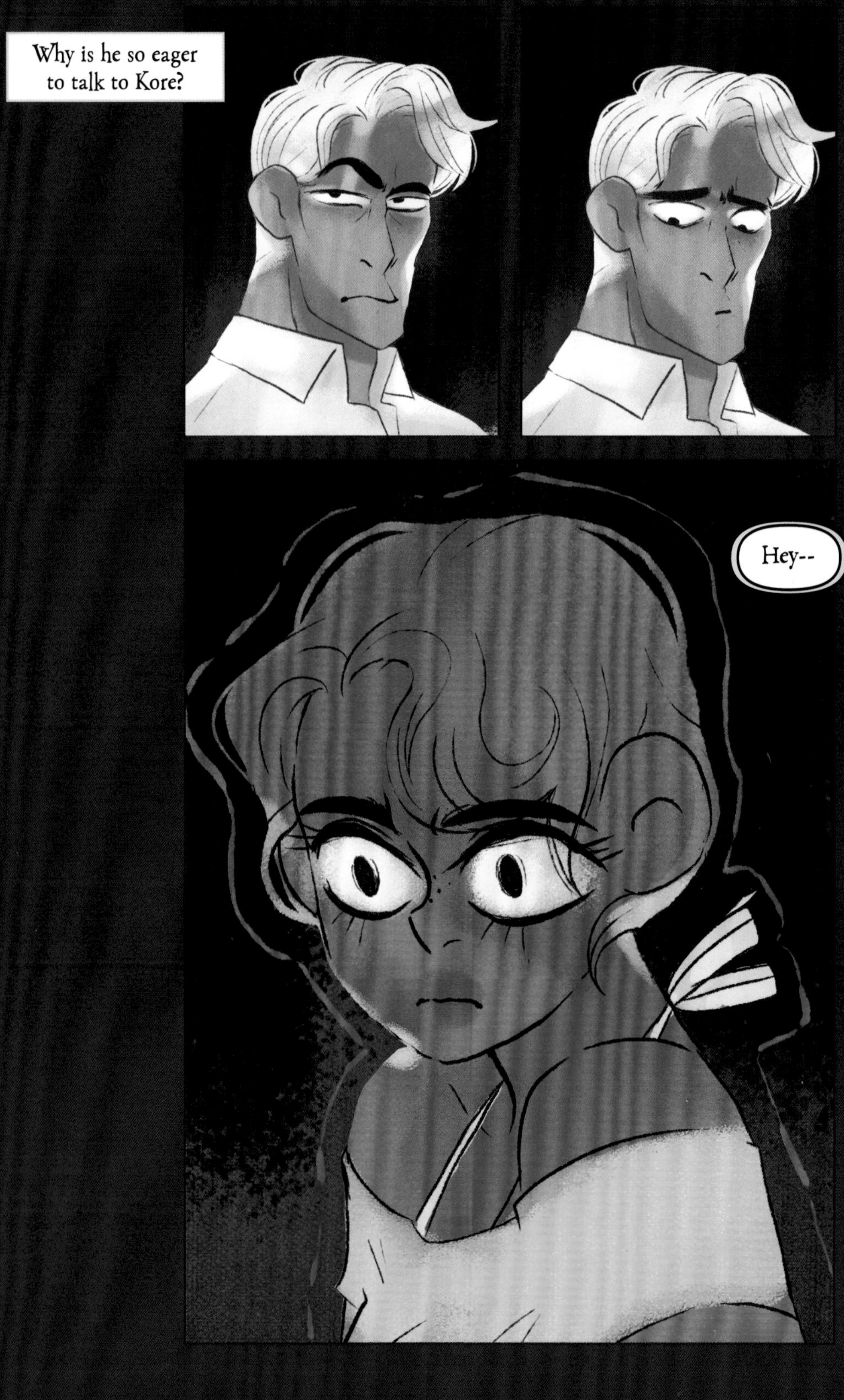
Why is he so eager to talk to Kore?
Hey--

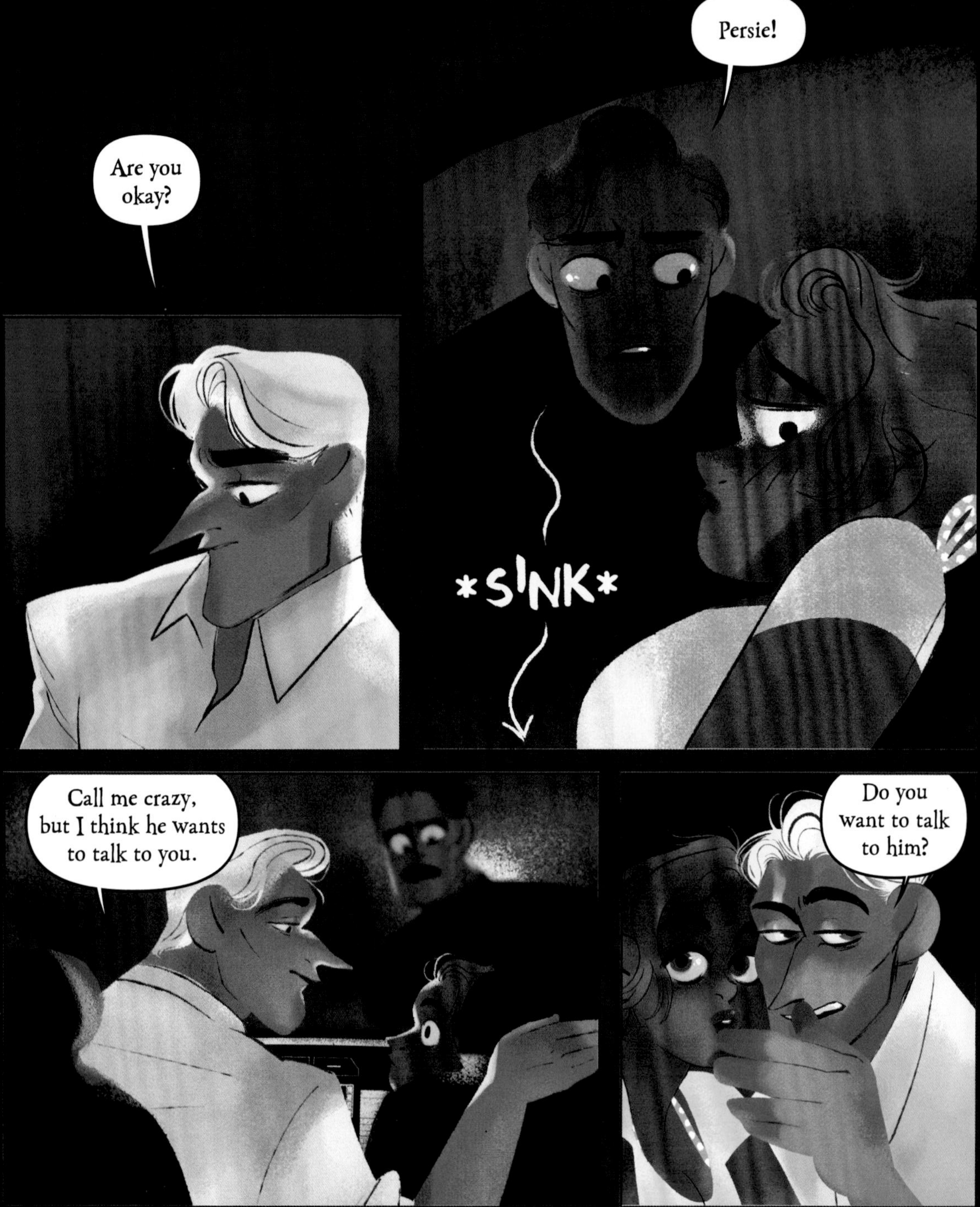
Are you okay?
Persie!
SINK
Call me crazy, but I think he wants to talk to you.
Do you want to talk to him?

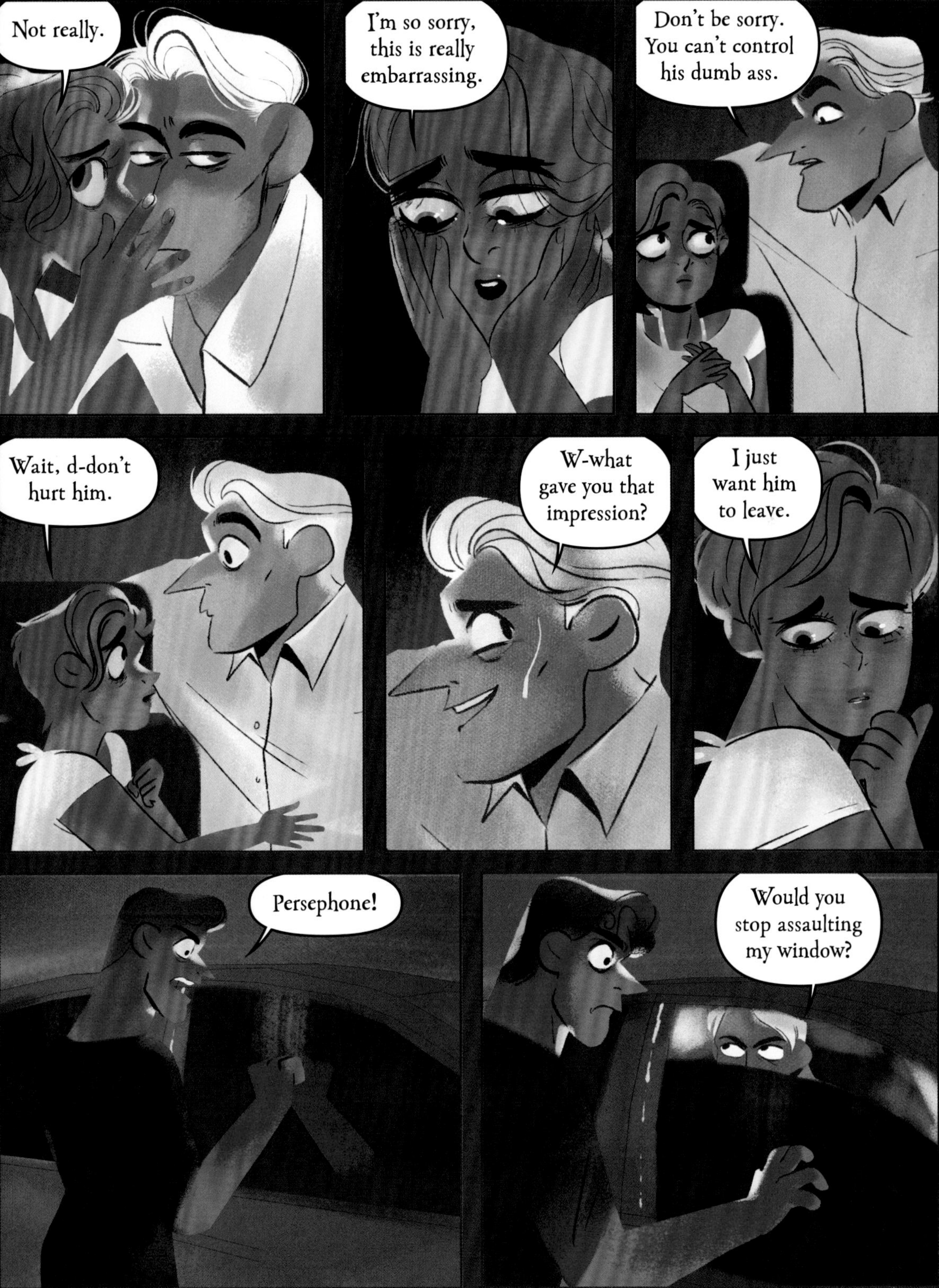
Not really.
I'm so sorry, this is really embarrassing.
Don't be sorry. You can't control his dumb ass.
Wait, d-don't hurt him.
W-what gave you that impression?
I just want him to leave.
Persephone!
Would you stop assaulting my window?

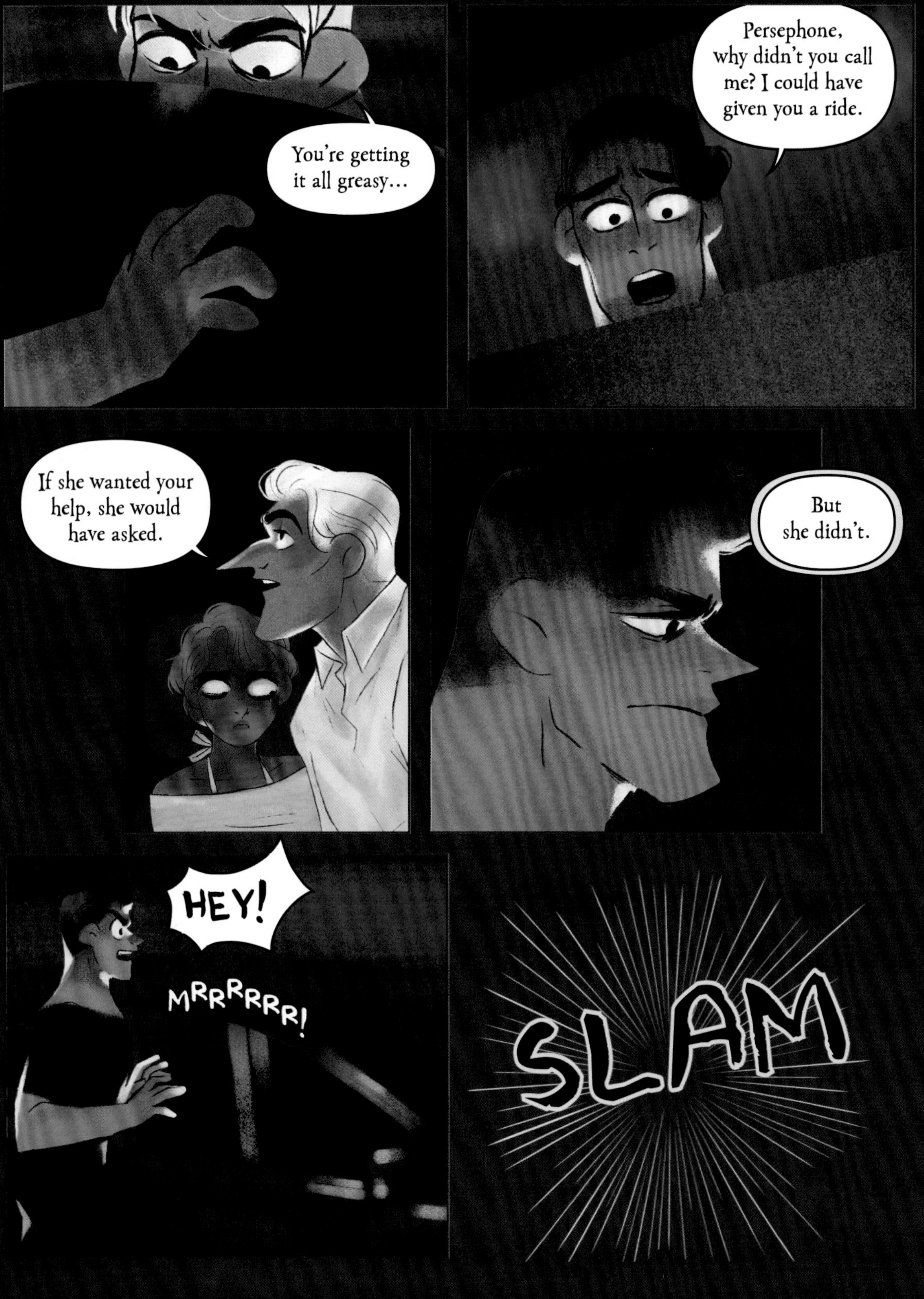
You're getting it all greasy…
Persephone, why didn't you call me? I could have given you a ride.
If she wanted your help, she would have asked.
But she didn't.
HEY!
MRRRRRRR!
SLAM

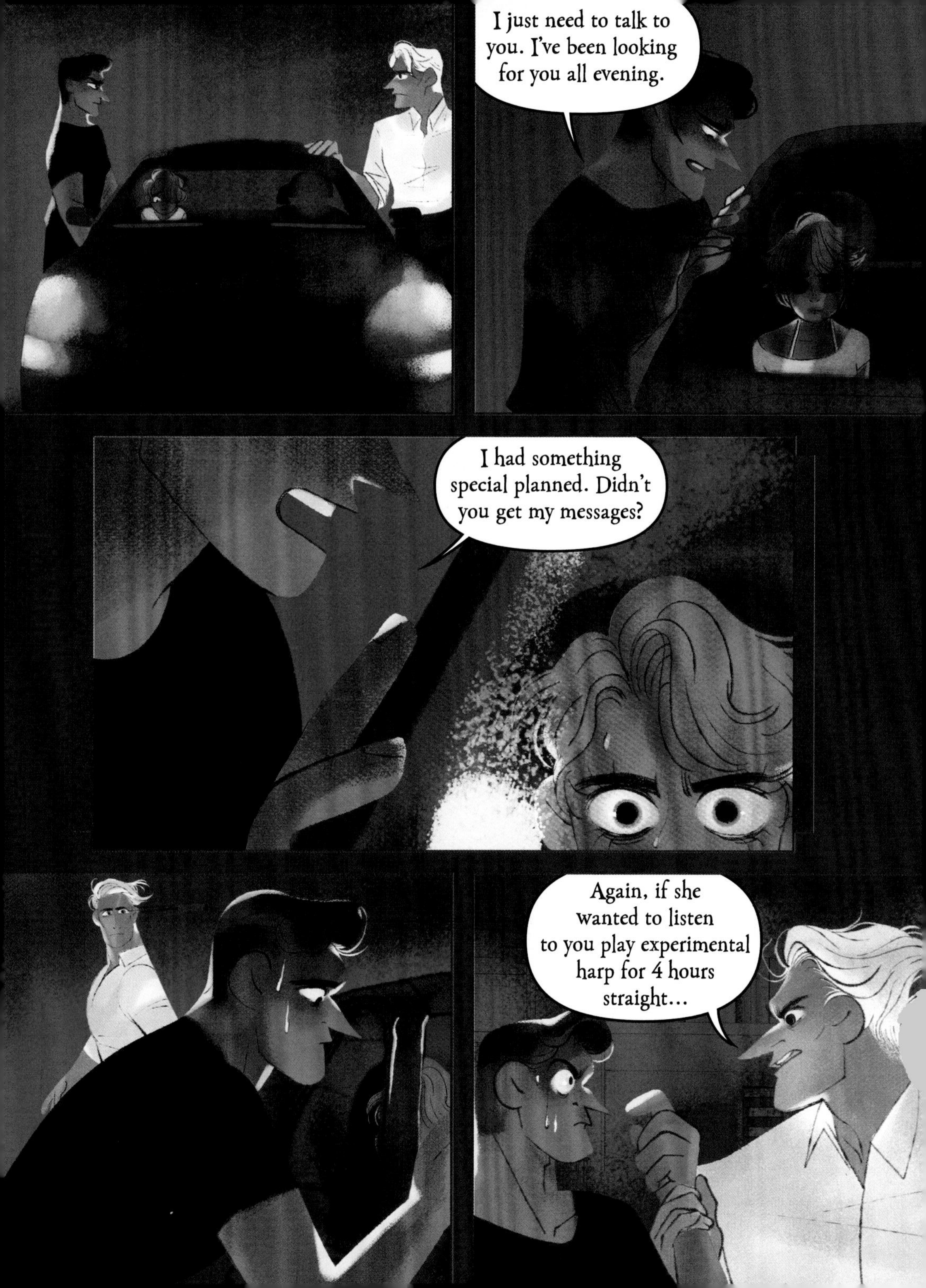
I just need to talk to you. I've been looking for you all evening.
I had something special planned. Didn't you get my messages?
Again, if she wanted to listen to you play experimental harp for 4 hours straight...

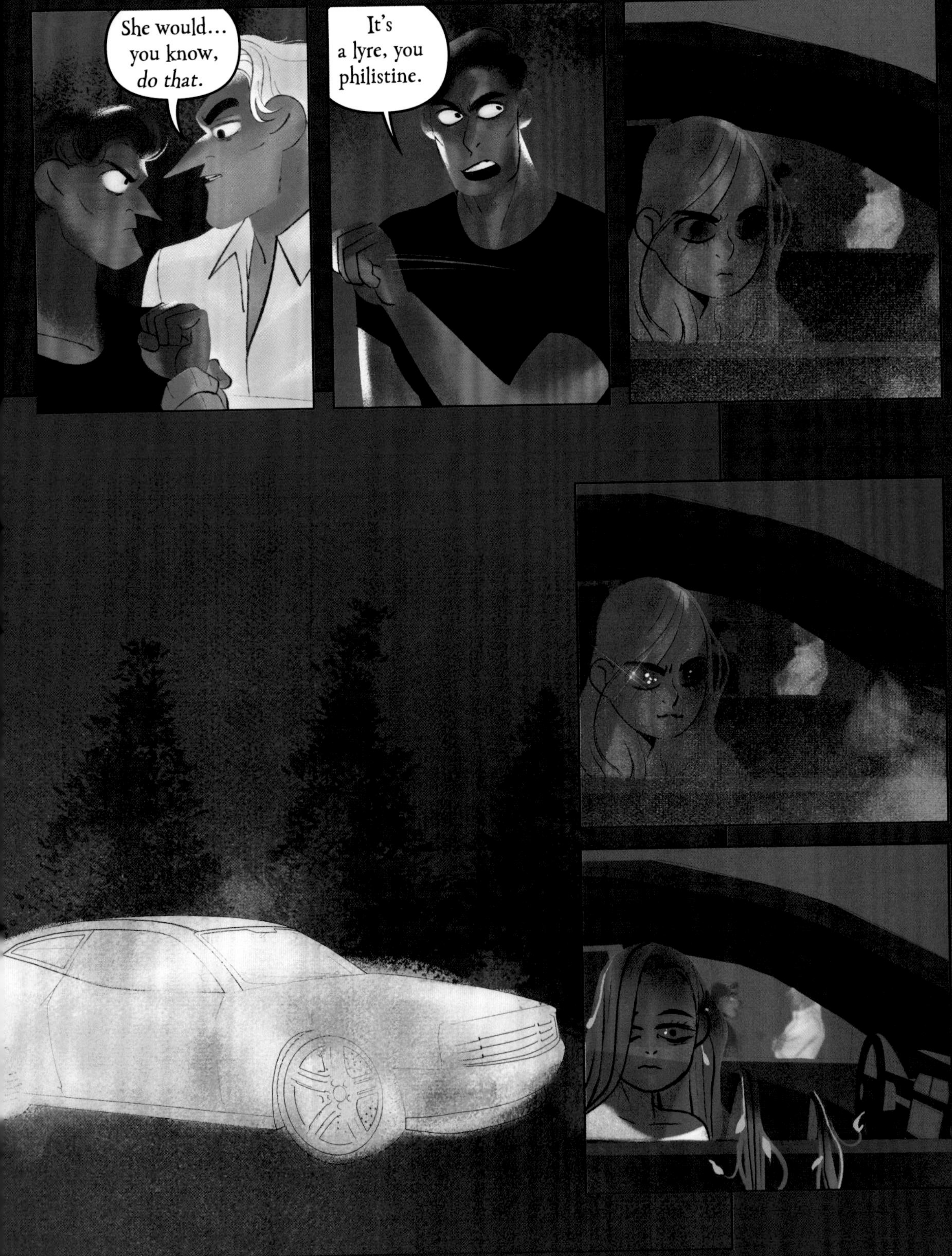
She would… you know, *do that*.
It's a lyre, you philistine.

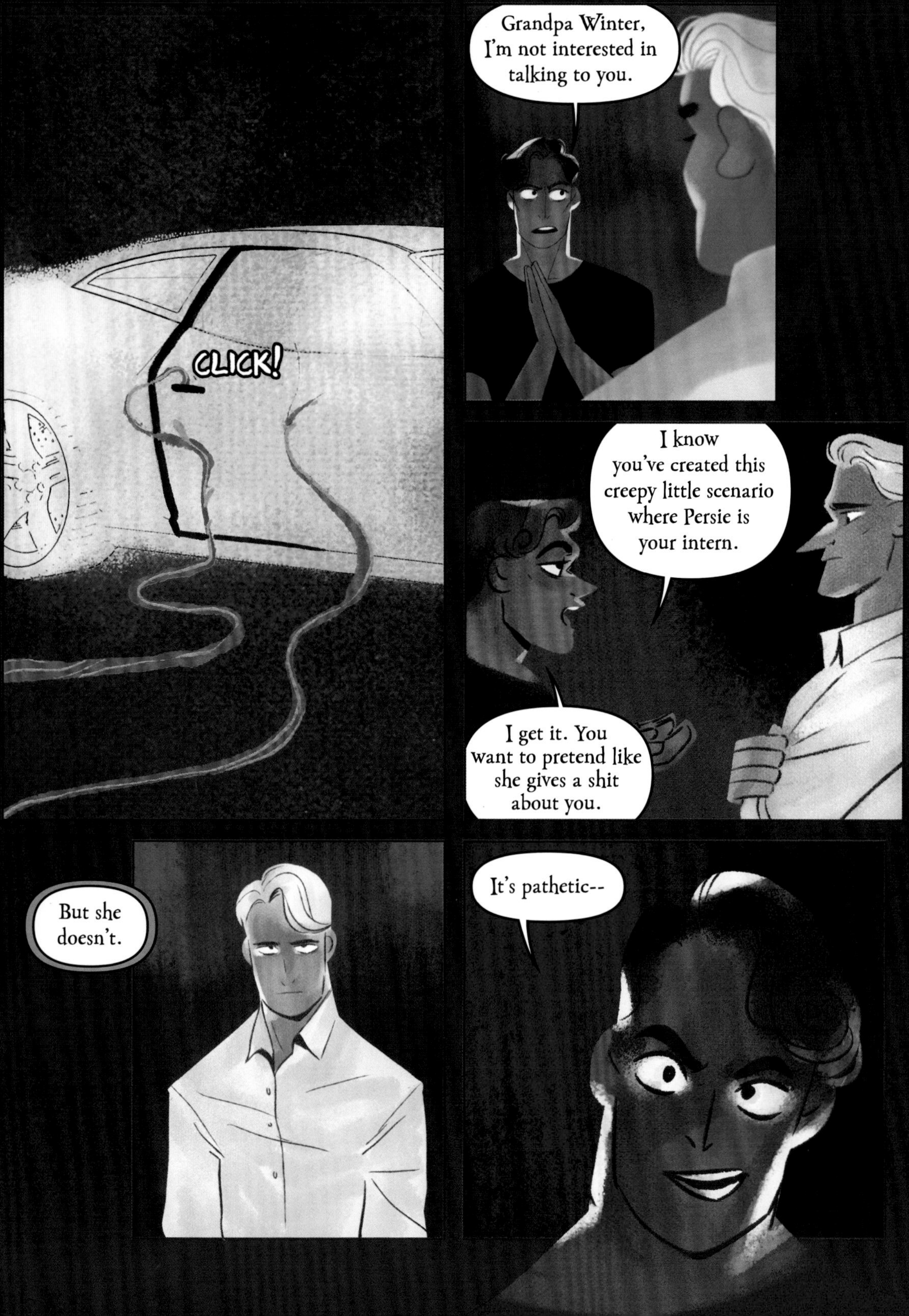
CLICK!
Grandpa Winter, I'm not interested in talking to you.
I know you've created this creepy little scenario where Persie is your intern.
I get it. You want to pretend like she gives a shit about you.
But she doesn't.
It's pathetic--

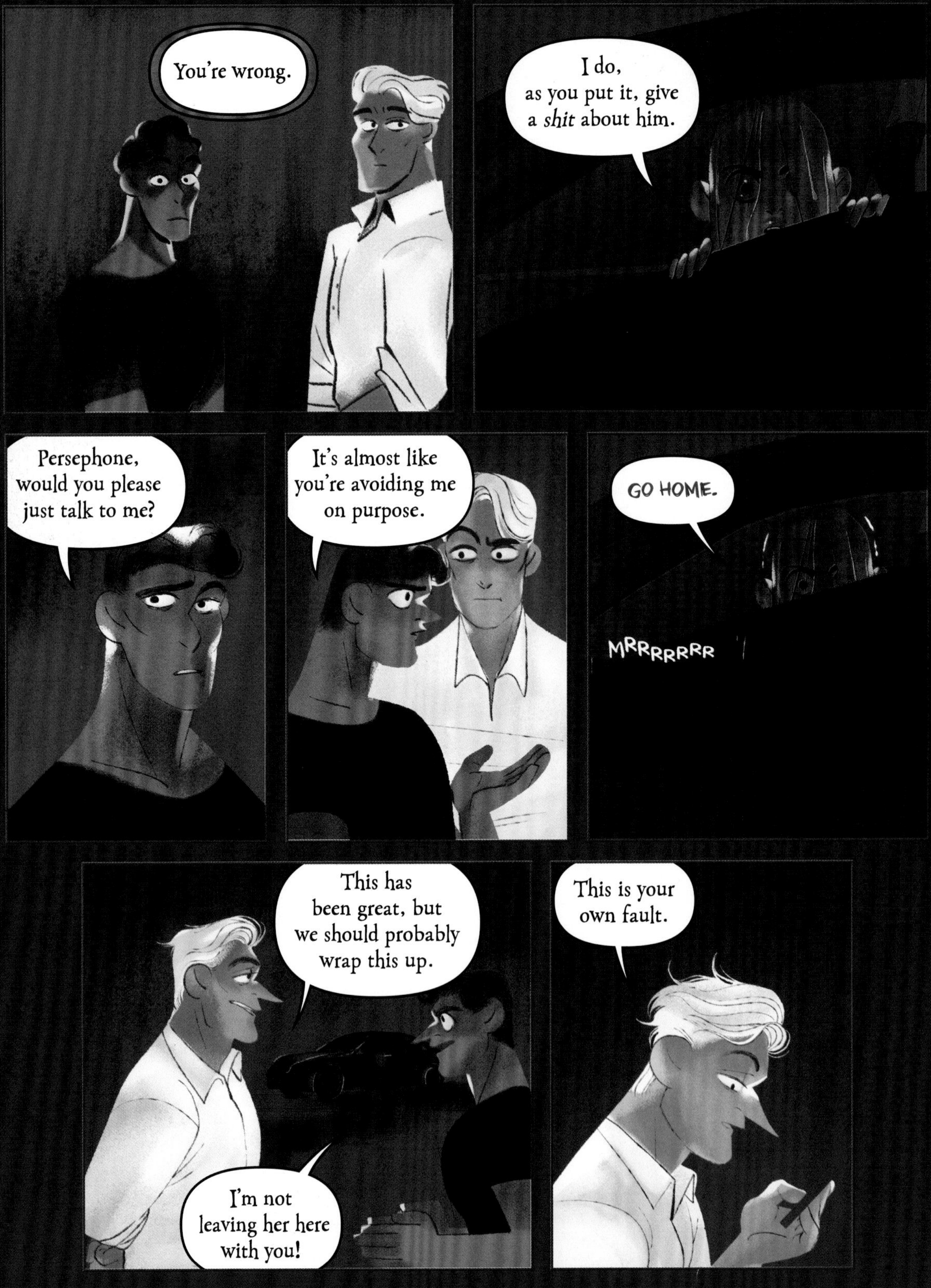
You're wrong.
I do, as you put it, give a *shit* about him.
Persephone, would you please just talk to me?
It's almost like you're avoiding me on purpose.
GO HOME.
MRRRRRRR
This has been great, but we should probably wrap this up.
I'm not leaving her here with you!
This is your own fault.

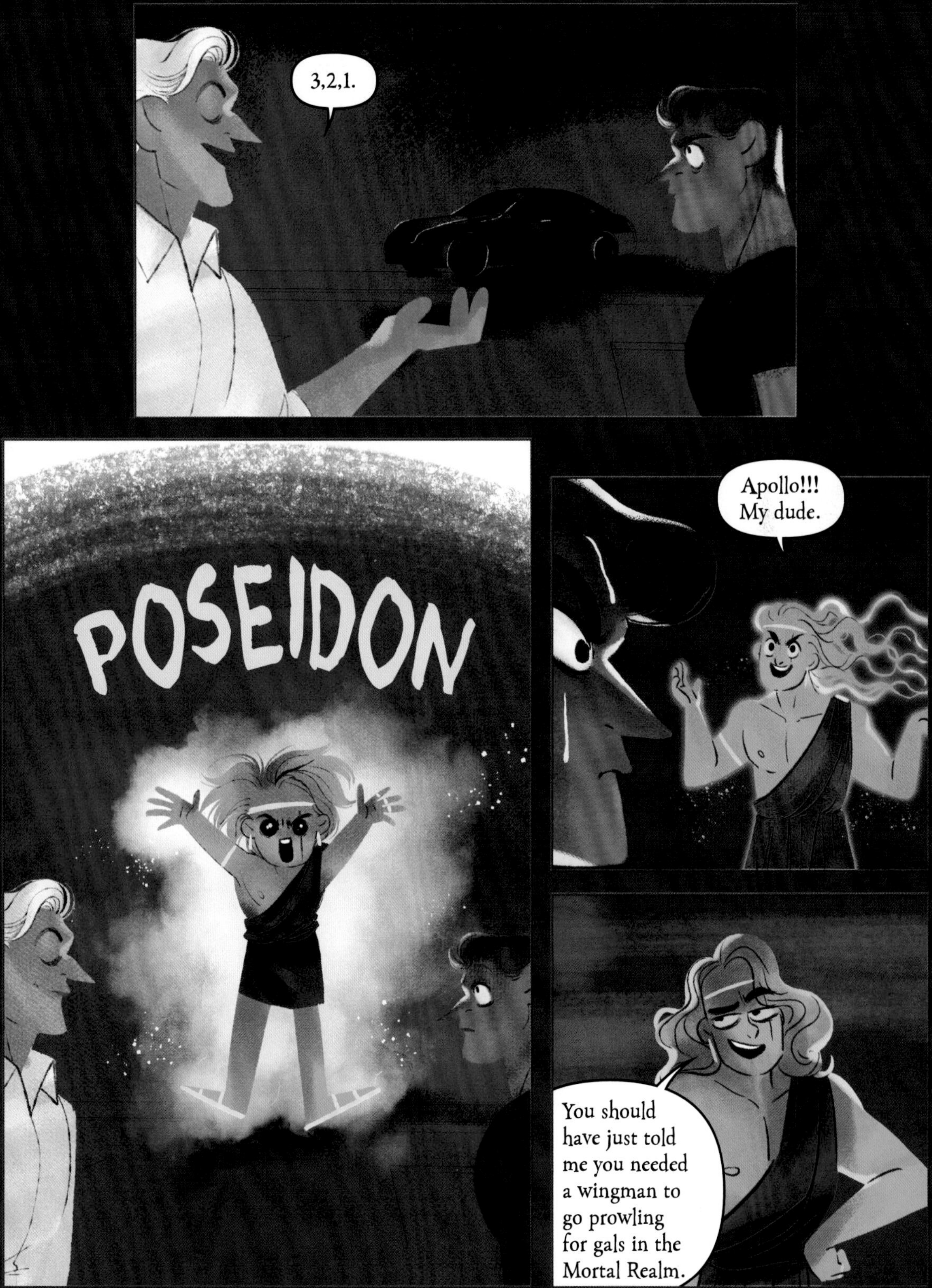
3,2,1.
POSEIDON
Apollo!!! My dude.
You should have just told me you needed a wingman to go prowling for gals in the Mortal Realm.

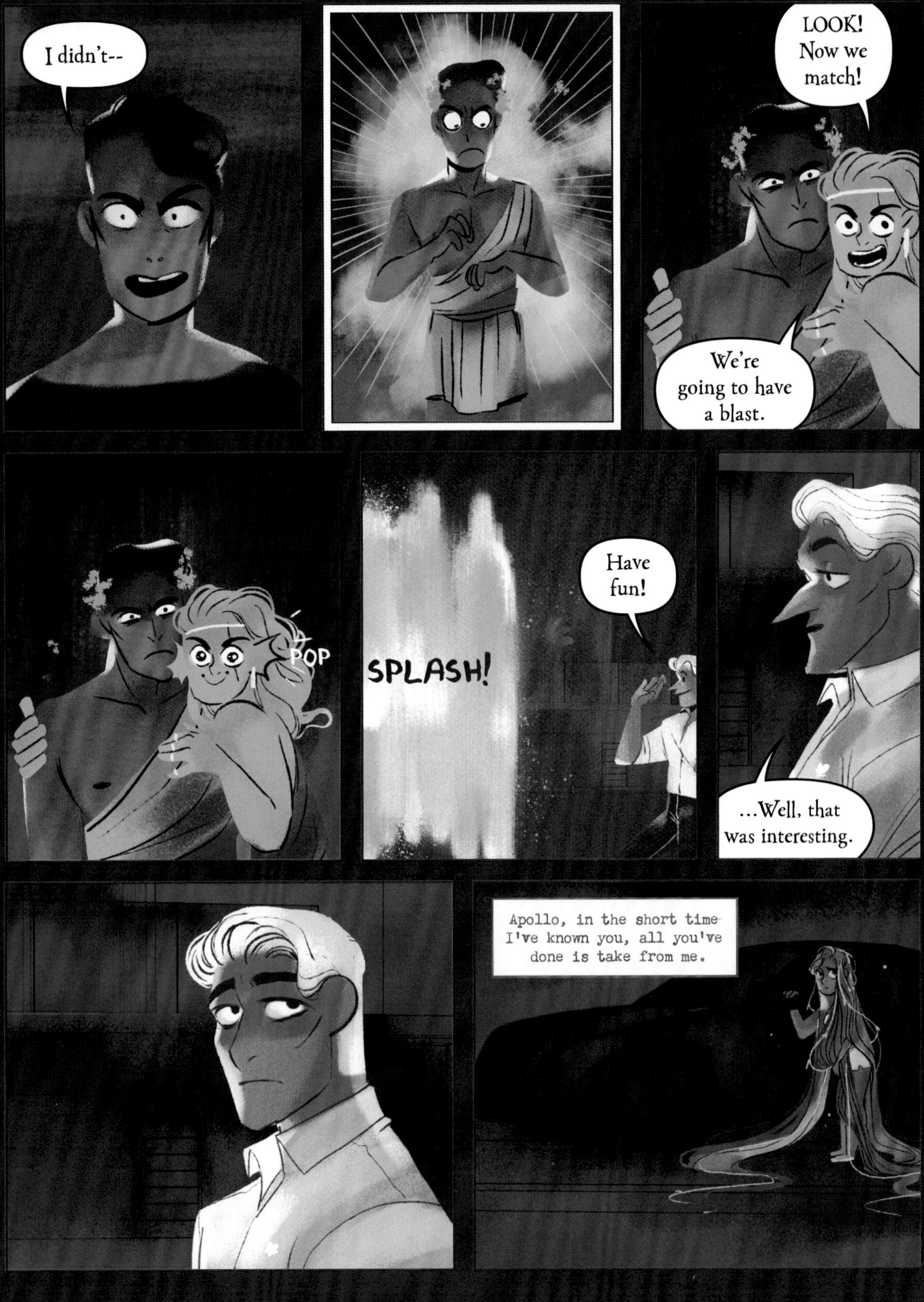
I didn't--
LOOK! Now we match!
We're going to have a blast.
POP
SPLASH!
Have fun!
...Well, that was interesting.
Apollo, in the short time I've known you, all you've done is take from me.

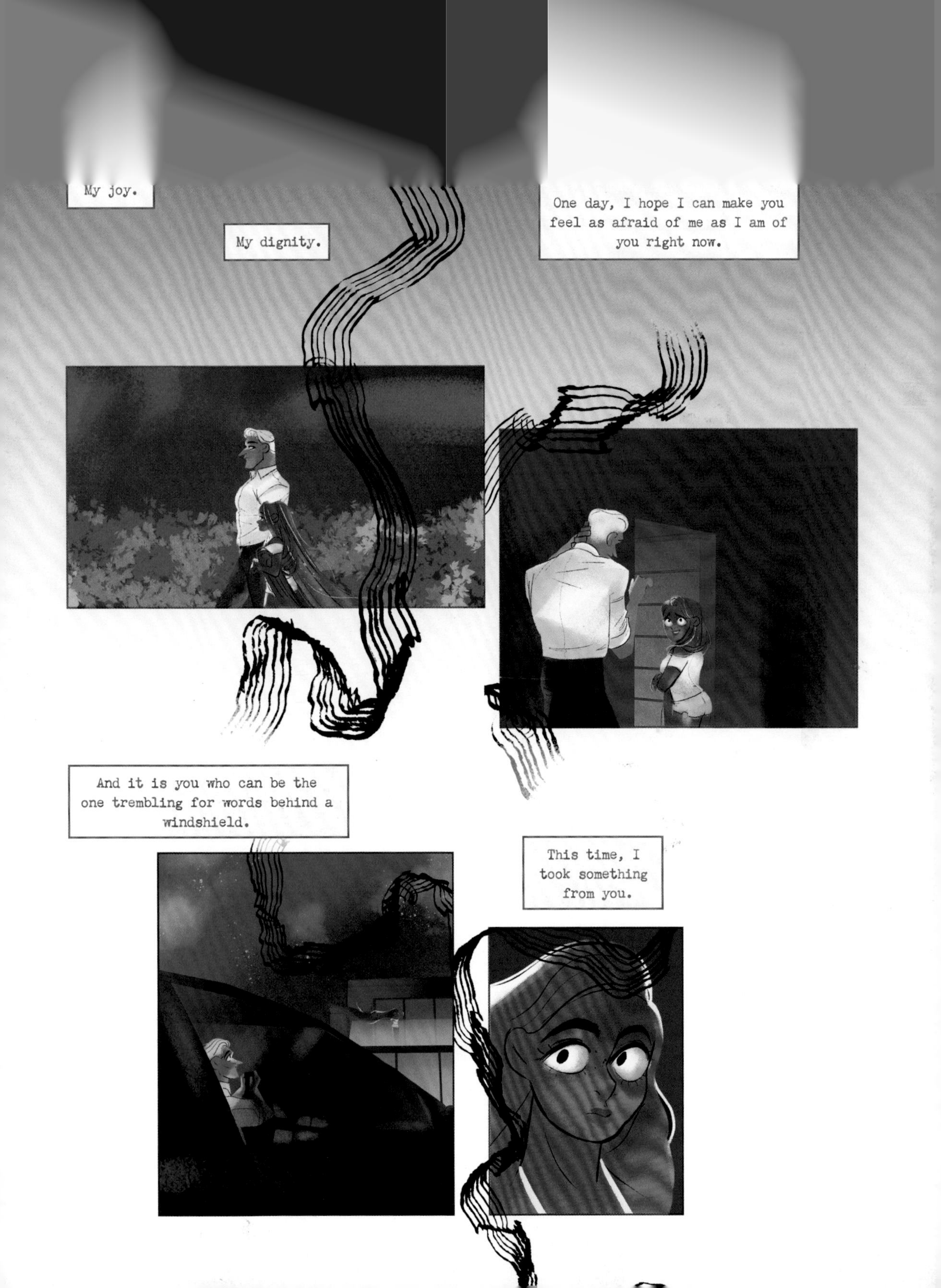
My joy.
My dignity.
One day, I hope I can make you feel as afraid of me as I am of you right now.
And it is you who can be the one trembling for words behind a windshield.
This time, I took something from you.

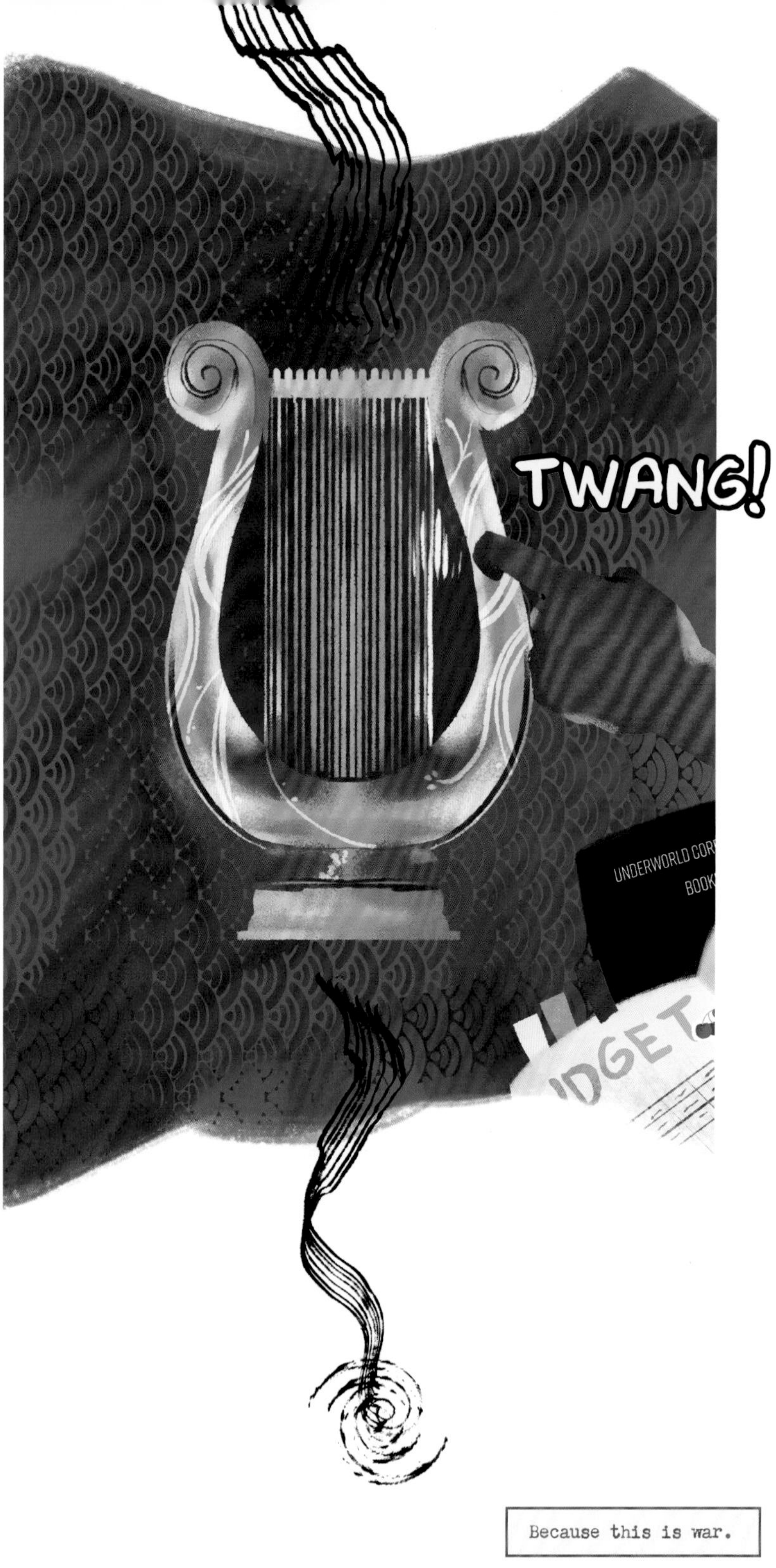
TWANG!
Because this is war.

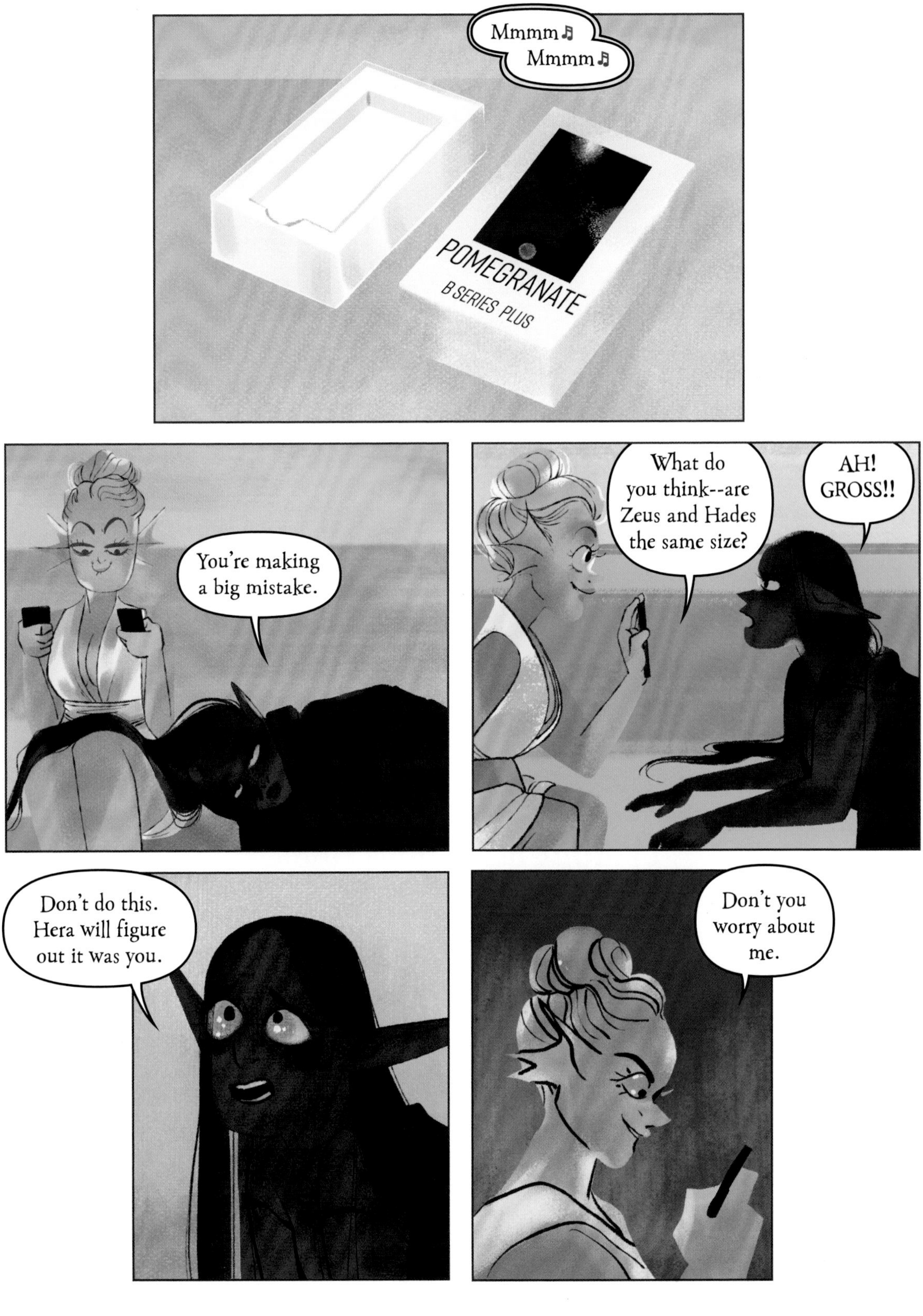
Mmmm♫ Mmmm♫
POMEGRANATE
B SERIES PLUS
You're making a big mistake.
What do you think--are Zeus and Hades the same size?
AH! GROSS!!
Don't do this. Hera will figure out it was you.
Don't you worry about me.

EPISODE 82: SAY MY NAME

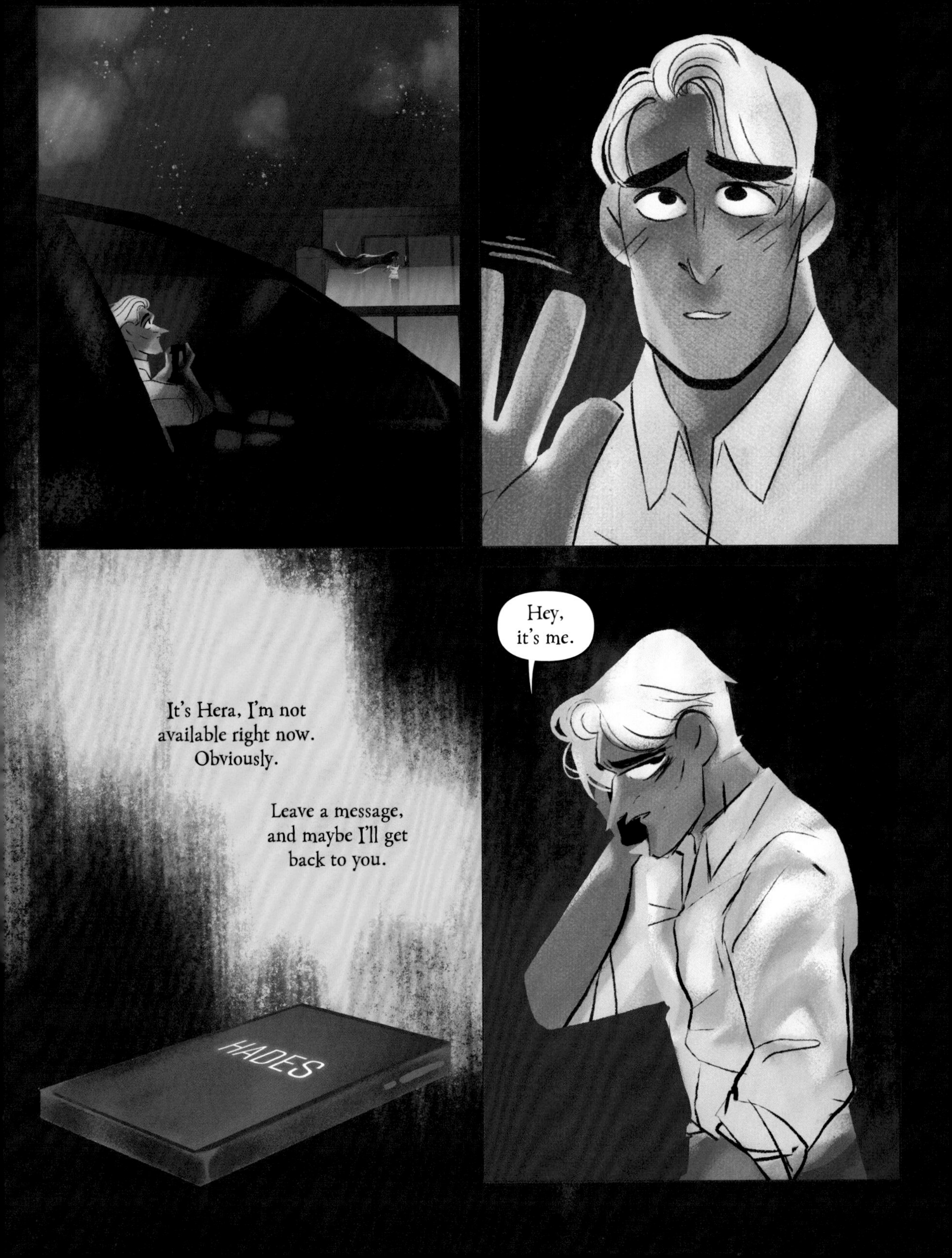
It's Hera, I'm not available right now. Obviously.
Leave a message, and maybe I'll get back to you.
HADES
Hey, it's me.

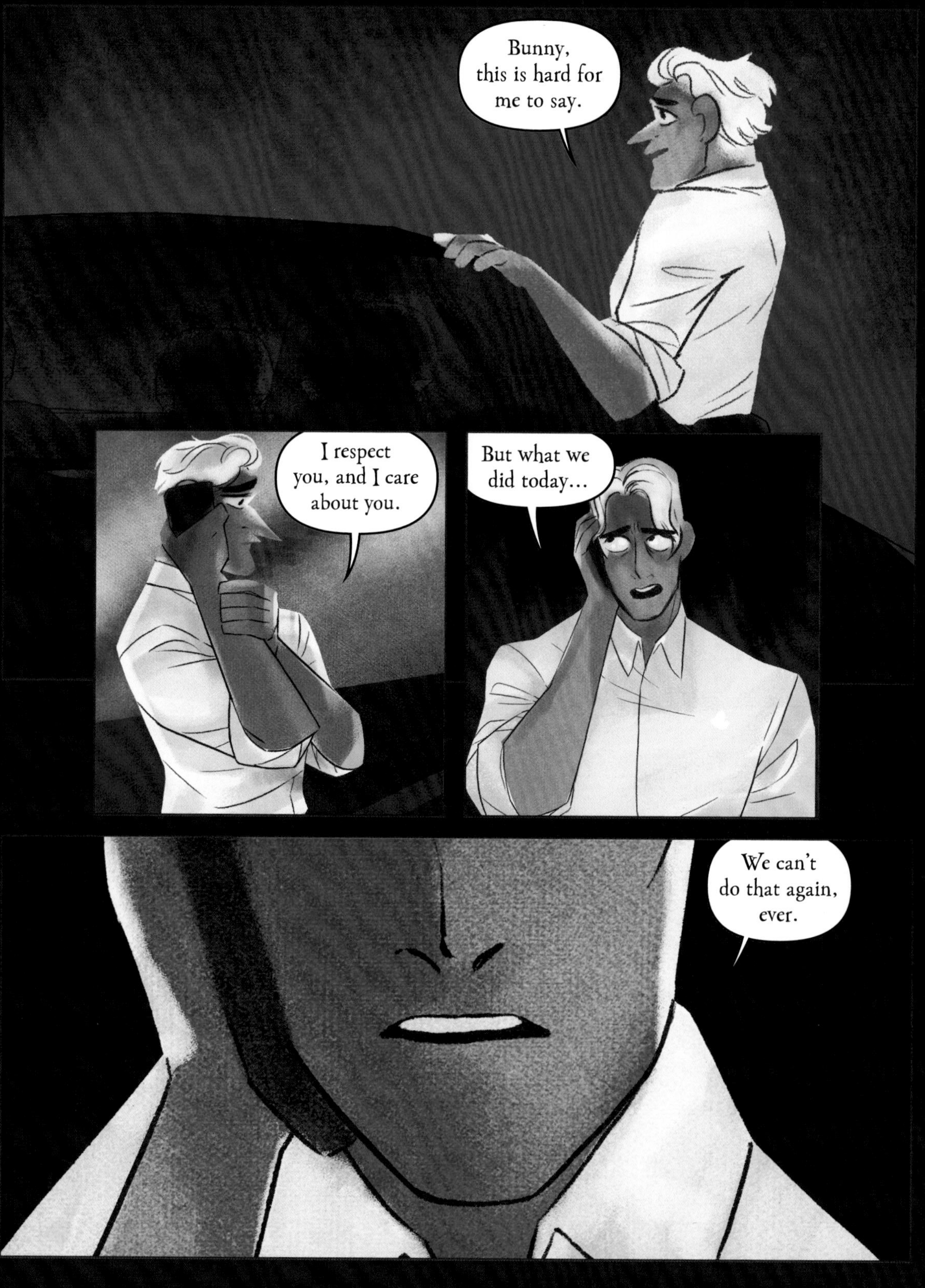
Bunny, this is hard for me to say.
I respect you, and I care about you.
But what we did today...
We can't do that again, ever.

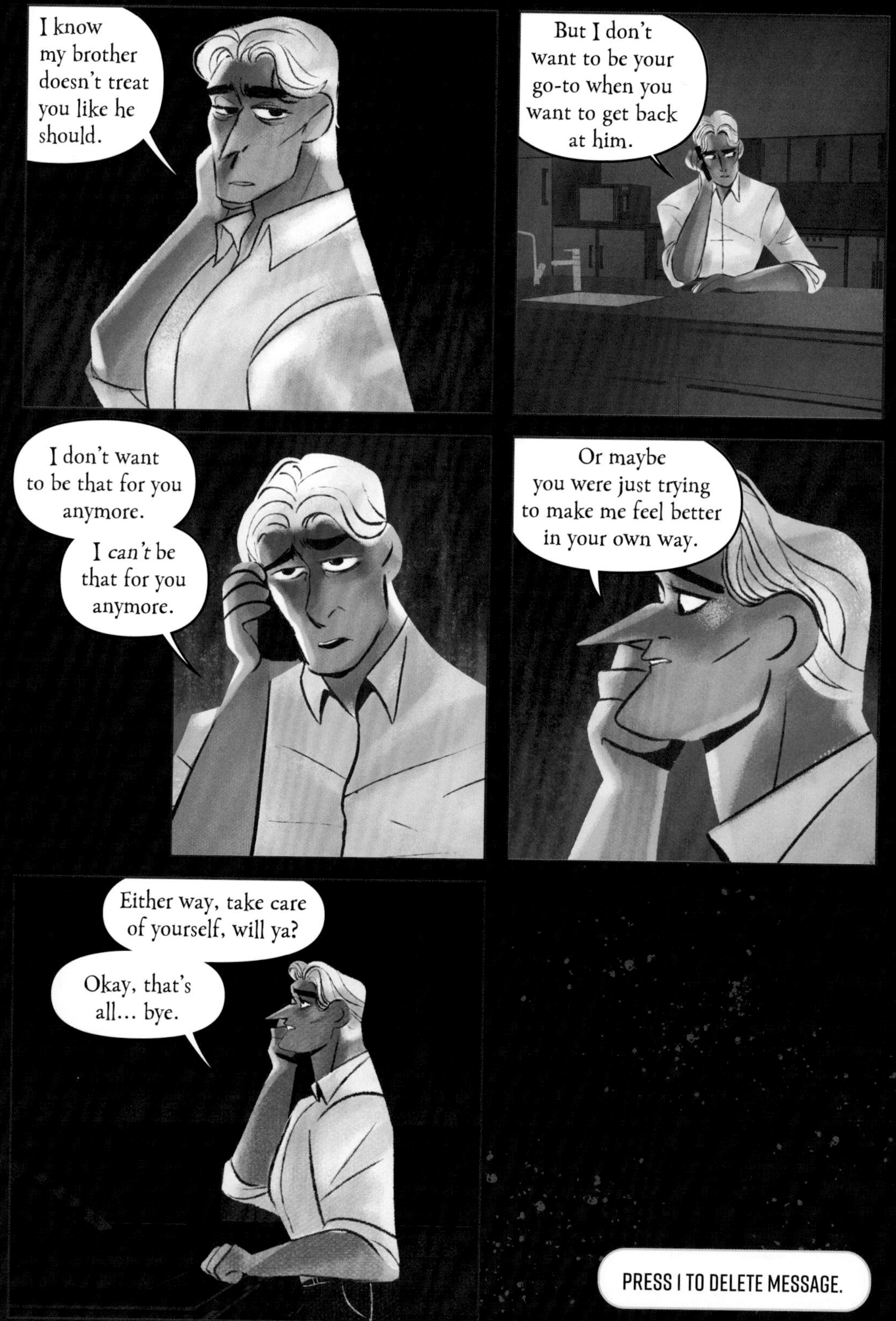
I know my brother doesn't treat you like he should.
But I don't want to be your go-to when you want to get back at him.
I don't want to be that for you anymore.
I *can't* be that for you anymore.
Or maybe you were just trying to make me feel better in your own way.
Either way, take care of yourself, will ya?
Okay, that's all... bye.
PRESS 1 TO DELETE MESSAGE.

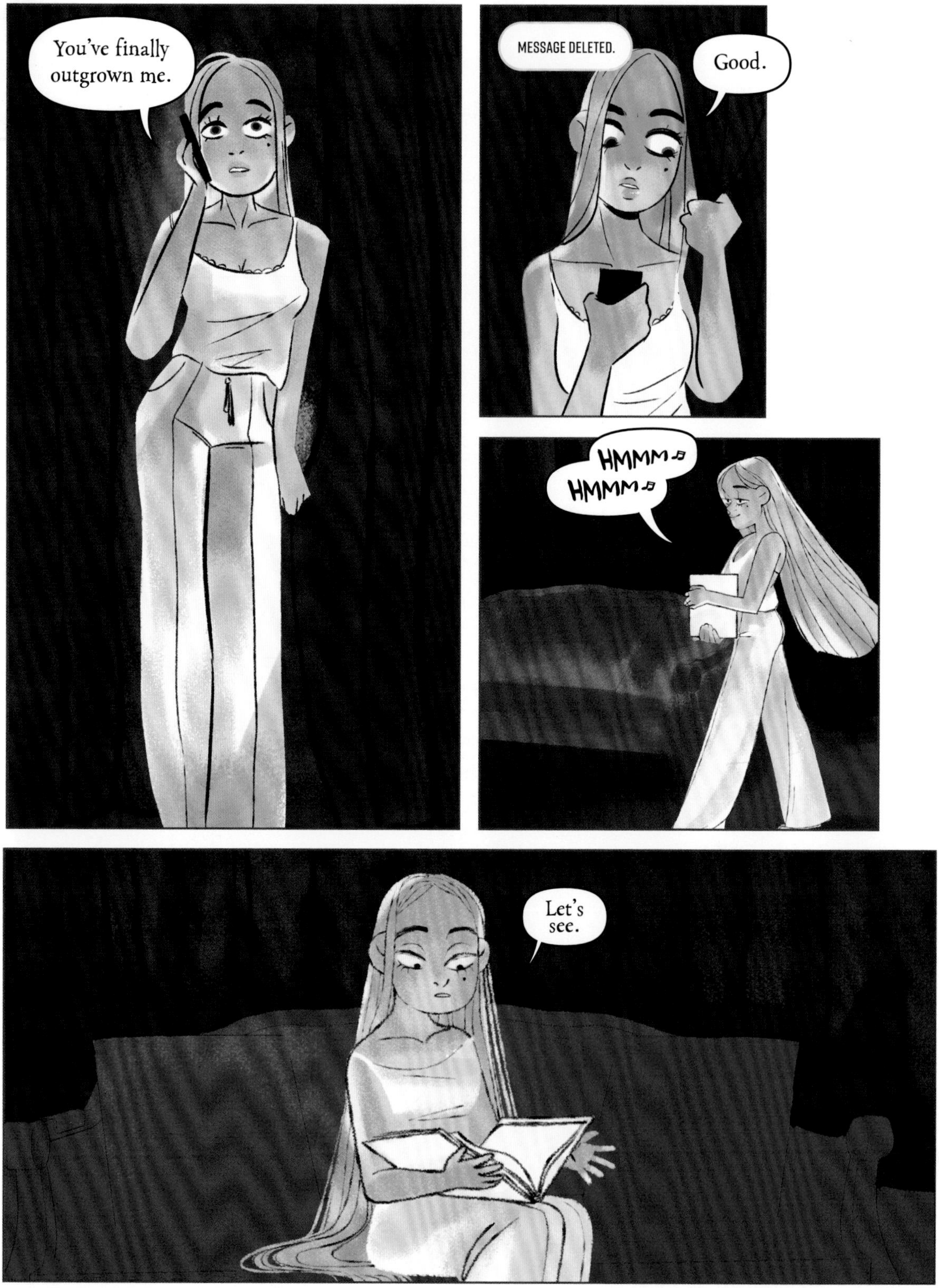
You've finally outgrown me.
MESSAGE DELETED.
Good.
HMMM♫ HMMM♫
Let's see.

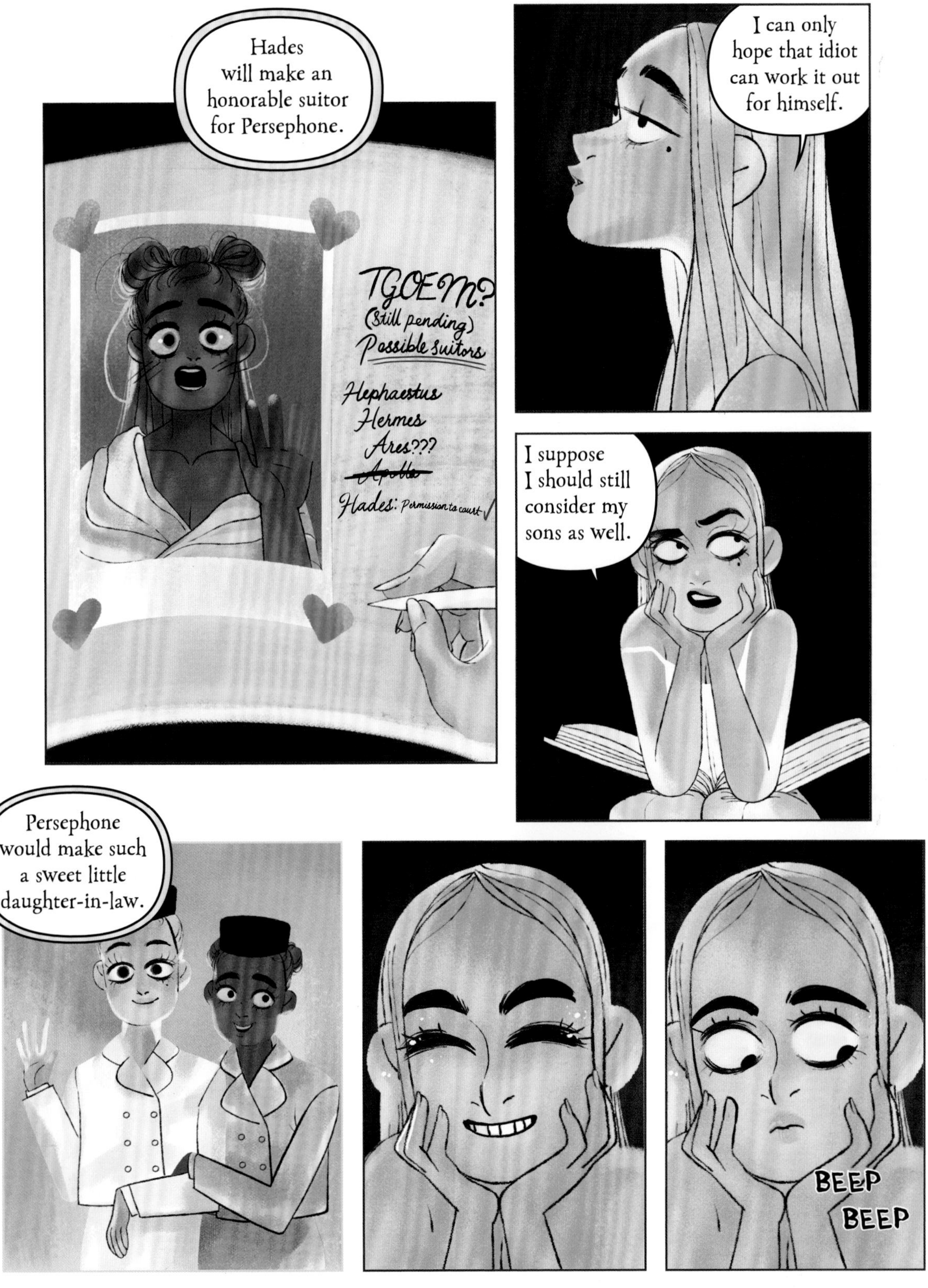
Hades will make an honorable suitor for Persephone.
TGOEM? (Still pending)
Possible suitors
Hephaestus
Hermes
Ares???
Apollo
Hades: Permission to court ✓
I can only hope that idiot can work it out for himself.
I suppose I should still consider my sons as well.
Persephone would make such a sweet little daughter-in-law.
BEEP
BEEP

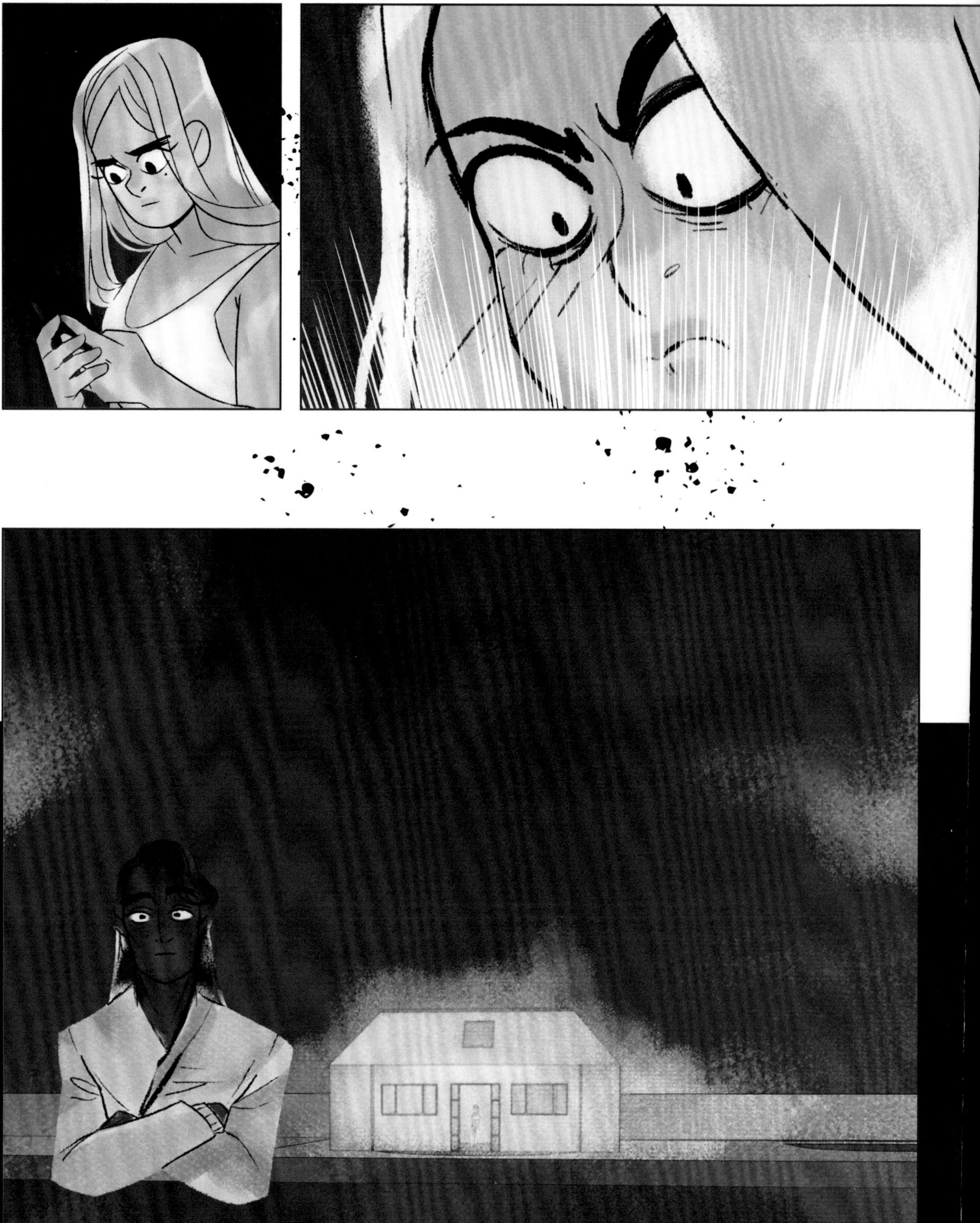

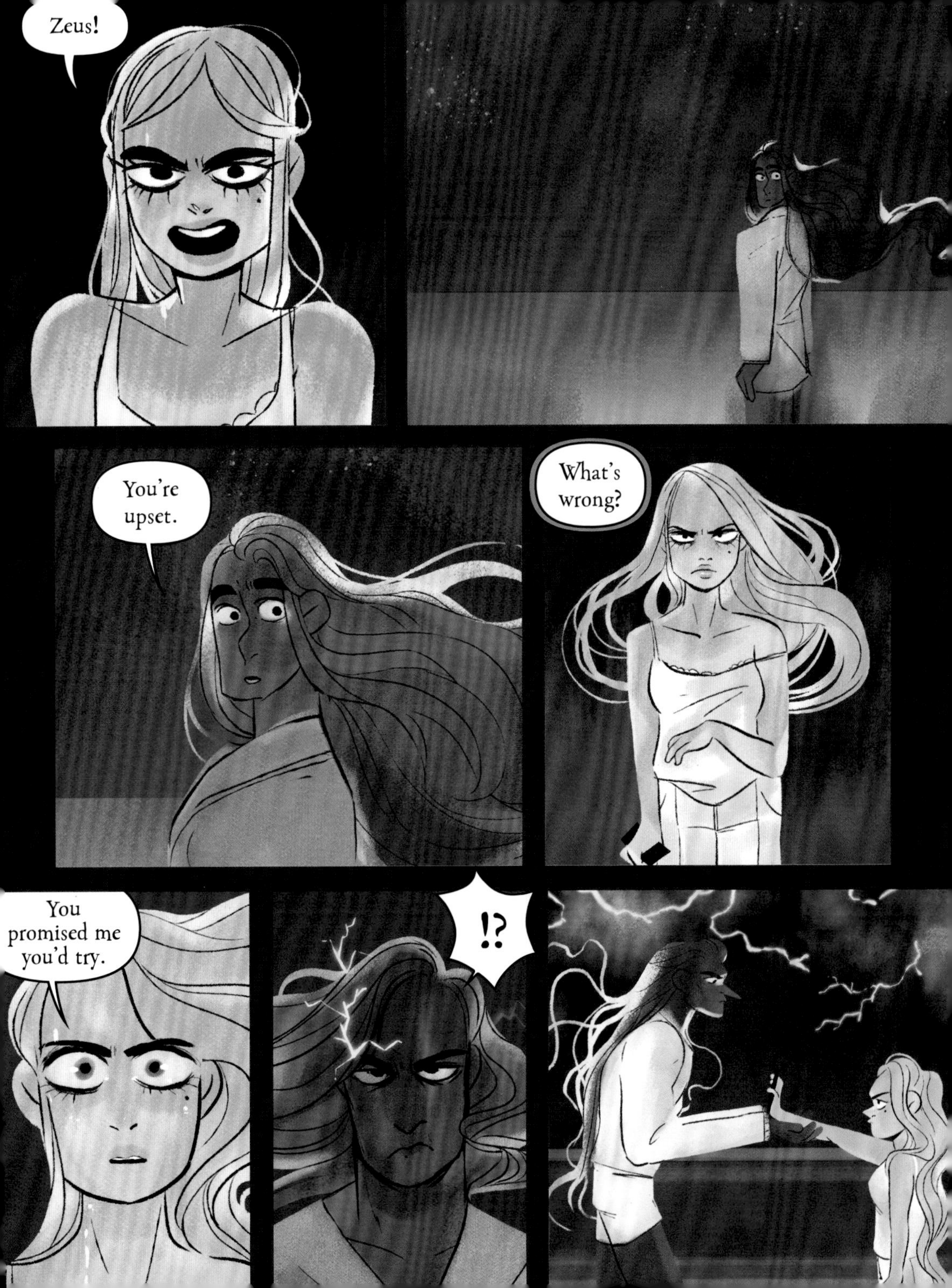
Zeus!
You're upset.
What's wrong?
You promised me you'd try.
!?

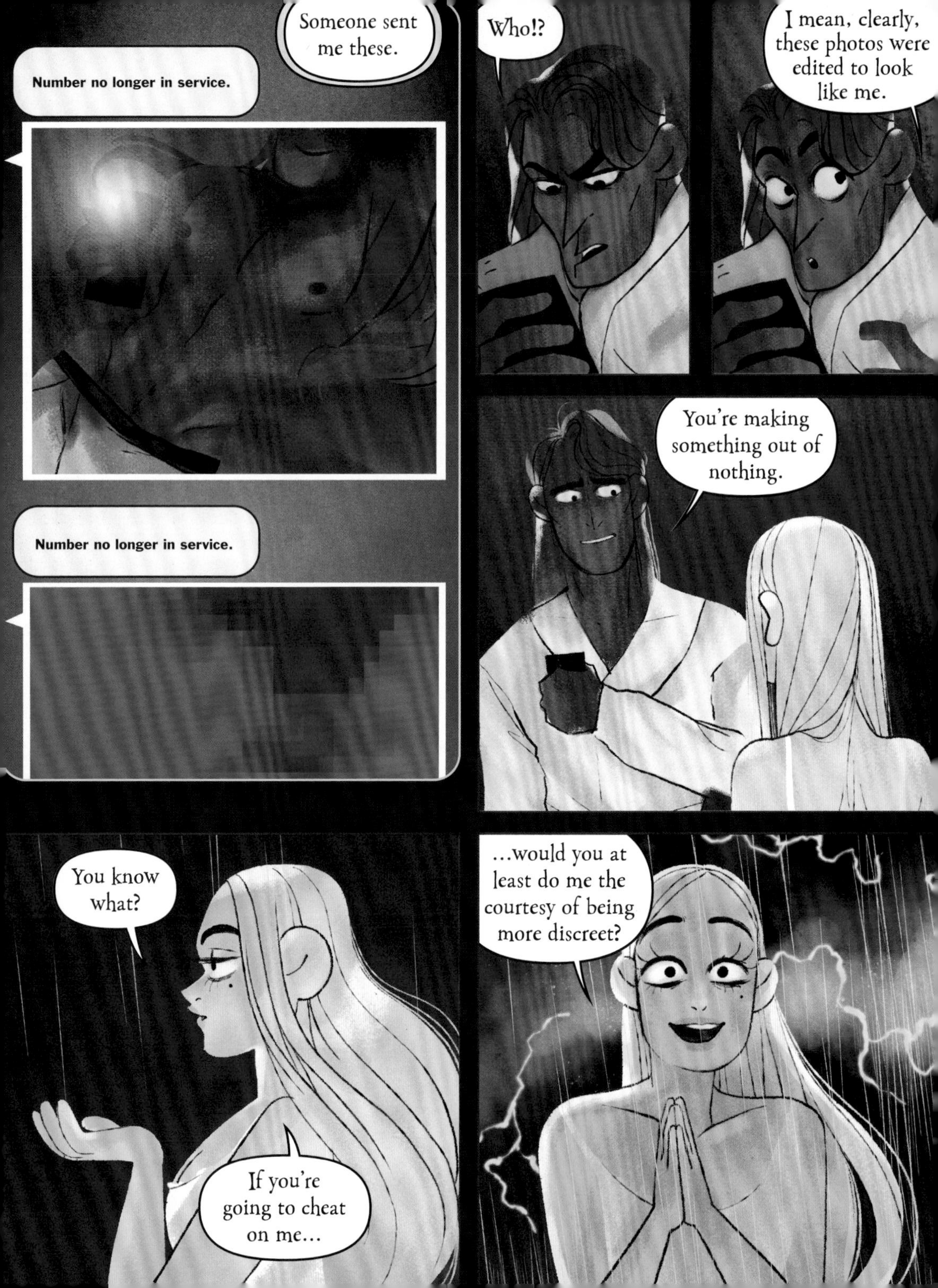
Someone sent me these.
Number no longer in service.
Number no longer in service.
Who!?
I mean, clearly, these photos were edited to look like me.
You're making something out of nothing.
You know what?
If you're going to cheat on me...
...would you at least do me the courtesy of being more discreet?

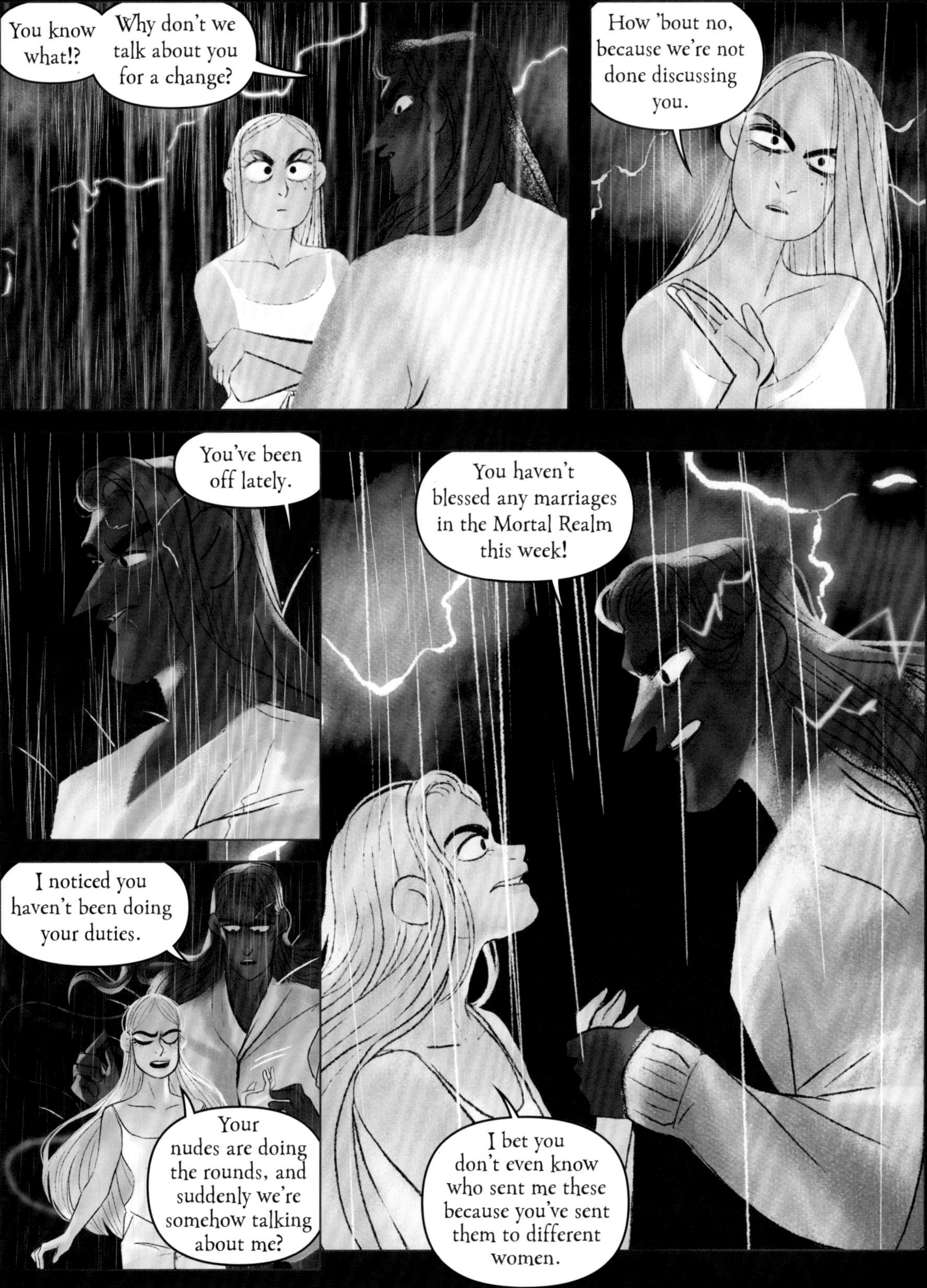
You know what!?
Why don't we talk about you for a change?
How 'bout no, because we're not done discussing you.
You've been off lately.
You haven't blessed any marriages in the Mortal Realm this week!
I noticed you haven't been doing your duties.
Your nudes are doing the rounds, and suddenly we're somehow talking about me?
I bet you don't even know who sent me these because you've sent them to different women.

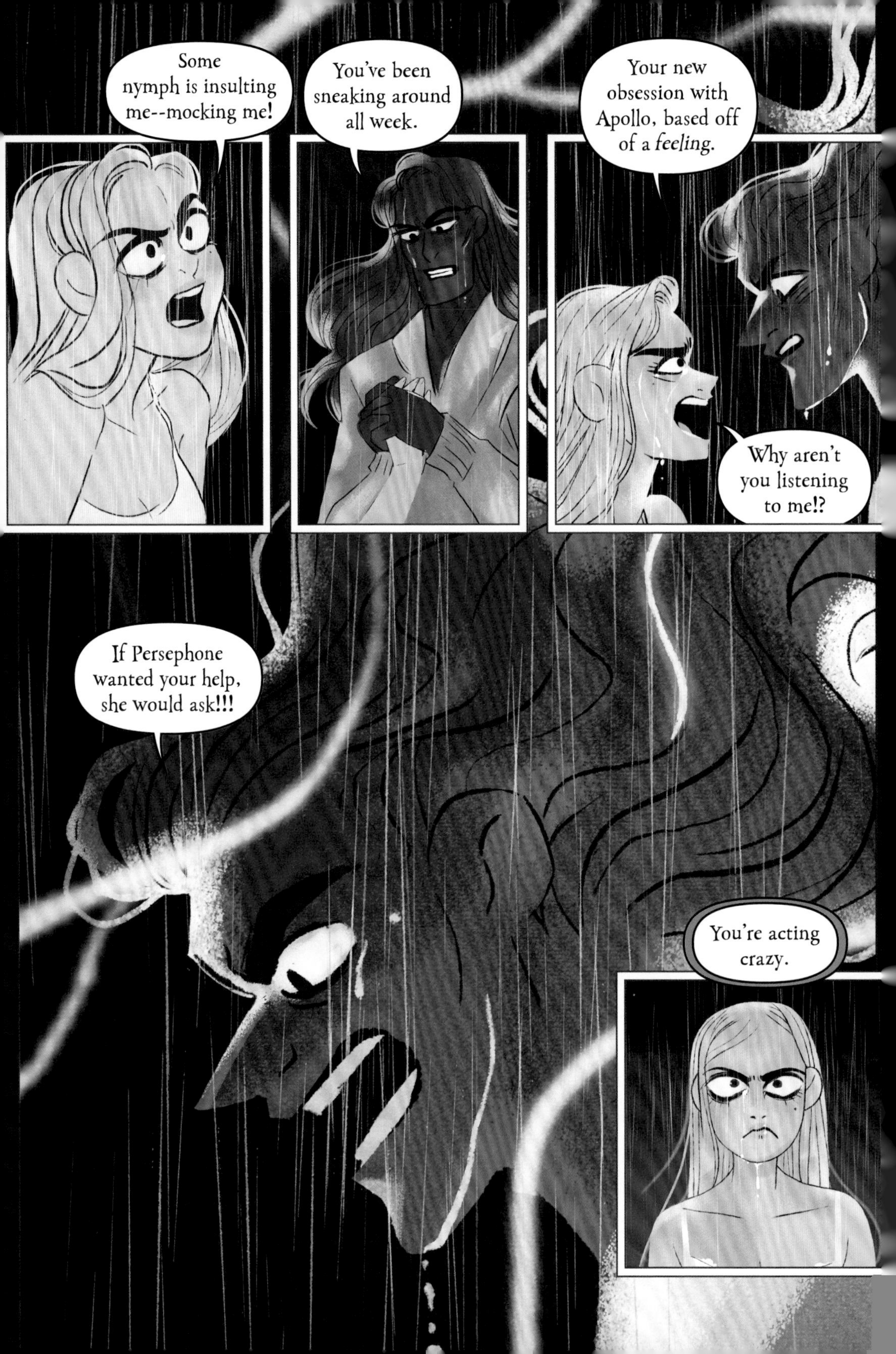
Some nymph is insulting me--mocking me!
You've been sneaking around all week.
Your new obsession with Apollo, based off of a *feeling*.
Why aren't you listening to me!?
If Persephone wanted your help, she would ask!!!
You're acting crazy.

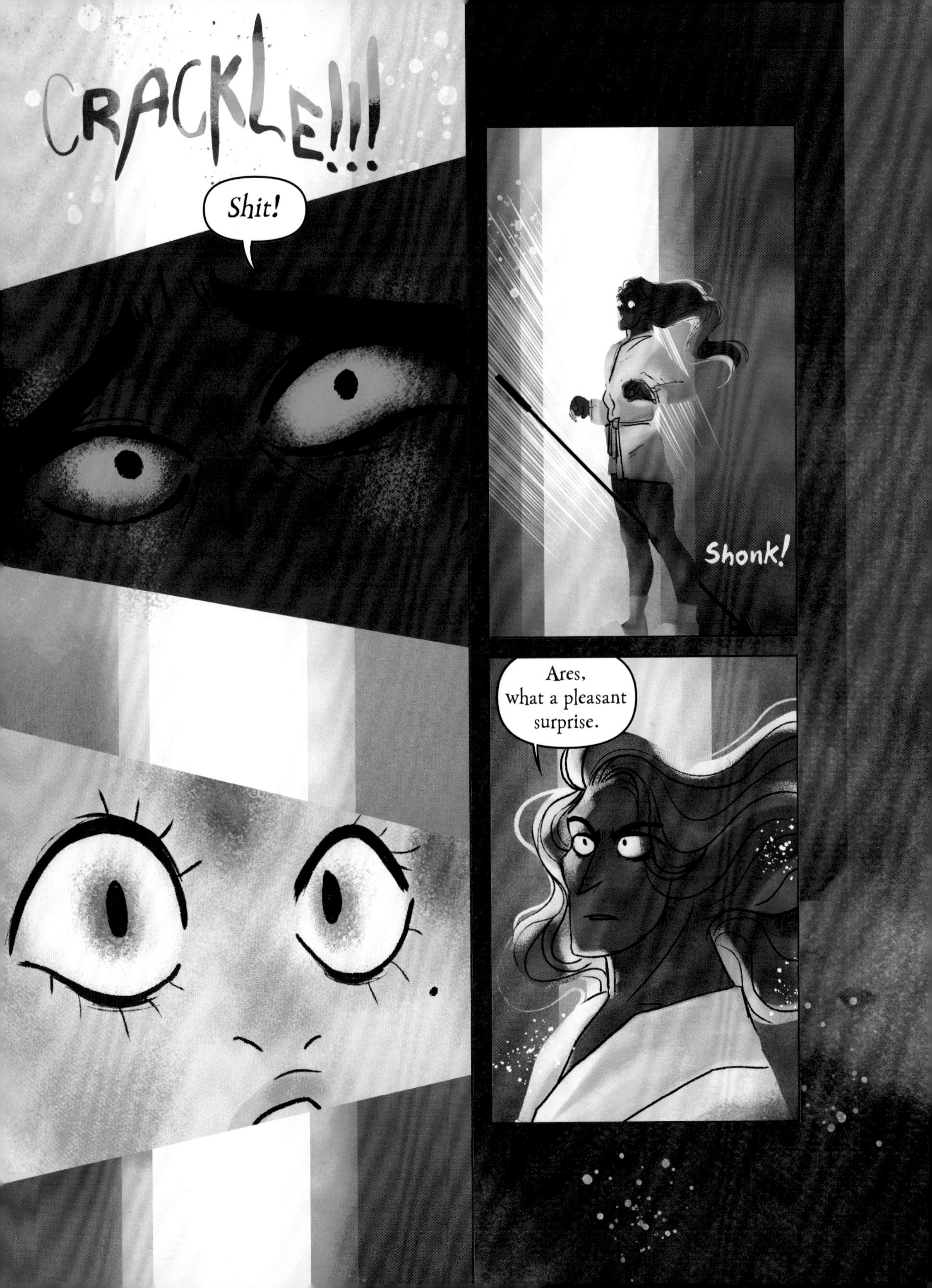
CRACKLE!!!
Shit!
Shonk!
Ares, what a pleasant surprise.

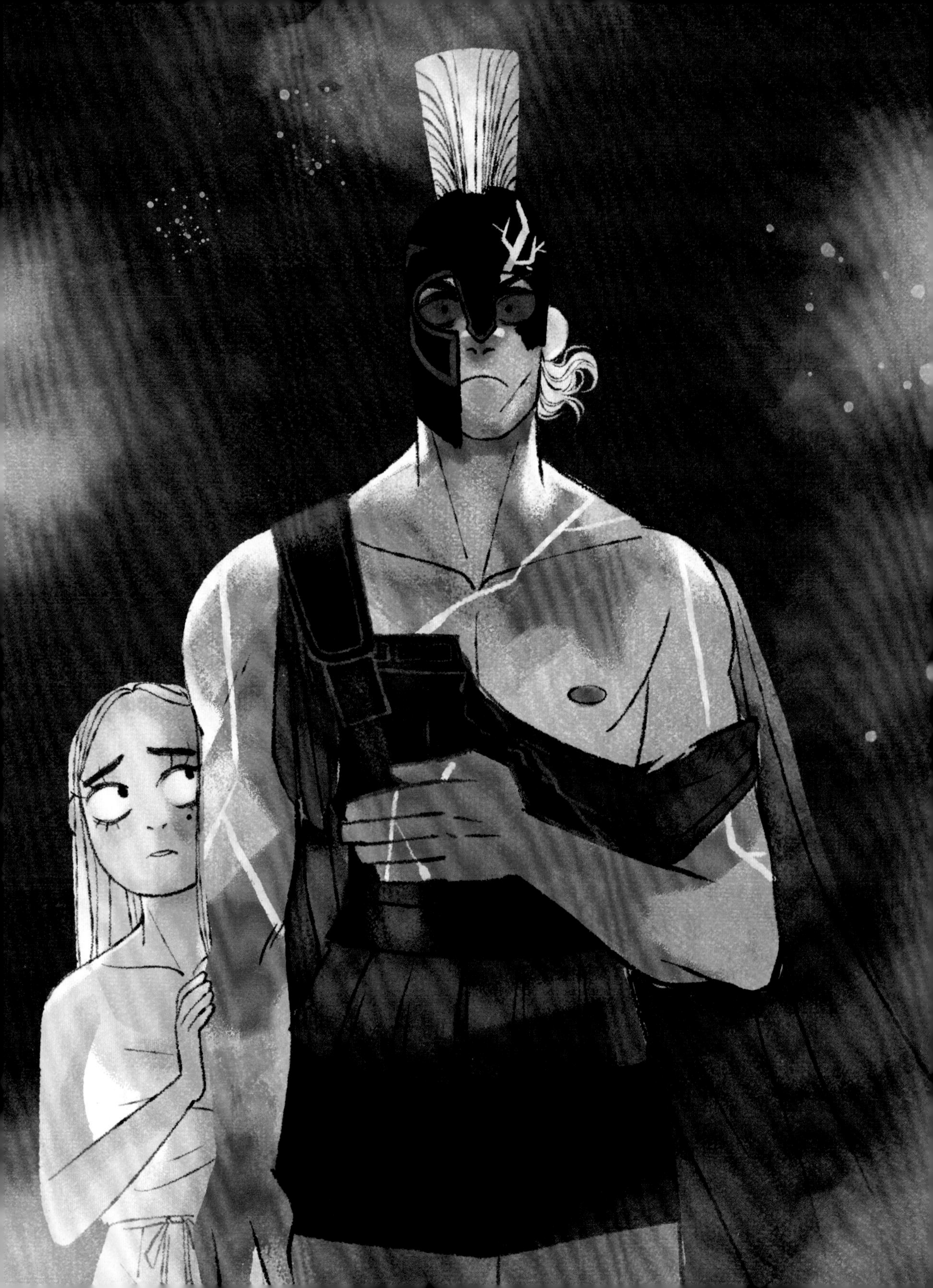

PREVIOUSLY ON LORE OLYMPUS

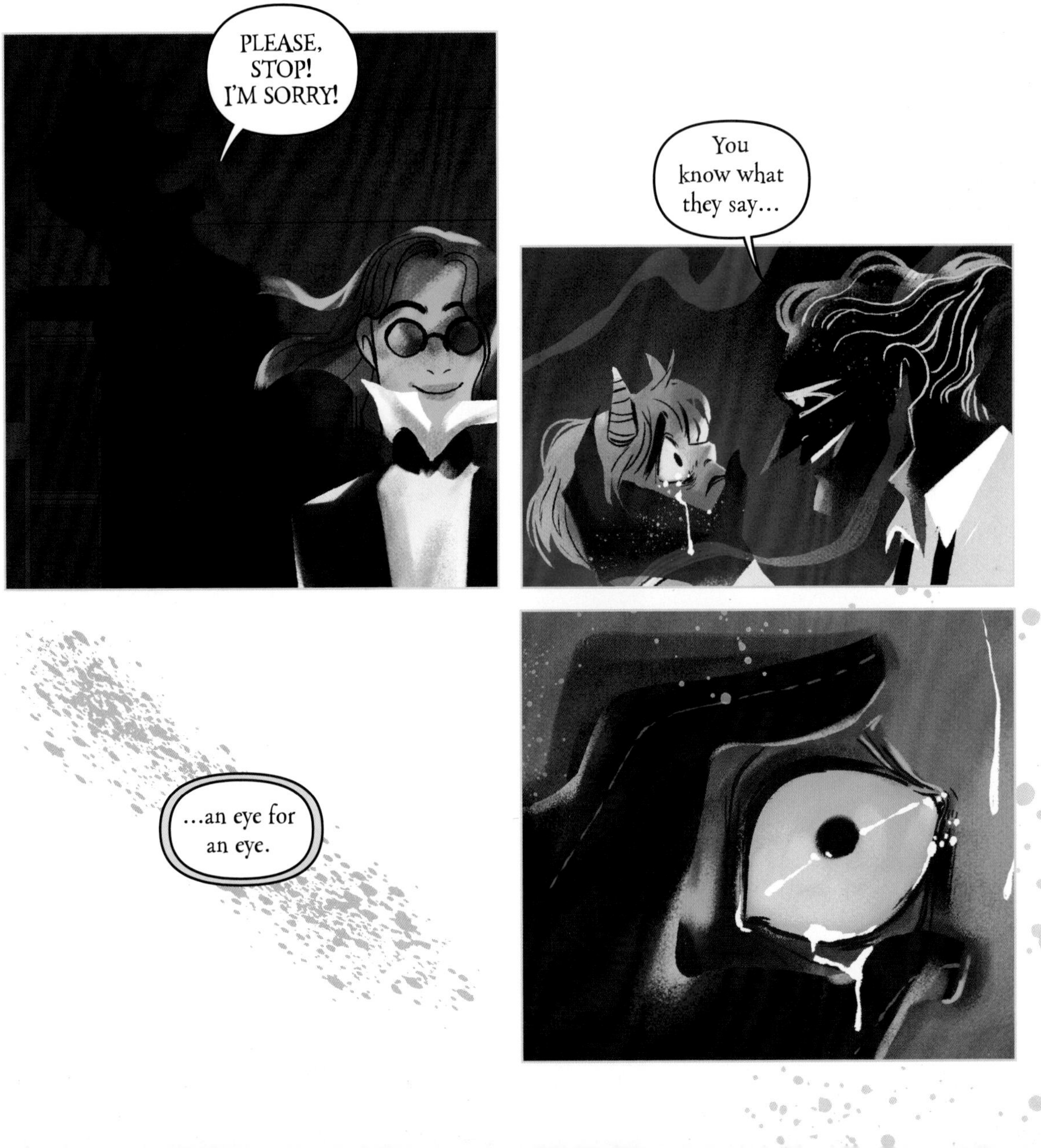
PLEASE, STOP! I'M SORRY!
You know what they say...
...an eye for an eye.

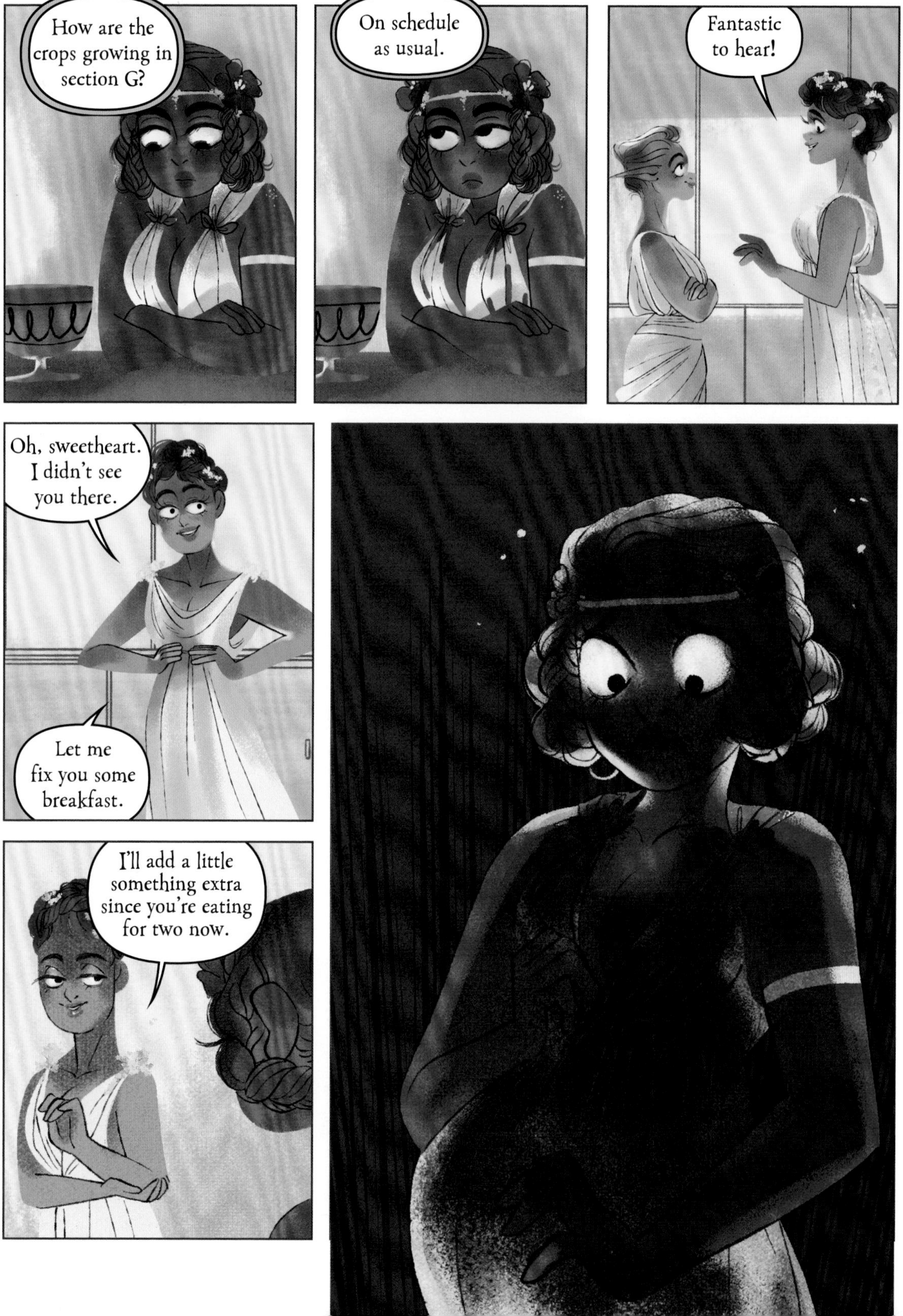
How are the crops growing in section G?
On schedule as usual.
Fantastic to hear!
Oh, sweetheart. I didn't see you there.
Let me fix you some breakfast.
I'll add a little something extra since you're eating for two now.

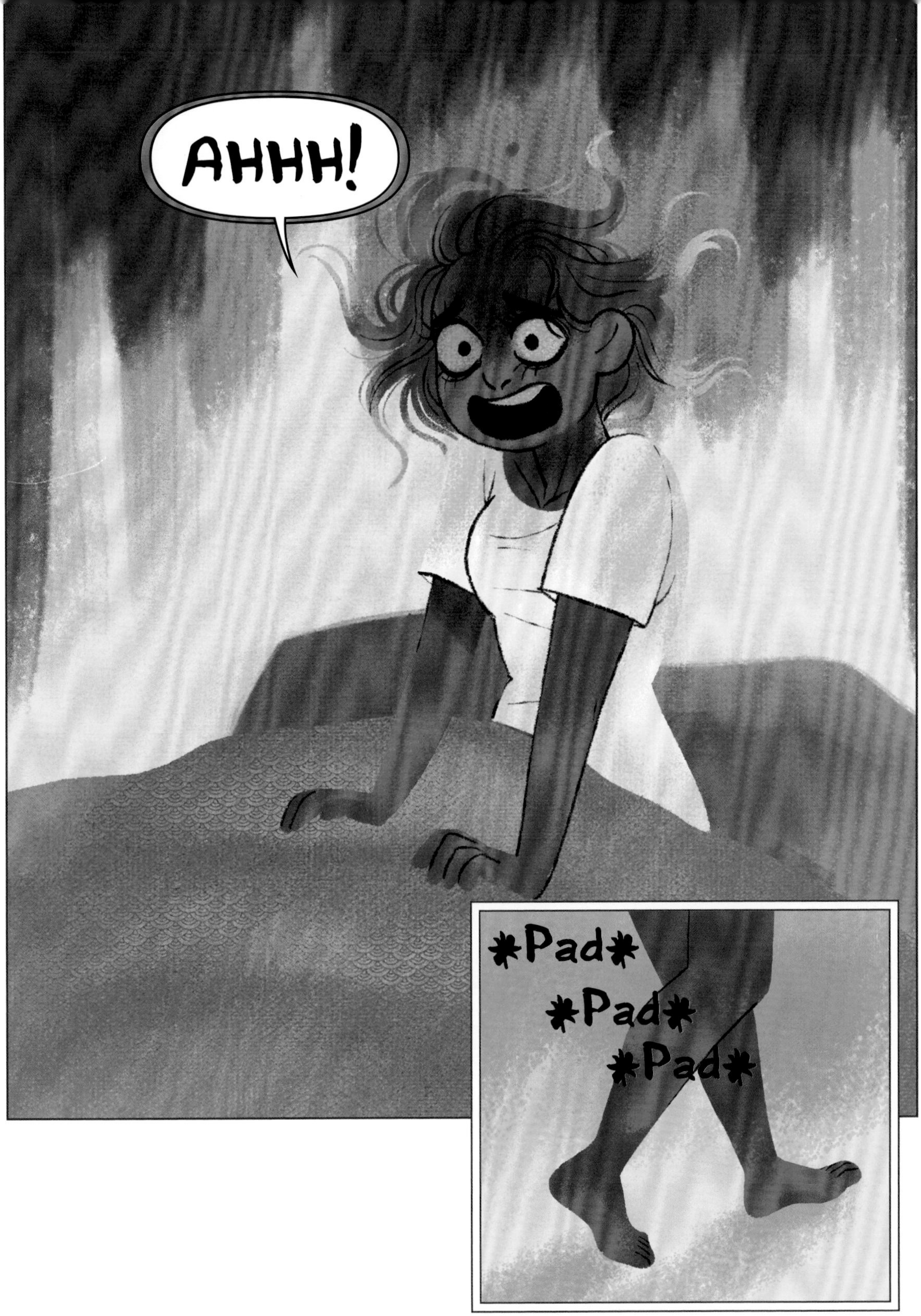
AHHH!
Pad
Pad
Pad

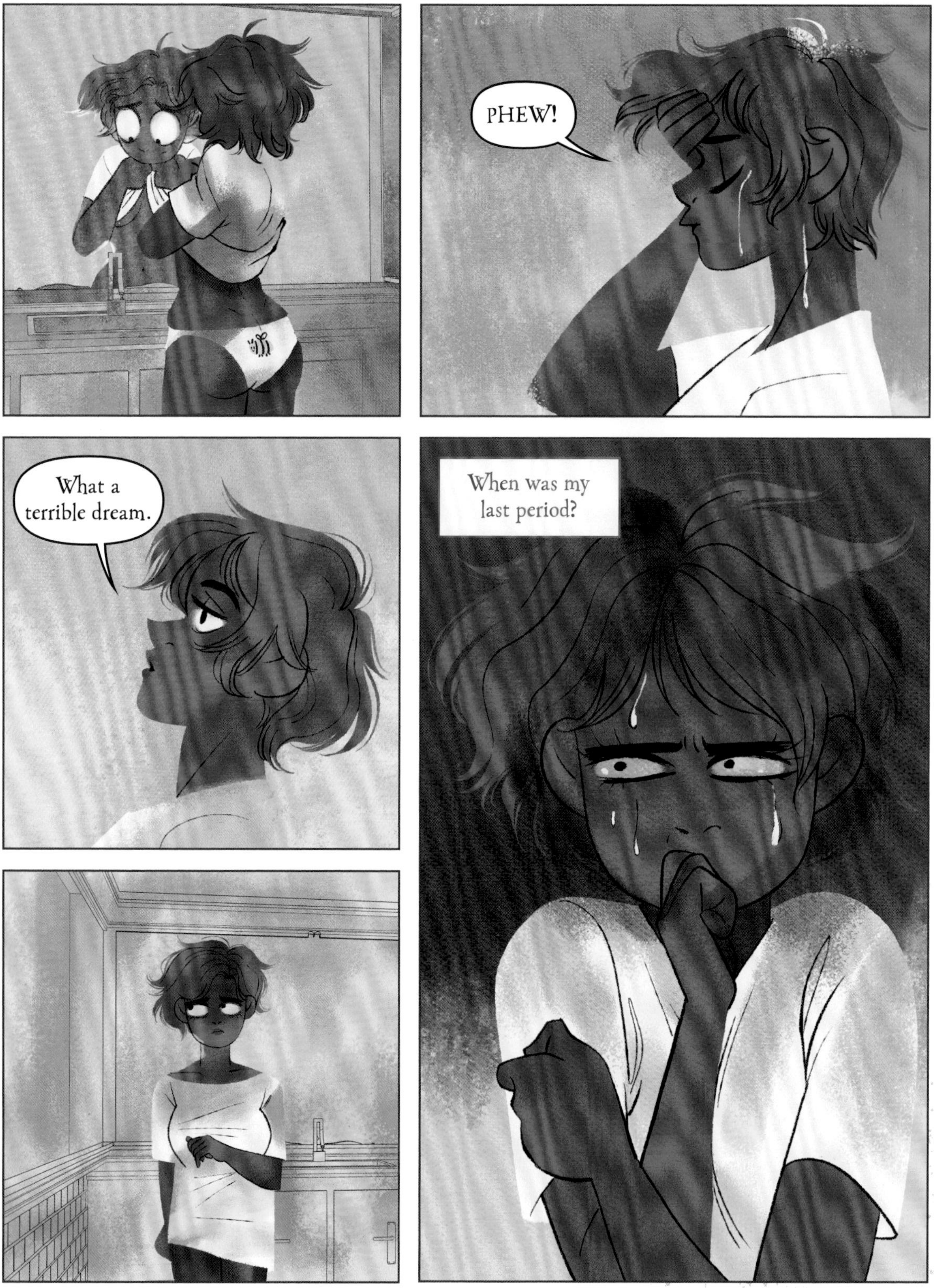
PHEW!
What a terrible dream.
When was my last period?

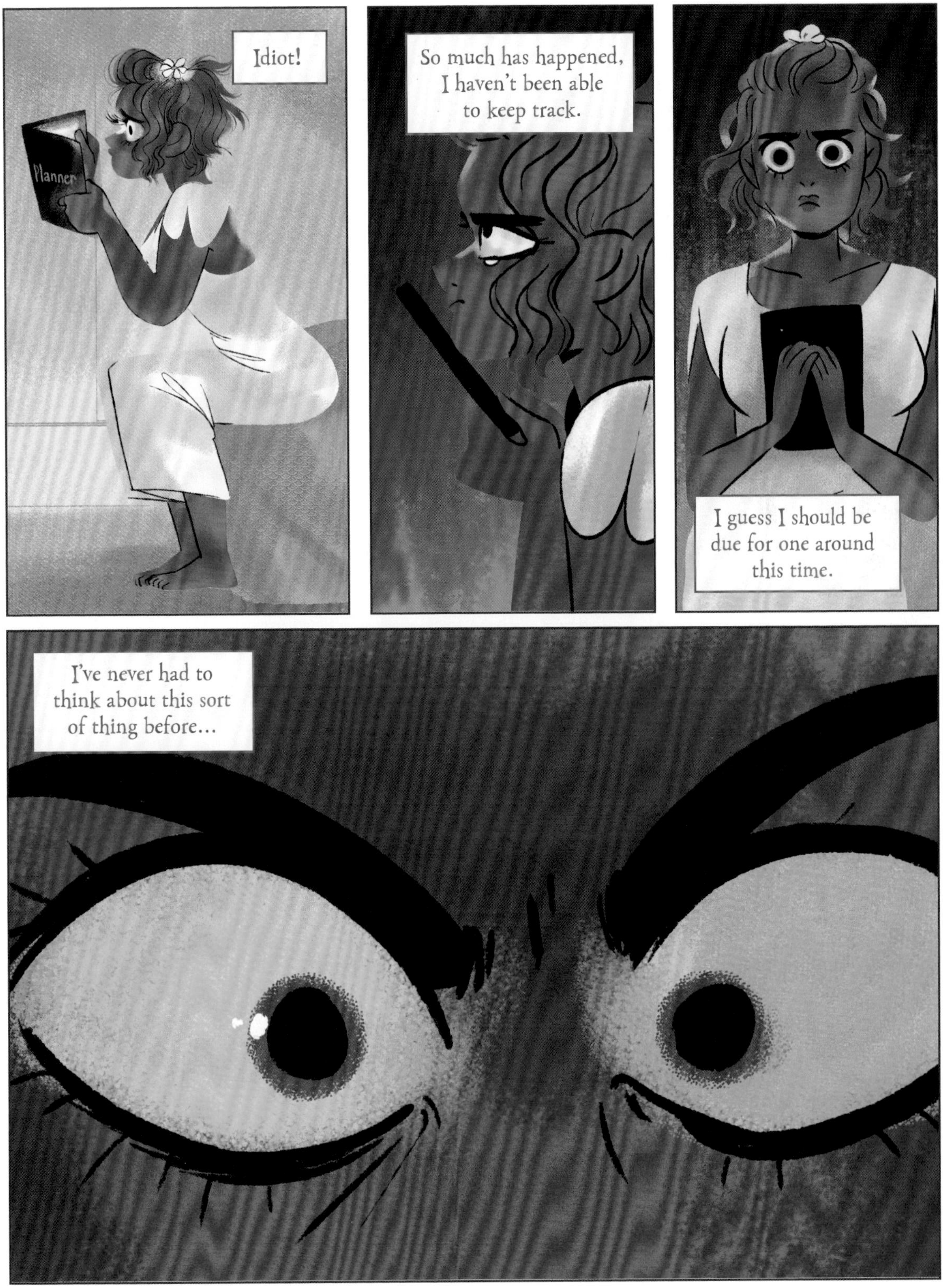
Idiot!
Planner
So much has happened, I haven't been able to keep track.
I guess I should be due for one around this time.
I've never had to think about this sort of thing before...

THUMP!

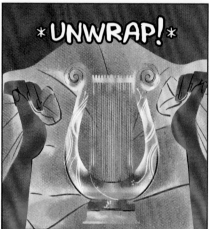

UNWRAP!

* GRIT! *

PULL!

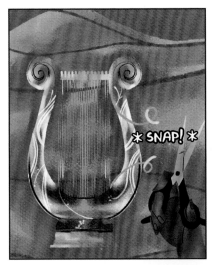

SNAP!

HUFF *HUFF*

I can find a better hiding place later.

BOOKS

I wonder how long it will take for him to notice it's missing.

BOOKS

His car is still there... But I don't see him.

This is not how I wanted to spend my Saturday.

EPISODE 83: PROSERPINA IS LATE

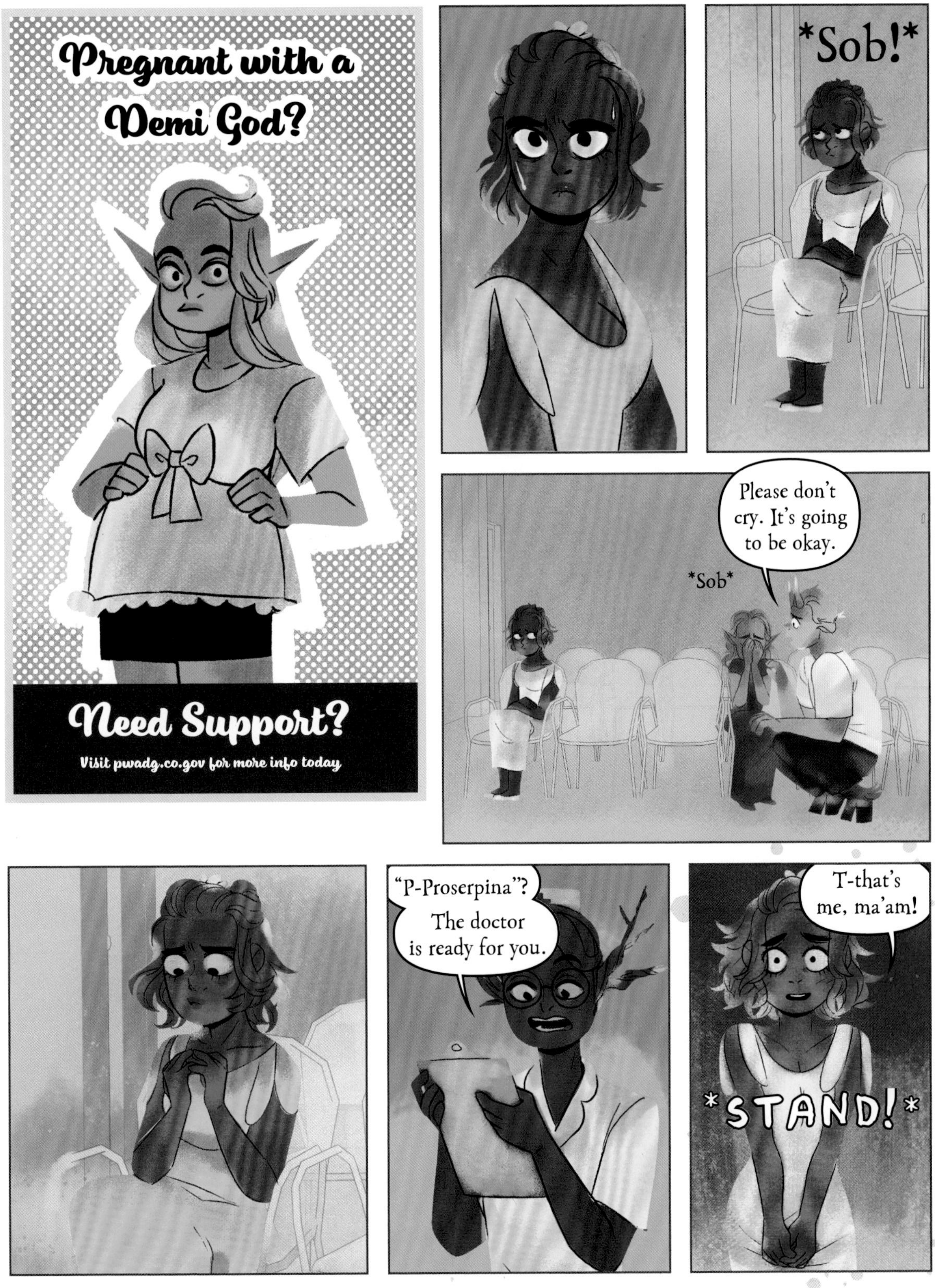
Pregnant with a Demi God?
Need Support?
Visit pwadg.co.gov for more info today
Sob!
Please don't cry. It's going to be okay.
Sob
"P-Proserpina"? The doctor is ready for you.
T-that's me, ma'am!
STAND!

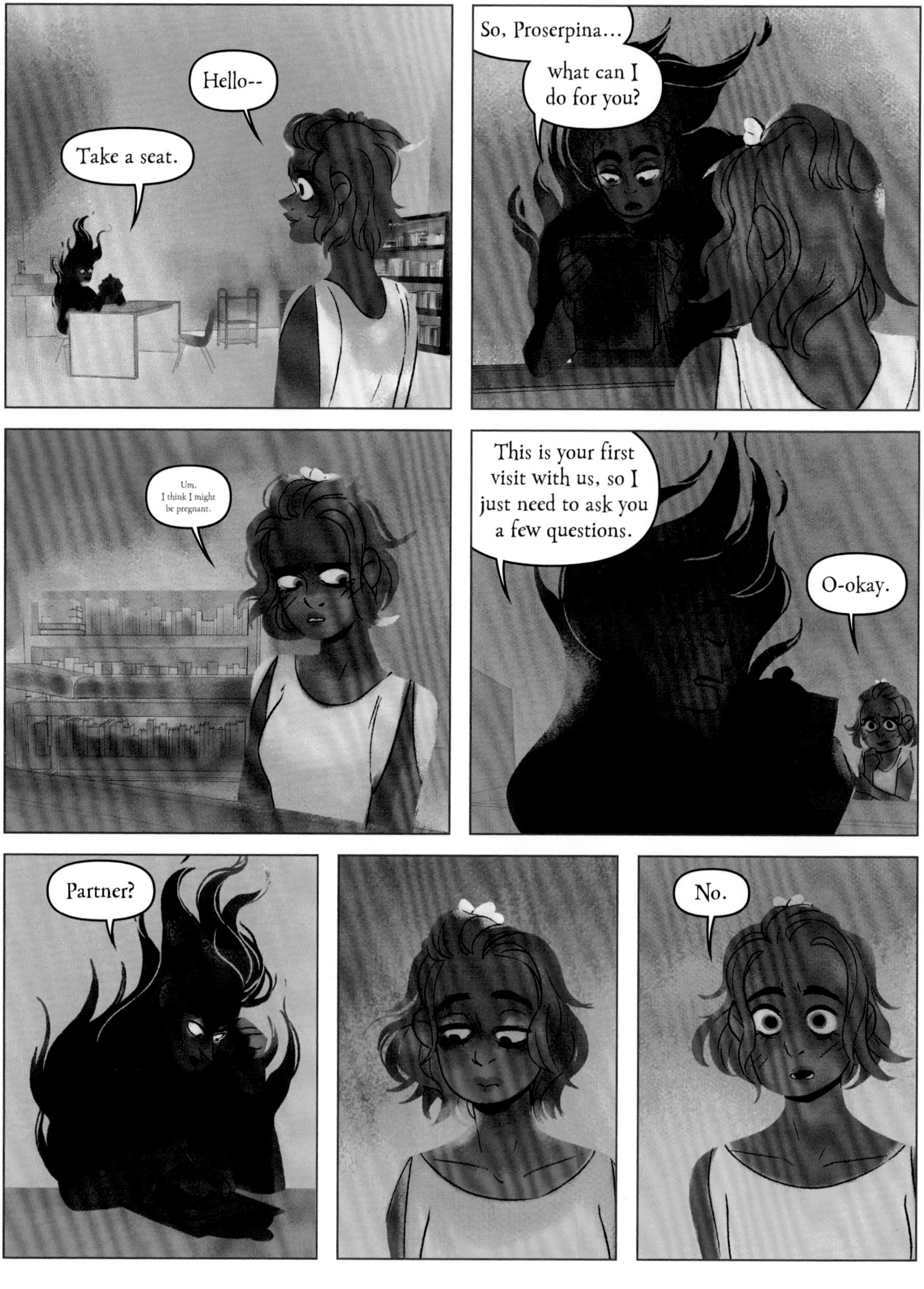
Hello--
Take a seat.
So, Proserpina...
what can I do for you?
Um, I think I might be pregnant.
This is your first visit with us, so I just need to ask you a few questions.
O-okay.
Partner?
No.

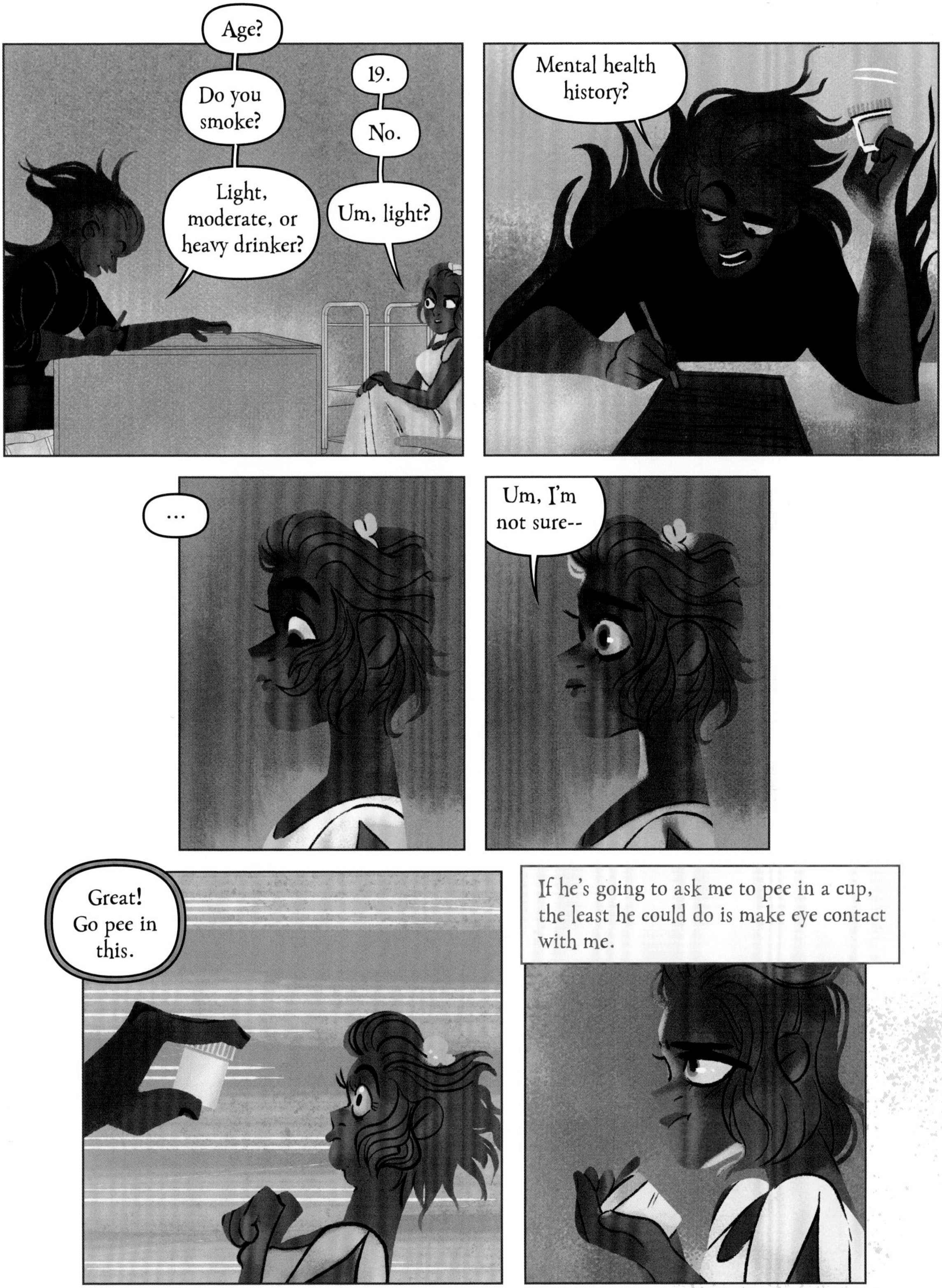
Age?
19.
Do you smoke?
No.
Light, moderate, or heavy drinker?
Um, light?
Mental health history?
...
Um, I'm not sure--
Great! Go pee in this.
If he's going to ask me to pee in a cup, the least he could do is make eye contact with me.

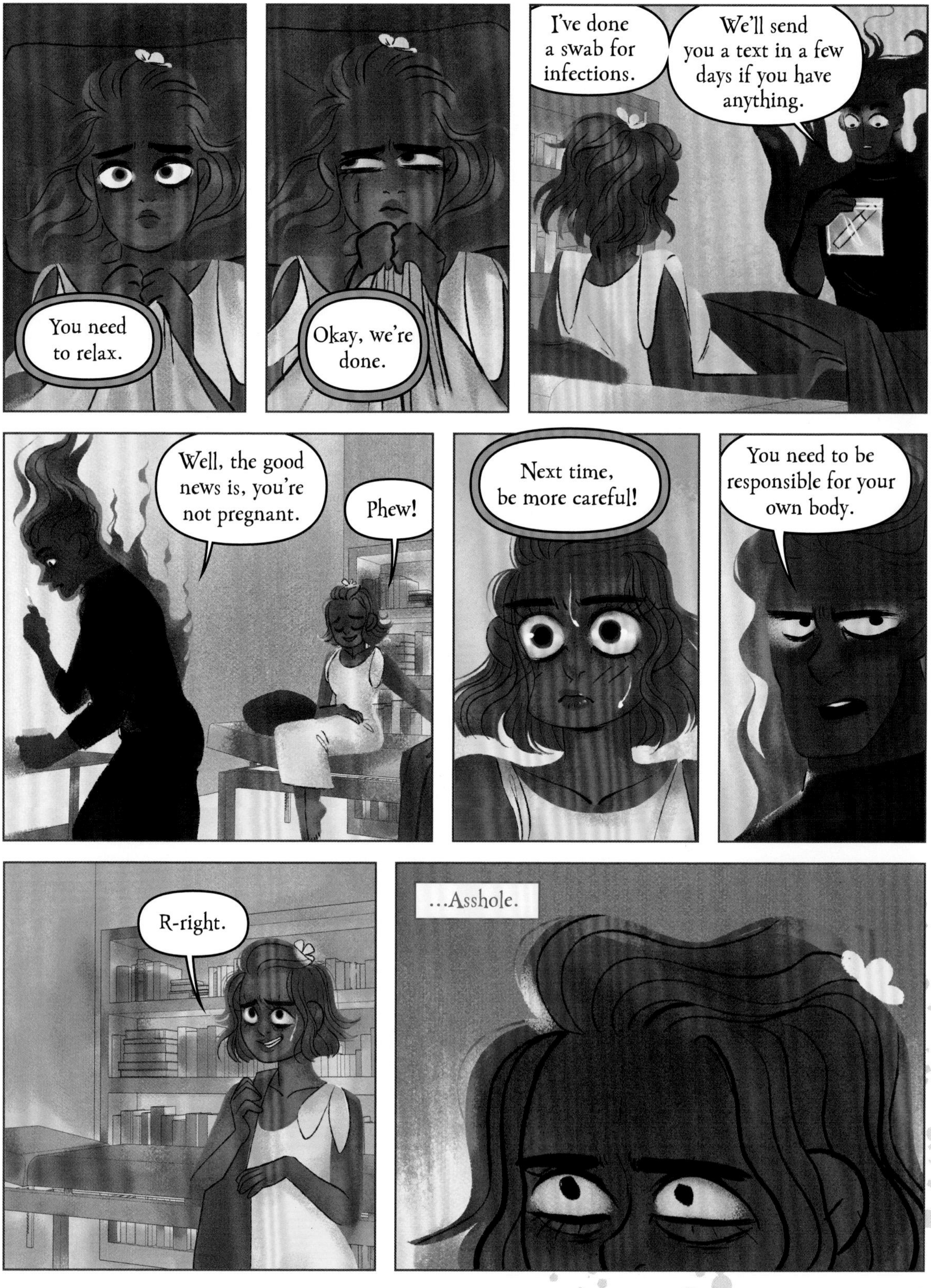
You need to relax.
Okay, we're done.
I've done a swab for infections.
We'll send you a text in a few days if you have anything.
Well, the good news is, you're not pregnant.
Phew!
Next time, be more careful!
You need to be responsible for your own body.
R-right.
...Asshole.

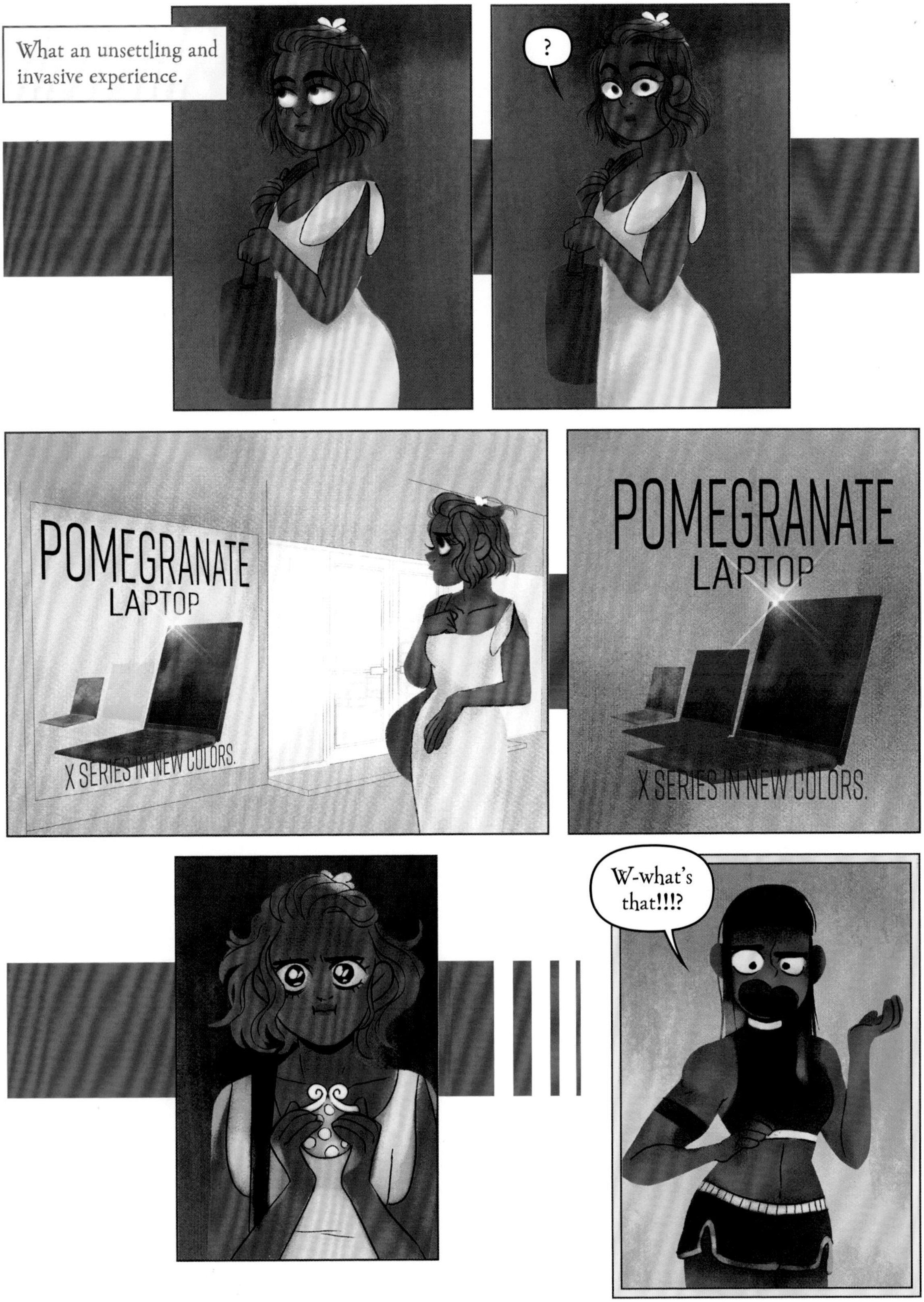
What an unsettling and invasive experience.
?
POMEGRANATE
LAPTOP
X SERIES IN NEW COLORS.
POMEGRANATE
LAPTOP
X SERIES IN NEW COLORS.
W-what's that!!!?

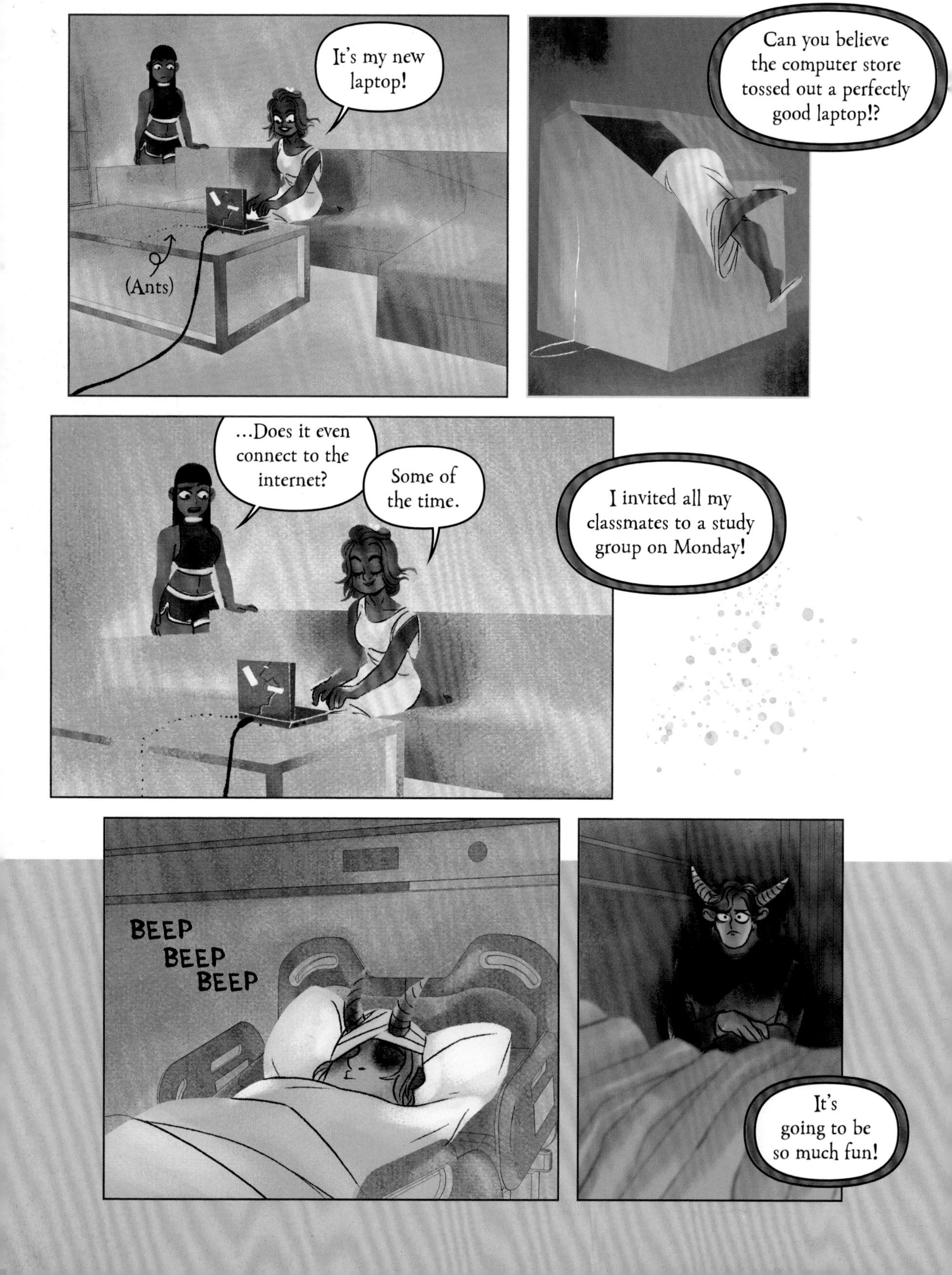
It's my new laptop!
(Ants)
Can you believe the computer store tossed out a perfectly good laptop!?
...Does it even connect to the internet?
Some of the time.
I invited all my classmates to a study group on Monday!
BEEP BEEP BEEP
It's going to be so much fun!

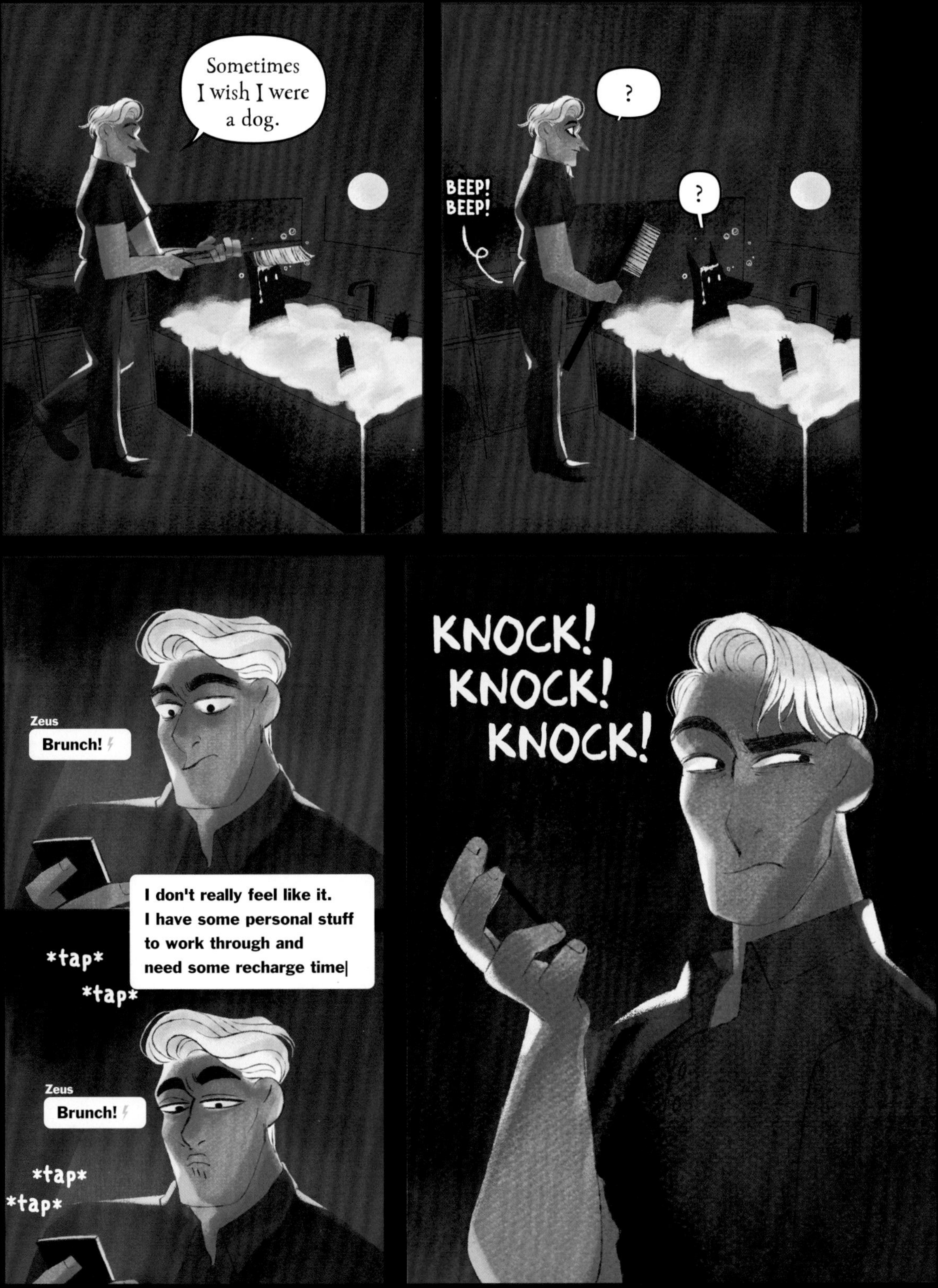
Sometimes I wish I were a dog.
?
BEEP! BEEP!
?
Zeus
Brunch!
I don't really feel like it. I have some personal stuff to work through and need some recharge time
tap
tap
Zeus
Brunch!
tap
tap
KNOCK! KNOCK! KNOCK!

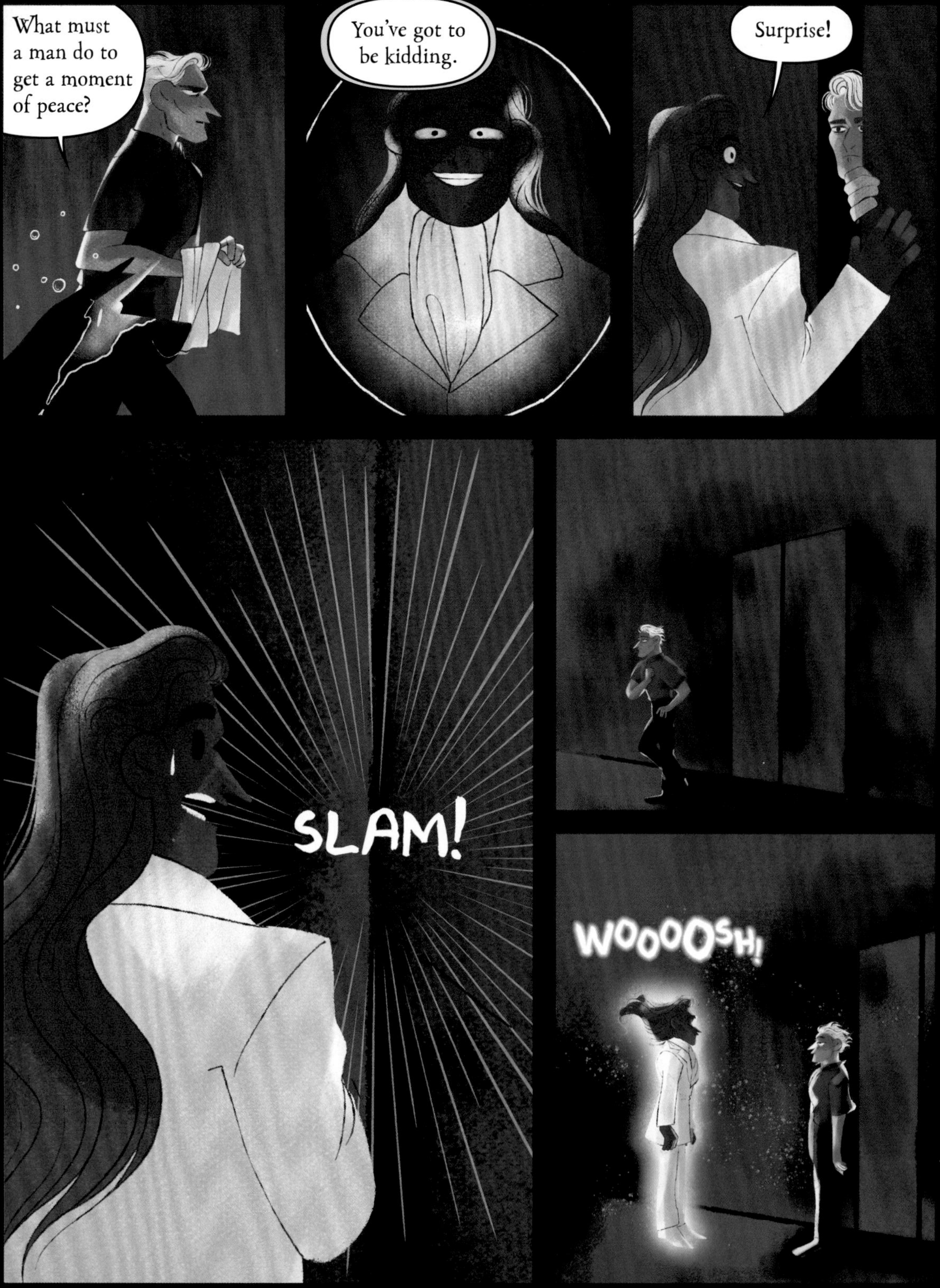
What must a man do to get a moment of peace?
You've got to be kidding.
Surprise!
SLAM!
WOOOOSH!

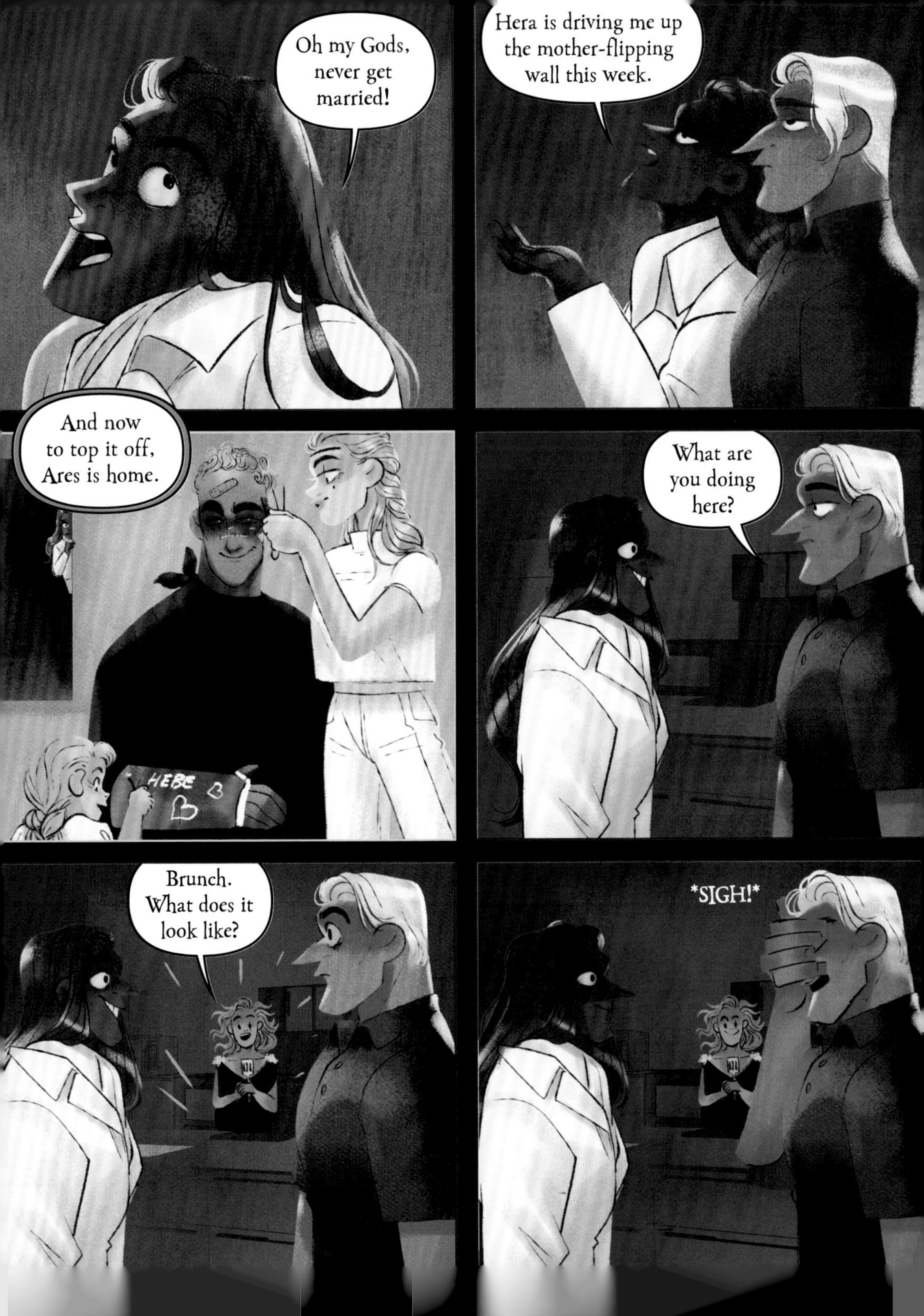
Oh my Gods, never get married!
Hera is driving me up the mother-flipping wall this week.
And now to top it off, Ares is home.
HEBE
What are you doing here?
Brunch. What does it look like?
SIGH!

EPISODE 84: PANCAKES

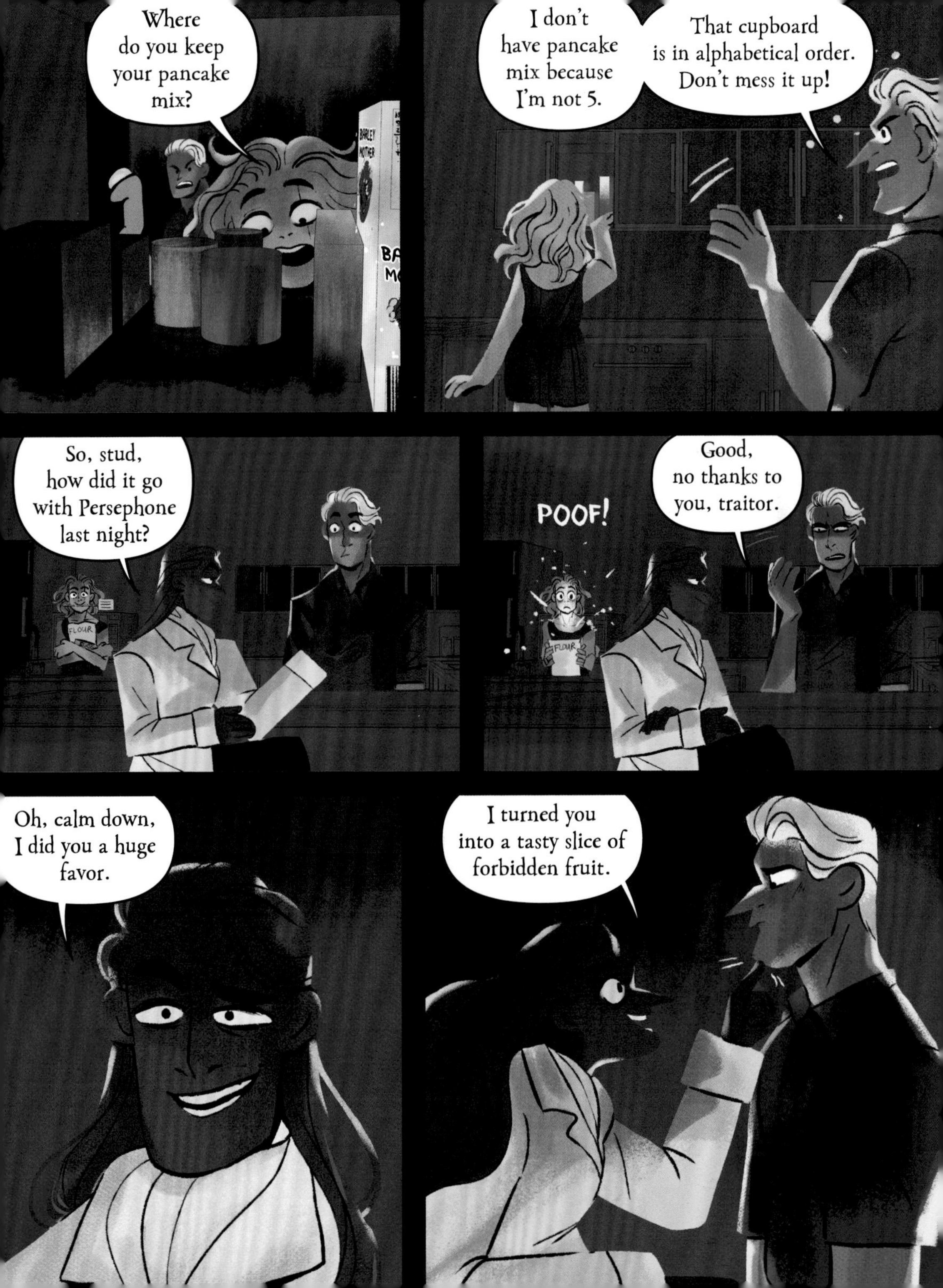
Where do you keep your pancake mix?
BARLEY MOTHER
I don't have pancake mix because I'm not 5.
That cupboard is in alphabetical order. Don't mess it up!
So, stud, how did it go with Persephone last night?
FLOUR
POOF!
Good, no thanks to you, traitor.
FLOUR
Oh, calm down, I did you a huge favor.
I turned you into a tasty slice of forbidden fruit.

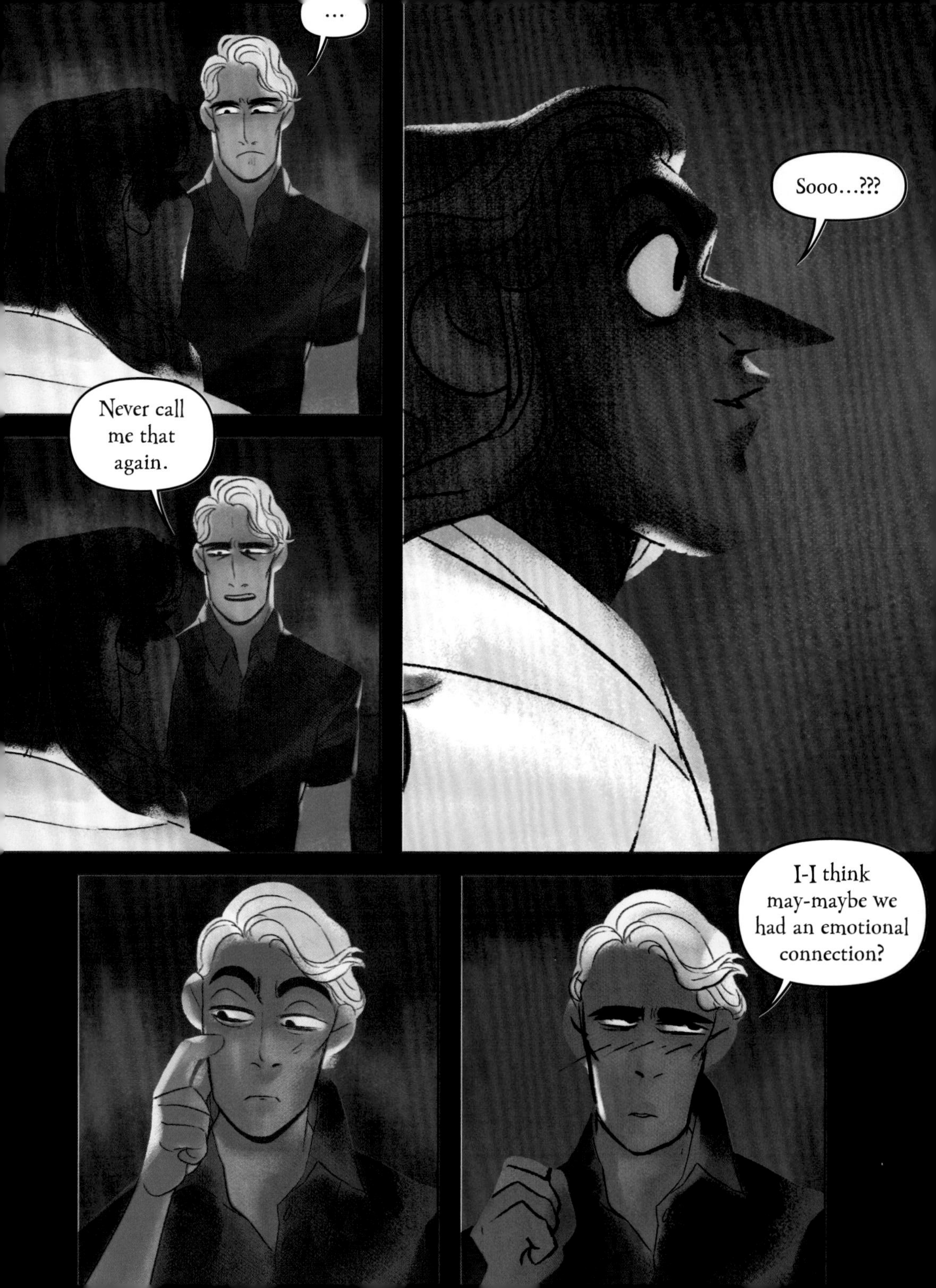
...
Sooo...???
Never call me that again.
I-I think may-maybe we had an emotional connection?

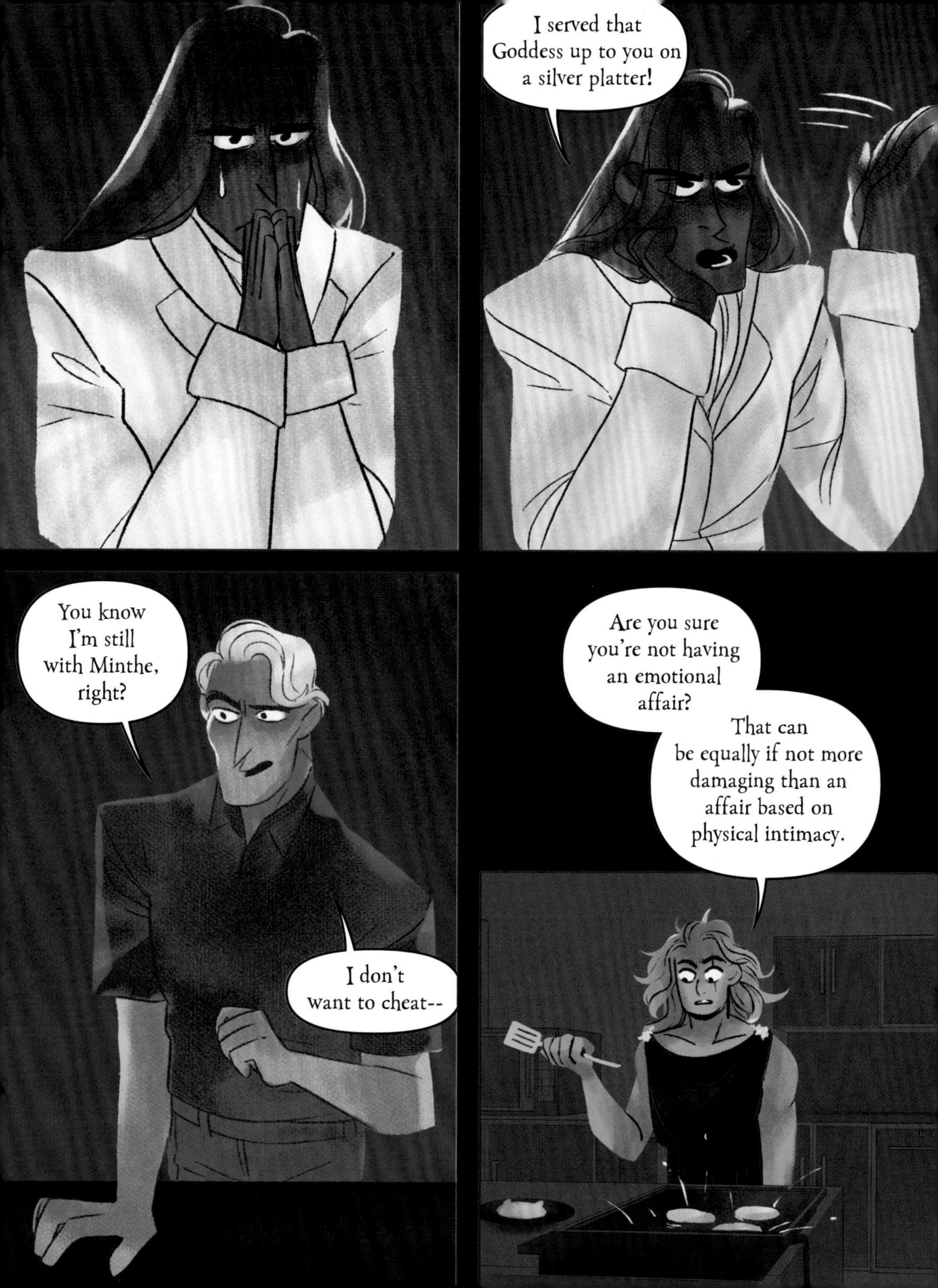
I served that Goddess up to you on a silver platter!
You know I'm still with Minthe, right?
I don't want to cheat--
Are you sure you're not having an emotional affair?
That can be equally if not more damaging than an affair based on physical intimacy.

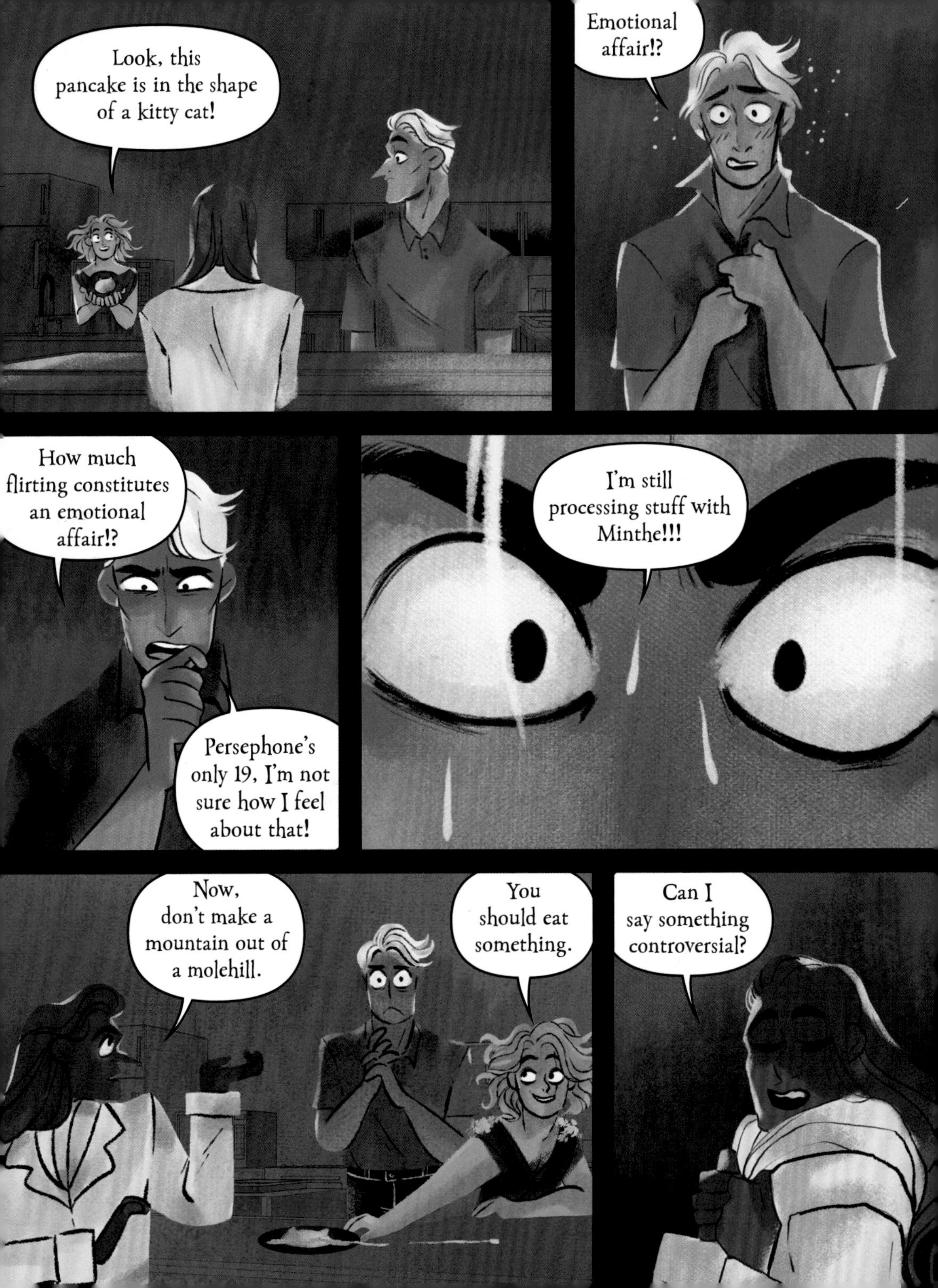
Look, this pancake is in the shape of a kitty cat!
Emotional affair!?
How much flirting constitutes an emotional affair!?
Persephone's only 19, I'm not sure how I feel about that!
I'm still processing stuff with Minthe!!!
Now, don't make a mountain out of a molehill.
You should eat something.
Can I say something controversial?

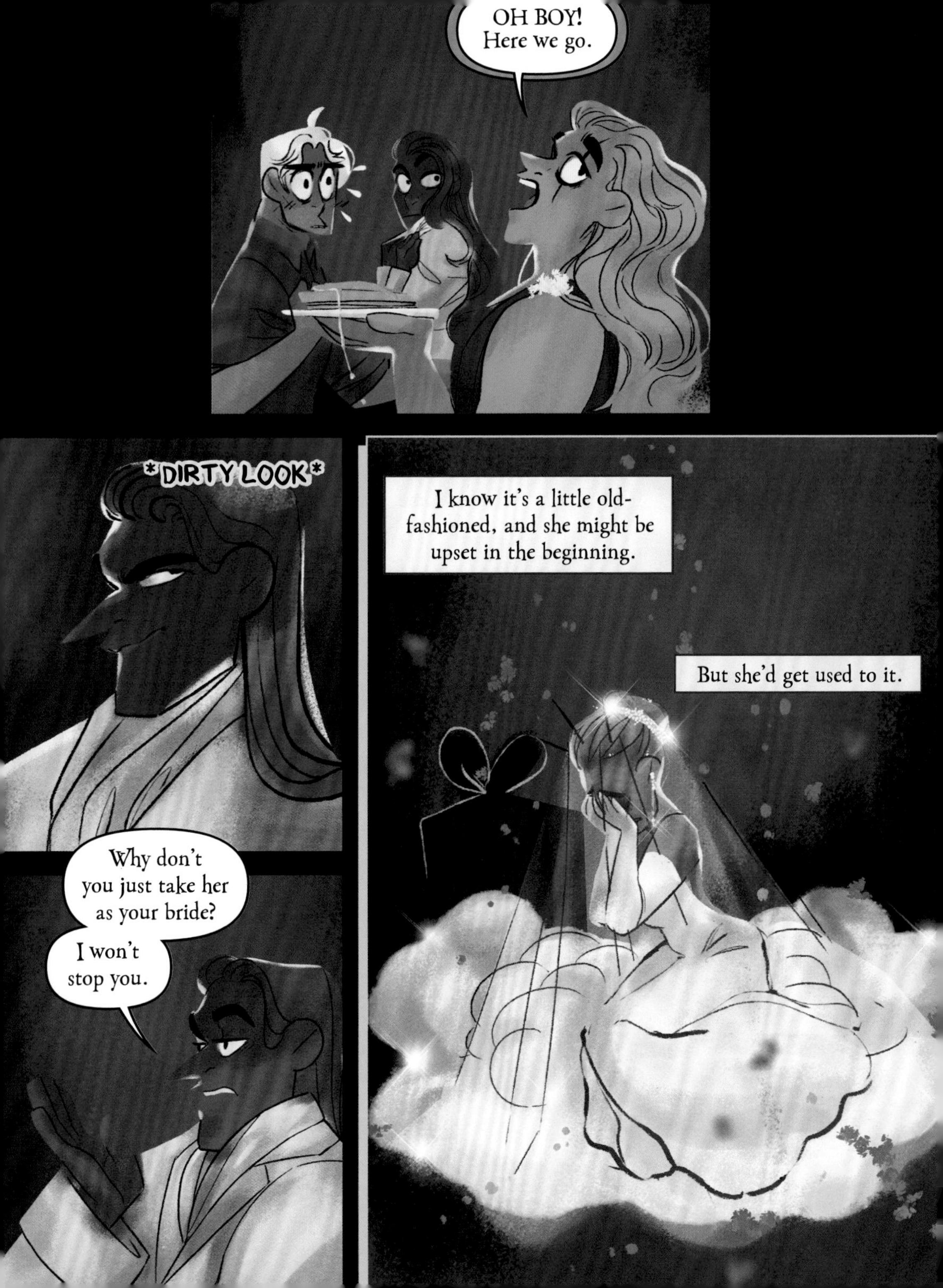
OH BOY!
Here we go.
DIRTY LOOK
Why don't you just take her as your bride?
I won't stop you.
I know it's a little old-fashioned, and she might be upset in the beginning.
But she'd get used to it.

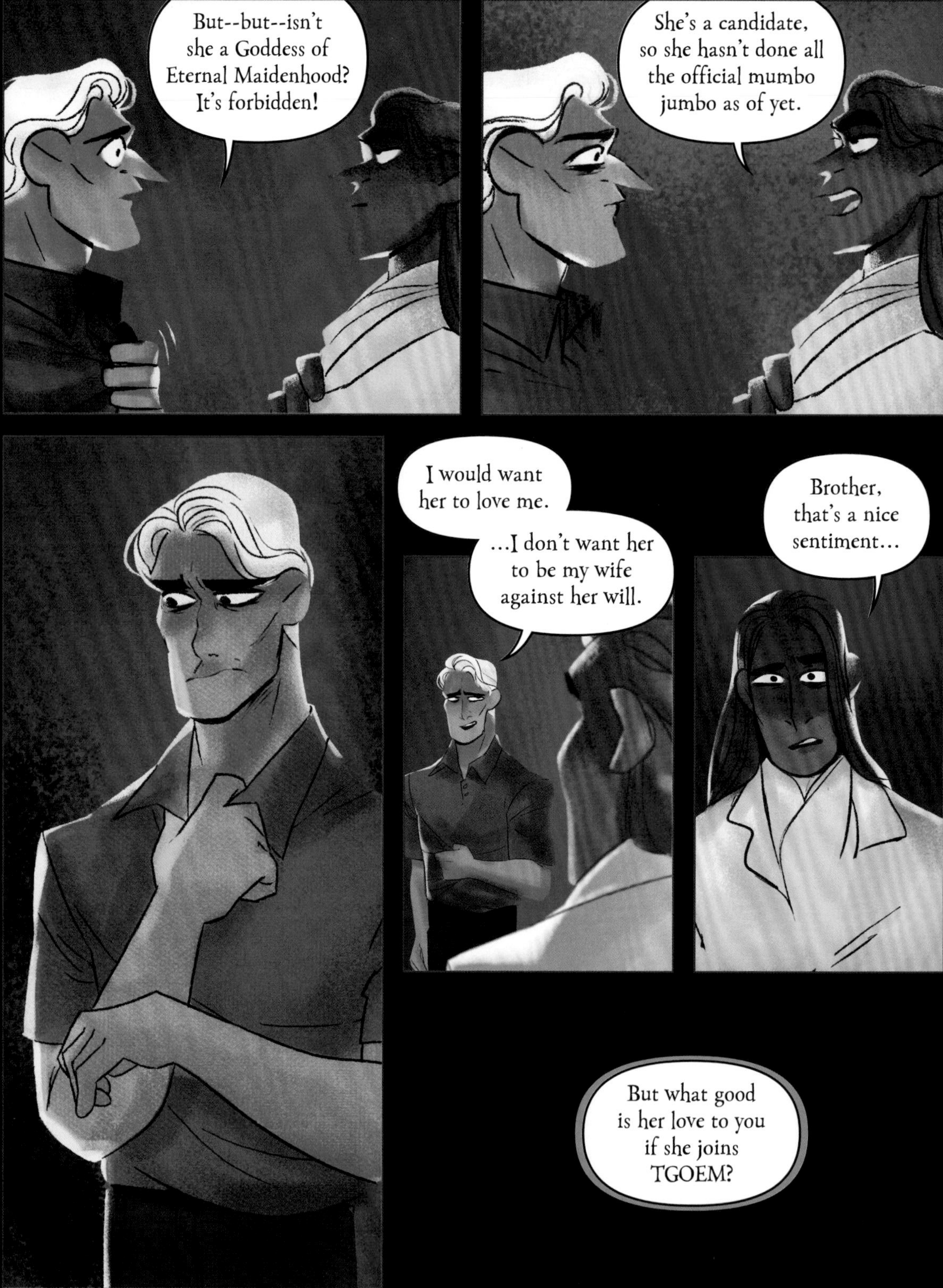
But--but--isn't she a Goddess of Eternal Maidenhood? It's forbidden!
She's a candidate, so she hasn't done all the official mumbo jumbo as of yet.
I would want her to love me.
...I don't want her to be my wife against her will.
Brother, that's a nice sentiment...
But what good is her love to you if she joins TGOEM?

THE NEXT DAY!

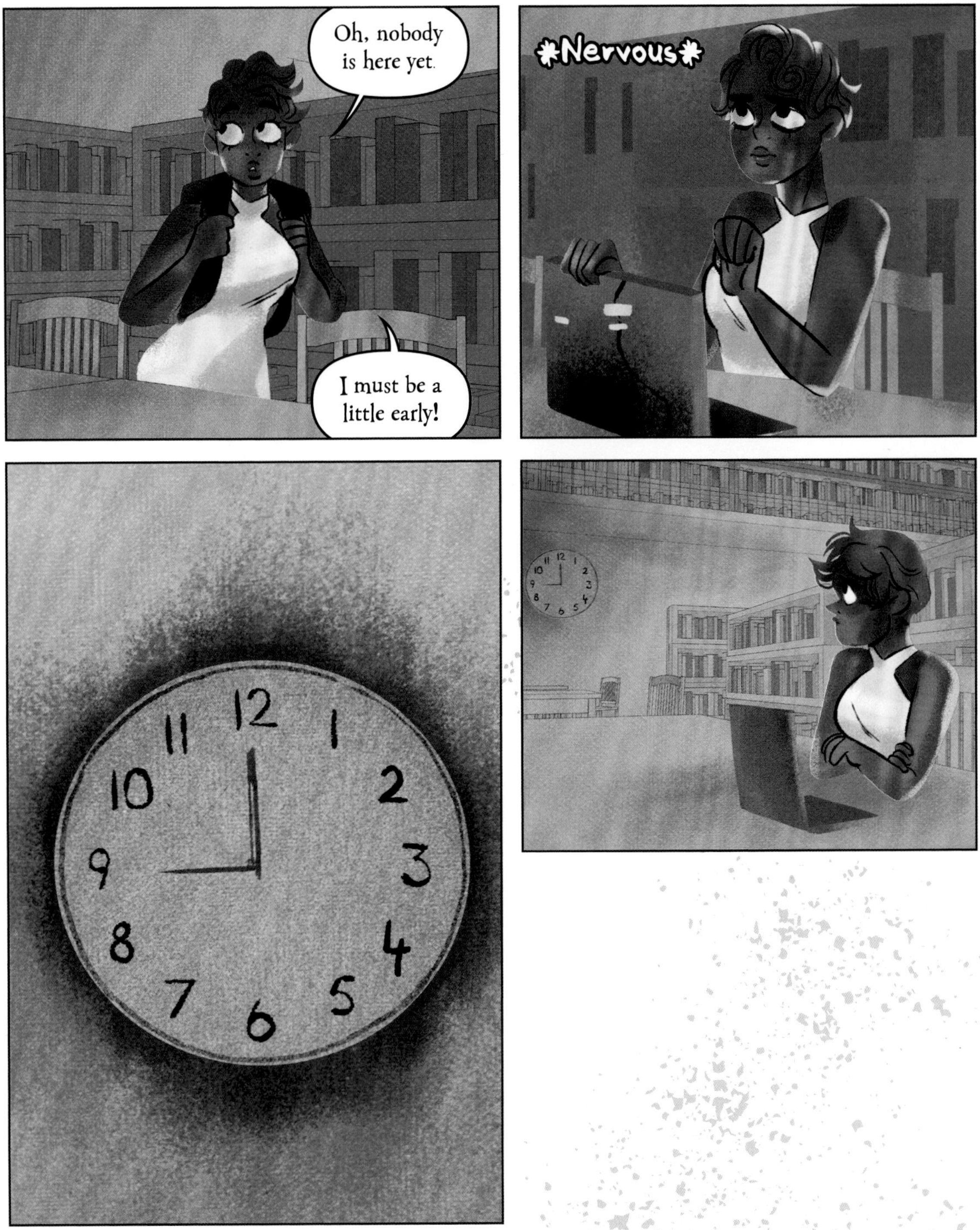
Oh, nobody is here yet.
I must be a little early!
Nervous

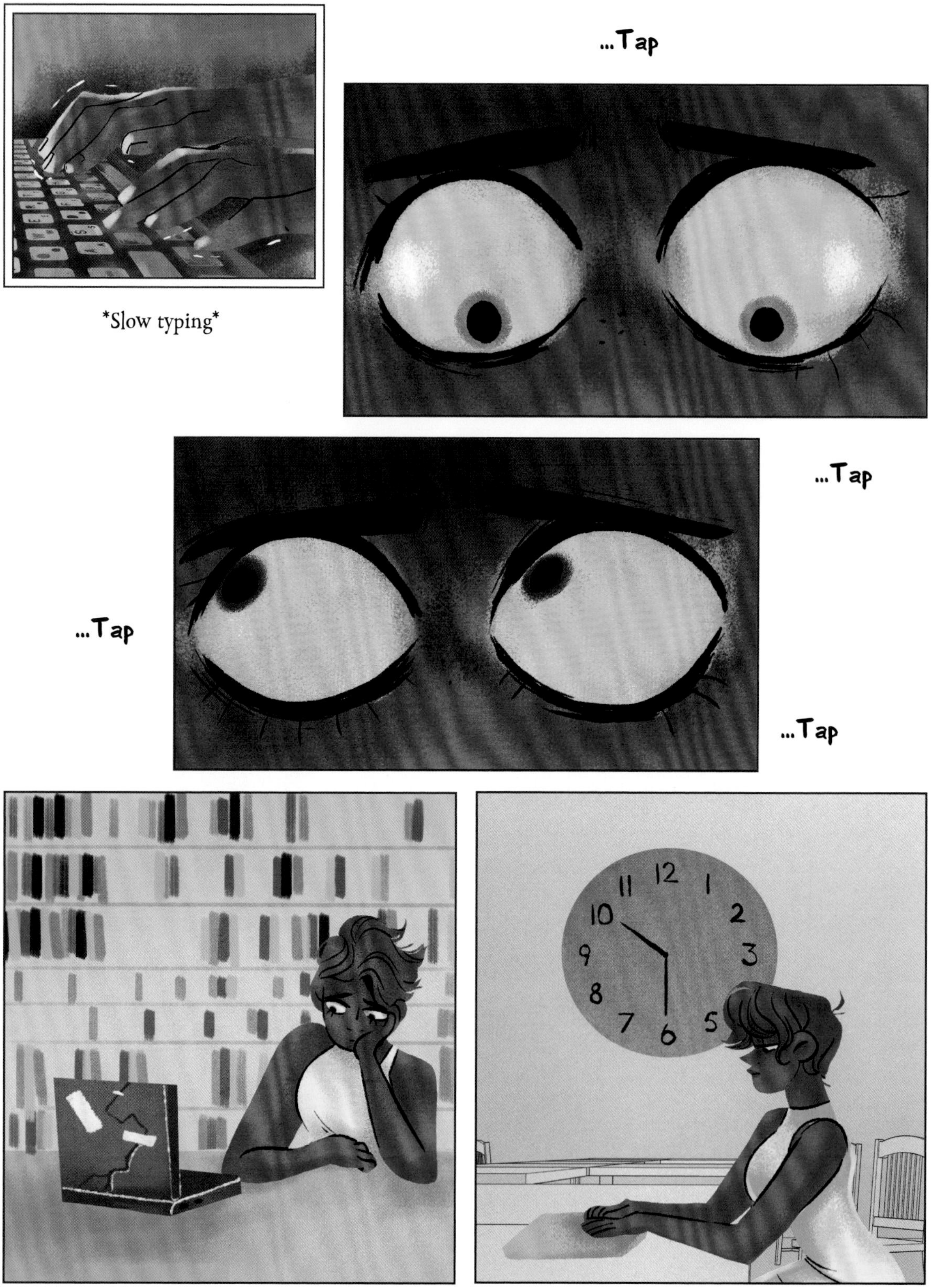
Slow typing
...Tap
...Tap
...Tap
...Tap

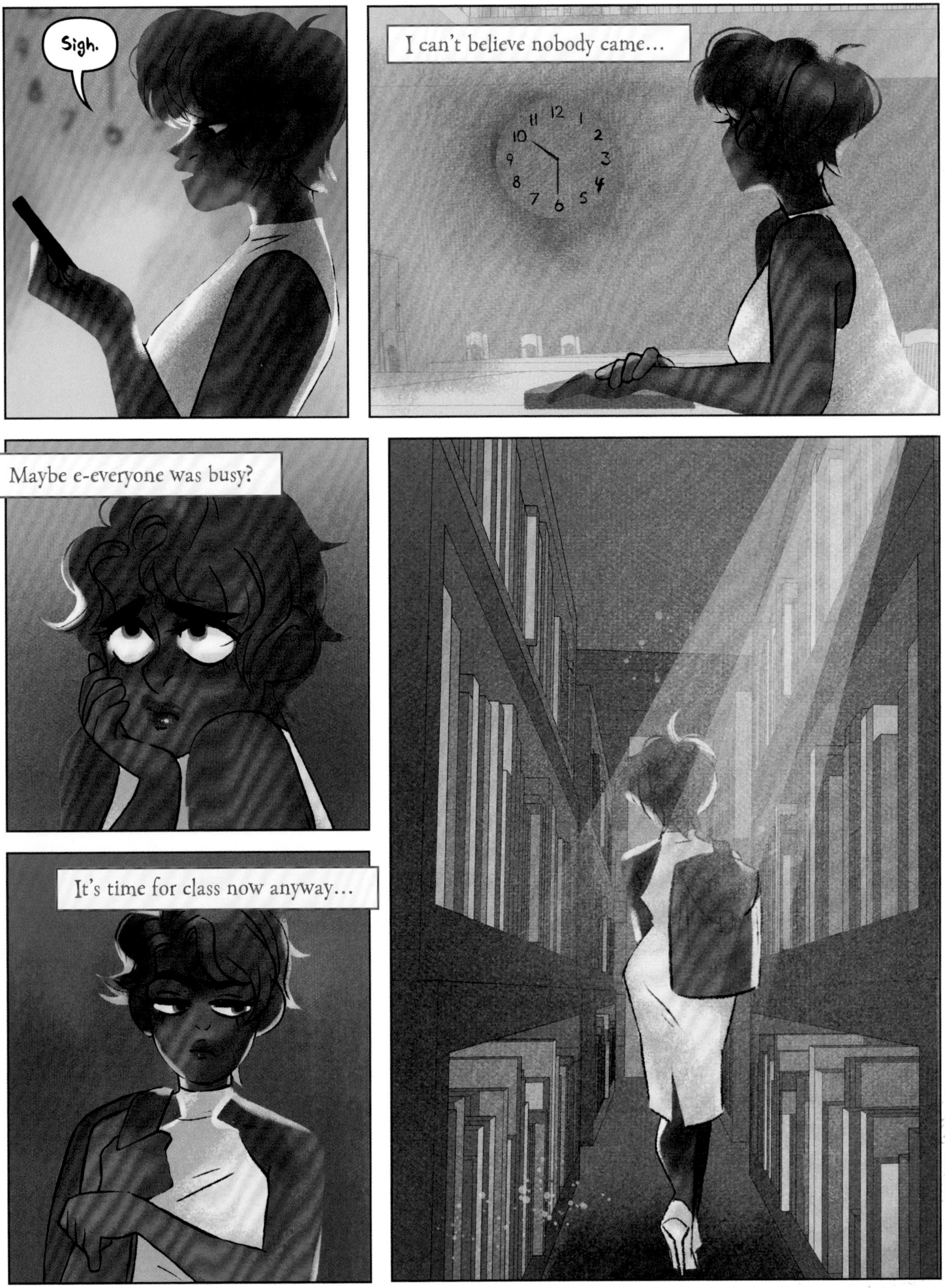
Sigh.
I can't believe nobody came...
Maybe e-everyone was busy?
It's time for class now anyway...

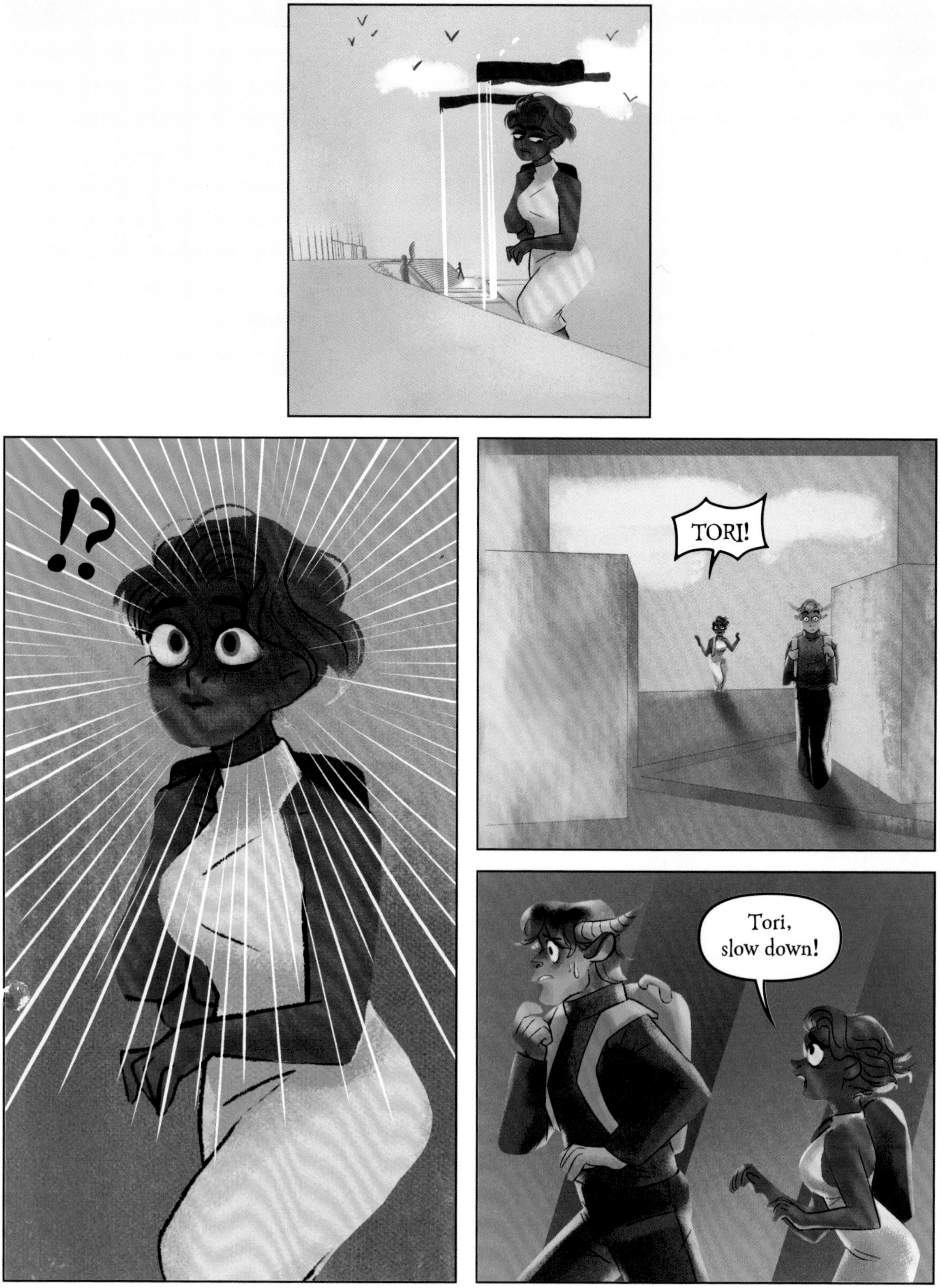
!?
TORI!
Tori, slow down!

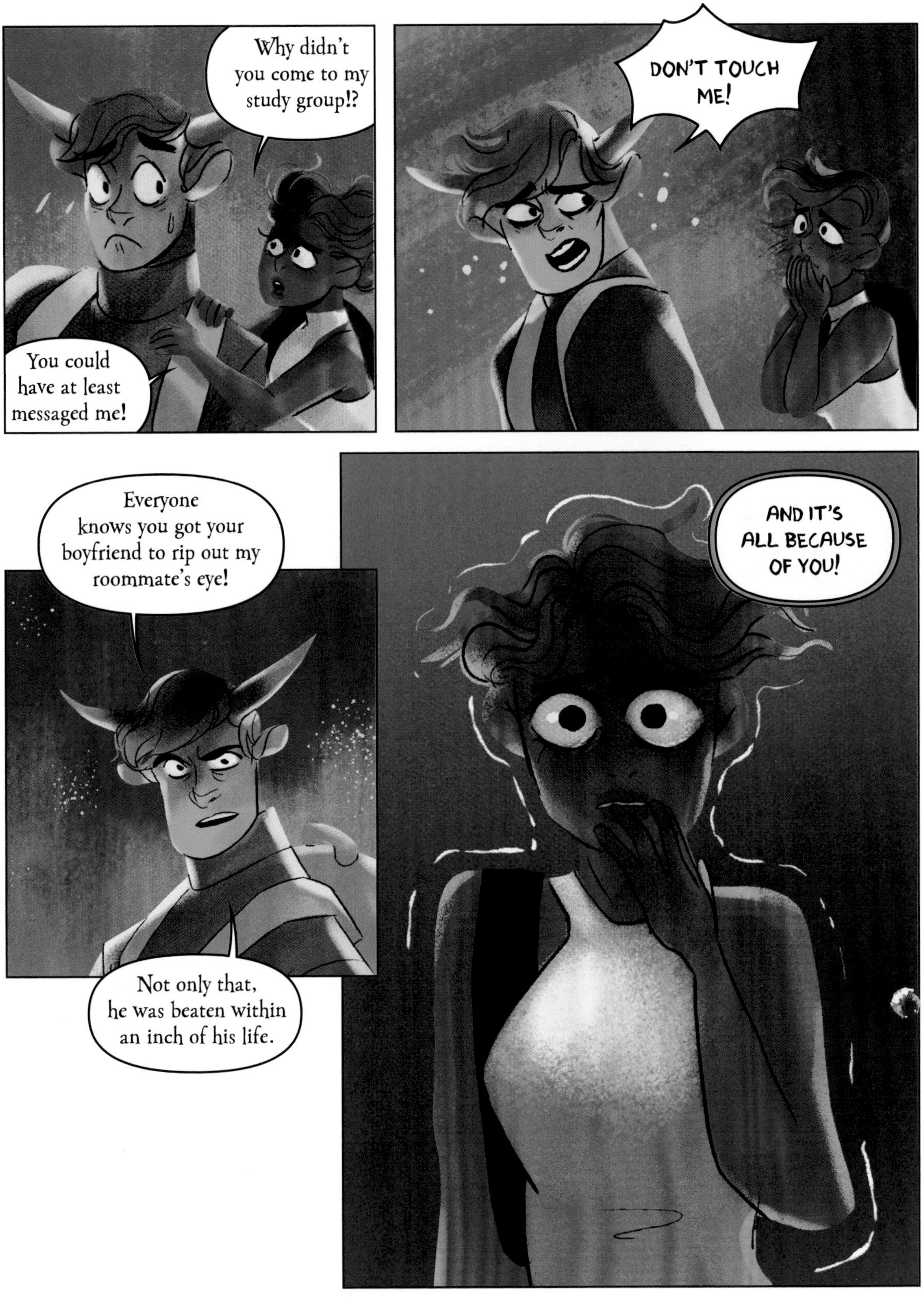
Why didn't you come to my study group!?
You could have at least messaged me!
DON'T TOUCH ME!
Everyone knows you got your boyfriend to rip out my roommate's eye!
Not only that, he was beaten within an inch of his life.
AND IT'S ALL BECAUSE OF YOU!

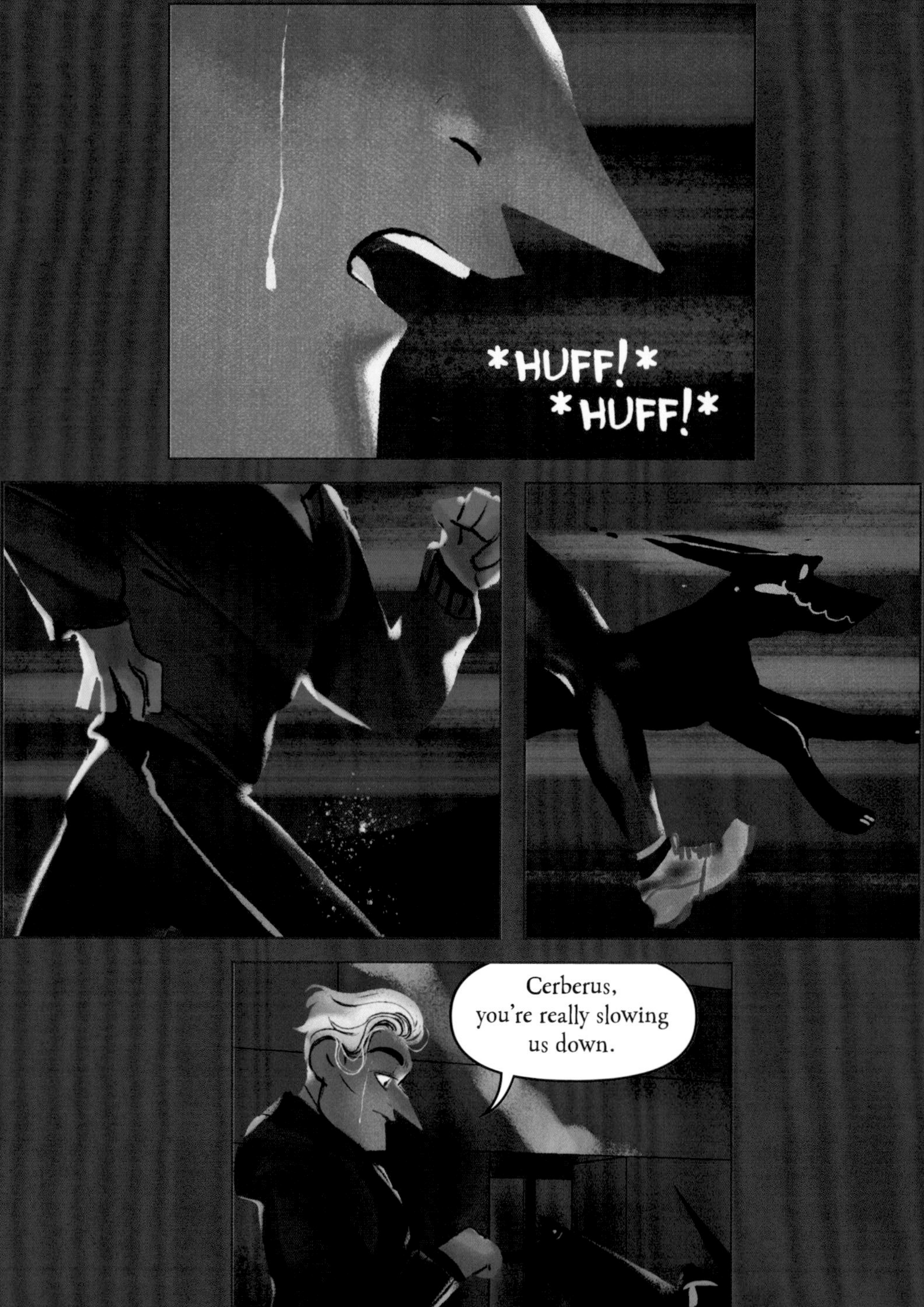
HUFF!
HUFF!
Cerberus, you're really slowing us down.

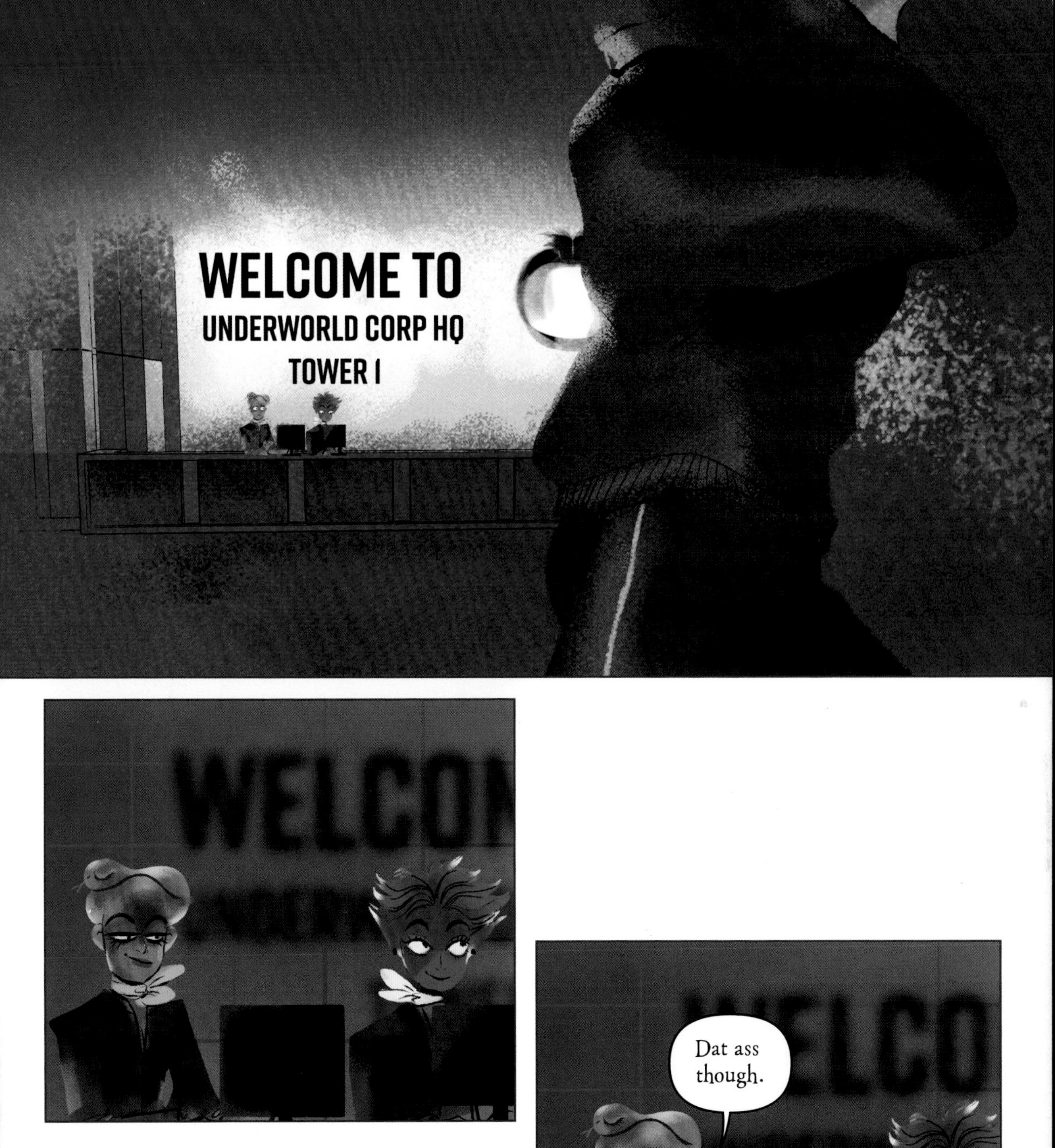
WELCOME TO
UNDERWORLD CORP HQ
TOWER 1
Dat ass though.

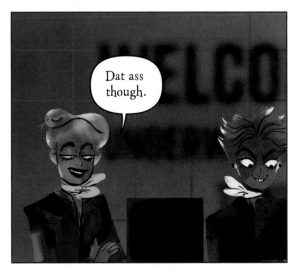

EPISODE 85: BETWEEN THE LINES

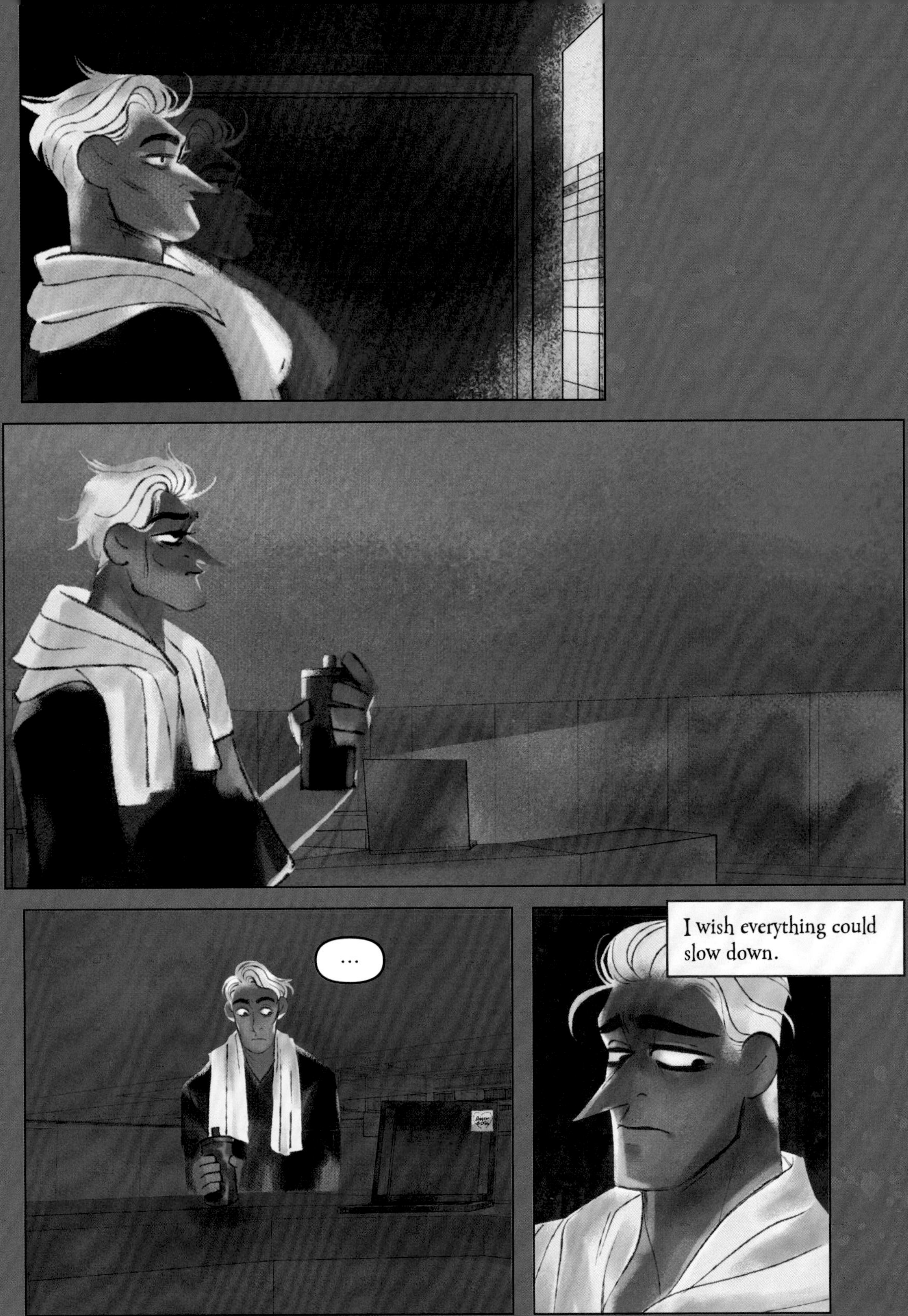
...
I wish everything could slow down.

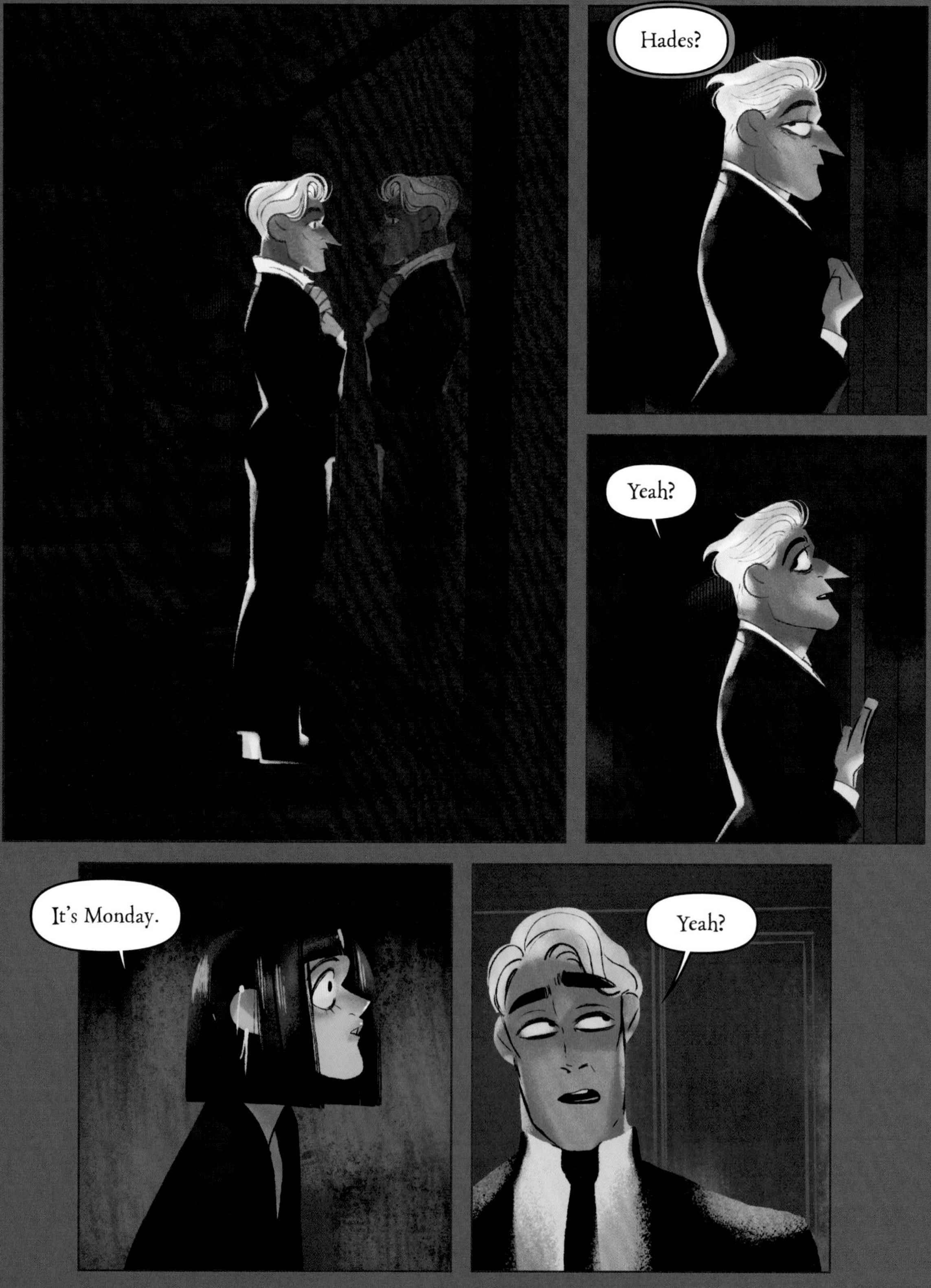
Hades?
Yeah?
It's Monday.
Yeah?

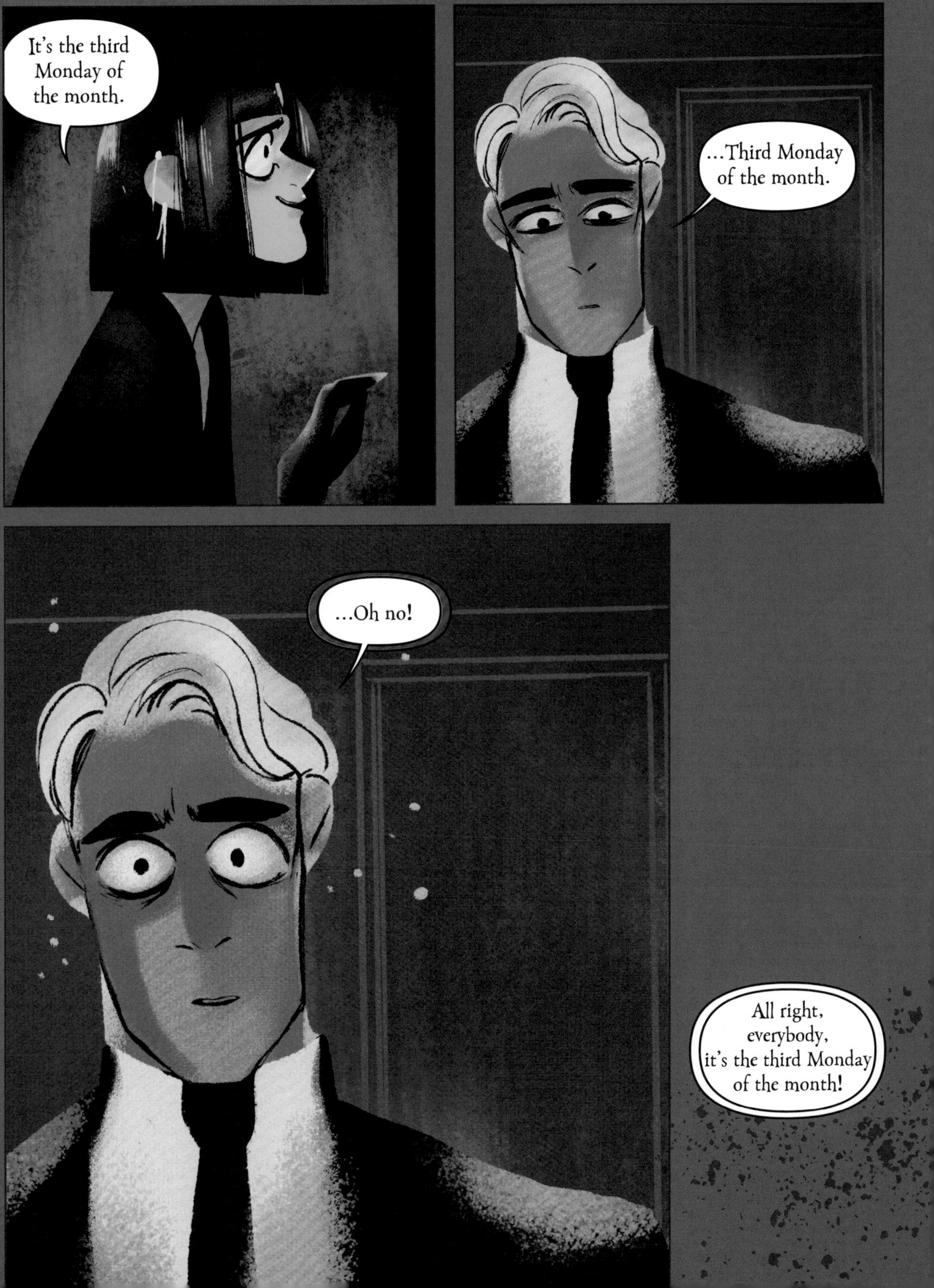
It's the third Monday of the month.
...Third Monday of the month.
...Oh no!
All right, everybody, it's the third Monday of the month!

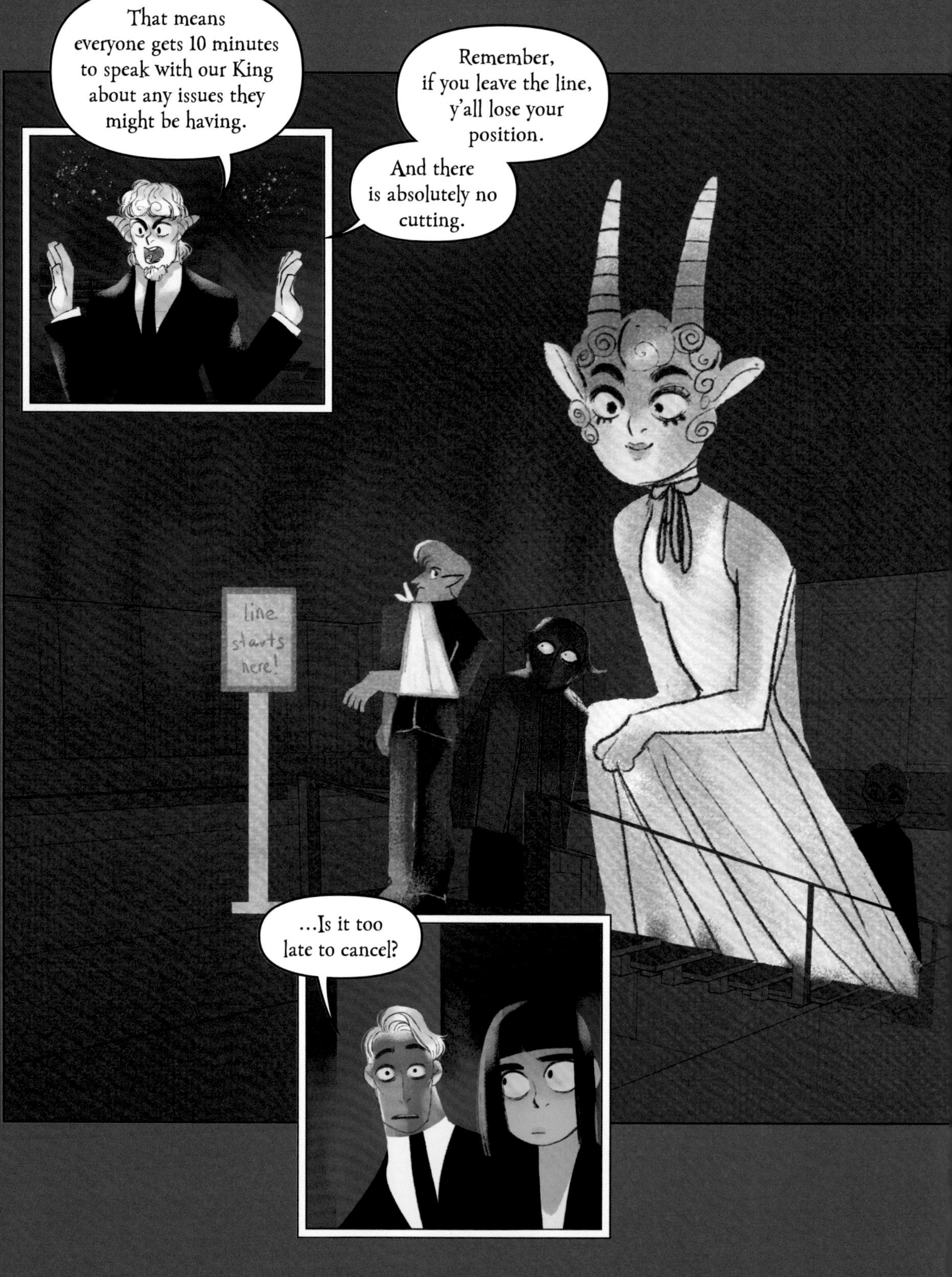
That means everyone gets 10 minutes to speak with our King about any issues they might be having.
Remember, if you leave the line, y'all lose your position.
And there is absolutely no cutting.
line starts here!
...Is it too late to cancel?

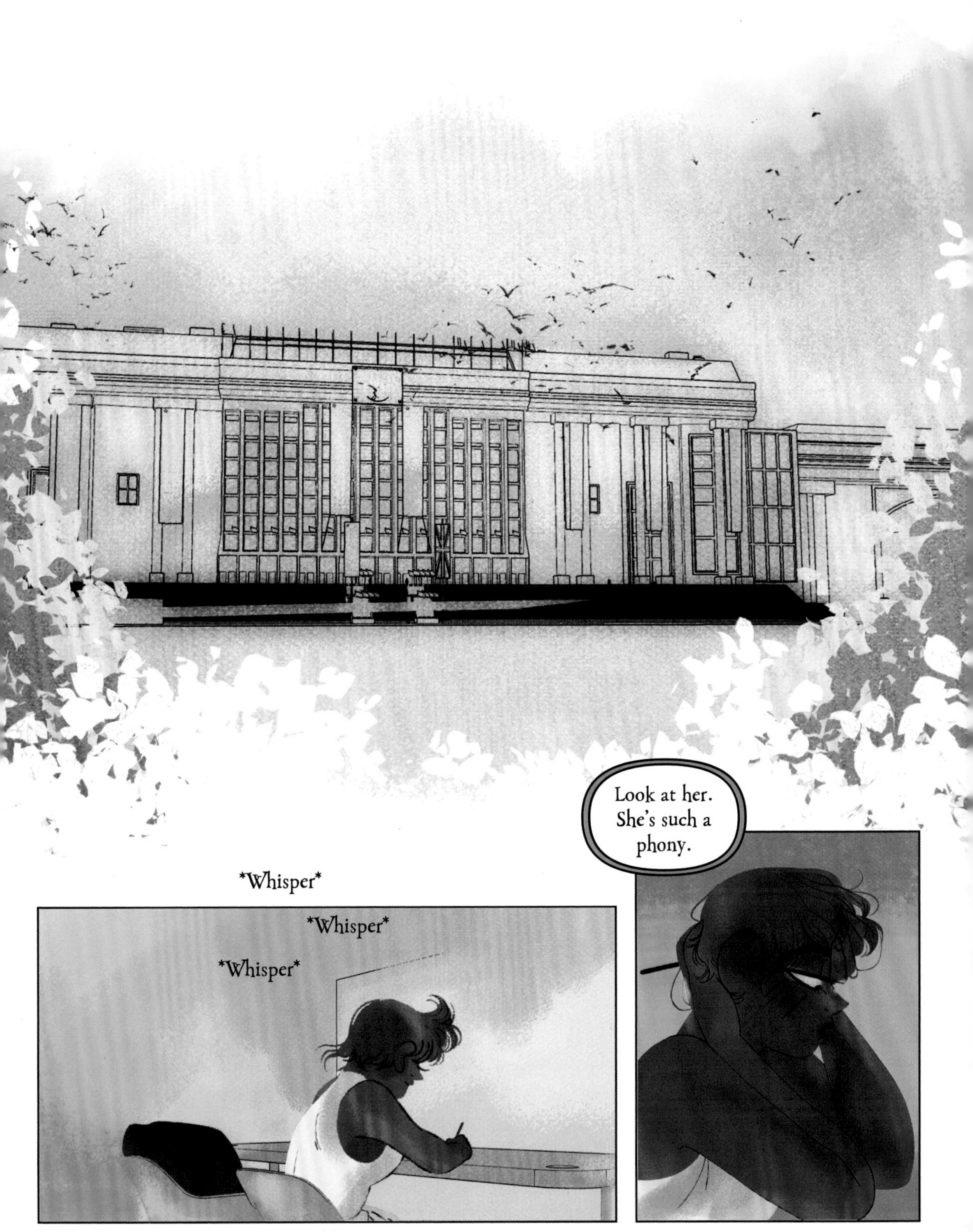
Whisper
Whisper
Whisper
Look at her. She's such a phony.

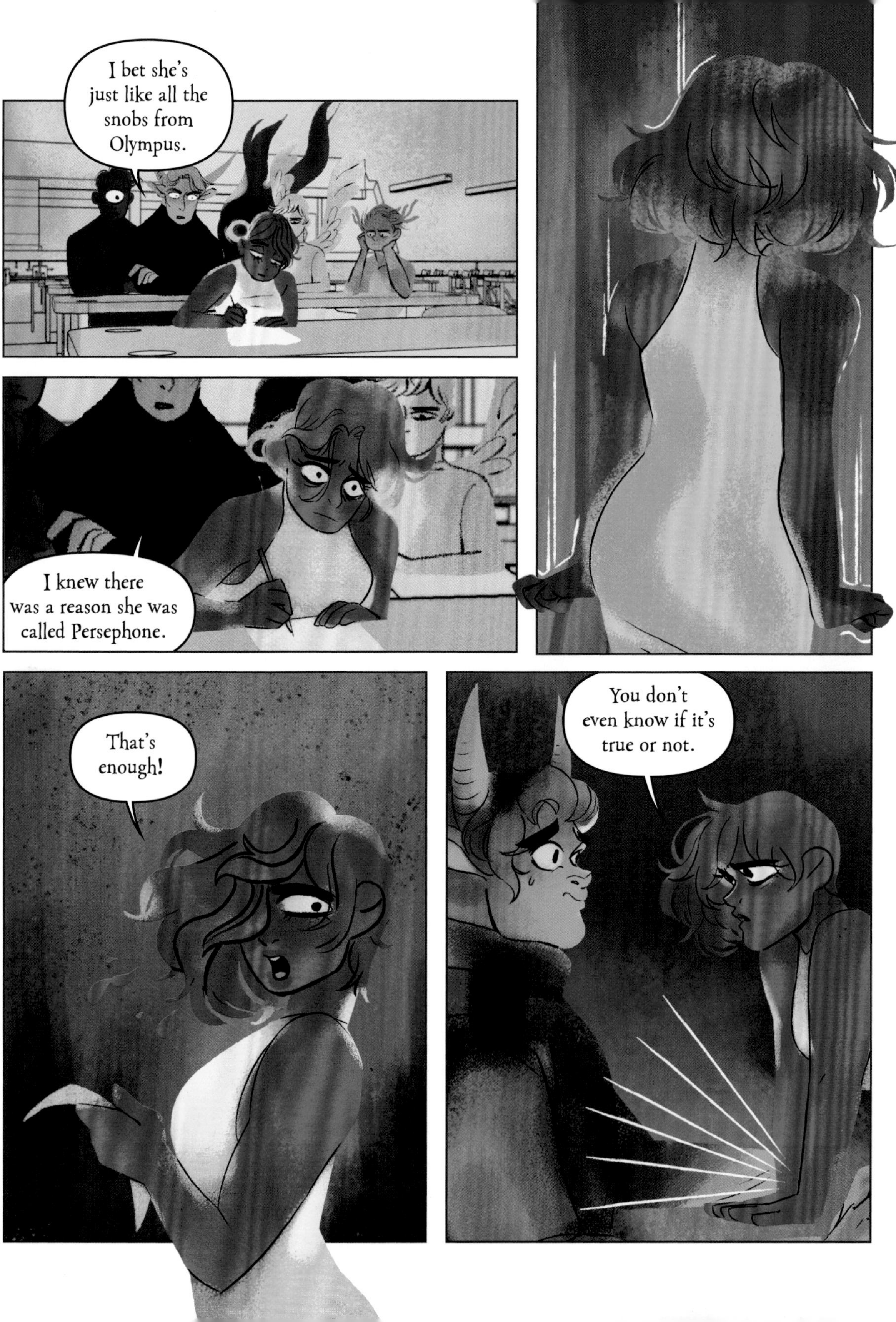
I bet she's just like all the snobs from Olympus.
I knew there was a reason she was called Persephone.
That's enough!
You don't even know if it's true or not.

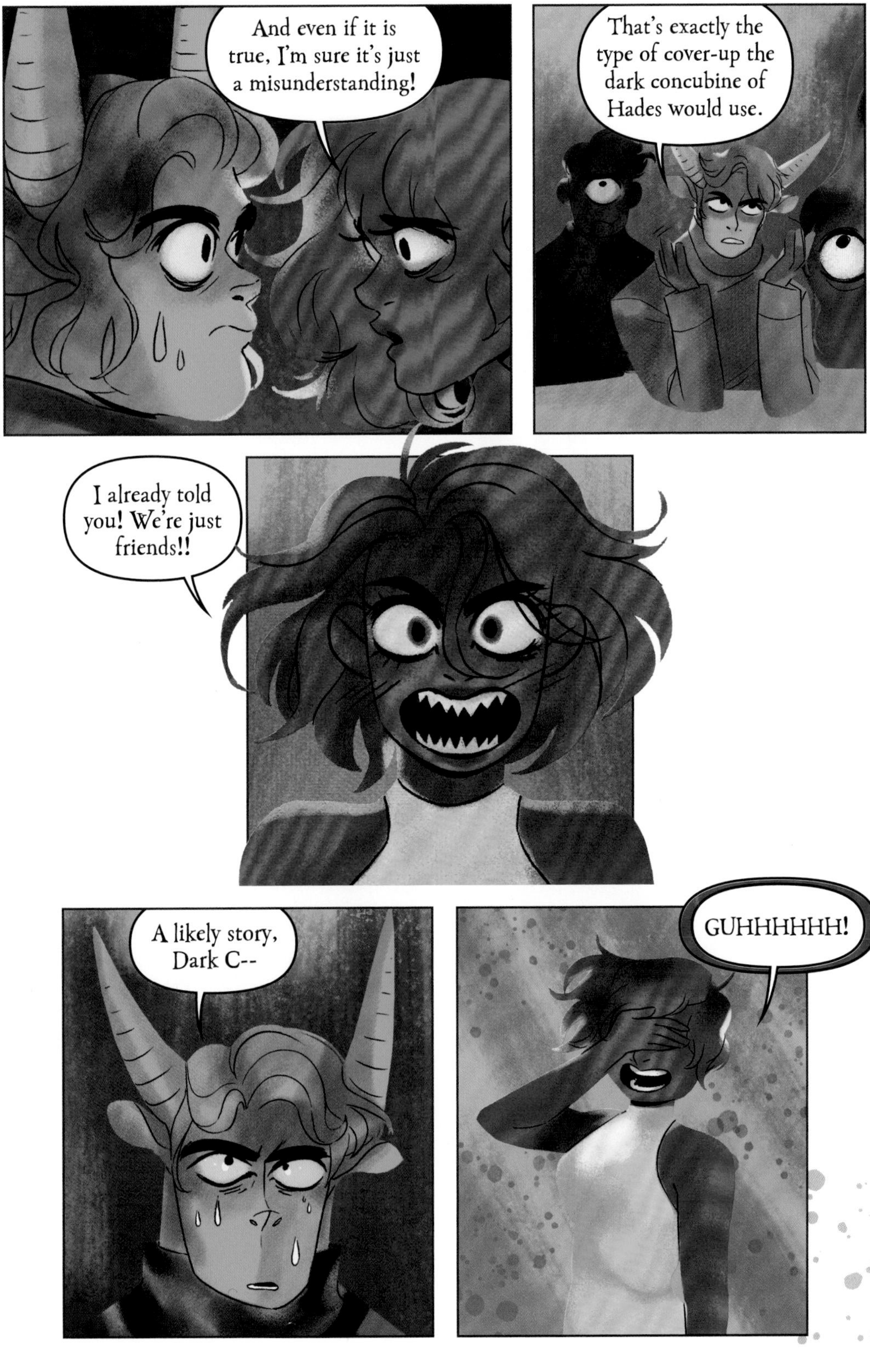

And even if it is true, I'm sure it's just a misunderstanding!
That's exactly the type of cover-up the dark concubine of Hades would use.
I already told you! We're just friends!!
A likely story, Dark C--
GUHHHHHH!

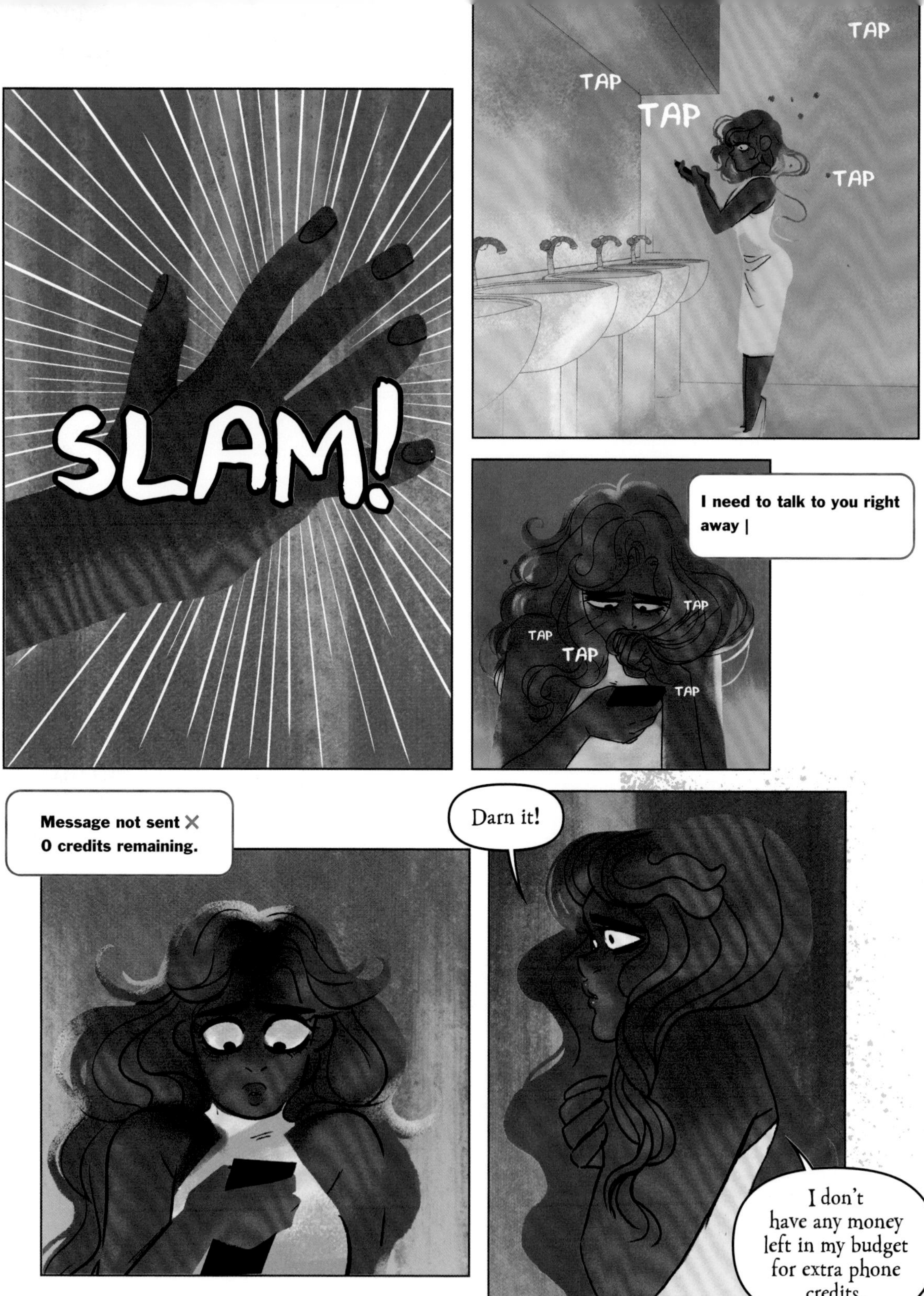
SLAM!
TAP
TAP
TAP
TAP
I need to talk to you right away |
TAP
TAP
TAP
TAP
Message not sent ✕
0 credits remaining.
Darn it!
I don't have any money left in my budget for extra phone credits.

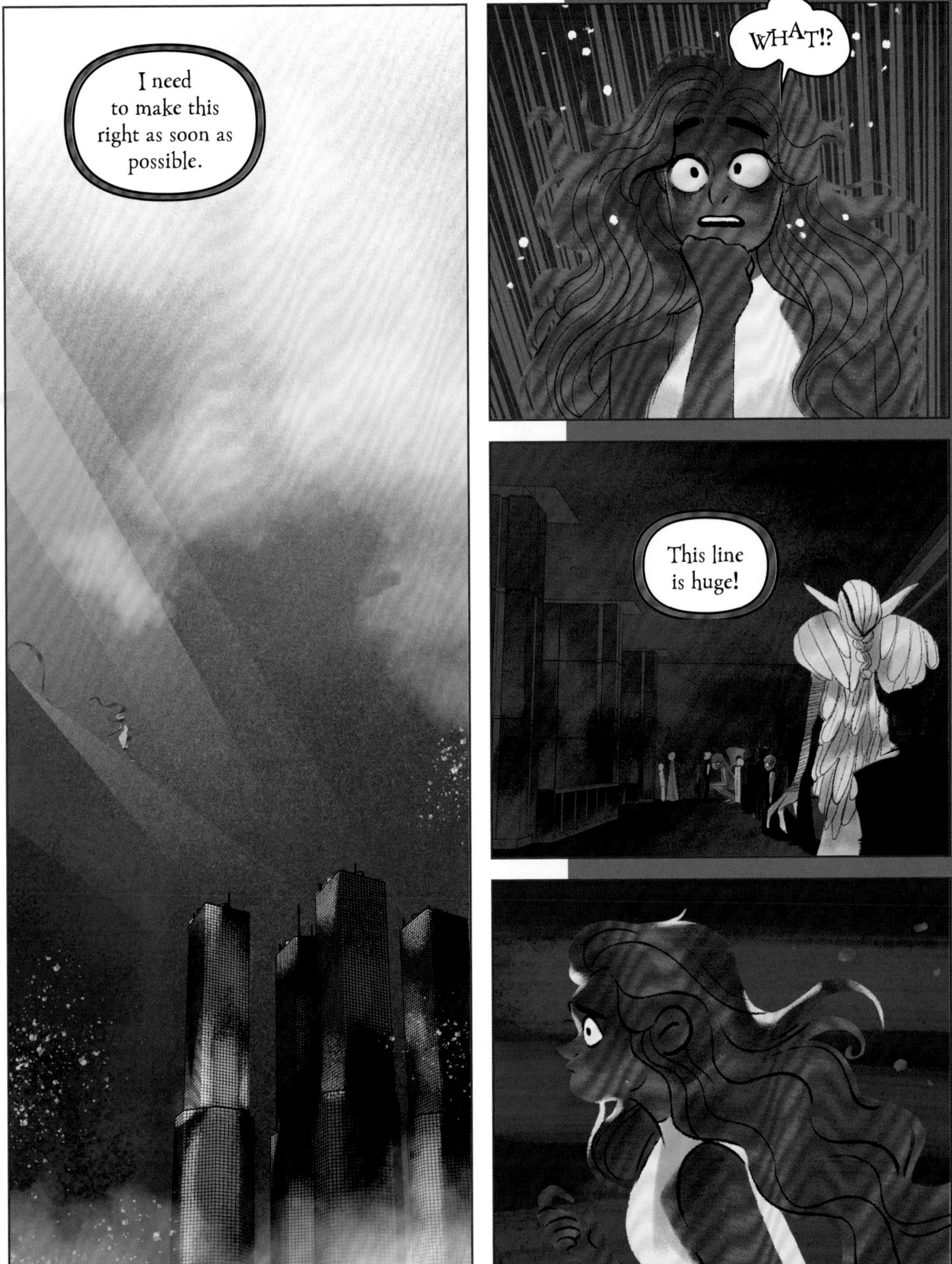
I need to make this right as soon as possible.
WHAT!?
This line is huge!

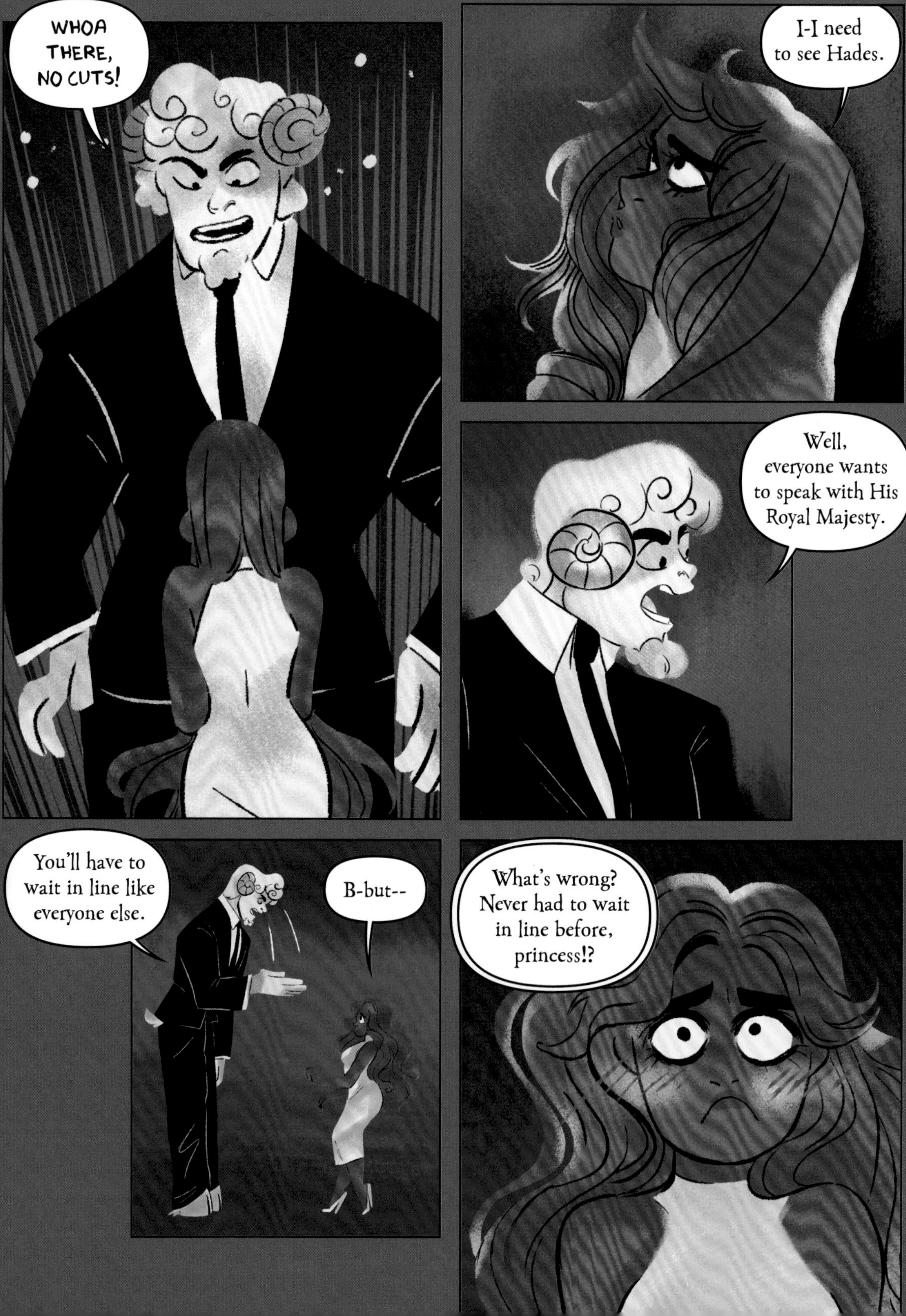
WHOA THERE, NO CUTS!
I-I need to see Hades.
Well, everyone wants to speak with His Royal Majesty.
You'll have to wait in line like everyone else.
B-but--
What's wrong? Never had to wait in line before, princess!?

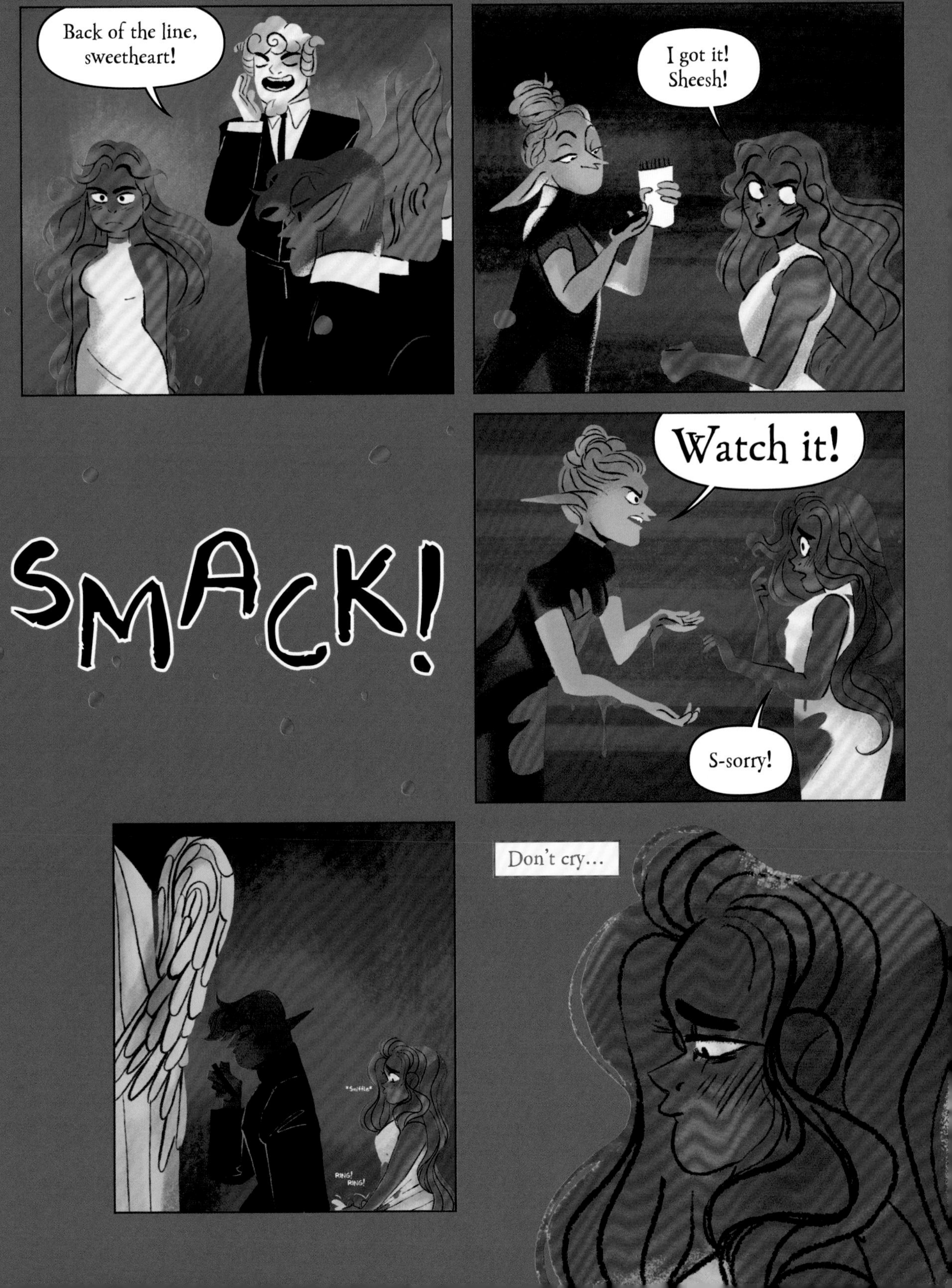
Back of the line, sweetheart!
I got it! Sheesh!
SMACK!
Watch it!
S-sorry!
Sniffle
RING! RING!
Don't cry…

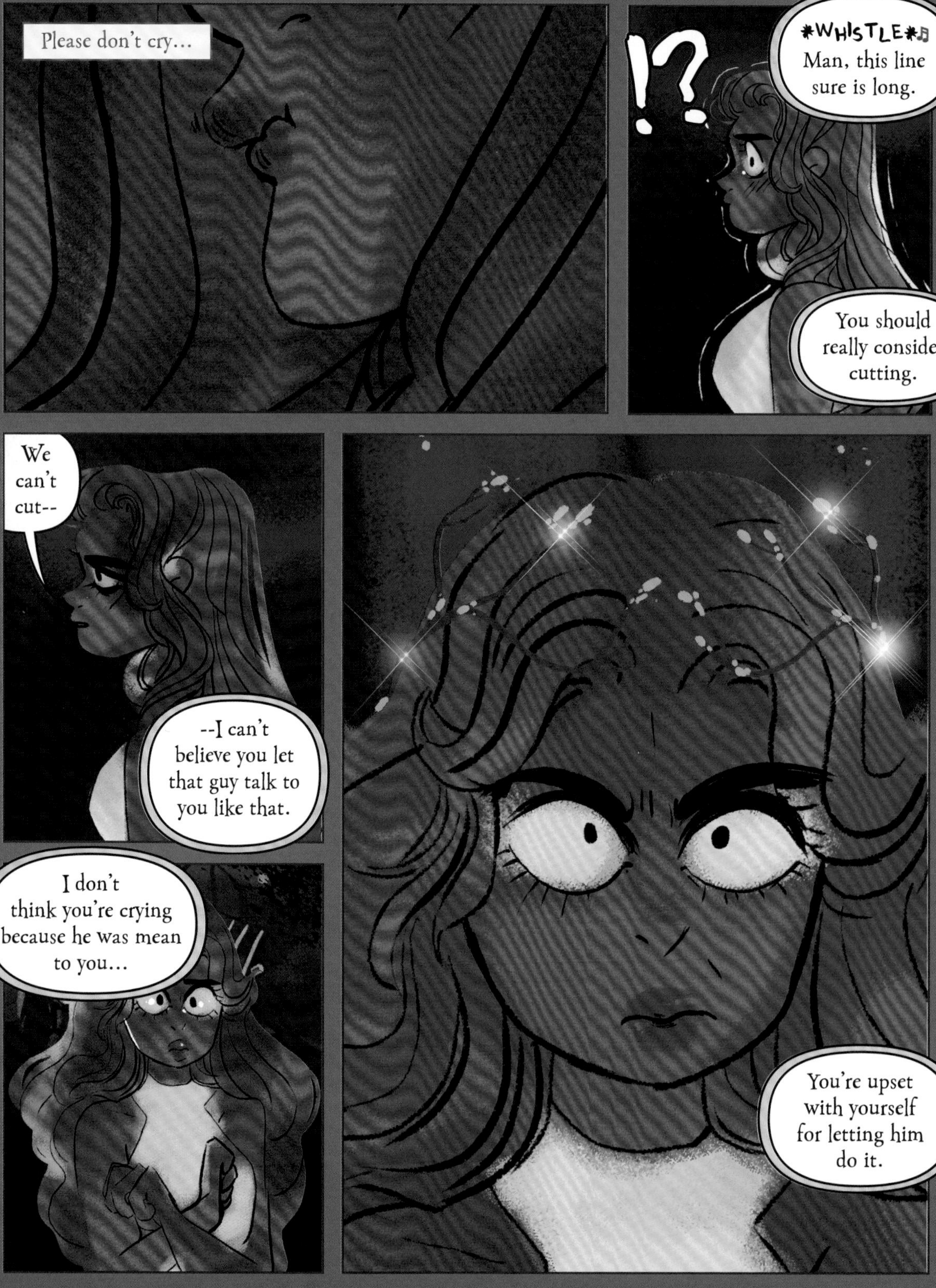
Please don't cry...
!?
WHISTLE♫ Man, this line sure is long.
You should really consider cutting.
We can't cut--
--I can't believe you let that guy talk to you like that.
I don't think you're crying because he was mean to you...
You're upset with yourself for letting him do it.

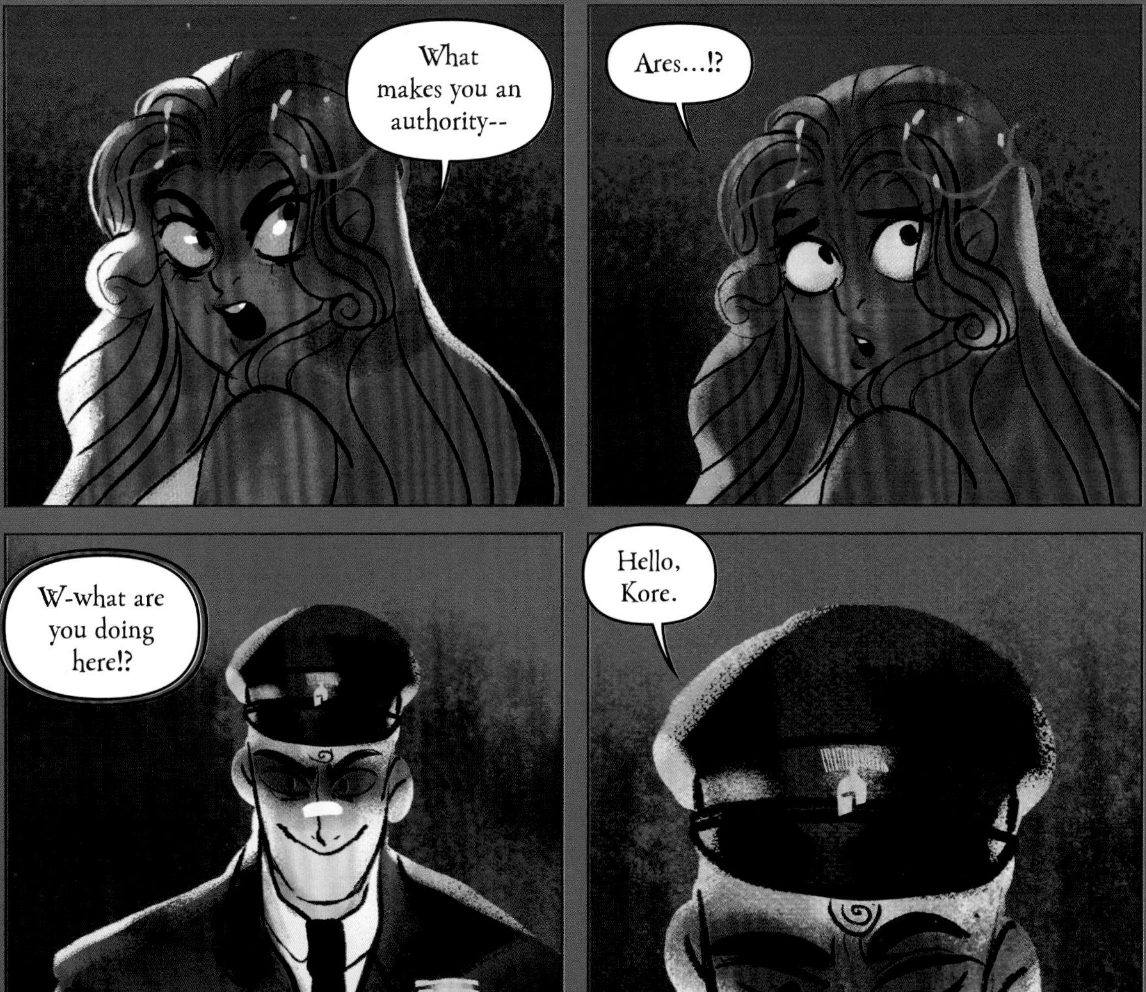
What makes you an authority--
Ares...!?
W-what are you doing here!?
Hello, Kore.
It's been a while.

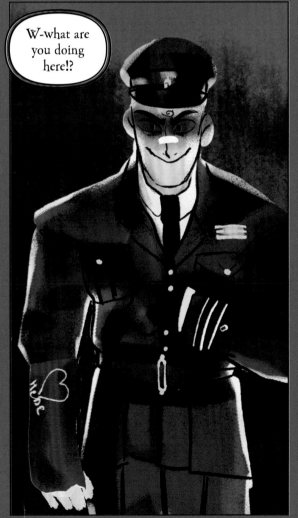

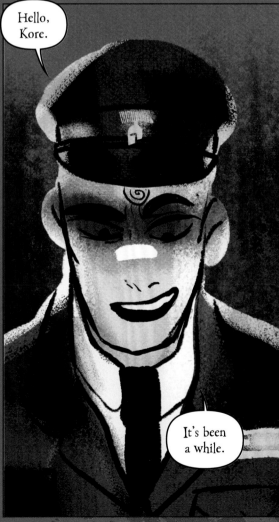

EPISODE 86: A FINE LINE

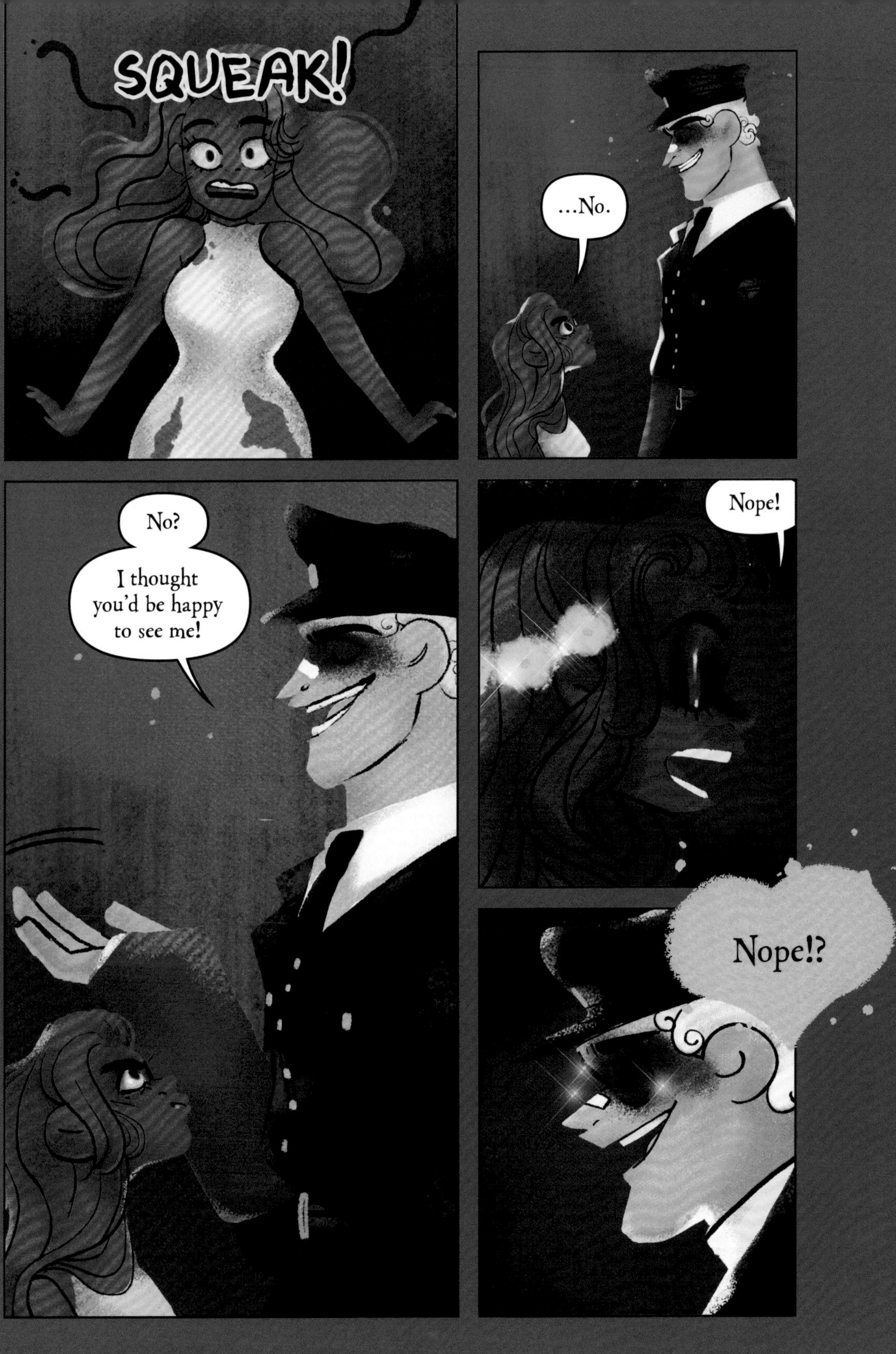
SQUEAK!
...No.
No?
I thought you'd be happy to see me!
Nope!
Nope!?

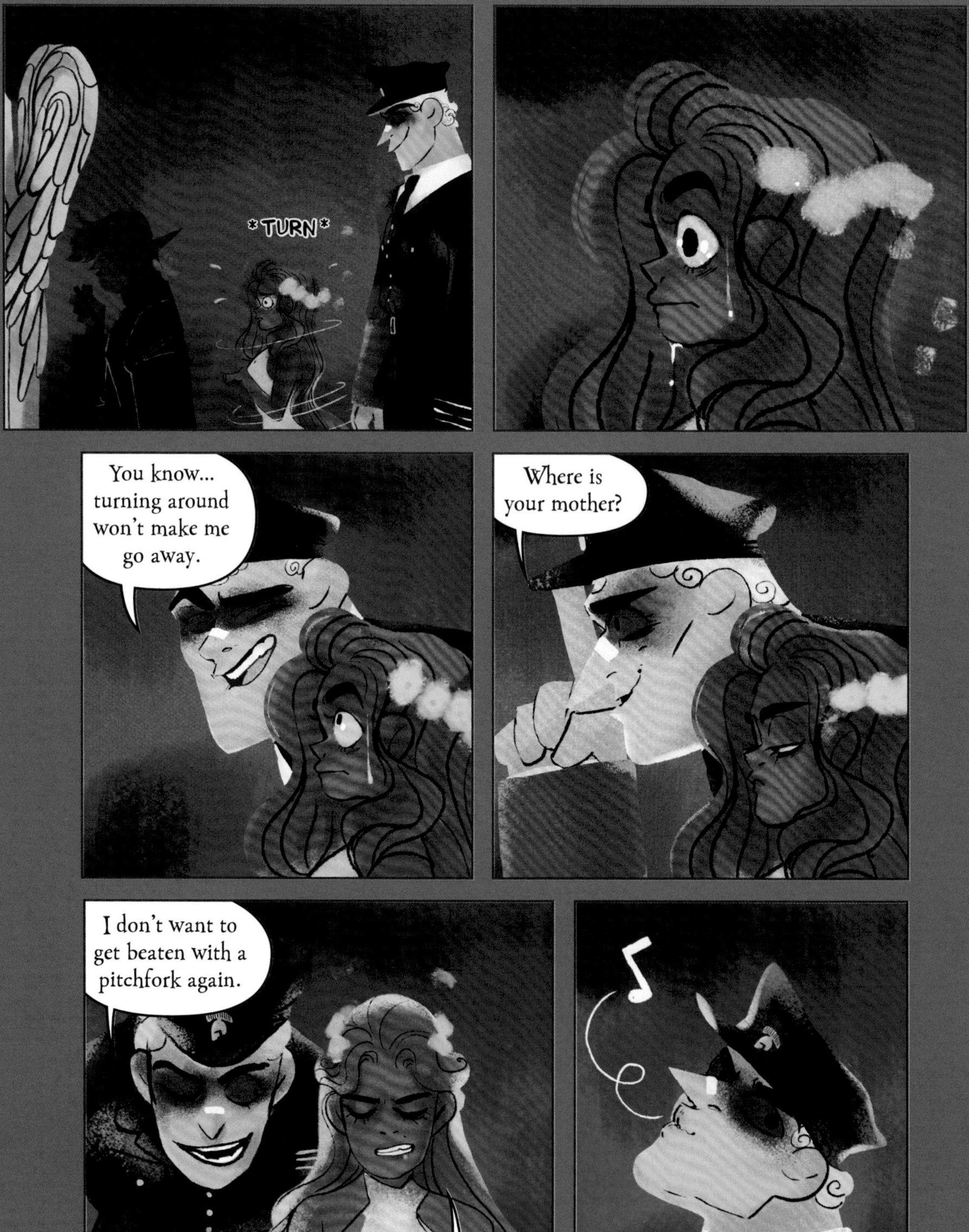
TURN
You know... turning around won't make me go away.
Where is your mother?
I don't want to get beaten with a pitchfork again.
She's not here.

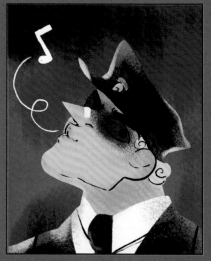

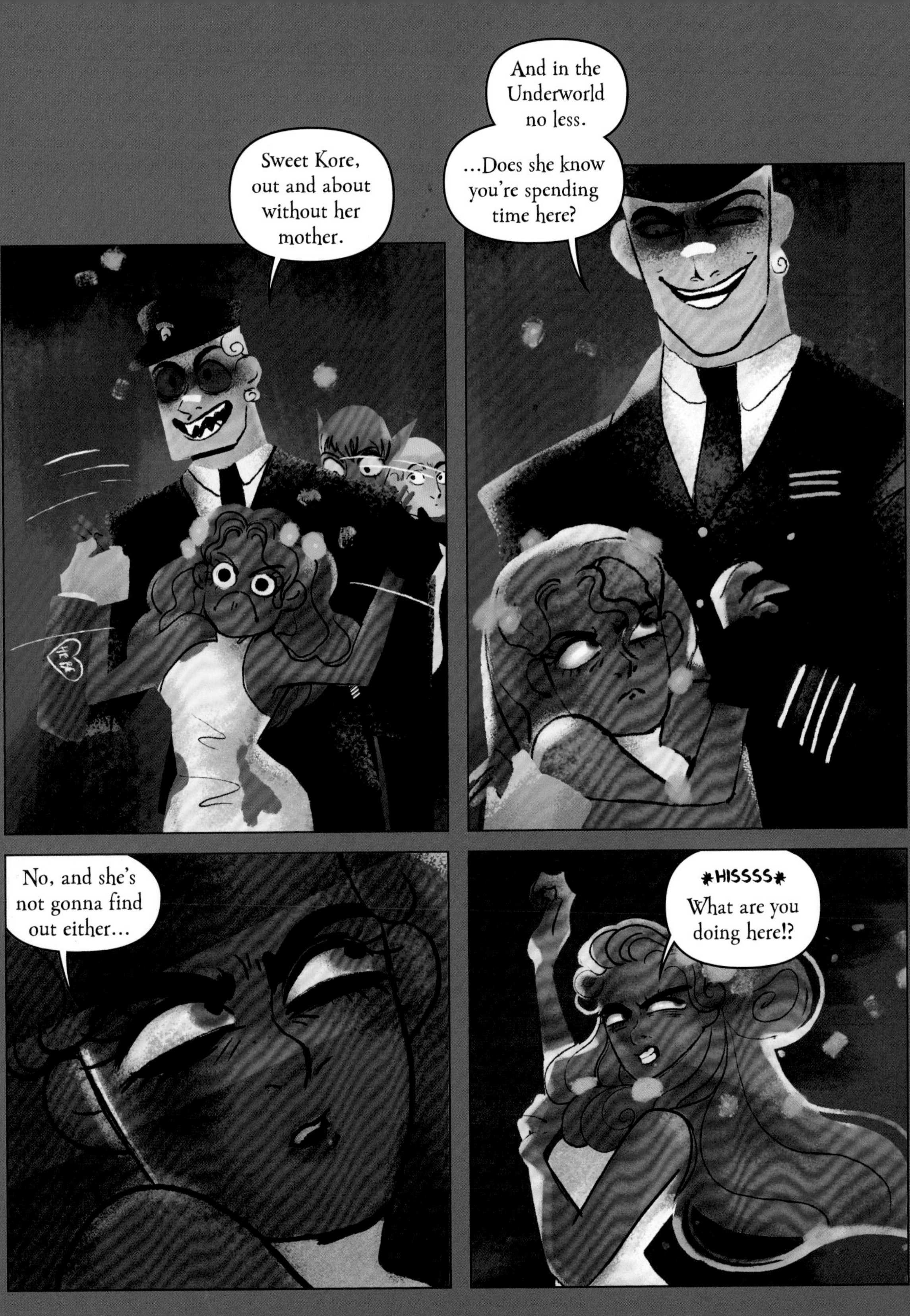
Sweet Kore, out and about without her mother.
And in the Underworld no less.
...Does she know you're spending time here?
No, and she's not gonna find out either...
HISSSS
What are you doing here!?

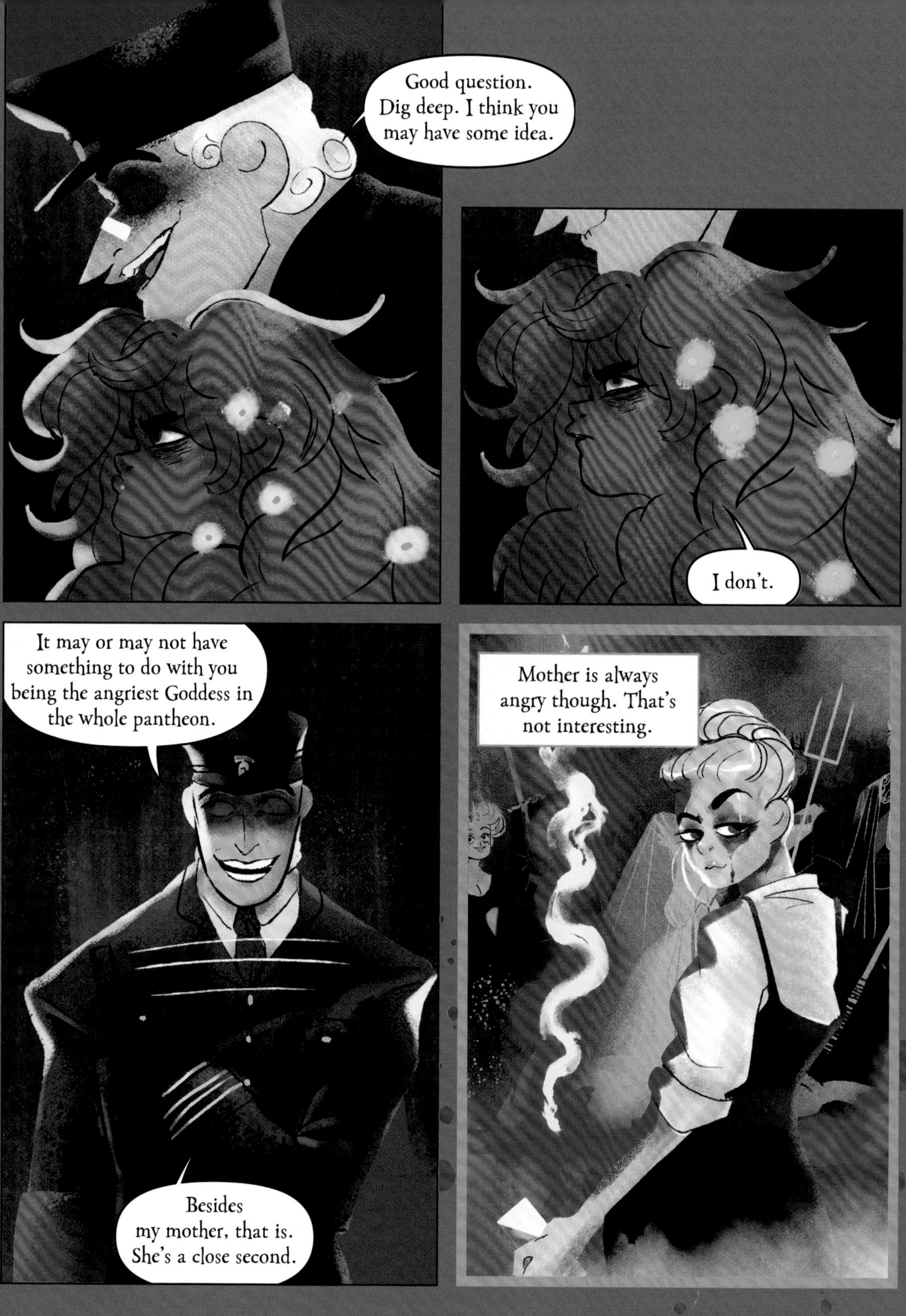

Good question. Dig deep. I think you may have some idea.
I don't.
It may or may not have something to do with you being the angriest Goddess in the whole pantheon.
Besides my mother, that is. She's a close second.
Mother is always angry though. That's not interesting.

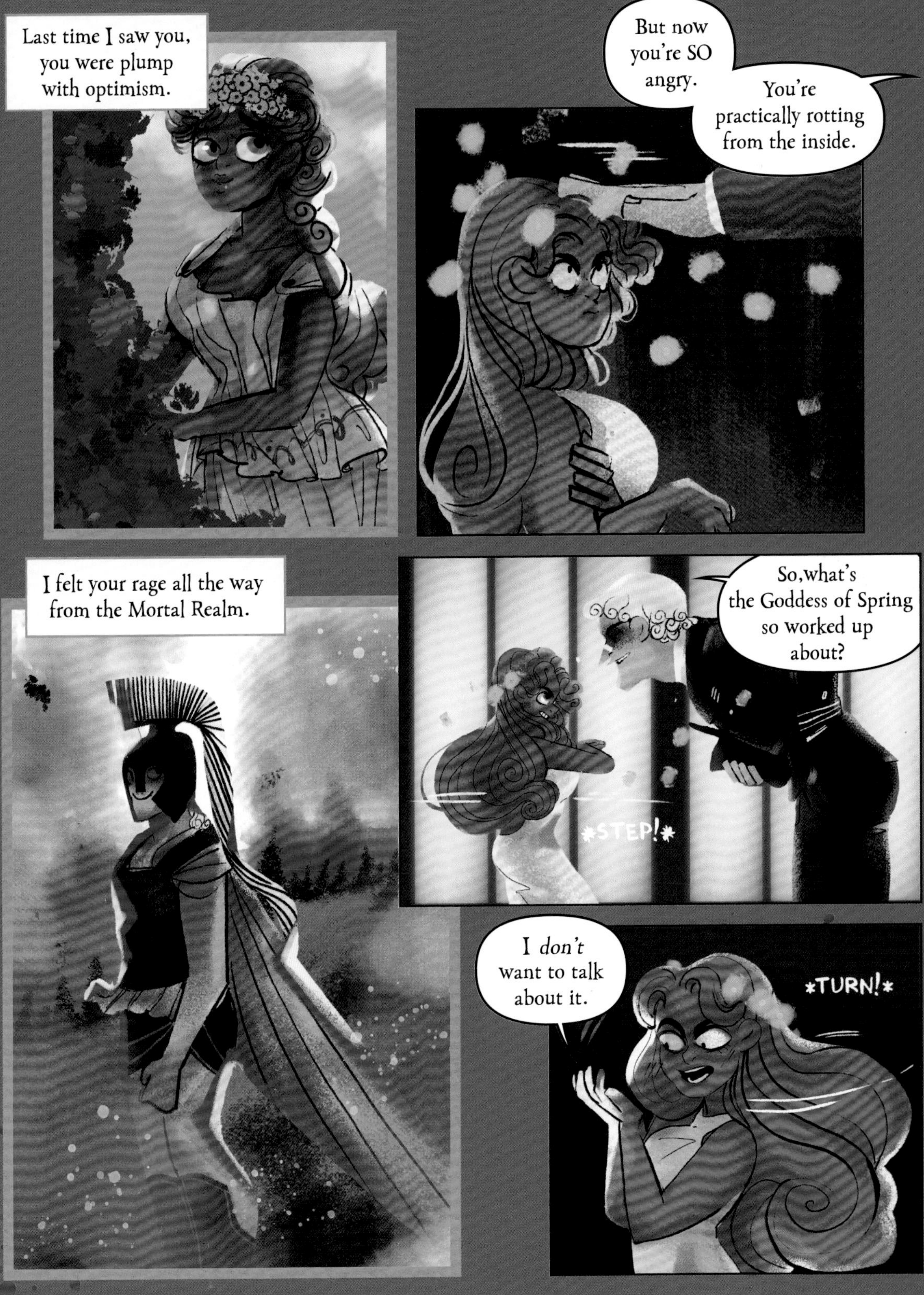
Last time I saw you, you were plump with optimism.
But now you're SO angry.
You're practically rotting from the inside.
I felt your rage all the way from the Mortal Realm.
So, what's the Goddess of Spring so worked up about?
STEP!
I *don't* want to talk about it.
TURN!

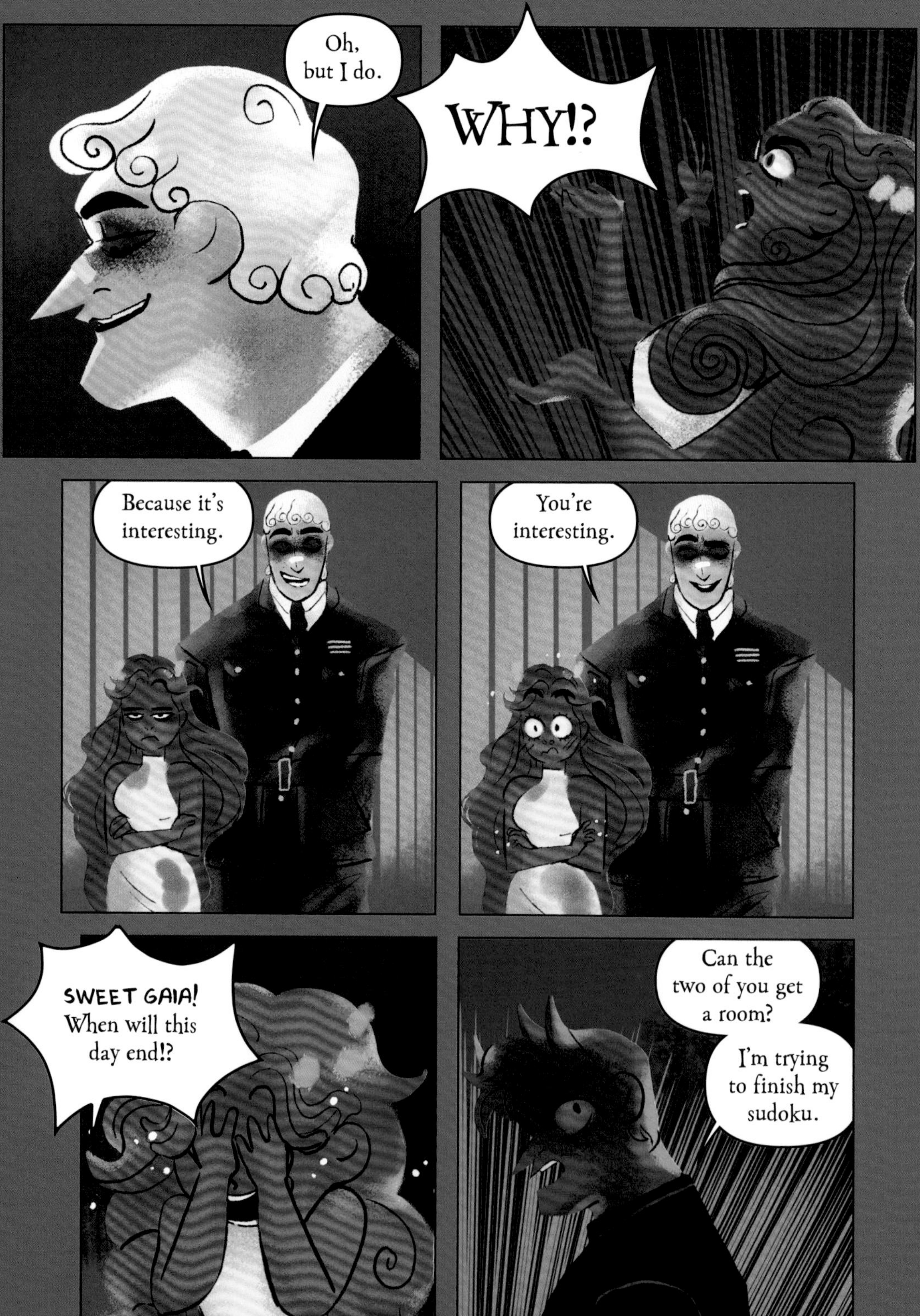
Oh, but I do.
WHY!?
Because it's interesting.
You're interesting.
SWEET GAIA! When will this day end!?
Can the two of you get a room?
I'm trying to finish my sudoku.

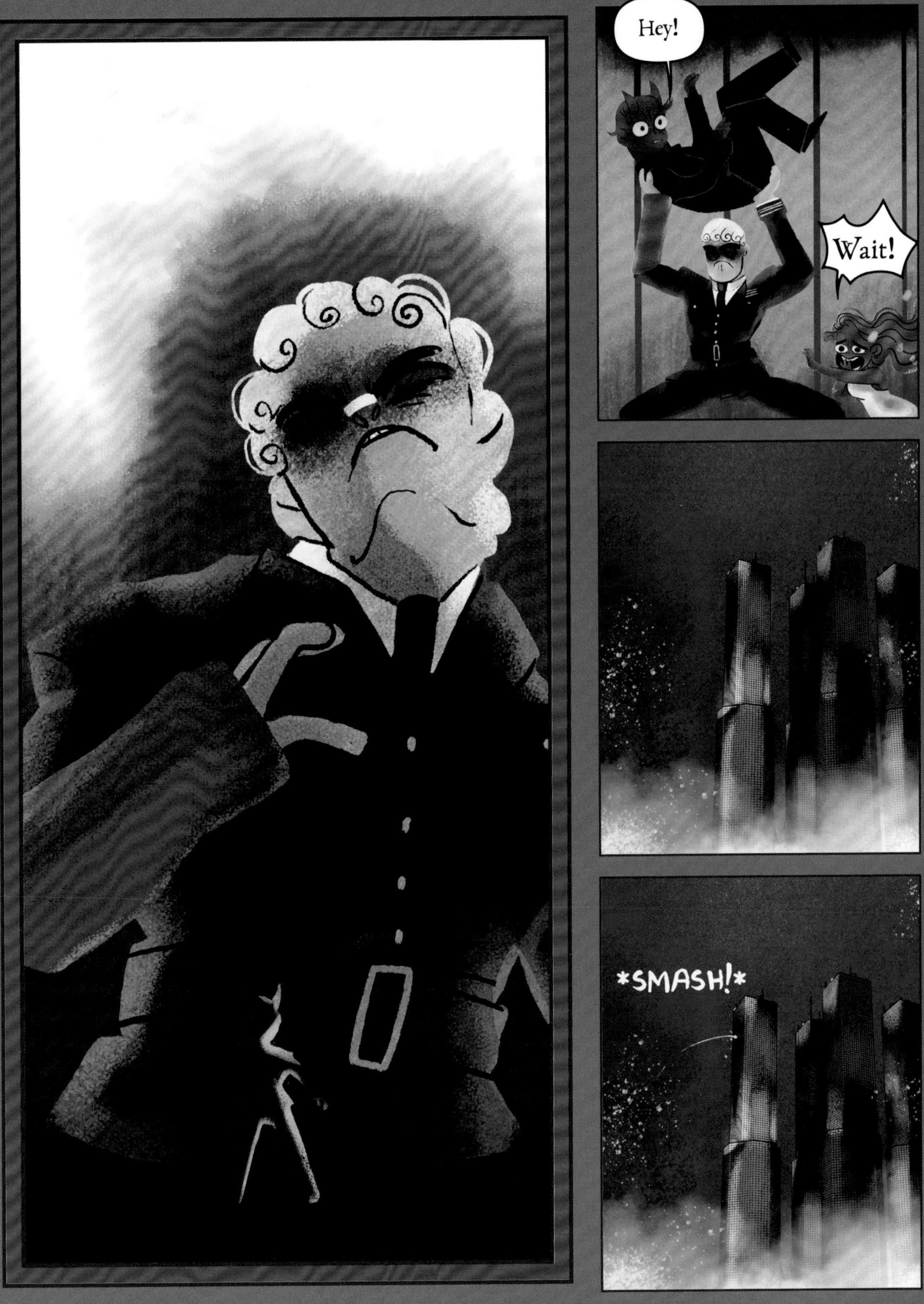
Hey!
Wait!
SMASH!

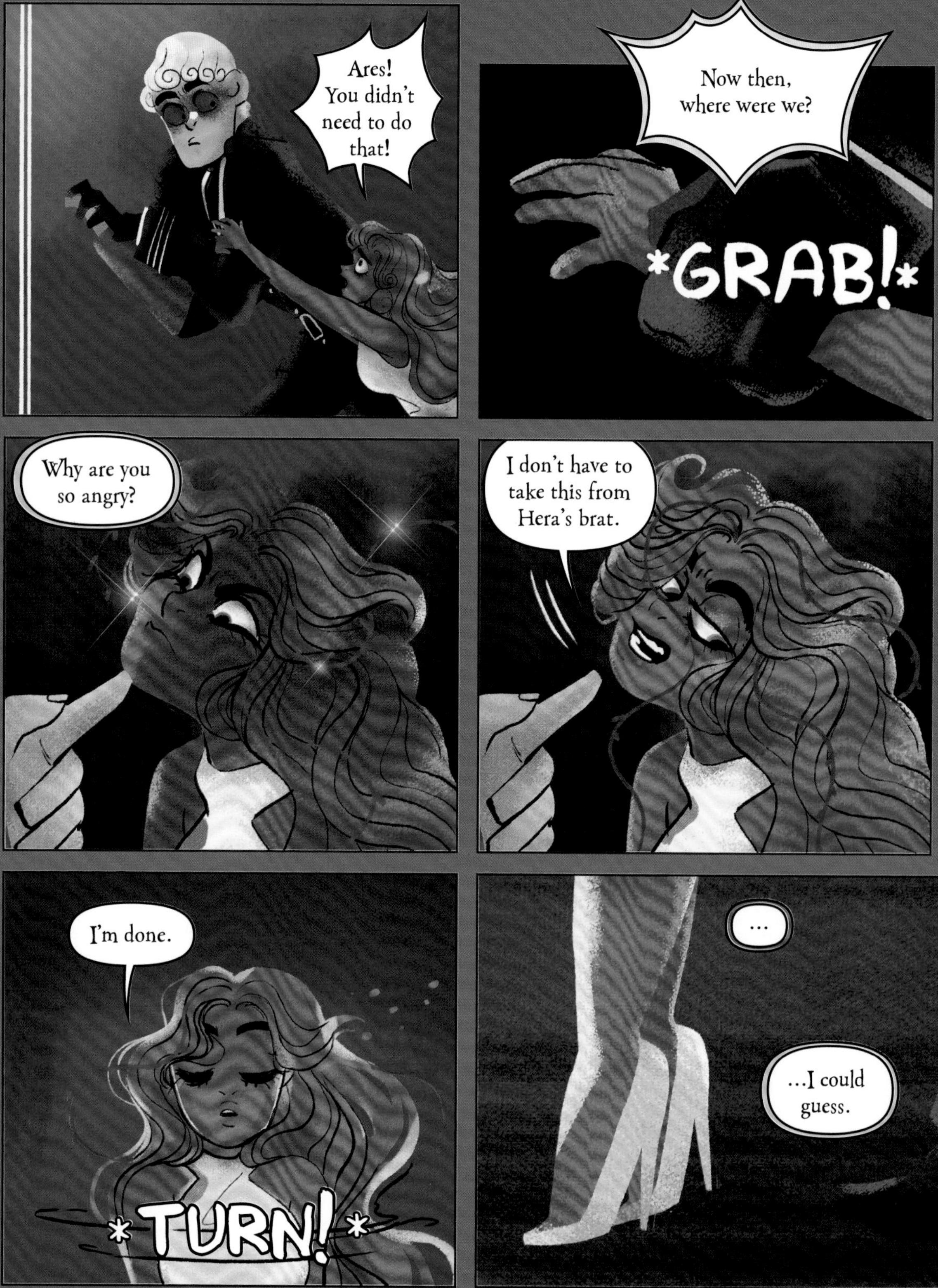
Ares! You didn't need to do that!
Now then, where were we?
GRAB!
Why are you so angry?
I don't have to take this from Hera's brat.
I'm done.
TURN!
...
...I could guess.

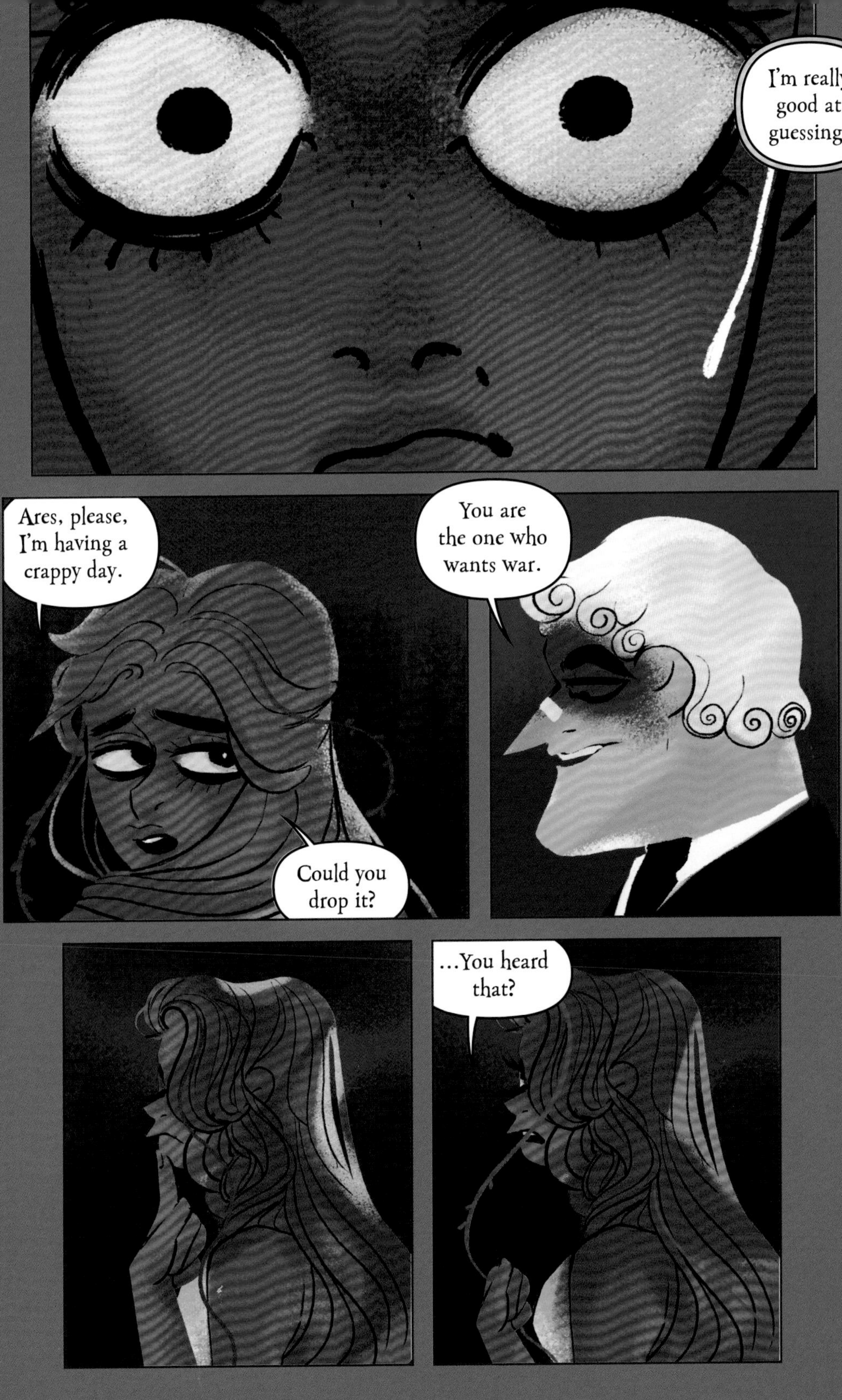
I'm really good at guessing.
Ares, please, I'm having a crappy day.
Could you drop it?
You are the one who wants war.
...You heard that?

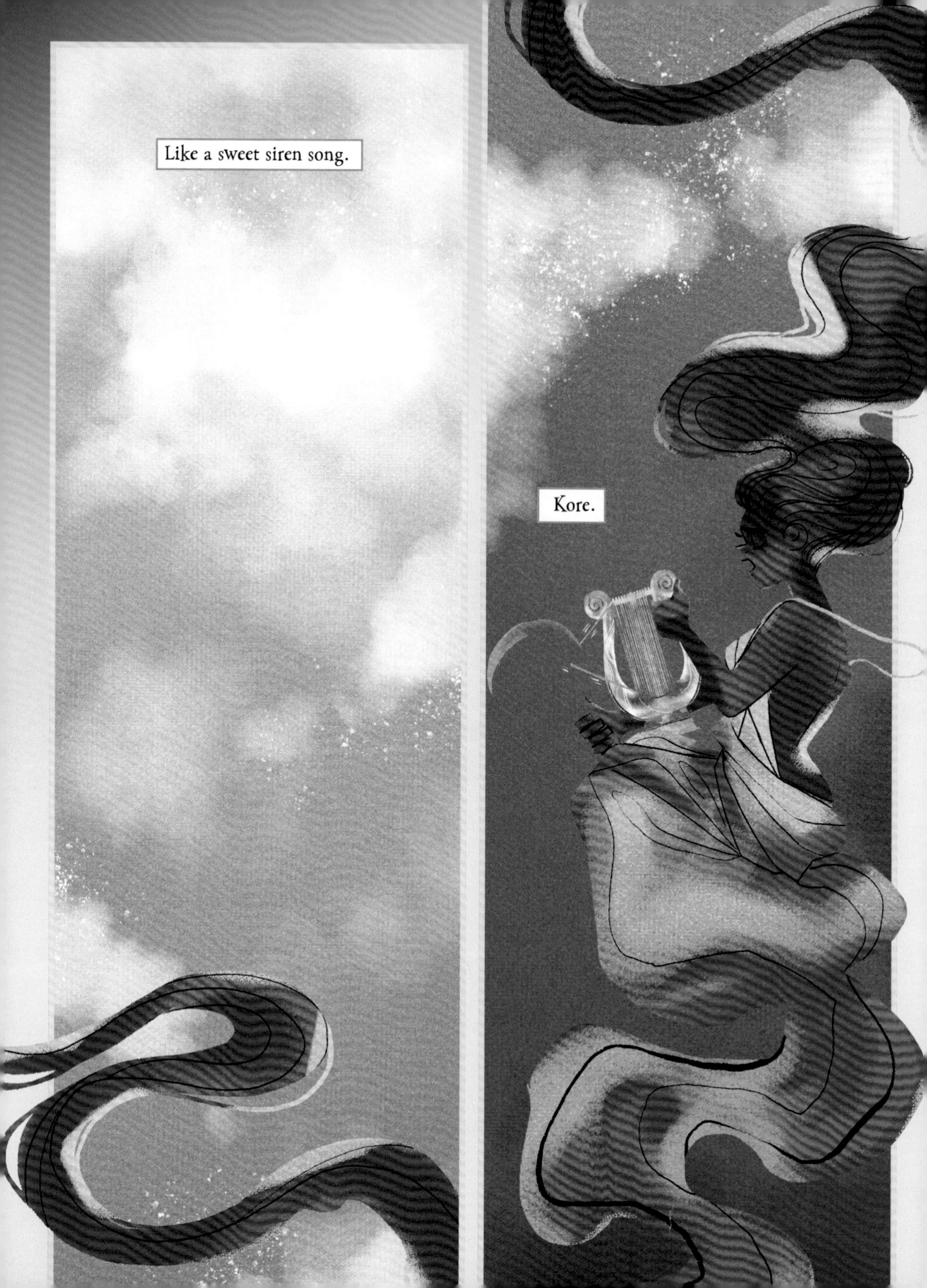
Like a sweet siren song.
Kore.

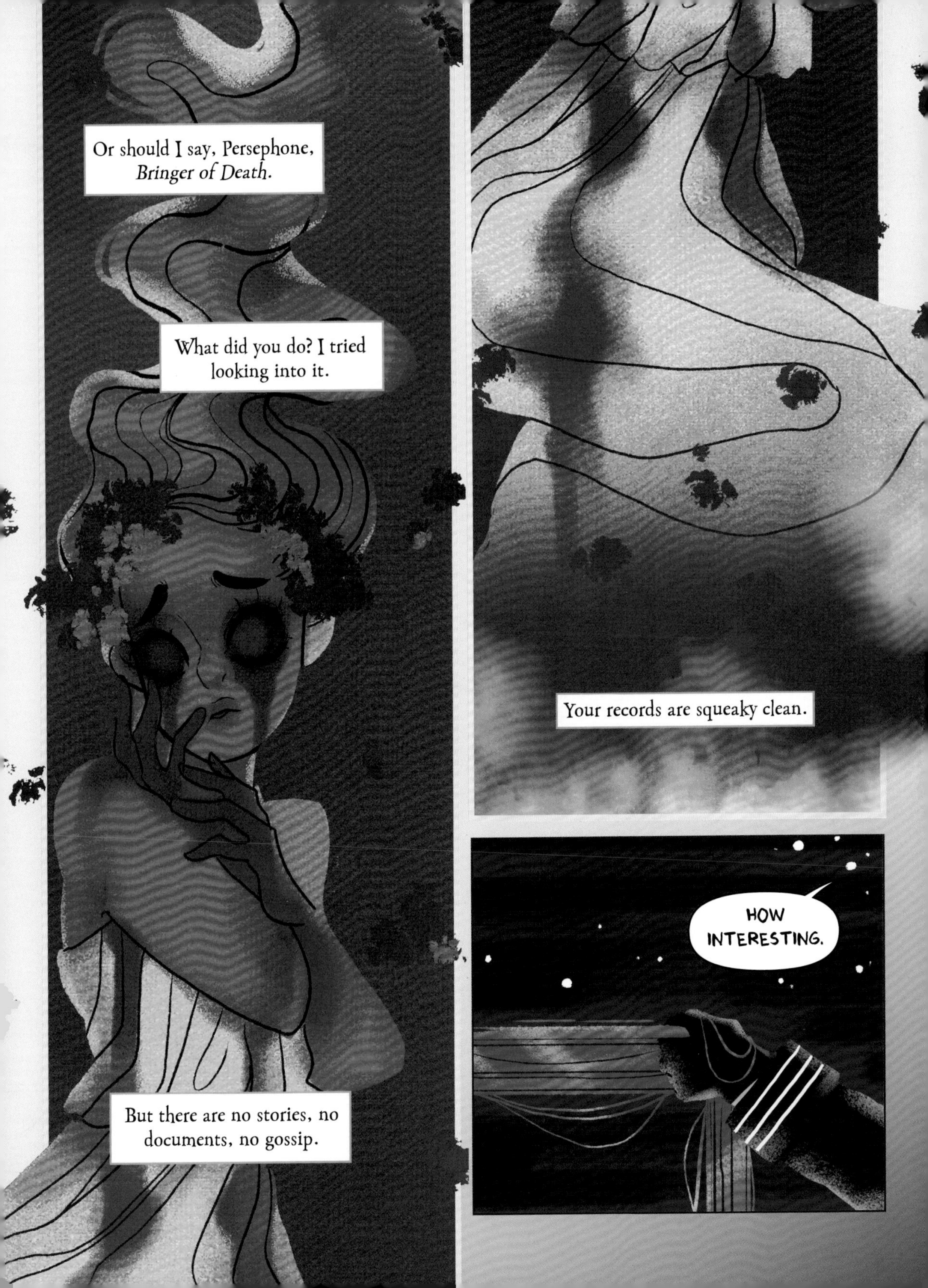
Or should I say, Persephone, *Bringer of Death*.
What did you do? I tried looking into it.
But there are no stories, no documents, no gossip.
Your records are squeaky clean.
HOW INTERESTING.

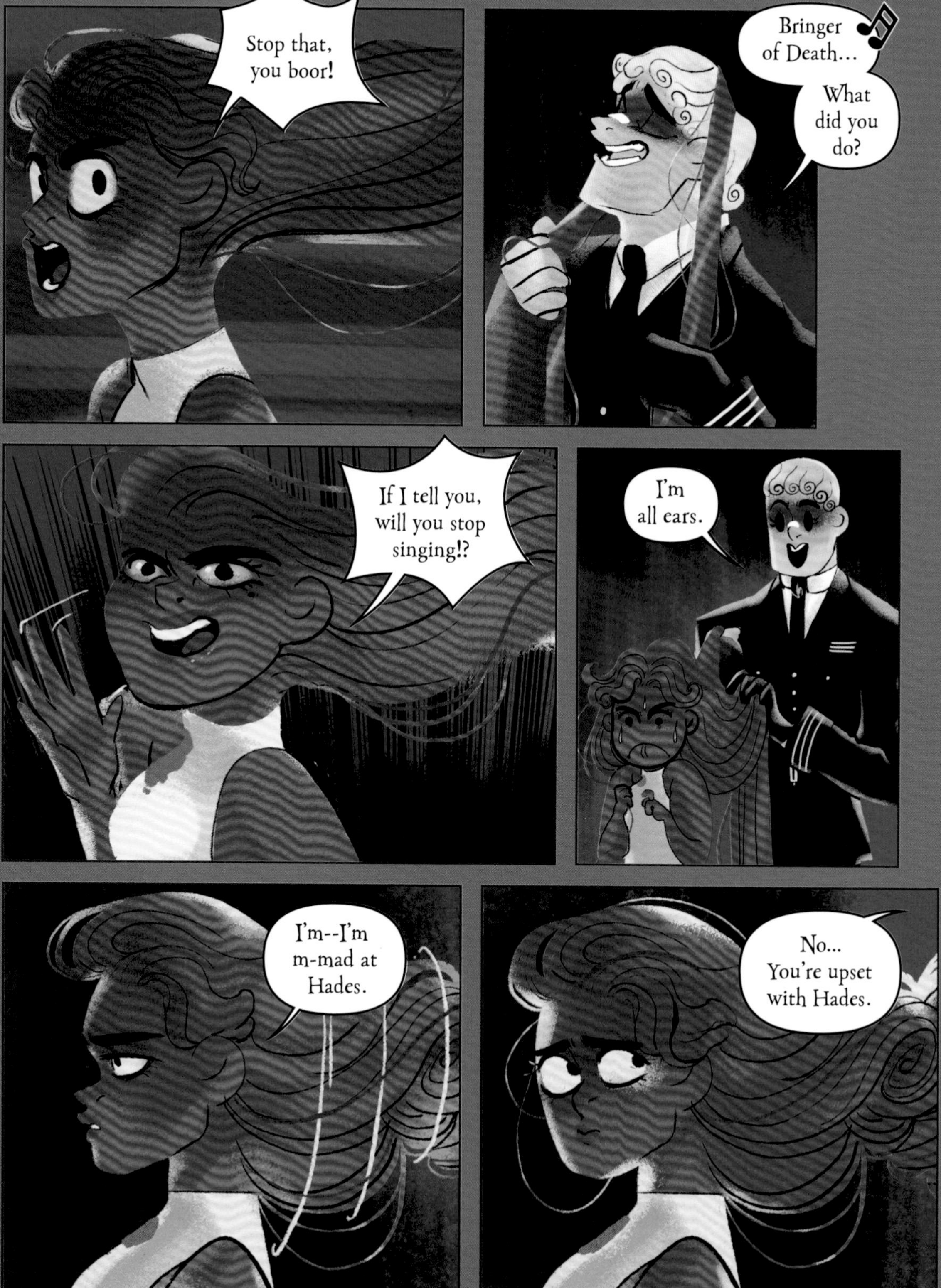
Stop that, you boor!
Bringer of Death...
What did you do?
If I tell you, will you stop singing!?
I'm all ears.
I'm--I'm m-mad at Hades.
No... You're upset with Hades.

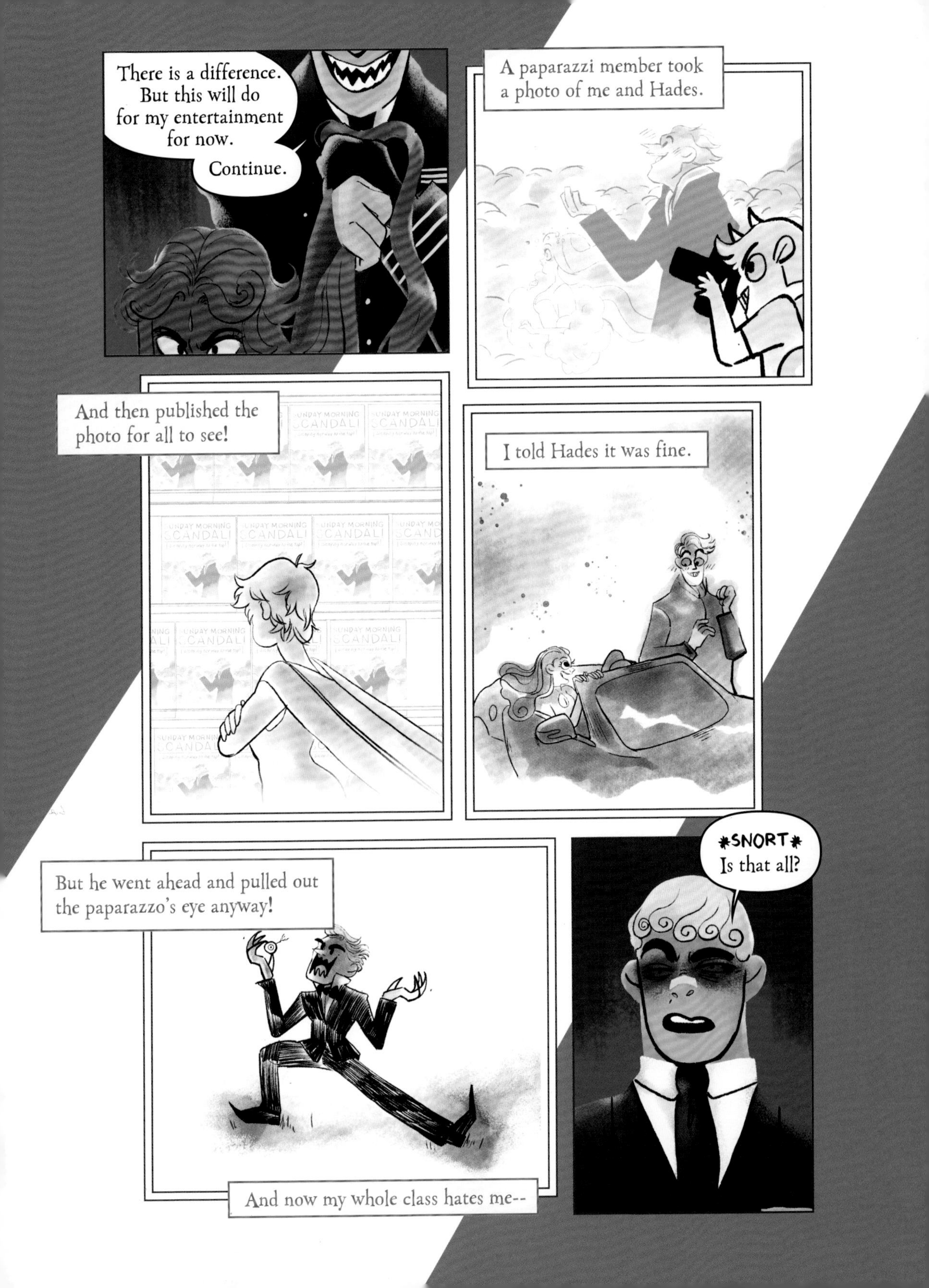
There is a difference. But this will do for my entertainment for now.
Continue.
A paparazzi member took a photo of me and Hades.
And then published the photo for all to see!
SUNDAY MORNING SCANDAL!
I told Hades it was fine.
But he went ahead and pulled out the paparazzo's eye anyway!
And now my whole class hates me--
SNORT
Is that all?

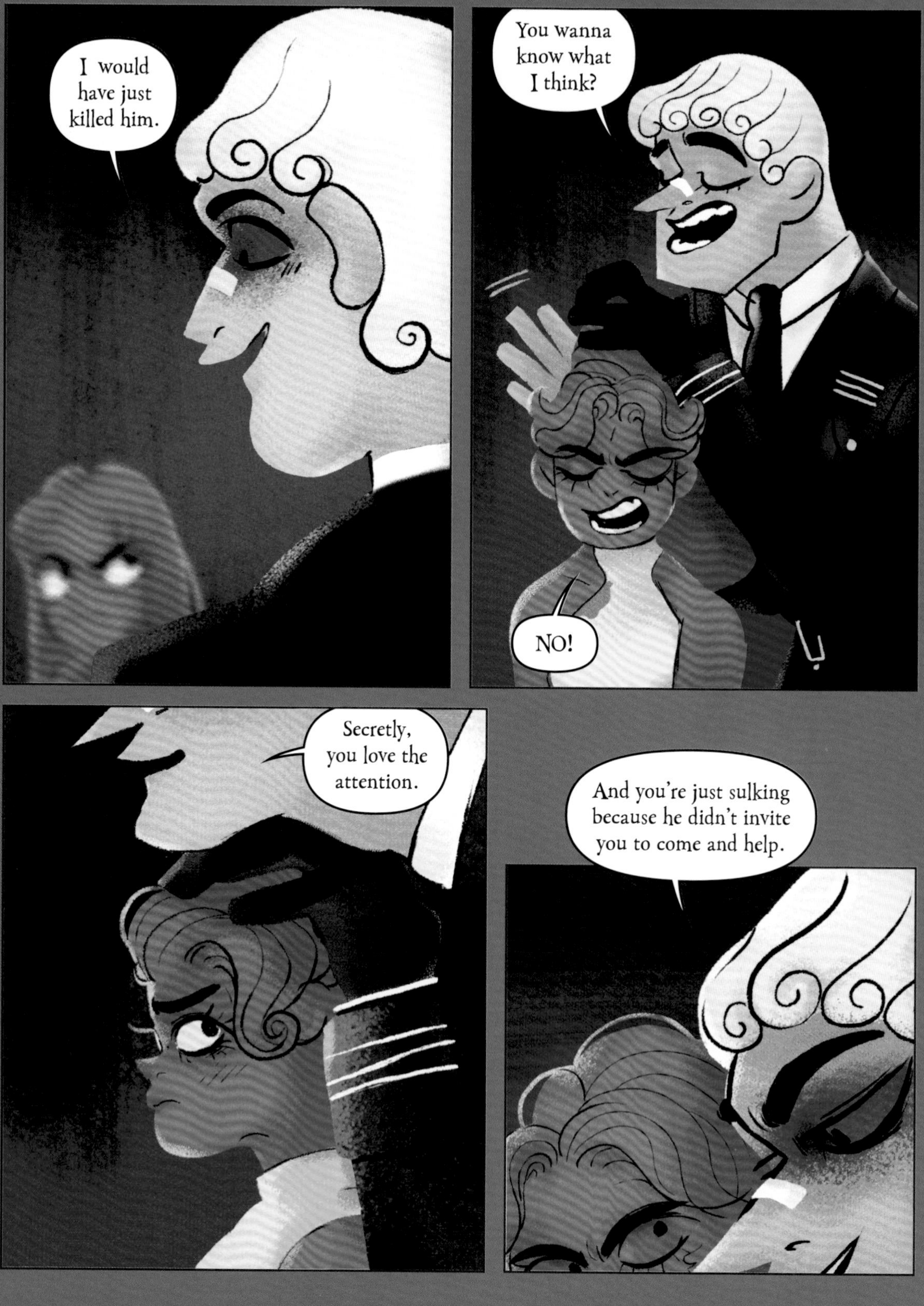
I would have just killed him.
You wanna know what I think?
NO!
Secretly, you love the attention.
And you're just sulking because he didn't invite you to come and help.

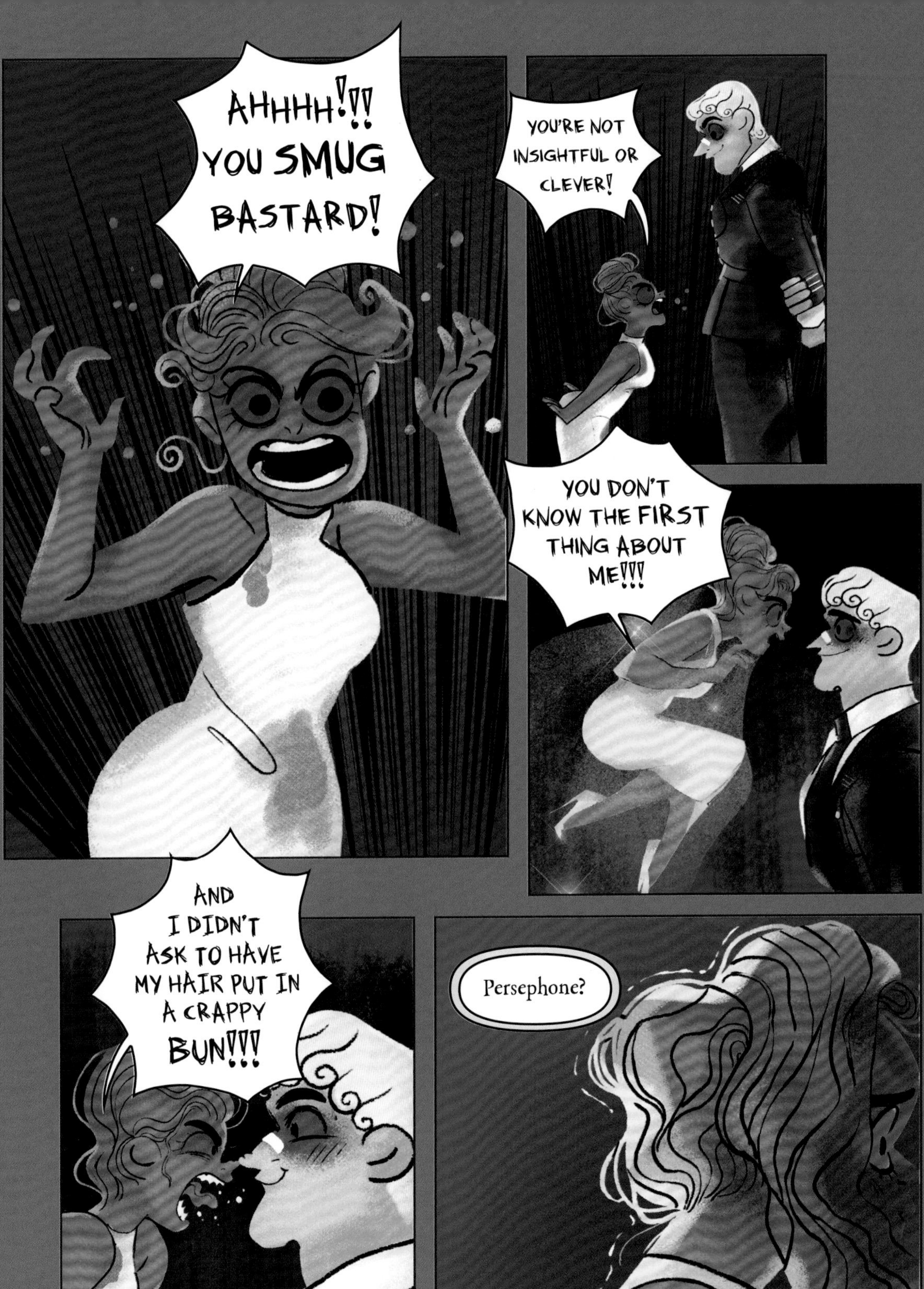
AHHHH!!! YOU SMUG BASTARD!
YOU'RE NOT INSIGHTFUL OR CLEVER!
YOU DON'T KNOW THE FIRST THING ABOUT ME!!!
AND I DIDN'T ASK TO HAVE MY HAIR PUT IN A CRAPPY BUN!!!
Persephone?

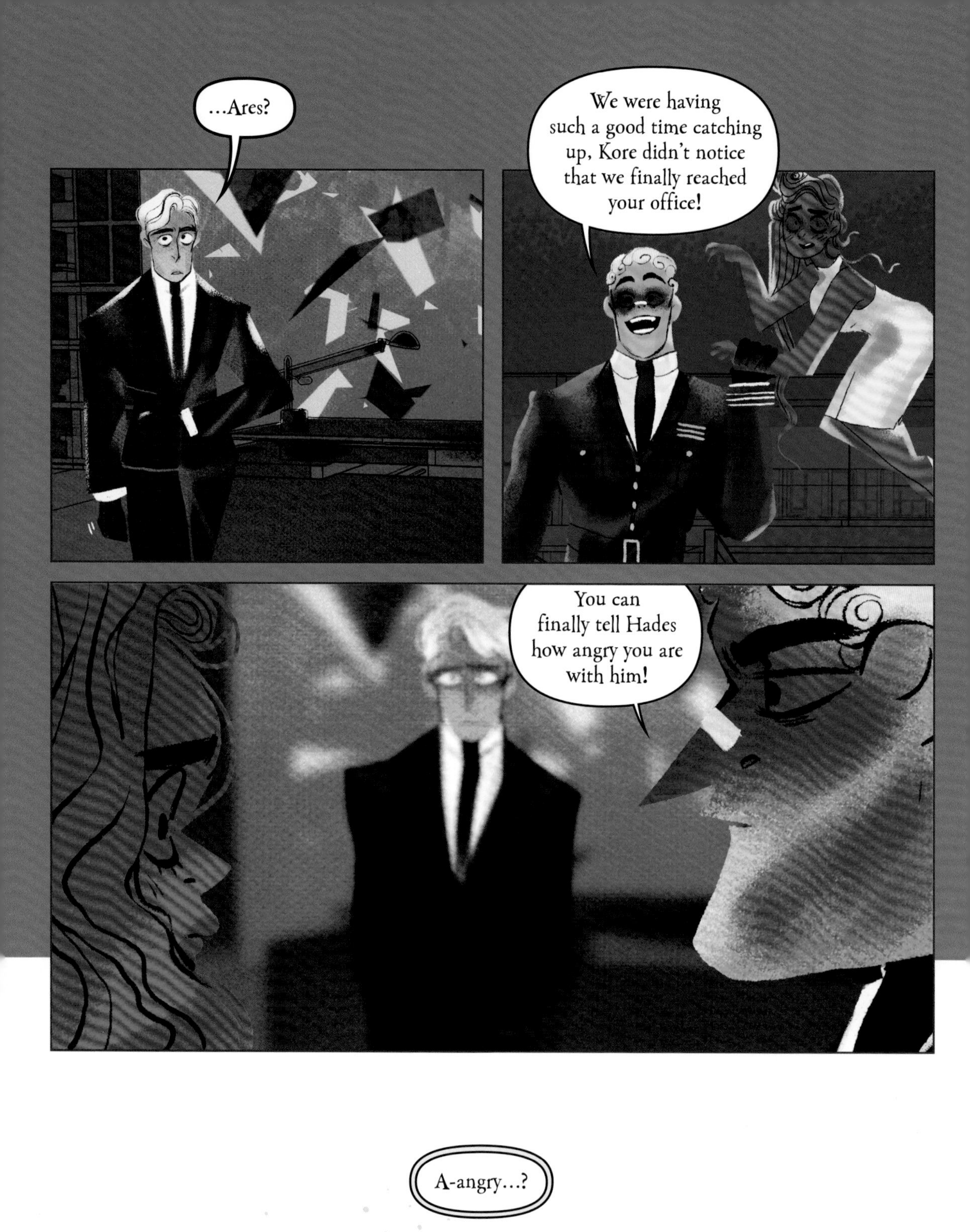
...Ares?
We were having such a good time catching up, Kore didn't notice that we finally reached your office!
You can finally tell Hades how angry you are with him!
A-angry...?

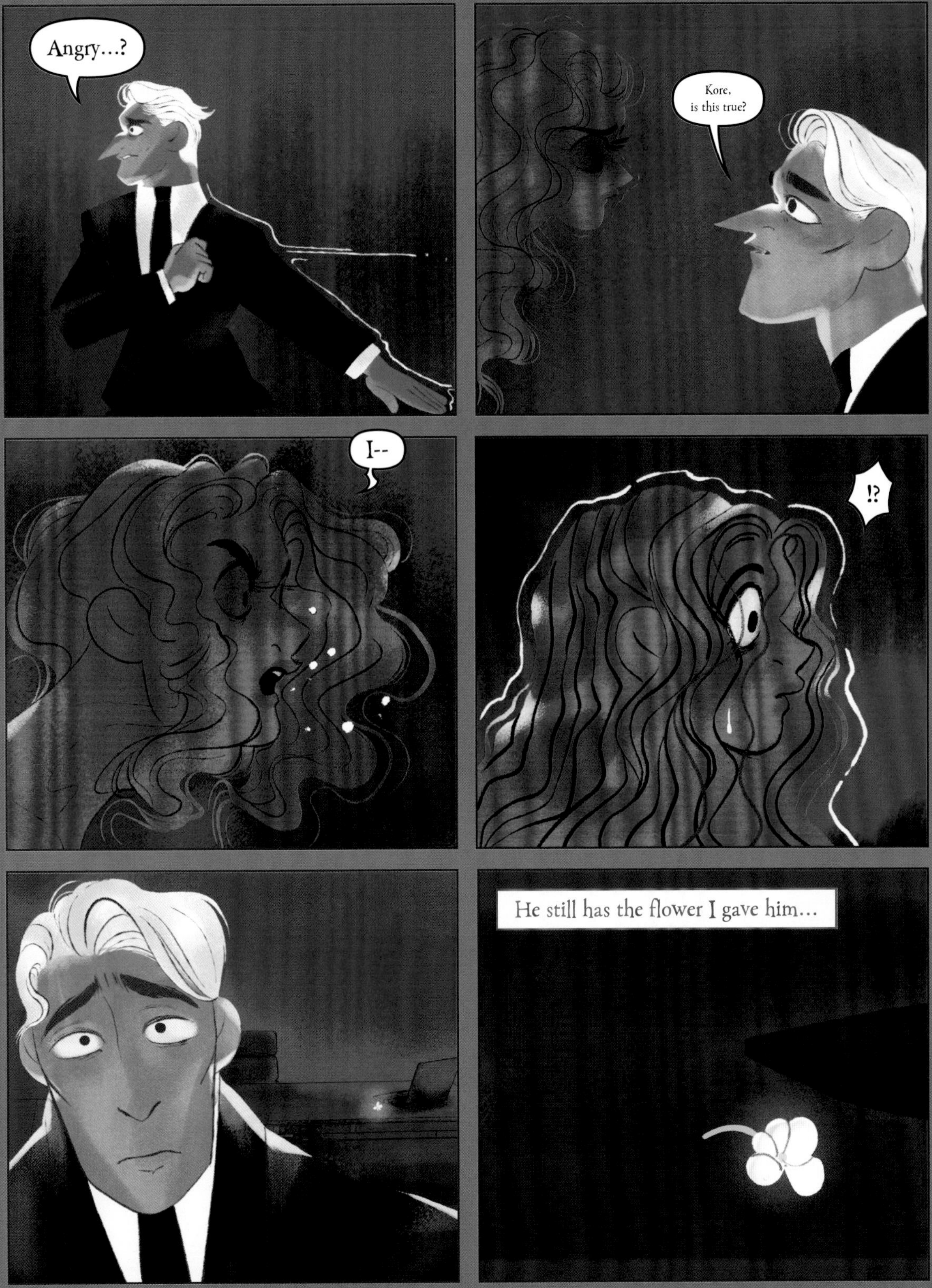
Angry...?
Kore, is this true?
I--
!?
He still has the flower I gave him...

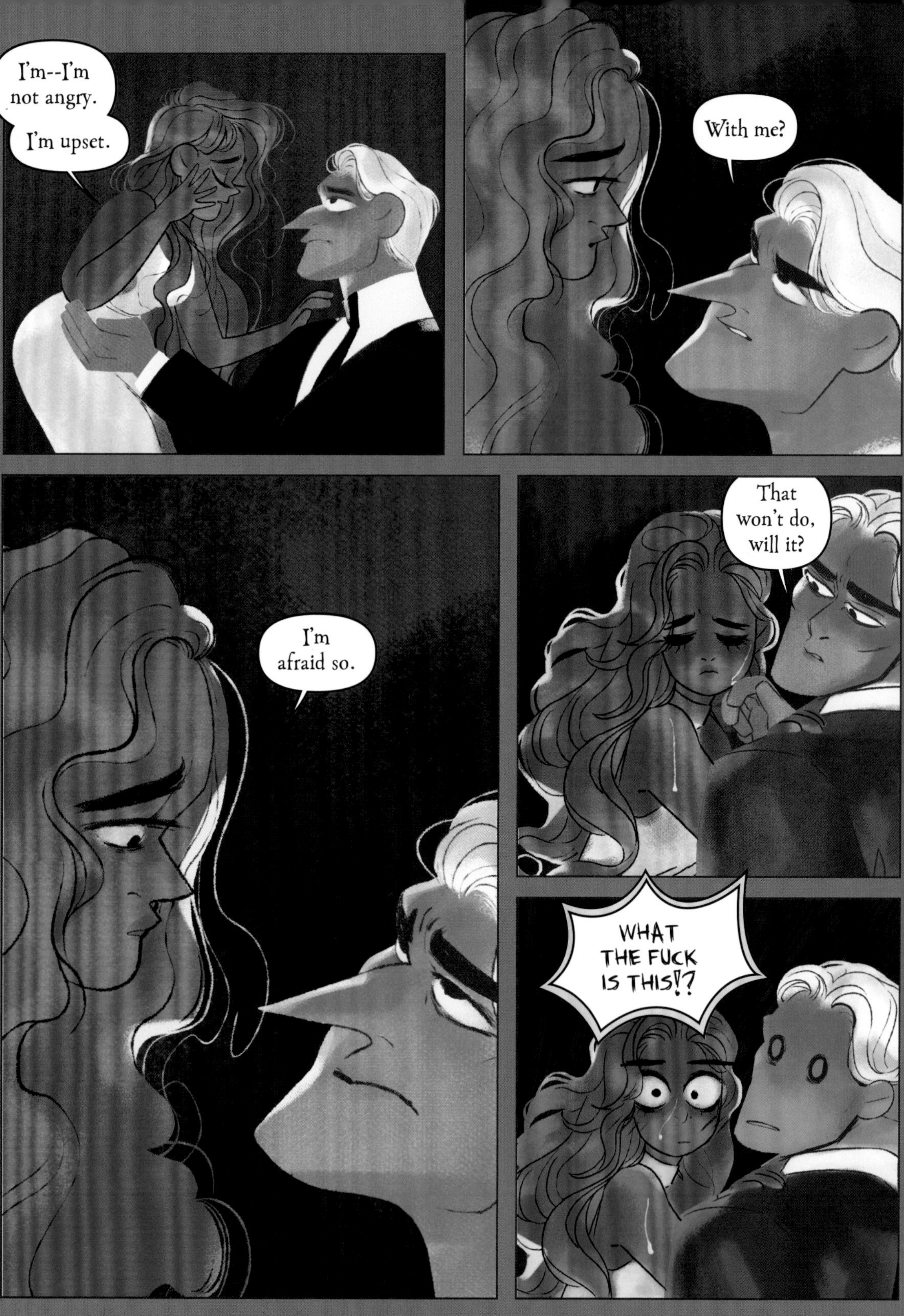
I'm--I'm not angry.
I'm upset.
With me?
I'm afraid so.
That won't do, will it?
WHAT THE FUCK IS THIS!?

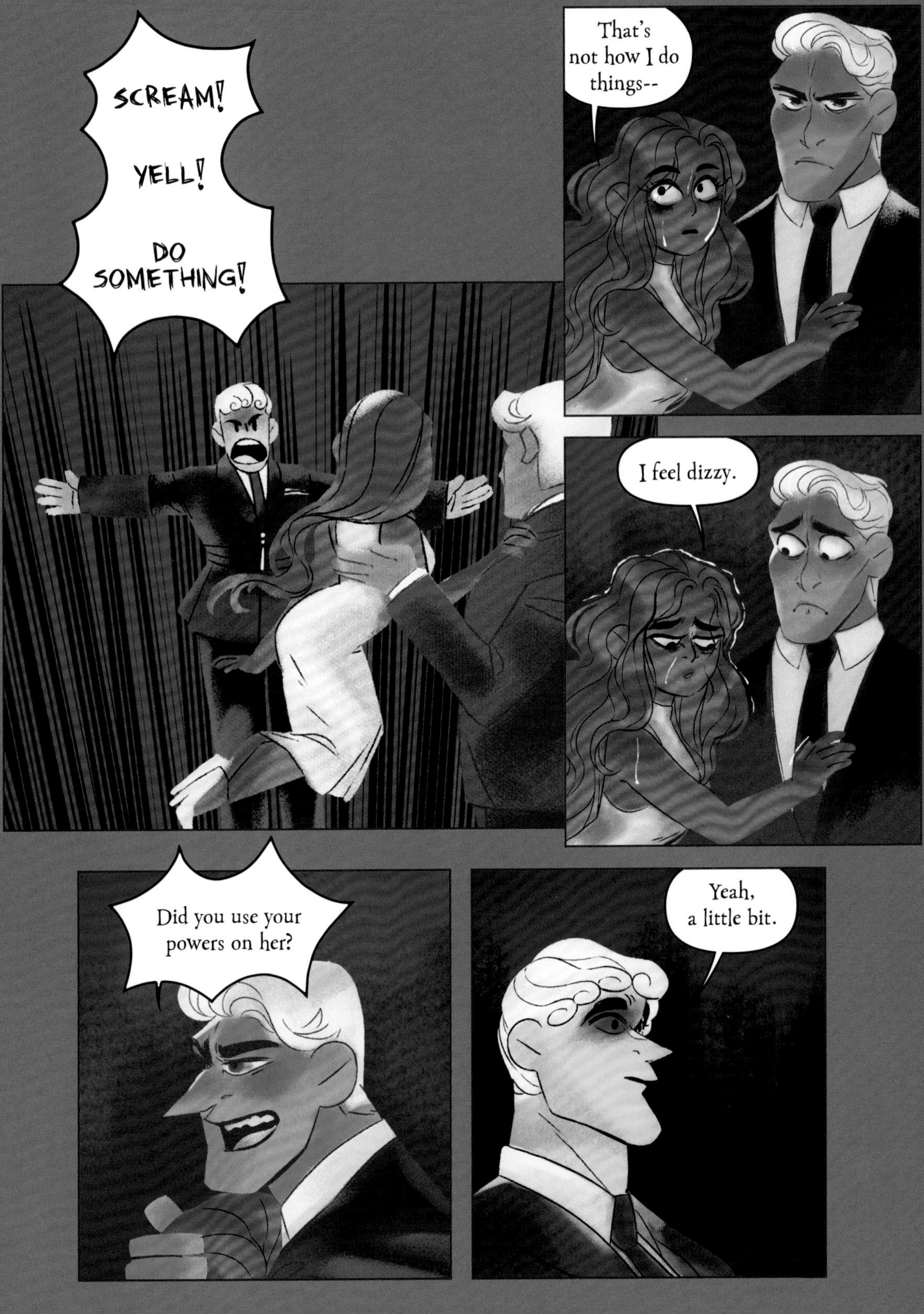
SCREAM!
YELL!
DO SOMETHING!
That's not how I do things--
I feel dizzy.
Did you use your powers on her?
Yeah, a little bit.

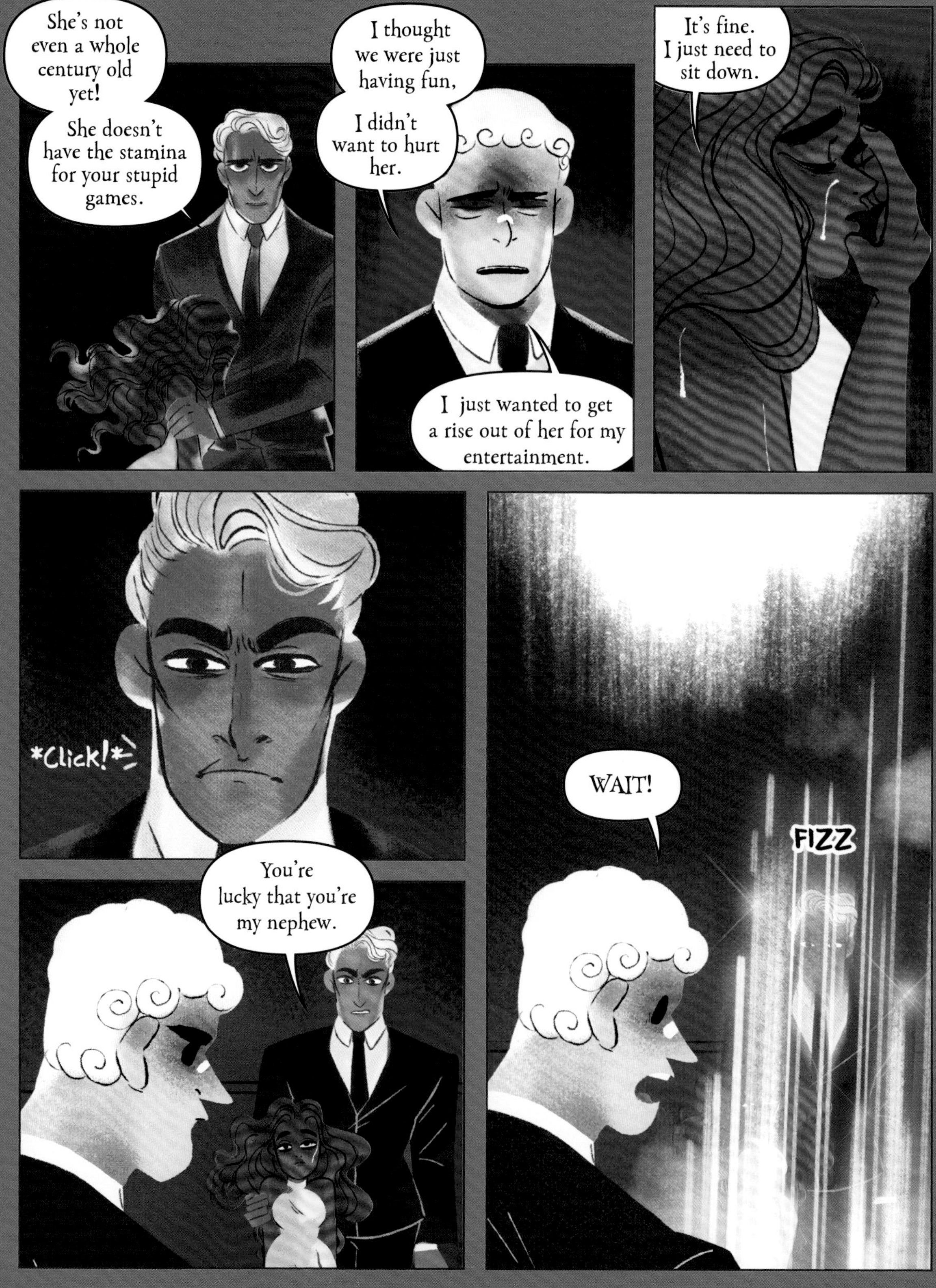
She's not even a whole century old yet!
She doesn't have the stamina for your stupid games.
I thought we were just having fun,
I didn't want to hurt her.
I just wanted to get a rise out of her for my entertainment.
It's fine. I just need to sit down.
Click!
You're lucky that you're my nephew.
WAIT!
FIZZ

EPISODE 87: IT'S ALL FUN AND GAMES UNTIL
SOMEONE LOSES AN EYE (PART I)

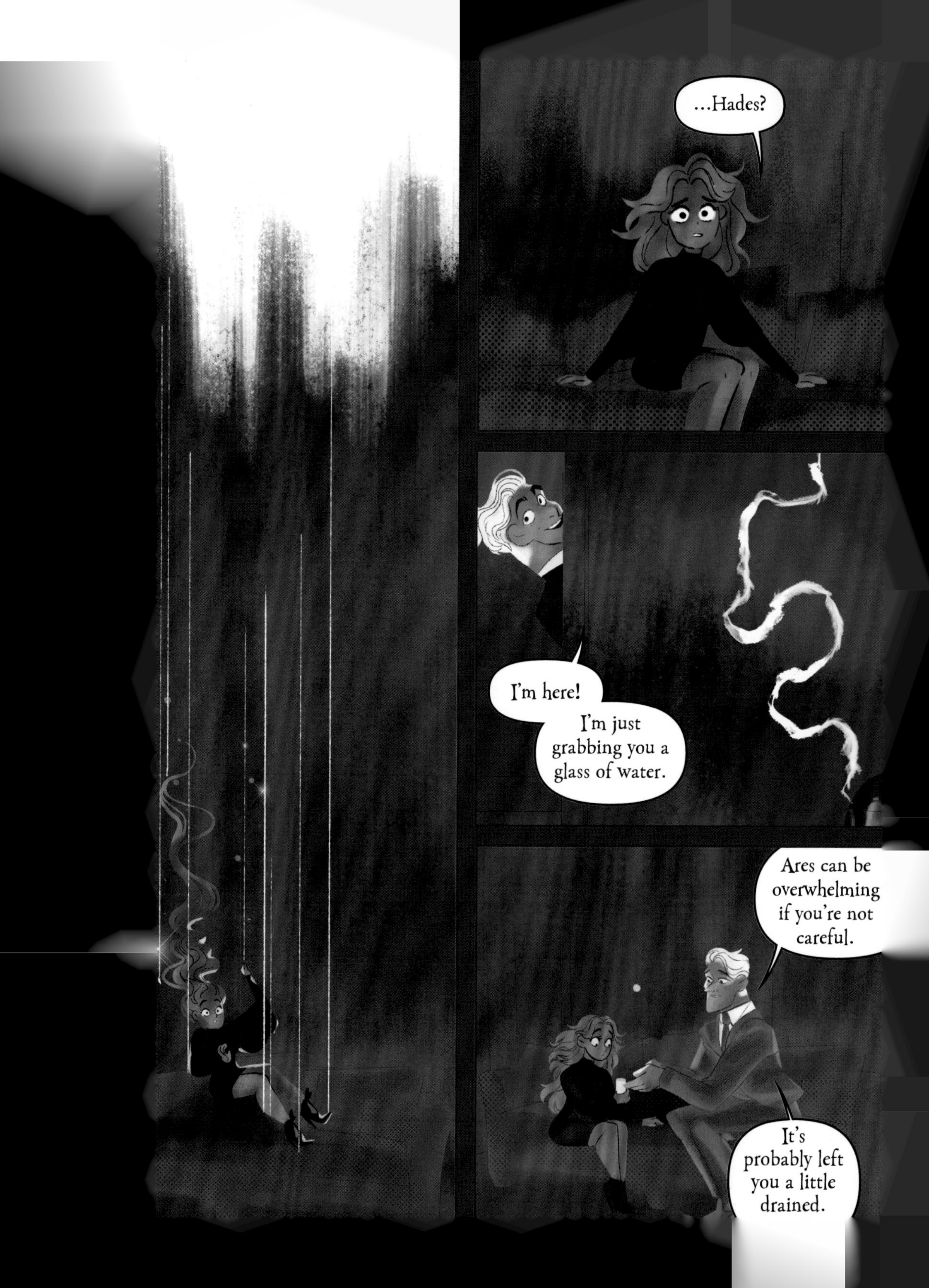
...Hades?
I'm here!
I'm just grabbing you a glass of water.
Ares can be overwhelming if you're not careful.
It's probably left you a little drained.

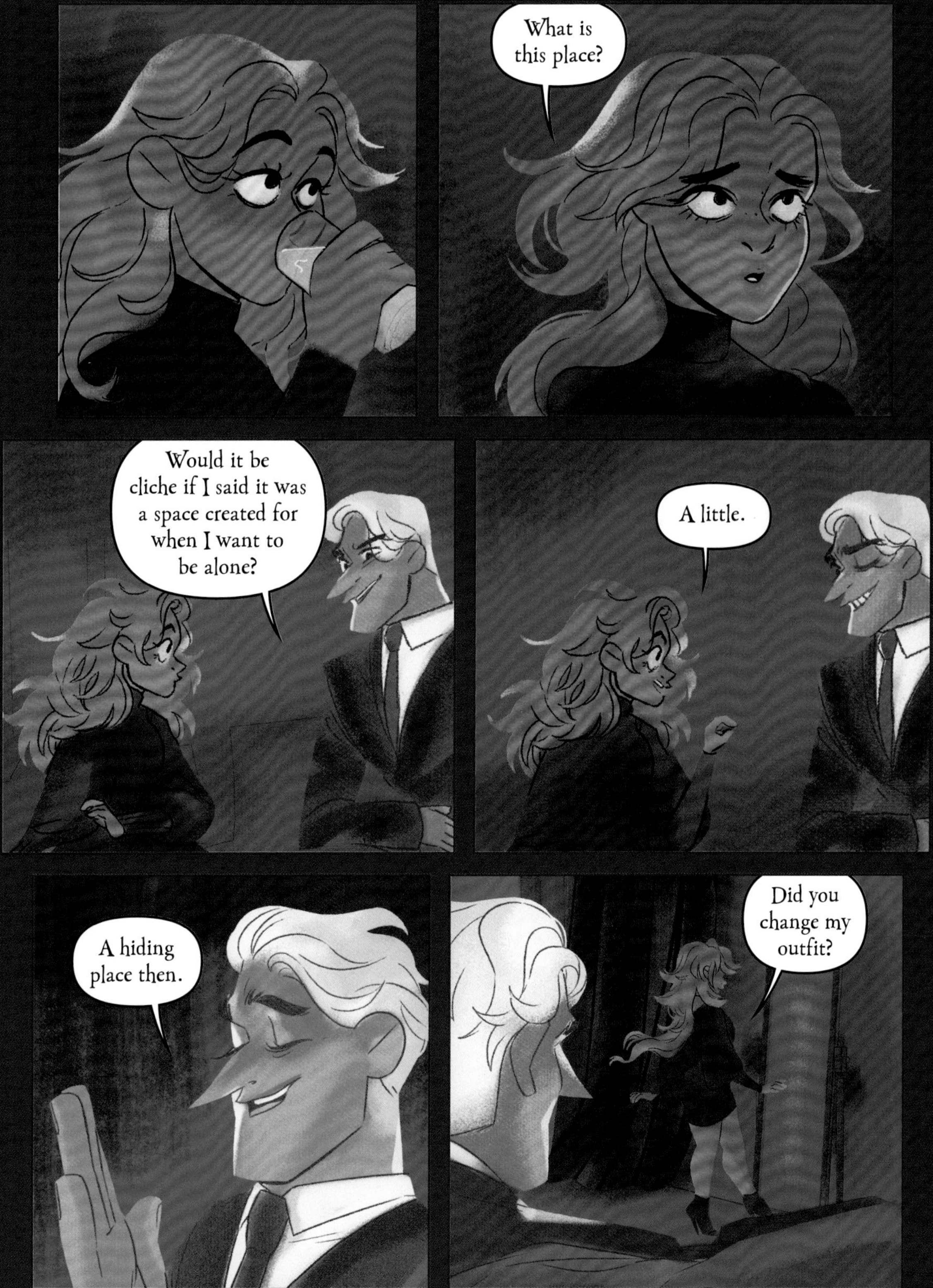
What is this place?
Would it be cliche if I said it was a space created for when I want to be alone?
A little.
A hiding place then.
Did you change my outfit?

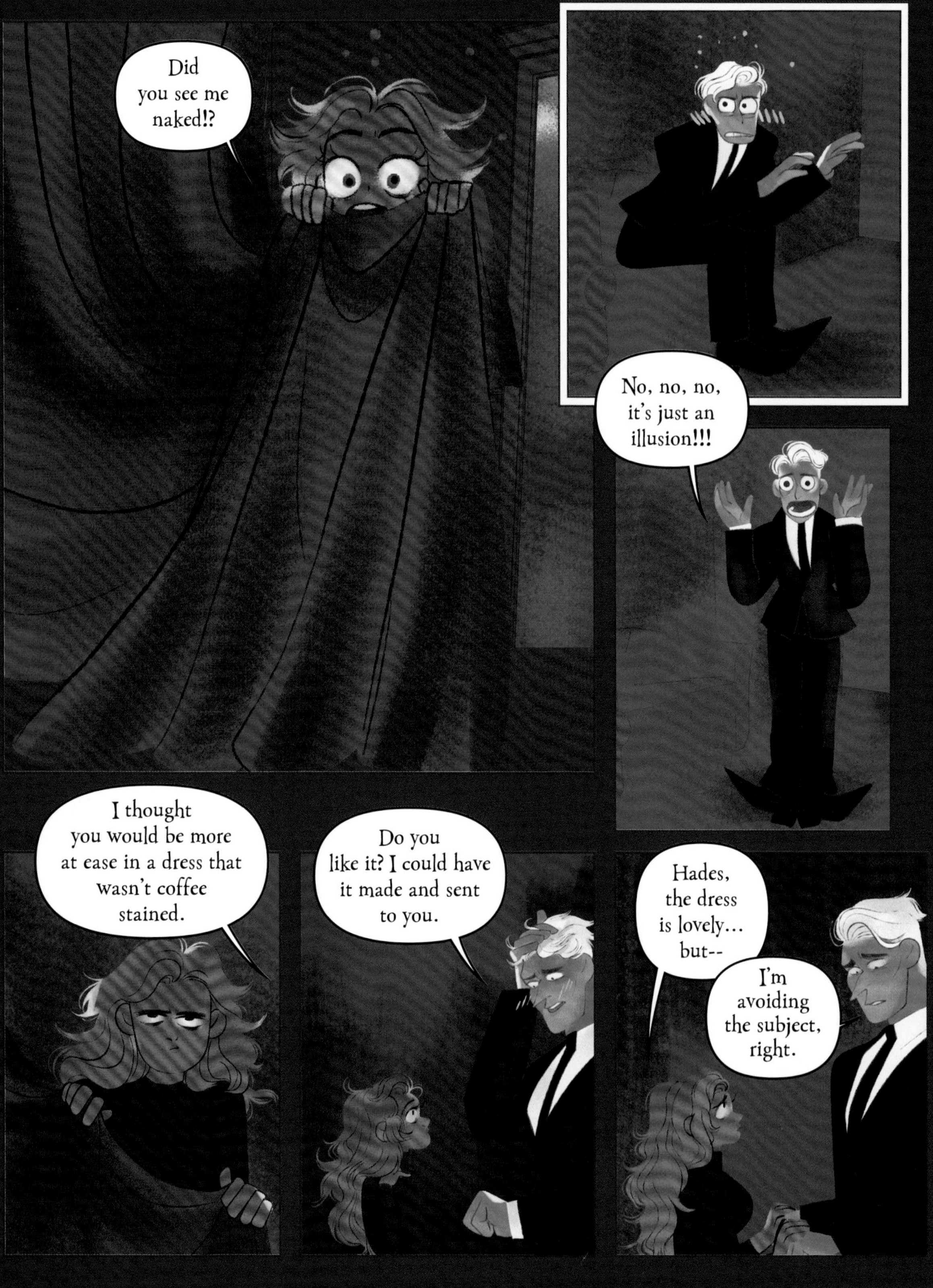
Did you see me naked!?
No, no, no, it's just an illusion!!!
I thought you would be more at ease in a dress that wasn't coffee stained.
Do you like it? I could have it made and sent to you.
Hades, the dress is lovely… but--
I'm avoiding the subject, right.

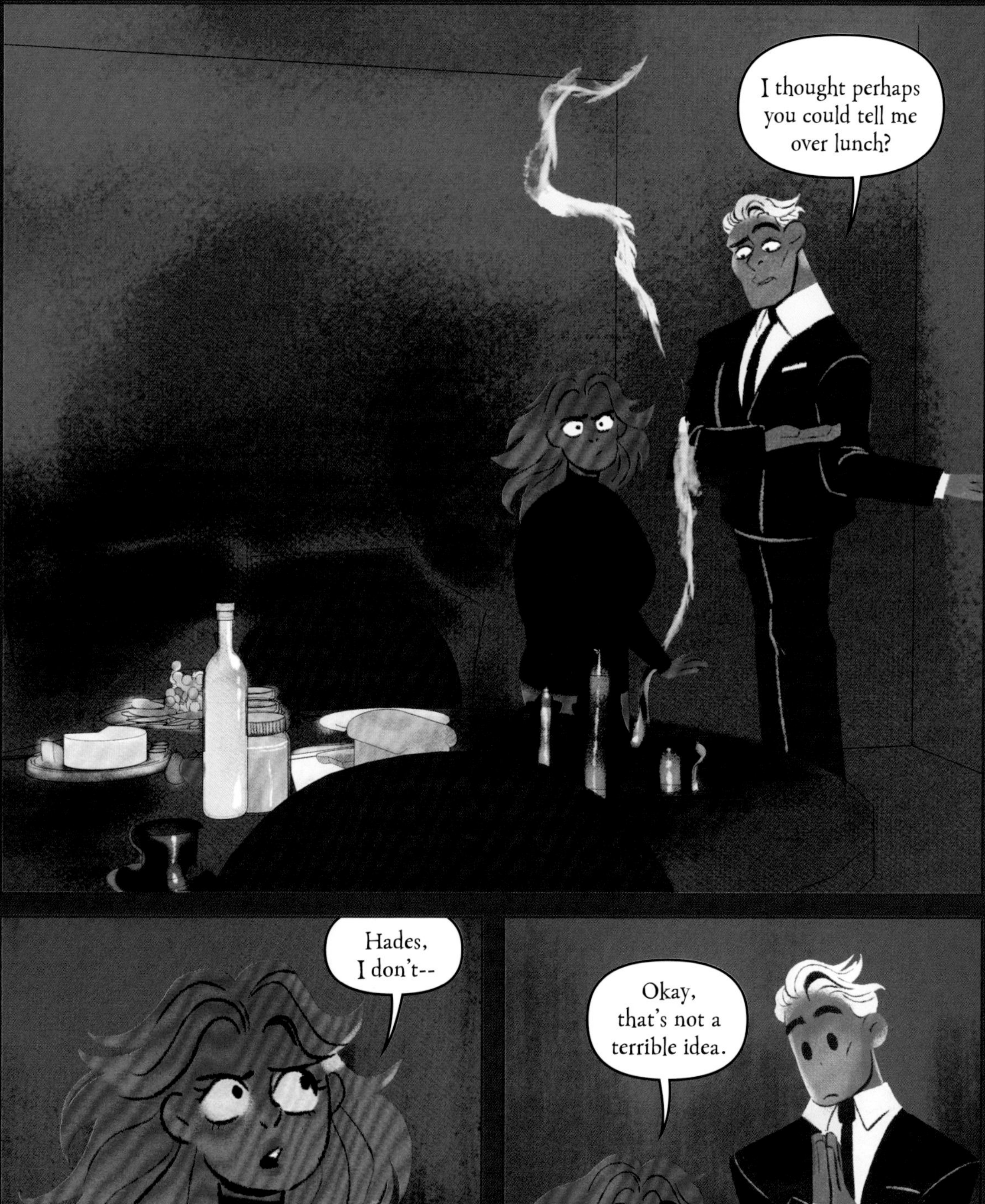
I thought perhaps you could tell me over lunch?
Hades, I don't--
Okay, that's not a terrible idea.
GRUMBLE

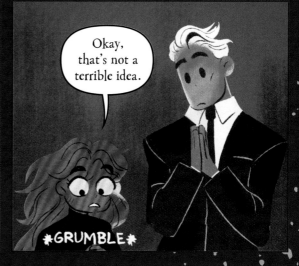

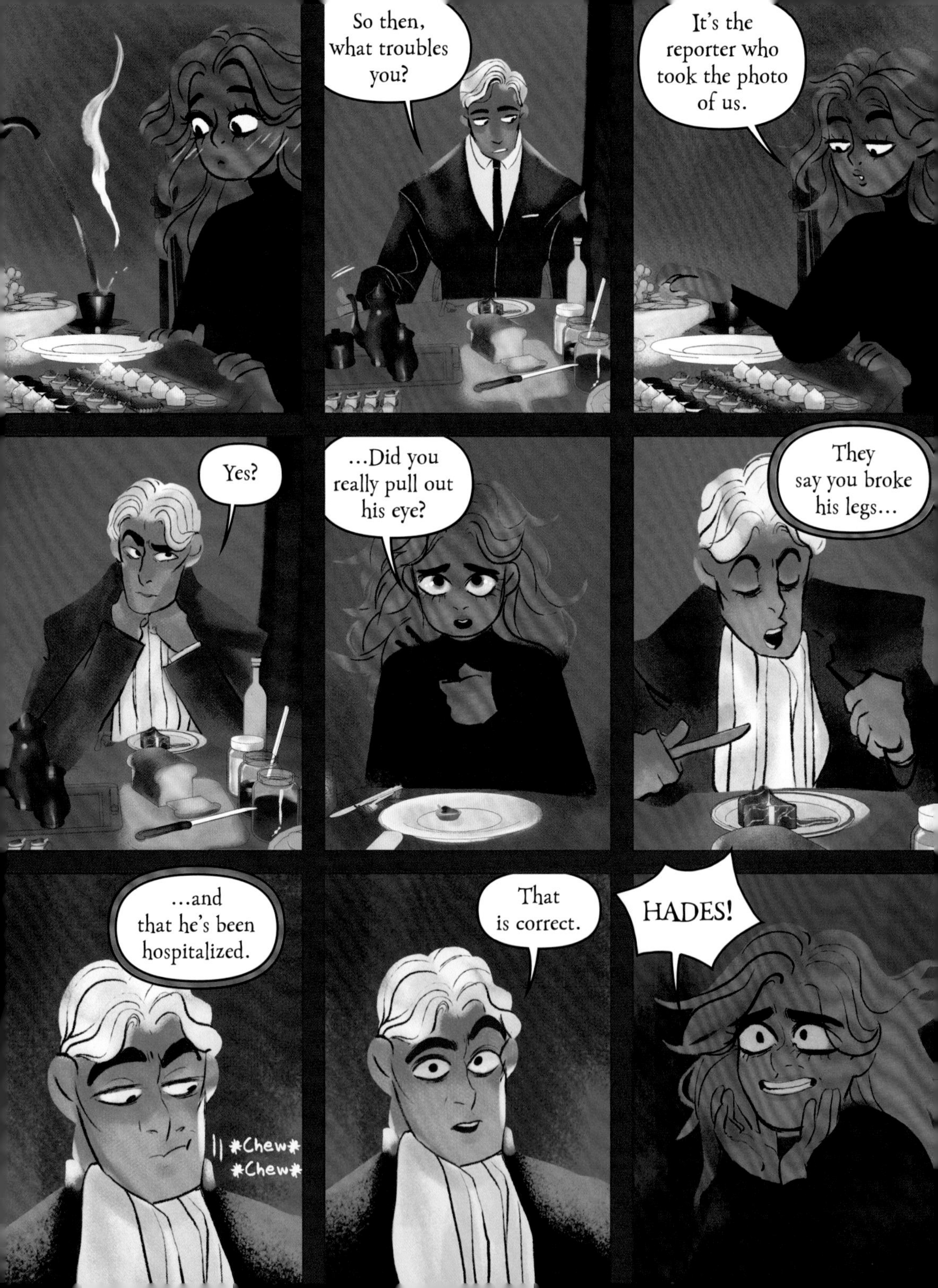
So then, what troubles you?
It's the reporter who took the photo of us.
Yes?
...Did you really pull out his eye?
They say you broke his legs...
...and that he's been hospitalized.
Chew *Chew*
That is correct.
HADES!

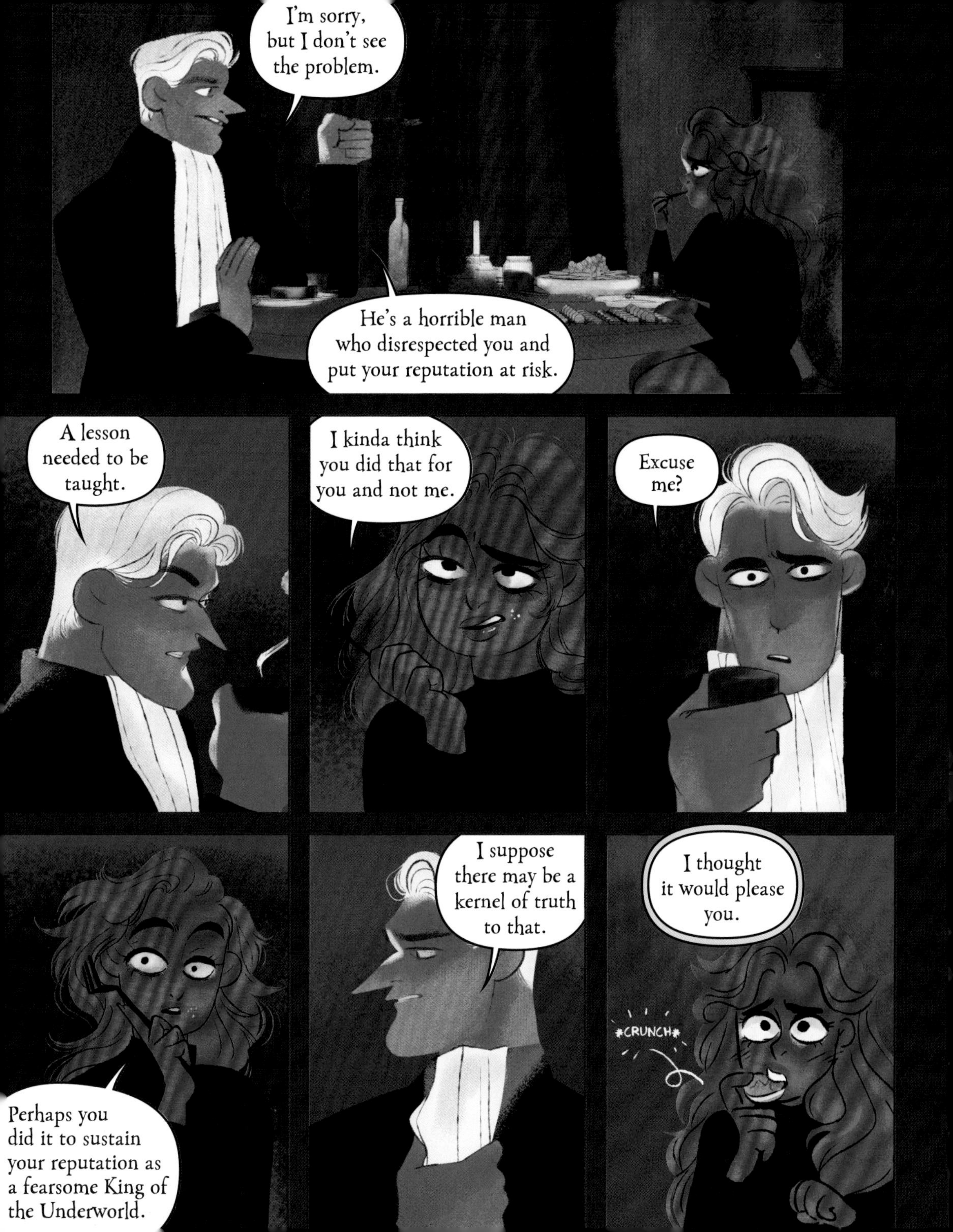
I'm sorry, but I don't see the problem.
He's a horrible man who disrespected you and put your reputation at risk.
A lesson needed to be taught.
I kinda think you did that for you and not me.
Excuse me?
Perhaps you did it to sustain your reputation as a fearsome King of the Underworld.
I suppose there may be a kernel of truth to that.
I thought it would please you.
CRUNCH

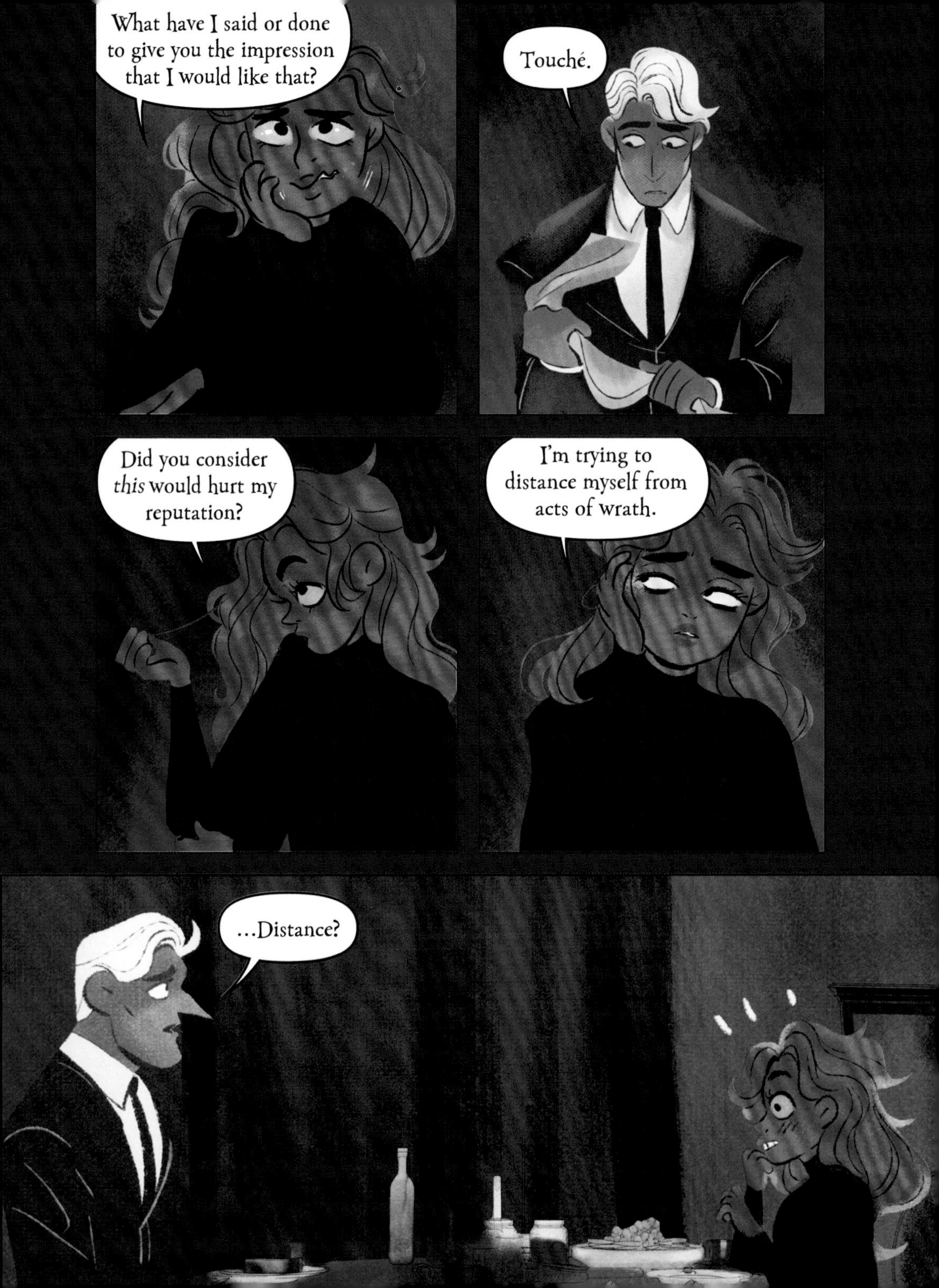

What have I said or done to give you the impression that I would like that?
Touché.
Did you consider *this* would hurt my reputation?
I'm trying to distance myself from acts of wrath.
...Distance?

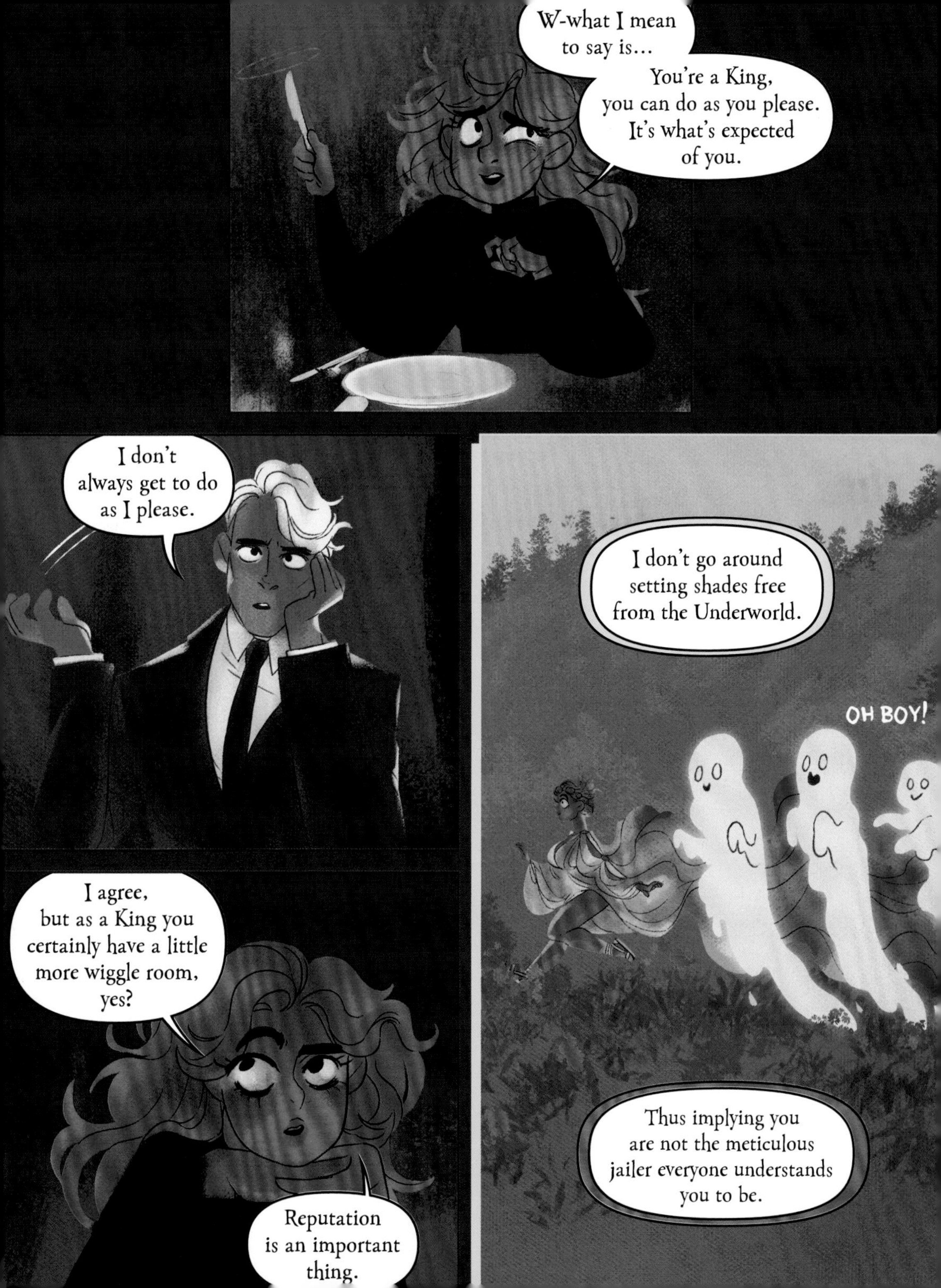
W-what I mean to say is...
You're a King, you can do as you please. It's what's expected of you.
I don't always get to do as I please.
I agree, but as a King you certainly have a little more wiggle room, yes?
Reputation is an important thing.
I don't go around setting shades free from the Underworld.
OH BOY!
Thus implying you are not the meticulous jailer everyone understands you to be.

All I'm saying is if you want to do something that involves me, could you talk to me first?

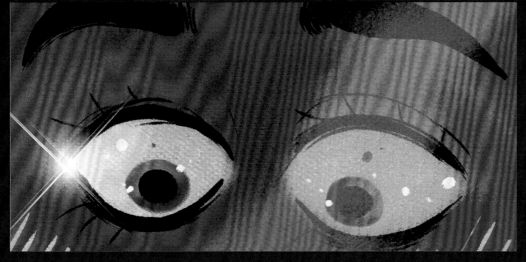

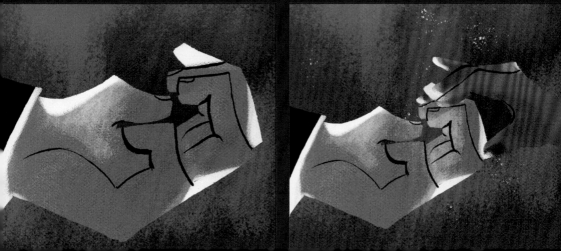

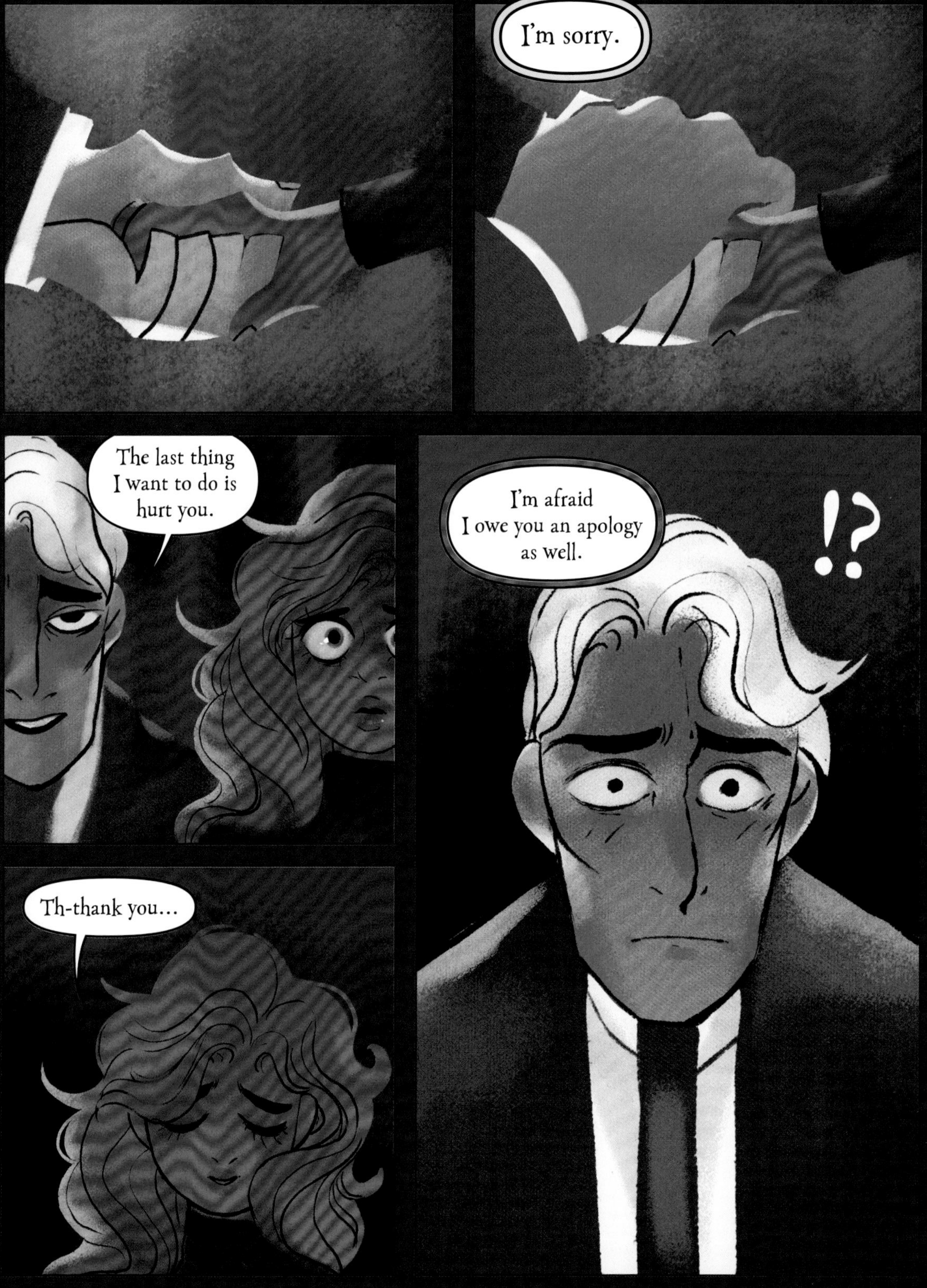
I'm sorry.
The last thing I want to do is hurt you.
Th-thank you...
I'm afraid I owe you an apology as well.
!?

EPISODE 88: IT'S ALL FUN AND GAMES UNTIL SOMEONE LOSES AN EYE (PART 2)

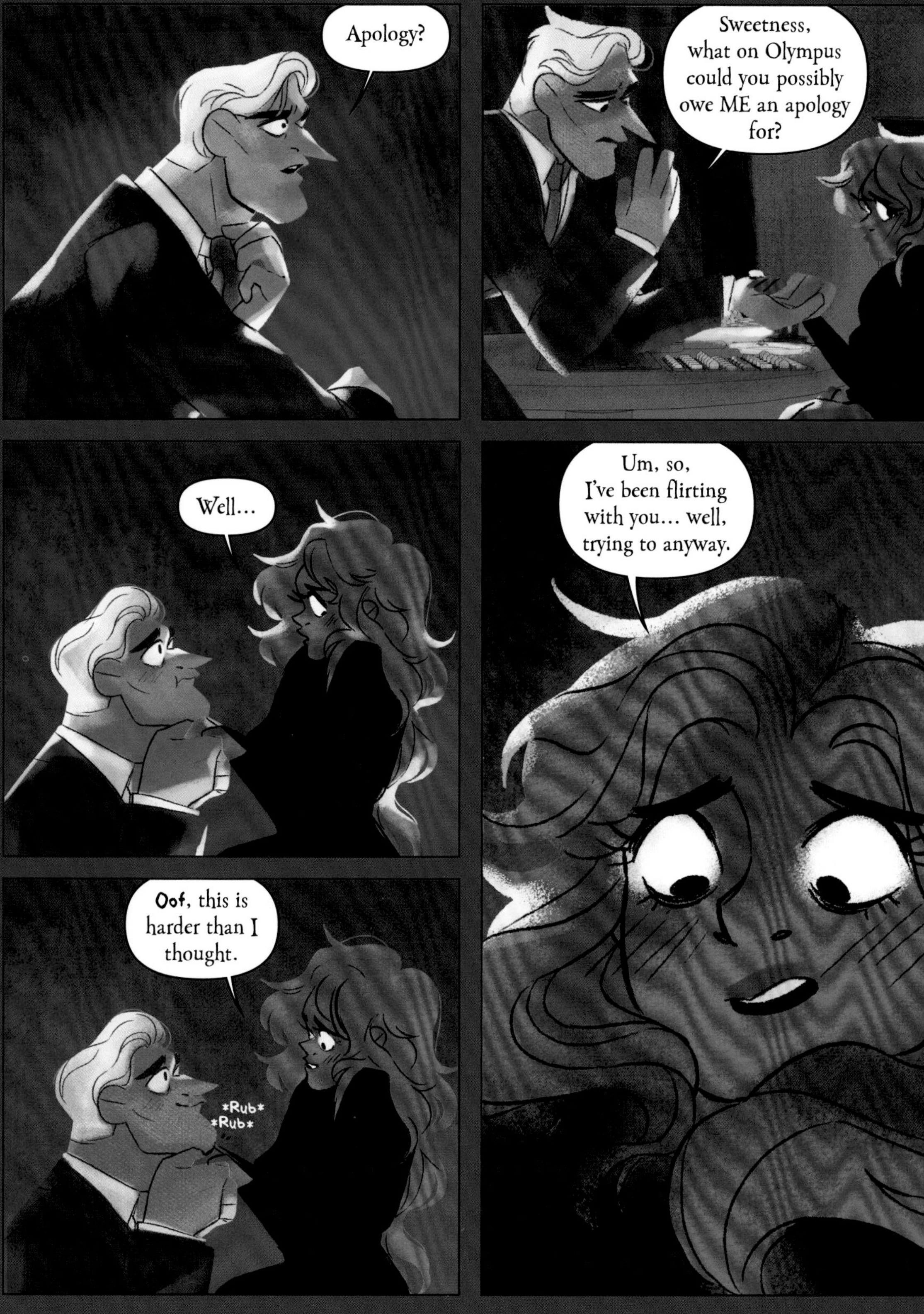
Apology?
Sweetness, what on Olympus could you possibly owe ME an apology for?
Well...
Oof, this is harder than I thought.
Rub *Rub*
Um, so, I've been flirting with you... well, trying to anyway.

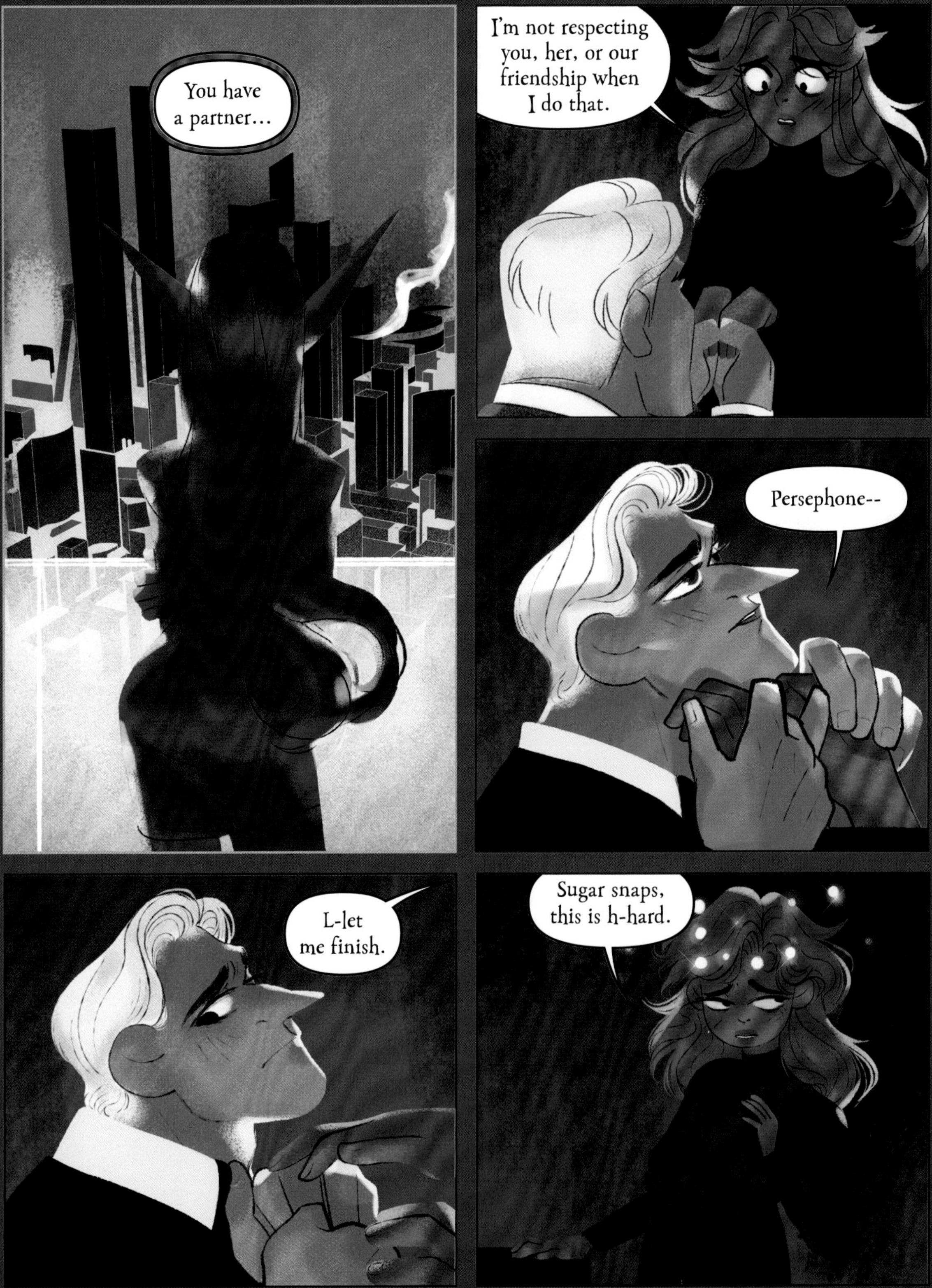
You have a partner...
I'm not respecting you, her, or our friendship when I do that.
Persephone--
L-let me finish.
Sugar snaps, this is h-hard.

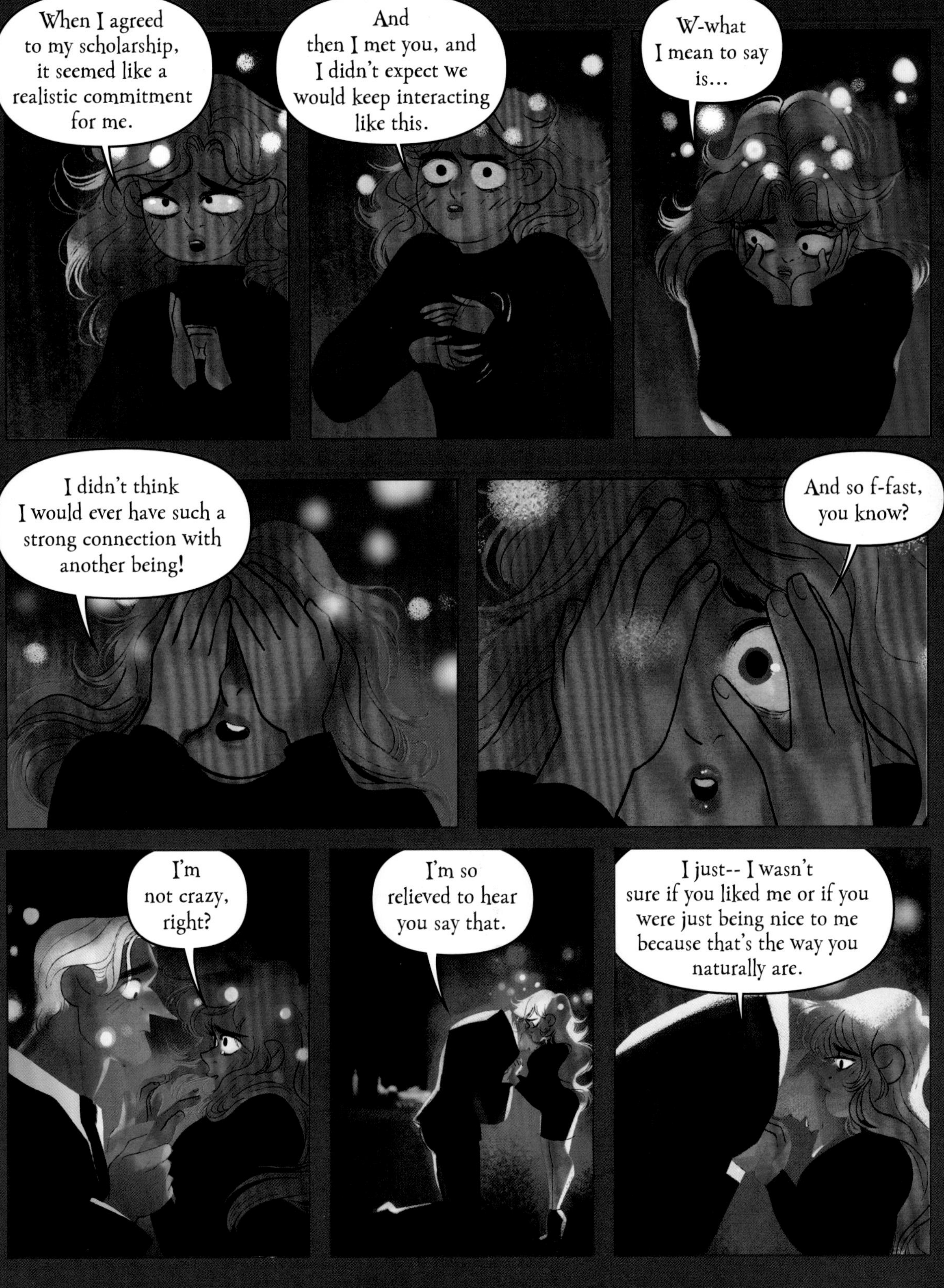

When I agreed to my scholarship, it seemed like a realistic commitment for me.
And then I met you, and I didn't expect we would keep interacting like this.
W-what I mean to say is...
I didn't think I would ever have such a strong connection with another being!
And so f-fast, you know?
I'm not crazy, right?
I'm so relieved to hear you say that.
I just-- I wasn't sure if you liked me or if you were just being nice to me because that's the way you naturally are.

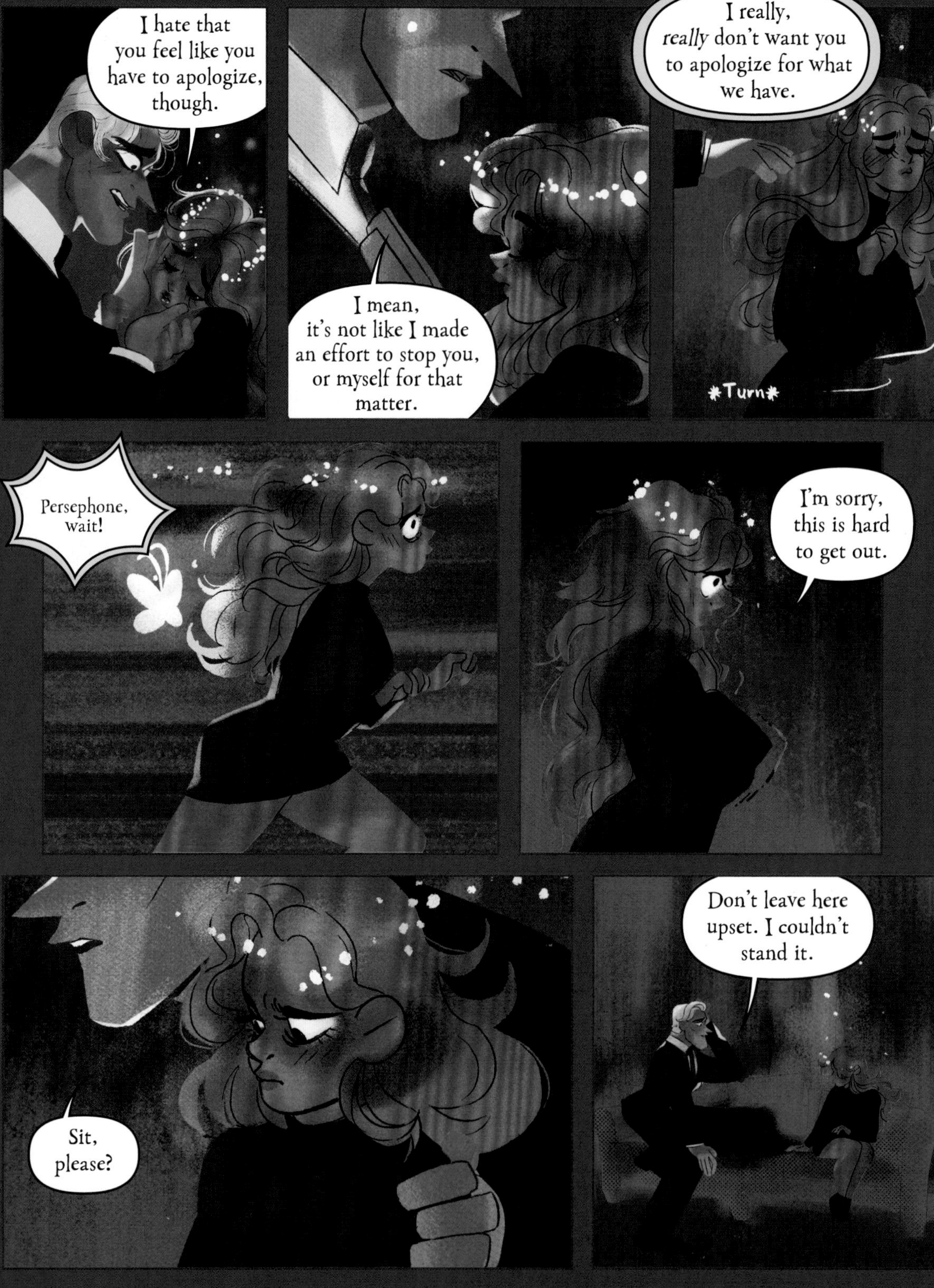
I hate that you feel like you have to apologize, though.
I mean, it's not like I made an effort to stop you, or myself for that matter.
I really, *really* don't want you to apologize for what we have.
Turn
Persephone, wait!
I'm sorry, this is hard to get out.
Sit, please?
Don't leave here upset. I couldn't stand it.

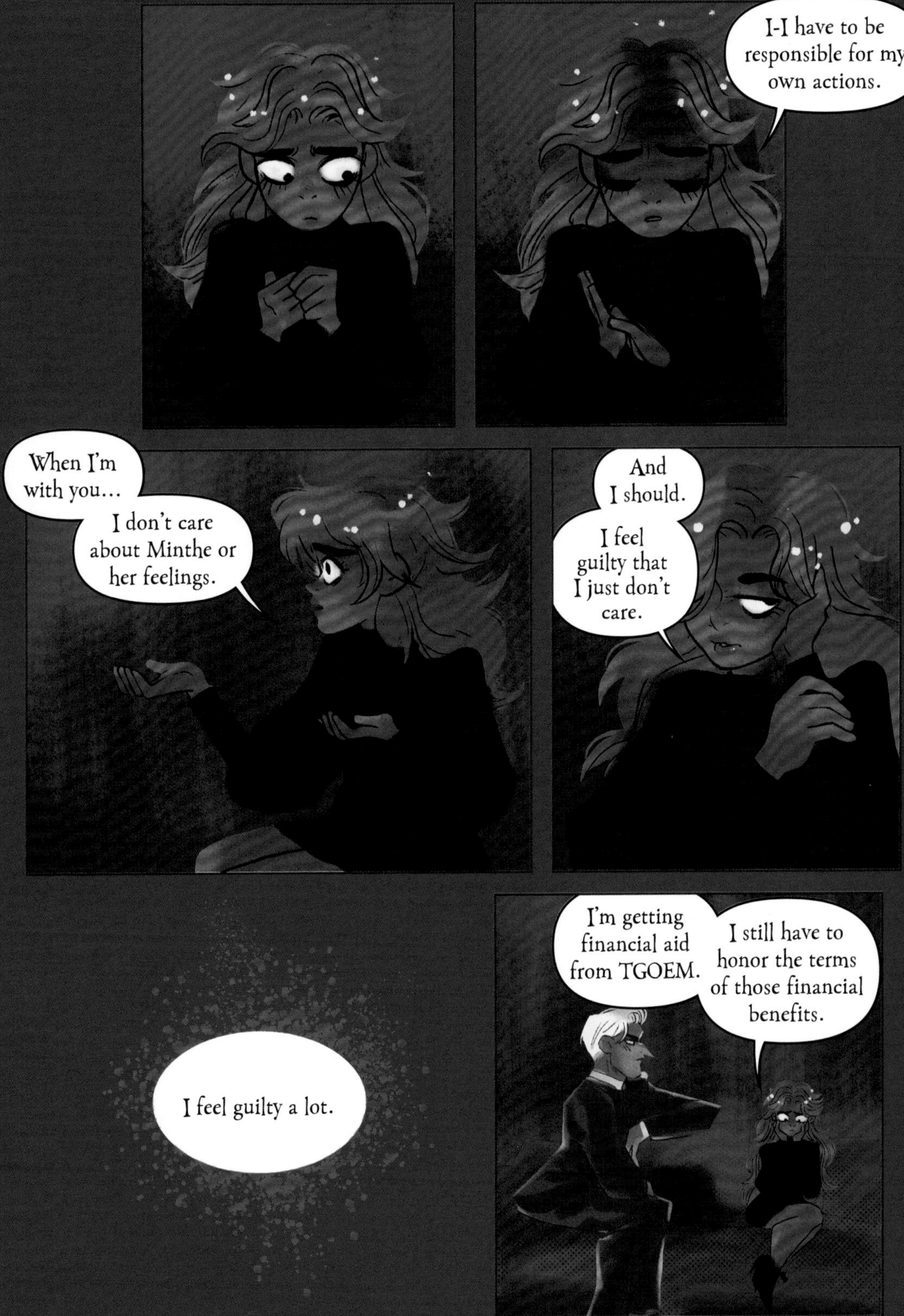
I-I have to be responsible for my own actions.
When I'm with you...
I don't care about Minthe or her feelings.
And I should.
I feel guilty that I just don't care.
I feel guilty a lot.
I'm getting financial aid from TGOEM.
I still have to honor the terms of those financial benefits.

I don't think having an intense hand-holding session with the King of the Underworld is what Hestia had in mind when she awarded me the scholarship.

Oh. Sorry.

You put a lot of pressure on yourself.

Out of everyone, you understand the importance of duty.

...

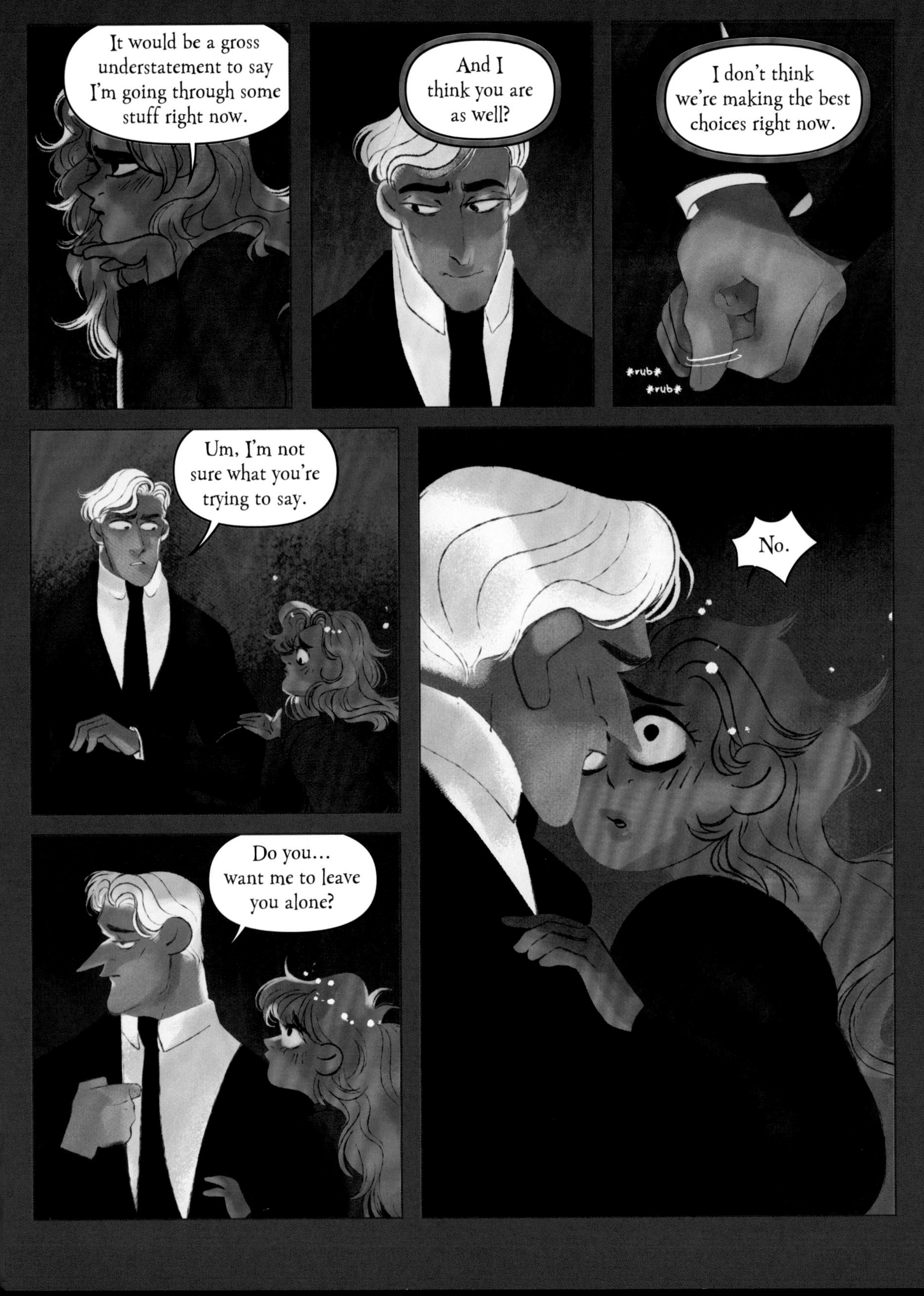
It would be a gross understatement to say I'm going through some stuff right now.
And I think you are as well?
I don't think we're making the best choices right now.
rub *rub*
Um, I'm not sure what you're trying to say.
Do you… want me to leave you alone?
No.

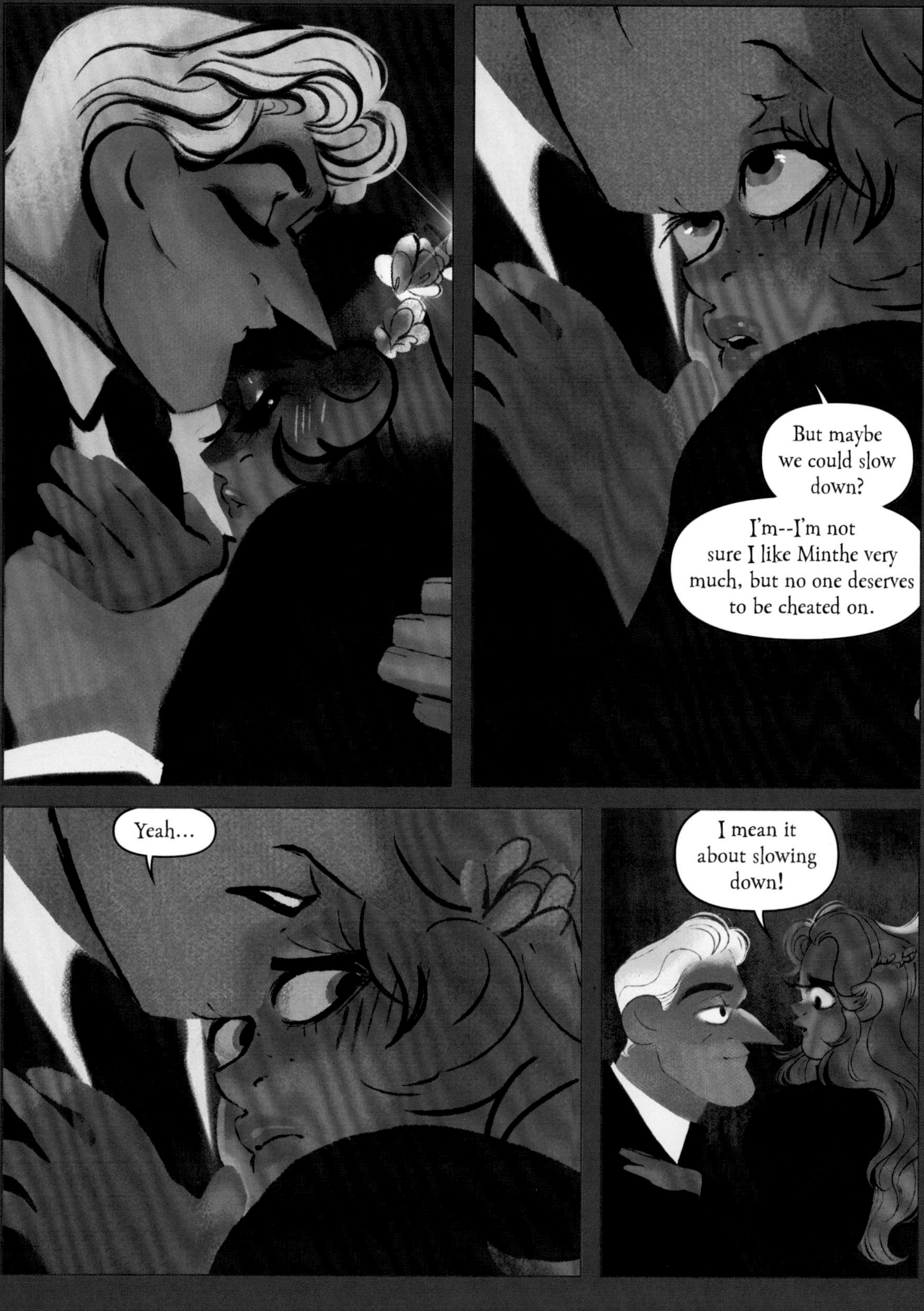
But maybe we could slow down?
I'm--I'm not sure I like Minthe very much, but no one deserves to be cheated on.
Yeah...
I mean it about slowing down!

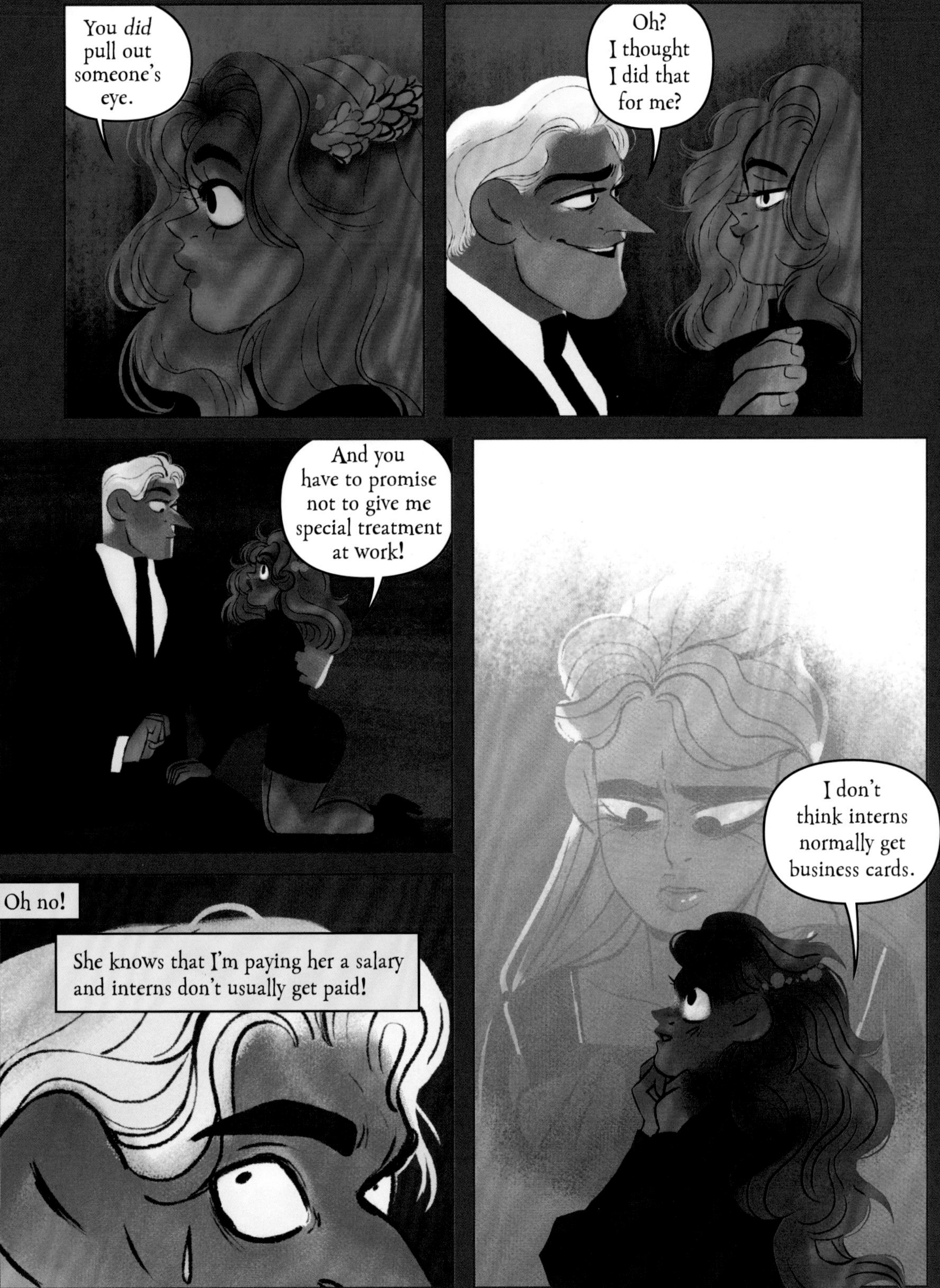
You *did* pull out someone's eye.
Oh? I thought I did that for me?
And you have to promise not to give me special treatment at work!
I don't think interns normally get business cards.
Oh no!
She knows that I'm paying her a salary and interns don't usually get paid!

Yes!
Getting away with it!
Okay, ya got me, no more special treatment.
...Wait! I might have one last teeny-weeny request.

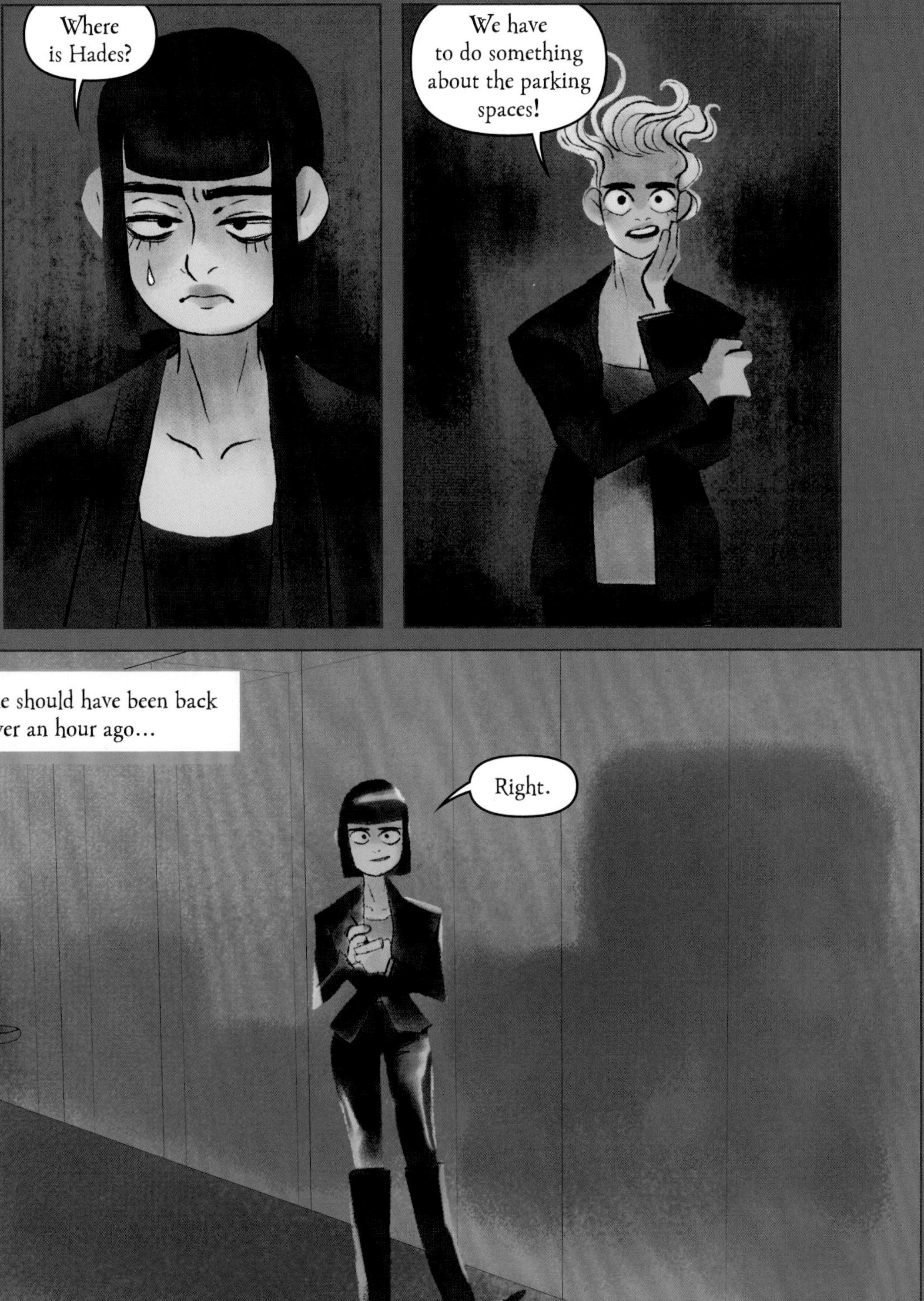
Where is Hades?
We have to do something about the parking spaces!
He should have been back over an hour ago...
Right.

Everyone needs to use their assigned spaces, otherwise, what's the point?

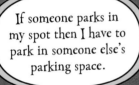

If someone parks in my spot then I have to park in someone else's parking space.

Got it.

What the--!?

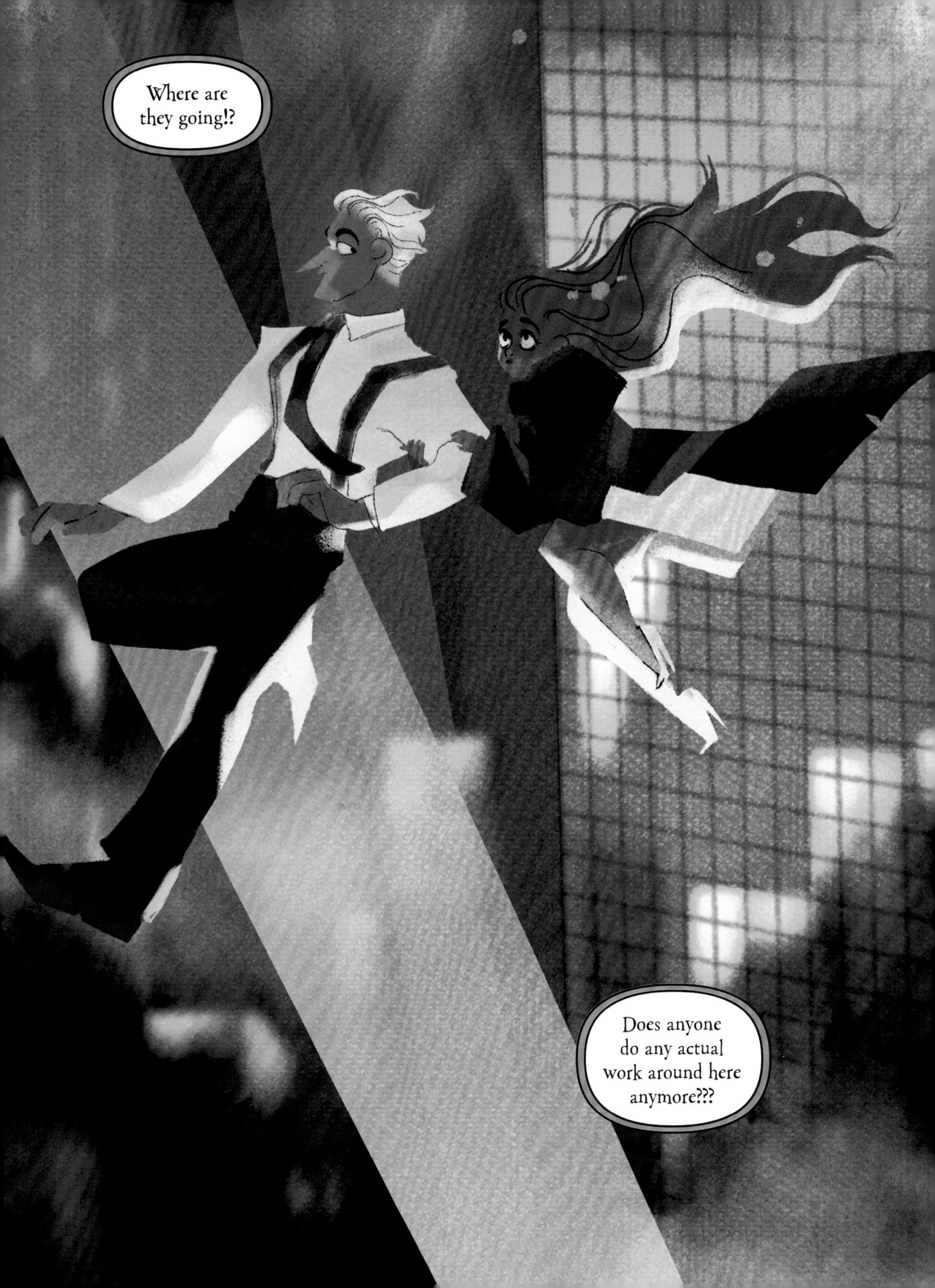
Where are they going!?
Does anyone do any actual work around here anymore???

EPISODE 89: IT'S ALL FUN AND GAMES UNTIL
SOMEONE LOSES AN EYE (PART 3)

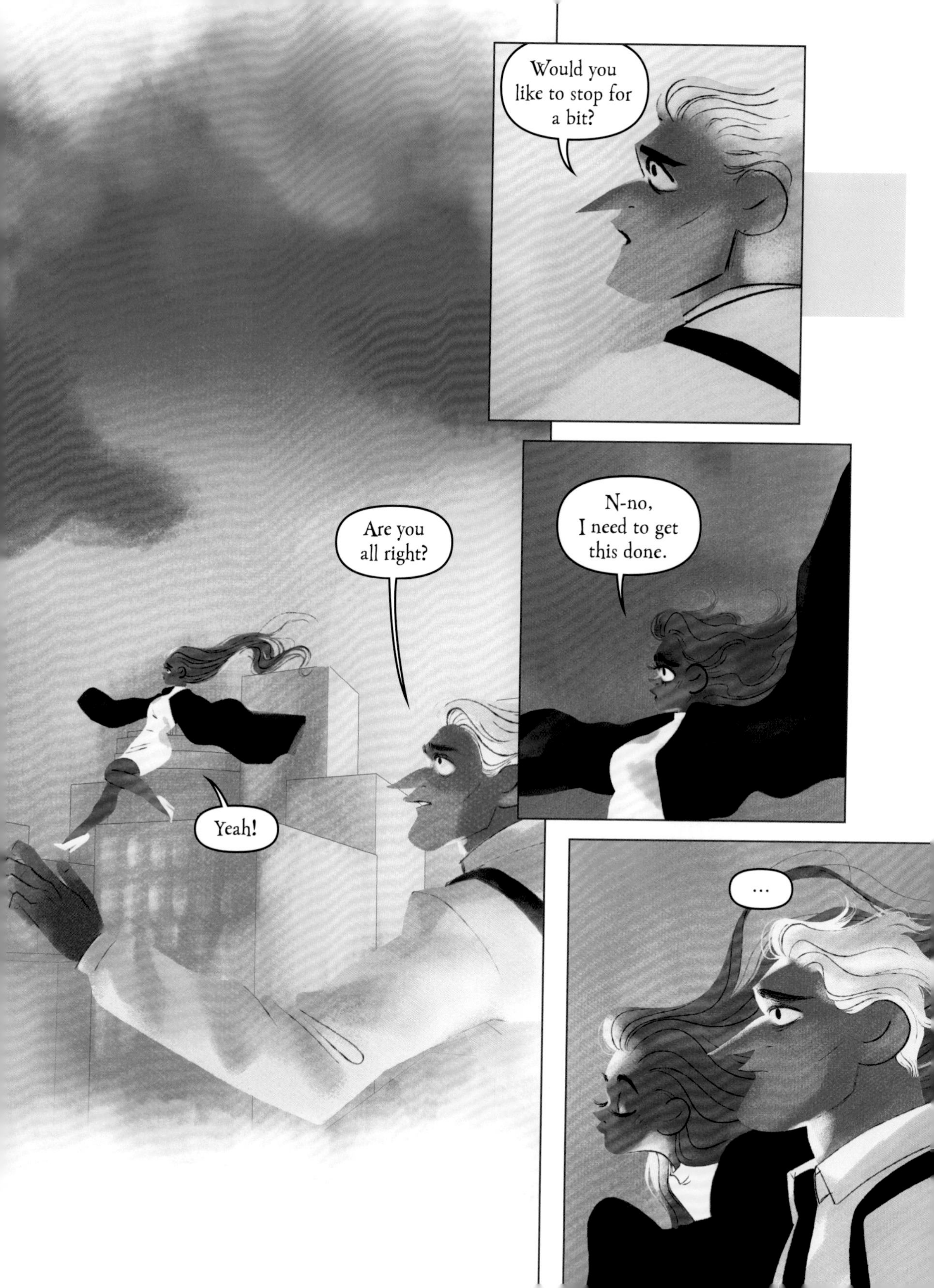
Would you like to stop for a bit?
Are you all right?
Yeah!
N-no, I need to get this done.
...

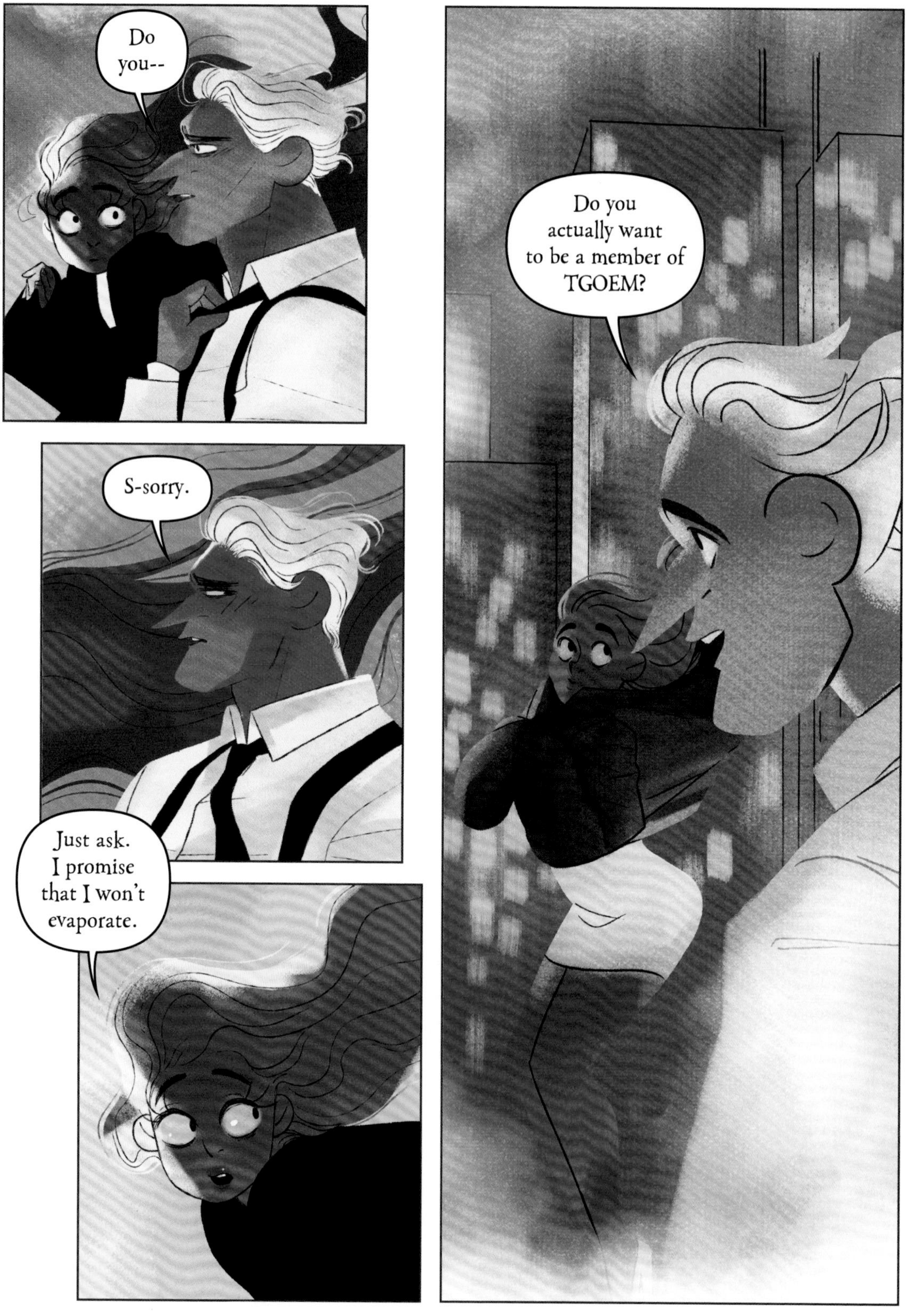
Do you--
S-sorry.
Just ask. I promise that I won't evaporate.
Do you actually want to be a member of TGOEM?

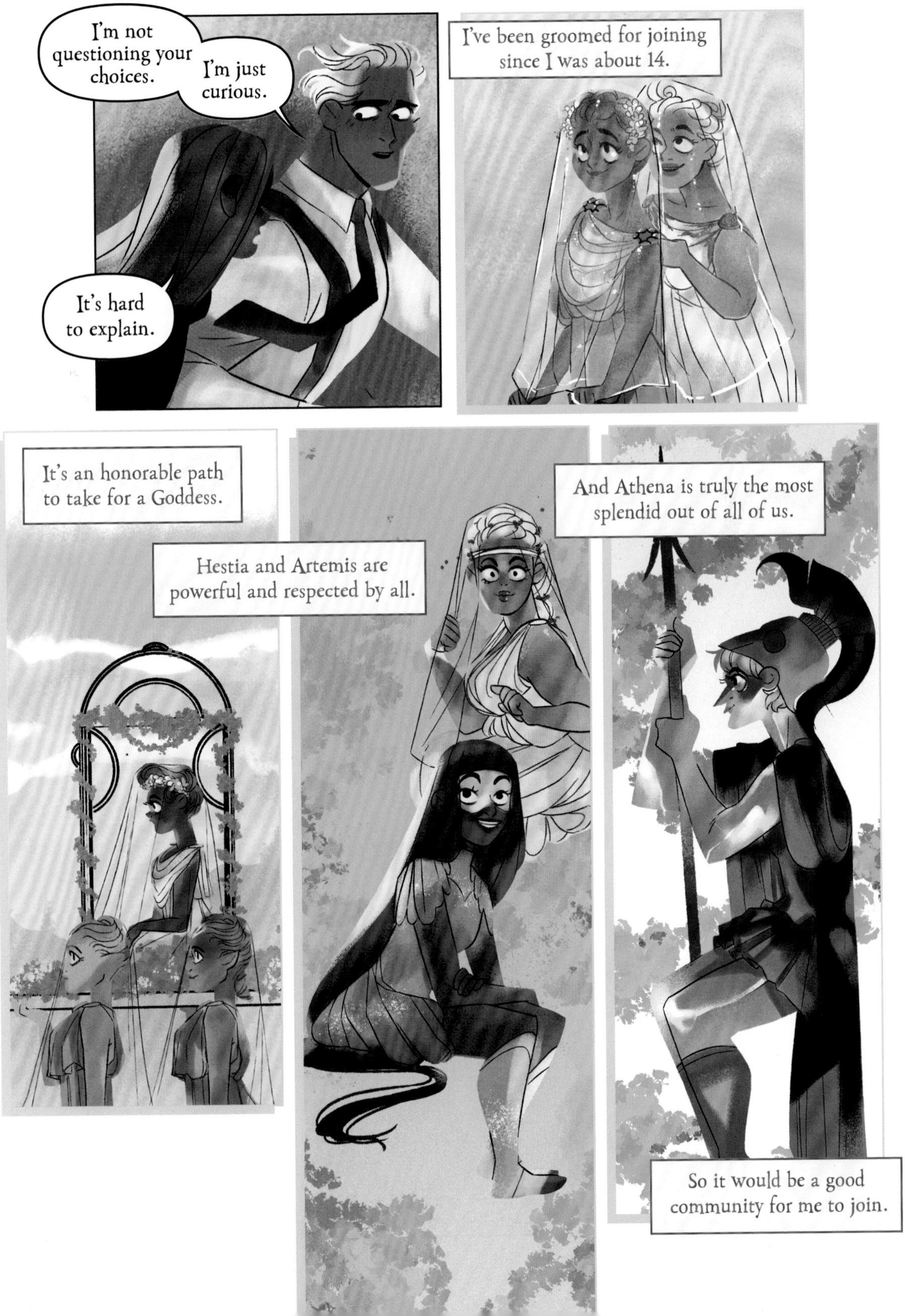
I'm not questioning your choices.
I'm just curious.
It's hard to explain.
I've been groomed for joining since I was about 14.
It's an honorable path to take for a Goddess.
Hestia and Artemis are powerful and respected by all.
And Athena is truly the most splendid out of all of us.
So it would be a good community for me to join.

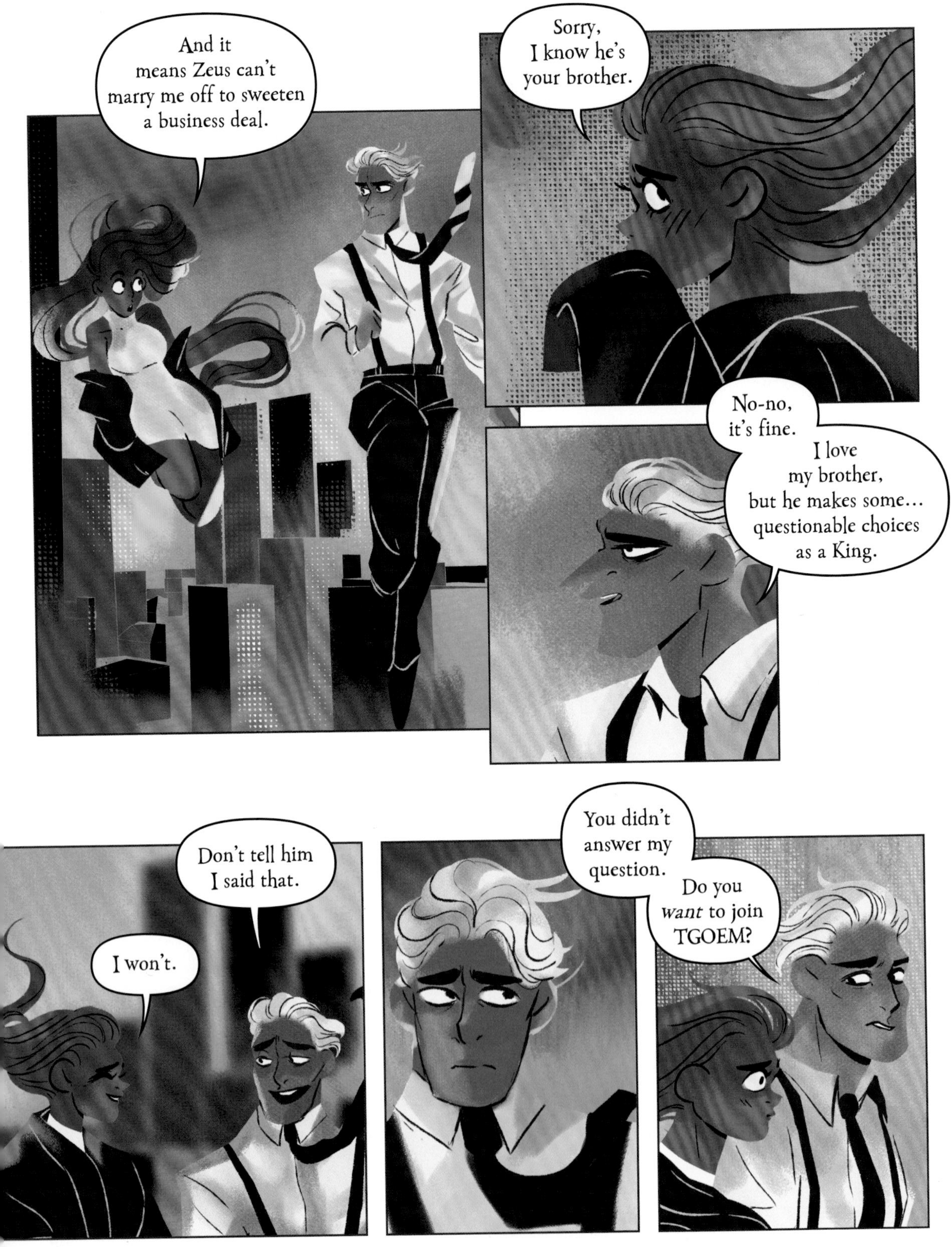
And it means Zeus can't marry me off to sweeten a business deal.
Sorry, I know he's your brother.
No-no, it's fine.
I love my brother, but he makes some... questionable choices as a King.
Don't tell him I said that.
I won't.
You didn't answer my question.
Do you *want* to join TGOEM?

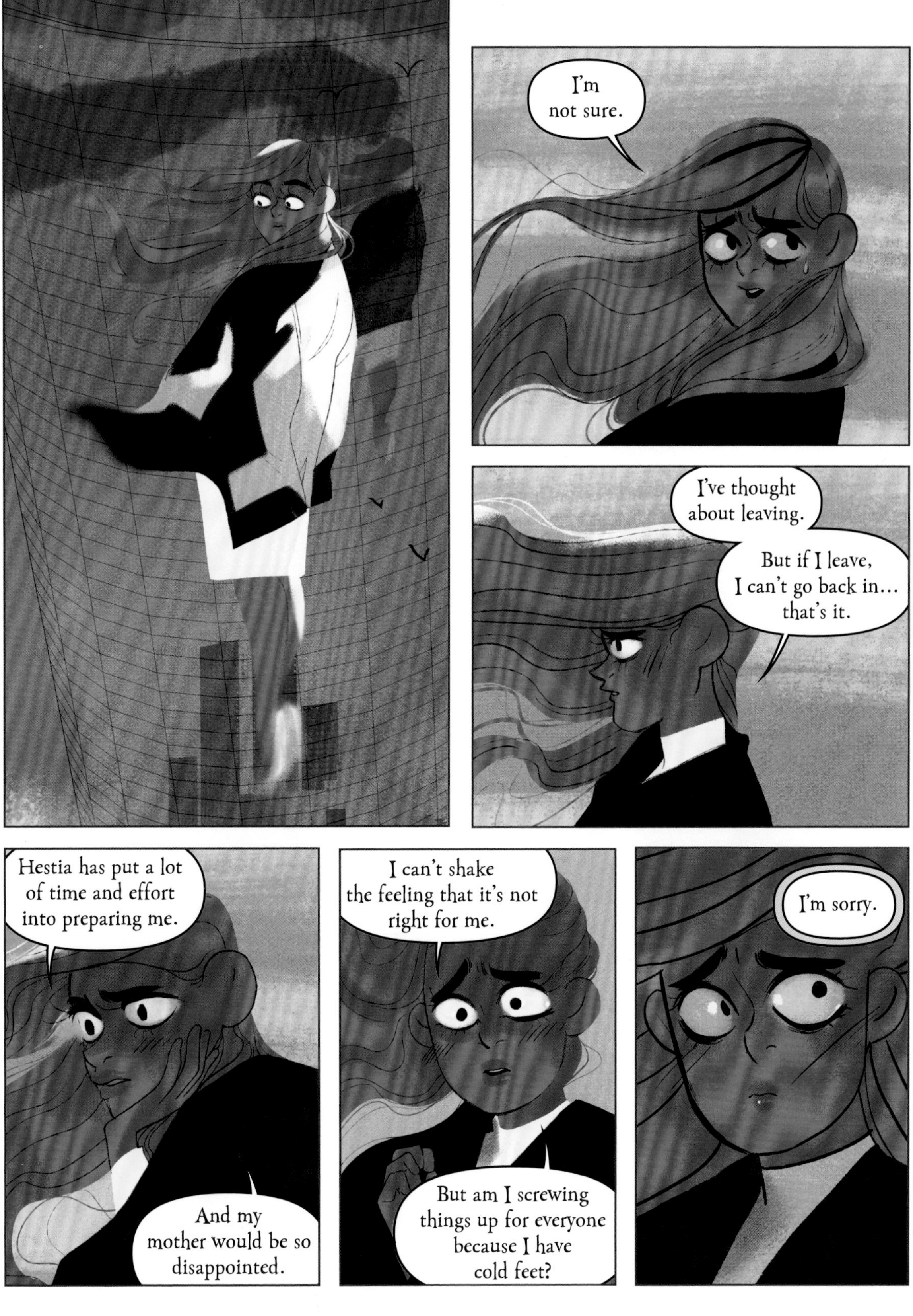
I'm not sure.
I've thought about leaving.
But if I leave, I can't go back in... that's it.
Hestia has put a lot of time and effort into preparing me.
And my mother would be so disappointed.
I can't shake the feeling that it's not right for me.
But am I screwing things up for everyone because I have cold feet?
I'm sorry.

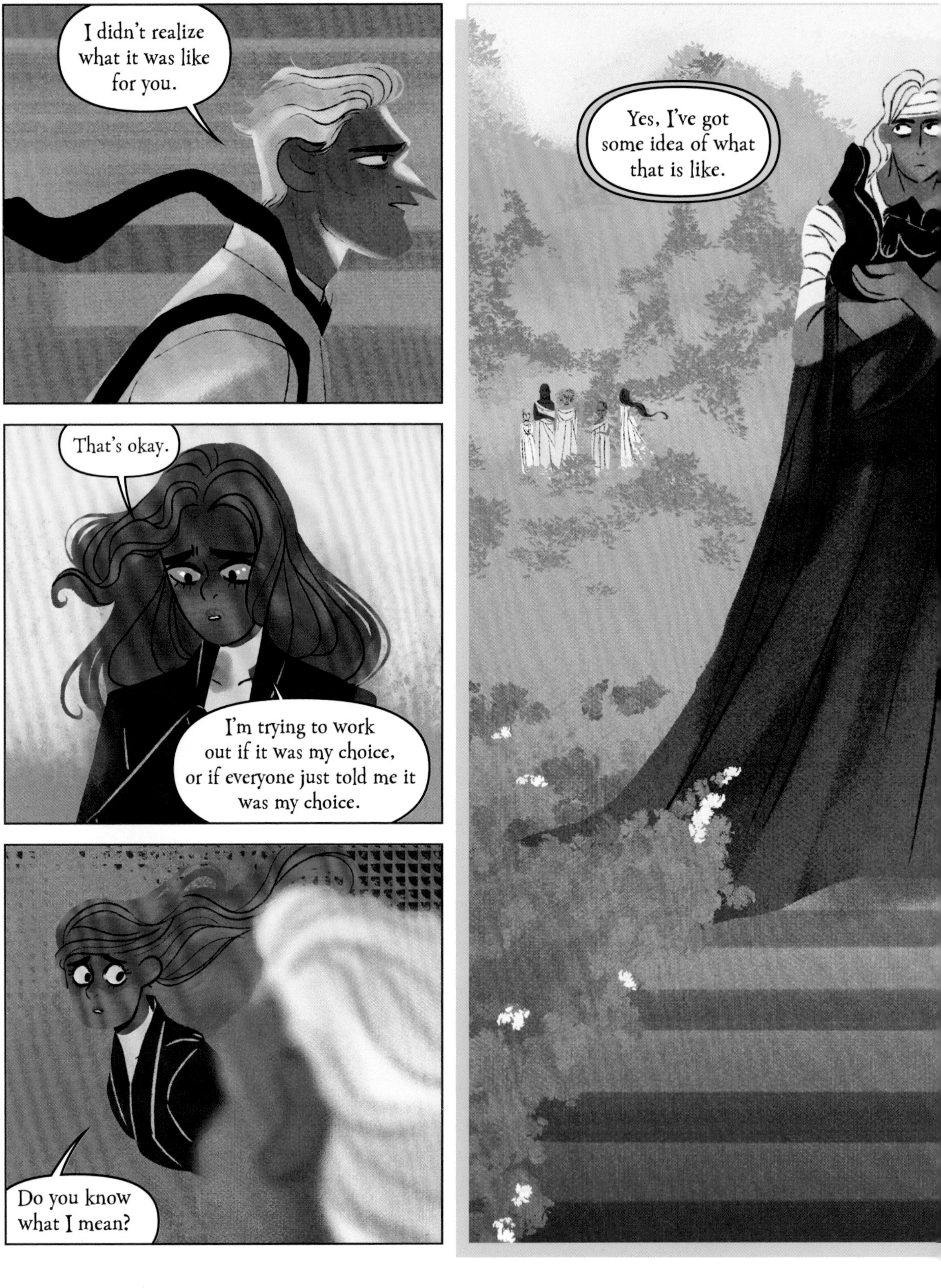
I didn't realize what it was like for you.
That's okay.
I'm trying to work out if it was my choice, or if everyone just told me it was my choice.
Do you know what I mean?
Yes, I've got some idea of what that is like.

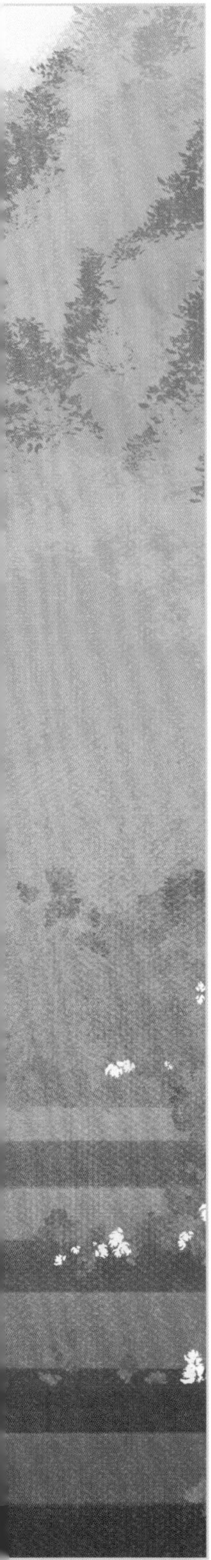

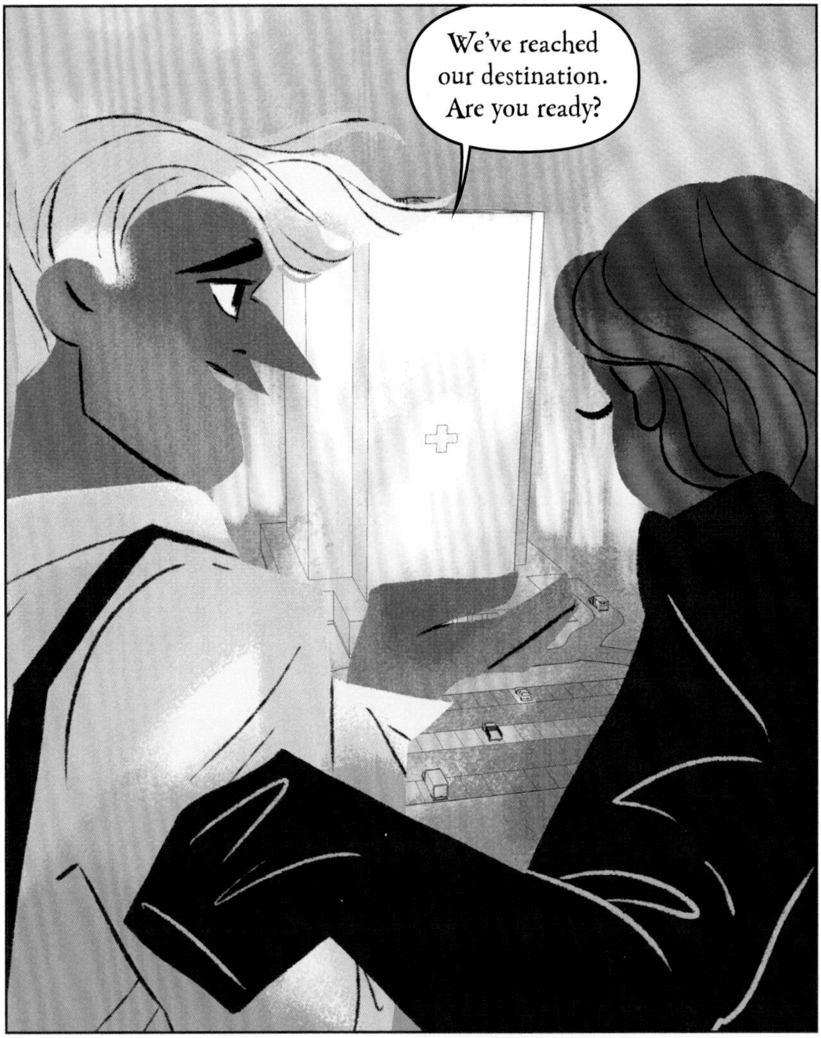
We've reached our destination. Are you ready?

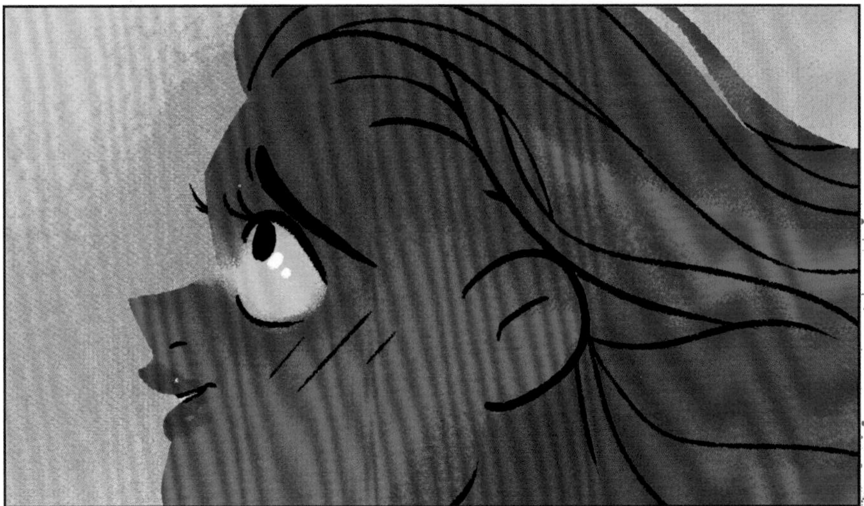

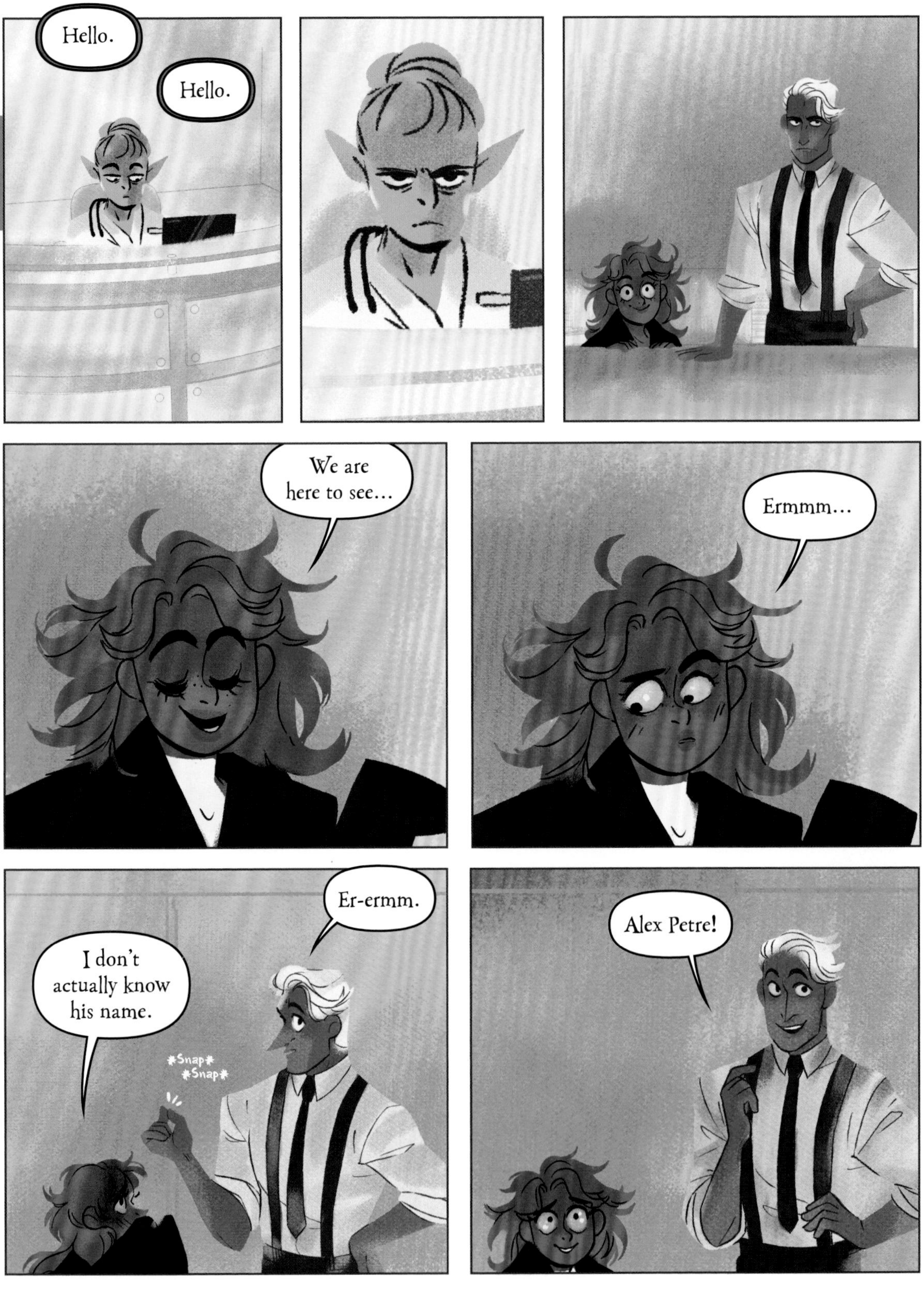
Hello.
Hello.
We are here to see…
Ermmm…
Er-ermm.
I don't actually know his name.
Snap *Snap*
Alex Petre!

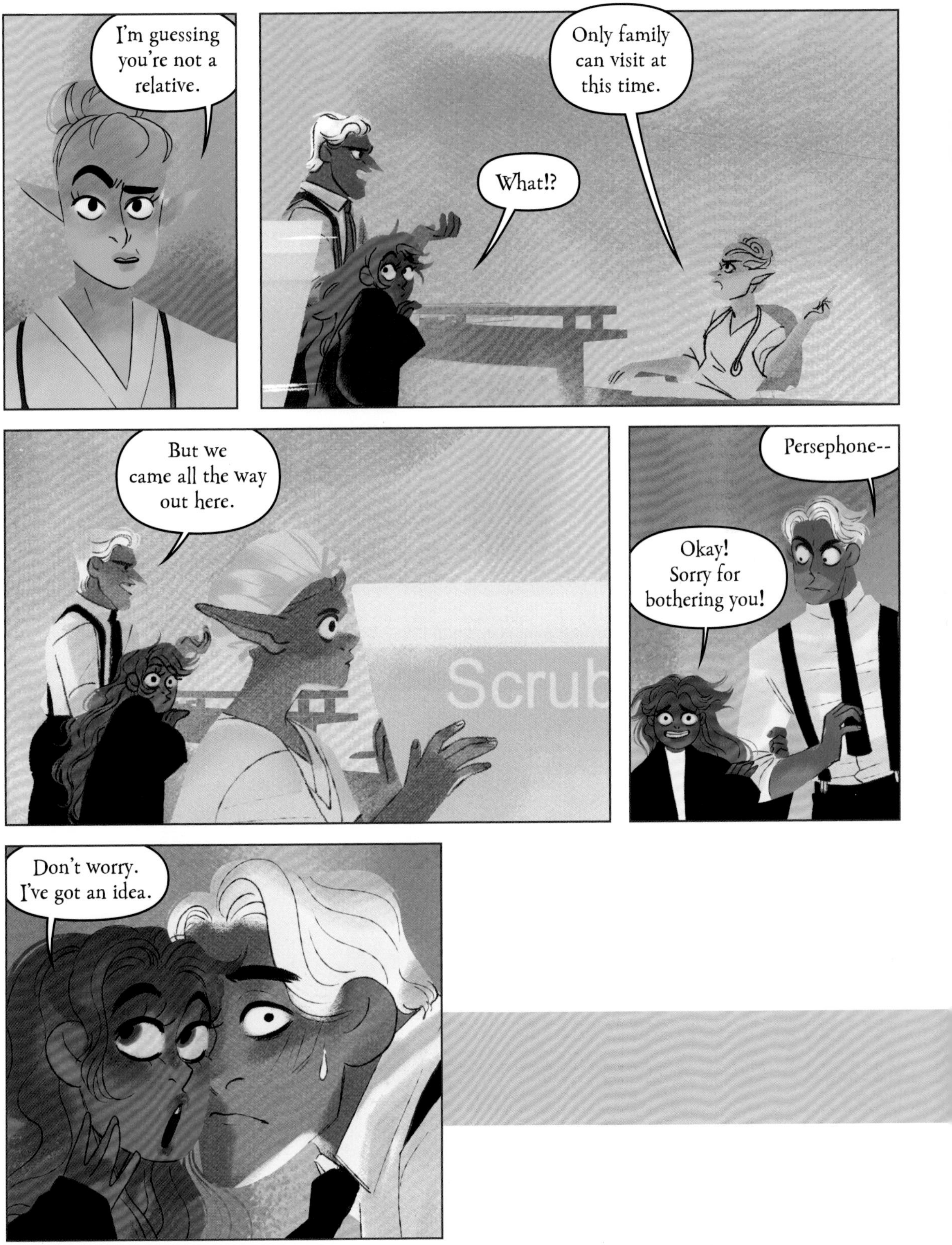
I'm guessing you're not a relative.
Only family can visit at this time.
What!?
But we came all the way out here.
Scrub
Persephone--
Okay! Sorry for bothering you!
Don't worry. I've got an idea.

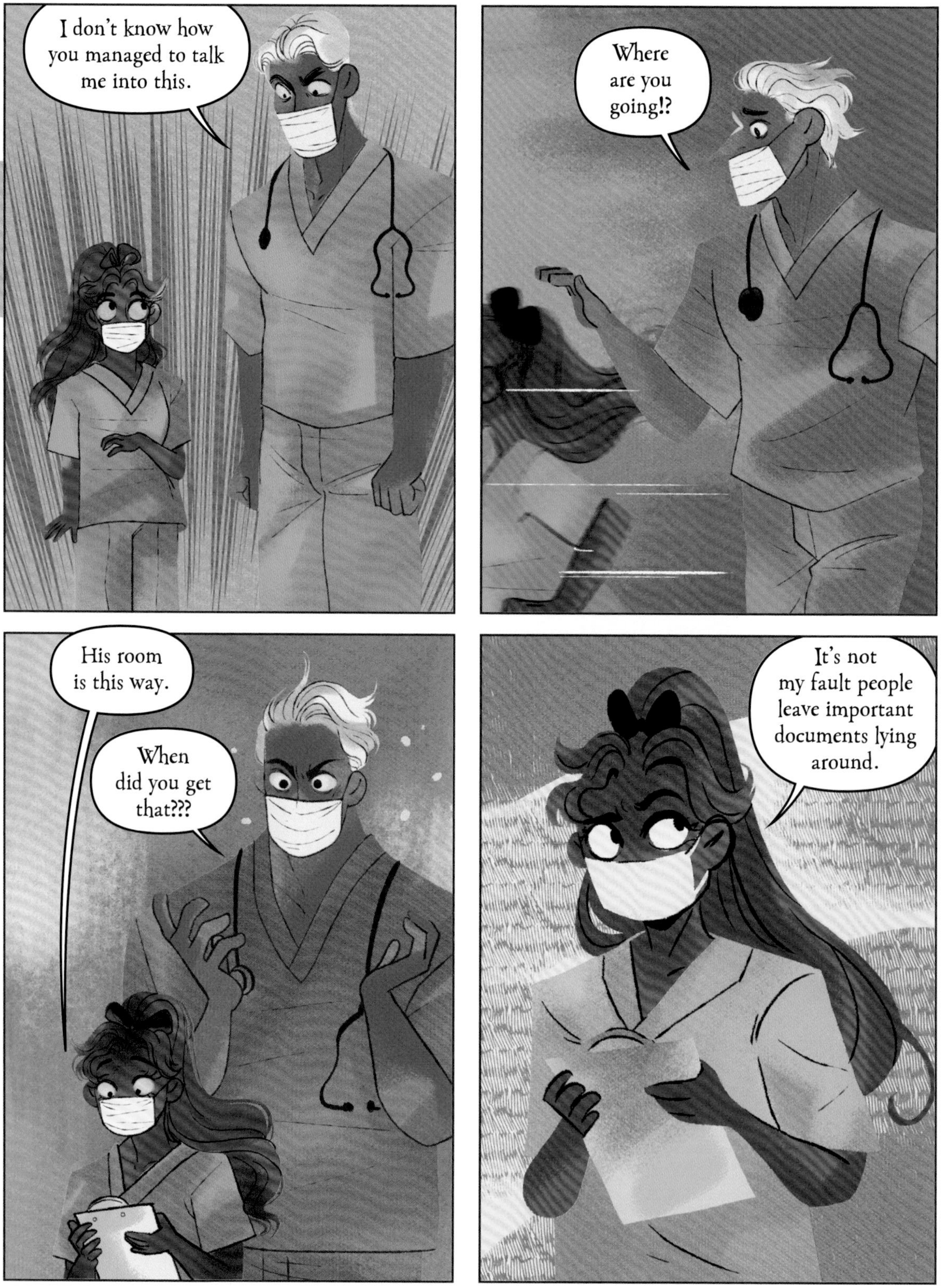
I don't know how you managed to talk me into this.
Where are you going!?
His room is this way.
When did you get that???
It's not my fault people leave important documents lying around.

SLIDE!

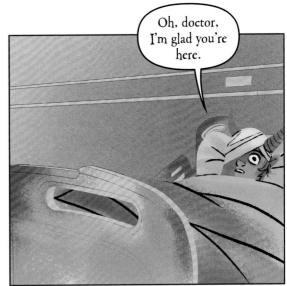

Oh, doctor, I'm glad you're here.

Surprise, it's us!!!

AHHHHHH! GET OUT!!!!

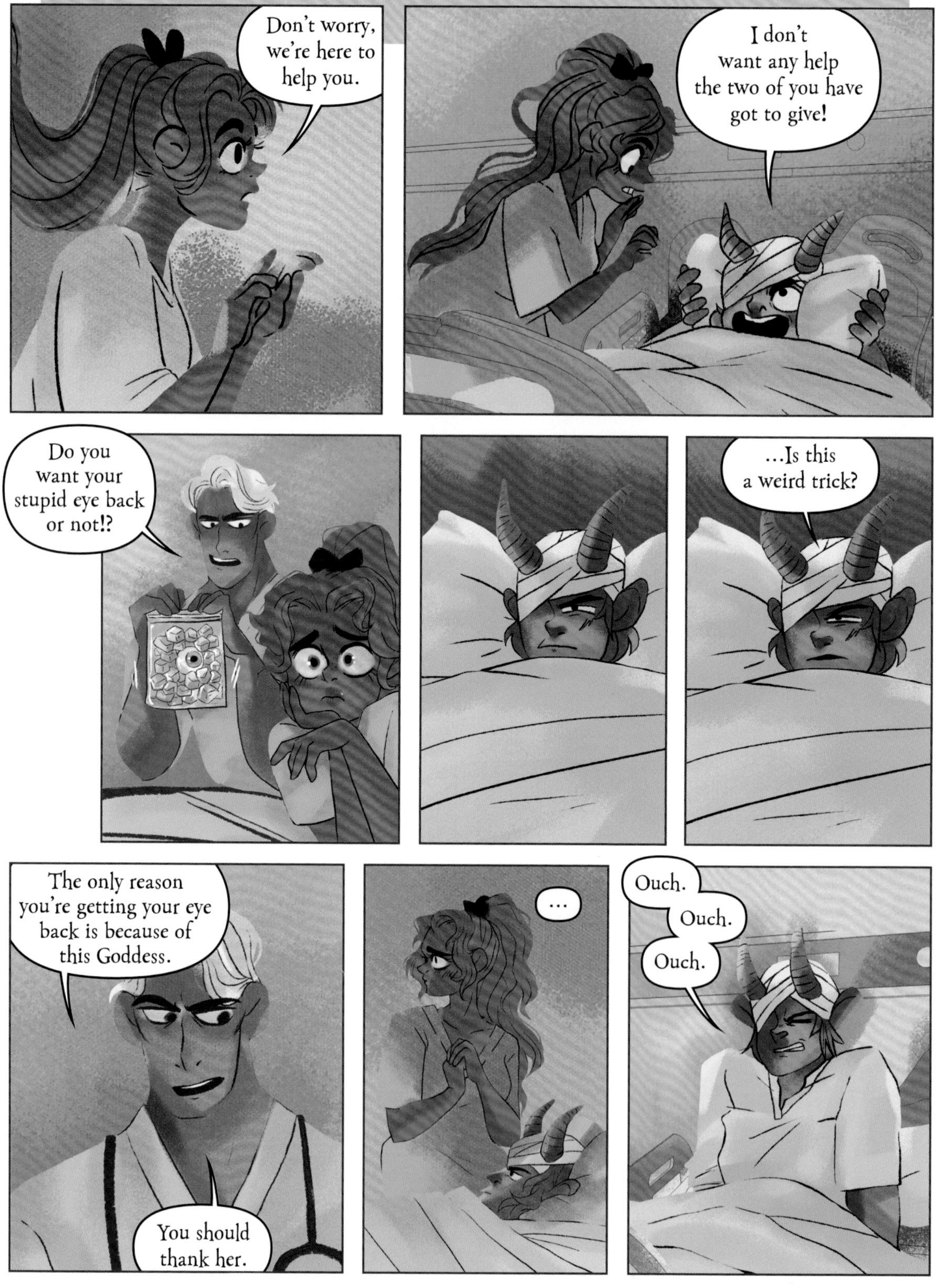
Don't worry, we're here to help you.
I don't want any help the two of you have got to give!
Do you want your stupid eye back or not!?
...Is this a weird trick?
The only reason you're getting your eye back is because of this Goddess.
You should thank her.
...
Ouch.
Ouch.
Ouch.

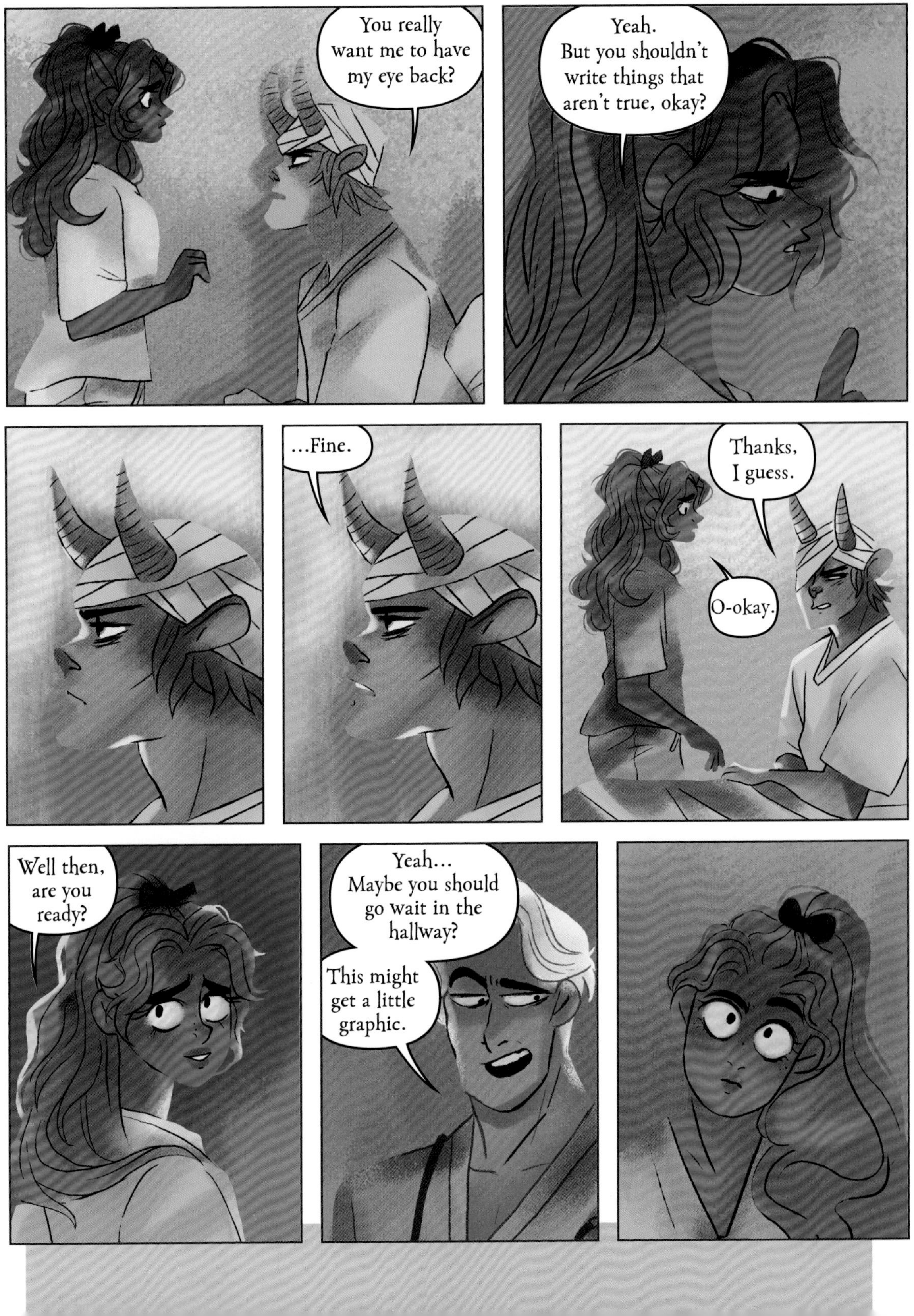
You really want me to have my eye back?
Yeah. But you shouldn't write things that aren't true, okay?
...Fine.
Thanks, I guess.
O-okay.
Well then, are you ready?
Yeah... Maybe you should go wait in the hallway?
This might get a little graphic.

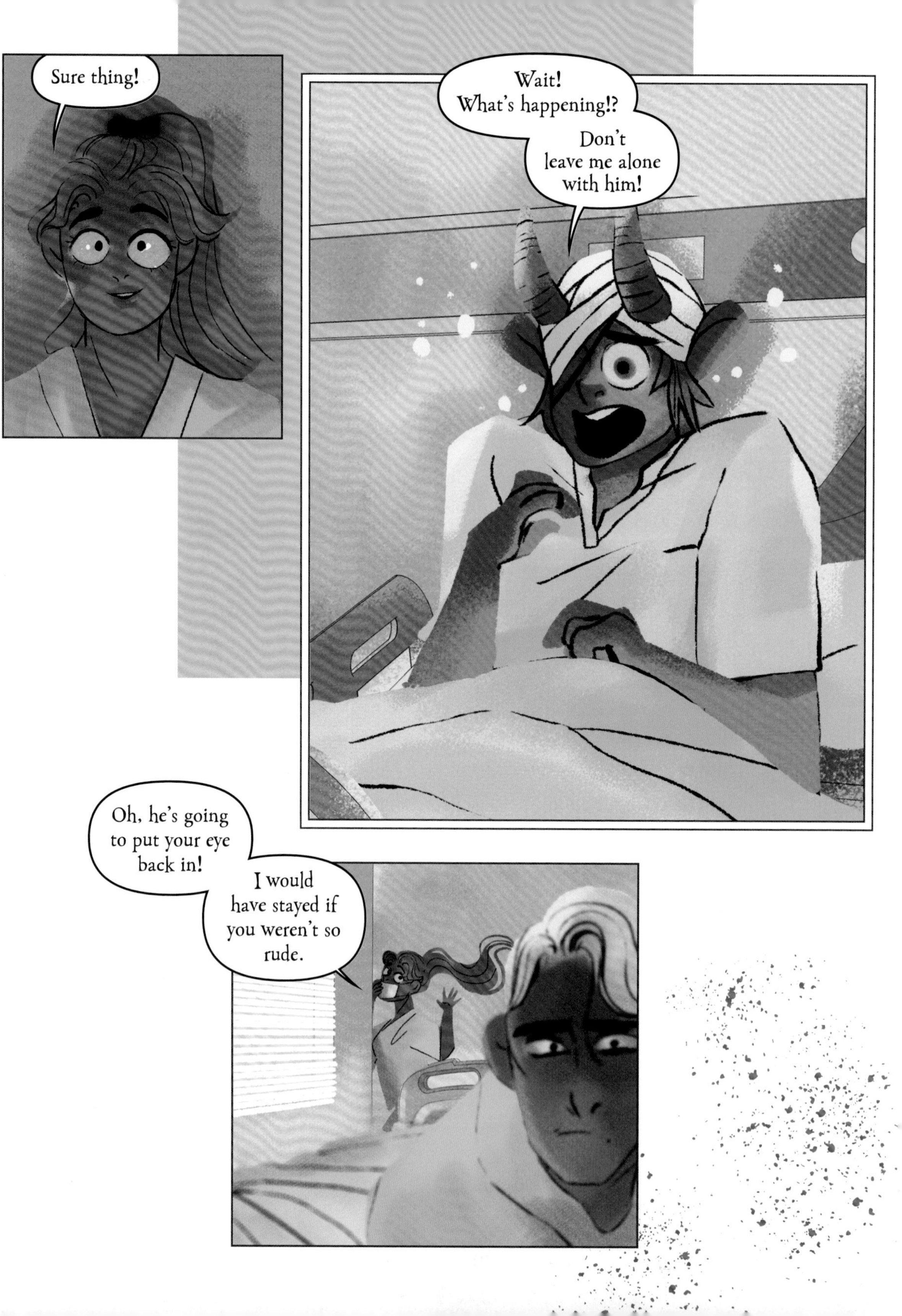
Sure thing!
Wait! What's happening!?
Don't leave me alone with him!
Oh, he's going to put your eye back in!
I would have stayed if you weren't so rude.

Gosh, it's taking a little longer than I thought.

I kinda wish I'd stayed. It can't be that gross.

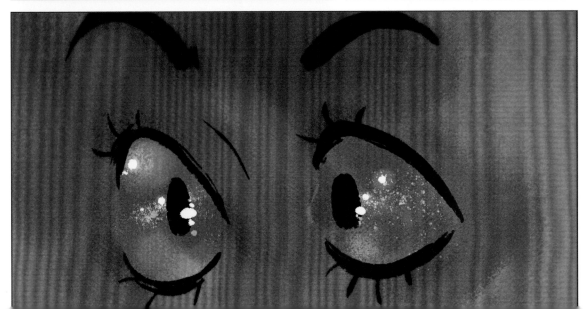

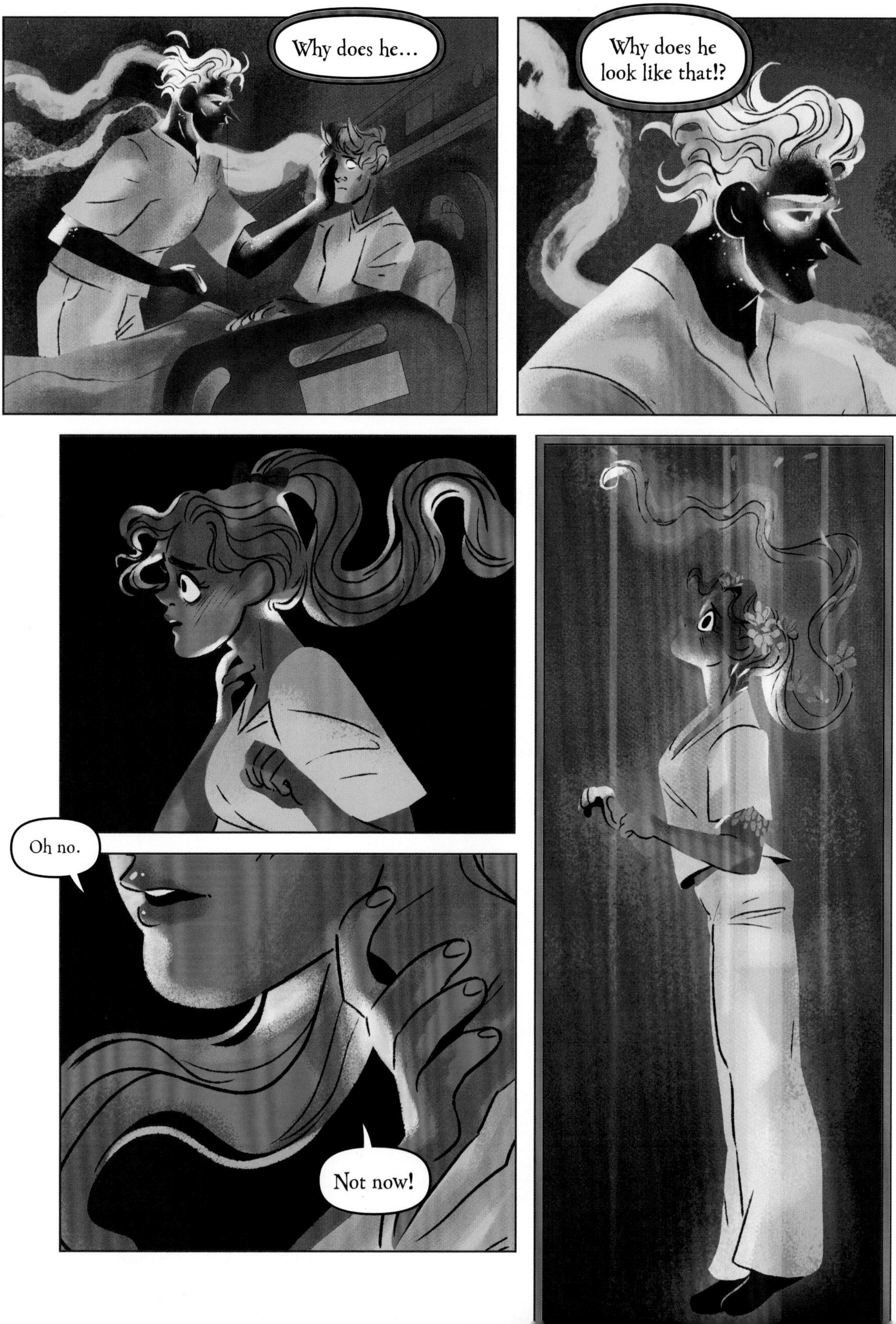
Why does he...
Why does he look like that!?
Oh no.
Not now!

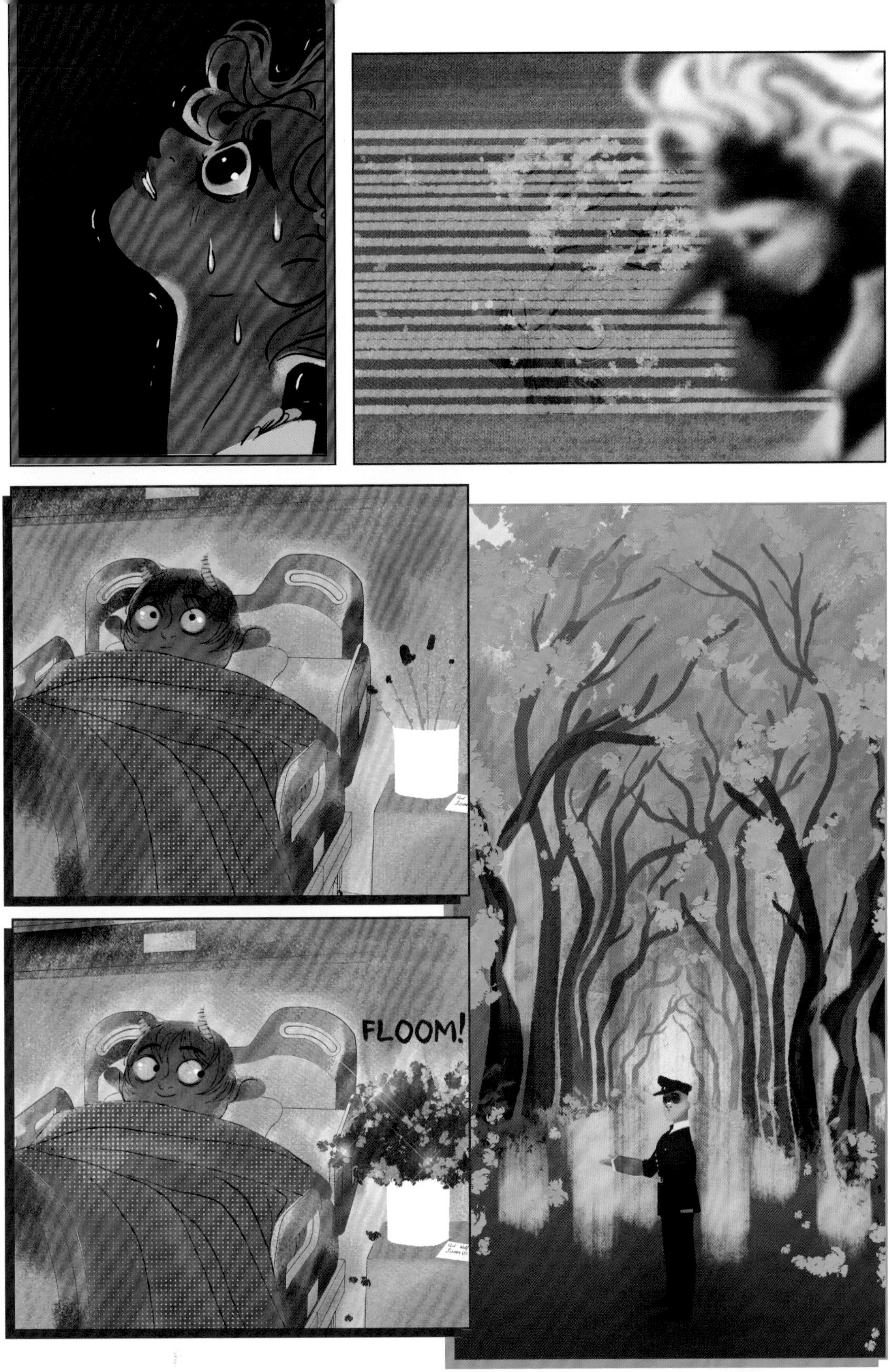
FLOOM!

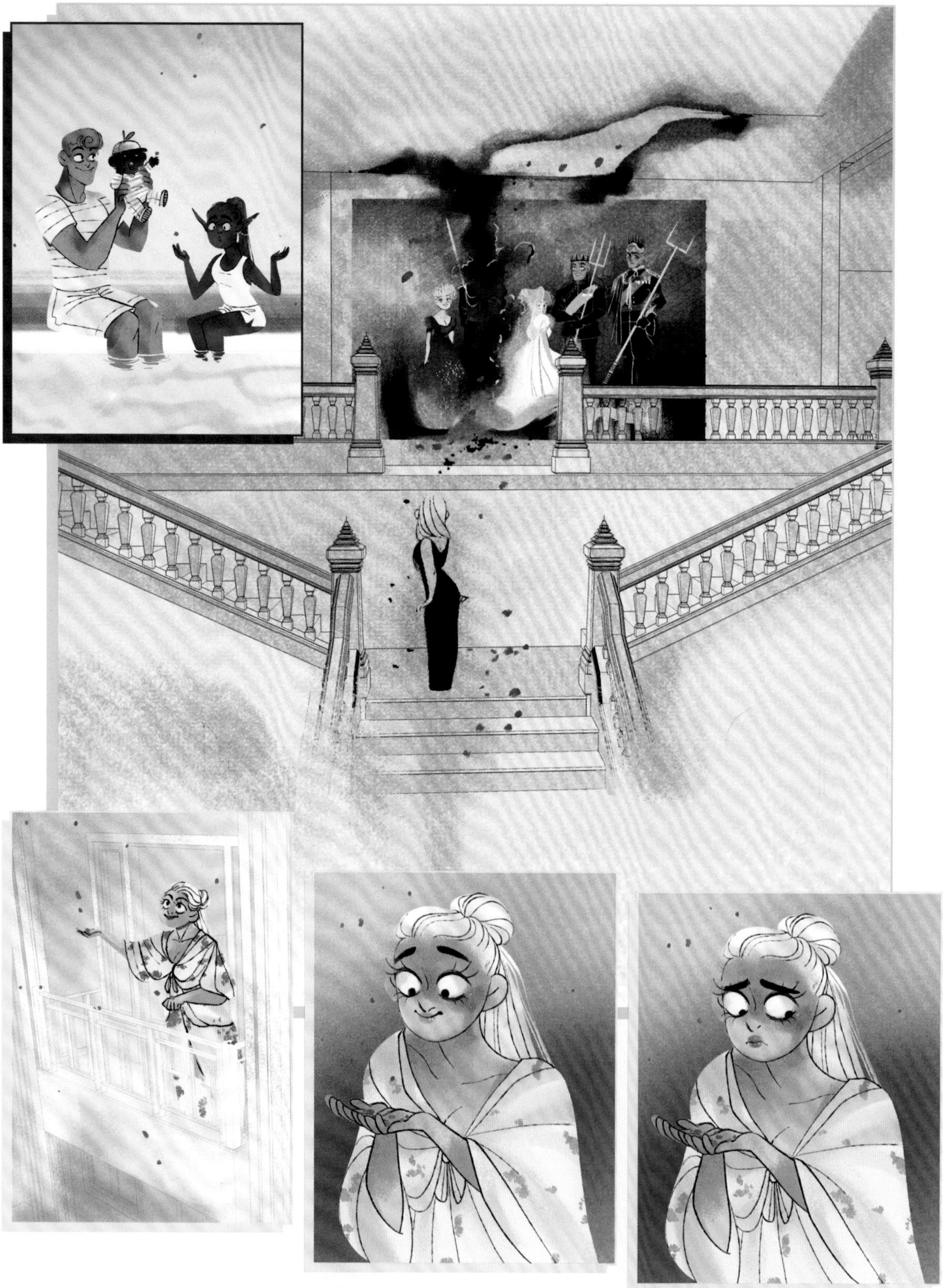

EPISODE 90: IT'S ALL FUN AND GAMES UNTIL SOMEONE LOSES AN EYE (PART 4)

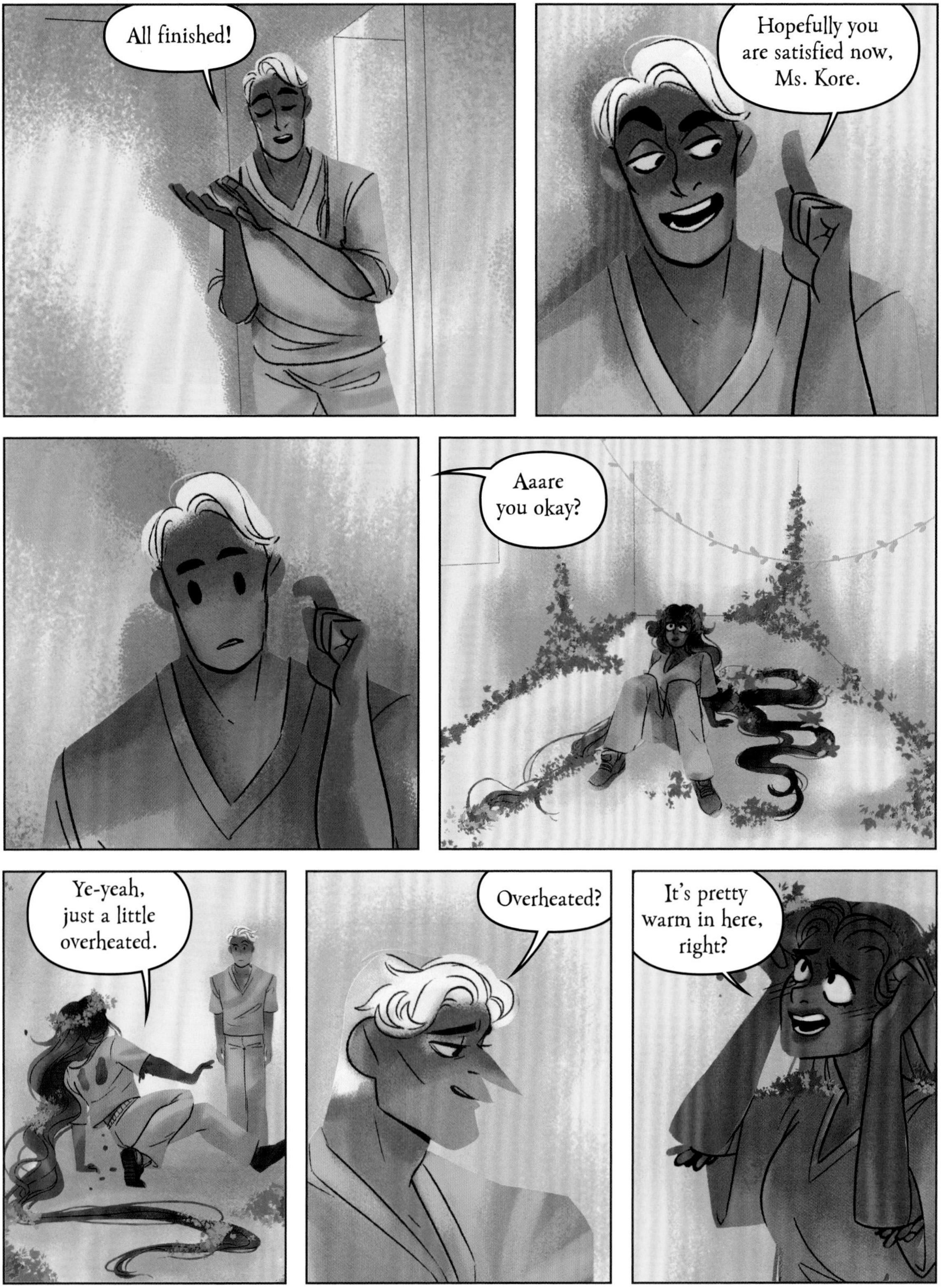
All finished!
Hopefully you are satisfied now, Ms. Kore.
Aaare you okay?
Ye-yeah, just a little overheated.
Overheated?
It's pretty warm in here, right?

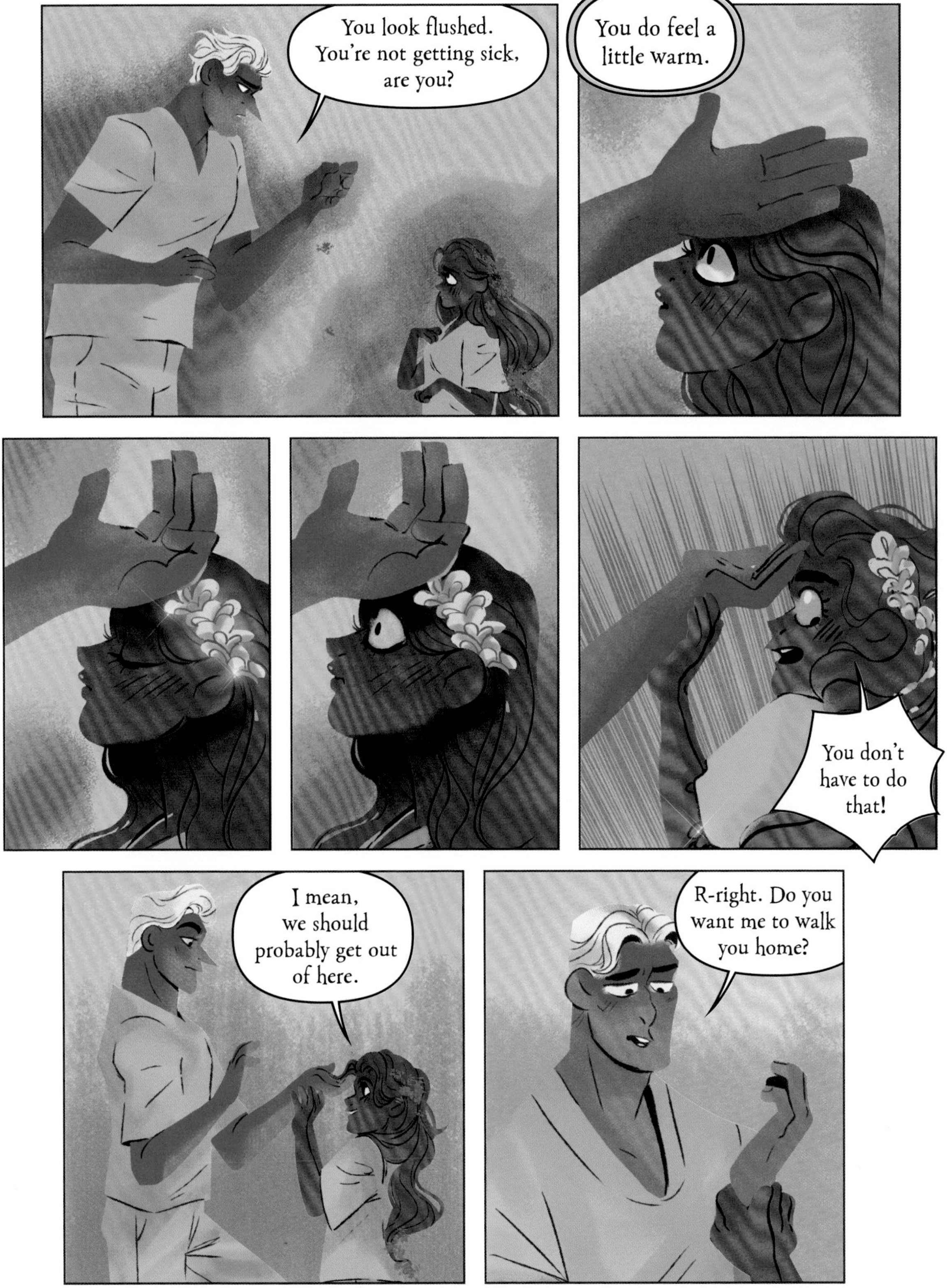
You look flushed. You're not getting sick, are you?
You do feel a little warm.
You don't have to do that!
I mean, we should probably get out of here.
R-right. Do you want me to walk you home?

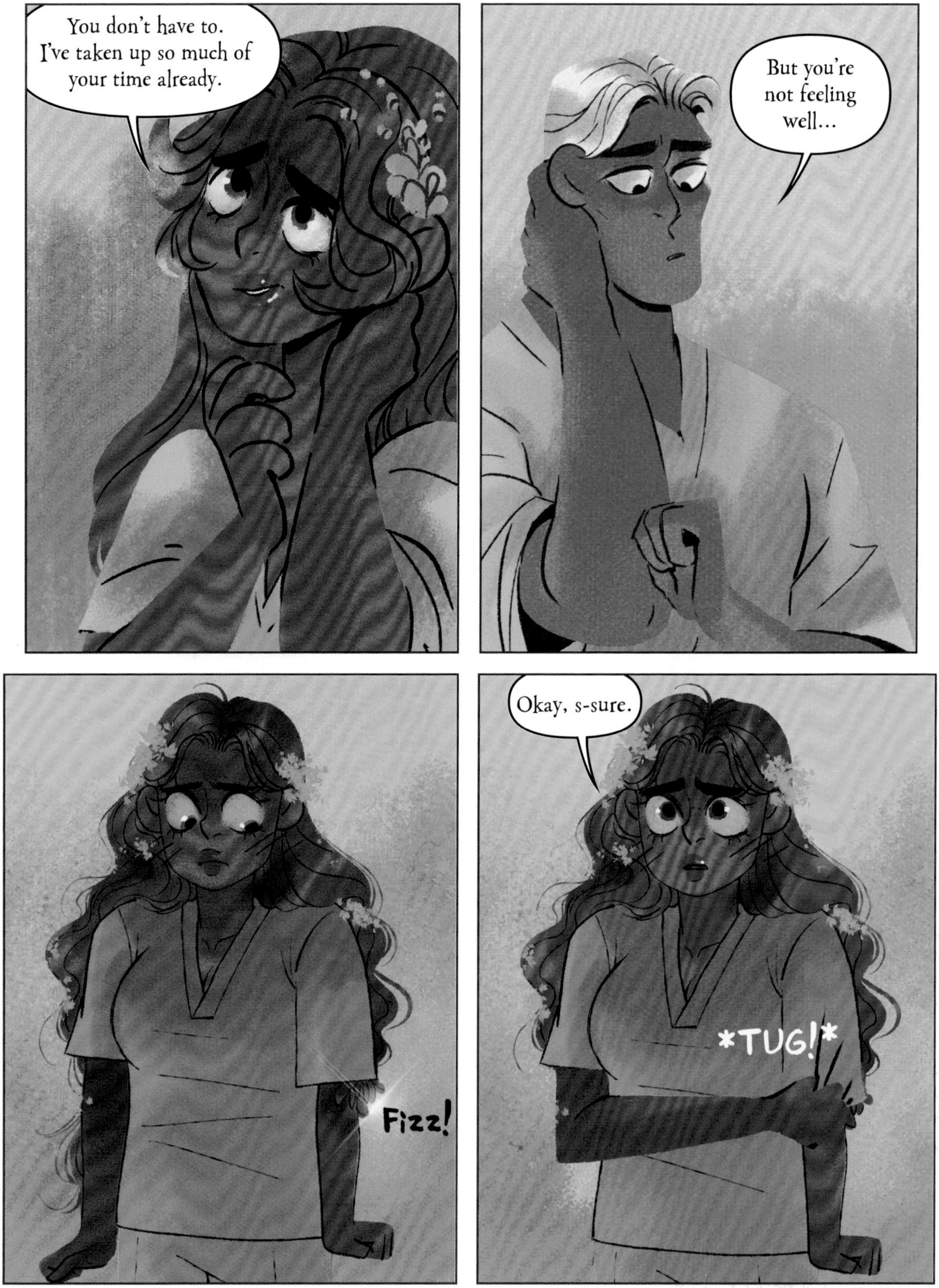
You don't have to. I've taken up so much of your time already.
But you're not feeling well...
Fizz!
Okay, s-sure.
TUG!

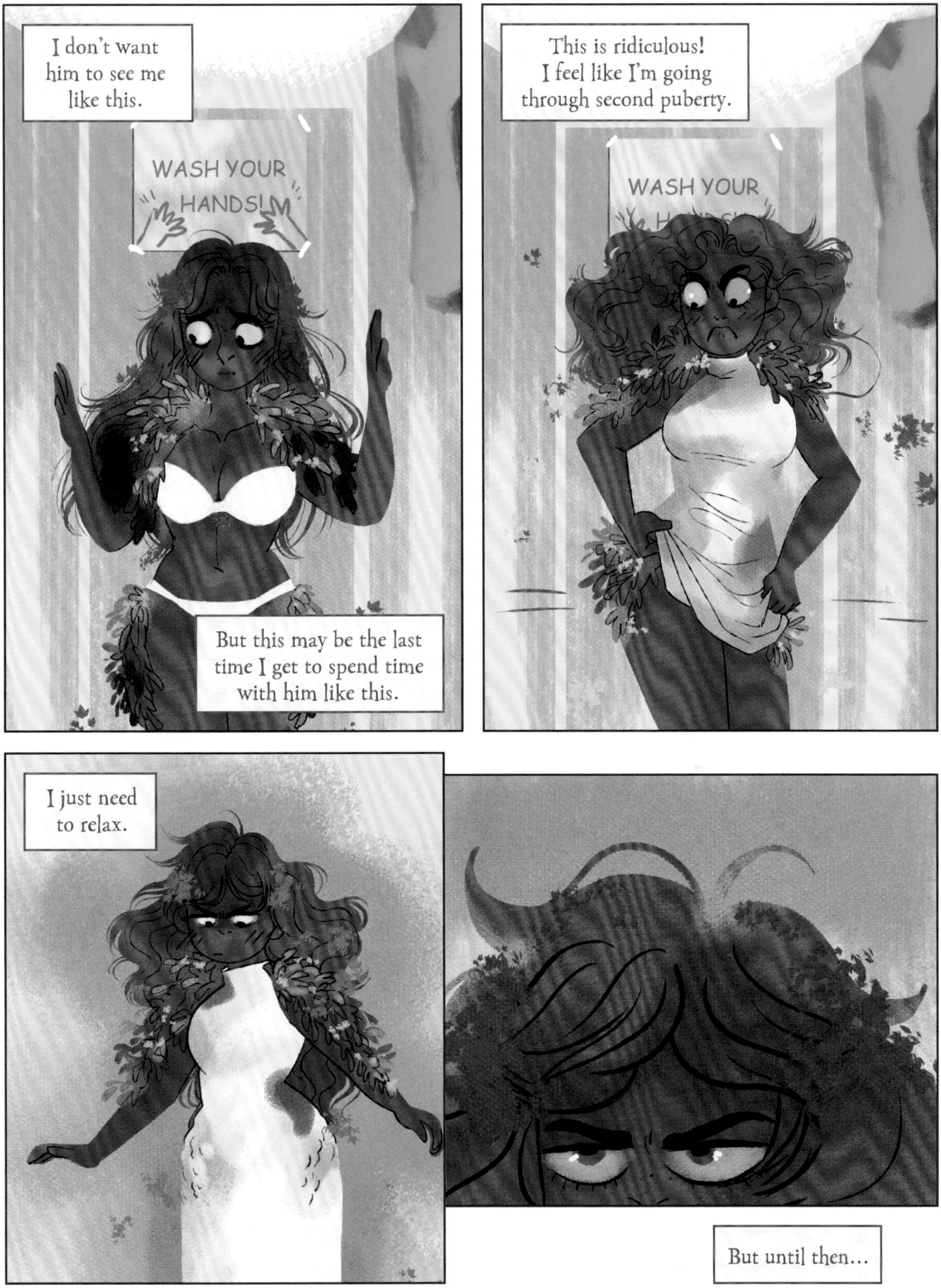
I don't want him to see me like this.
WASH YOUR HANDS!
But this may be the last time I get to spend time with him like this.
This is ridiculous! I feel like I'm going through second puberty.
WASH YOUR
I just need to relax.
But until then...

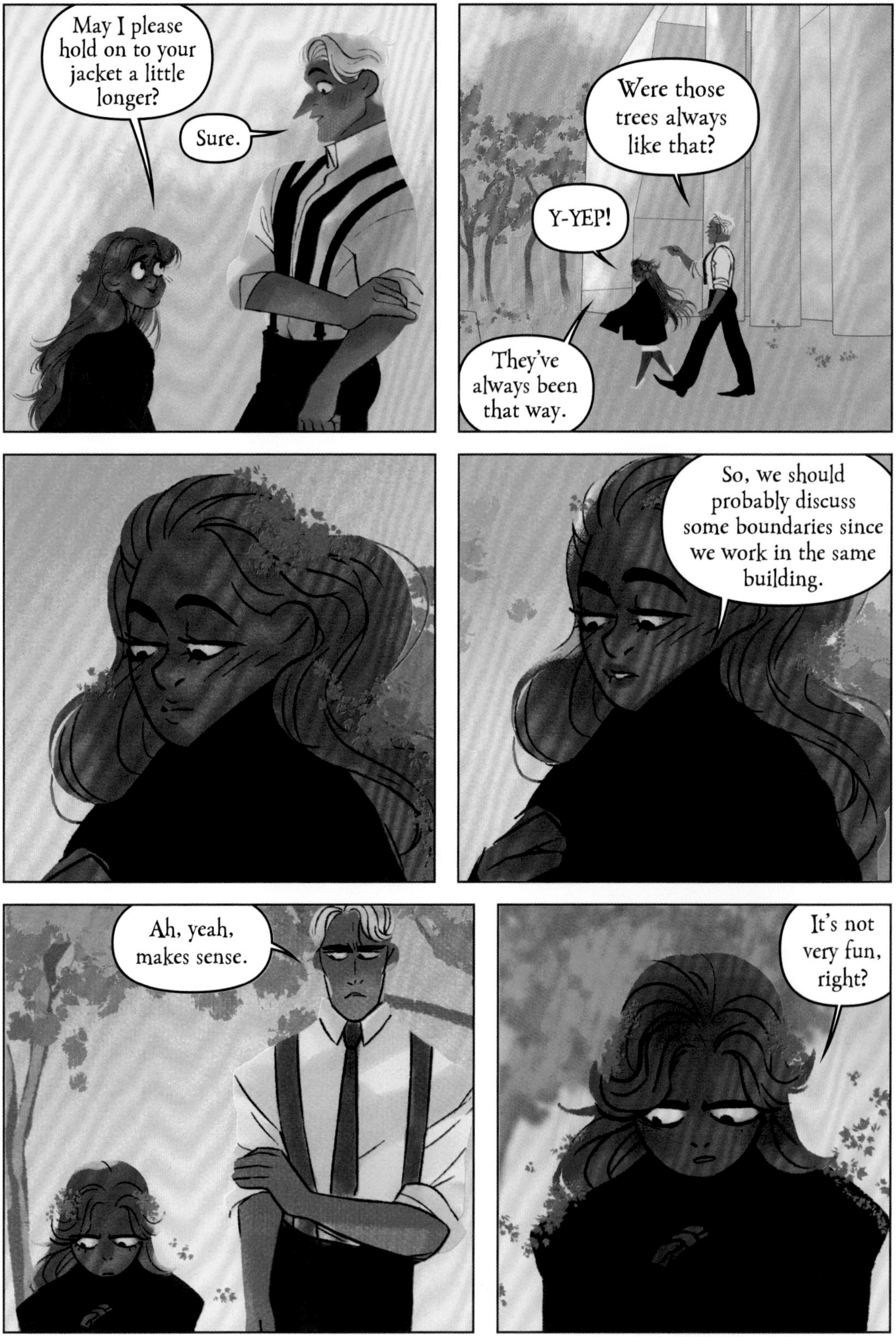

May I please hold on to your jacket a little longer?
Sure.
Were those trees always like that?
Y-YEP!
They've always been that way.
So, we should probably discuss some boundaries since we work in the same building.
Ah, yeah, makes sense.
It's not very fun, right?

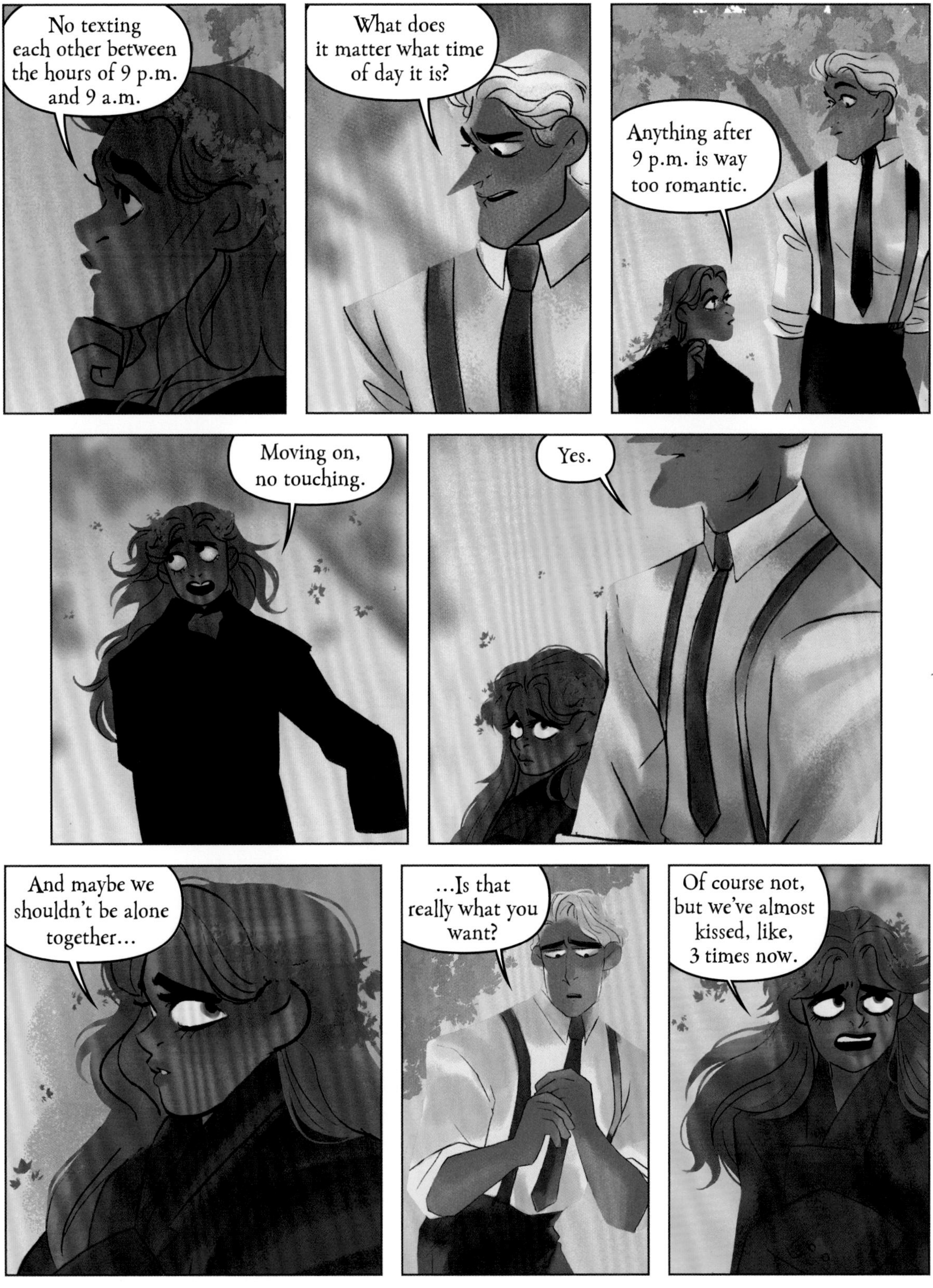
No texting each other between the hours of 9 p.m. and 9 a.m.
What does it matter what time of day it is?
Anything after 9 p.m. is way too romantic.
Moving on, no touching.
Yes.
And maybe we shouldn't be alone together...
...Is that really what you want?
Of course not, but we've almost kissed, like, 3 times now.

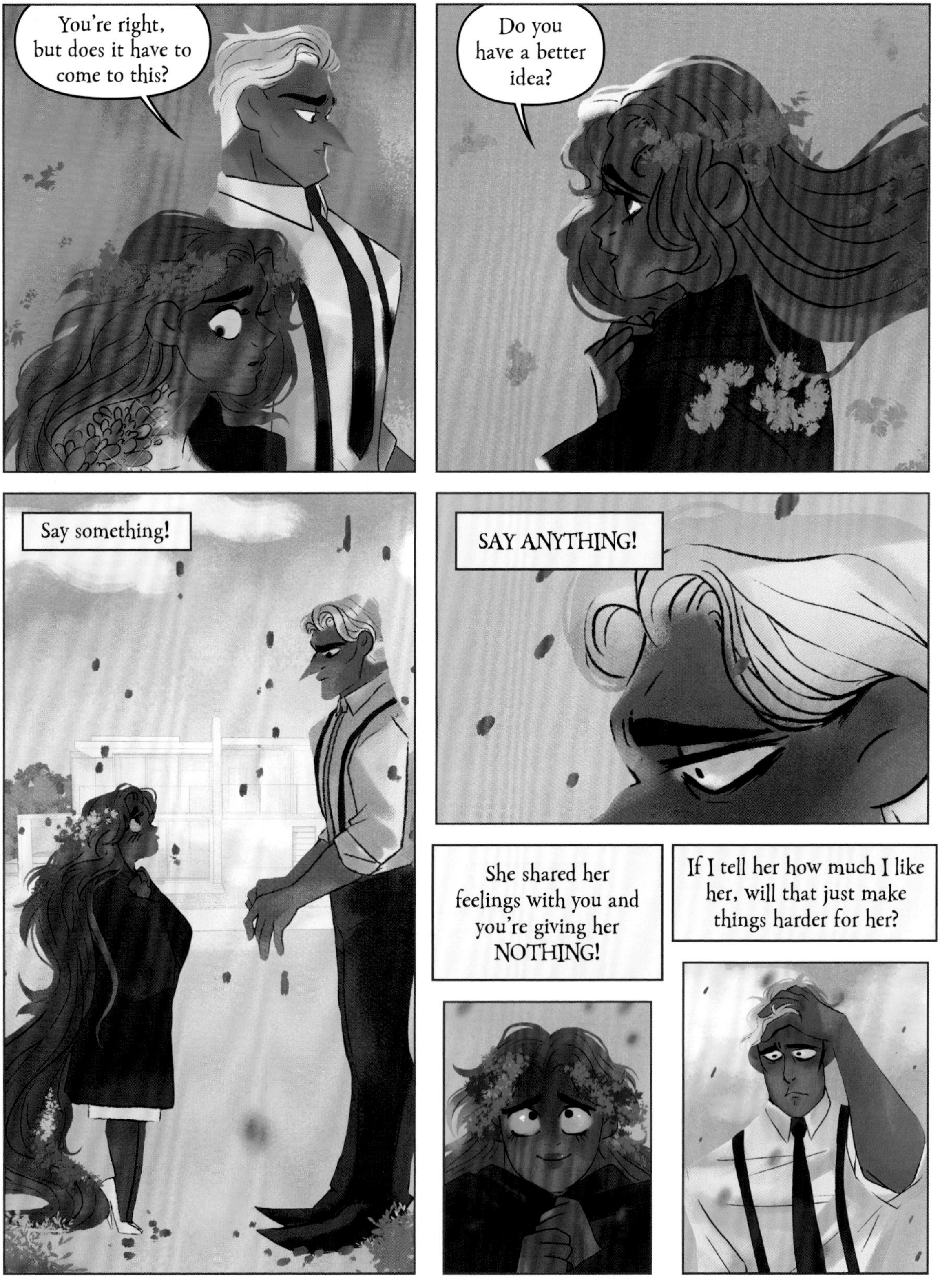
You're right, but does it have to come to this?
Do you have a better idea?
Say something!
SAY ANYTHING!
She shared her feelings with you and you're giving her NOTHING!
If I tell her how much I like her, will that just make things harder for her?

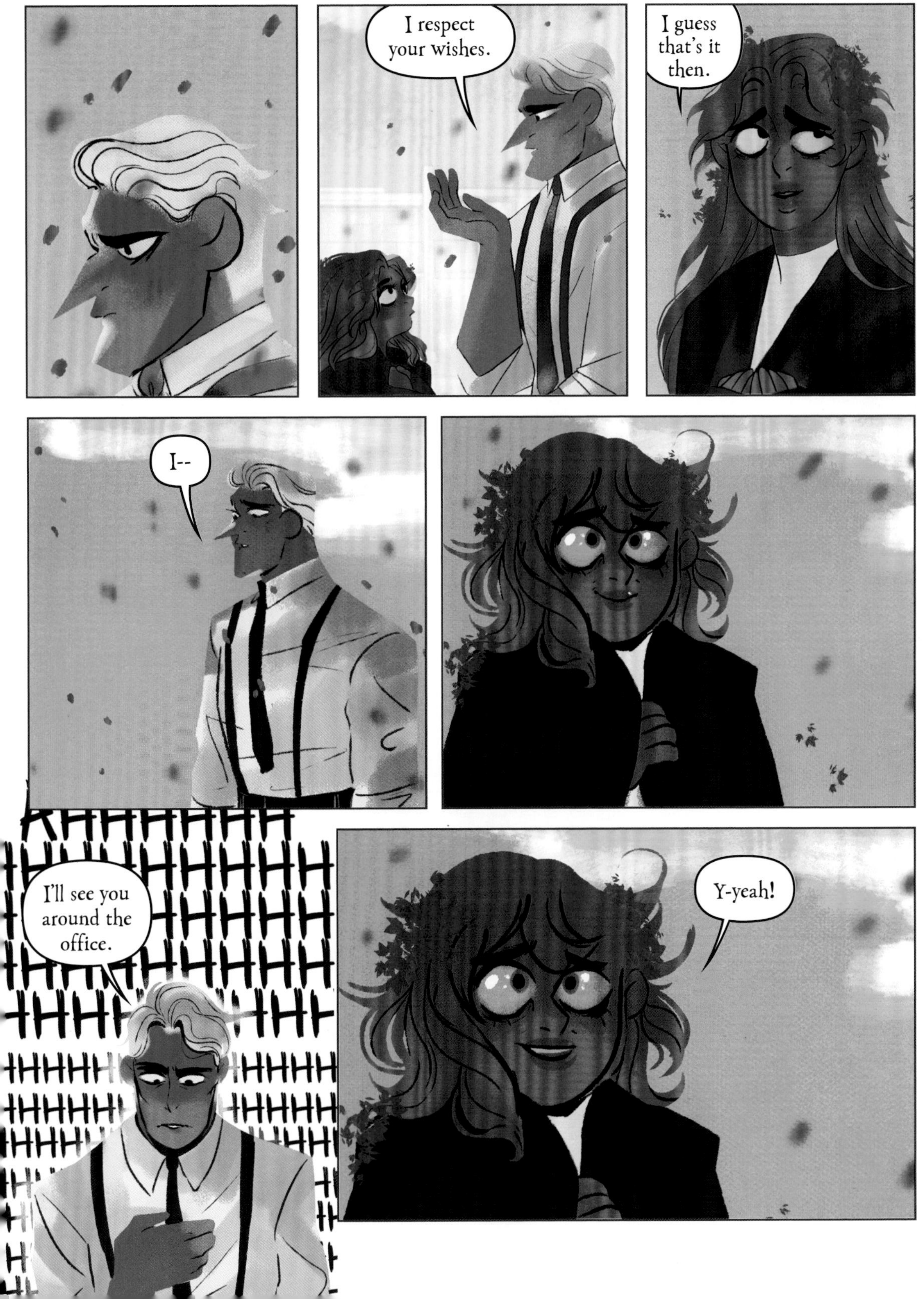
I respect your wishes.
I guess that's it then.
I--
I'll see you around the office.
Y-yeah!

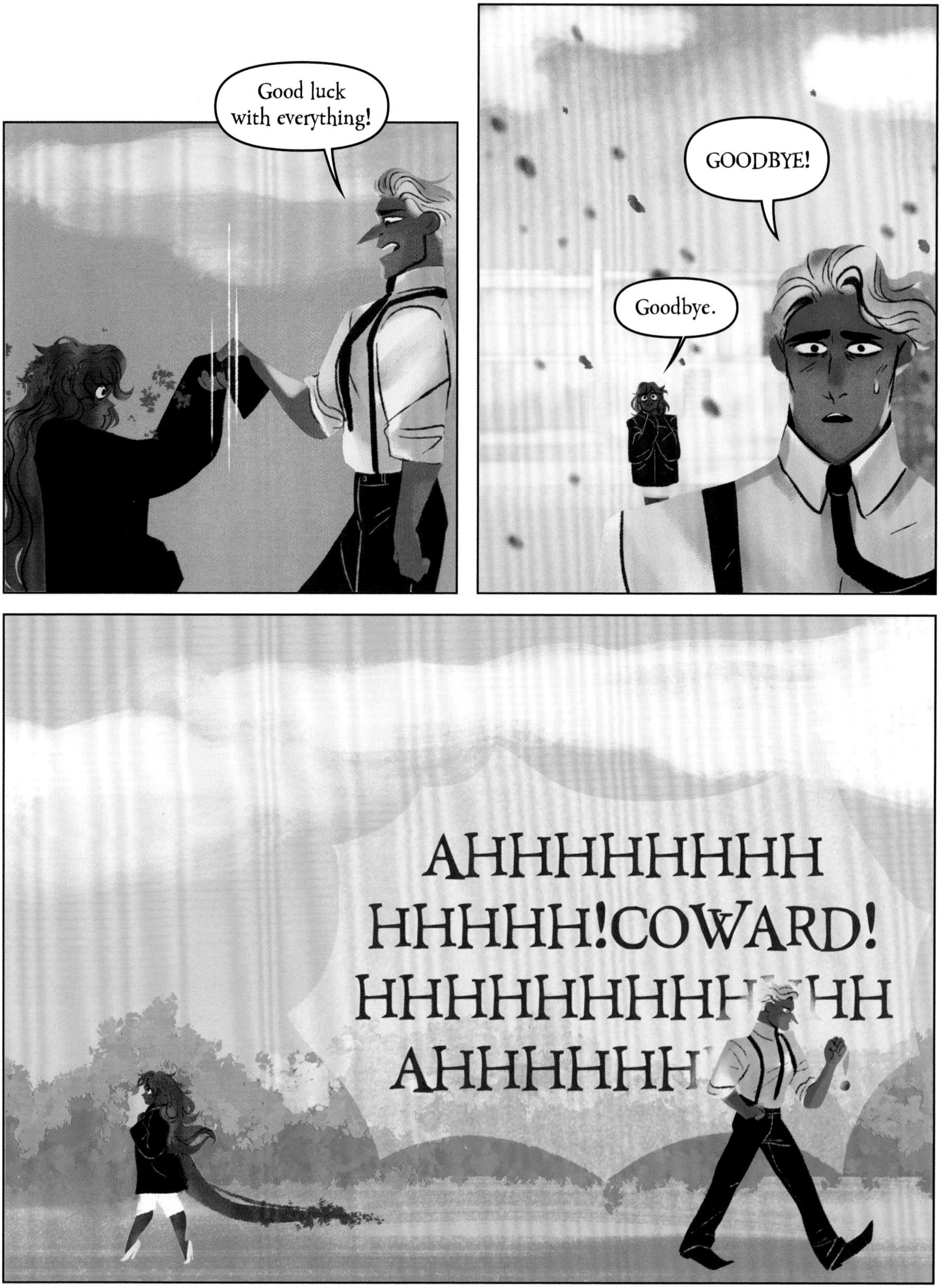
Good luck with everything!
GOODBYE!
Goodbye.
AHHHHHHHH
HHHHH!COWARD!
AHHHHHHH

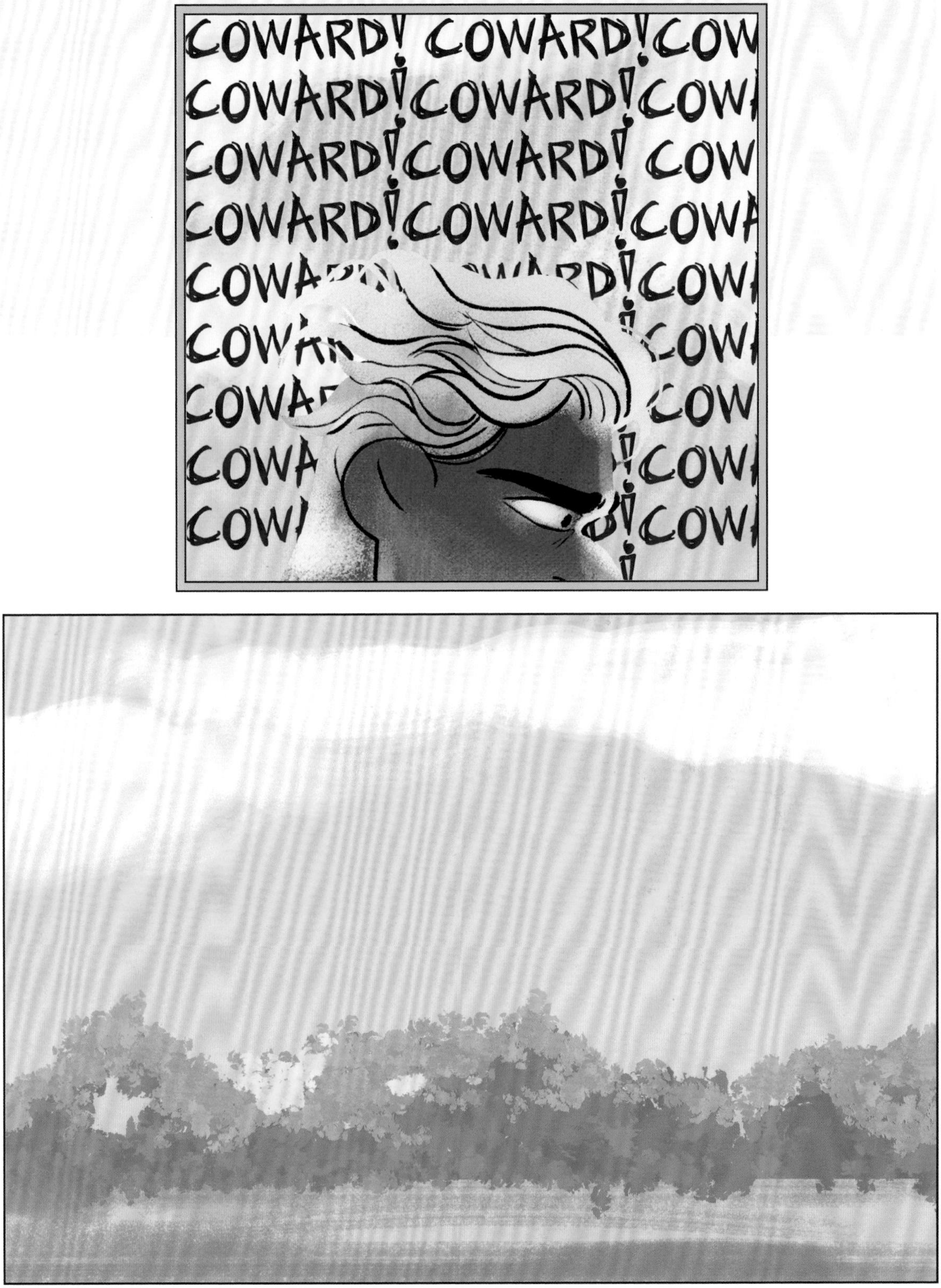
COWARD! COWARD! COW
COWARD! COWARD! COW
COWARD! COWARD! COW
COWARD! COWARD! COW

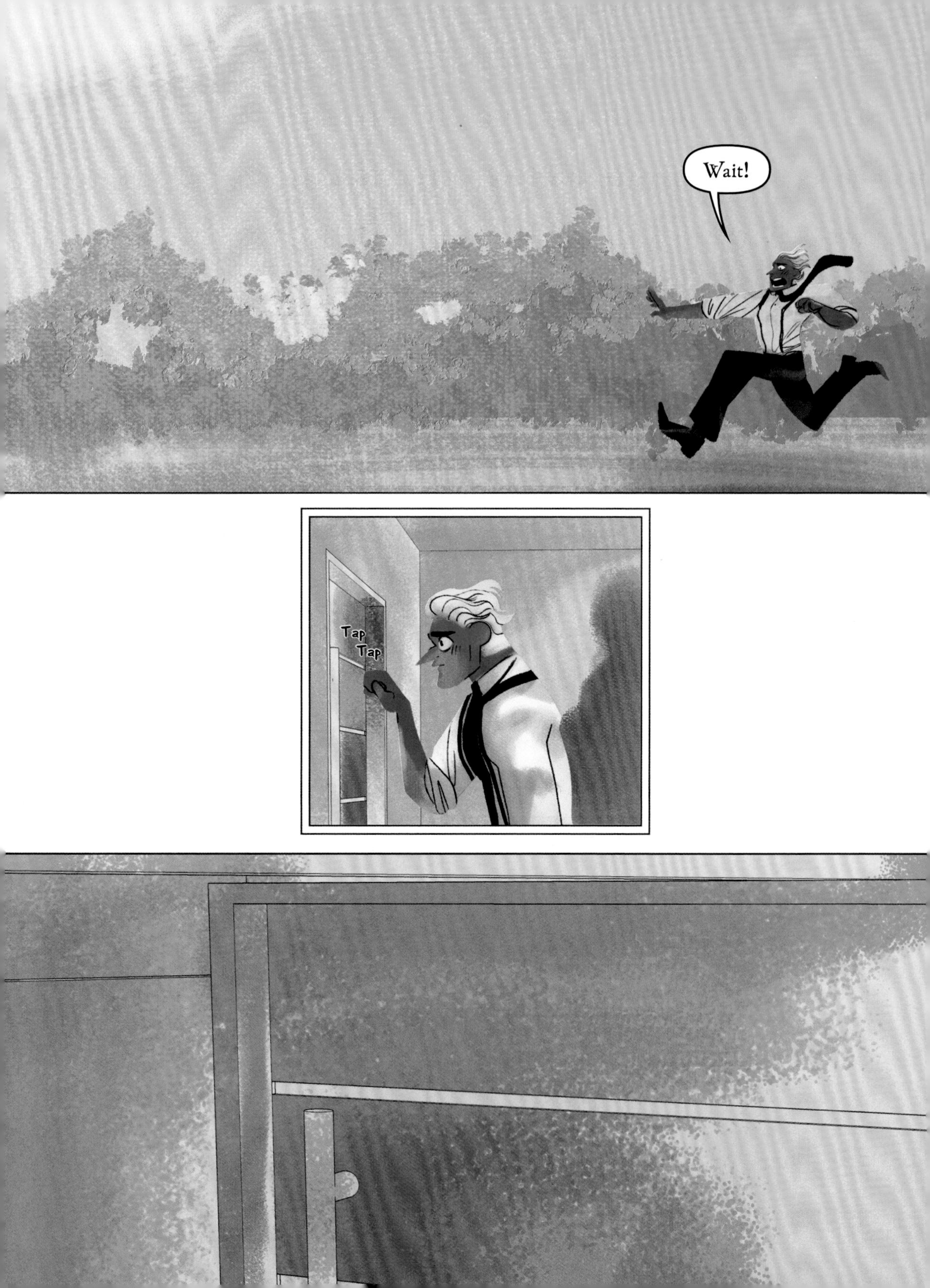
Wait!
Tap
Tap

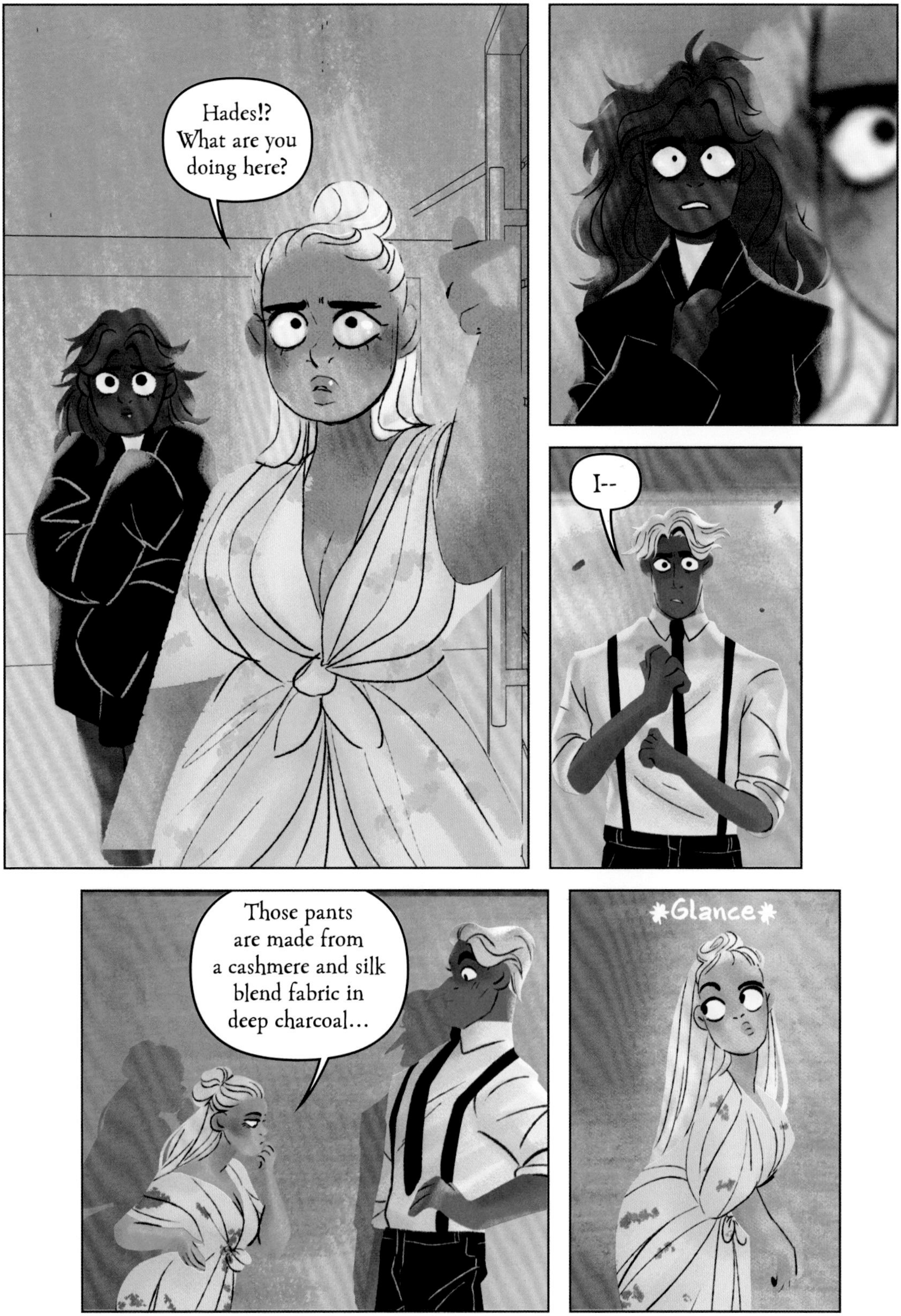
Hades!? What are you doing here?
I--
Those pants are made from a cashmere and silk blend fabric in deep charcoal...
Glance

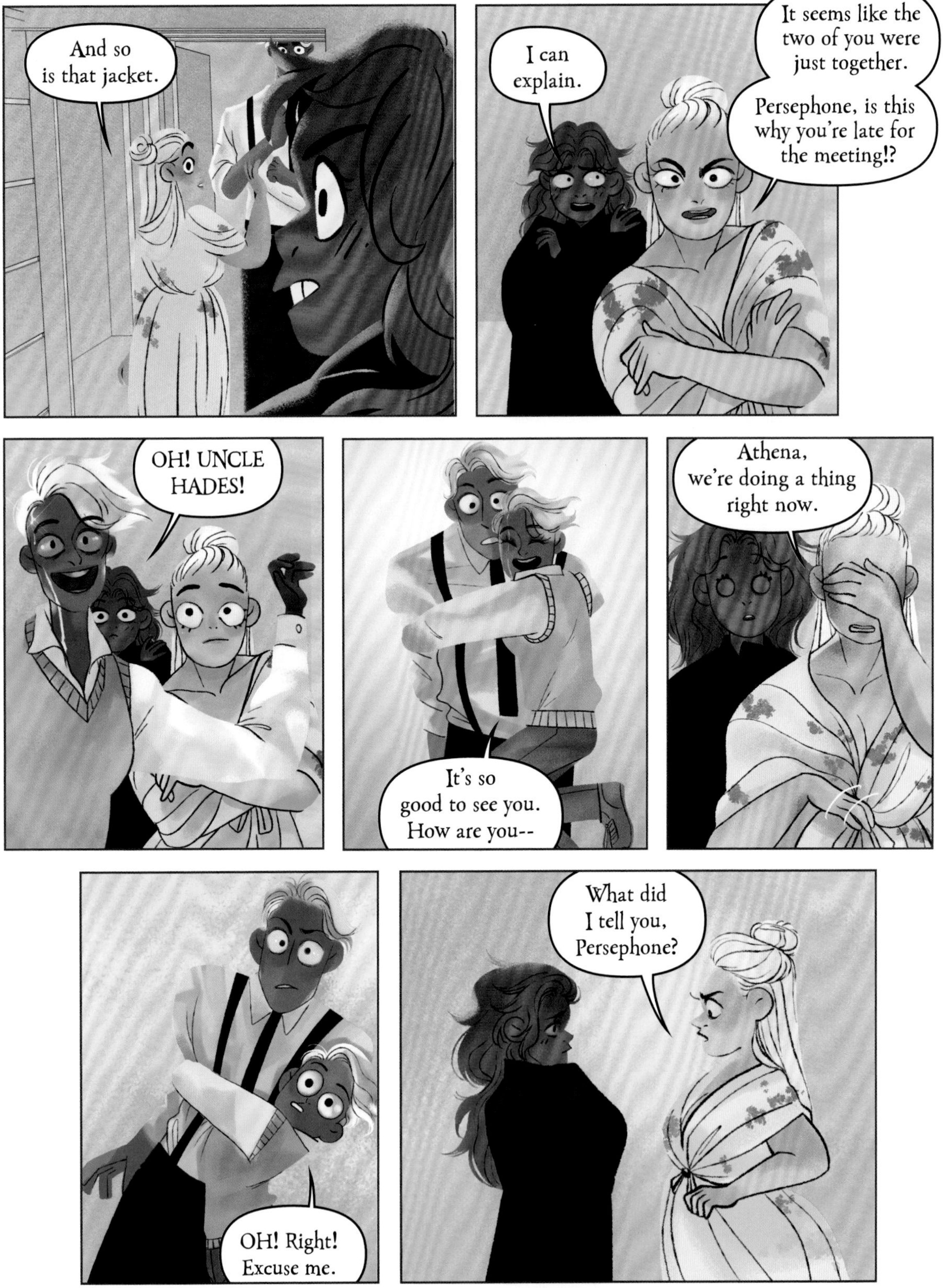
And so is that jacket.
I can explain.
It seems like the two of you were just together.
Persephone, is this why you're late for the meeting!?
OH! UNCLE HADES!
It's so good to see you. How are you--
Athena, we're doing a thing right now.
OH! Right! Excuse me.
What did I tell you, Persephone?

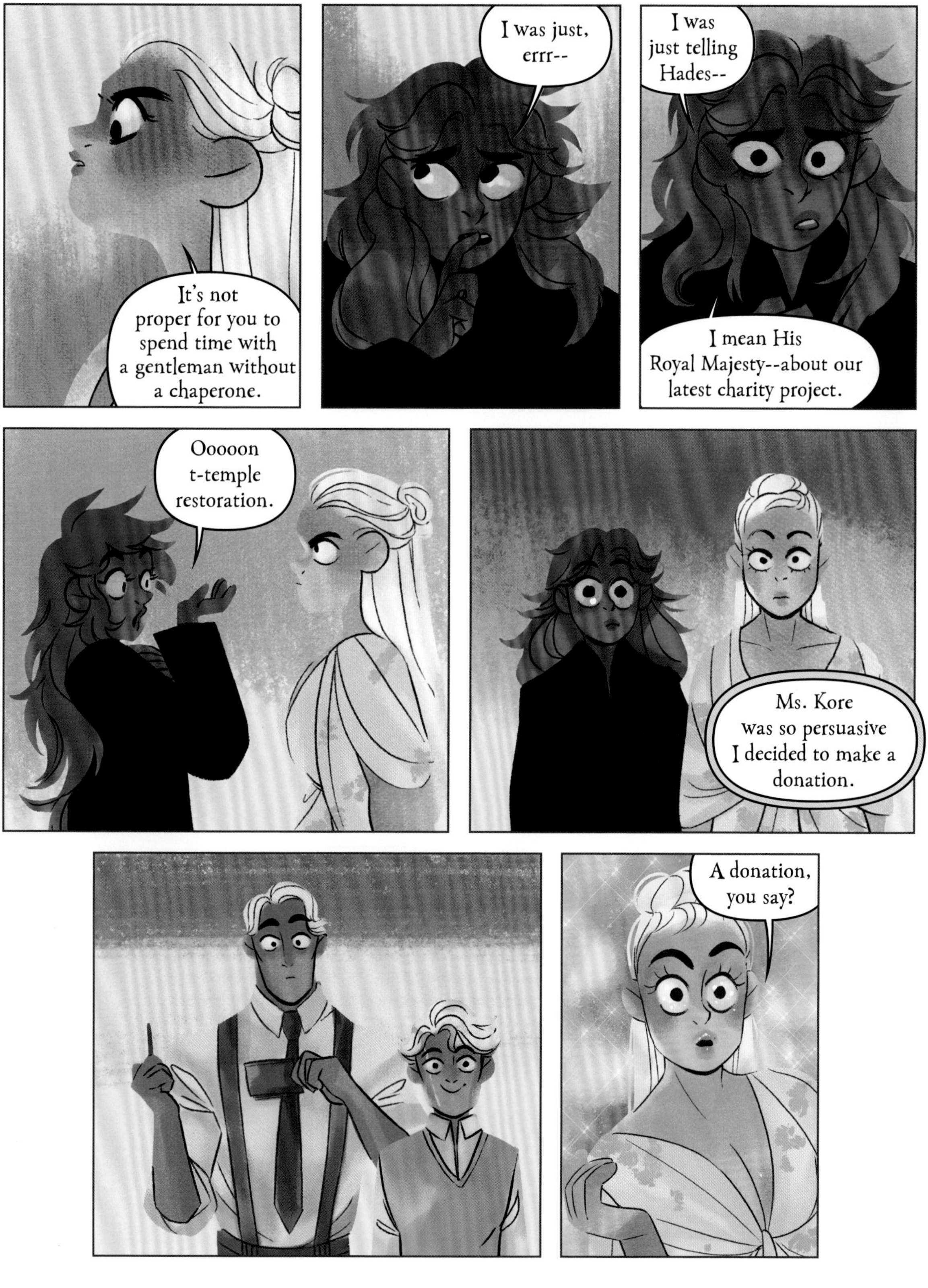
It's not proper for you to spend time with a gentleman without a chaperone.
I was just, errr--
I was just telling Hades--
I mean His Royal Majesty--about our latest charity project.
Oooooon t-temple restoration.
Ms. Kore was so persuasive I decided to make a donation.
A donation, you say?

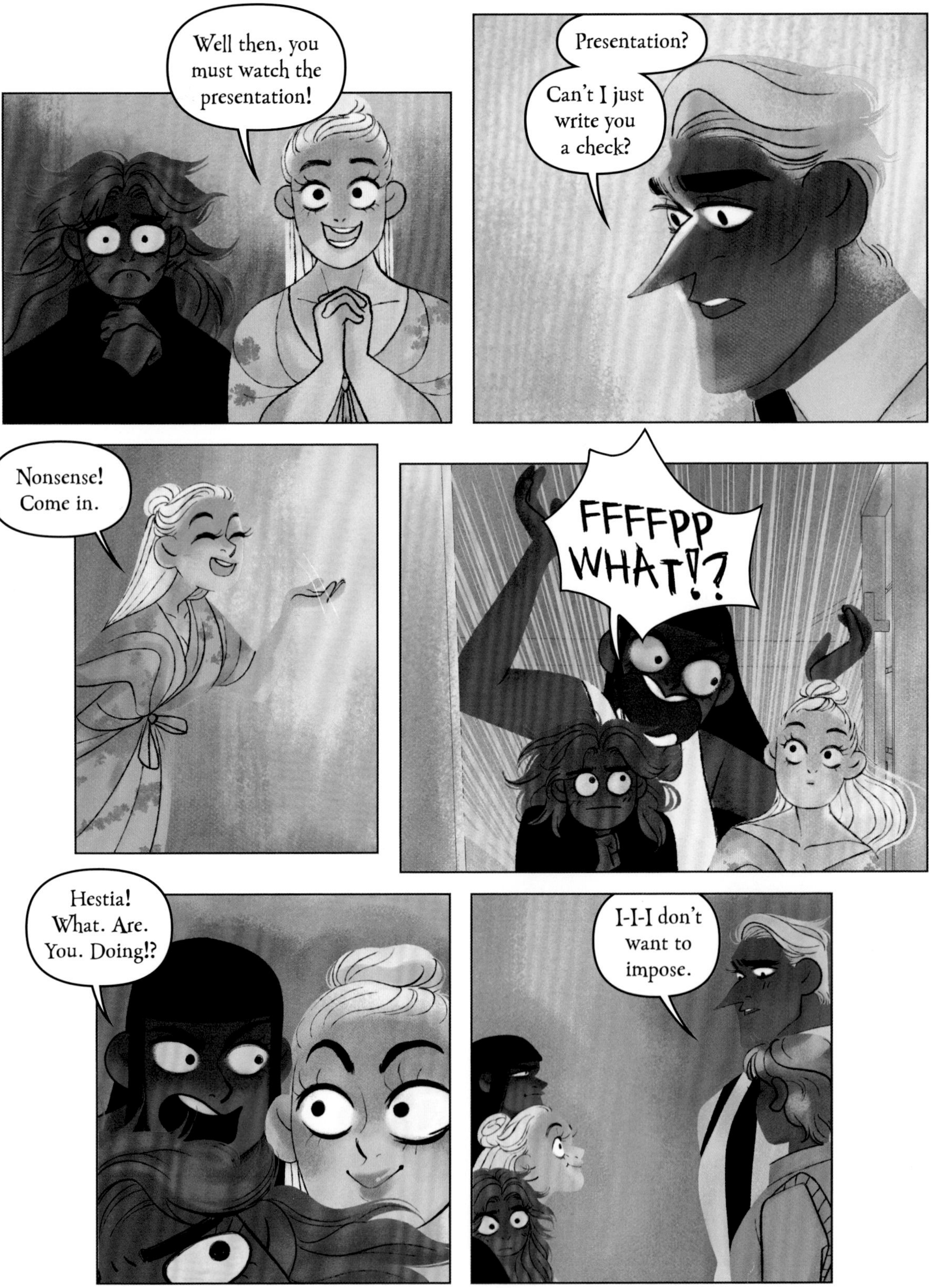
Well then, you must watch the presentation!
Presentation?
Can't I just write you a check?
Nonsense! Come in.
FFFFPP WHAT!?
Hestia! What. Are. You. Doing!?
I-I-I don't want to impose.

EPISODE 91: SLIDESHOW

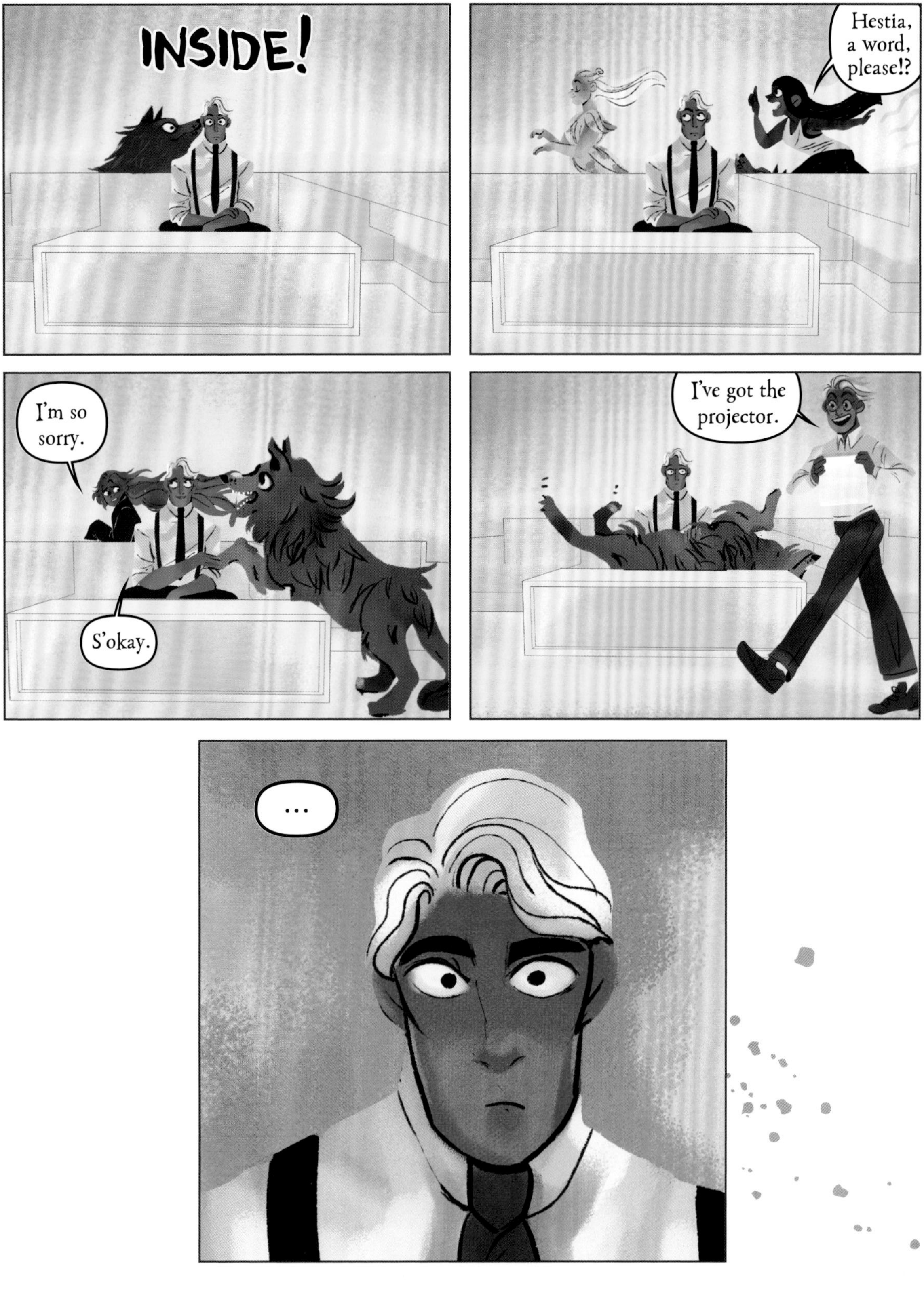
INSIDE!
Hestia, a word, please!?
I'm so sorry.
S'okay.
I've got the projector.
...

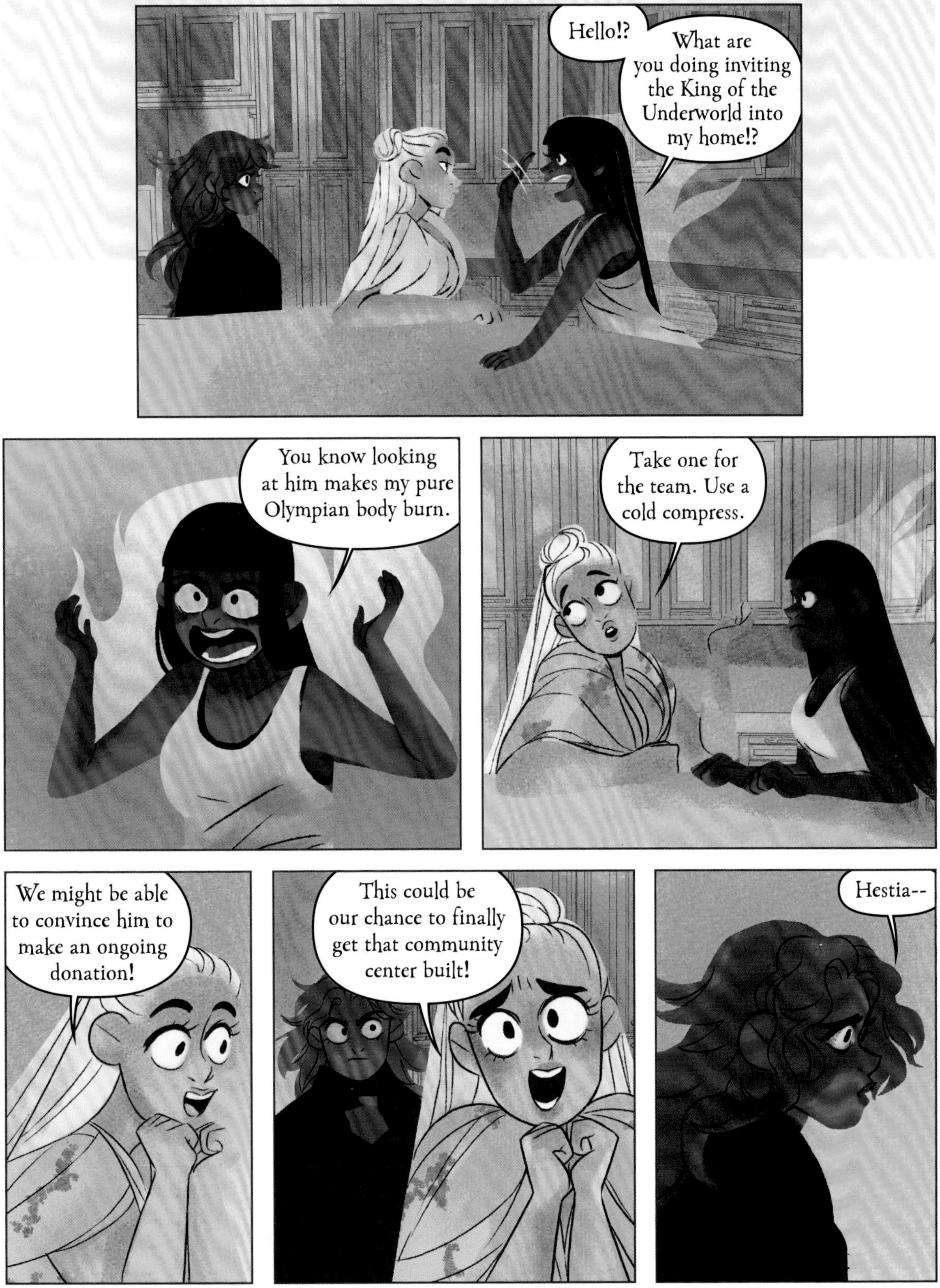
Hello!?
What are you doing inviting the King of the Underworld into my home!?
You know looking at him makes my pure Olympian body burn.
Take one for the team. Use a cold compress.
We might be able to convince him to make an ongoing donation!
This could be our chance to finally get that community center built!
Hestia--

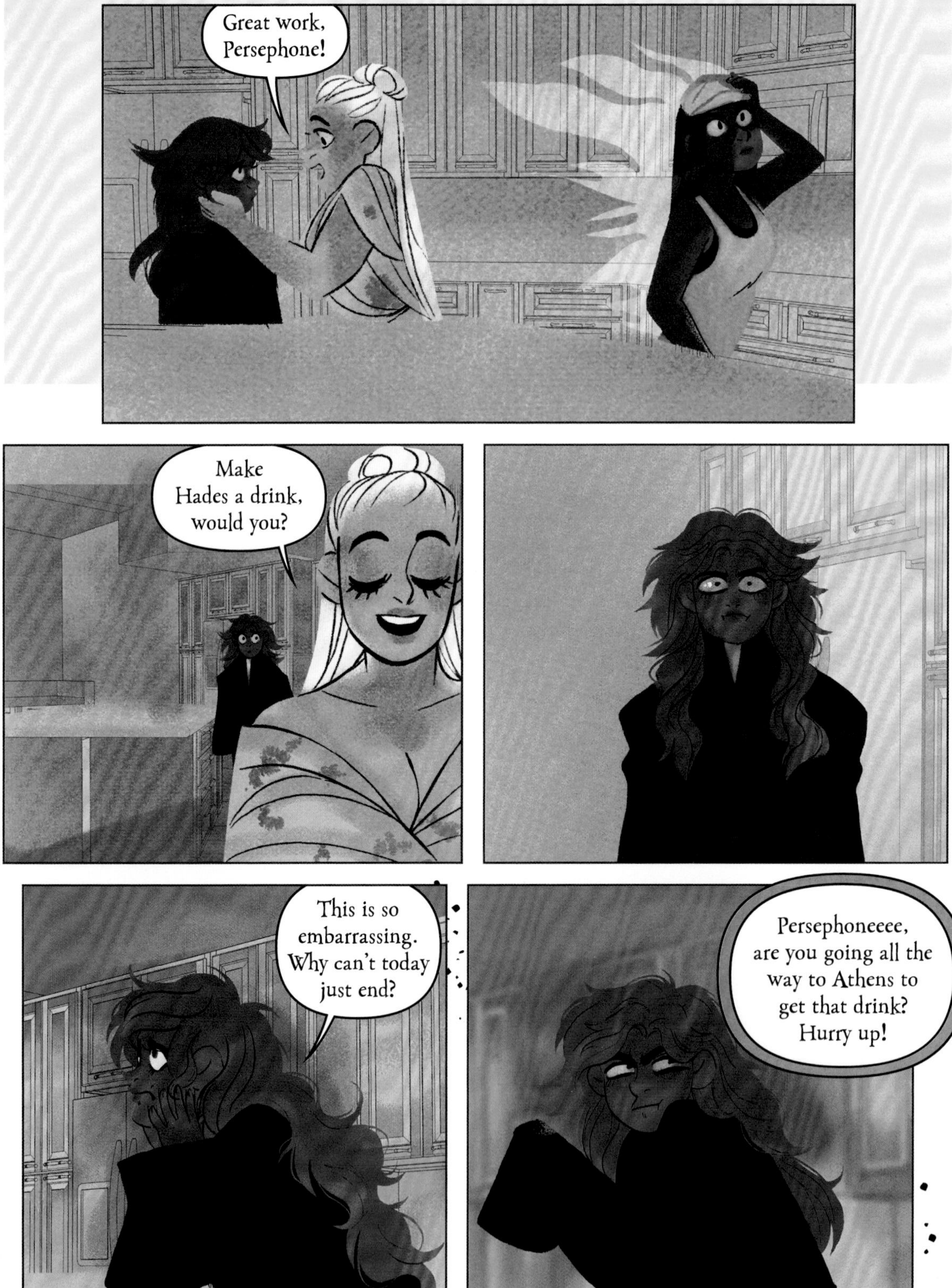
Great work, Persephone!
Make Hades a drink, would you?
This is so embarrassing. Why can't today just end?
Persephoneeee, are you going all the way to Athens to get that drink? Hurry up!

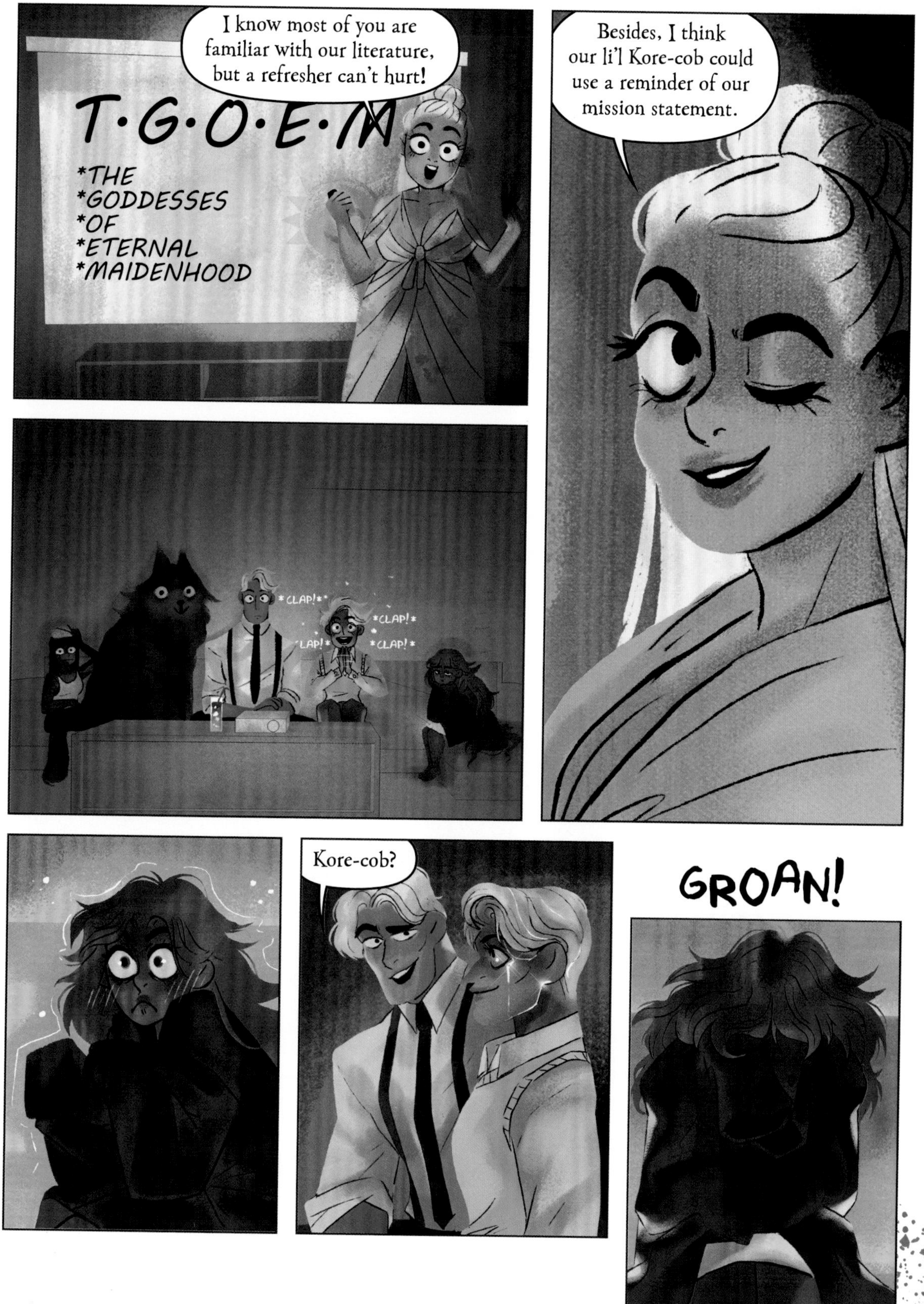
I know most of you are familiar with our literature, but a refresher can't hurt!
T·G·O·E·M
*THE
*GODDESSES
*OF
*ETERNAL
*MAIDENHOOD
Besides, I think our li'l Kore-cob could use a reminder of our mission statement.
CLAP!
CLAP!
CLAP!
CLAP!
Kore-cob?
GROAN!

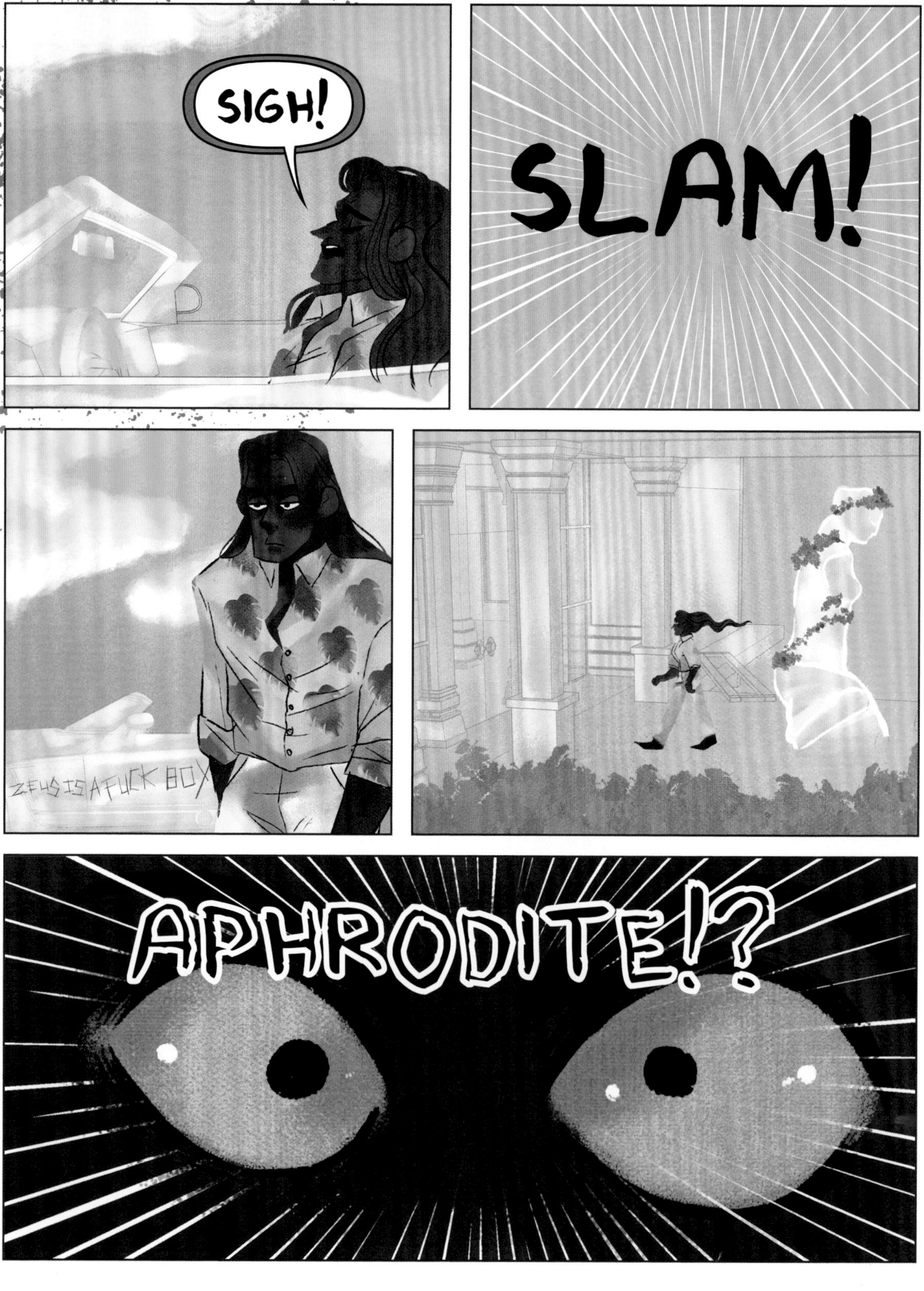
SIGH!
SLAM!
ZEUS IS A FUCK BOY
APHRODITE!?

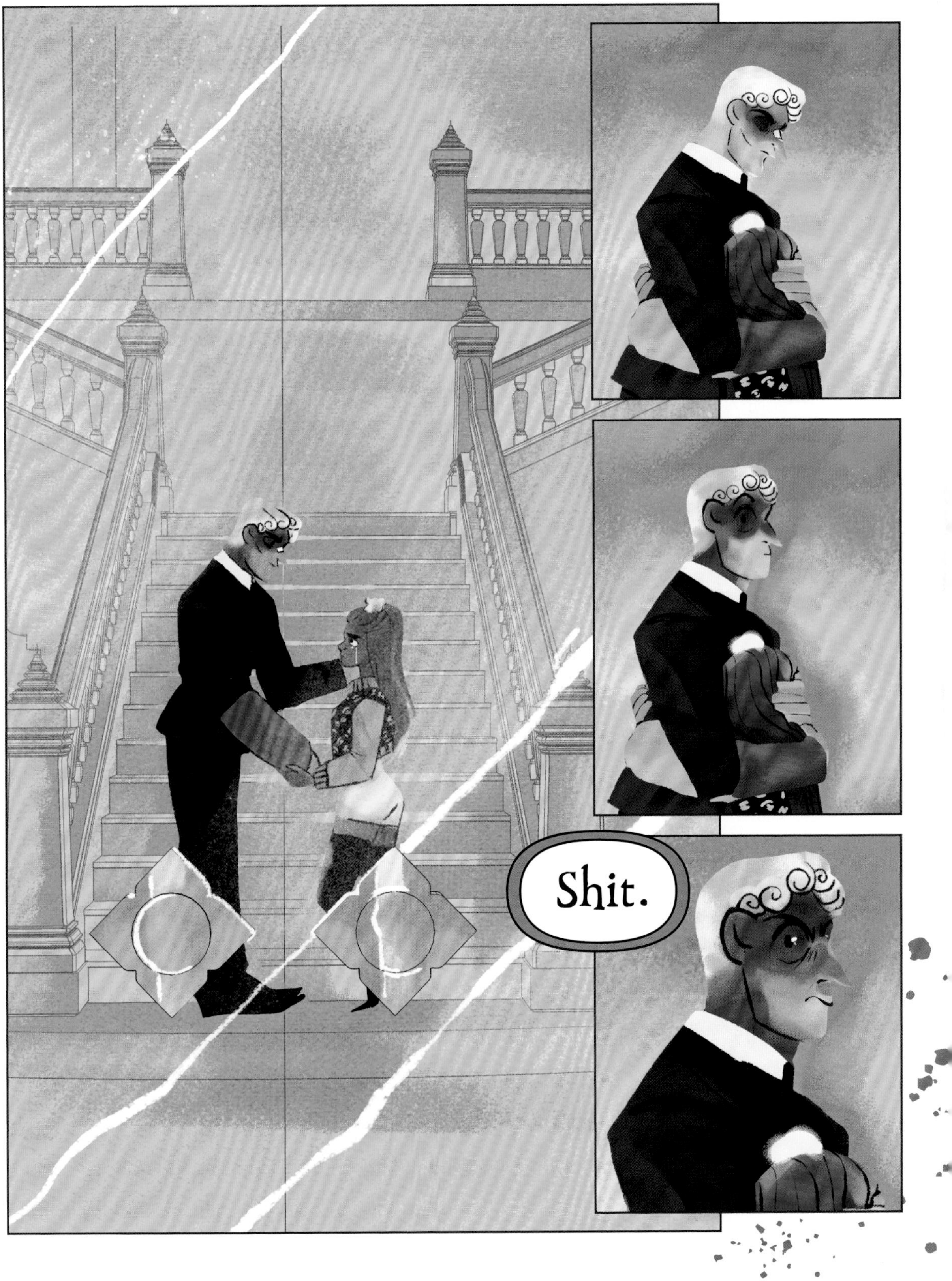
Shit.

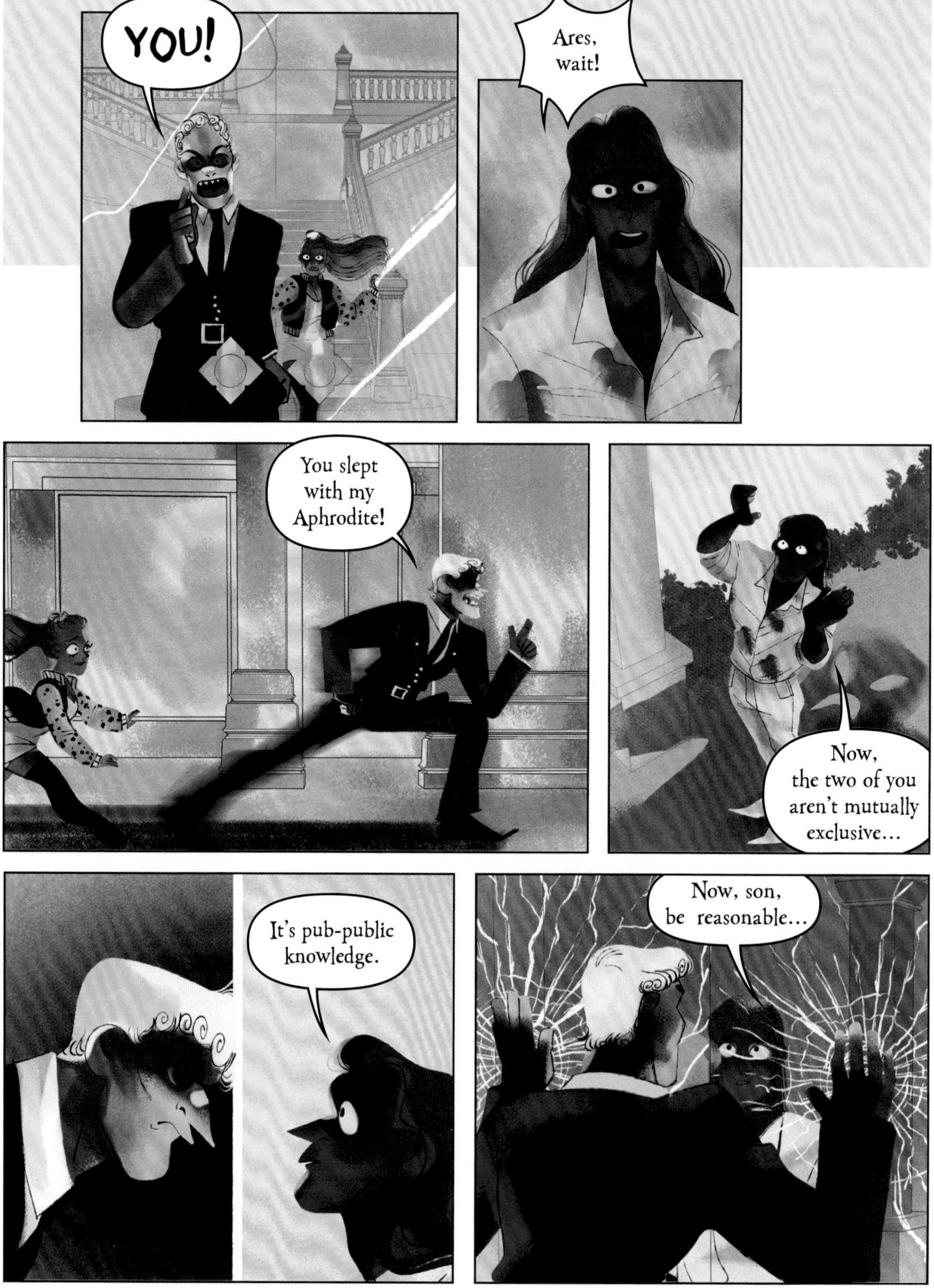
YOU!
Ares, wait!
You slept with my Aphrodite!
Now, the two of you aren't mutually exclusive...
It's pub-public knowledge.
Now, son, be reasonable...

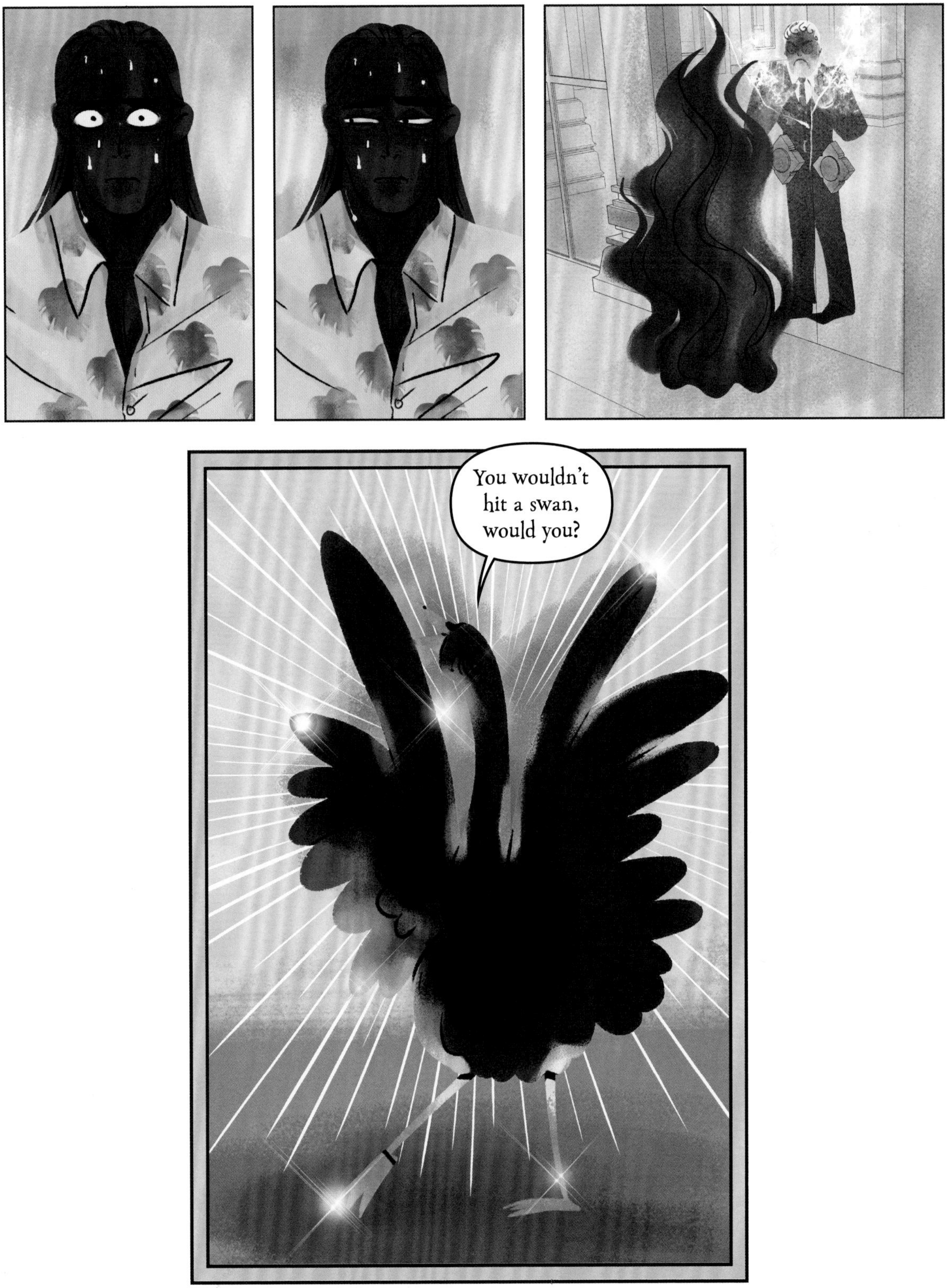
You wouldn't hit a swan, would you?

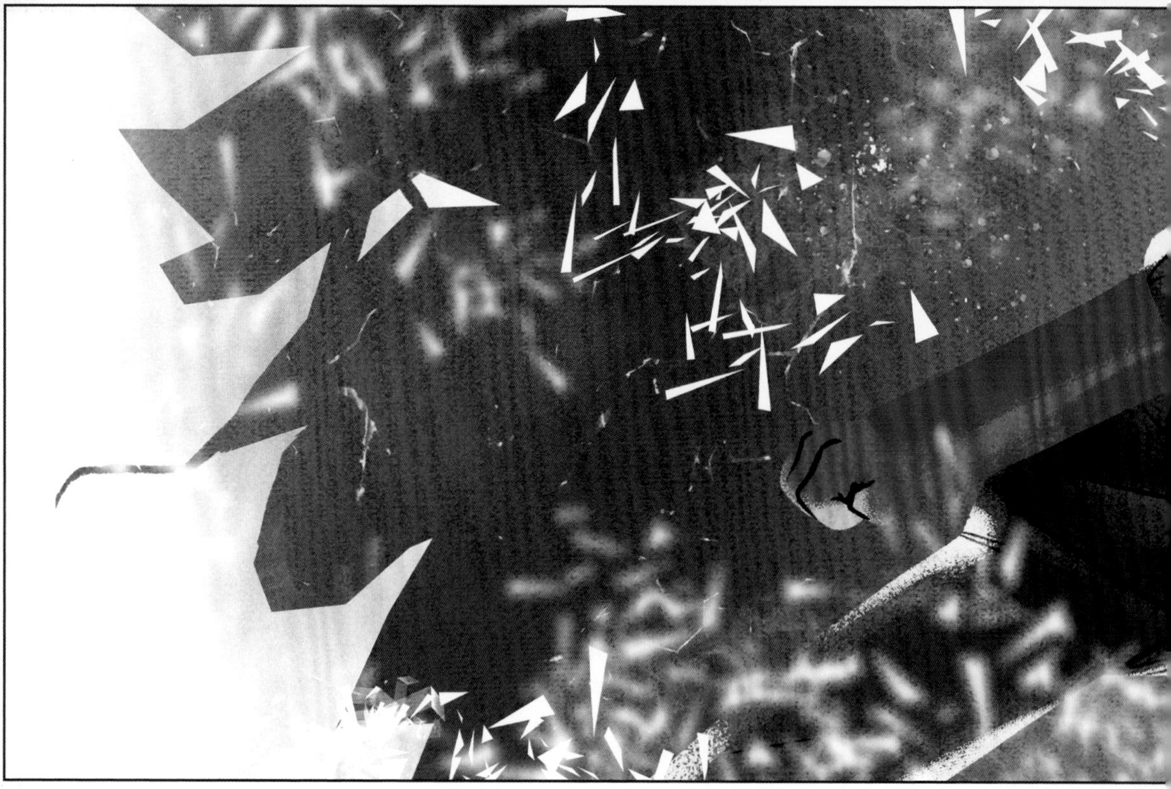

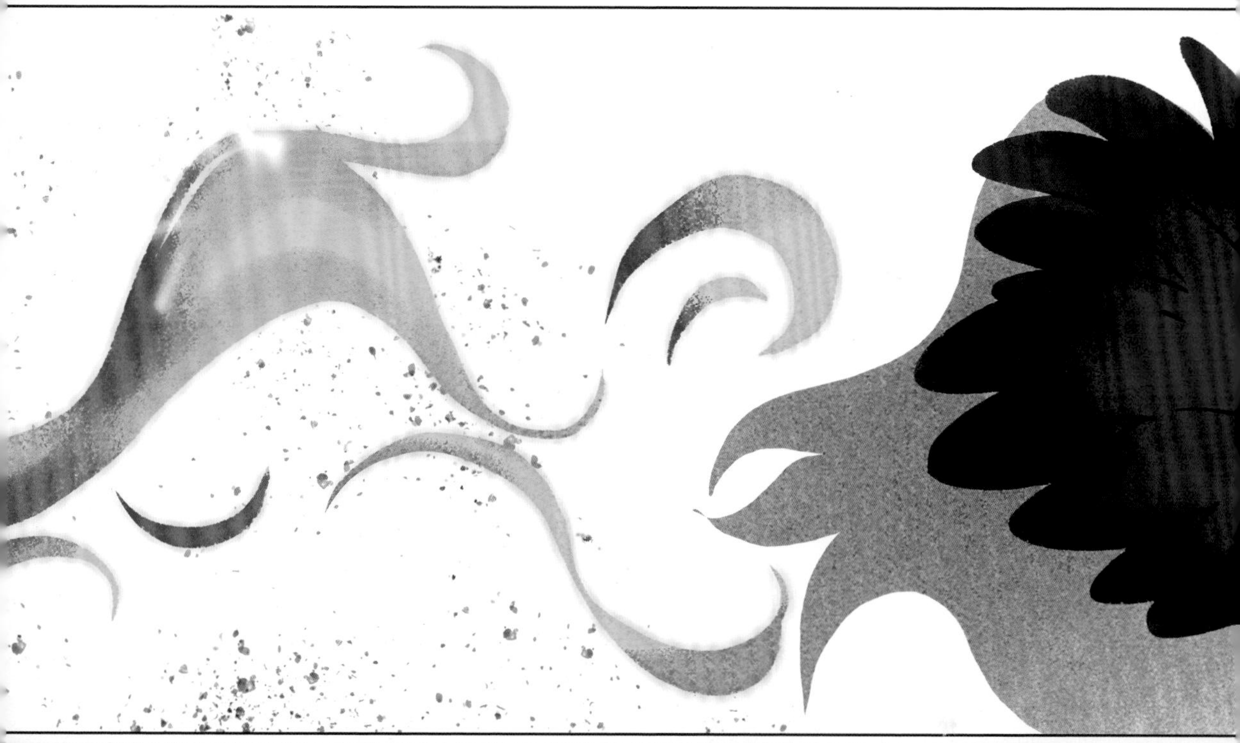

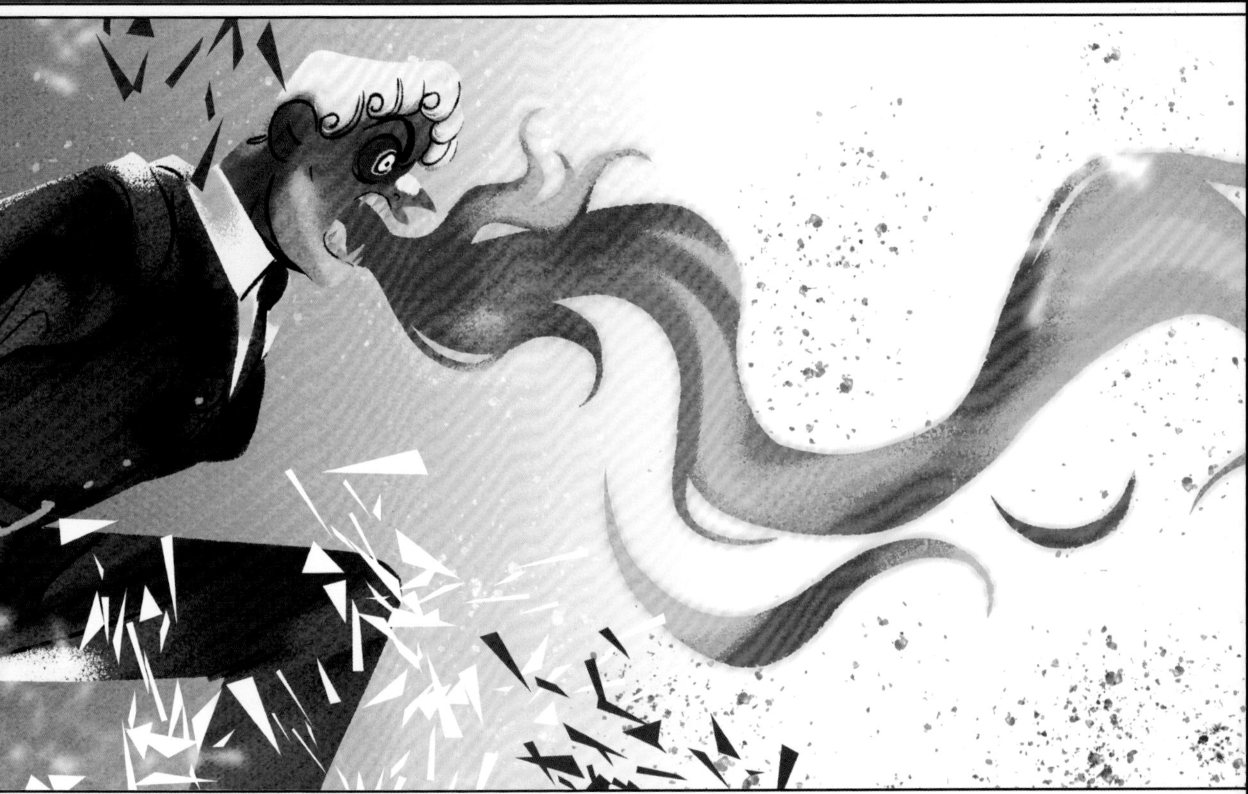

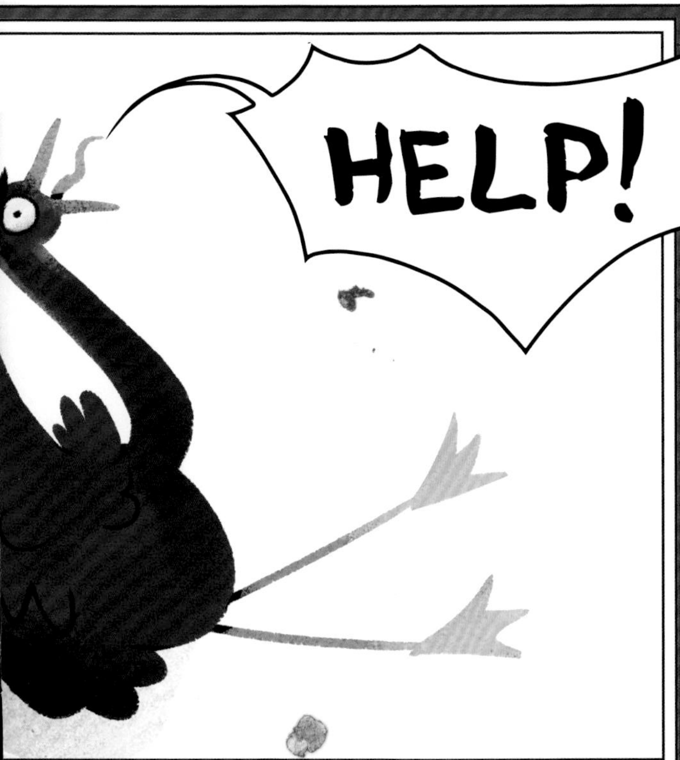
HELP!

EPISODE 92: FRONT LAWN

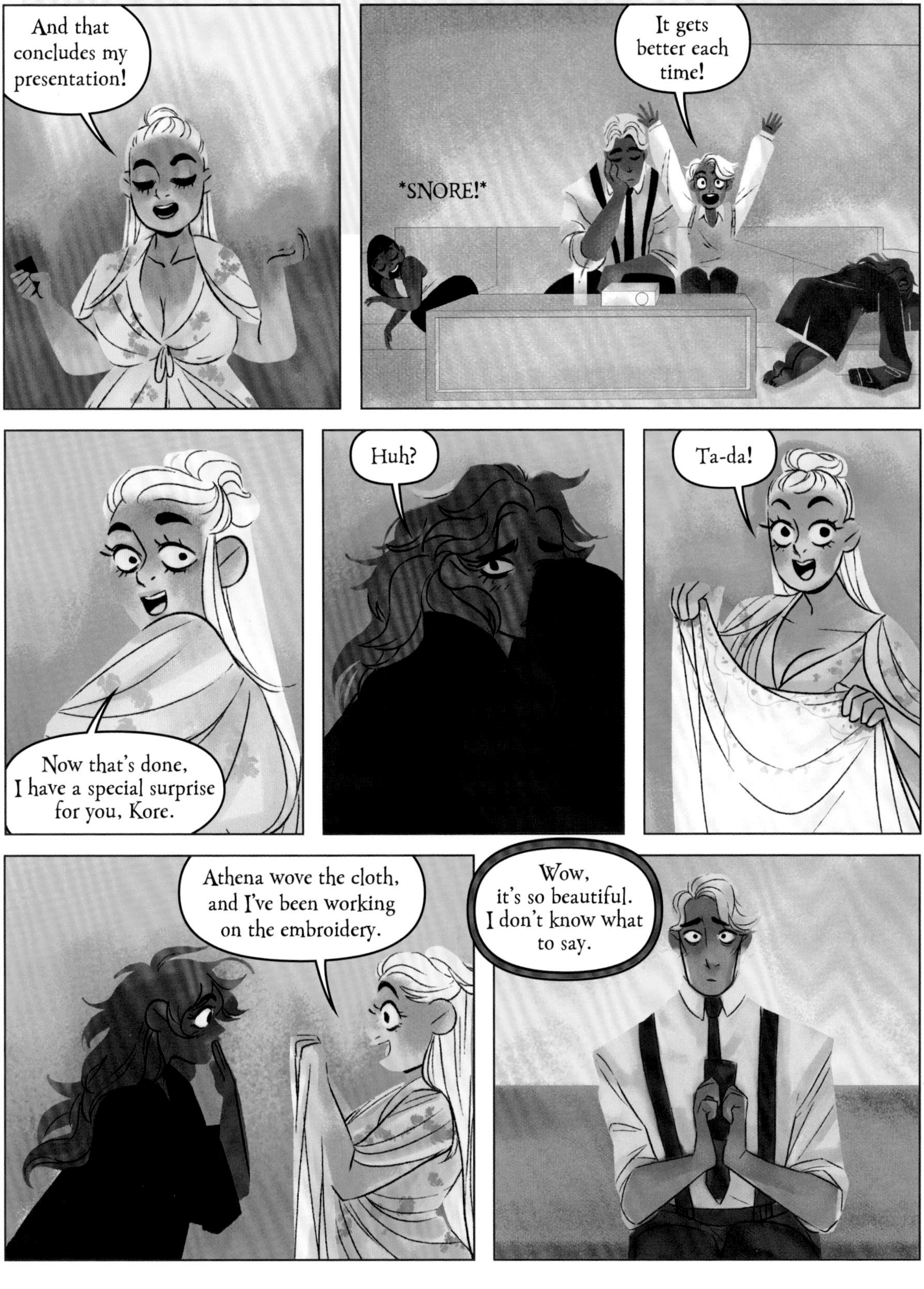
And that concludes my presentation!
SNORE!
It gets better each time!
Now that's done, I have a special surprise for you, Kore.
Huh?
Ta-da!
Athena wove the cloth, and I've been working on the embroidery.
Wow, it's so beautiful. I don't know what to say.

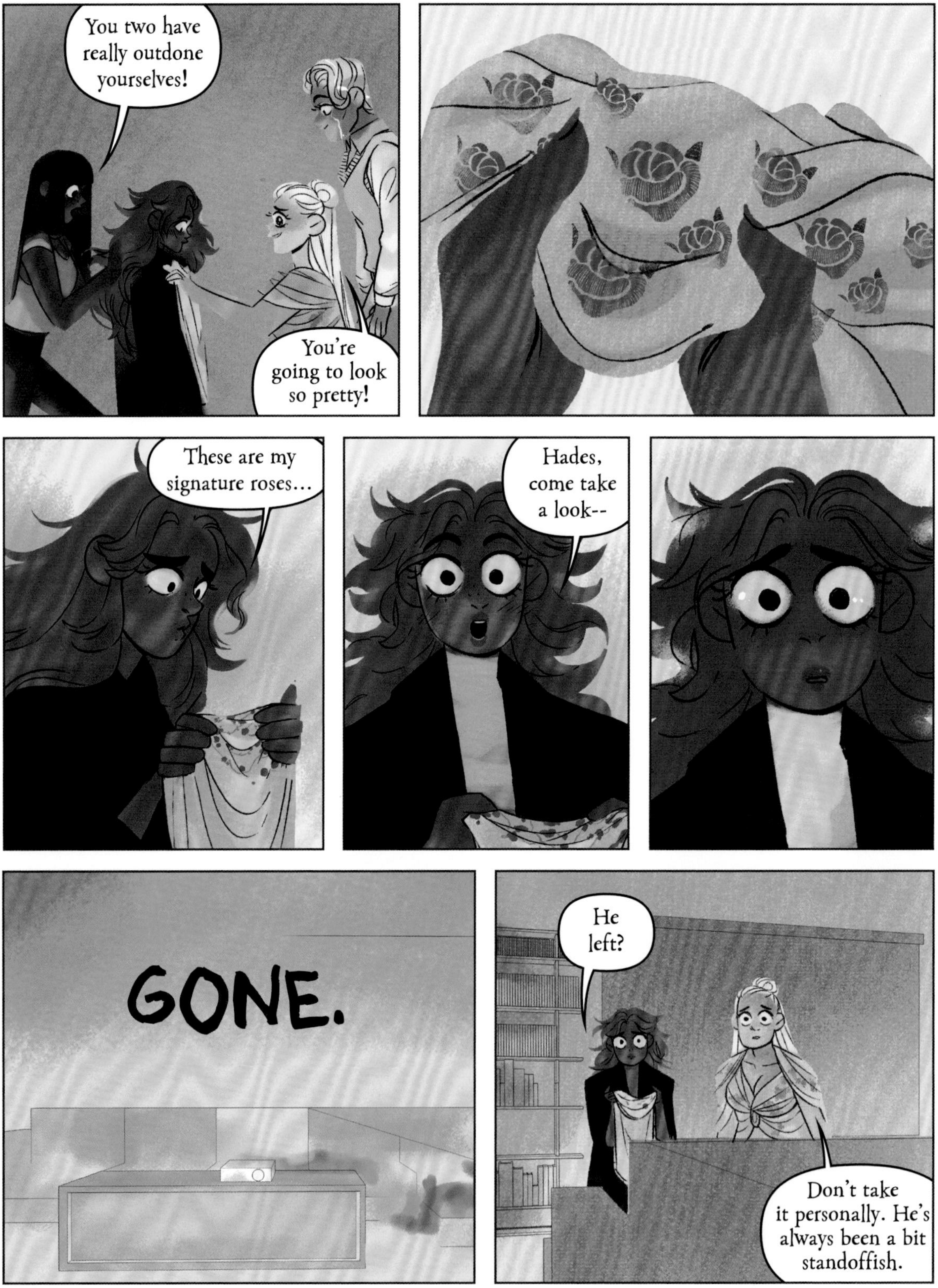
You two have really outdone yourselves!
You're going to look so pretty!
These are my signature roses...
Hades, come take a look--
GONE.
He left?
Don't take it personally. He's always been a bit standoffish.

At least he still wrote the check.

He made it out to you and not TGOEM.

I trust you to sort this out. Okay?

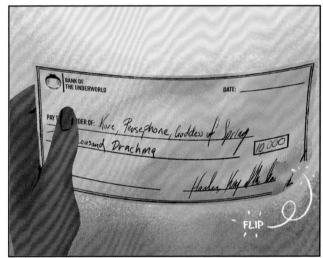

BANK OF
THE UNDERWORLD

DATE:

PAY TO THE ORDER OF: Kore, Persephone, Goddess of Spring

Thousand Drachma   10,000

Hades King of the Dead

FLIP

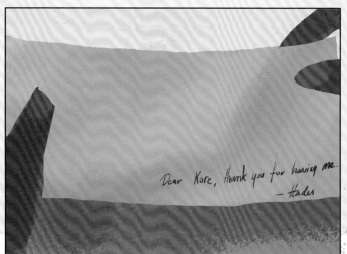

Dear Kore, thank you for having me.
— Hades

Guh, why won't today just end!?

BEEP-A-BEEP

Oh snap!

ZEUS

CODE RED

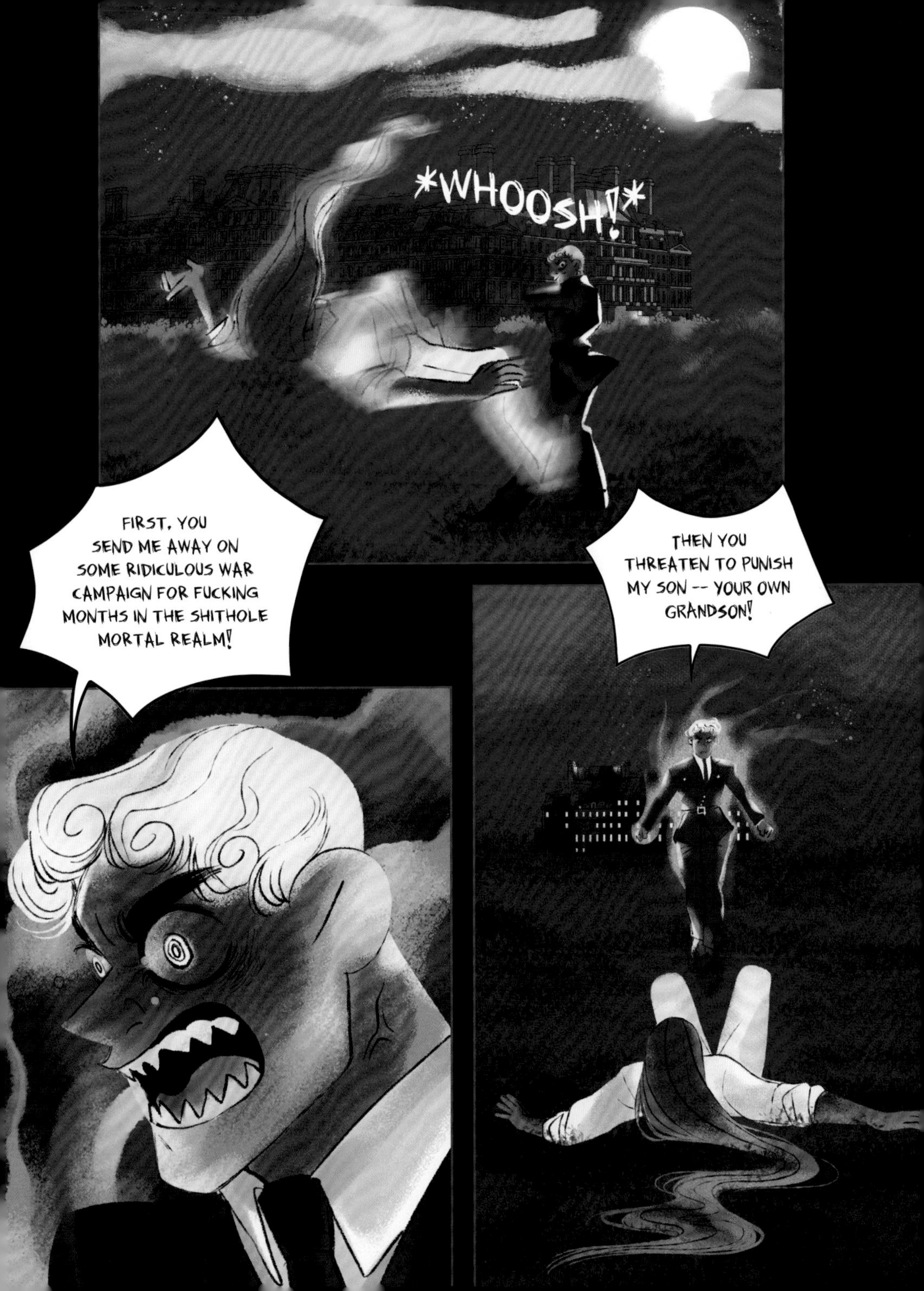
WHOOSH!
FIRST, YOU SEND ME AWAY ON SOME RIDICULOUS WAR CAMPAIGN FOR FUCKING MONTHS IN THE SHITHOLE MORTAL REALM!
THEN YOU THREATEN TO PUNISH MY SON -- YOUR OWN GRANDSON!

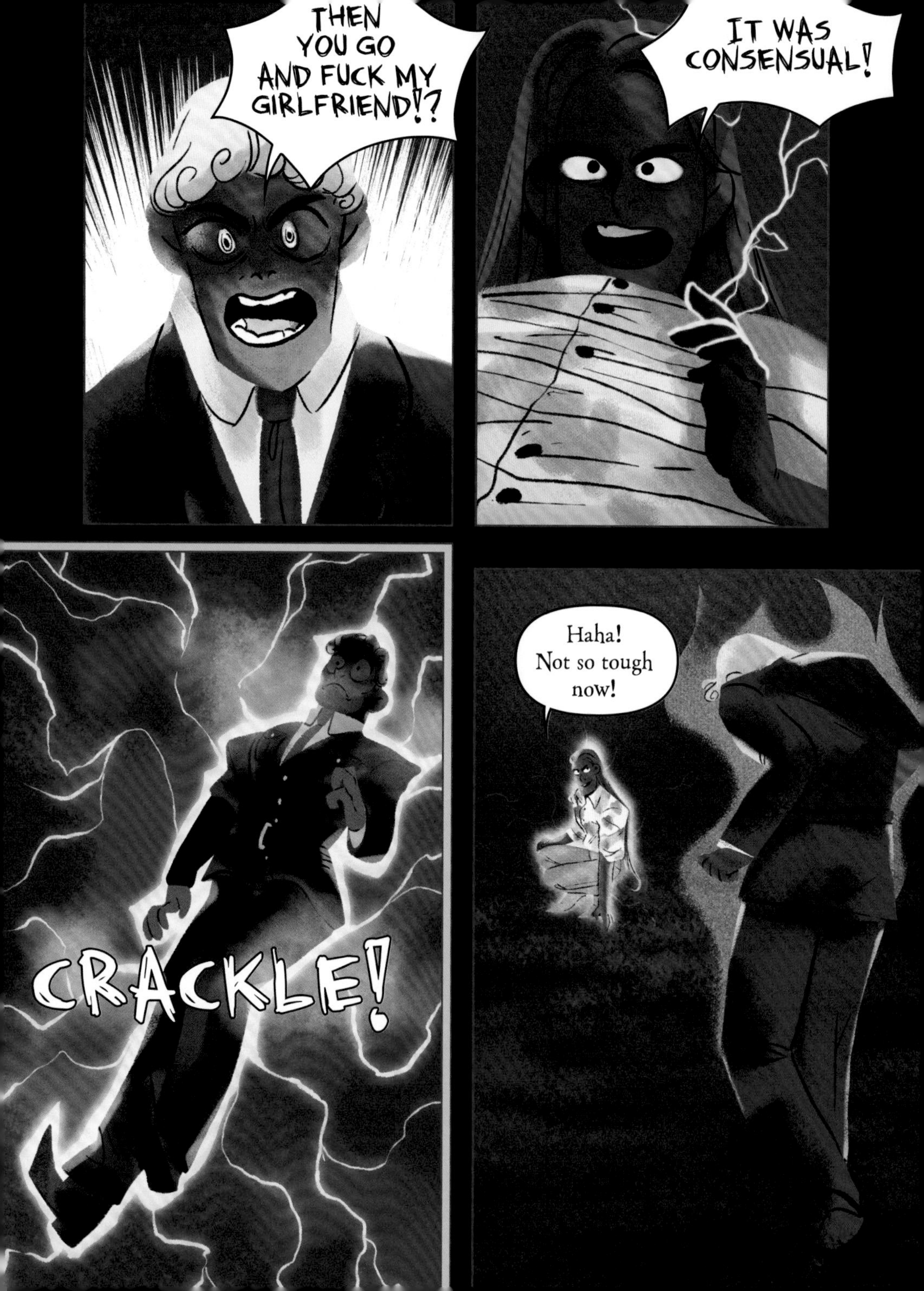
THEN YOU GO AND FUCK MY GIRLFRIEND!?
IT WAS CONSENSUAL!
CRACKLE!
Haha! Not so tough now!

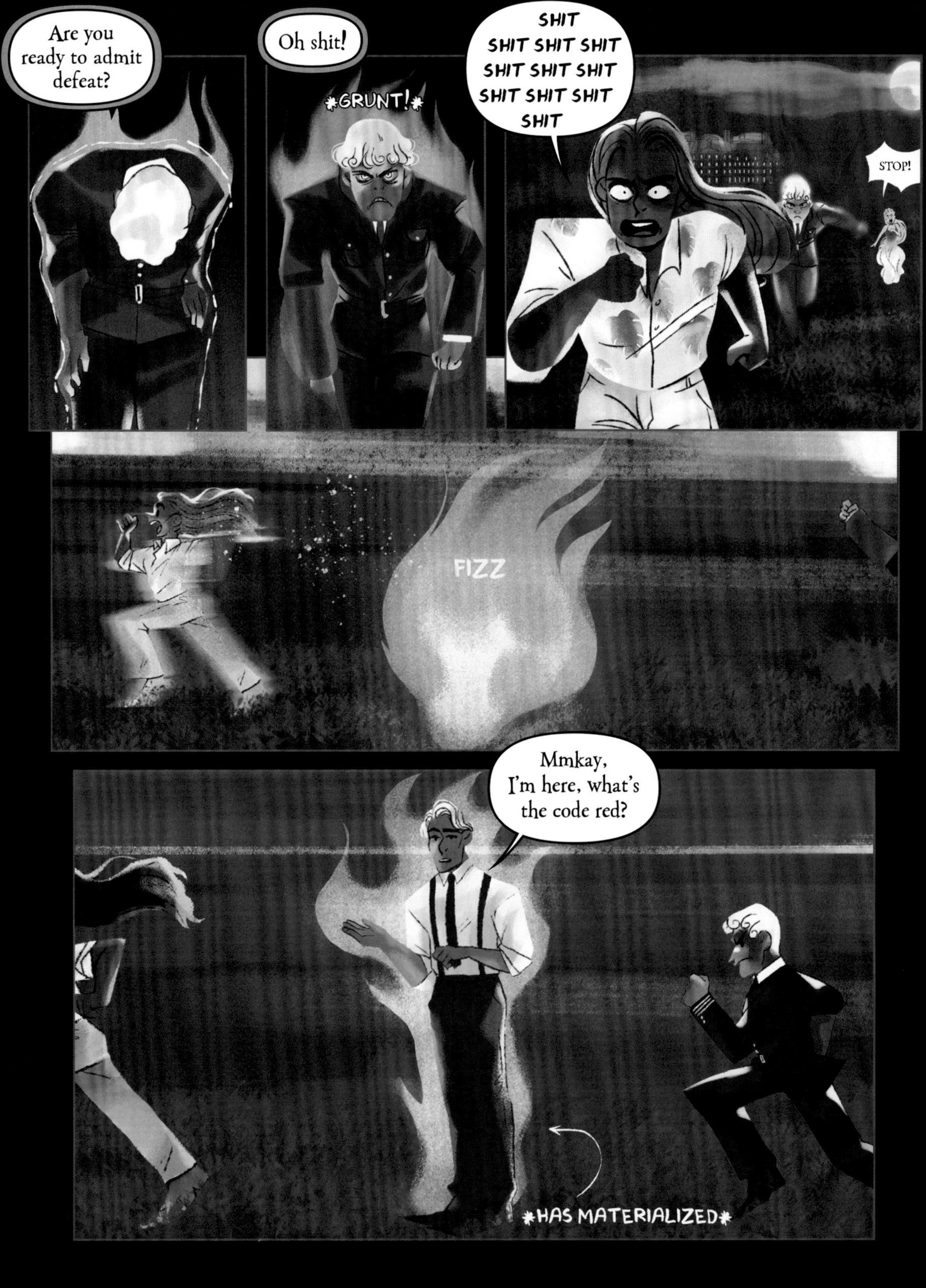
Are you ready to admit defeat?
Oh shit!
GRUNT!
SHIT SHIT SHIT SHIT SHIT SHIT SHIT SHIT SHIT SHIT SHIT
STOP!
FIZZ
Mmkay, I'm here, what's the code red?
HAS MATERIALIZED

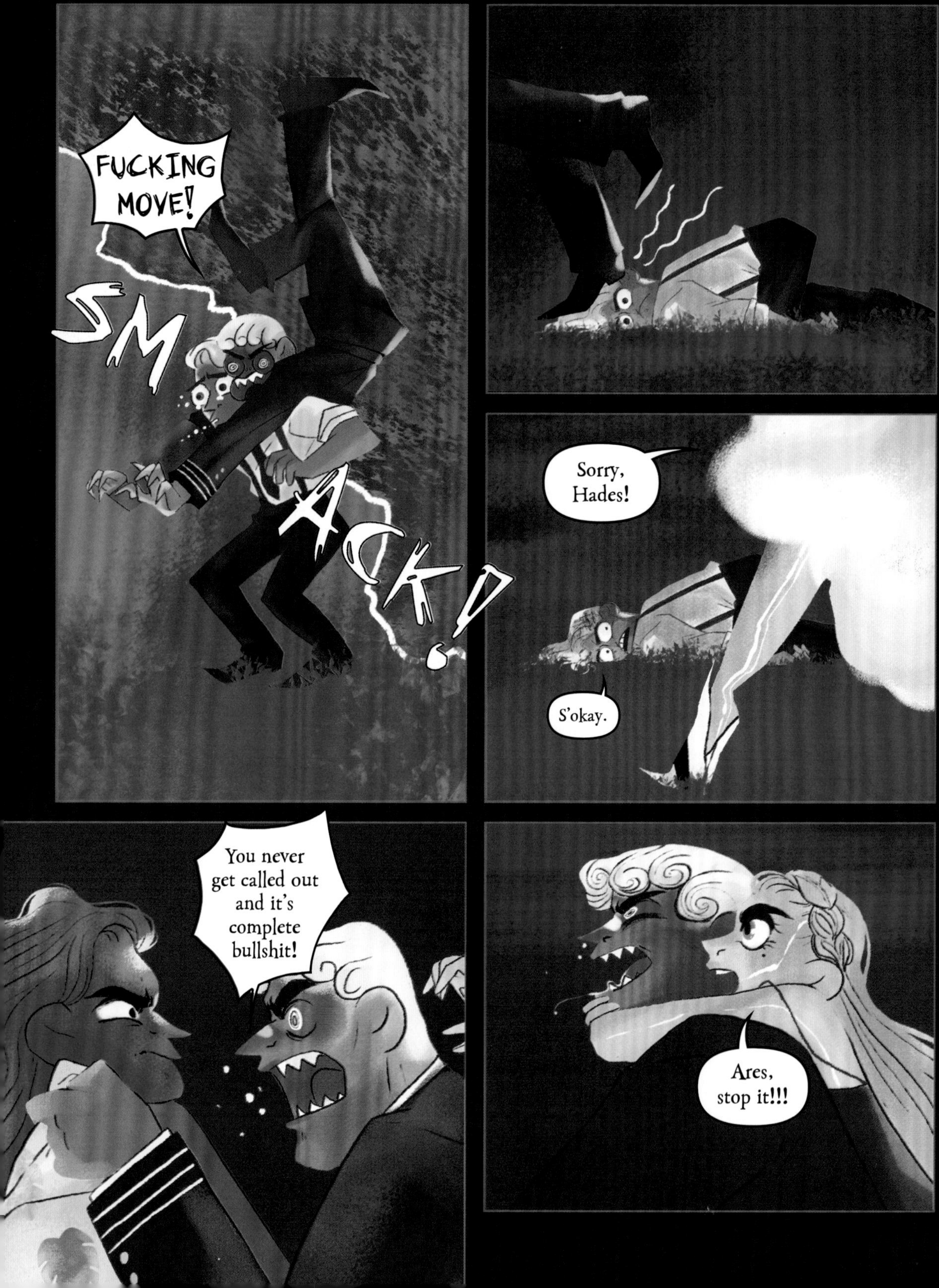
FUCKING MOVE!
SMACK!
Sorry, Hades!
S'okay.
You never get called out and it's complete bullshit!
Ares, stop it!!!

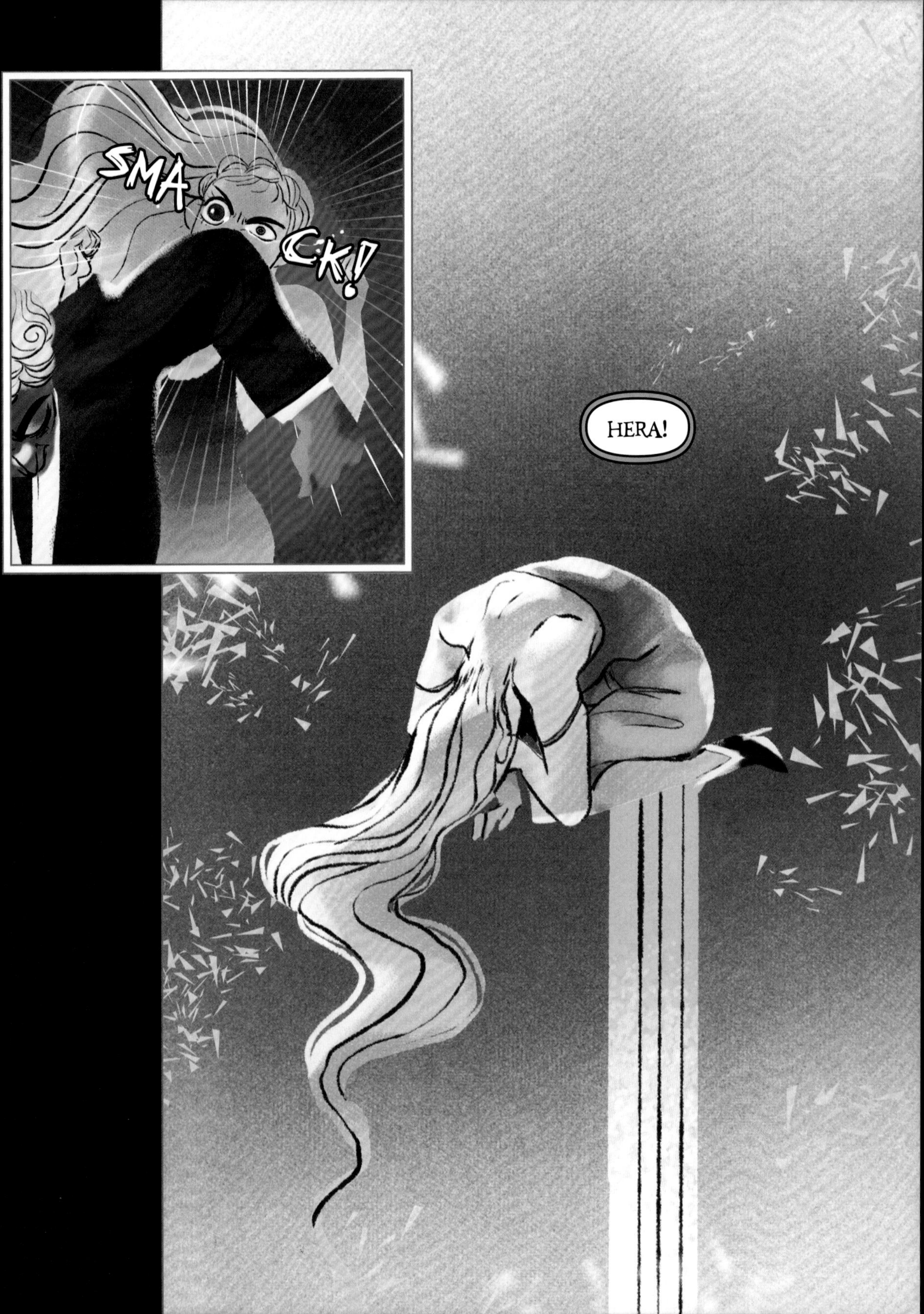
SMACK!
HERA!

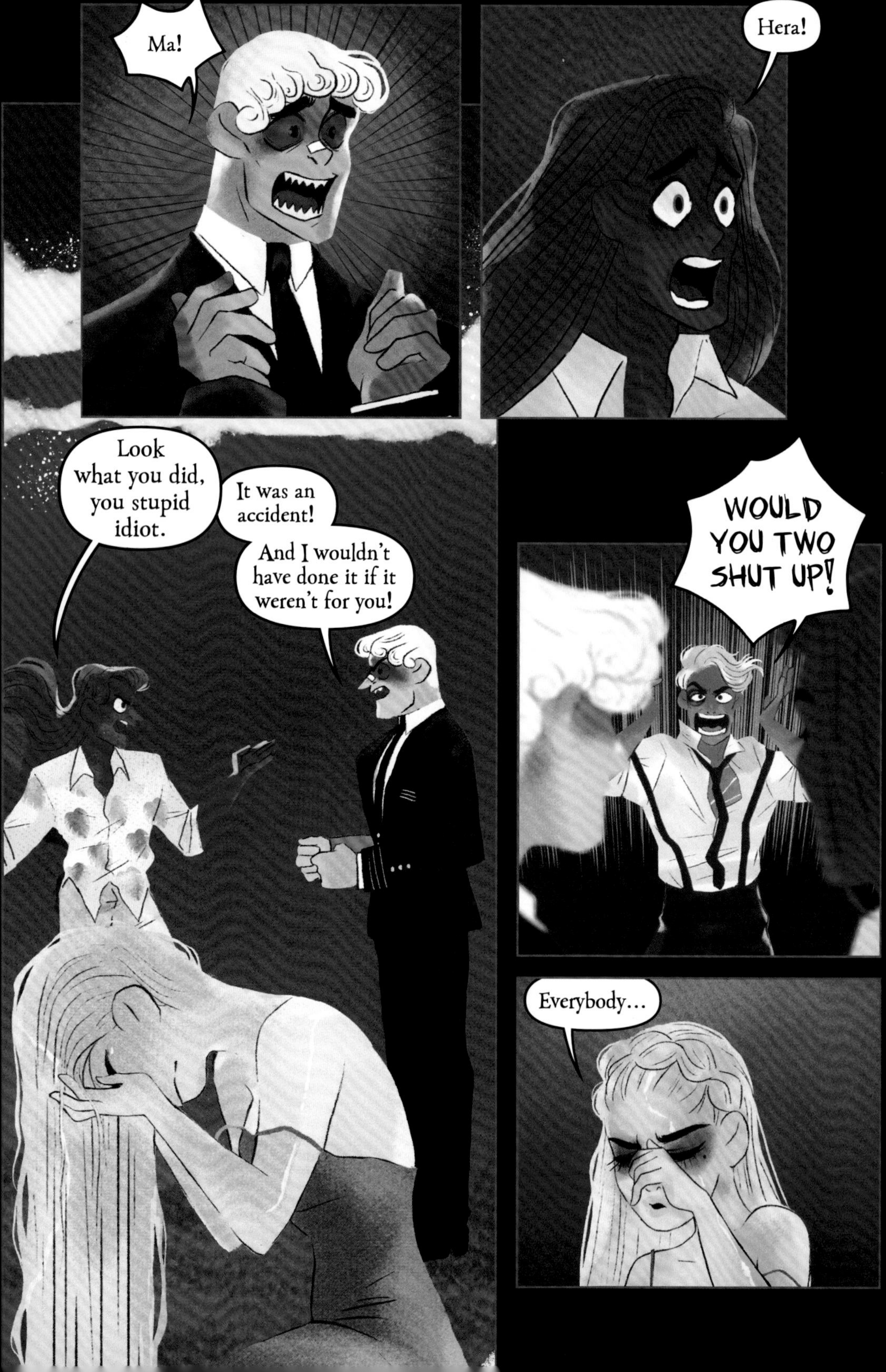

Ma!
Hera!
Look what you did, you stupid idiot.
It was an accident!
And I wouldn't have done it if it weren't for you!
WOULD YOU TWO SHUT UP!
Everybody...

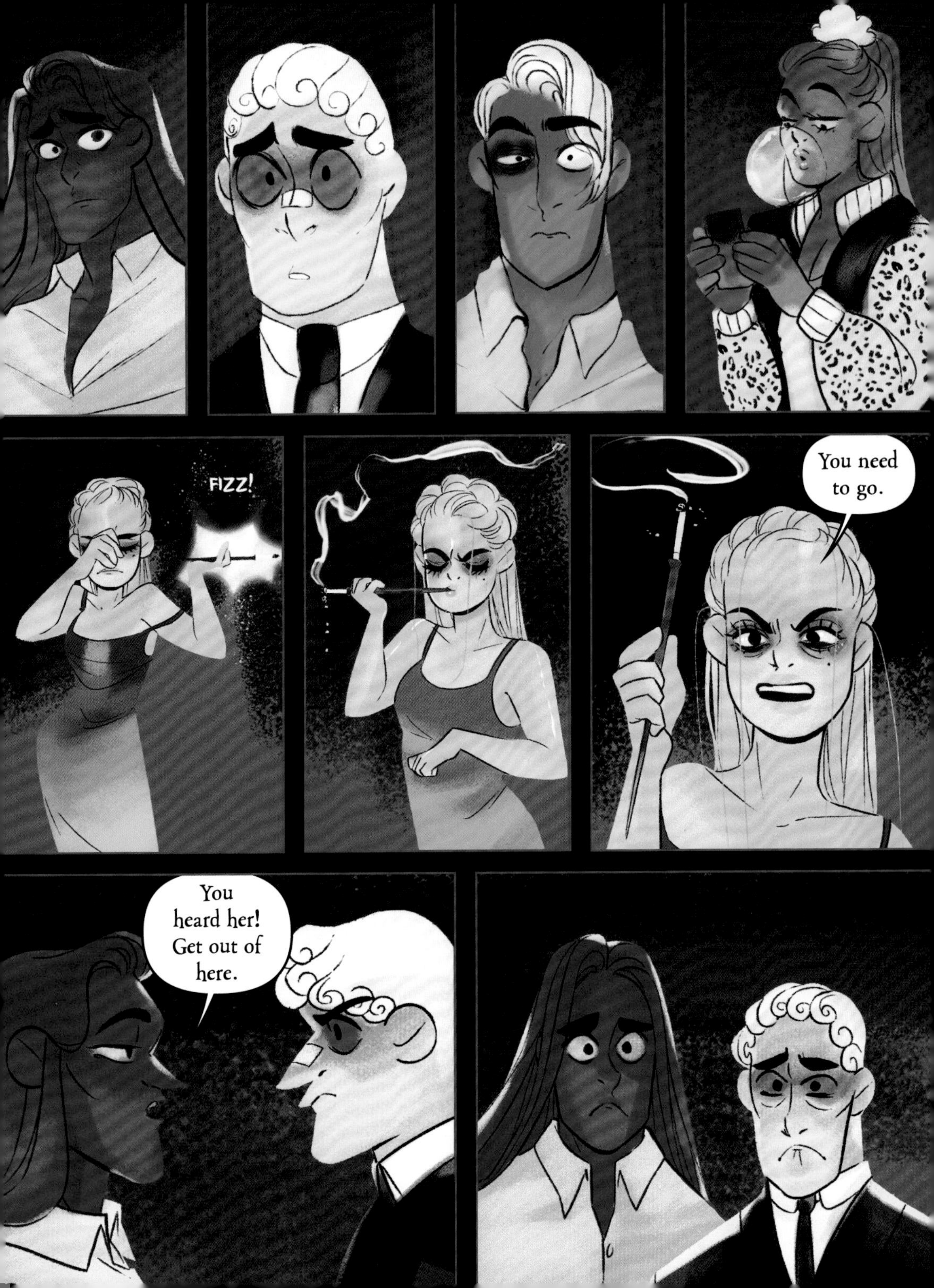
FIZZ!
You need to go.
You heard her! Get out of here.

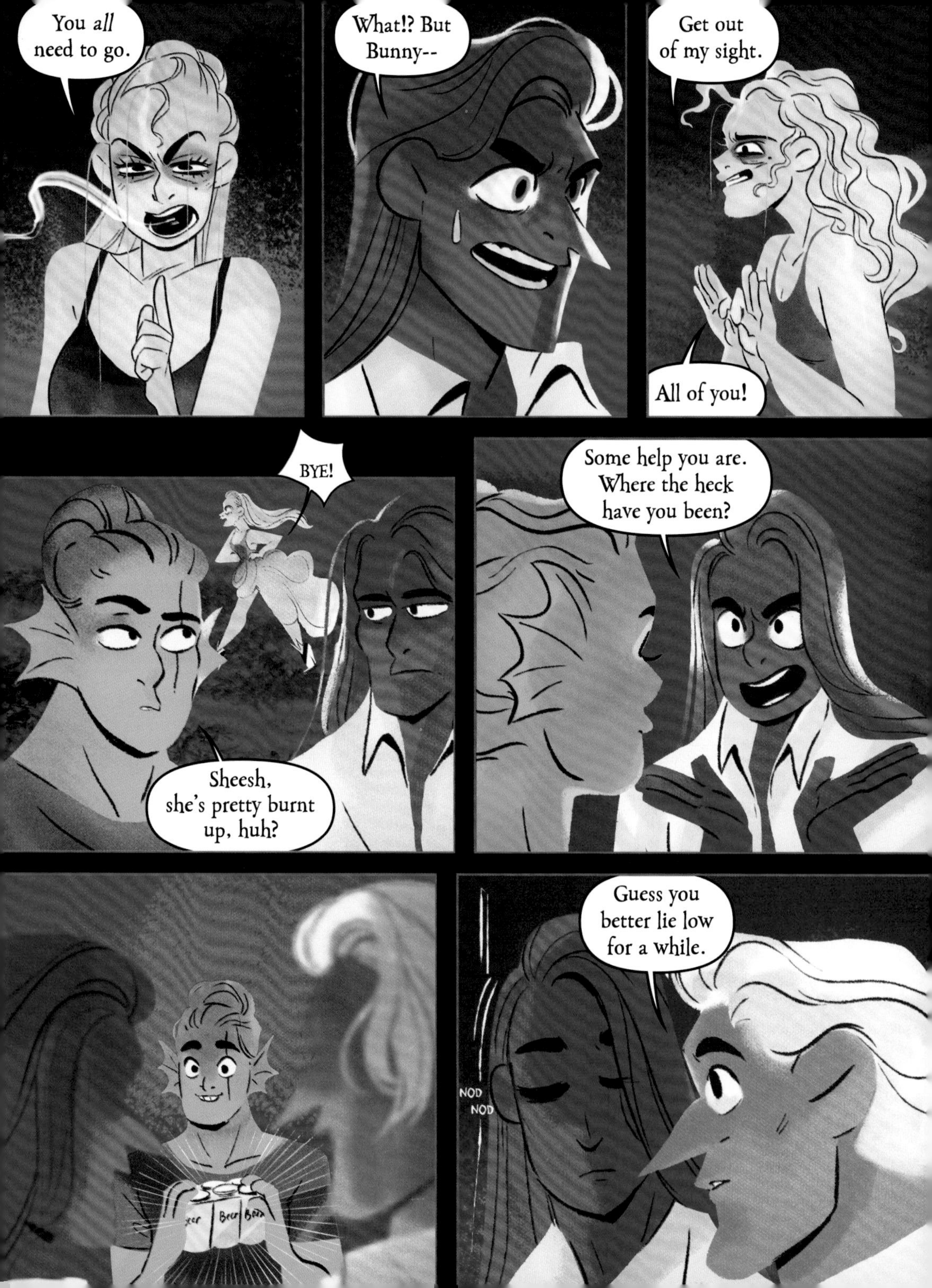
You *all* need to go.
What!? But Bunny--
Get out of my sight.
All of you!
BYE!
Sheesh, she's pretty burnt up, huh?
Some help you are. Where the heck have you been?
Beer Beer Beer
Guess you better lie low for a while.
NOD NOD

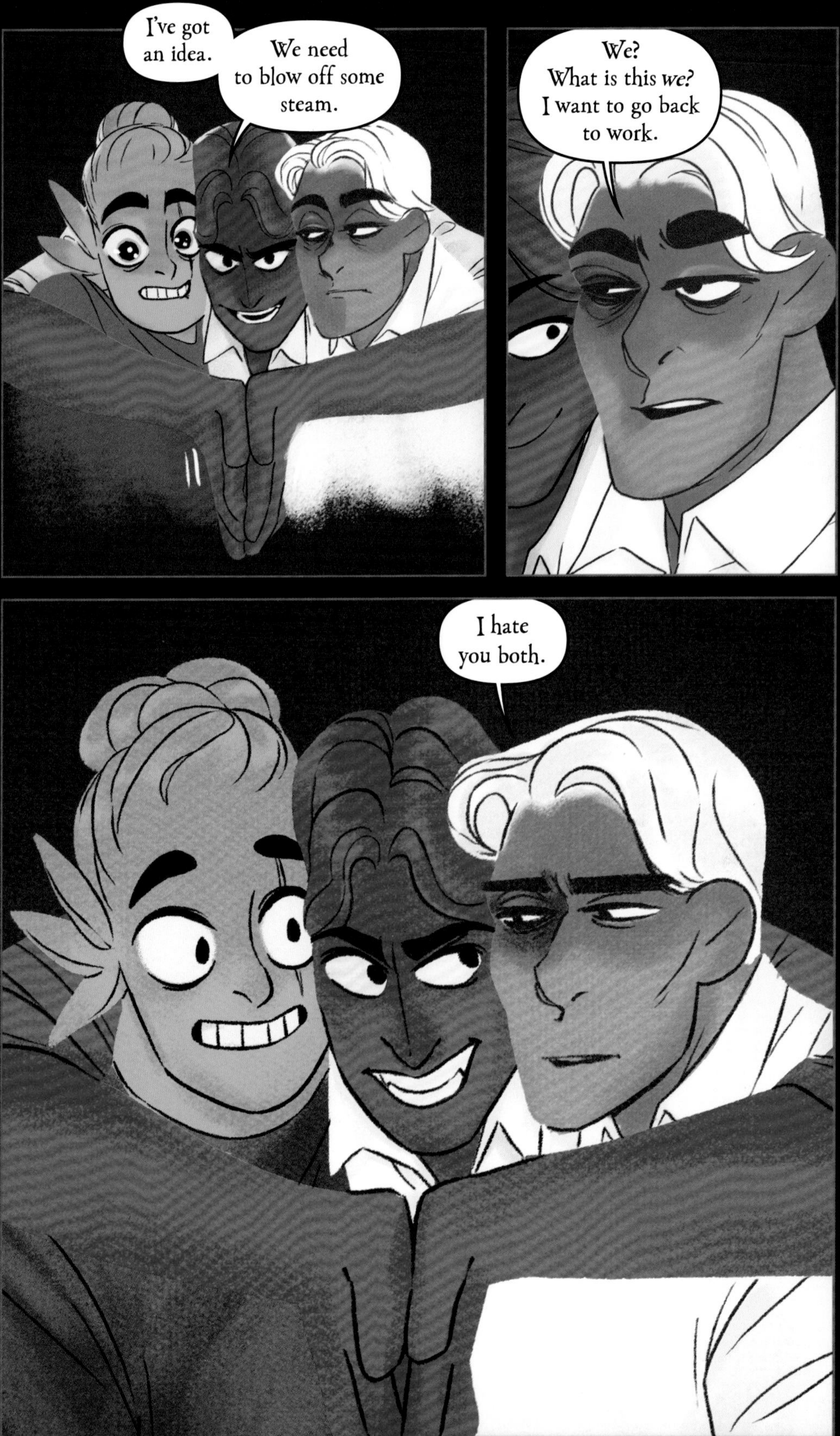
I've got an idea.
We need to blow off some steam.
We? What is this *we?* I want to go back to work.
I hate you both.

EPISODE 93: SEMELE

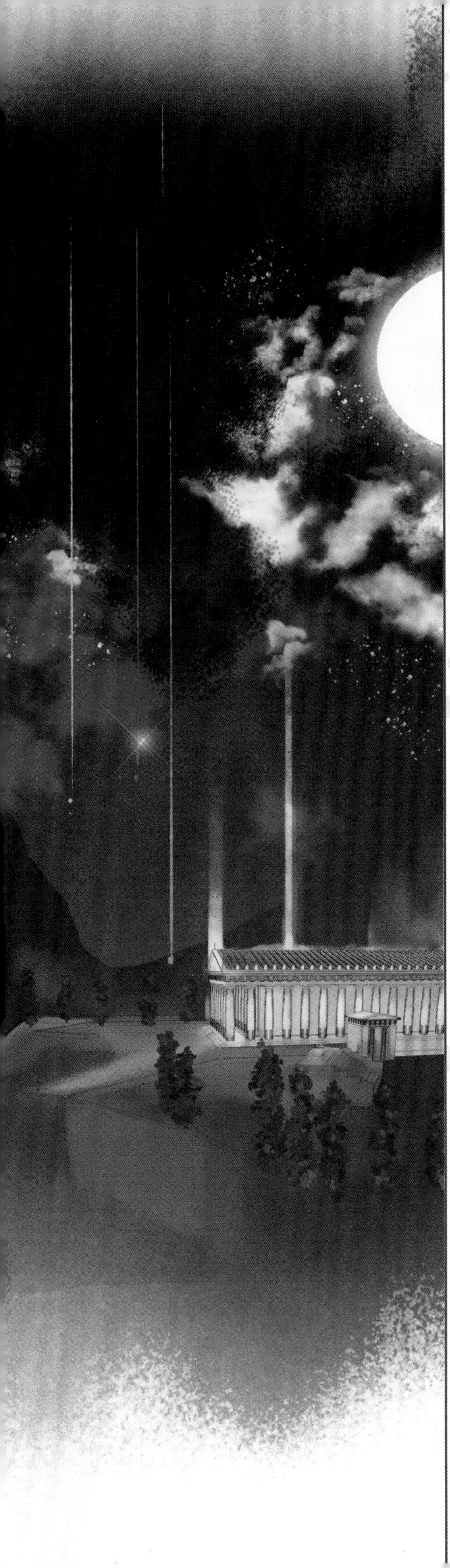

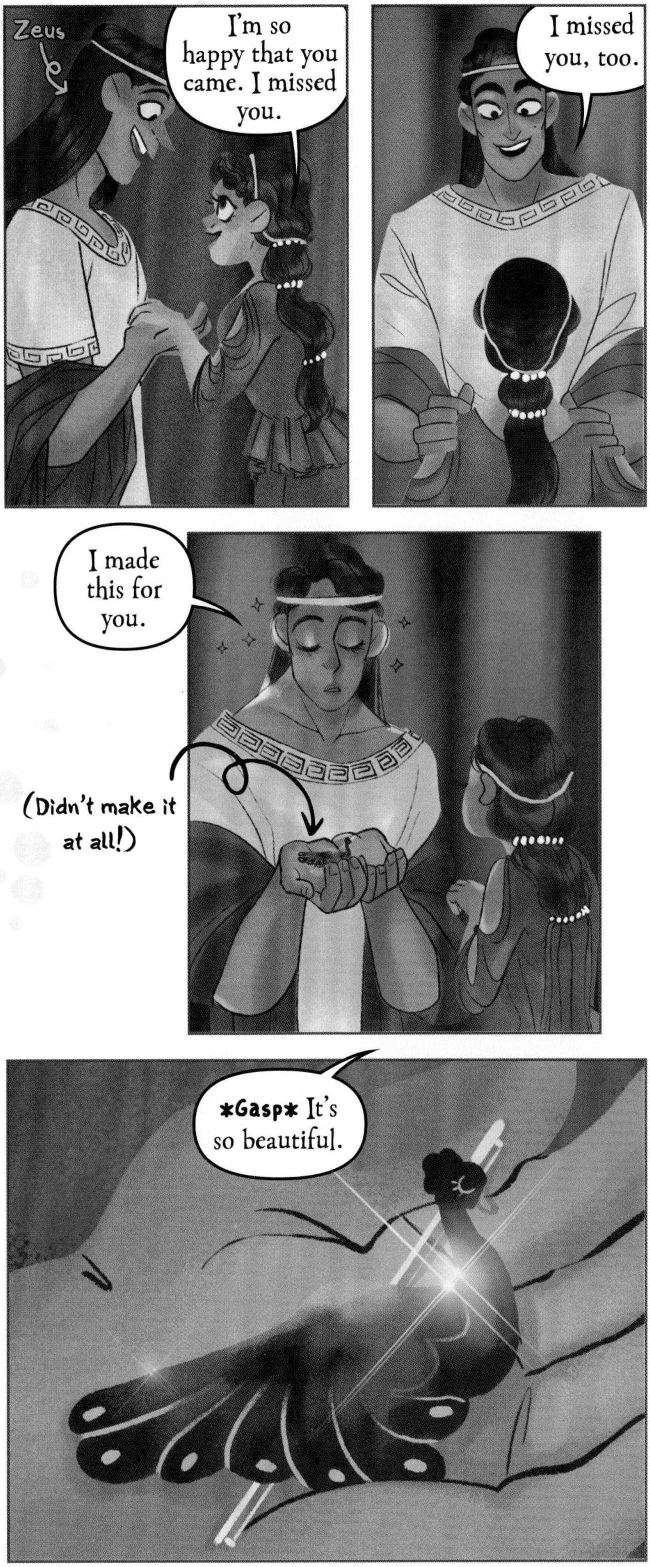
Zeus
I'm so happy that you came. I missed you.
I missed you, too.
I made this for you.
(Didn't make it at all!)
Gasp It's so beautiful.

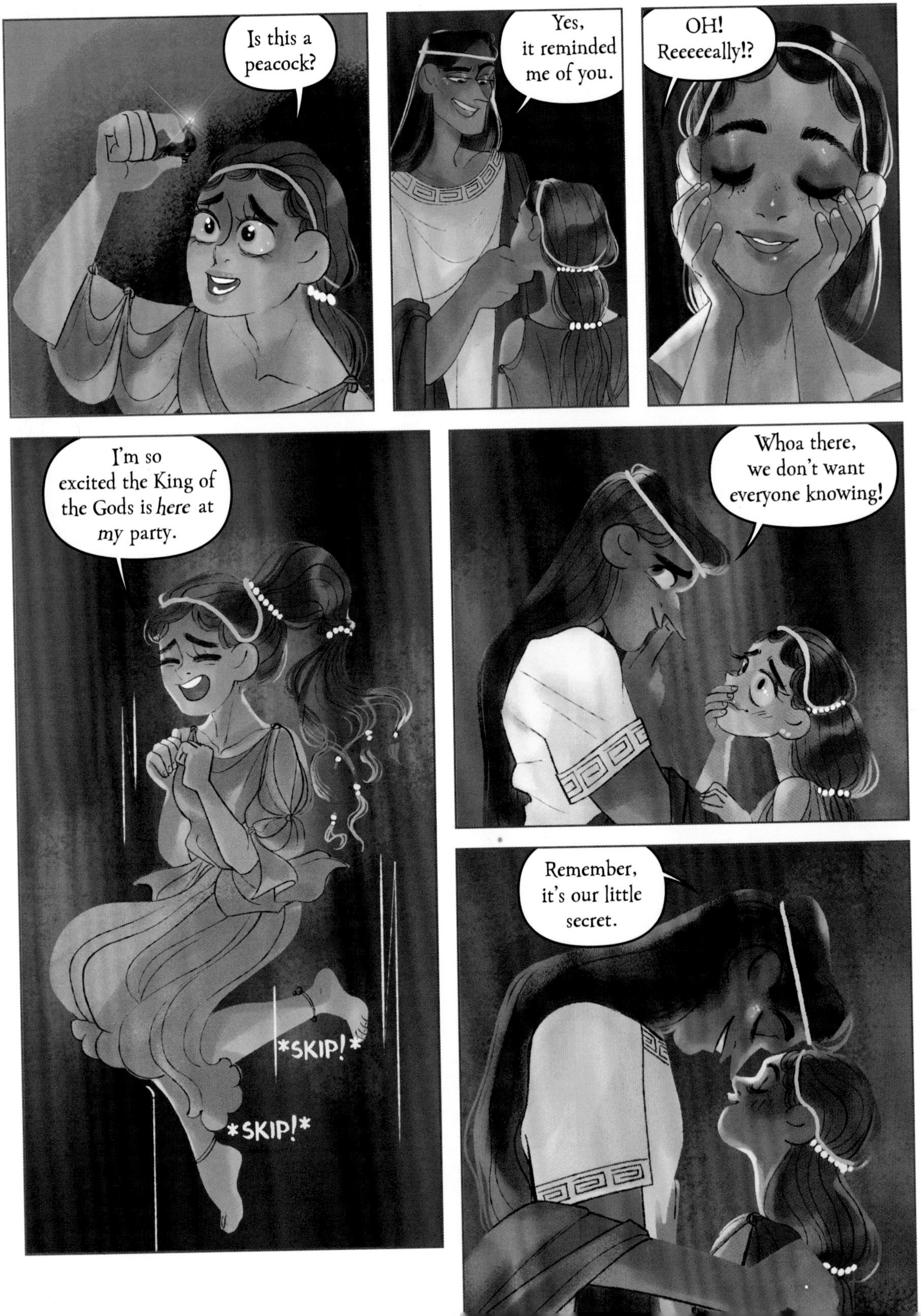
Is this a peacock?
Yes, it reminded me of you.
OH! Reeeeeally!?
I'm so excited the King of the Gods is *here* at *my* party.
Whoa there, we don't want everyone knowing!
SKIP!
SKIP!
Remember, it's our little secret.

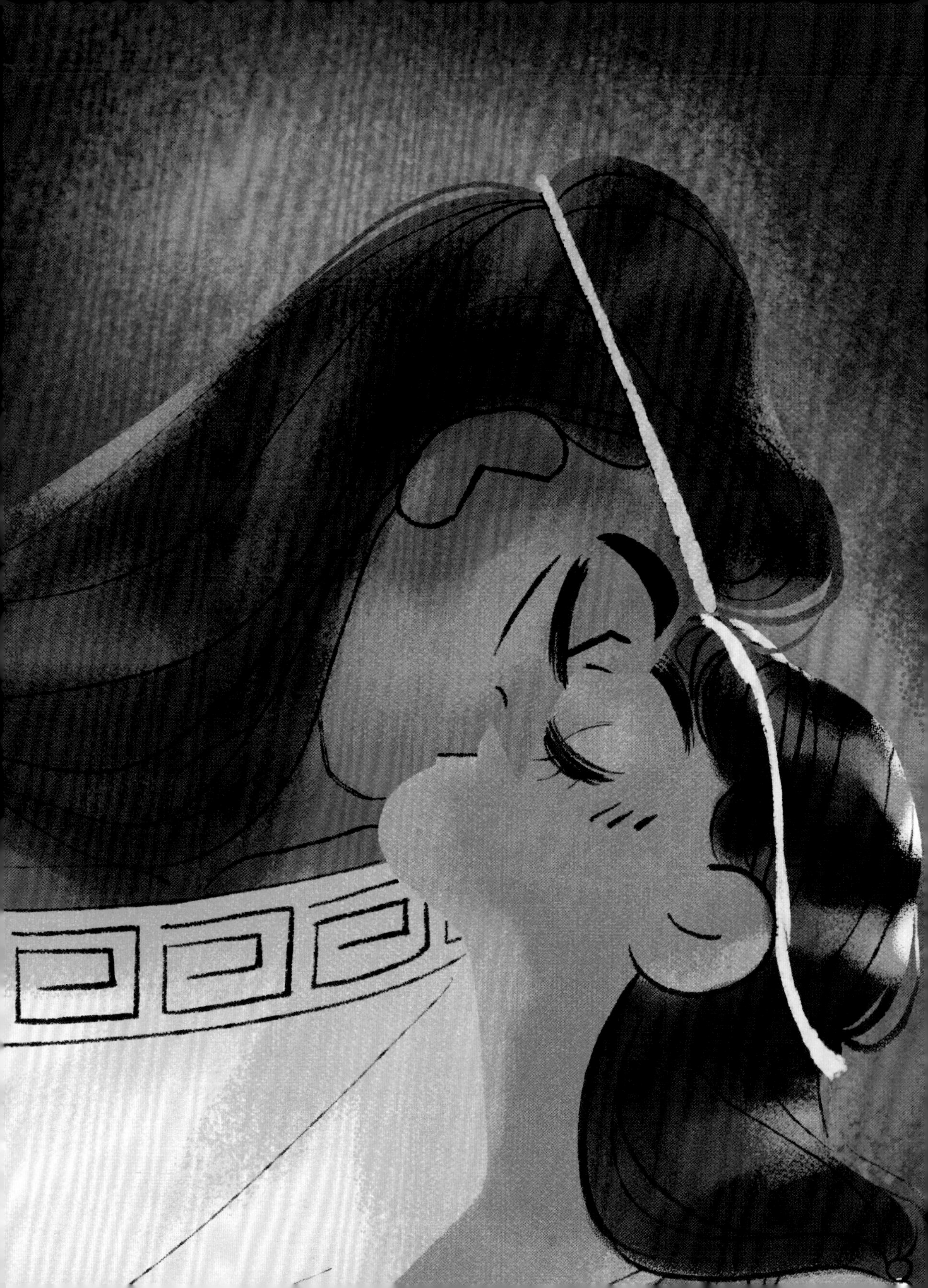

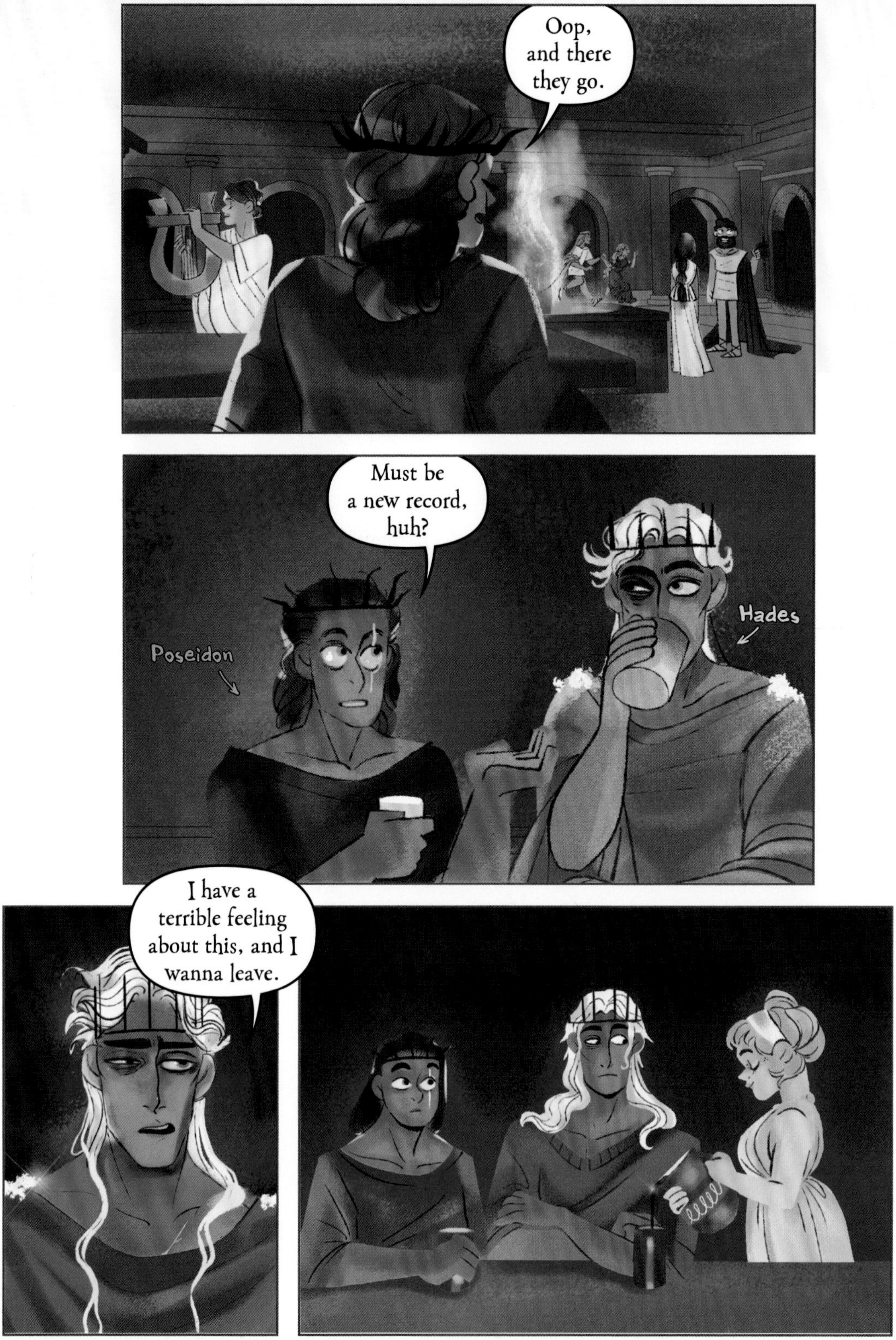
Oop, and there they go.
Must be a new record, huh?
Poseidon
Hades
I have a terrible feeling about this, and I wanna leave.

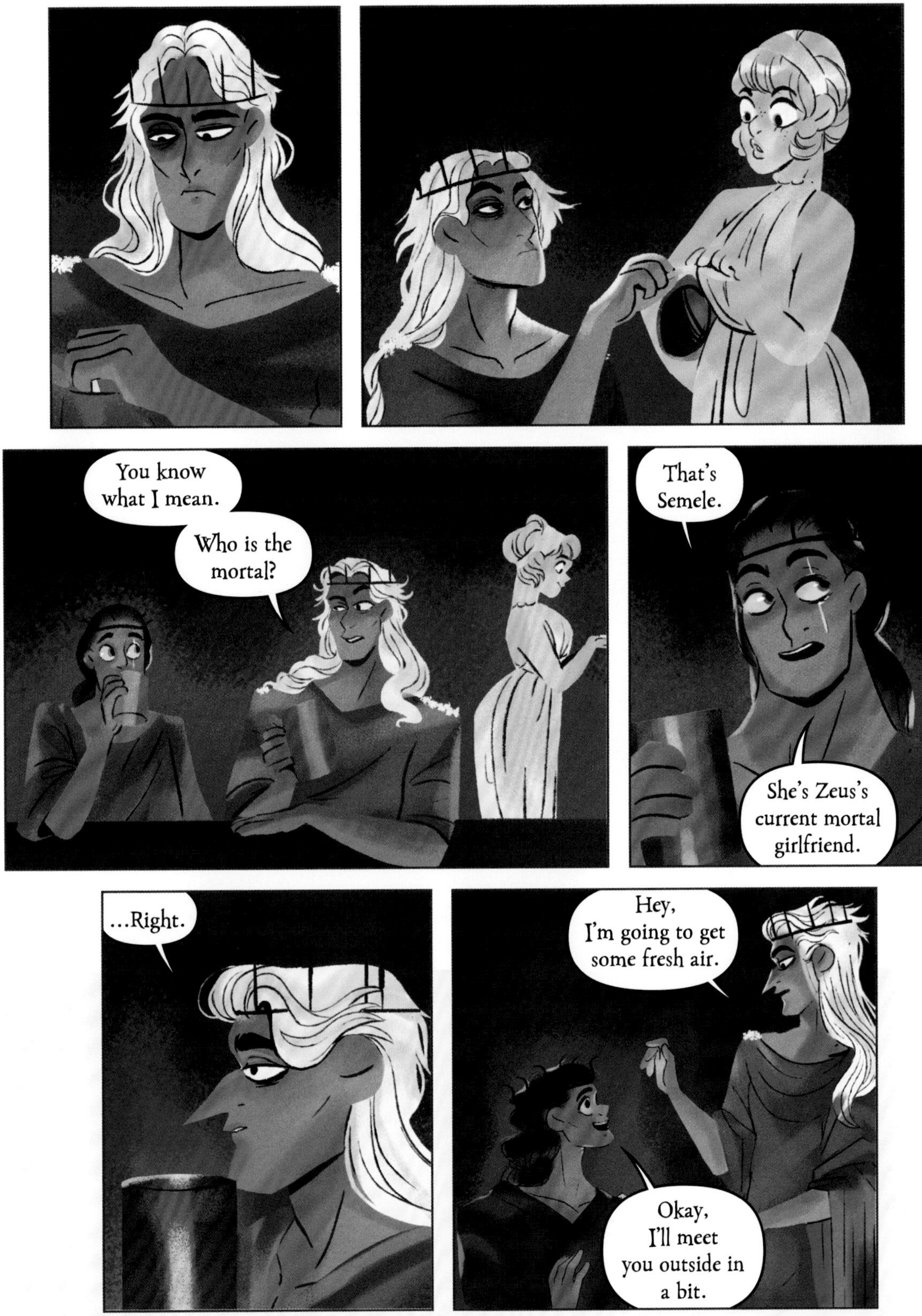

You know what I mean.
Who is the mortal?
That's Semele.
She's Zeus's current mortal girlfriend.
...Right.
Hey, I'm going to get some fresh air.
Okay, I'll meet you outside in a bit.

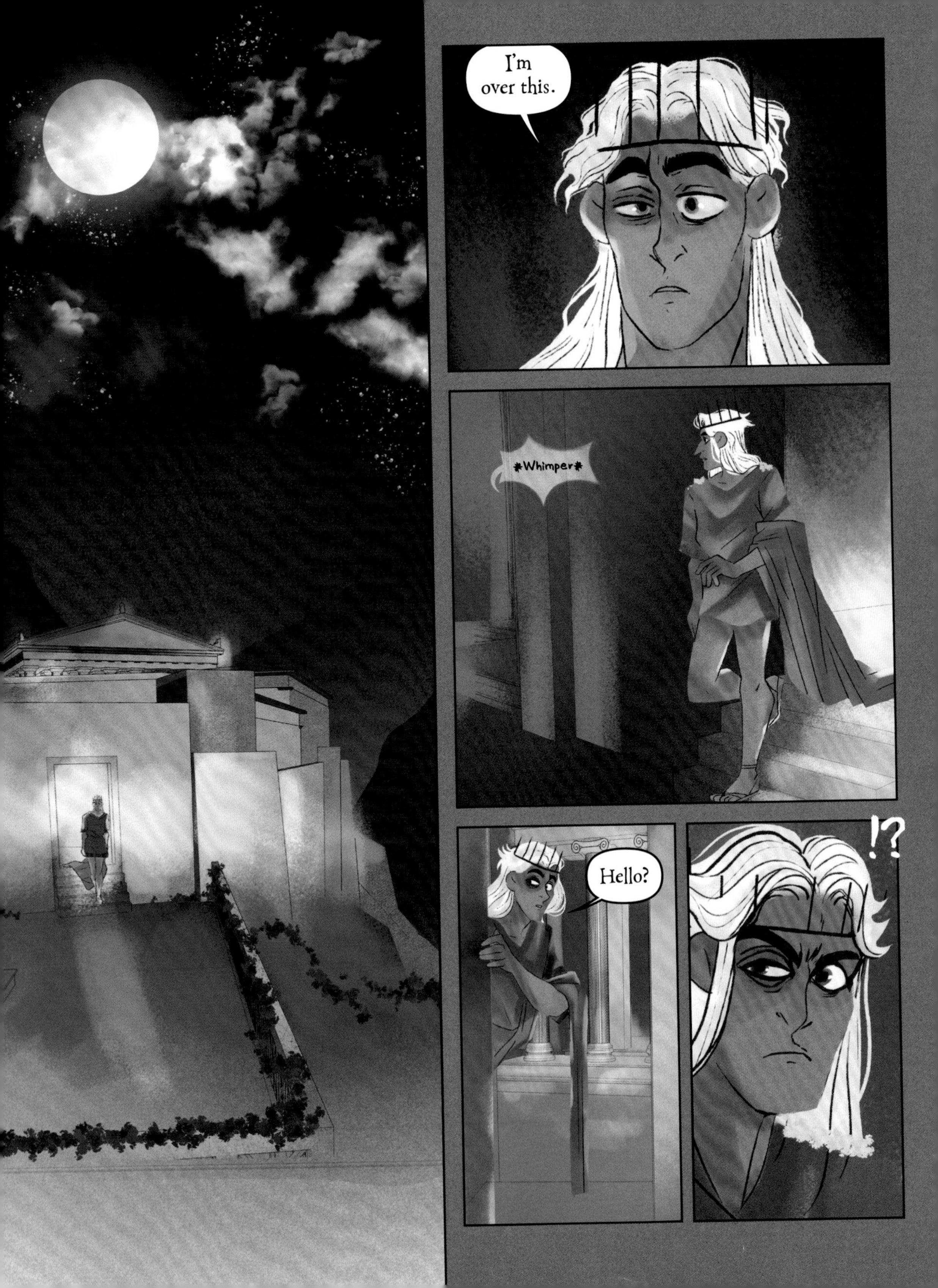
I'm over this.
Whimper
Hello?
!?

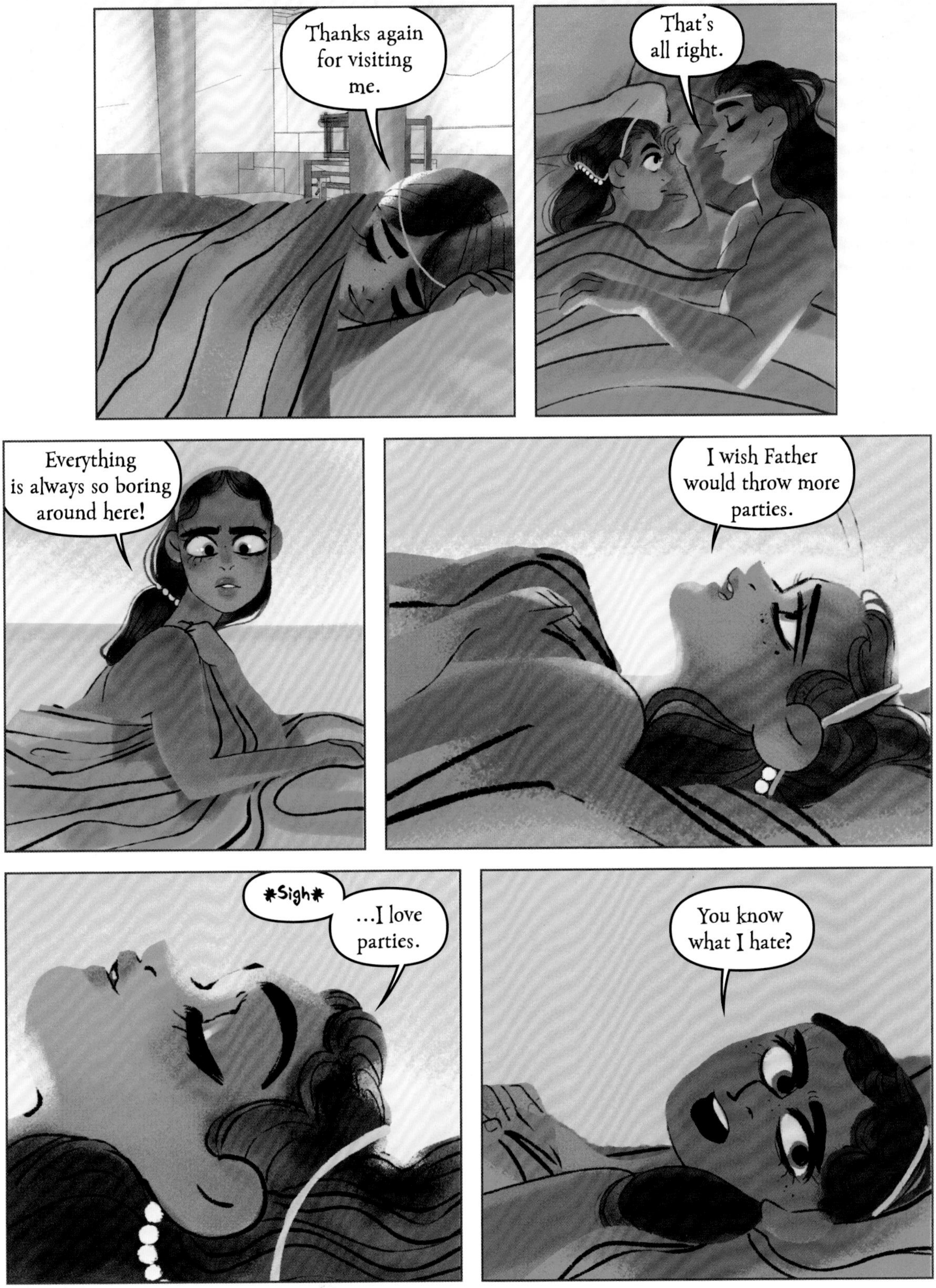

Thanks again for visiting me.
That's all right.
Everything is always so boring around here!
I wish Father would throw more parties.
Sigh
...I love parties.
You know what I hate?

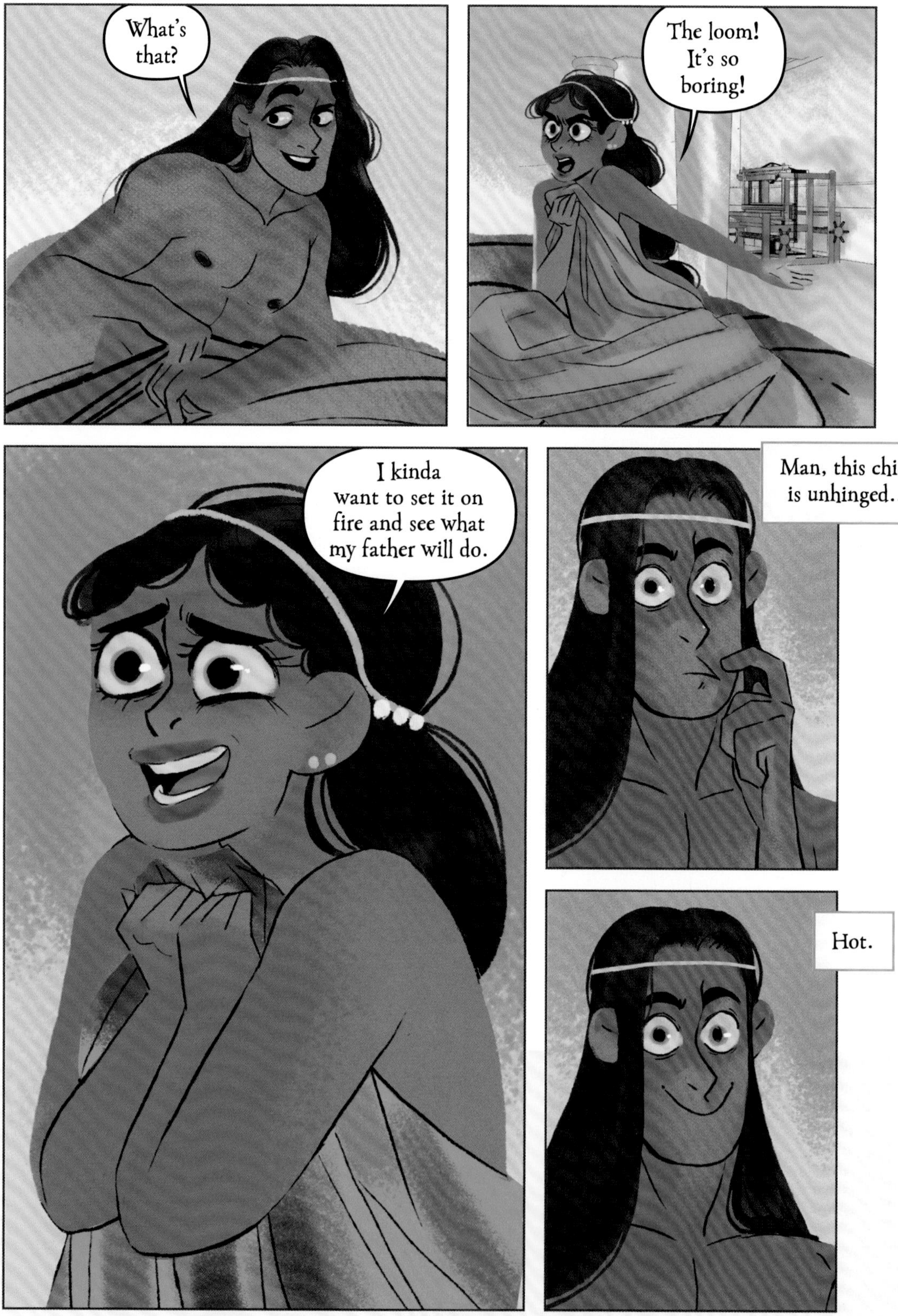
What's that?
The loom! It's so boring!
I kinda want to set it on fire and see what my father will do.
Man, this chick is unhinged...
Hot.

EPISODE 94: LITTLE BROTHER

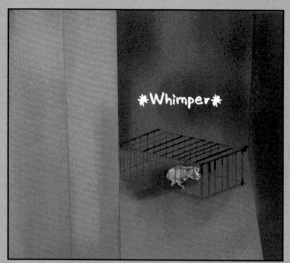

Whimper

…A dog?

A cage isn't a very nice place to be, is it?

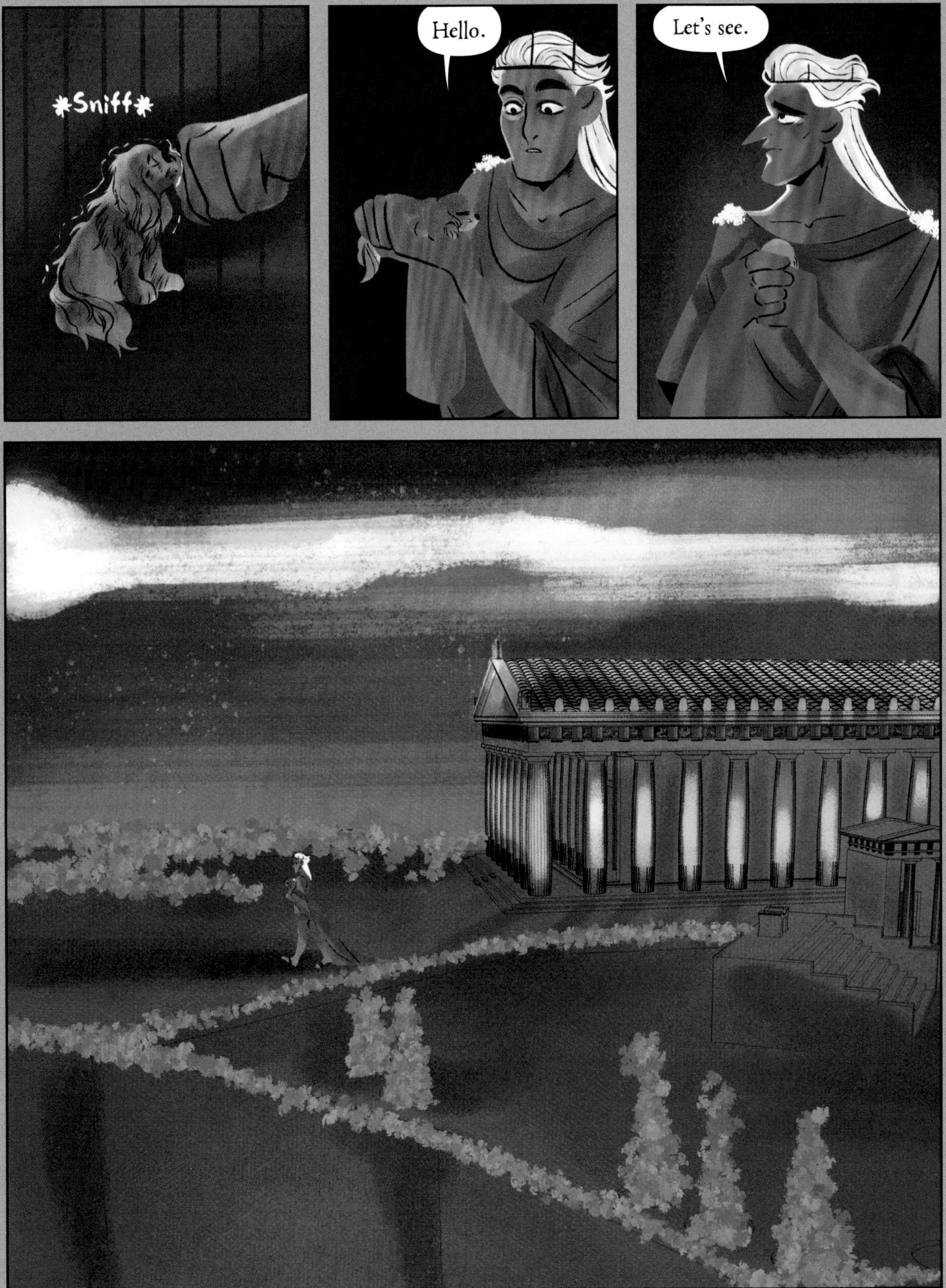
Sniff
Hello.
Let's see.

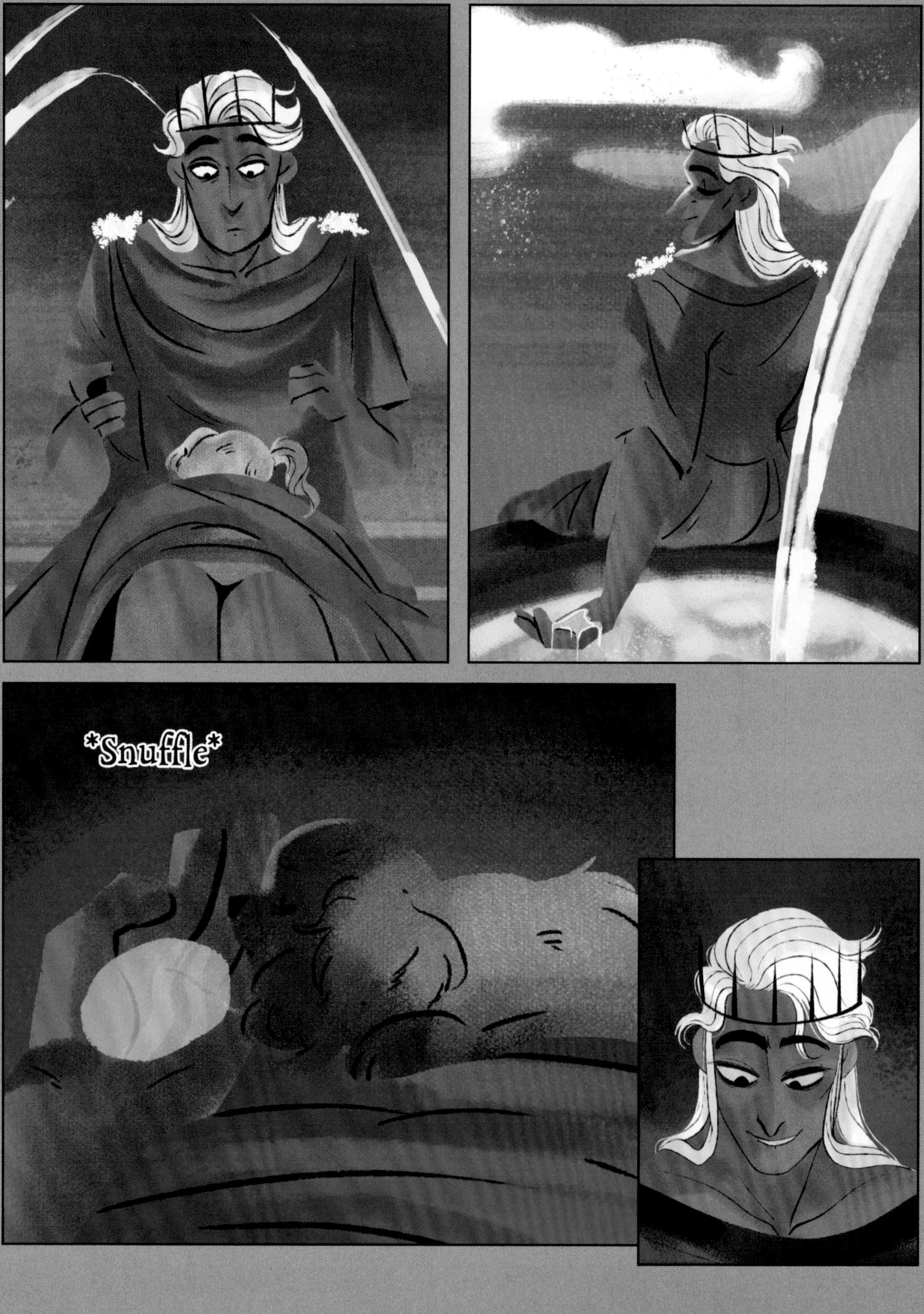
Snuffle

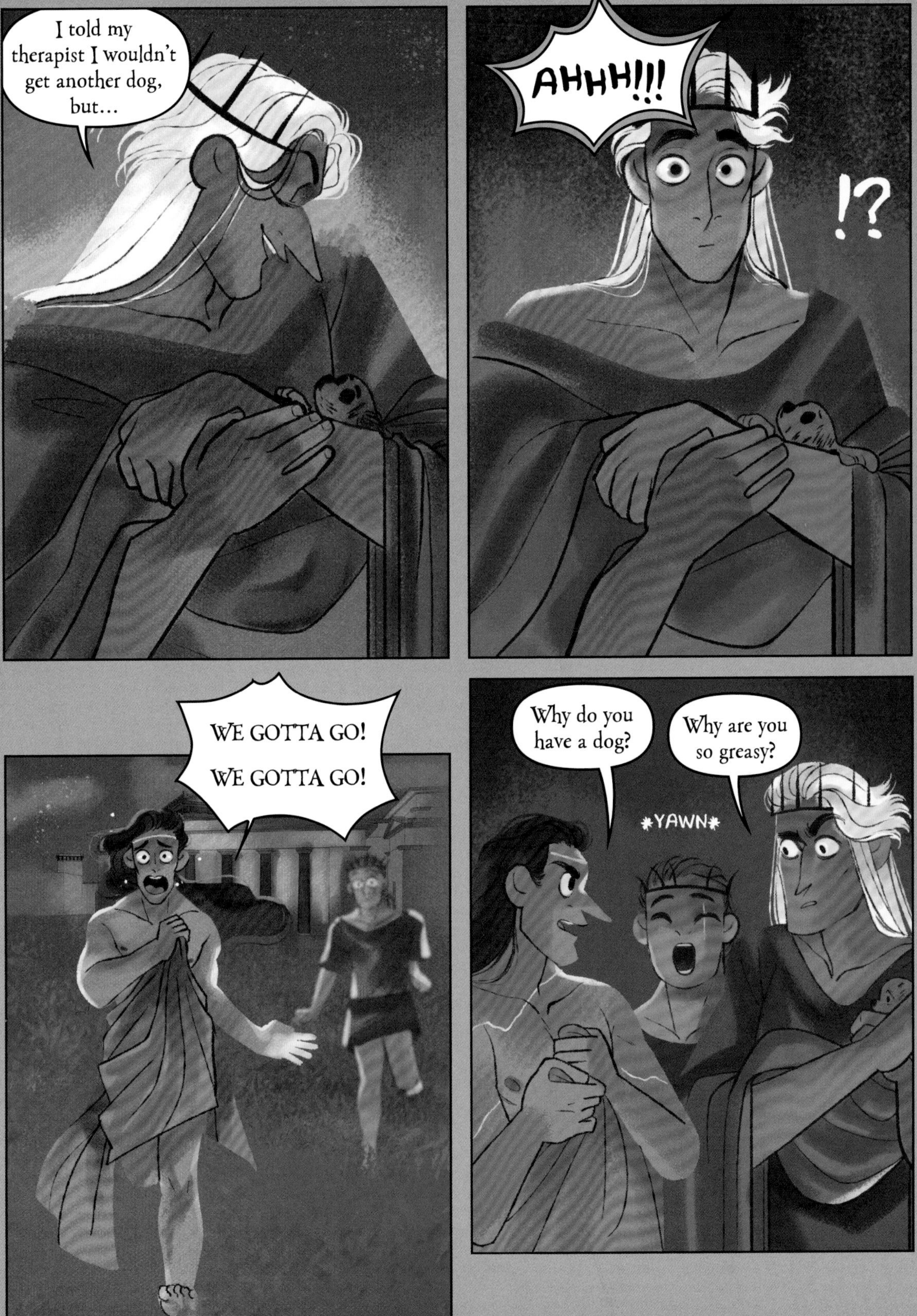
I told my therapist I wouldn't get another dog, but…
AHHH!!!
!?
WE GOTTA GO! WE GOTTA GO!
Why do you have a dog?
Why are you so greasy?
YAWN

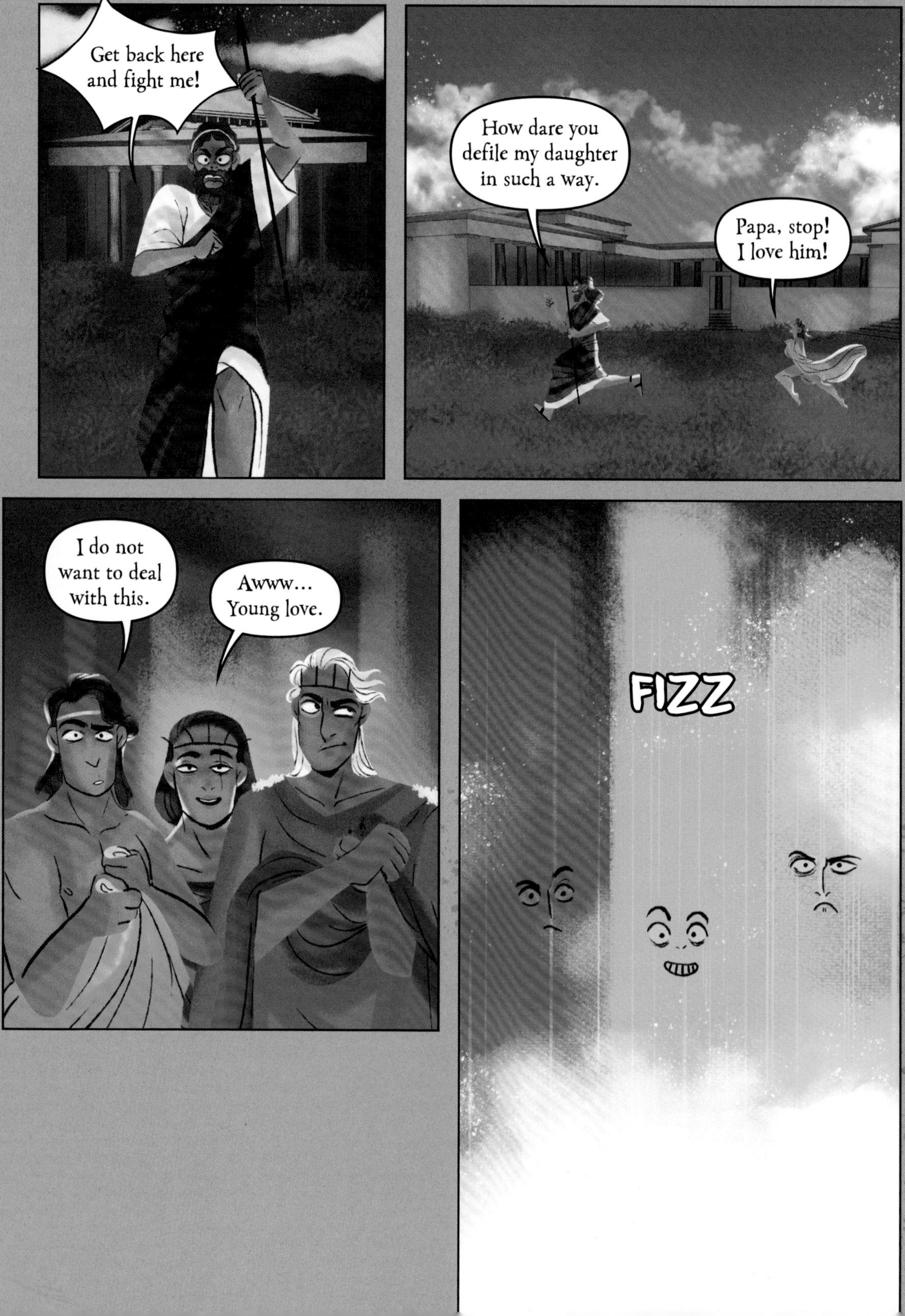
Get back here and fight me!
How dare you defile my daughter in such a way.
Papa, stop! I love him!
I do not want to deal with this.
Awww... Young love.
FIZZ

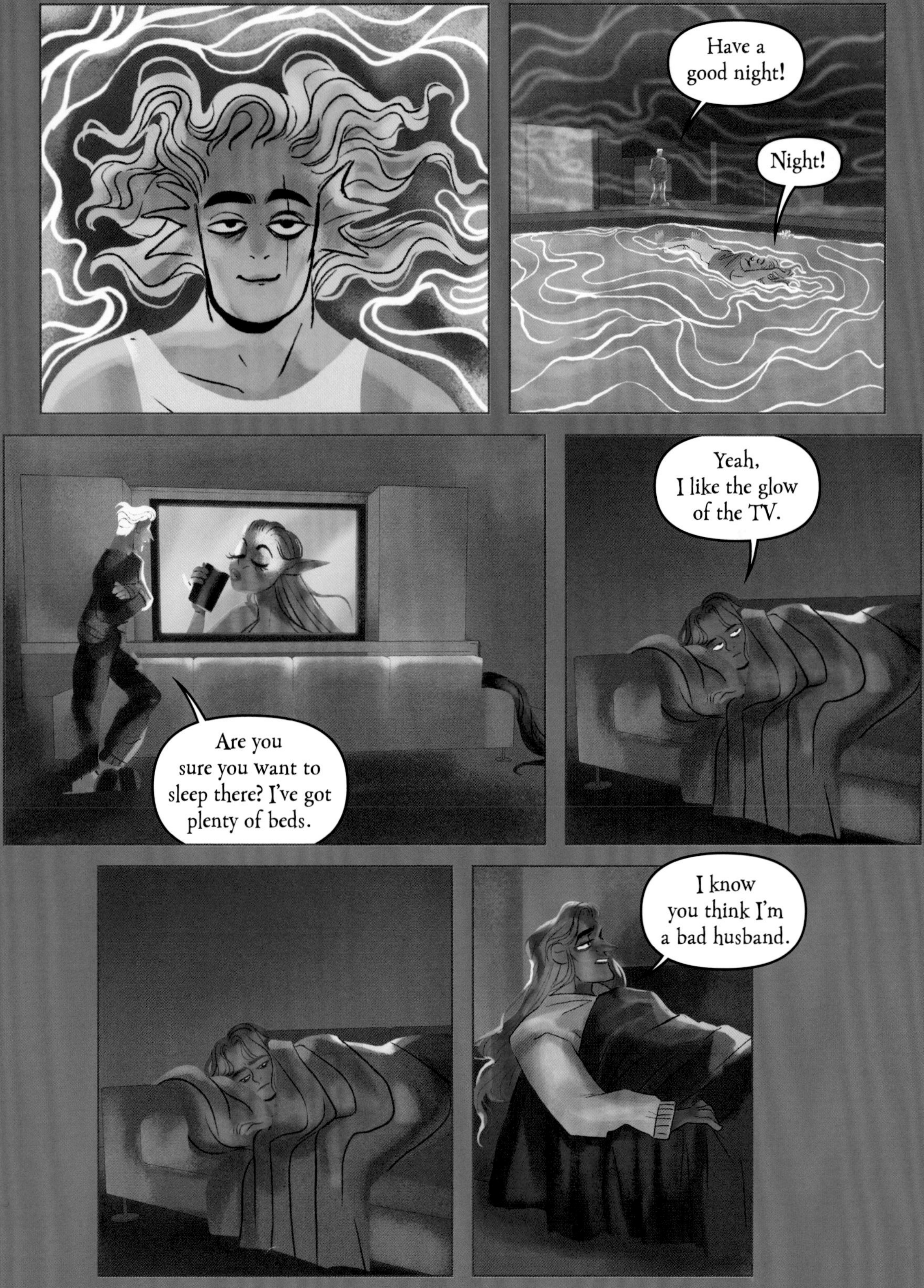
Have a good night!
Night!
Are you sure you want to sleep there? I've got plenty of beds.
Yeah, I like the glow of the TV.
I know you think I'm a bad husband.

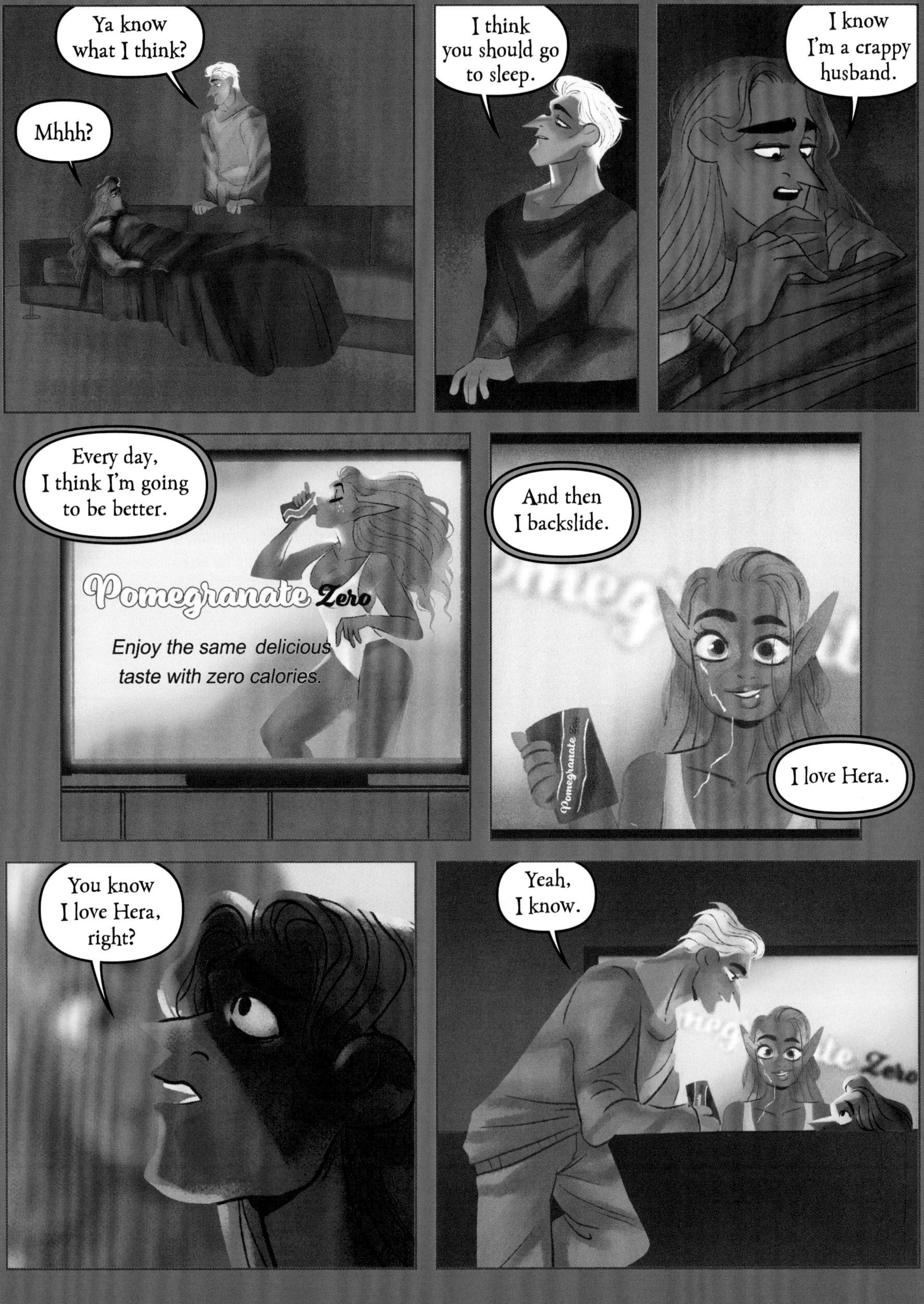
Ya know what I think?
Mhhh?
I think you should go to sleep.
I know I'm a crappy husband.
Every day, I think I'm going to be better.
Pomegranate Zero
Enjoy the same delicious taste with zero calories.
And then I backslide.
Pomegranate Zero
I love Hera.
You know I love Hera, right?
Yeah, I know.

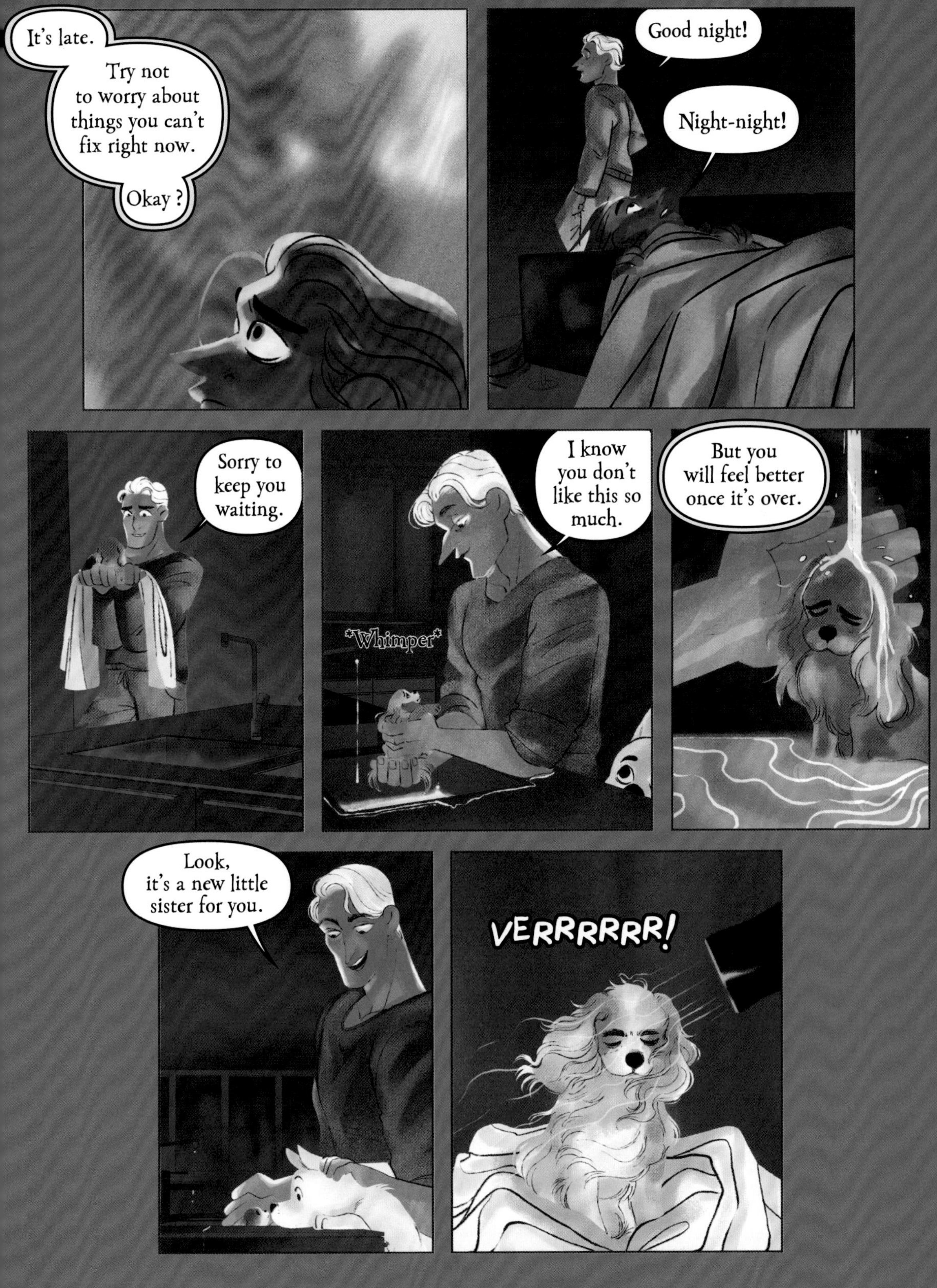
It's late.
Try not to worry about things you can't fix right now.
Okay ?
Good night!
Night-night!
Sorry to keep you waiting.
I know you don't like this so much.
Whimper
But you will feel better once it's over.
Look, it's a new little sister for you.
VERRRRRR!

There, all finished.

Ah, I bet Persephone would love you!

I probably shouldn't text her right now...

FLOP!

I forgot about that stuff.

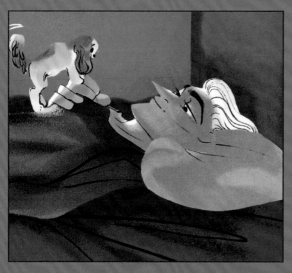

SMALLER FLOP!

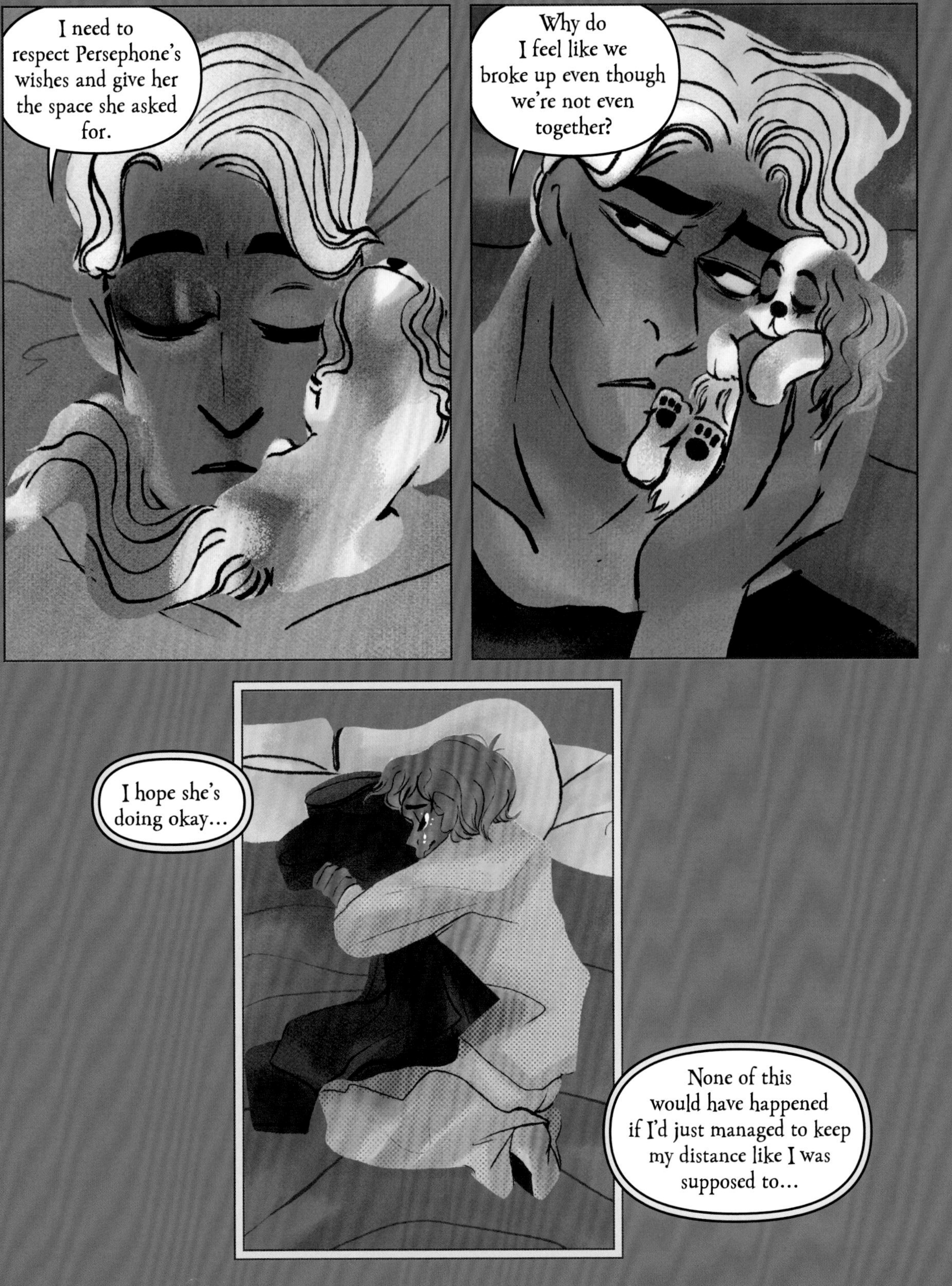
I need to respect Persephone's wishes and give her the space she asked for.
Why do I feel like we broke up even though we're not even together?
I hope she's doing okay...
None of this would have happened if I'd just managed to keep my distance like I was supposed to...

One thing is still really bothering me, though.

Persephone is frightened of Apollo.

Why?

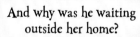

And why was he waiting outside her home?

Was it a one-time thing?

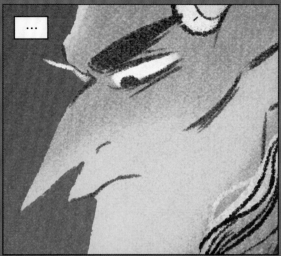

...

...Or does it happen all the time?

Apollo
Today at 11:15 a.m.

Get to hang with this cutie today! 🥰🥰🥰 #Blessed

Daphne
Lucky!

Persephone
Can you take this down?

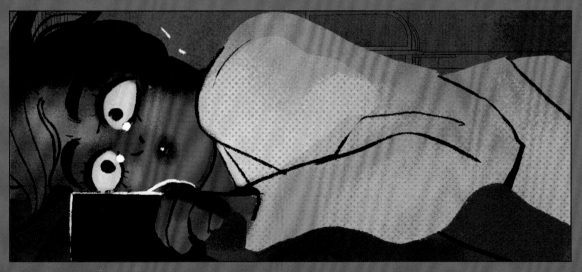

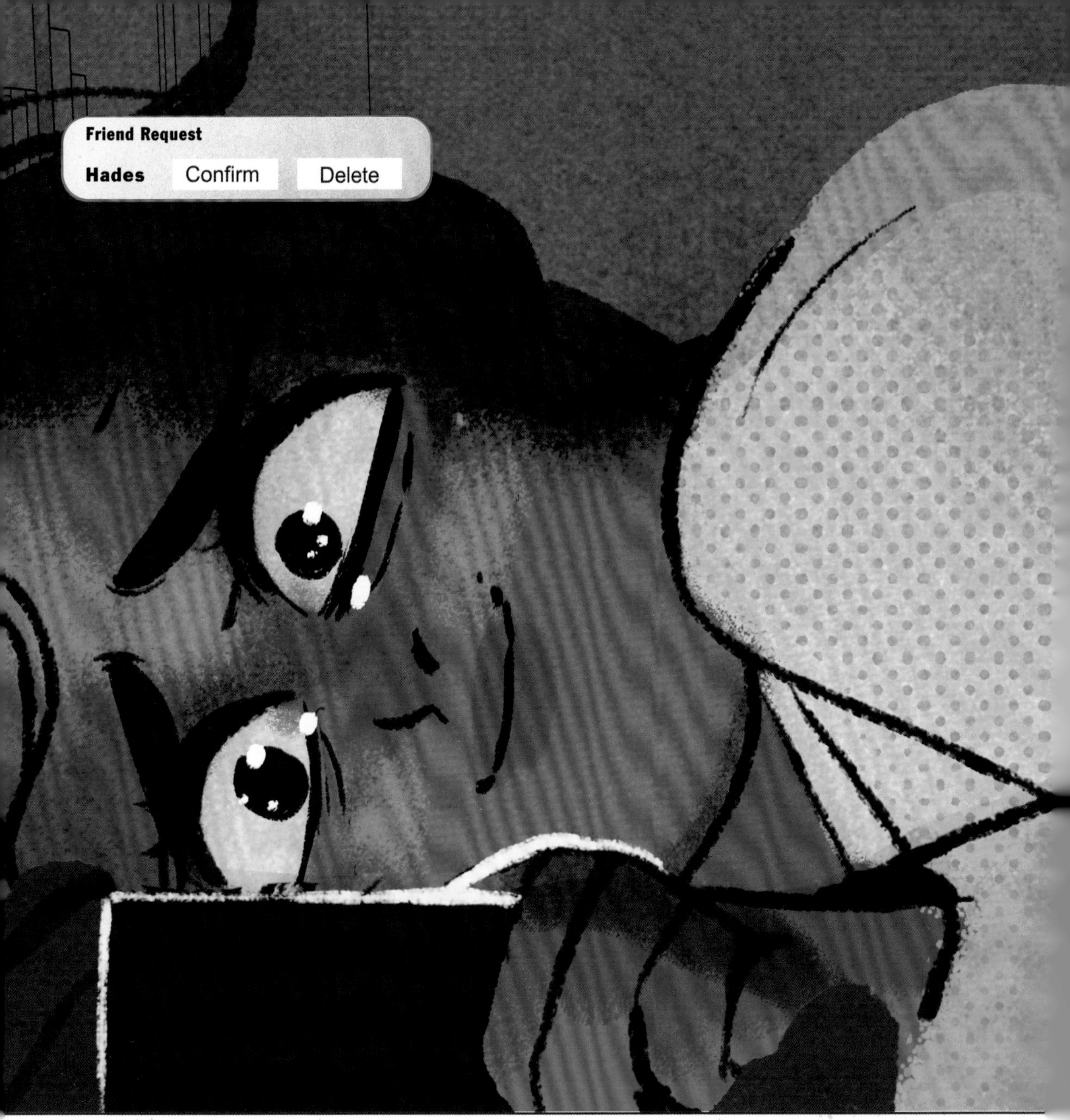
Friend Request
Hades Confirm Delete

I hope she still knows
I would help her, no
matter what.

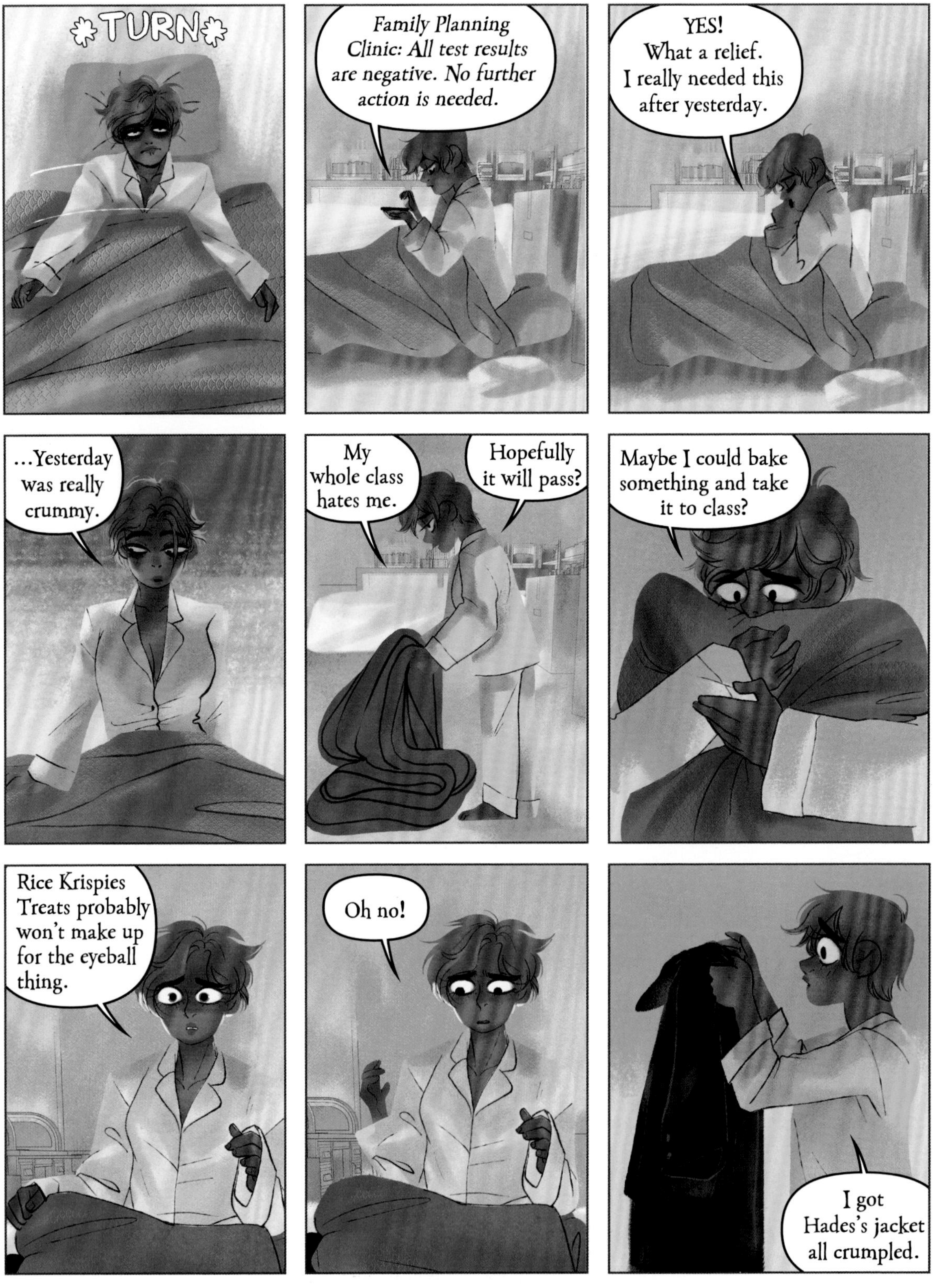
TURN
Family Planning Clinic: All test results are negative. No further action is needed.
YES! What a relief. I really needed this after yesterday.
...Yesterday was really crummy.
My whole class hates me.
Hopefully it will pass?
Maybe I could bake something and take it to class?
Rice Krispies Treats probably won't make up for the eyeball thing.
Oh no!
I got Hades's jacket all crumpled.

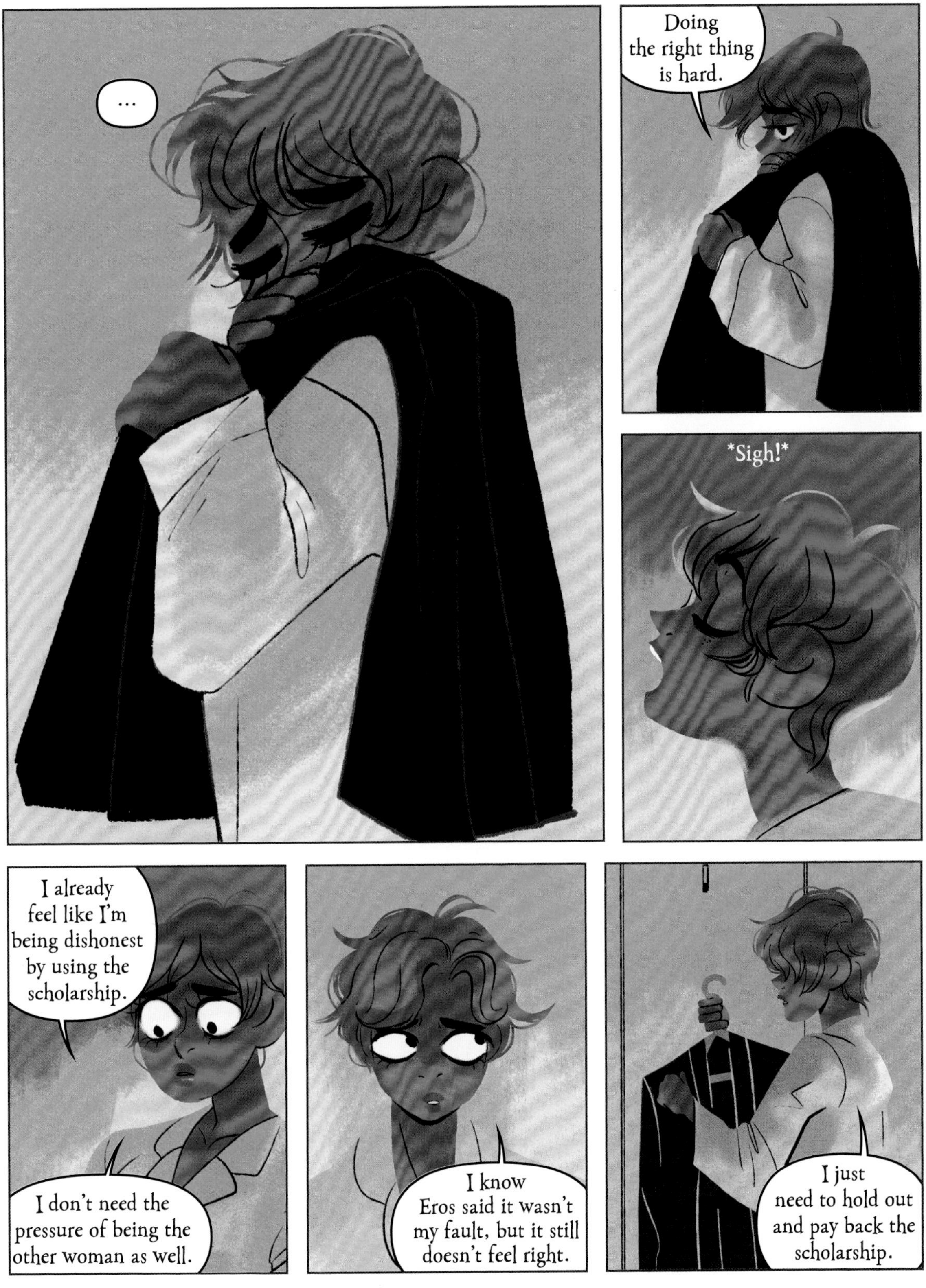
...
Doing the right thing is hard.
Sigh!
I already feel like I'm being dishonest by using the scholarship.
I don't need the pressure of being the other woman as well.
I know Eros said it wasn't my fault, but it still doesn't feel right.
I just need to hold out and pay back the scholarship.

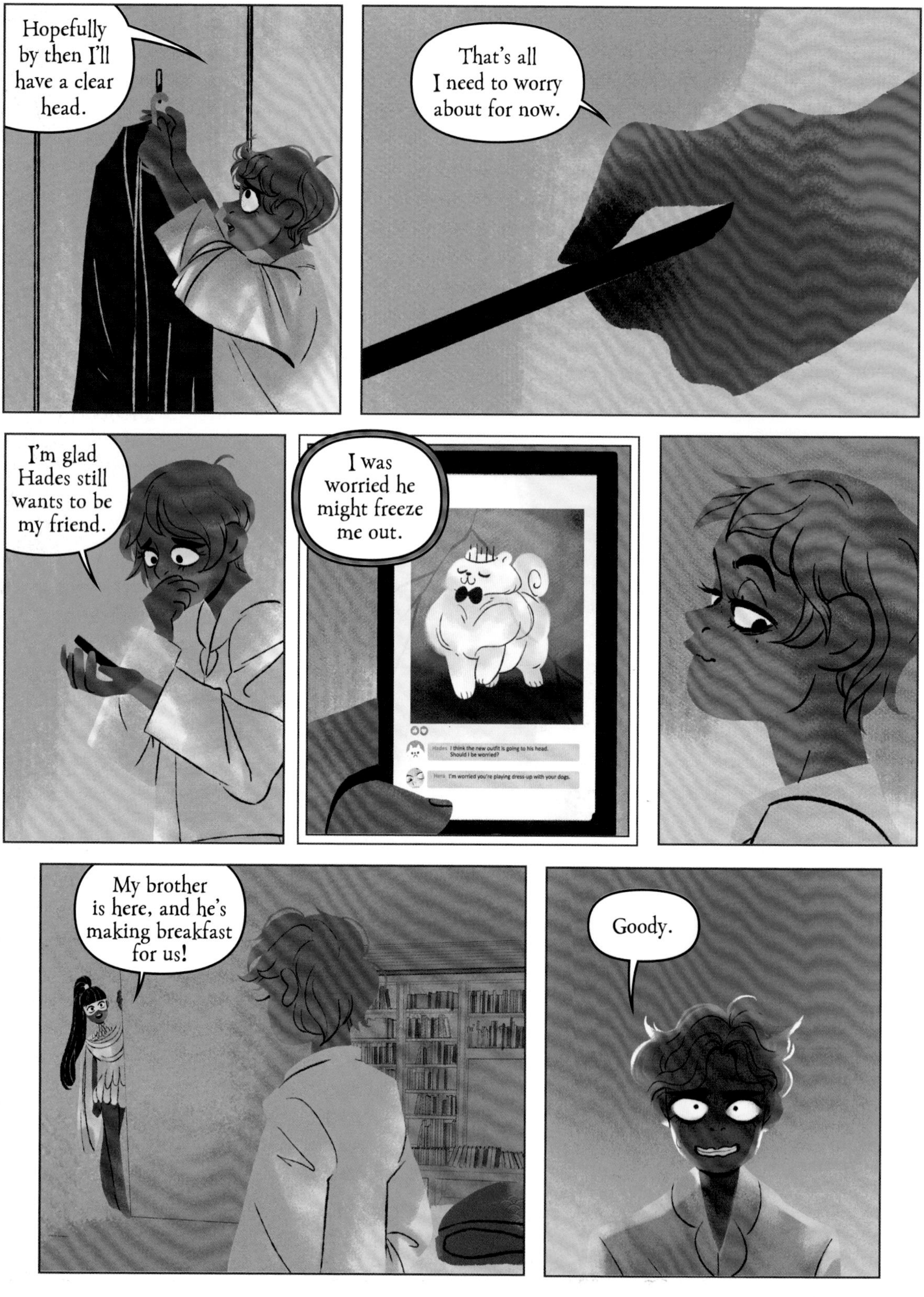
Hopefully by then I'll have a clear head.
That's all I need to worry about for now.
I'm glad Hades still wants to be my friend.
I was worried he might freeze me out.
Hades I think the new outfit is going to his head. Should I be worried?
Hera I'm worried you're playing dress-up with your dogs.
My brother is here, and he's making breakfast for us!
Goody.

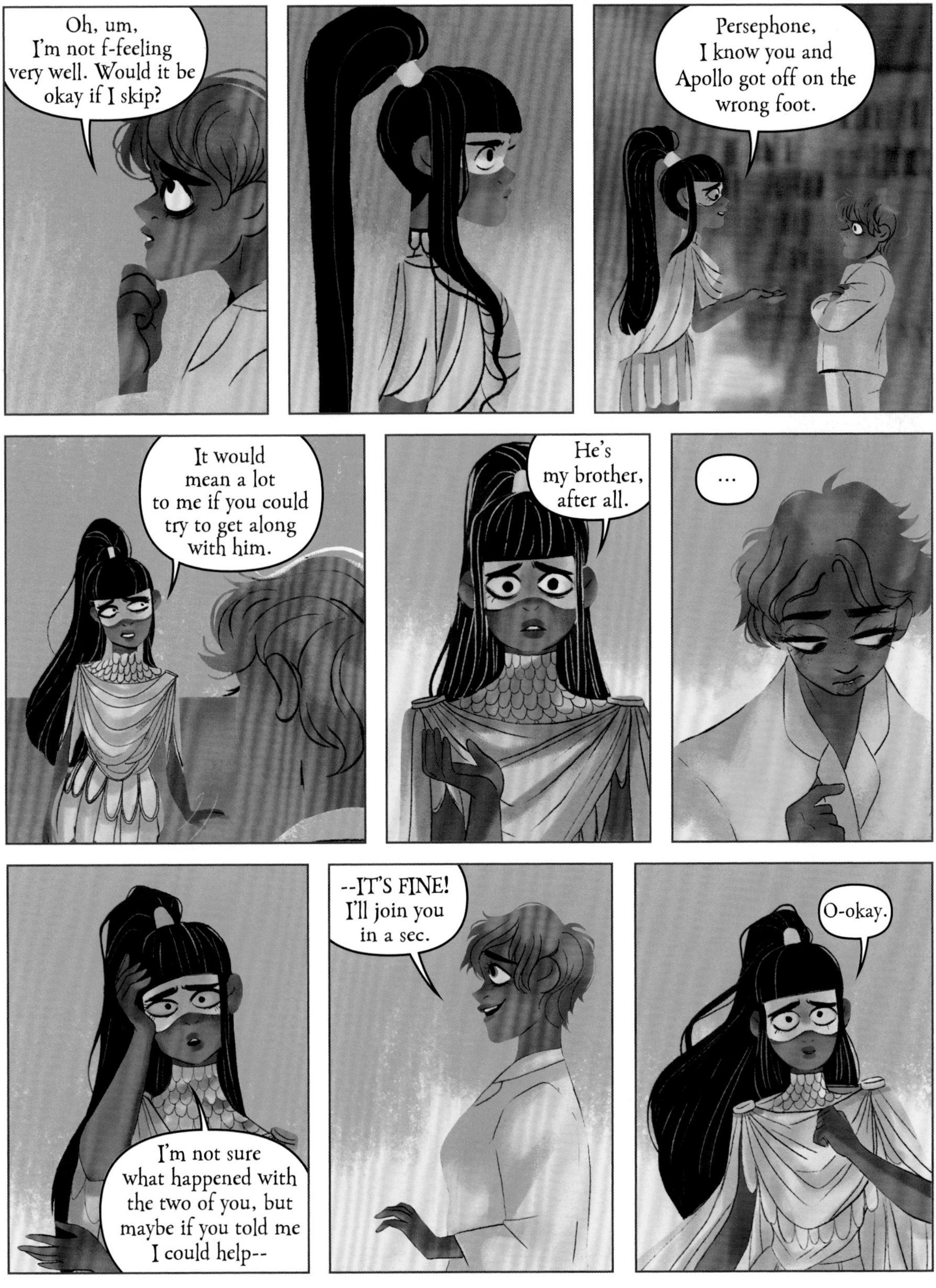
Oh, um, I'm not f-feeling very well. Would it be okay if I skip?
Persephone, I know you and Apollo got off on the wrong foot.
It would mean a lot to me if you could try to get along with him.
He's my brother, after all.
...
I'm not sure what happened with the two of you, but maybe if you told me I could help--
--IT'S FINE! I'll join you in a sec.
O-okay.

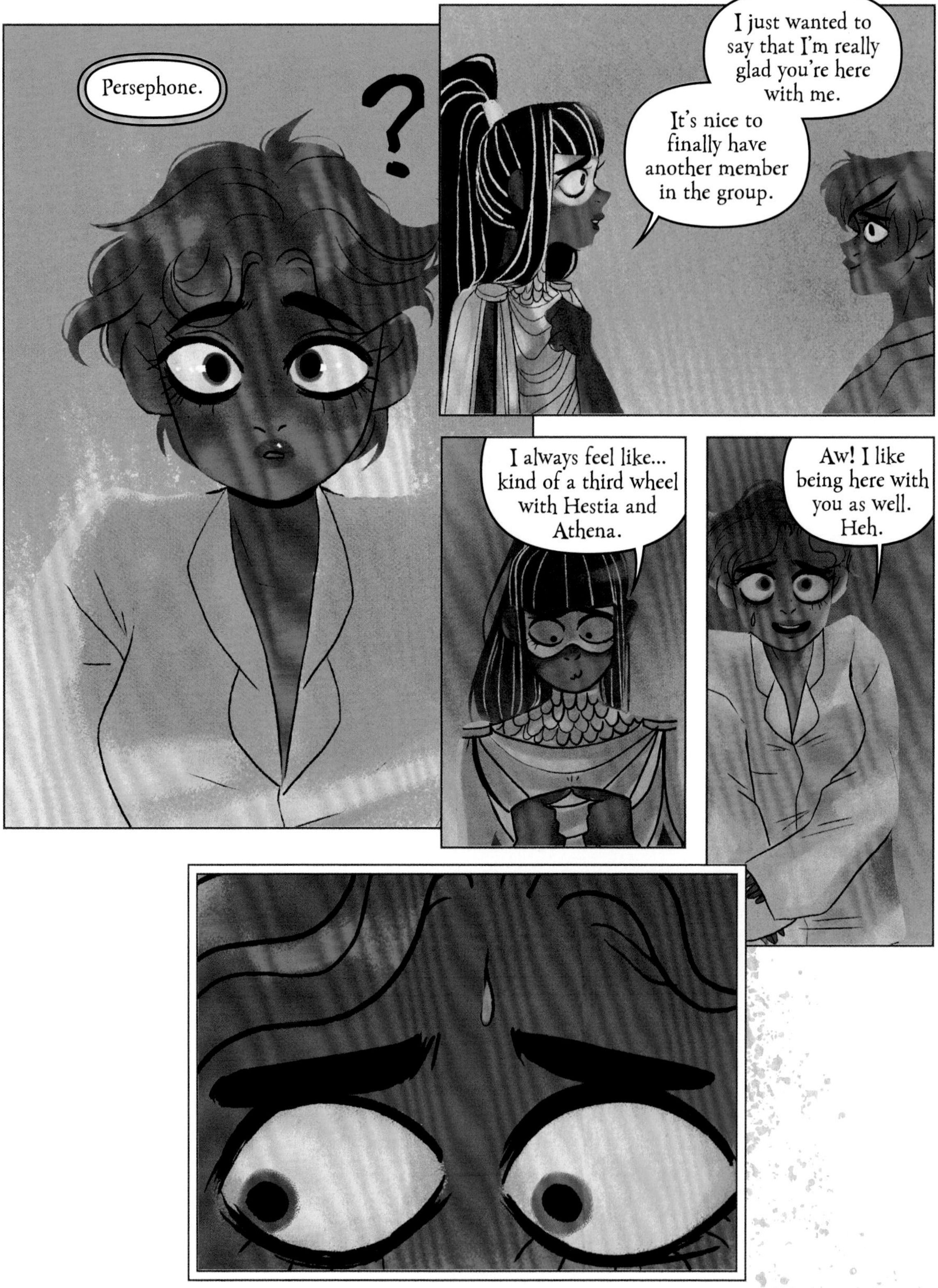
Persephone.
?
I just wanted to say that I'm really glad you're here with me.
It's nice to finally have another member in the group.
I always feel like... kind of a third wheel with Hestia and Athena.
Aw! I like being here with you as well. Heh.

EPISODE 95: AUDACITY

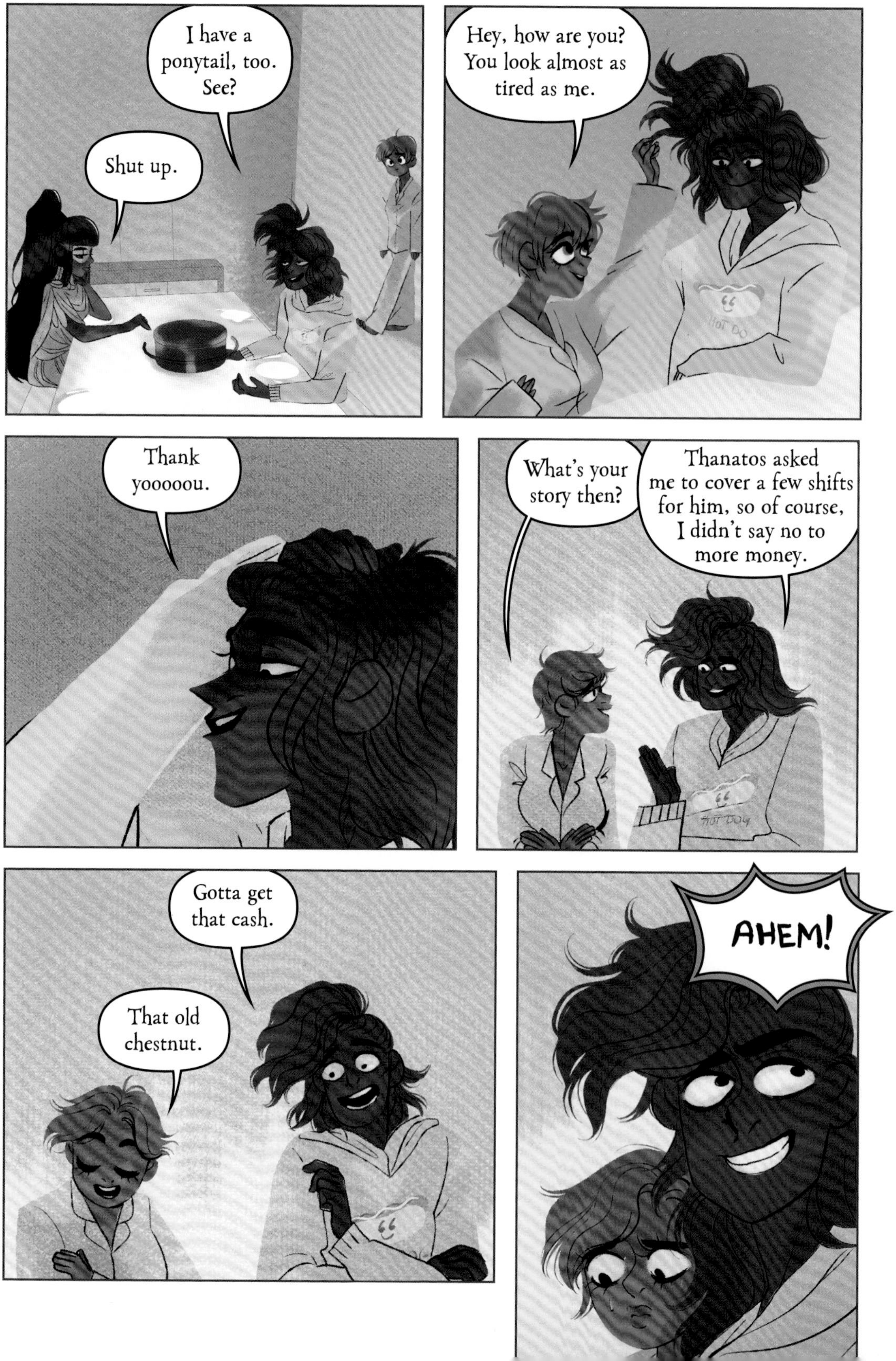
I have a ponytail, too. See?
Shut up.
Hey, how are you? You look almost as tired as me.
Thank yoooou.
What's your story then?
Thanatos asked me to cover a few shifts for him, so of course, I didn't say no to more money.
Gotta get that cash.
That old chestnut.
AHEM!

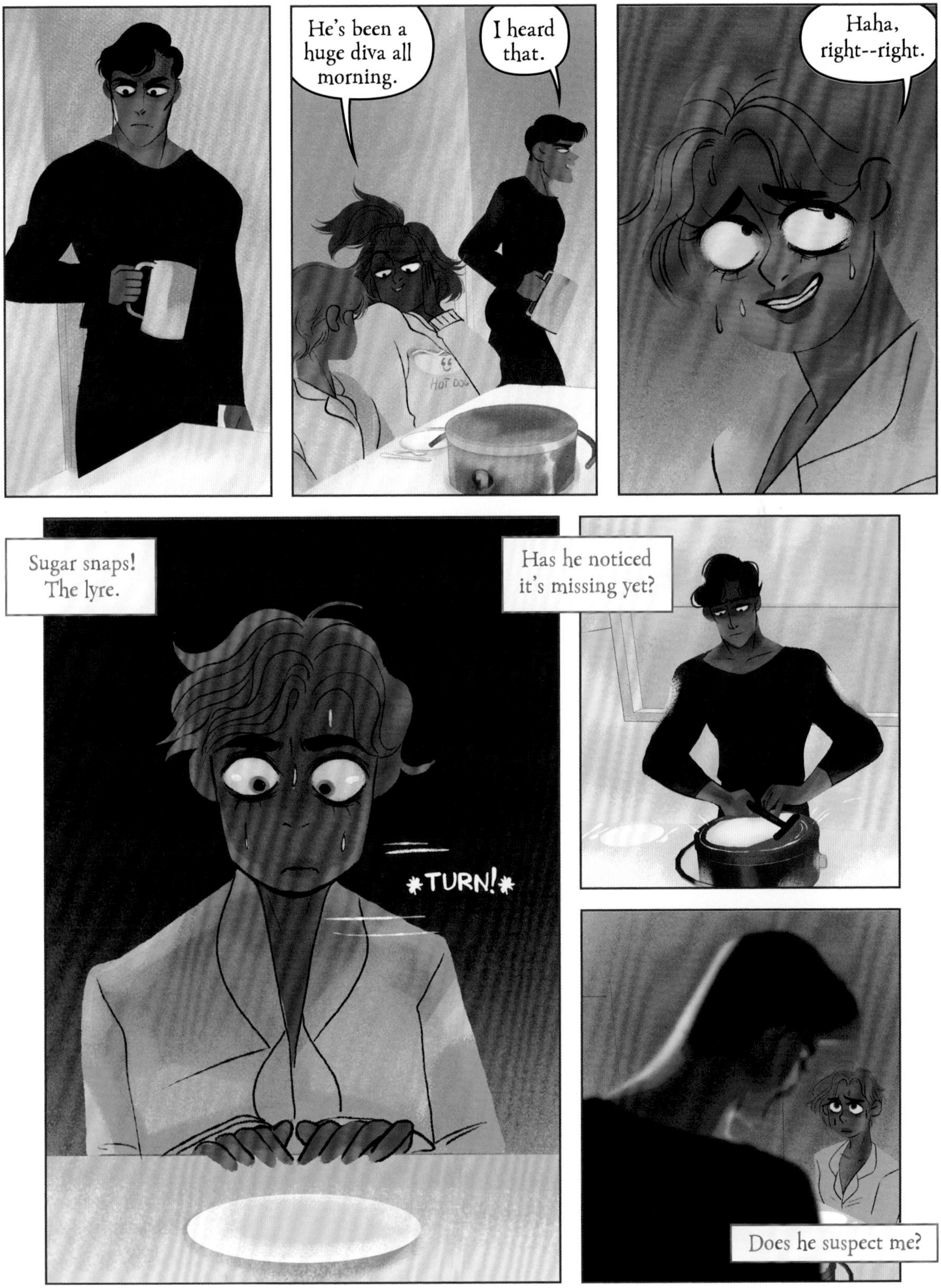
He's been a huge diva all morning.
I heard that.
HOT DOG
Haha, right--right.
Sugar snaps! The lyre.
TURN!
Has he noticed it's missing yet?
Does he suspect me?

This is weird.

GLANCE

Don't look so concerned. It's just a crepe.

Th-thanks.

...Maybe he is just trying to be nice?

All I have to do is eat this stupid crepe and then I can leave.

So good!

You can deal with this...

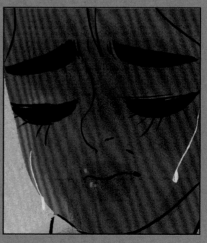

Chew

Chew

So good, right?

My brother is a man of many talents.

SWALLOW!

Yeah, de-delicious.

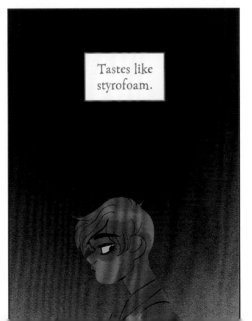

Tastes like styrofoam.

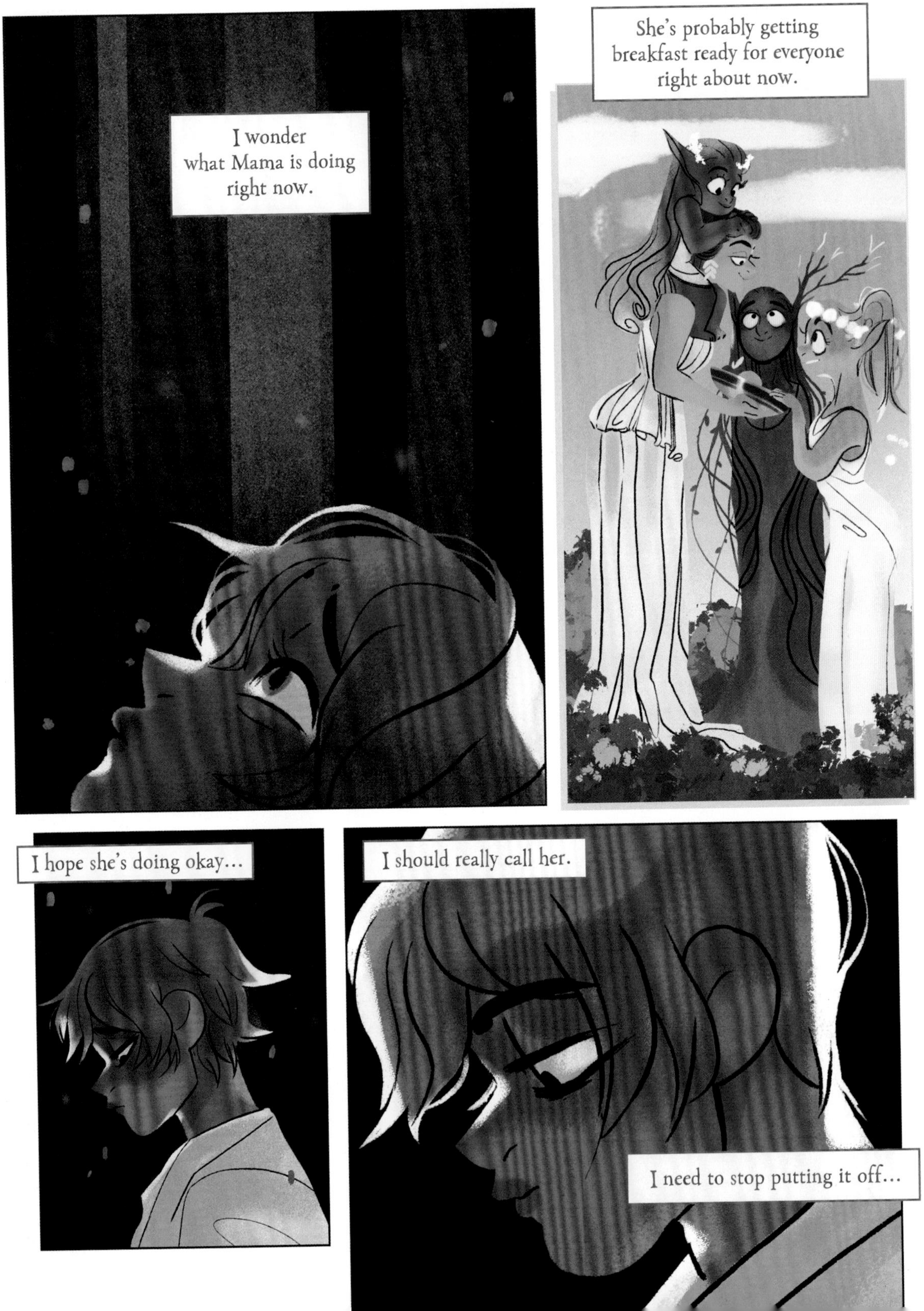
I wonder what Mama is doing right now.
She's probably getting breakfast ready for everyone right about now.
I hope she's doing okay...
I should really call her.
I need to stop putting it off...

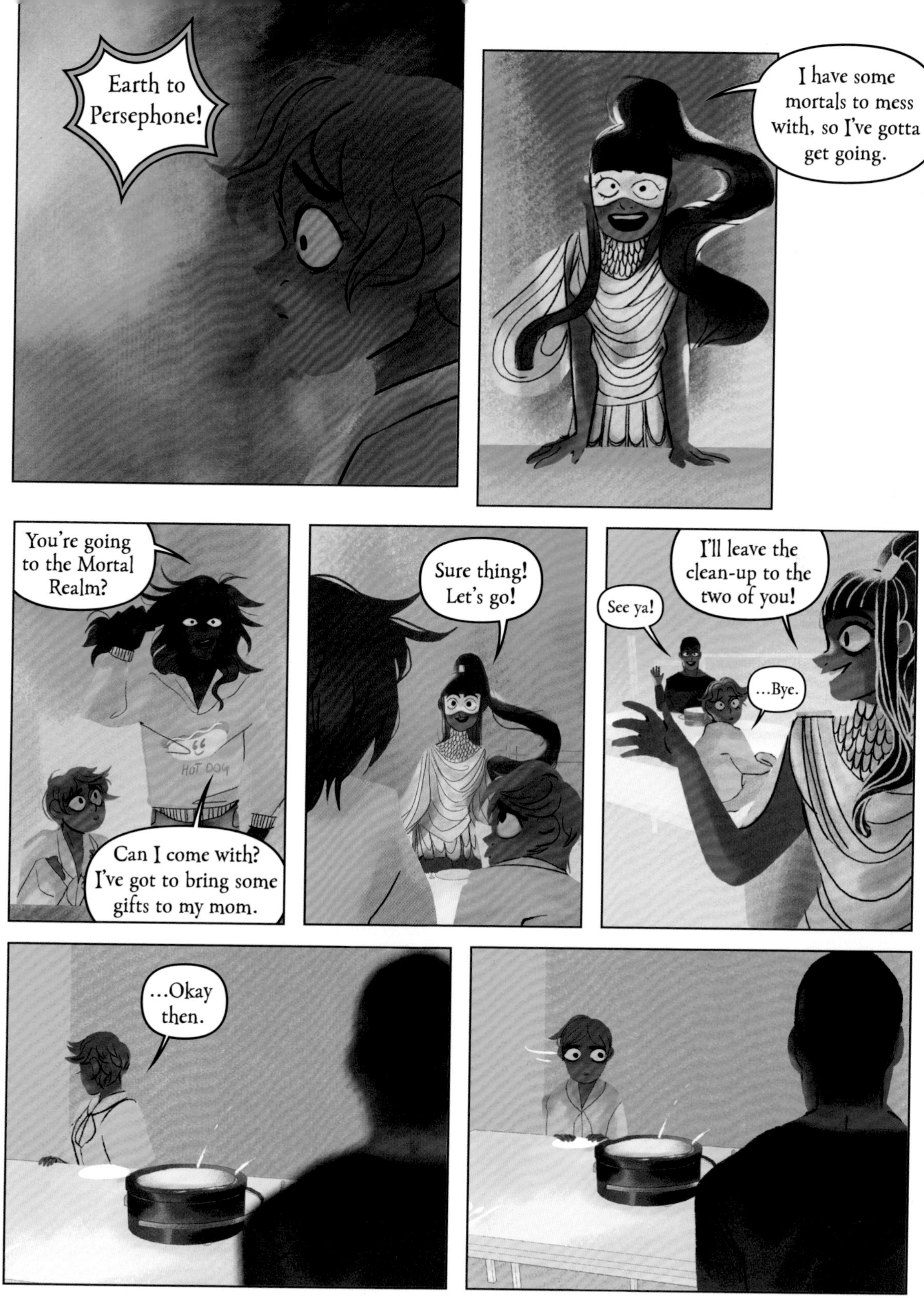
Earth to Persephone!
I have some mortals to mess with, so I've gotta get going.
You're going to the Mortal Realm?
HOT DOG
Can I come with? I've got to bring some gifts to my mom.
Sure thing! Let's go!
I'll leave the clean-up to the two of you!
See ya!
...Bye.
...Okay then.

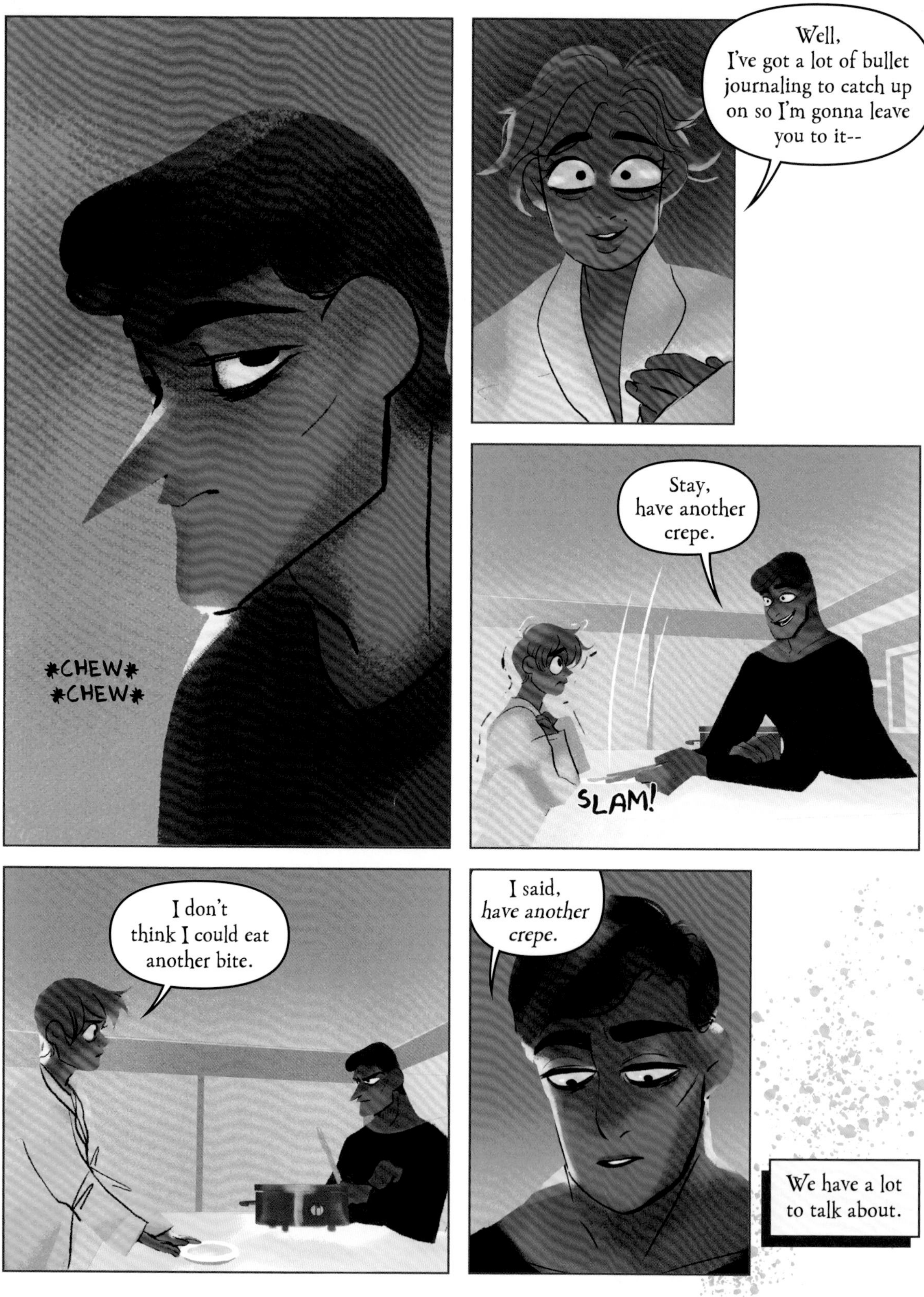
CHEW
CHEW
Well,
I've got a lot of bullet journaling to catch up on so I'm gonna leave you to it--
Stay, have another crepe.
SLAM!
I don't think I could eat another bite.
I said, *have another crepe.*
We have a lot to talk about.

EPISODE 96: MAMA

What should I do?

...What would Mama do?

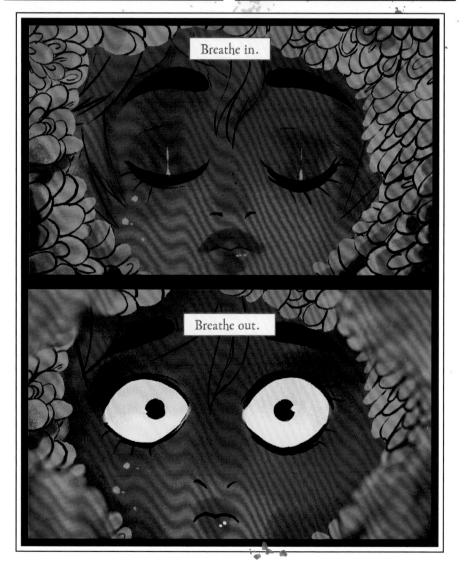

Breathe in.

Breathe out.

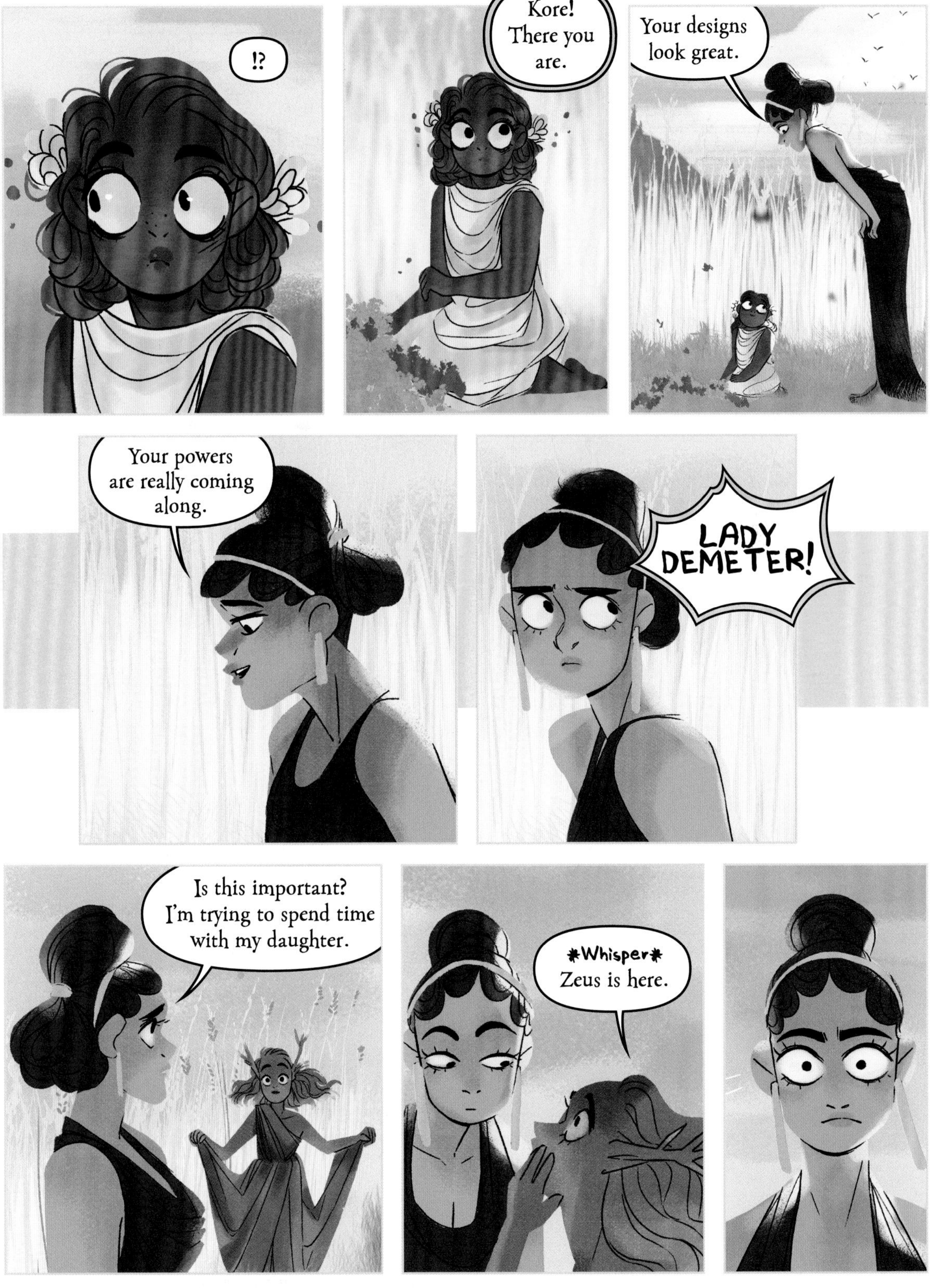
!?
Kore! There you are.
Your designs look great.
Your powers are really coming along.
LADY DEMETER!
Is this important? I'm trying to spend time with my daughter.
Whisper Zeus is here.

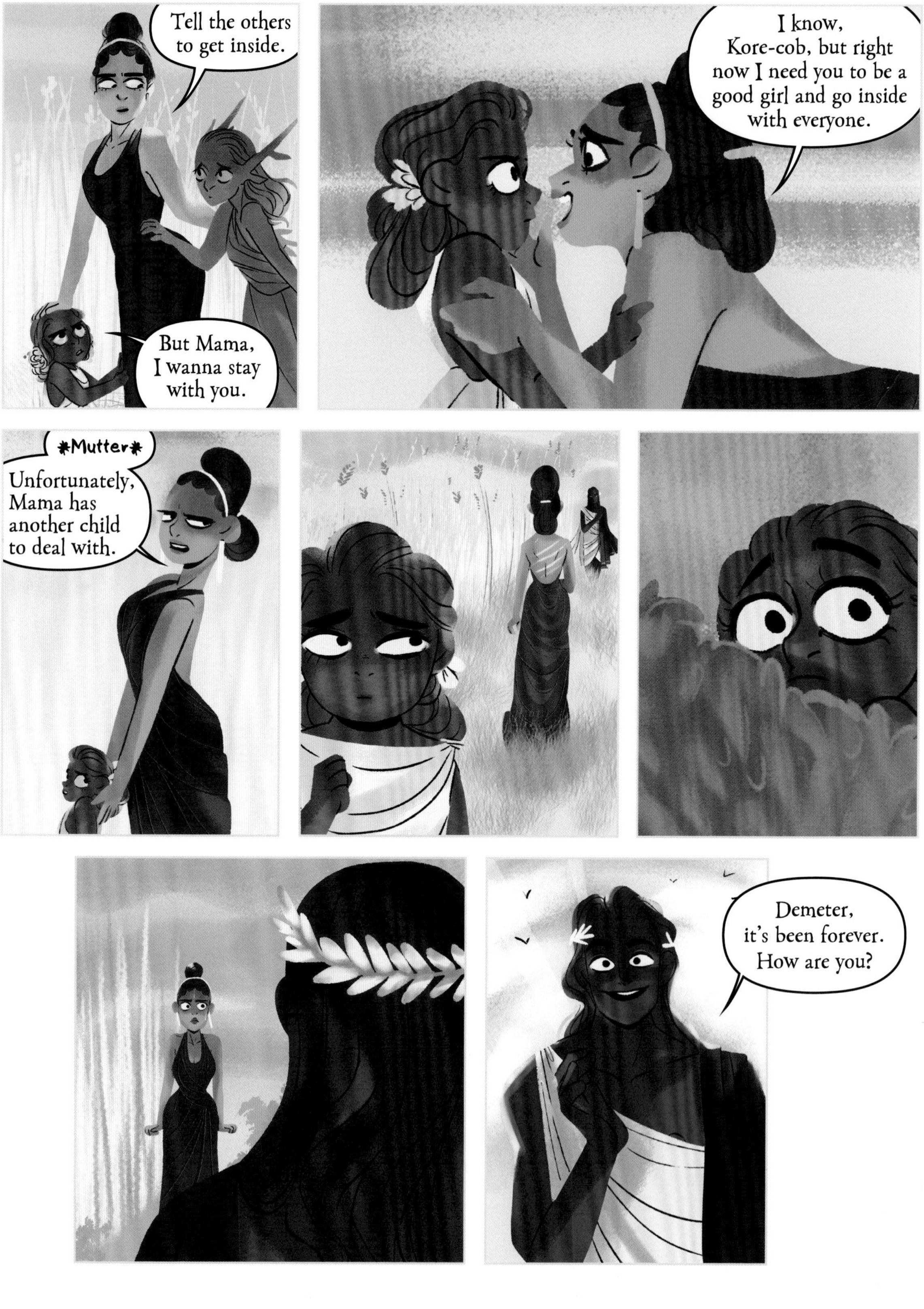
Tell the others to get inside.
But Mama, I wanna stay with you.
I know, Kore-cob, but right now I need you to be a good girl and go inside with everyone.
Mutter
Unfortunately, Mama has another child to deal with.
Demeter, it's been forever. How are you?

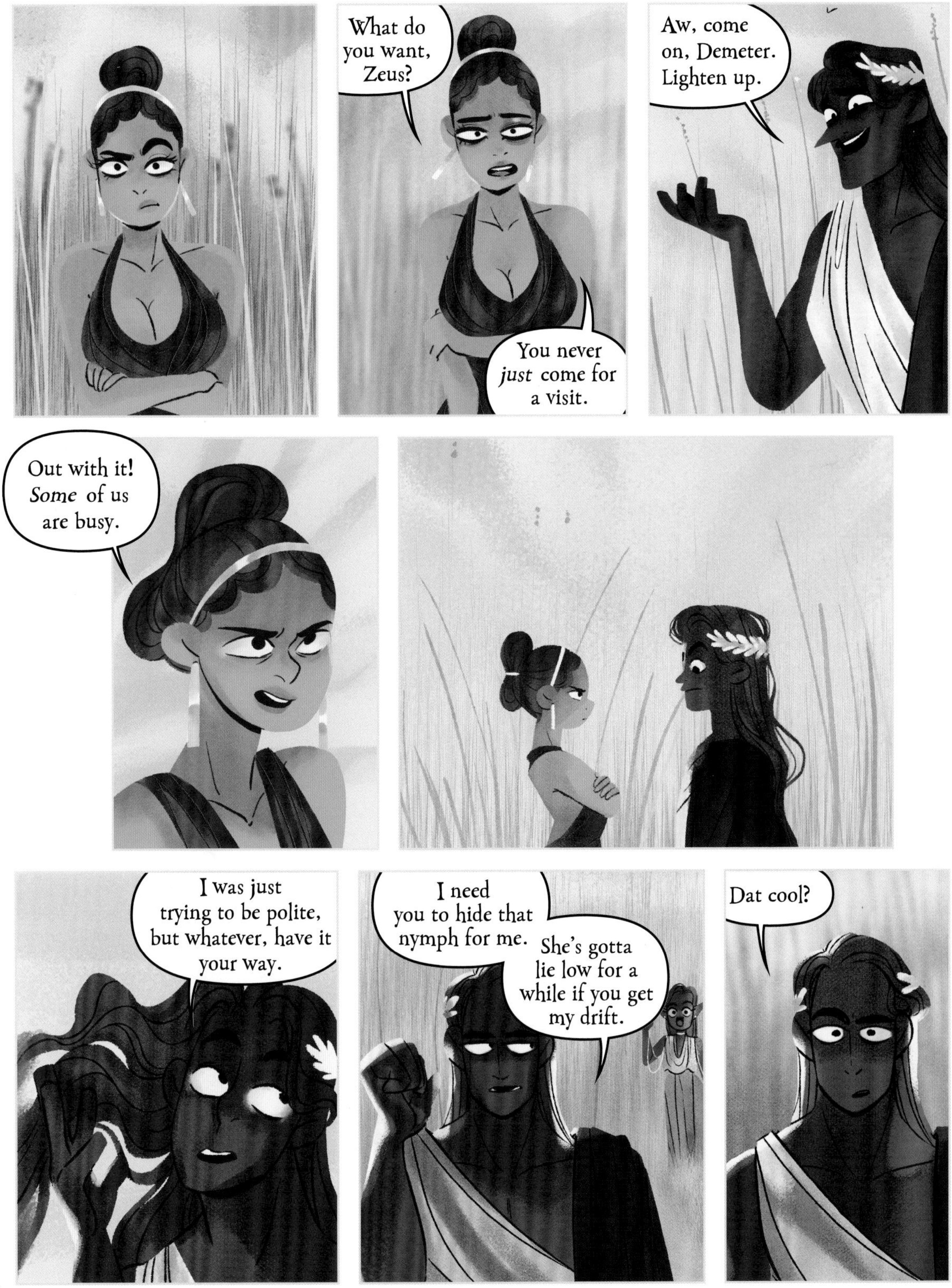
What do you want, Zeus?
You never *just* come for a visit.
Aw, come on, Demeter. Lighten up.
Out with it! *Some* of us are busy.
I was just trying to be polite, but whatever, have it your way.
I need you to hide that nymph for me.
She's gotta lie low for a while if you get my drift.
Dat cool?

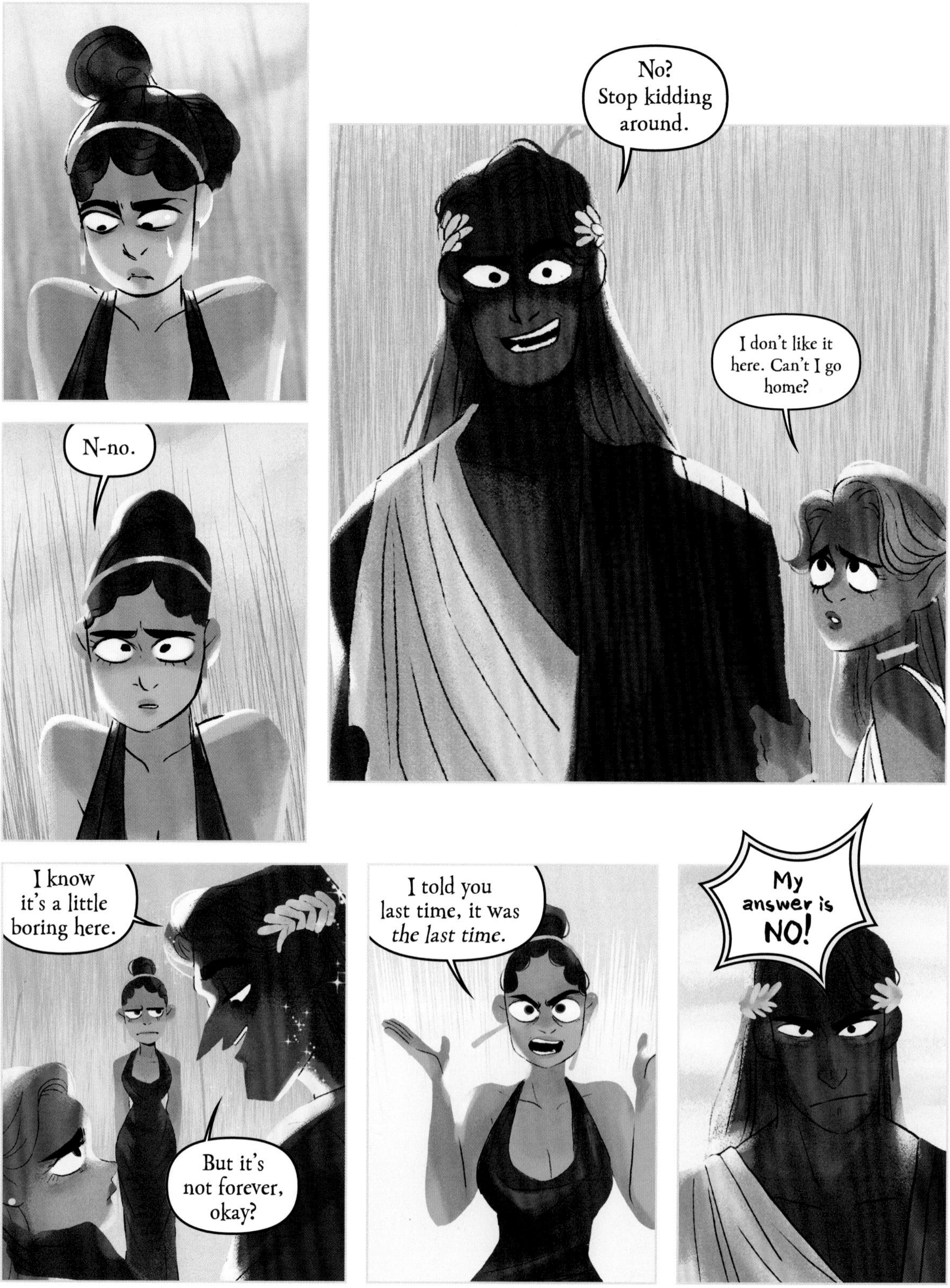
N-no.
No? Stop kidding around.
I don't like it here. Can't I go home?
I know it's a little boring here.
But it's not forever, okay?
I told you last time, it was *the last time.*
My answer is NO!

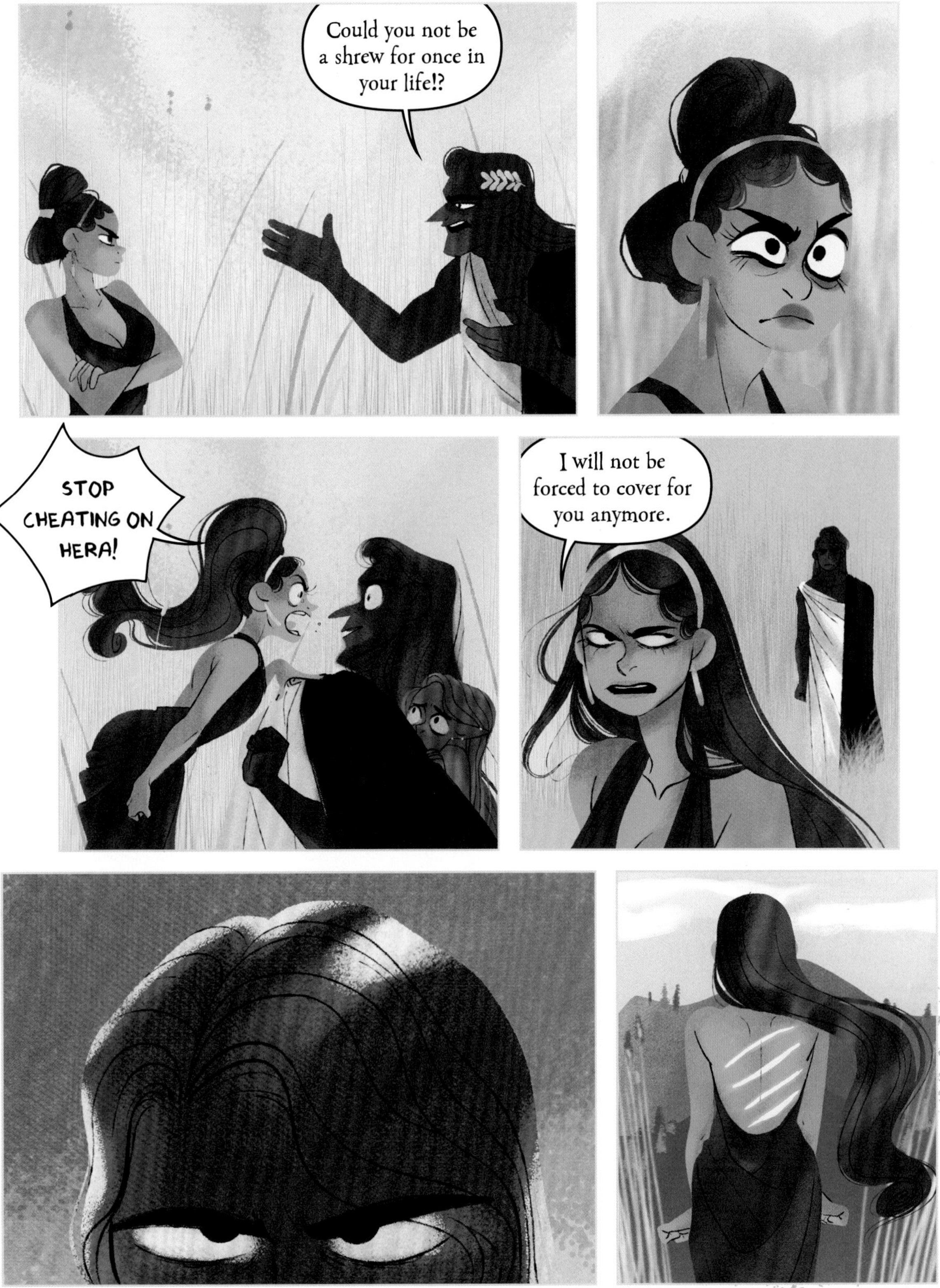
Could you not be a shrew for once in your life!?
STOP CHEATING ON HERA!
I will not be forced to cover for you anymore.

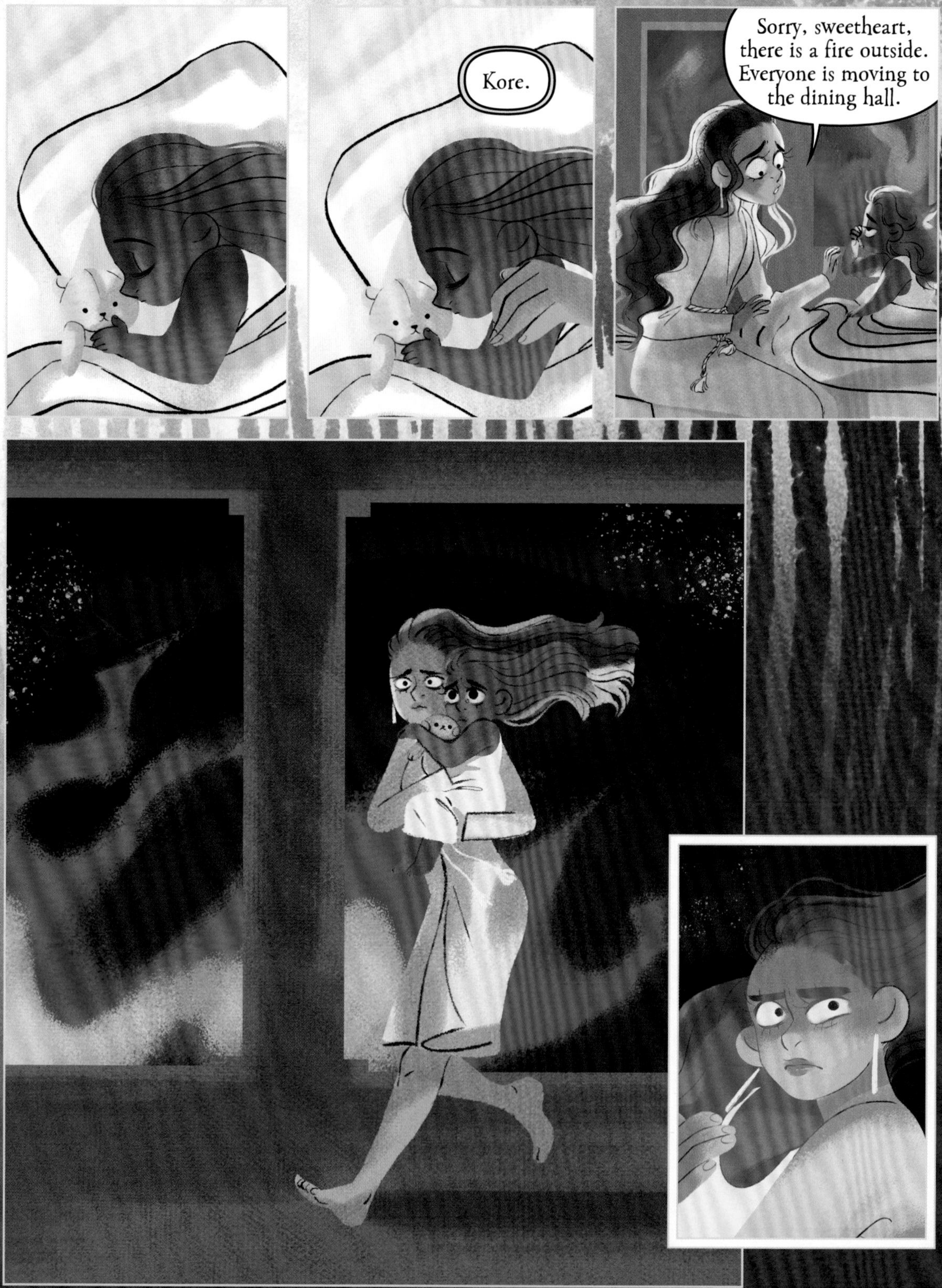
Kore.
Sorry, sweetheart, there is a fire outside. Everyone is moving to the dining hall.

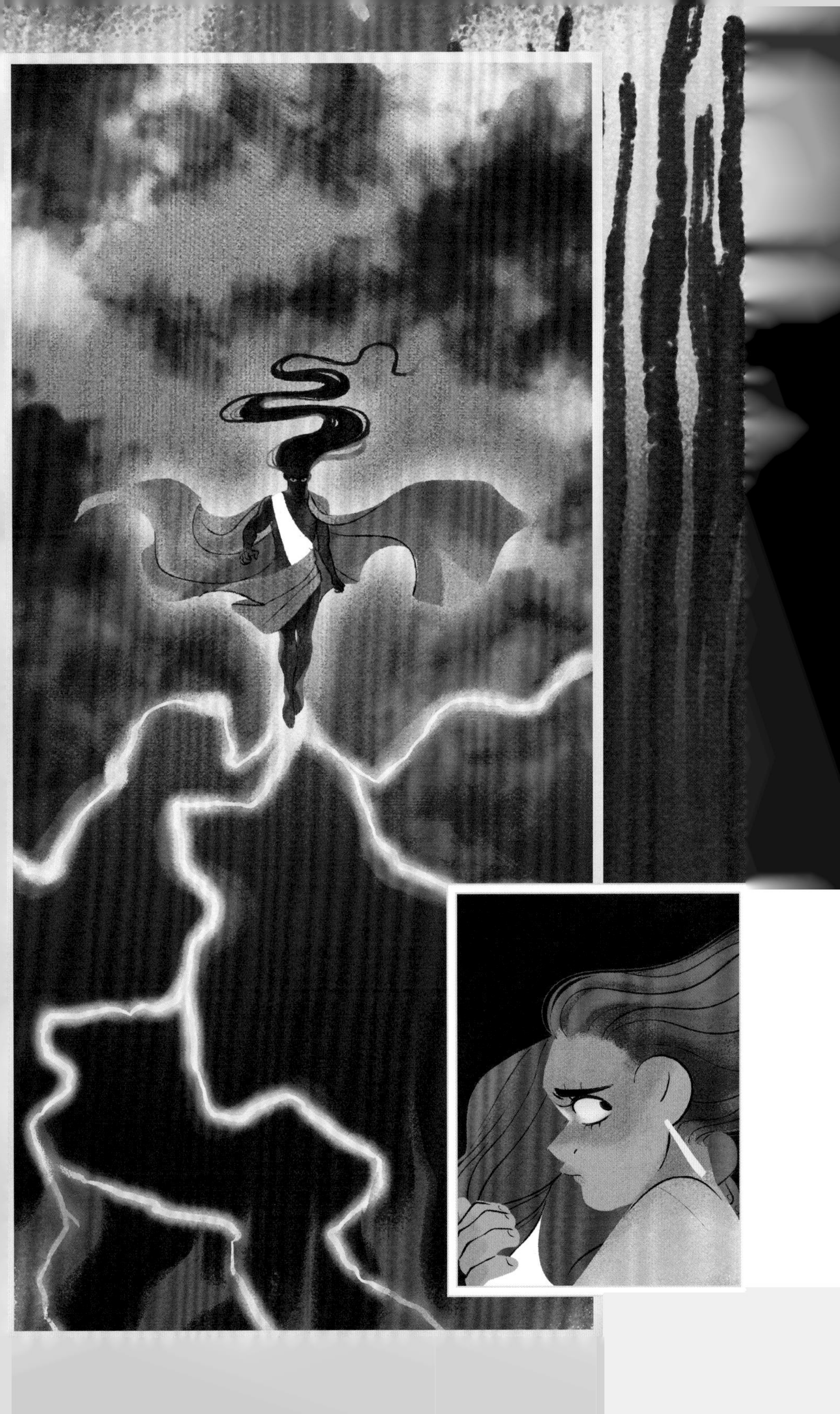

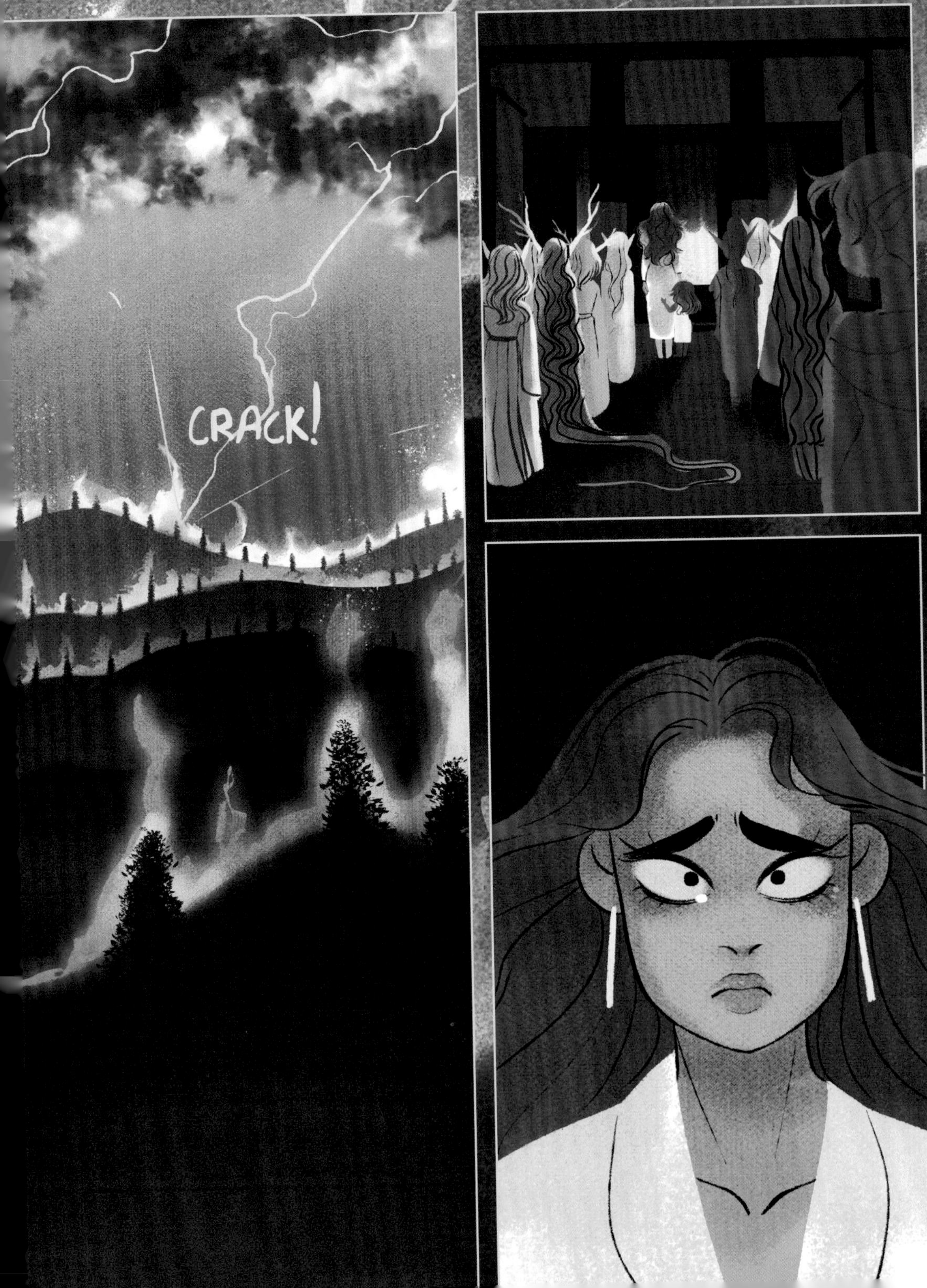
CRACK!

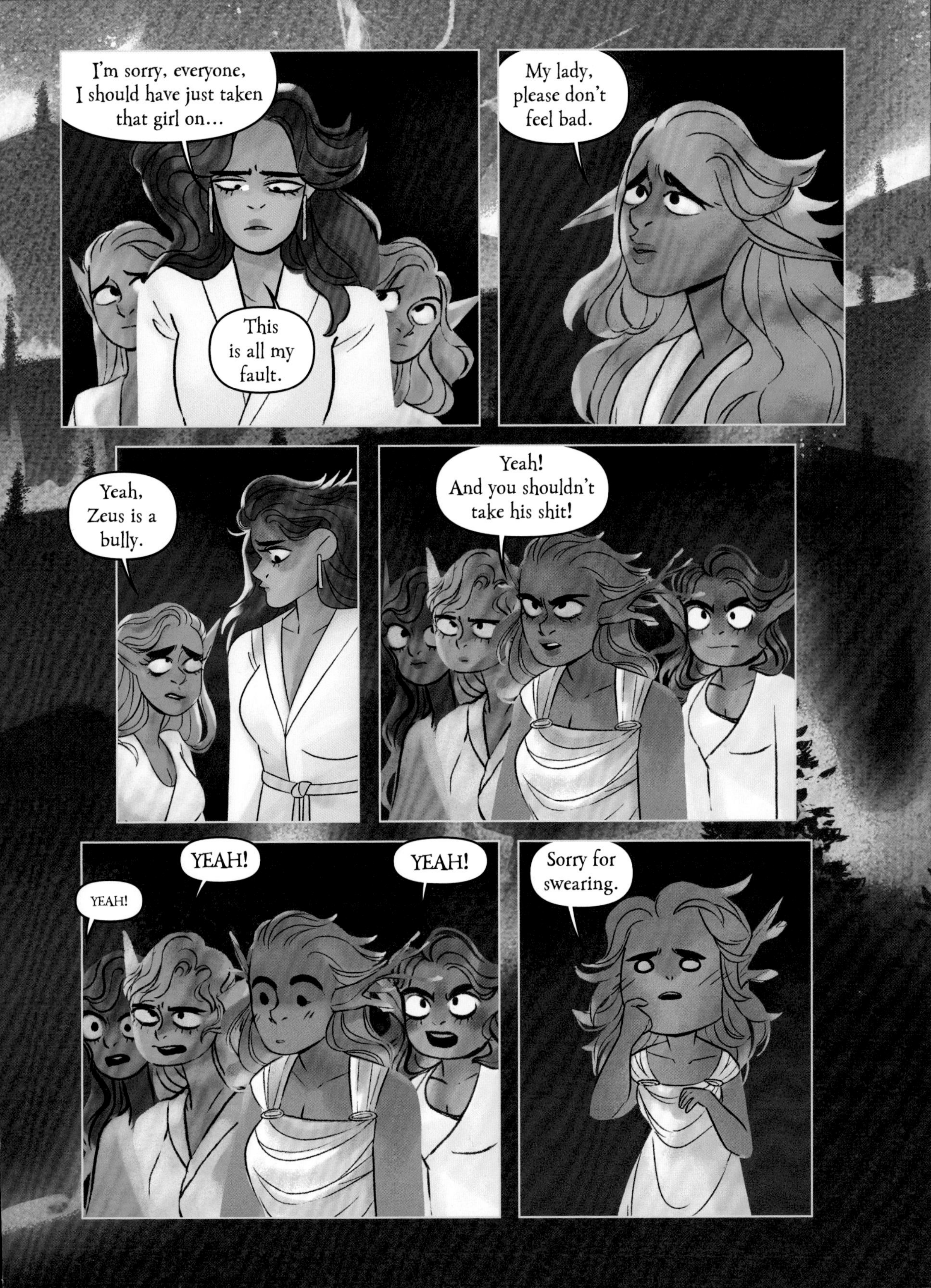
I'm sorry, everyone, I should have just taken that girl on...
This is all my fault.
My lady, please don't feel bad.
Yeah, Zeus is a bully.
Yeah! And you shouldn't take his shit!
YEAH!
YEAH!
YEAH!
Sorry for swearing.

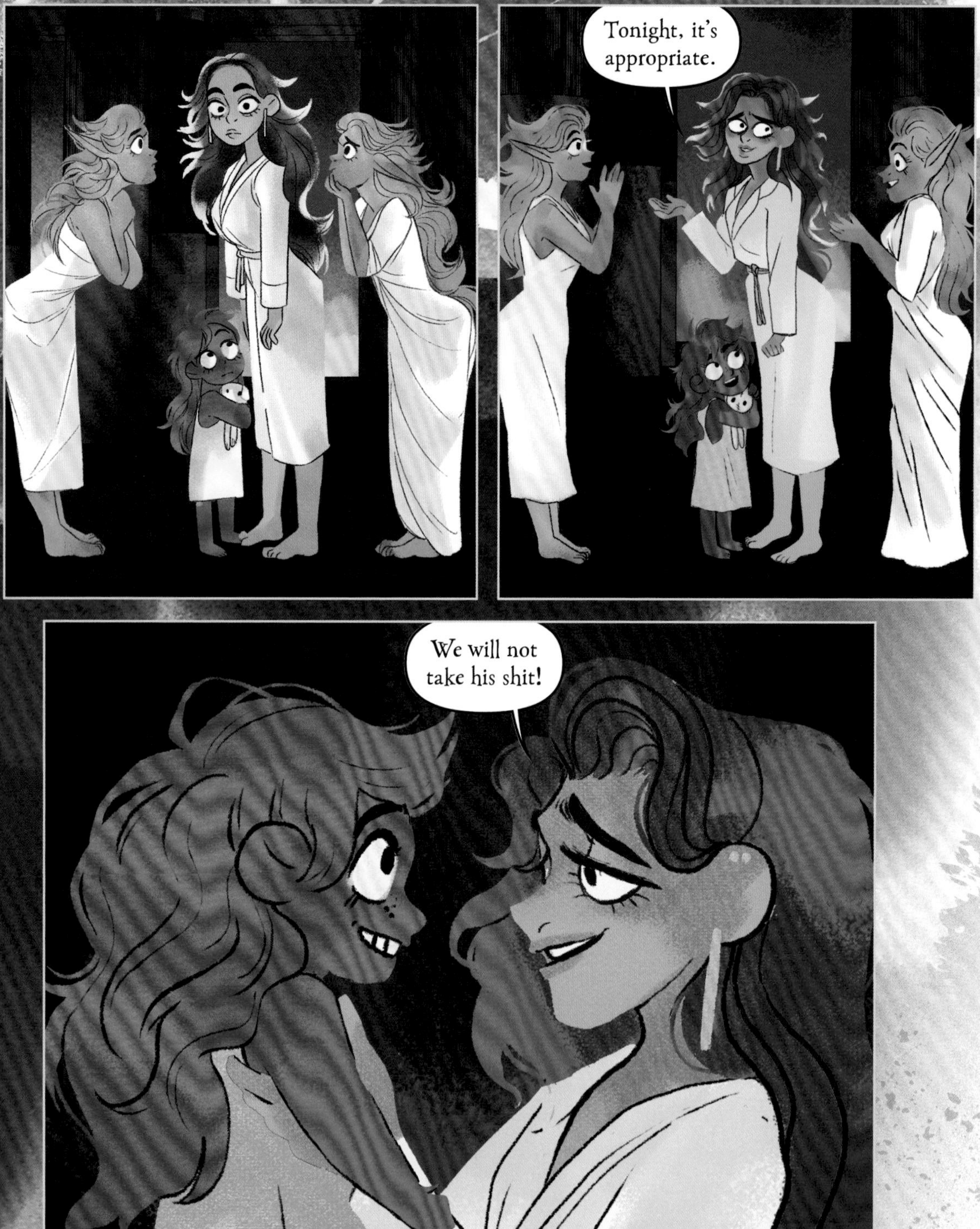
Tonight, it's
appropriate.
We will not
take his shit!

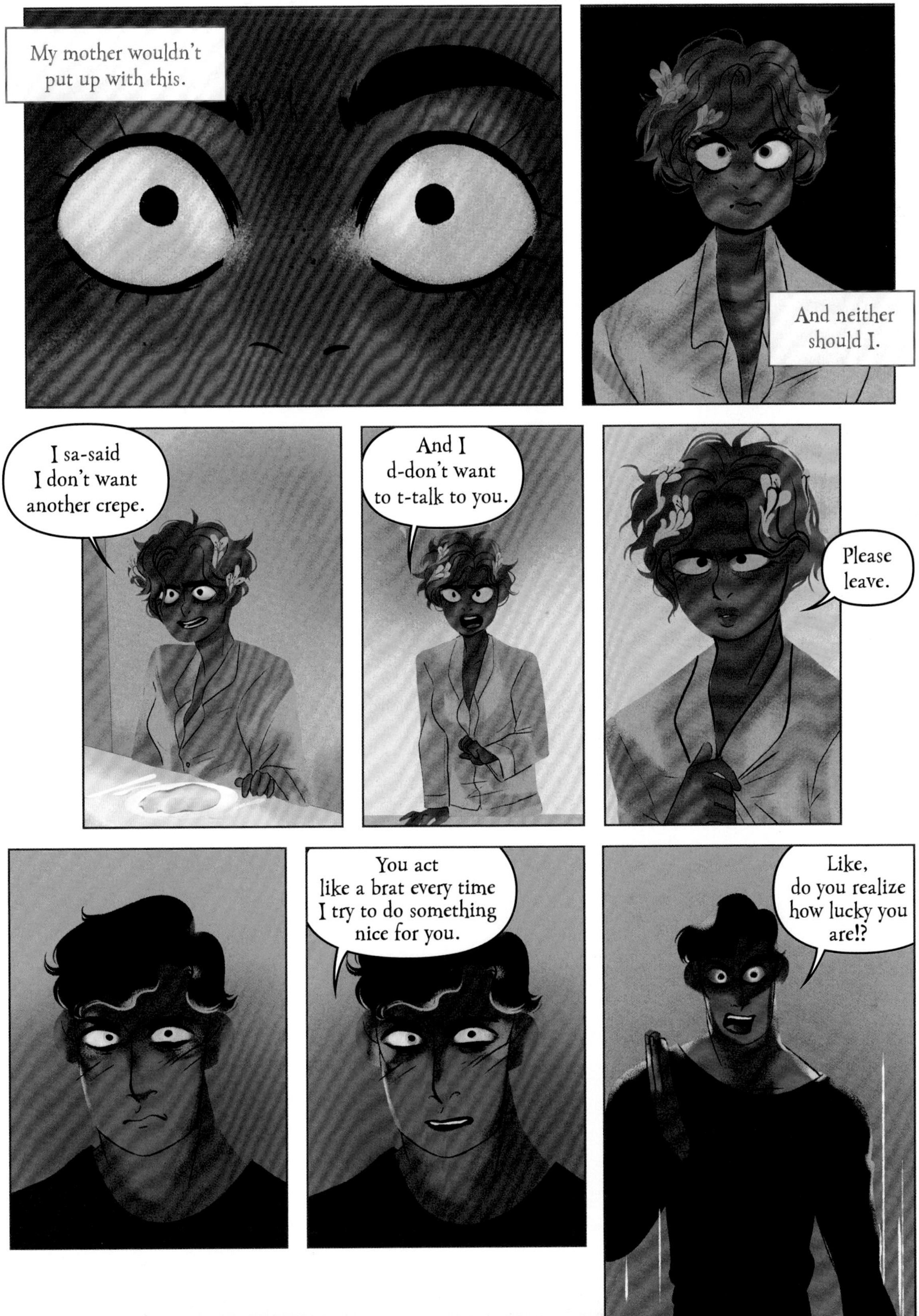
My mother wouldn't put up with this.
And neither should I.
I sa-said I don't want another crepe.
And I d-don't want to t-talk to you.
Please leave.
You act like a brat every time I try to do something nice for you.
Like, do you realize how lucky you are!?

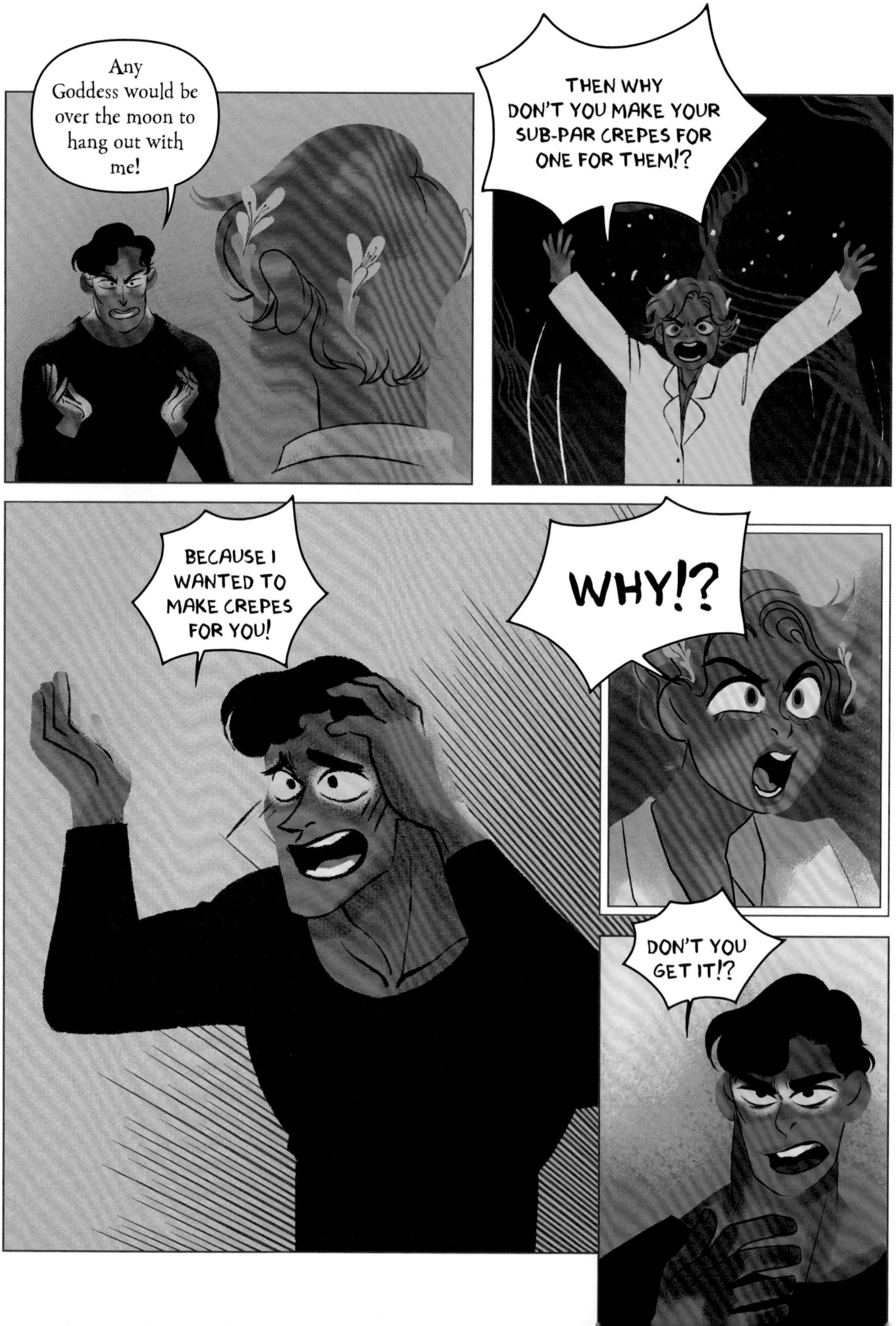
Any Goddess would be over the moon to hang out with me!
THEN WHY DON'T YOU MAKE YOUR SUB-PAR CREPES FOR ONE FOR THEM!?
BECAUSE I WANTED TO MAKE CREPES FOR YOU!
WHY!?
DON'T YOU GET IT!?

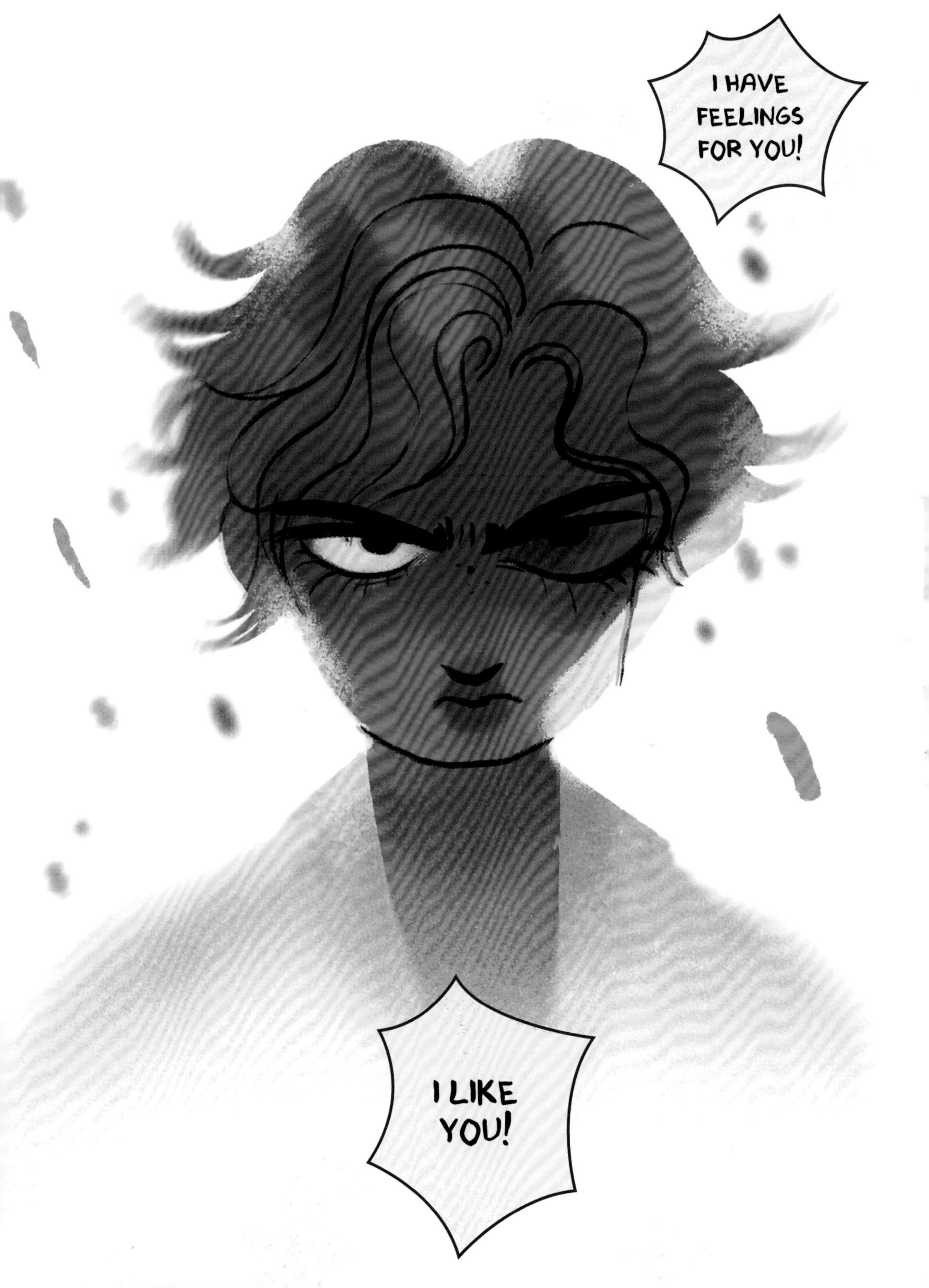
I HAVE FEELINGS FOR YOU!
I LIKE YOU!

EPISODE 97: WE ARE NOTHING

At first I thought what we had was just a one-time fling.

But, what we had was truly special, and I can't think of anyone else but you.

I have feelings for you.

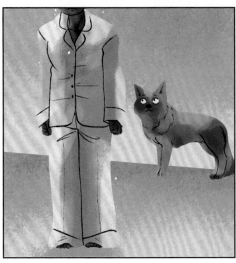

whimper

I've been trying and trying to talk to you.

But you're making it impossible.

I've been thinking, and I've worked it out.

I know you're angry with me because I said we should keep our relationship on the down-low.

TUG!

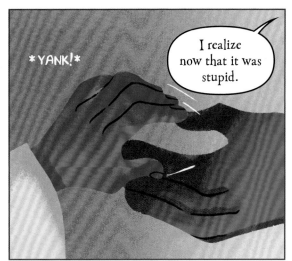

YANK!

I realize now that it was stupid.

I'm sorry.

I was thinking we should make it official.

Make what official?

You and me.

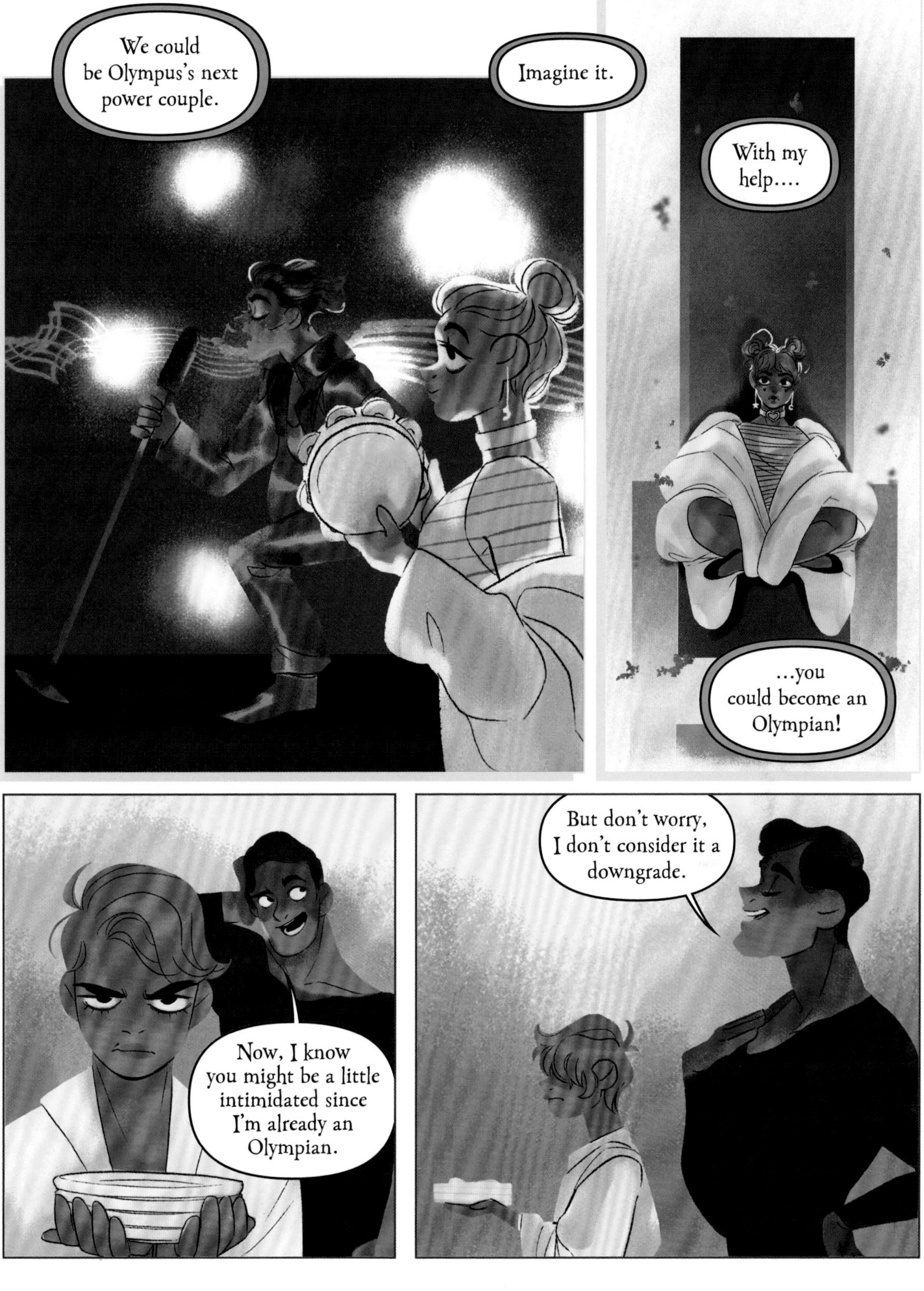
We could be Olympus's next power couple.
Imagine it.
With my help....
...you could become an Olympian!
Now, I know you might be a little intimidated since I'm already an Olympian.
But don't worry, I don't consider it a downgrade.

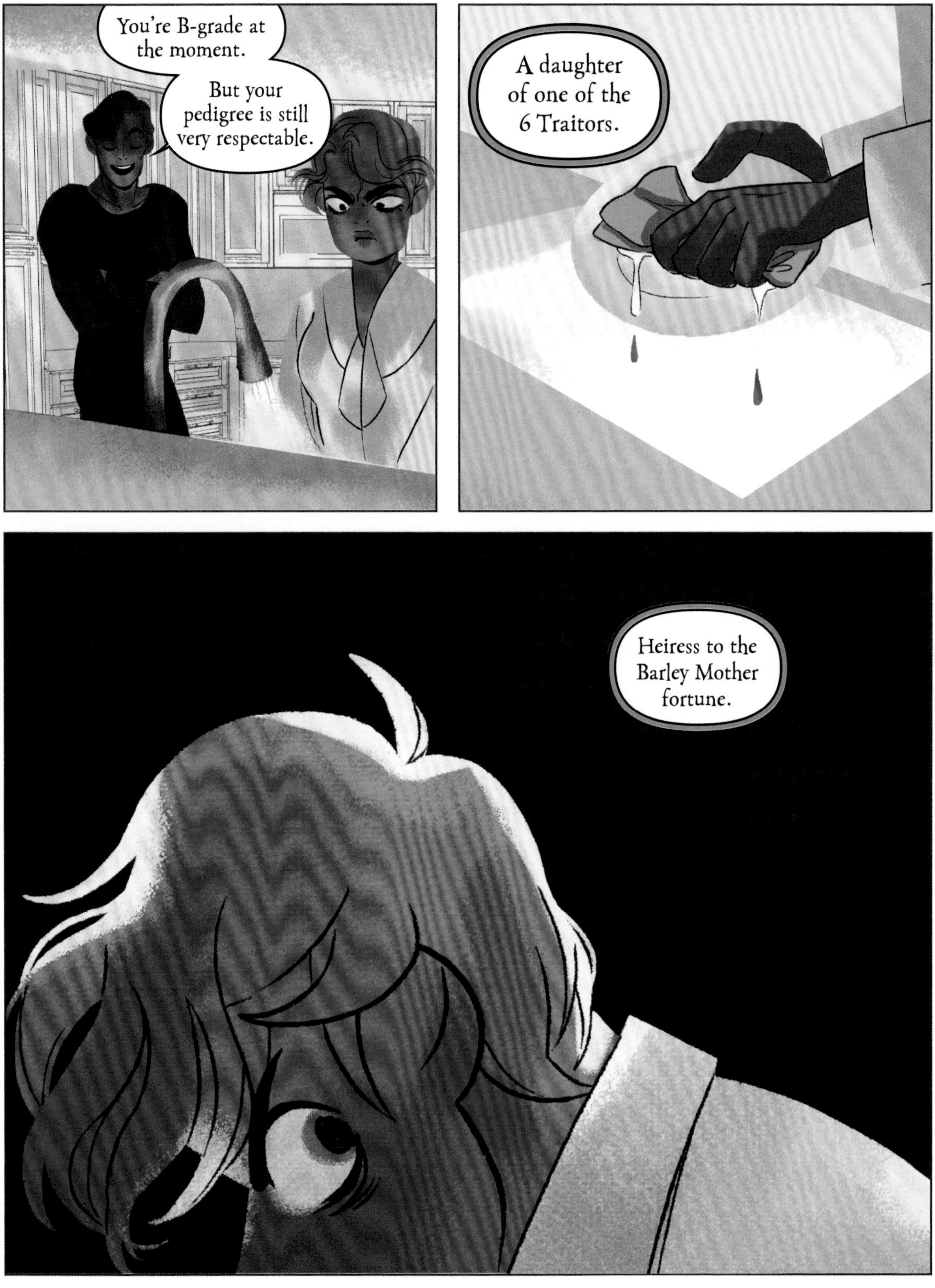

You're B-grade at the moment.
But your pedigree is still very respectable.
A daughter of one of the 6 Traitors.
Heiress to the Barley Mother fortune.

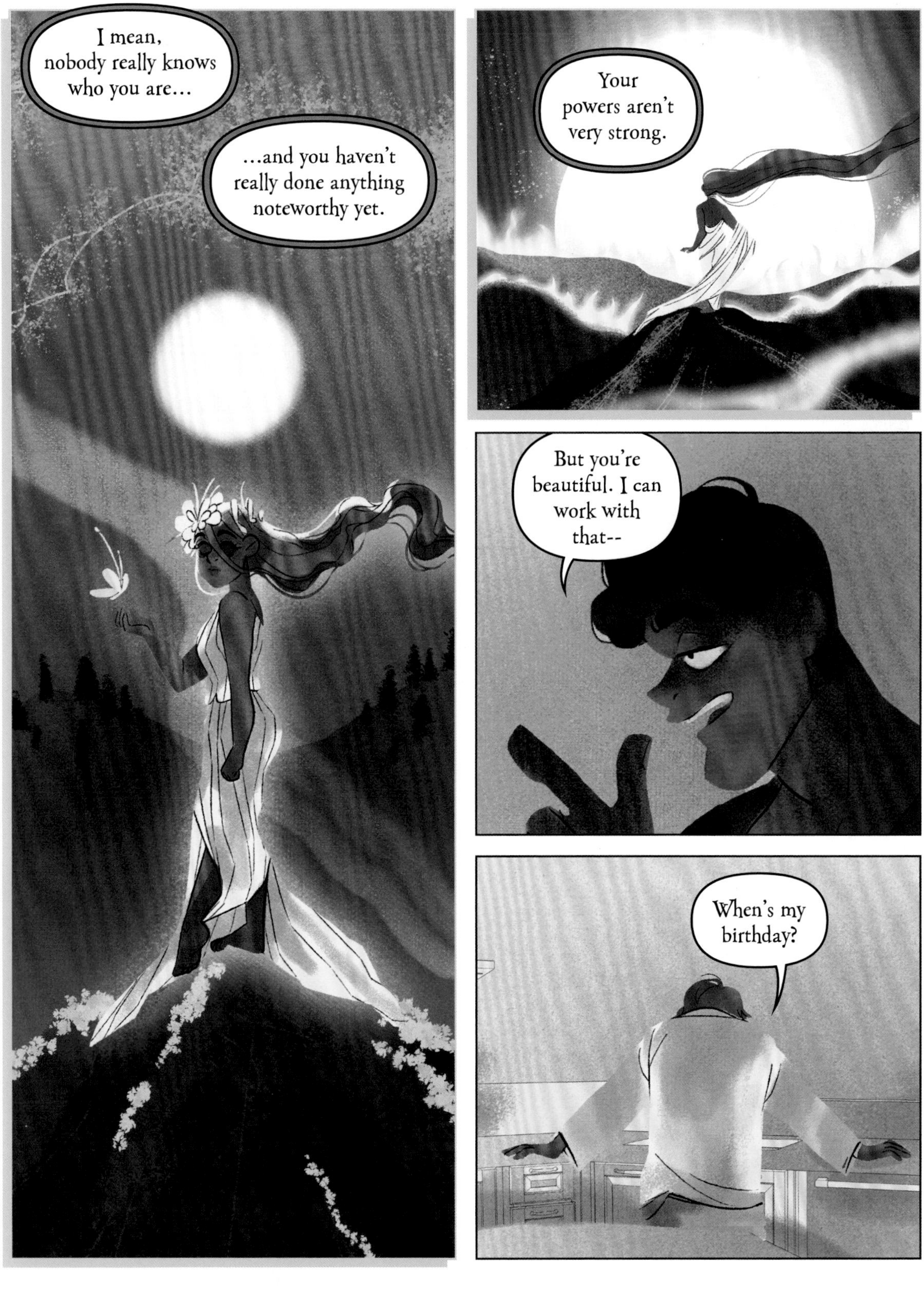
I mean, nobody really knows who you are...
...and you haven't really done anything noteworthy yet.
Your powers aren't very strong.
But you're beautiful. I can work with that--
When's my birthday?

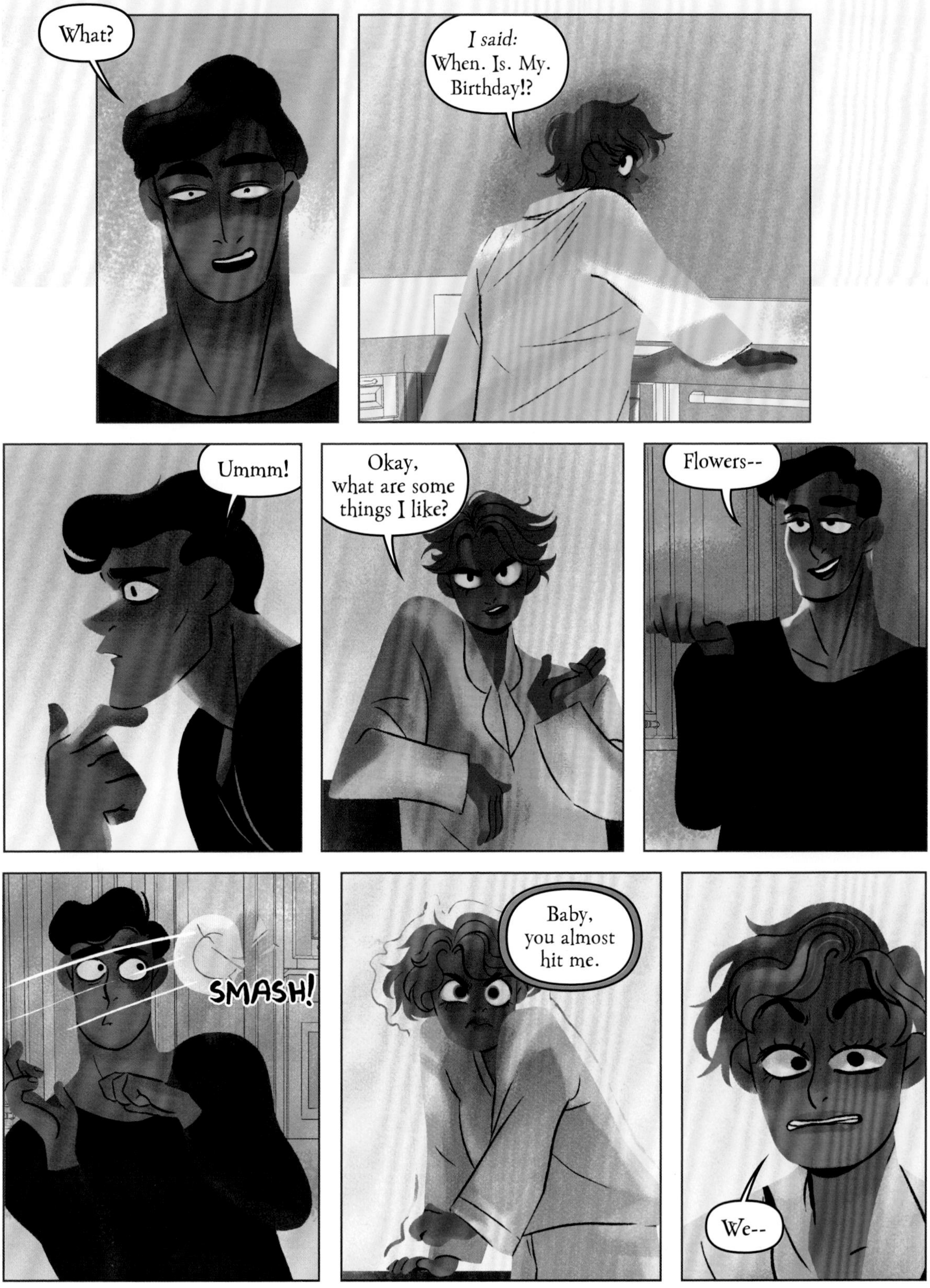
What?
I said: When. Is. My. Birthday!?
Ummm!
Okay, what are some things I like?
Flowers--
SMASH!
Baby, you almost hit me.
We--

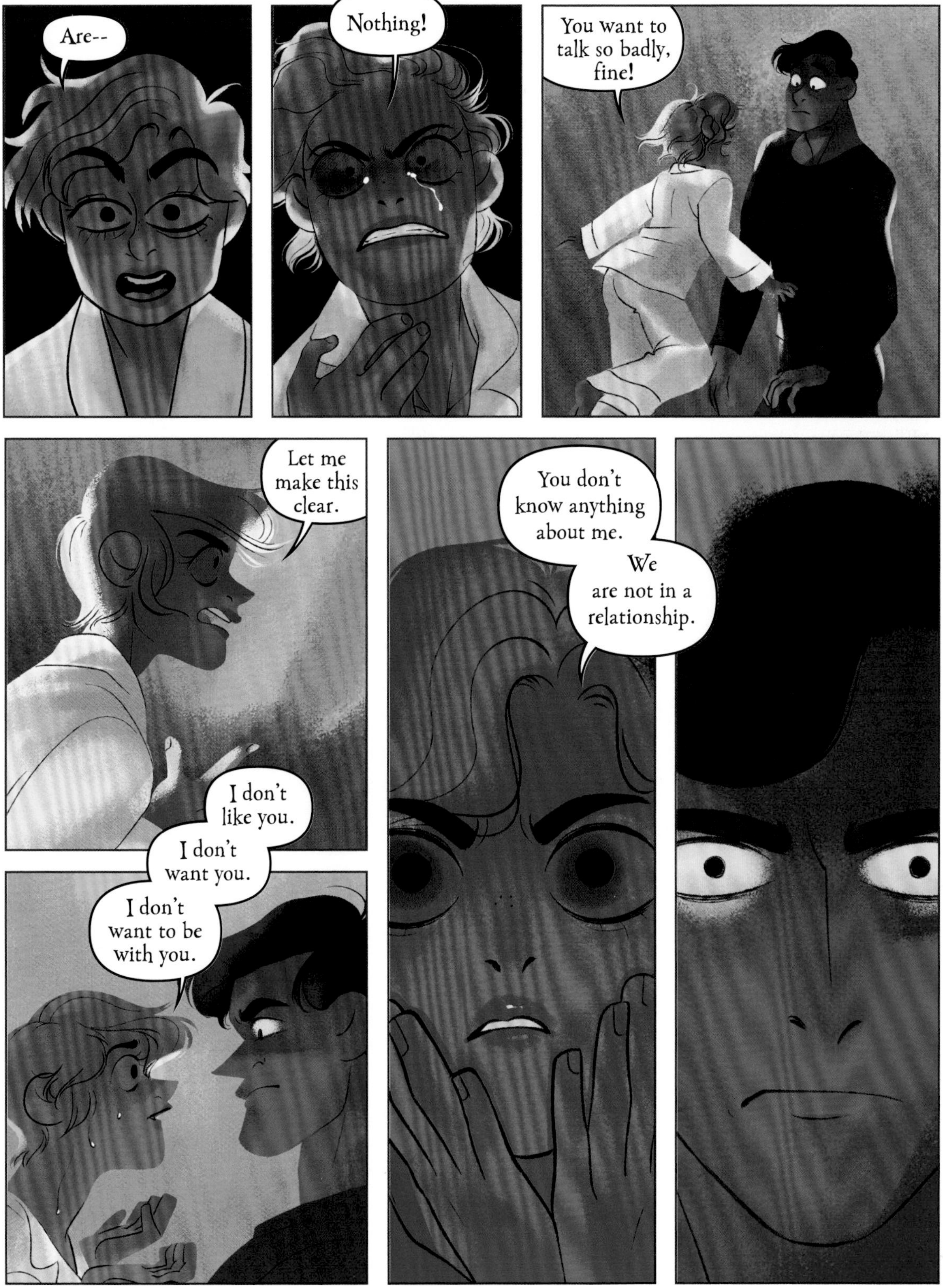
Are--
Nothing!
You want to talk so badly, fine!
Let me make this clear.
I don't like you.
I don't want you.
I don't want to be with you.
You don't know anything about me.
We are not in a relationship.

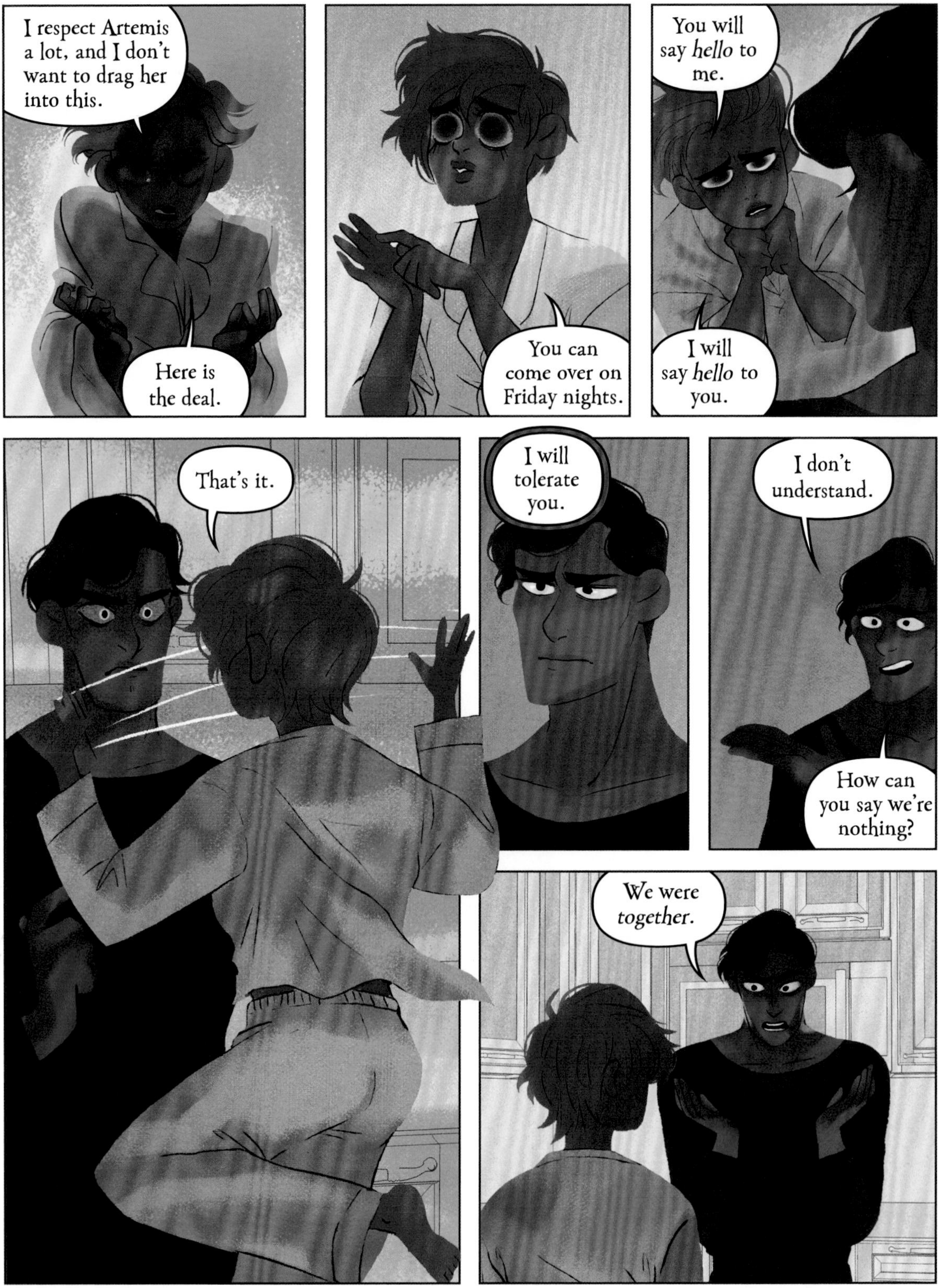
I respect Artemis a lot, and I don't want to drag her into this.
Here is the deal.
You can come over on Friday nights.
You will say *hello* to me.
I will say *hello* to you.
That's it.
I will tolerate you.
I don't understand.
How can you say we're nothing?
We were *together*.

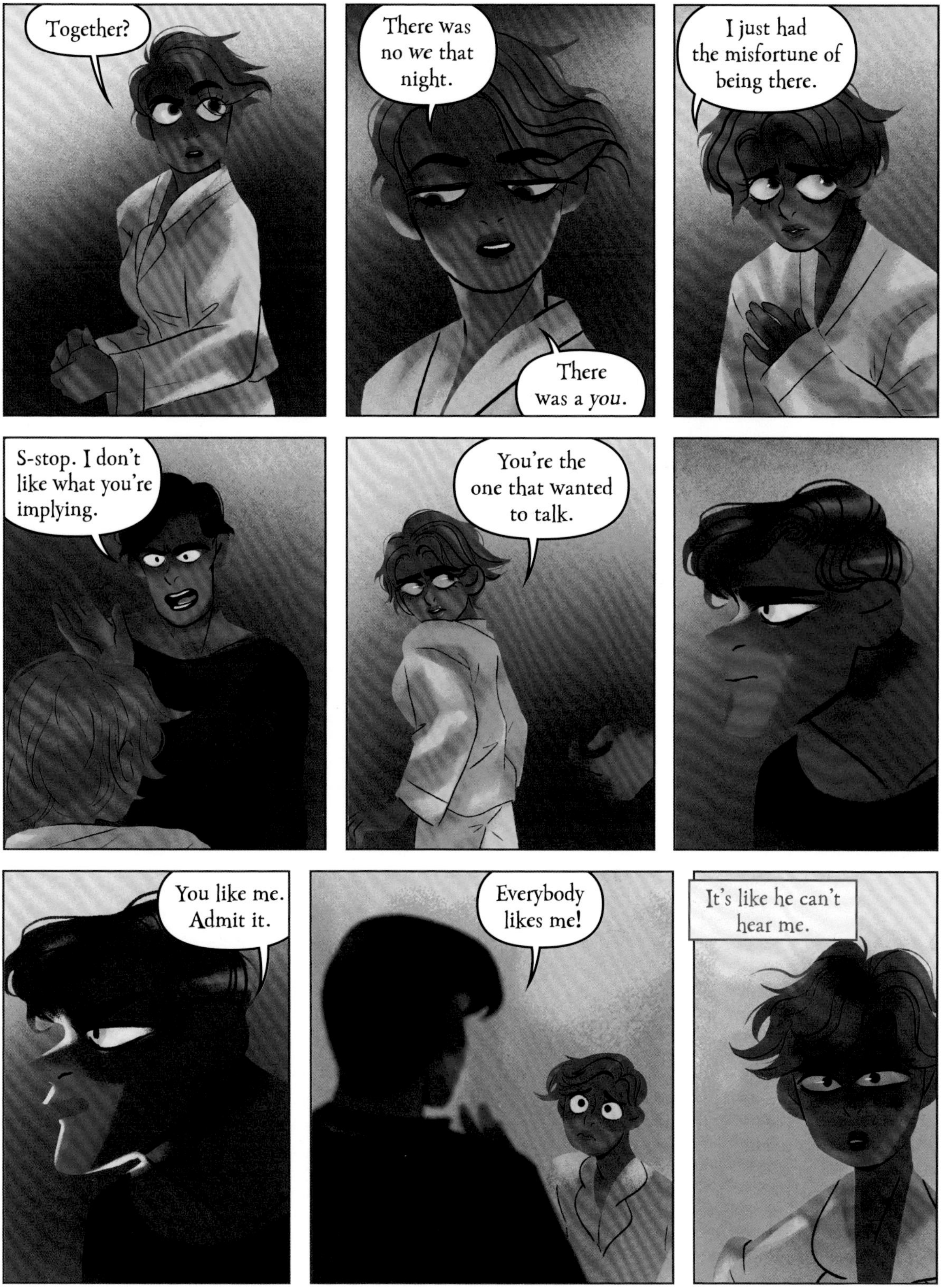
Together?
There was no we that night.
There was a you.
I just had the misfortune of being there.
S-stop. I don't like what you're implying.
You're the one that wanted to talk.
You like me. Admit it.
Everybody likes me!
It's like he can't hear me.

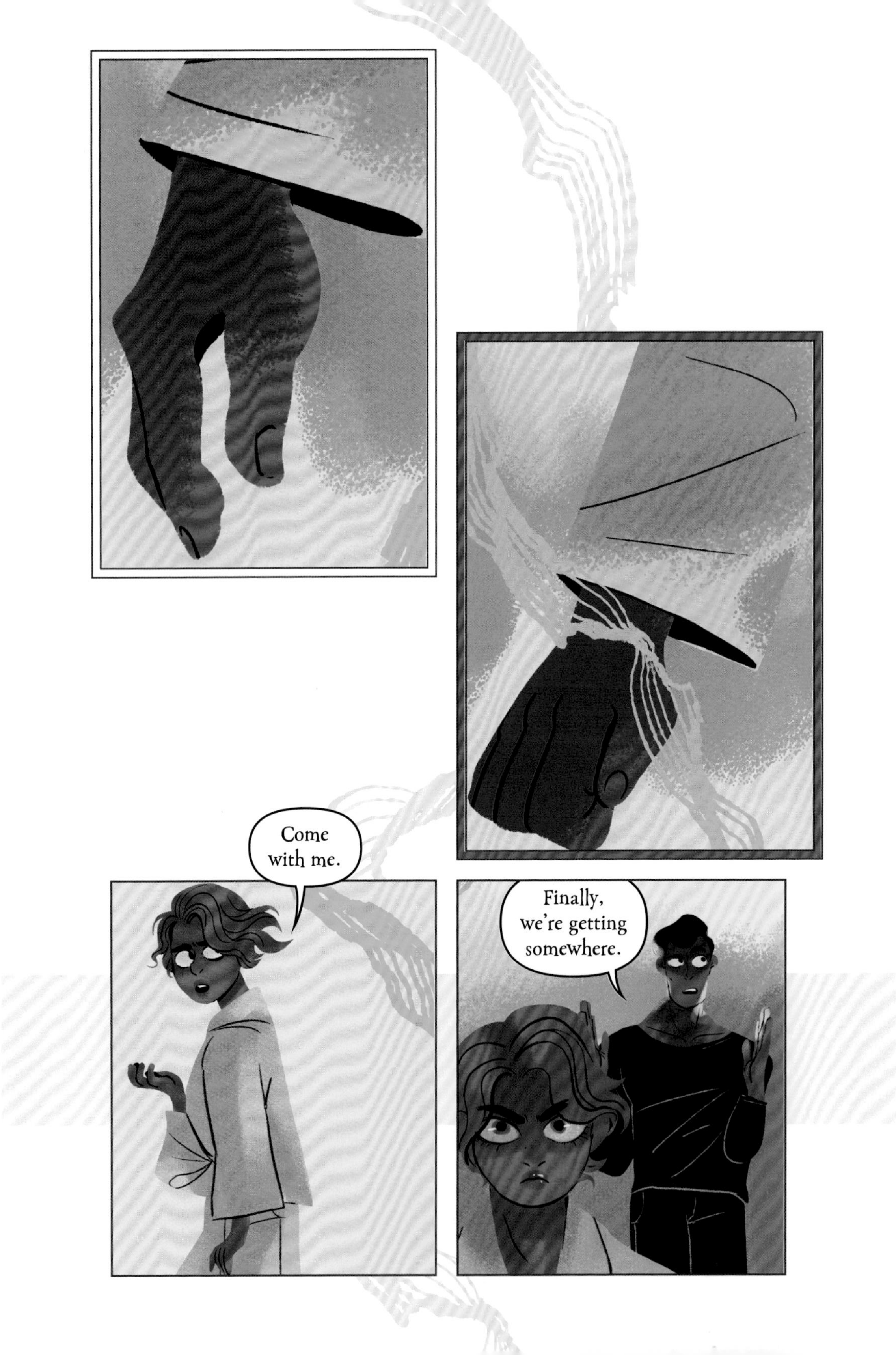

Come with me.
Finally, we're getting somewhere.

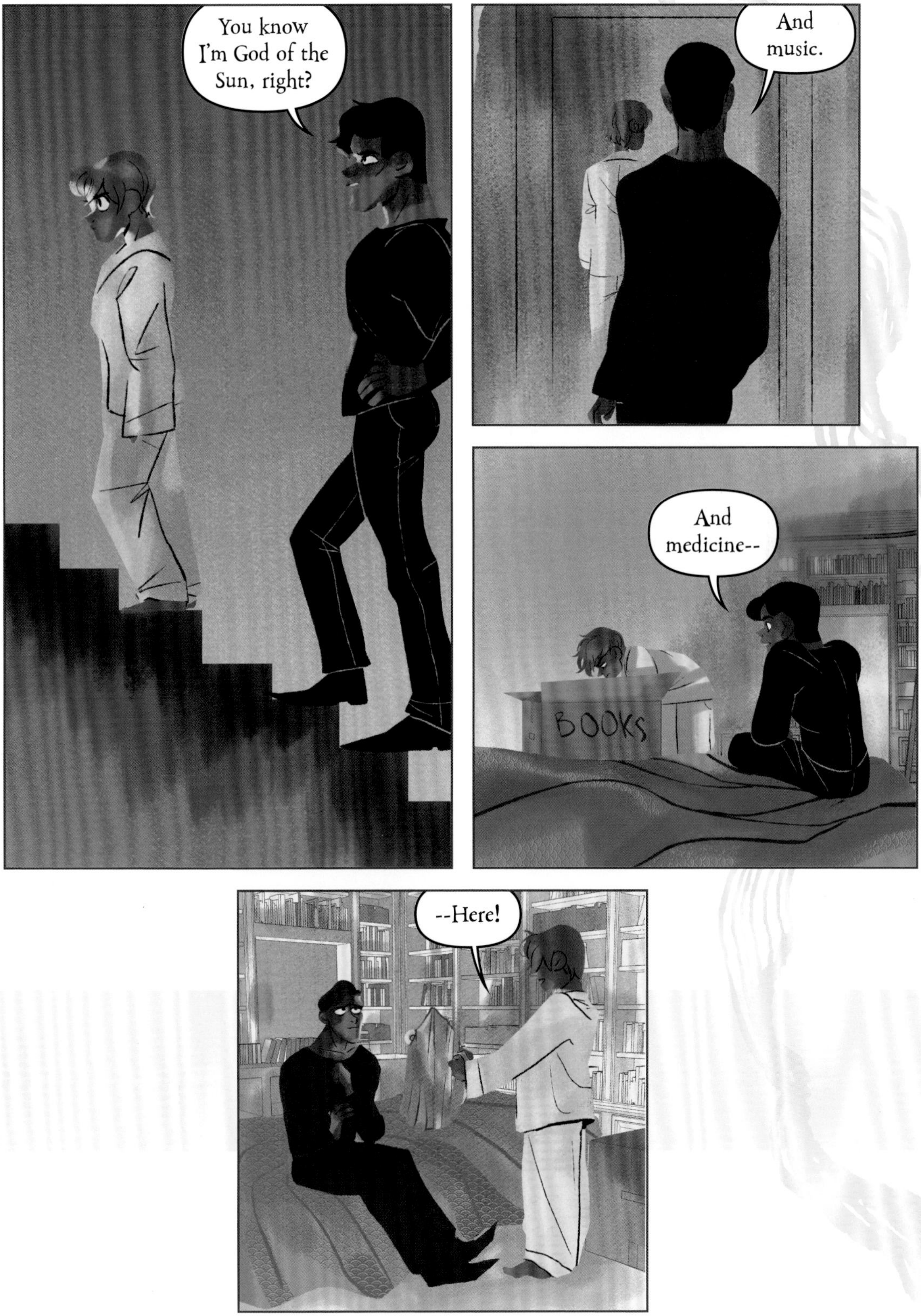
You know I'm God of the Sun, right?
And music.
And medicine--
BOOKS
--Here!

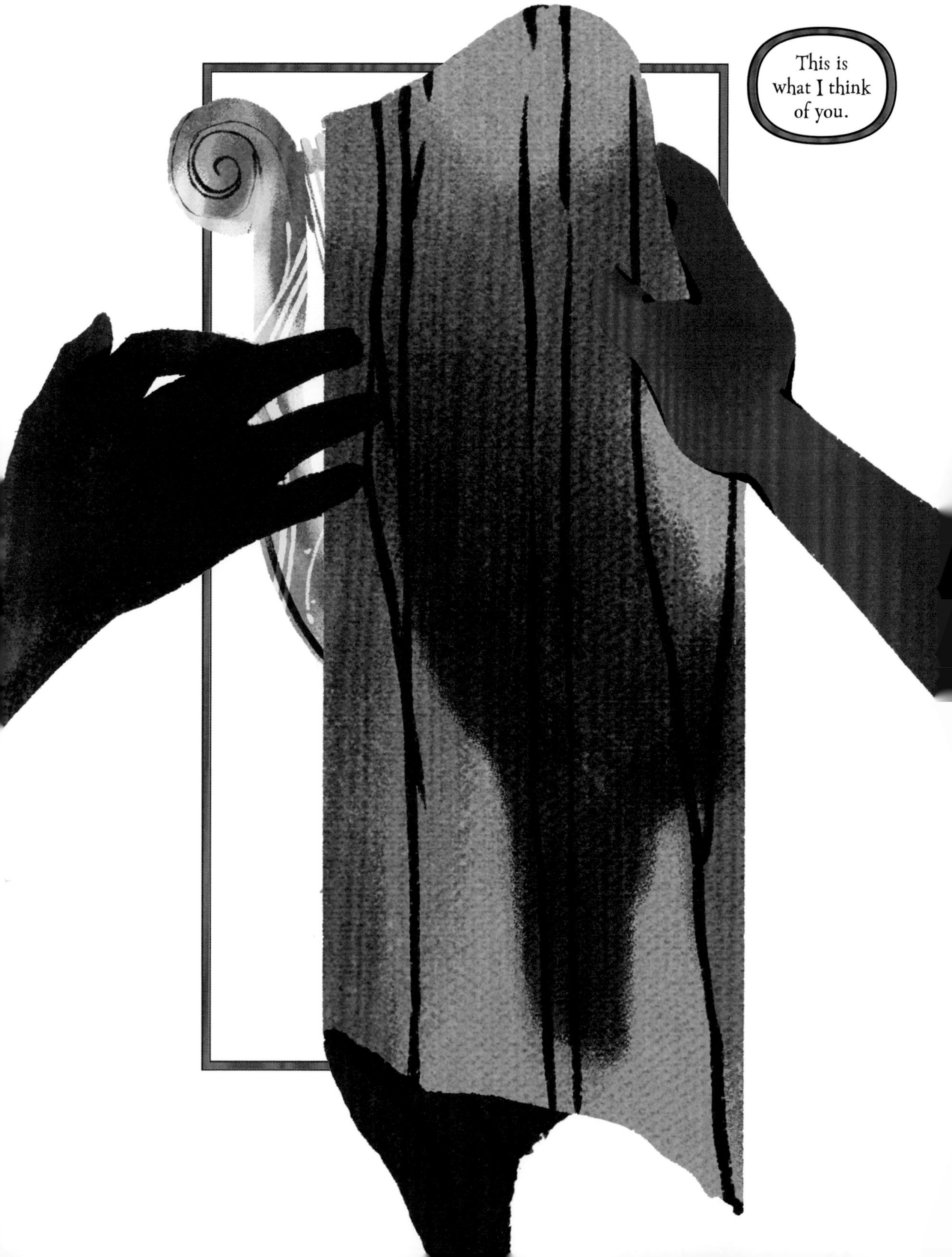
This is what I think of you.

EPISODE 98: NOT YOUR OLYMPIAN

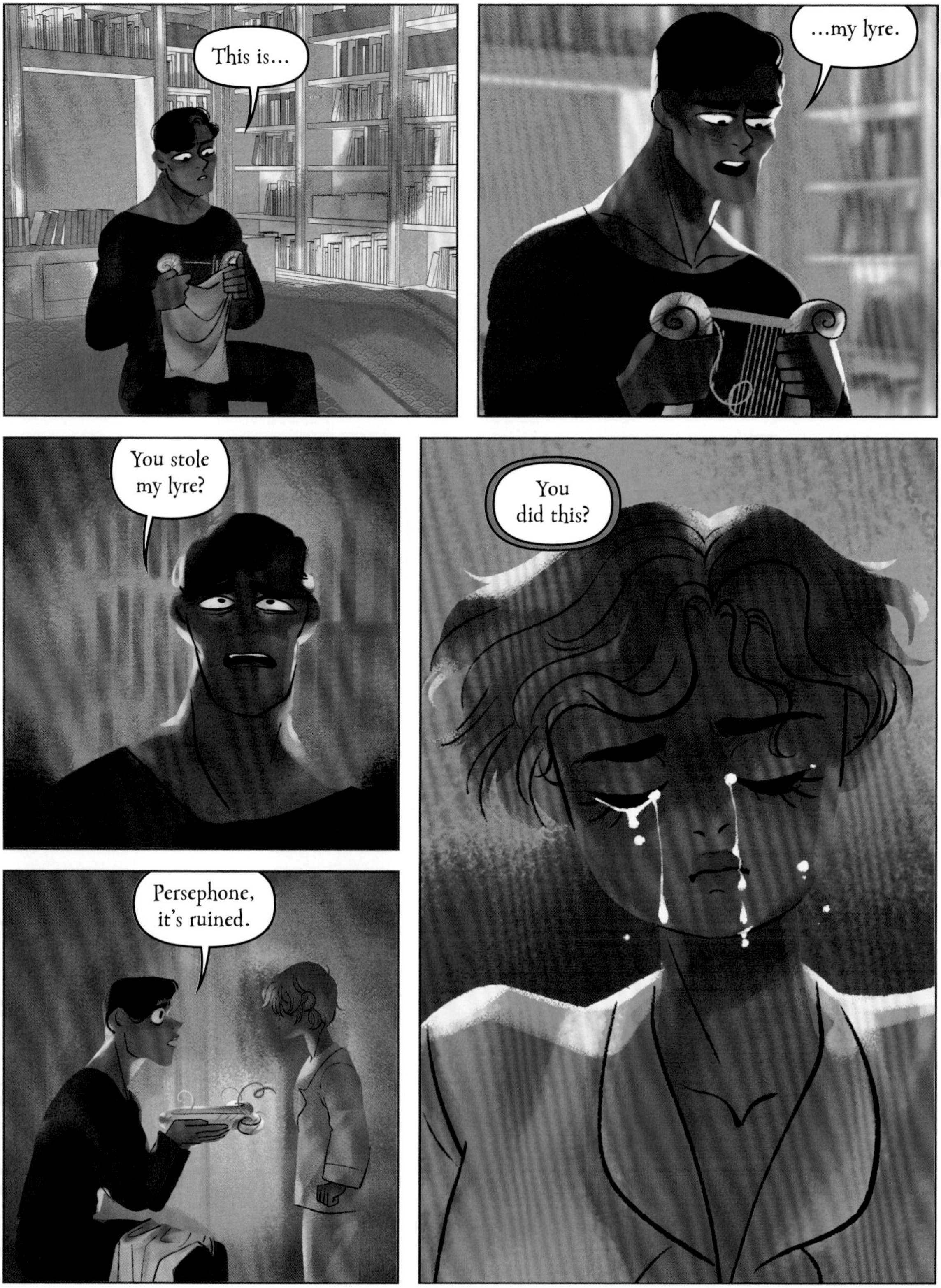

This is...
...my lyre.
You stole my lyre?
Persephone, it's ruined.
You did this?

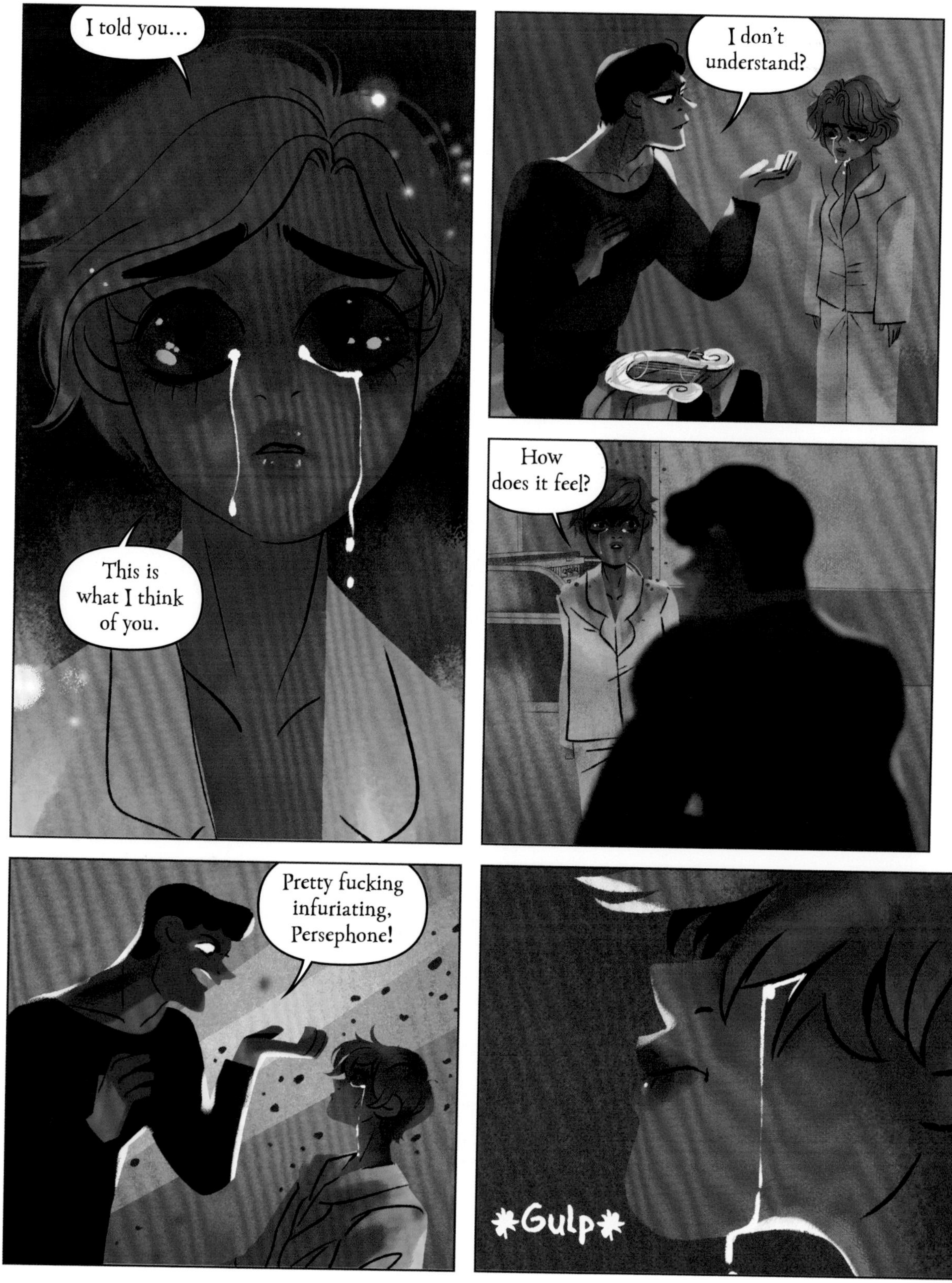
I told you...
This is what I think of you.
I don't understand?
How does it feel?
Pretty fucking infuriating, Persephone!
Gulp

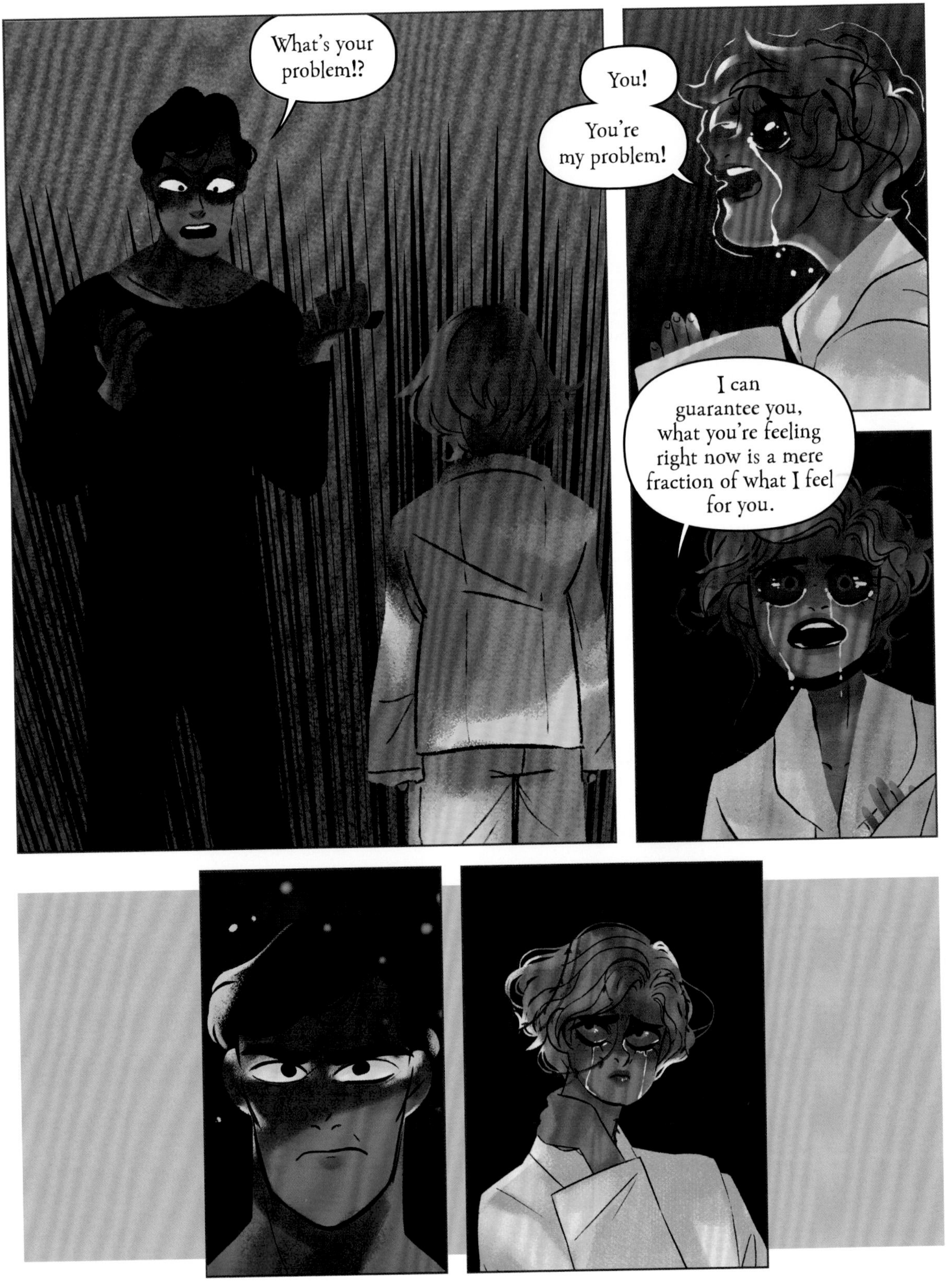
What's your problem!?
You!
You're my problem!
I can guarantee you, what you're feeling right now is a mere fraction of what I feel for you.

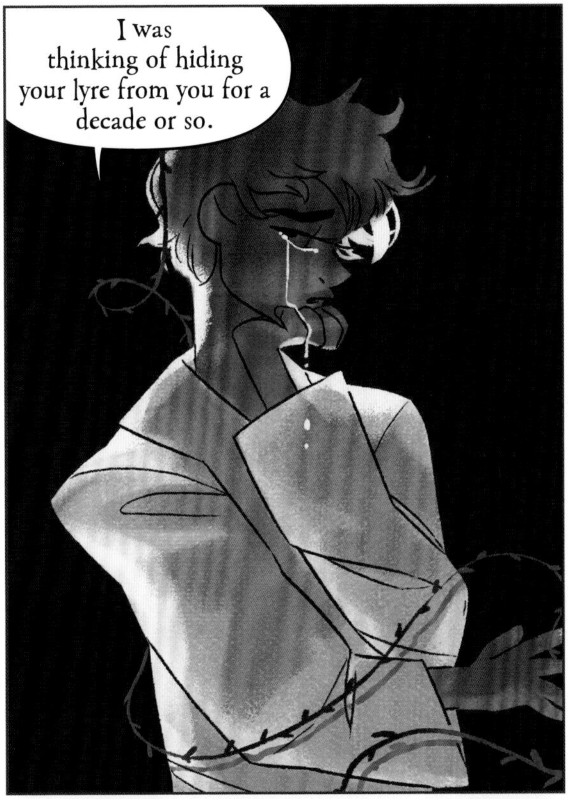
I was thinking of hiding your lyre from you for a decade or so.

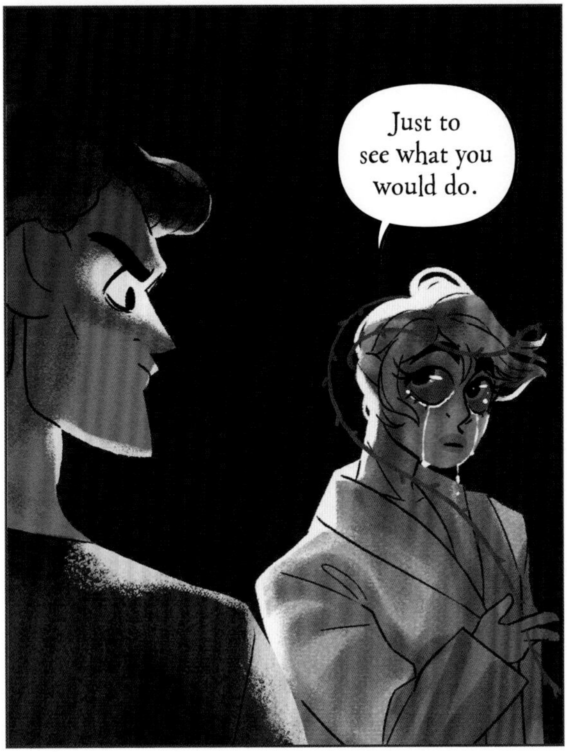
Just to see what you would do.

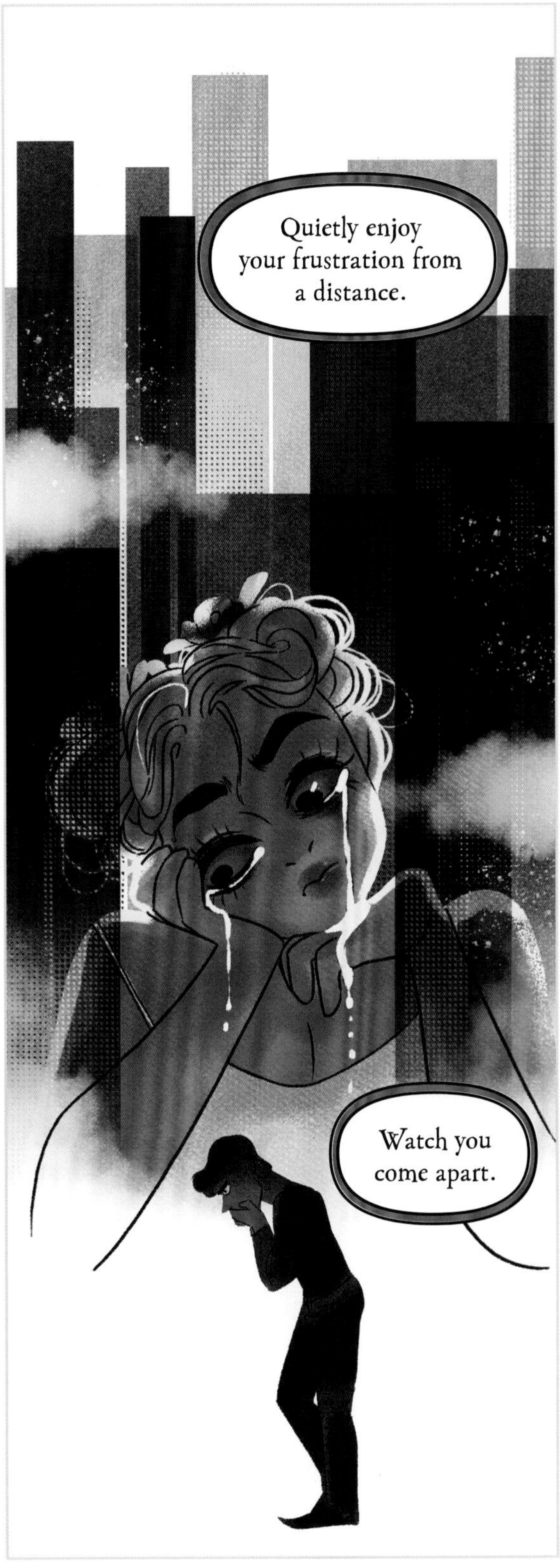
Quietly enjoy your frustration from a distance.
Watch you come apart.

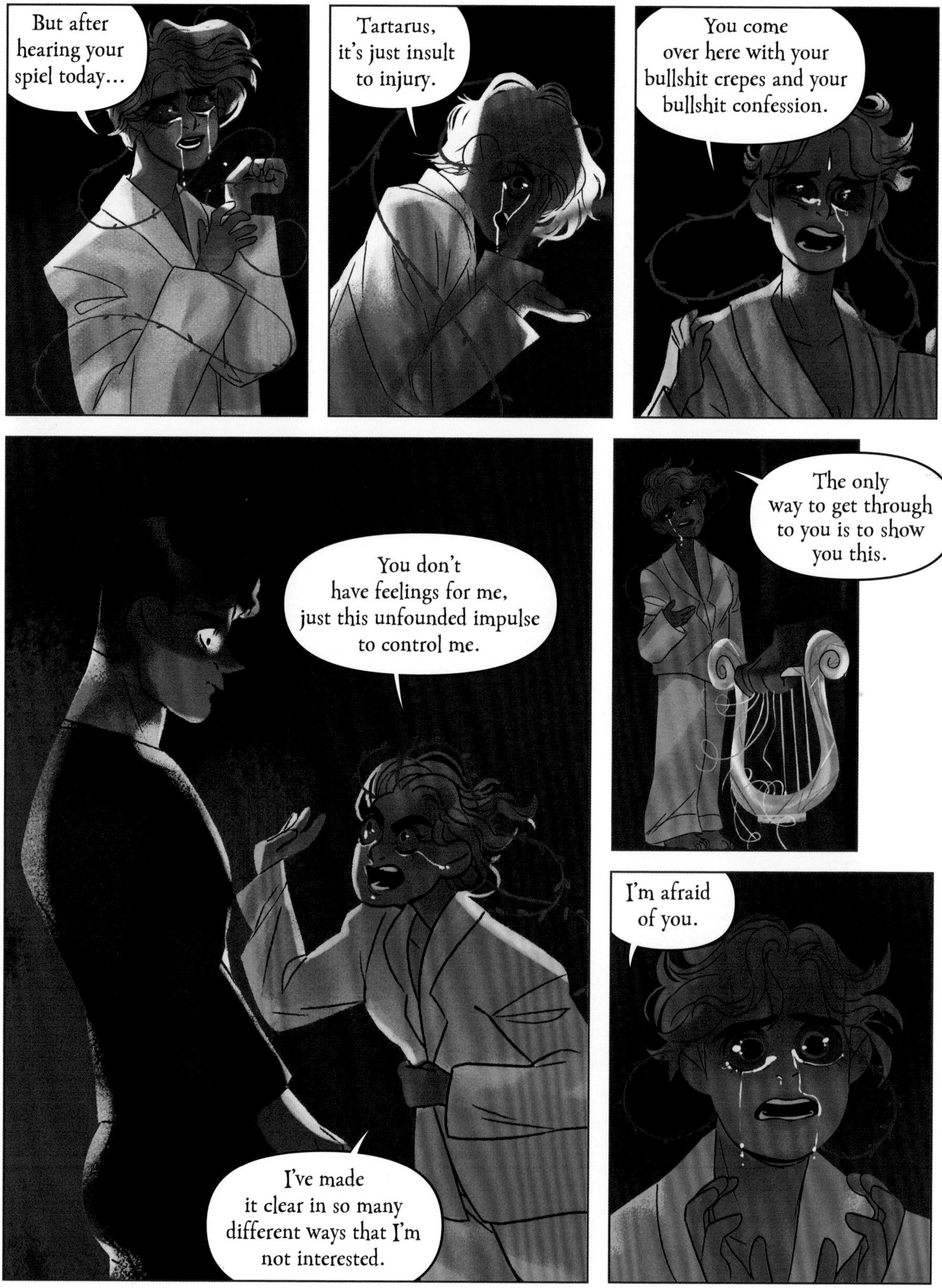
But after hearing your spiel today...
Tartarus, it's just insult to injury.
You come over here with your bullshit crepes and your bullshit confession.
You don't have feelings for me, just this unfounded impulse to control me.
I've made it clear in so many different ways that I'm not interested.
The only way to get through to you is to show you this.
I'm afraid of you.

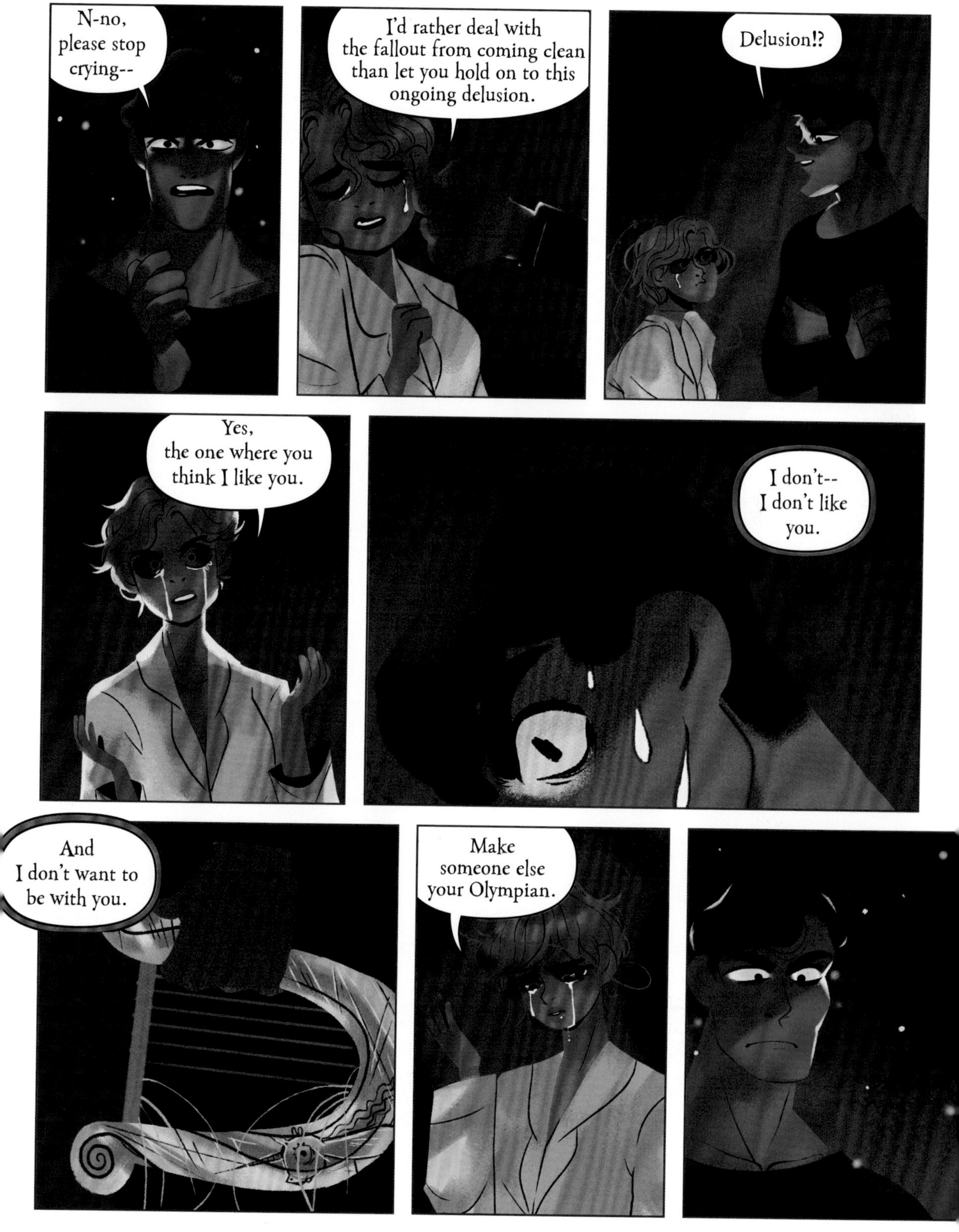
N-no, please stop crying--
I'd rather deal with the fallout from coming clean than let you hold on to this ongoing delusion.
Delusion!?
Yes, the one where you think I like you.
I don't-- I don't like you.
And I don't want to be with you.
Make someone else your Olympian.

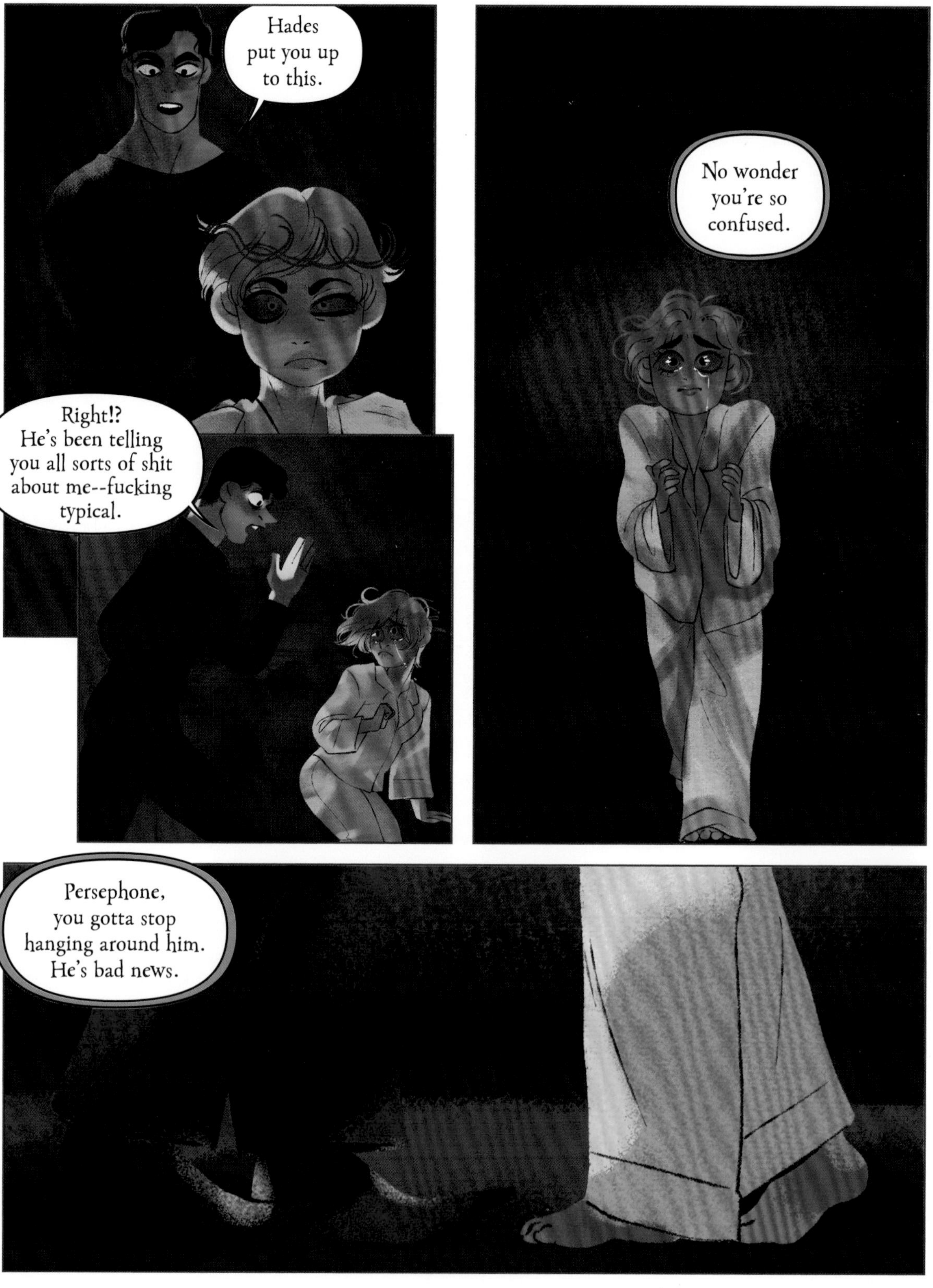
Hades put you up to this.
Right!? He's been telling you all sorts of shit about me--fucking typical.
No wonder you're so confused.
Persephone, you gotta stop hanging around him. He's bad news.

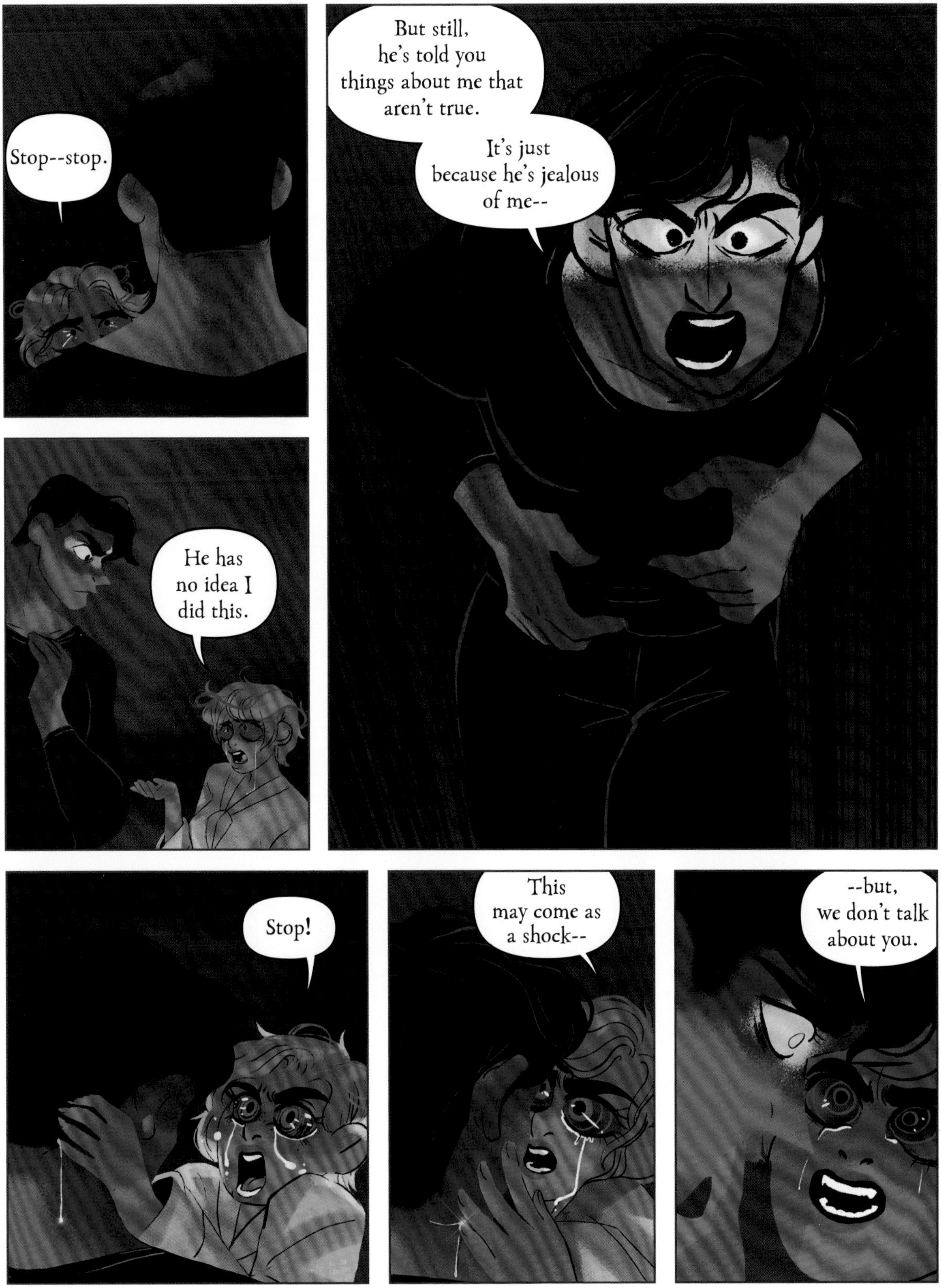
Stop--stop.
But still, he's told you things about me that aren't true.
It's just because he's jealous of me--
He has no idea I did this.
Stop!
This may come as a shock--
--but, we don't talk about you.

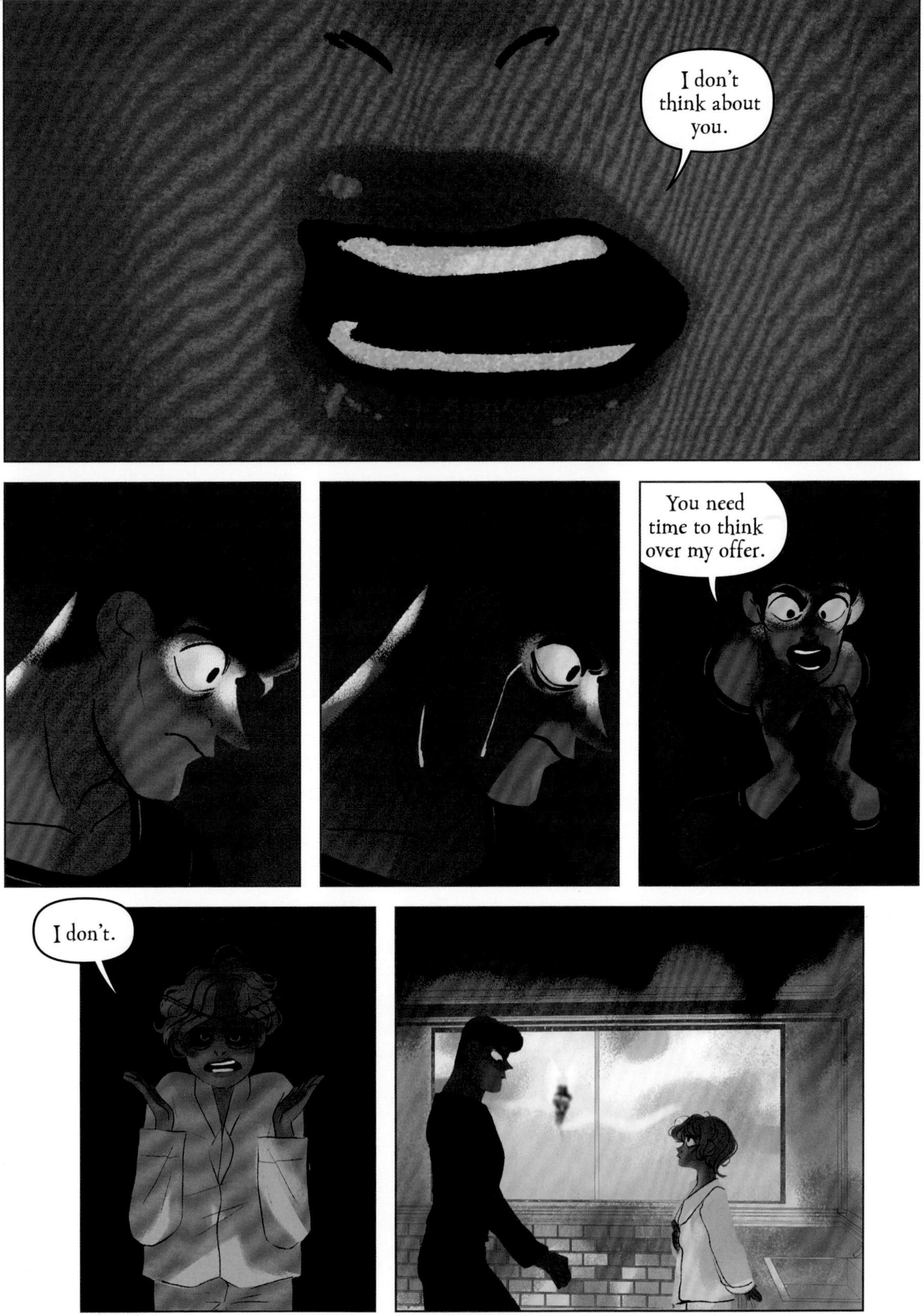

I don't think about you.
You need time to think over my offer.
I don't.

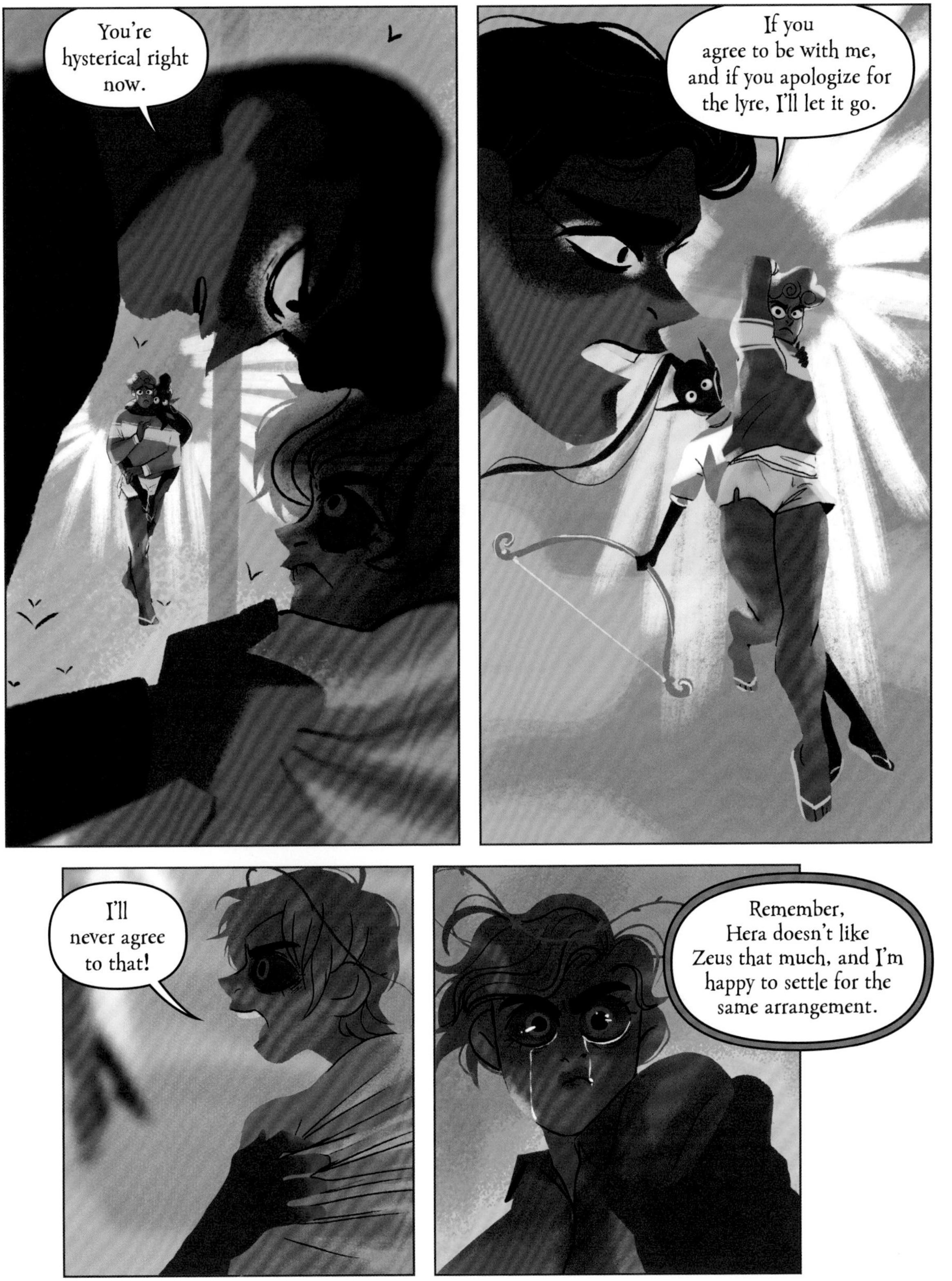
You're hysterical right now.
If you agree to be with me, and if you apologize for the lyre, I'll let it go.
I'll never agree to that!
Remember, Hera doesn't like Zeus that much, and I'm happy to settle for the same arrangement.

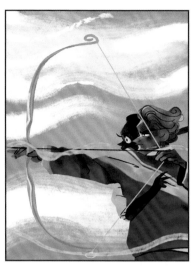

I don't need you to like me to be my wife.

I know more about you than you realize--

SMASH!

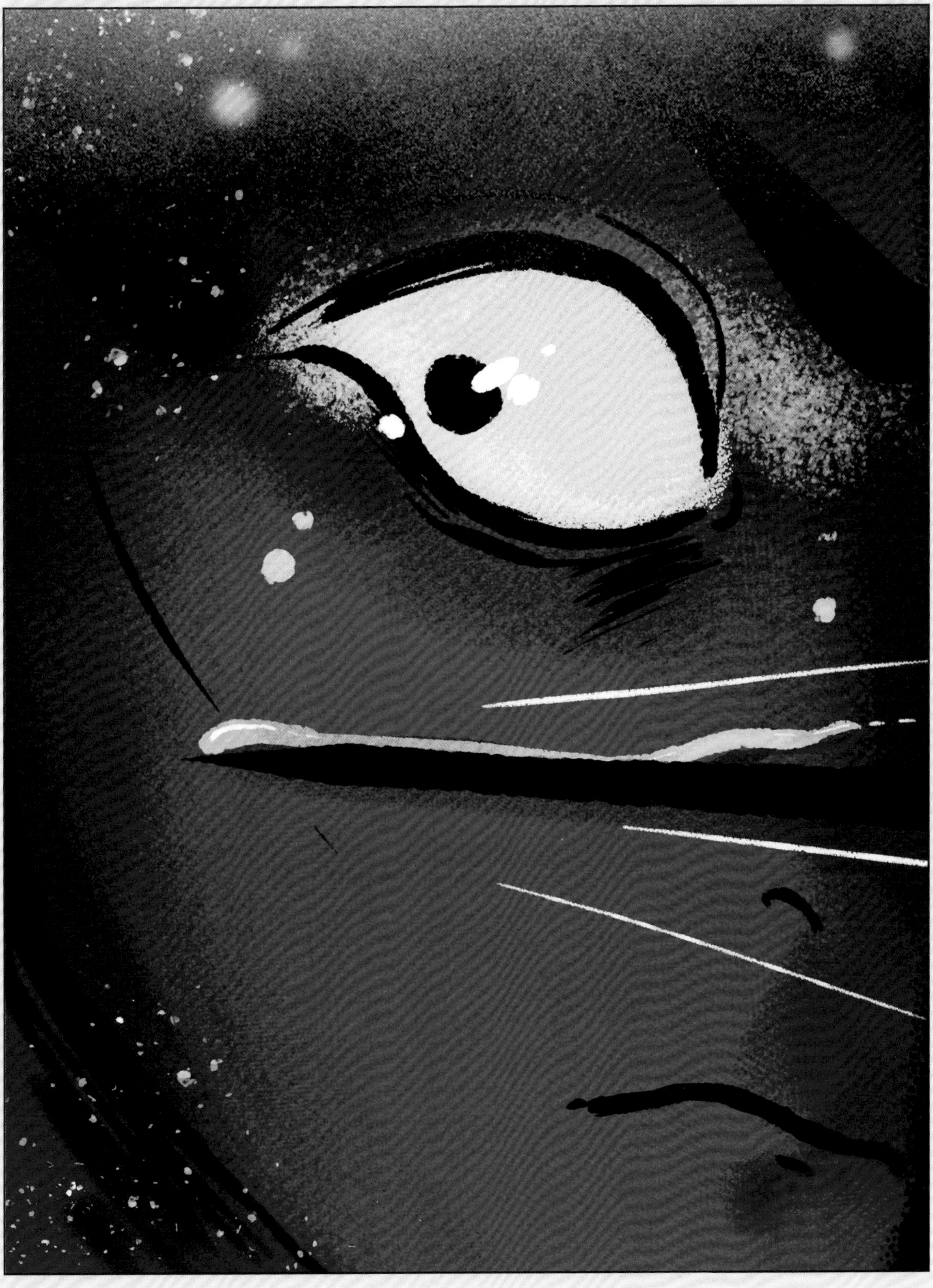

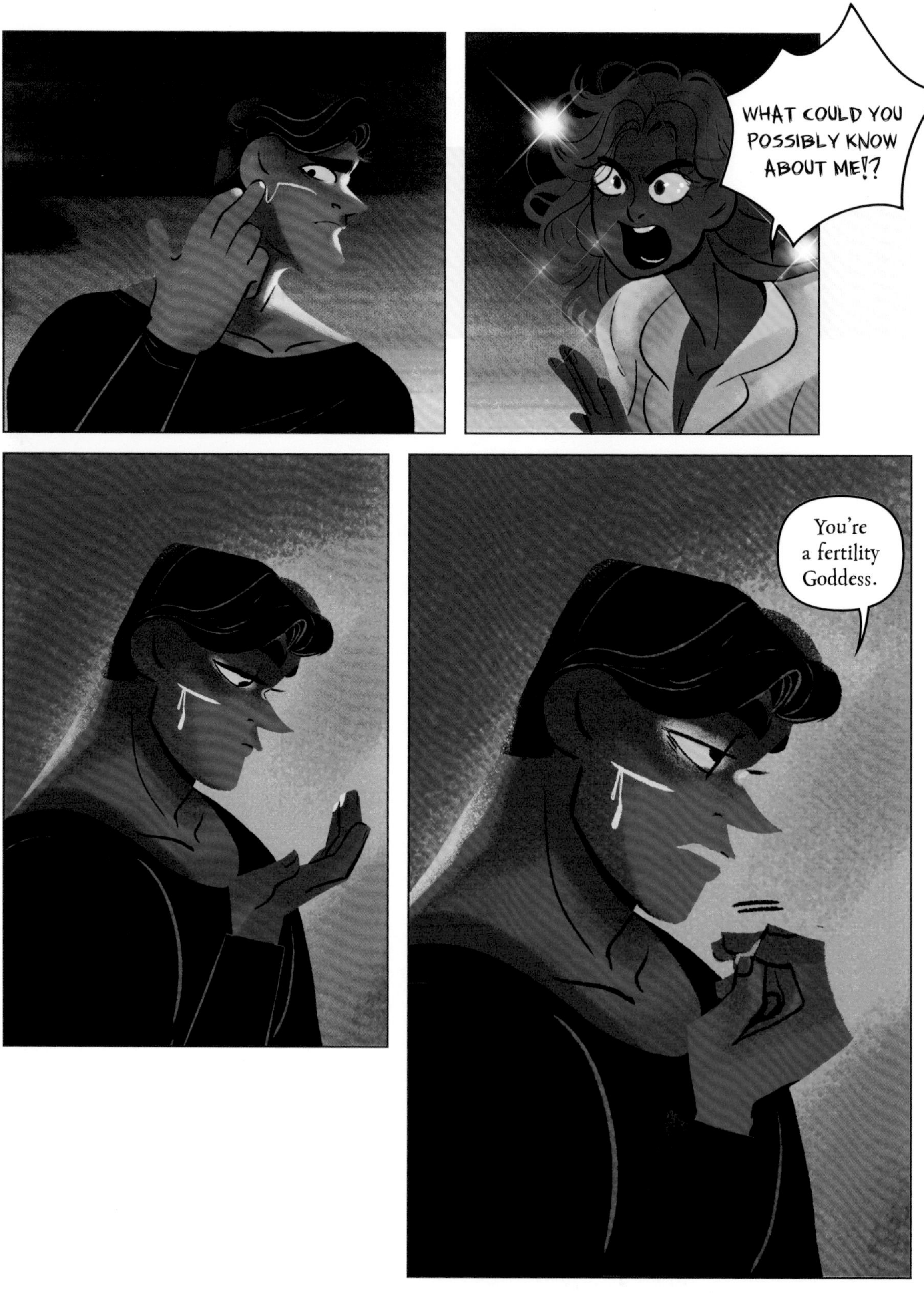
WHAT COULD YOU POSSIBLY KNOW ABOUT ME!?
You're a fertility Goddess.

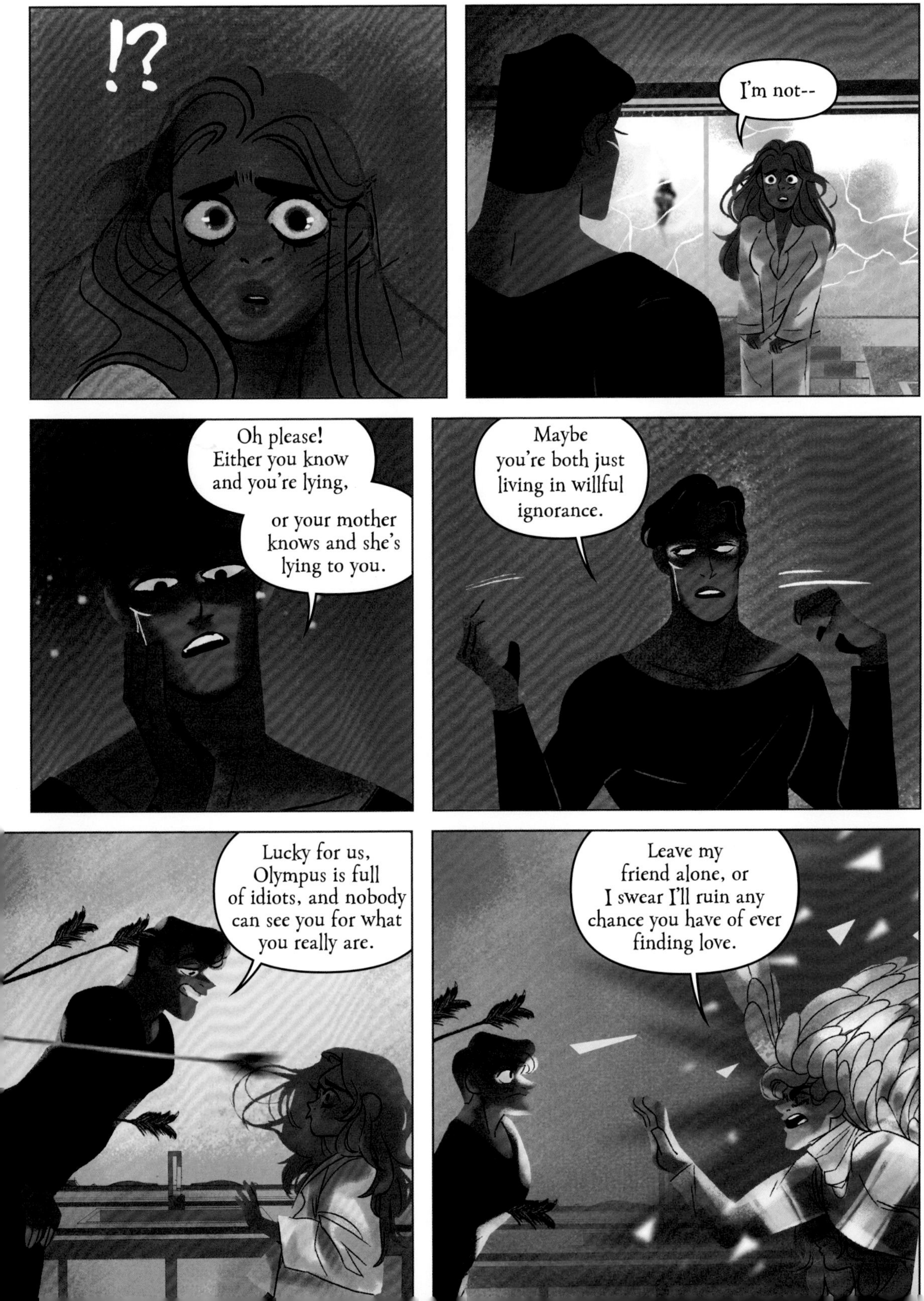
!?
I'm not--
Oh please! Either you know and you're lying,
or your mother knows and she's lying to you.
Maybe you're both just living in willful ignorance.
Lucky for us, Olympus is full of idiots, and nobody can see you for what you really are.
Leave my friend alone, or I swear I'll ruin any chance you have of ever finding love.

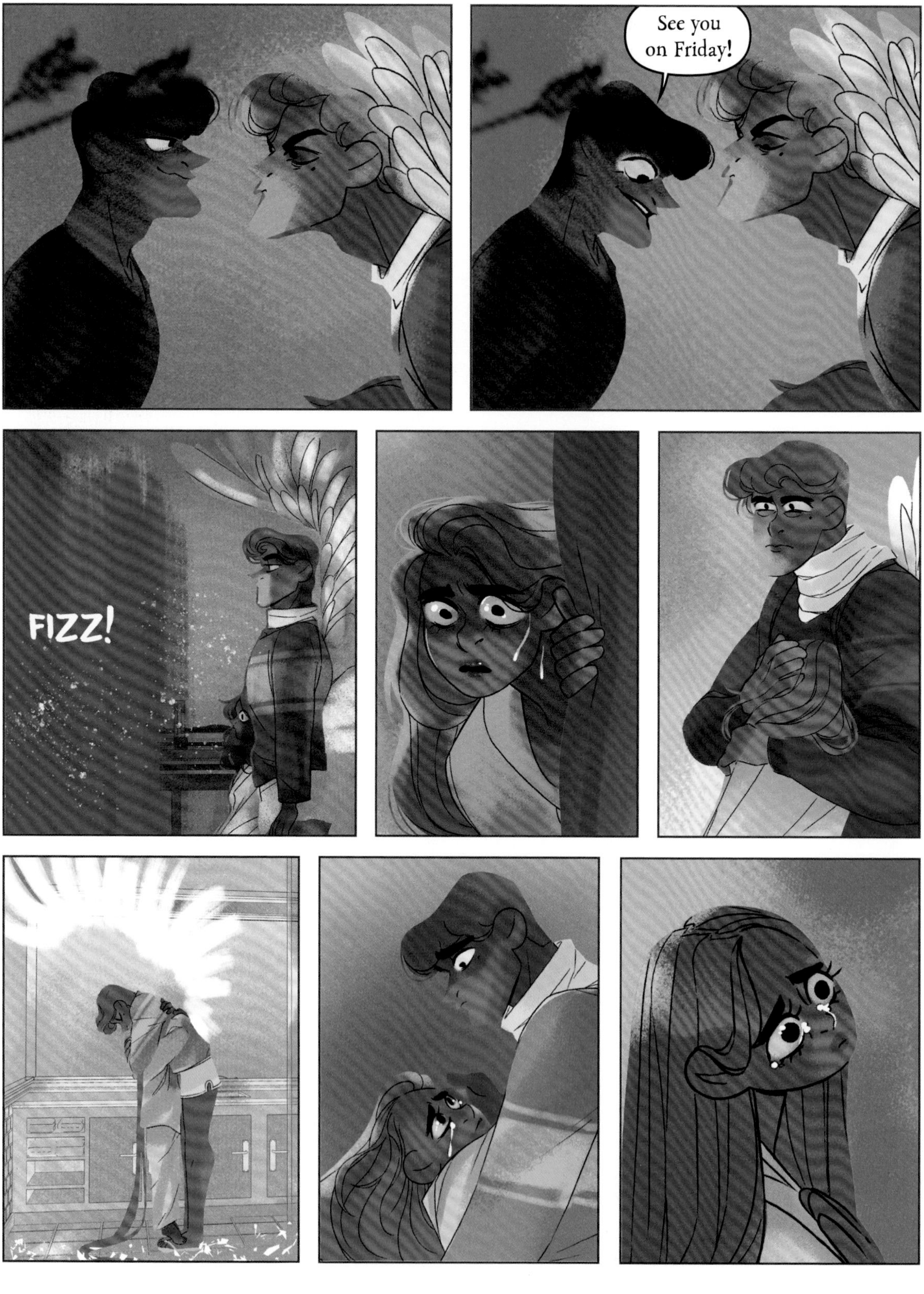
See you on Friday!
FIZZ!

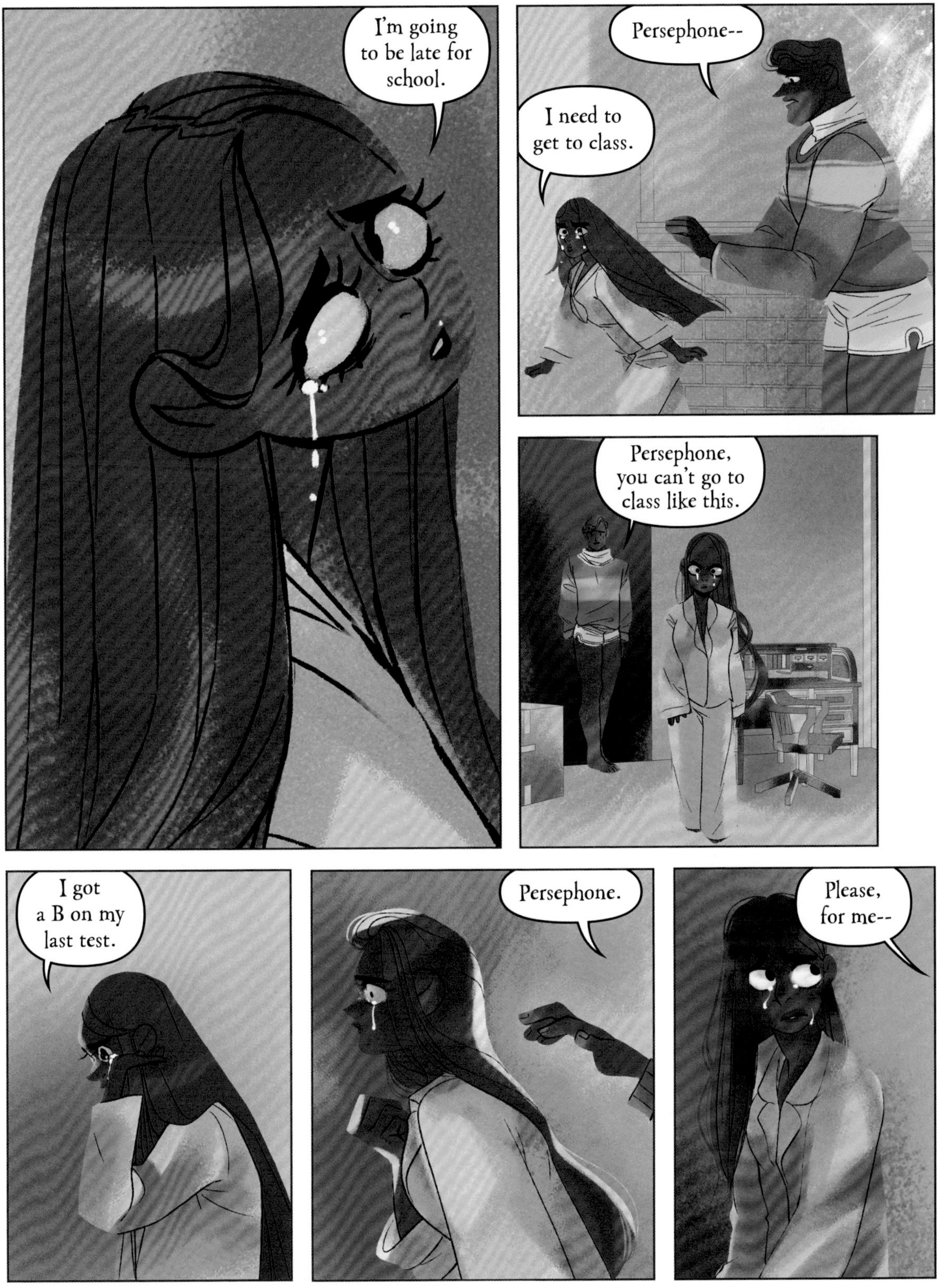
I'm going to be late for school.
Persephone--
I need to get to class.
Persephone, you can't go to class like this.
I got a B on my last test.
Persephone.
Please, for me--

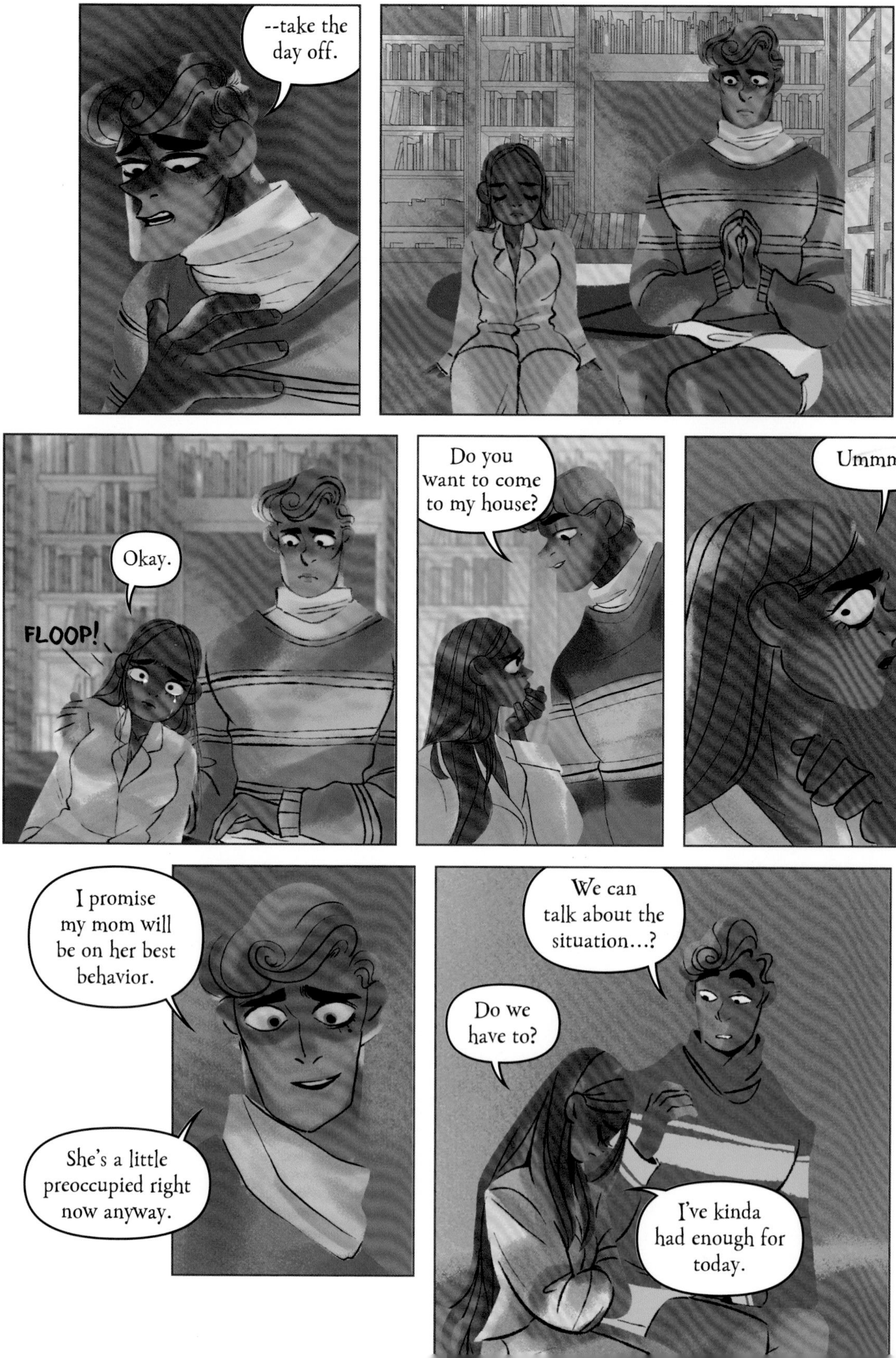
--take the day off.
Okay.
FLOOP!
Do you want to come to my house?
Ummm...
I promise my mom will be on her best behavior.
She's a little preoccupied right now anyway.
We can talk about the situation...?
Do we have to?
I've kinda had enough for today.

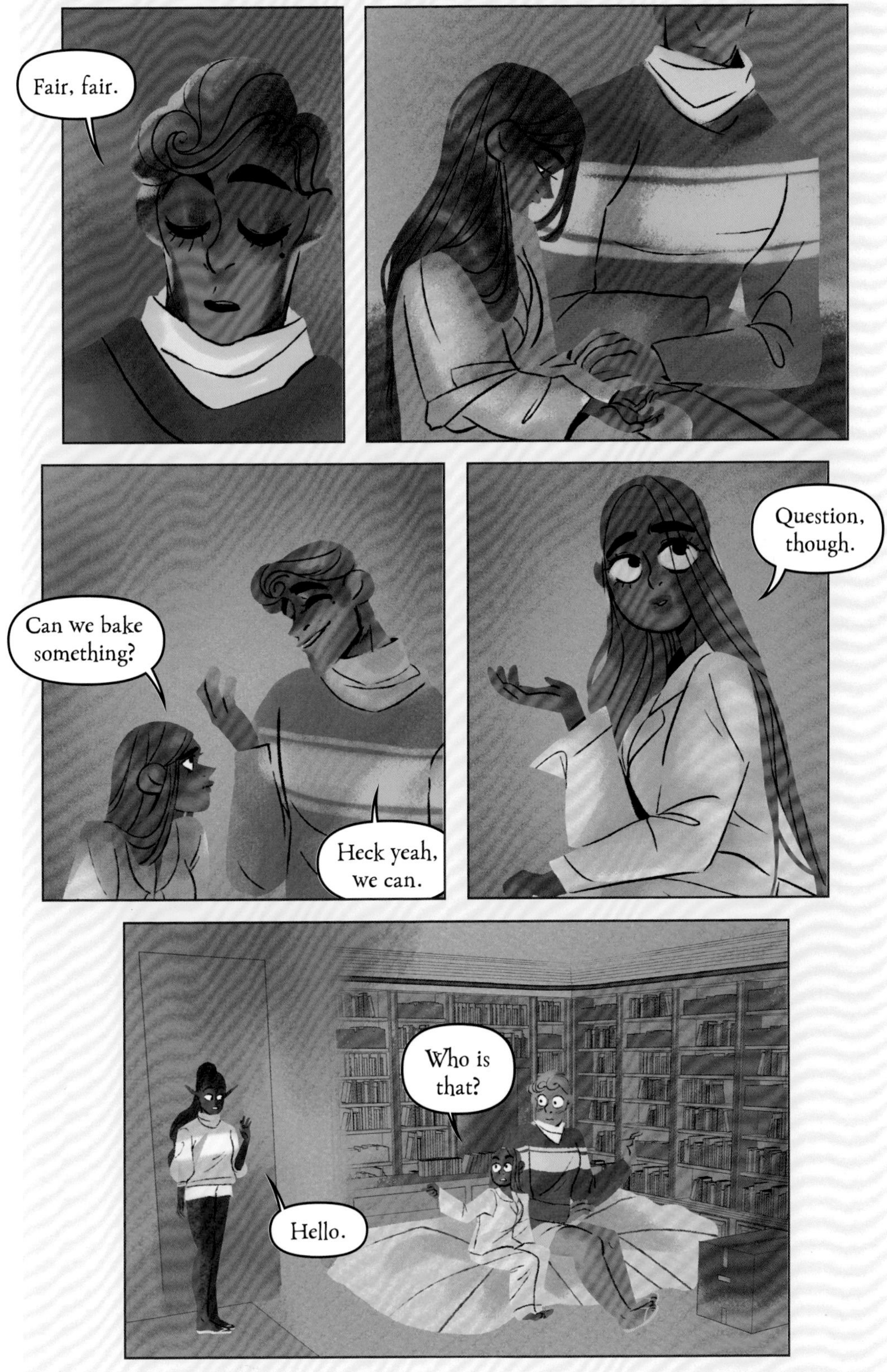
Fair, fair.
Can we bake something?
Heck yeah, we can.
Question, though.
Who is that?
Hello.

EPISODE 99: CUPID'S ARROW

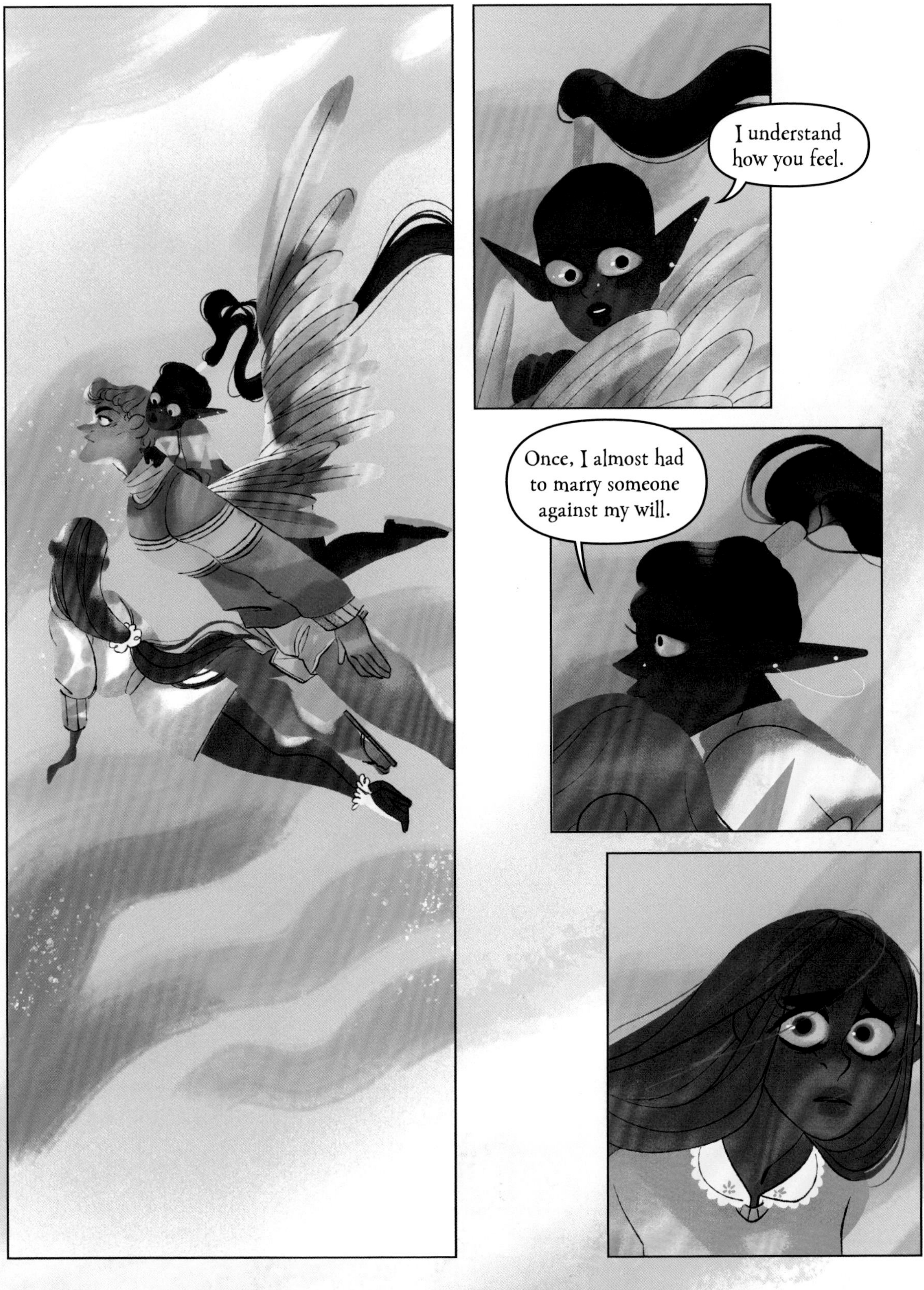
I understand how you feel.
Once, I almost had to marry someone against my will.

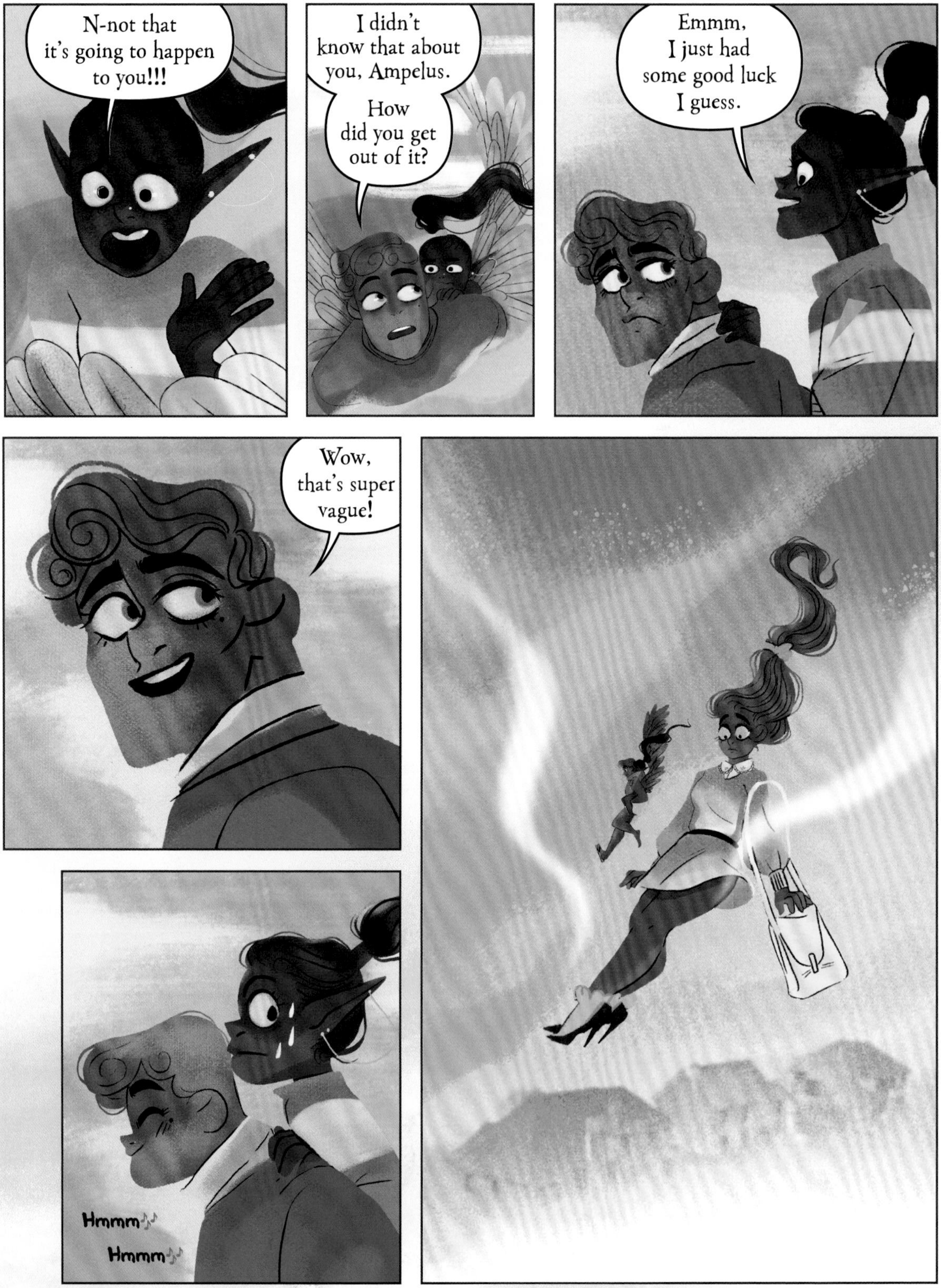
N-not that it's going to happen to you!!!
I didn't know that about you, Ampelus.
How did you get out of it?
Emmm, I just had some good luck I guess.
Wow, that's super vague!
Hmmm♪
Hmmm♪

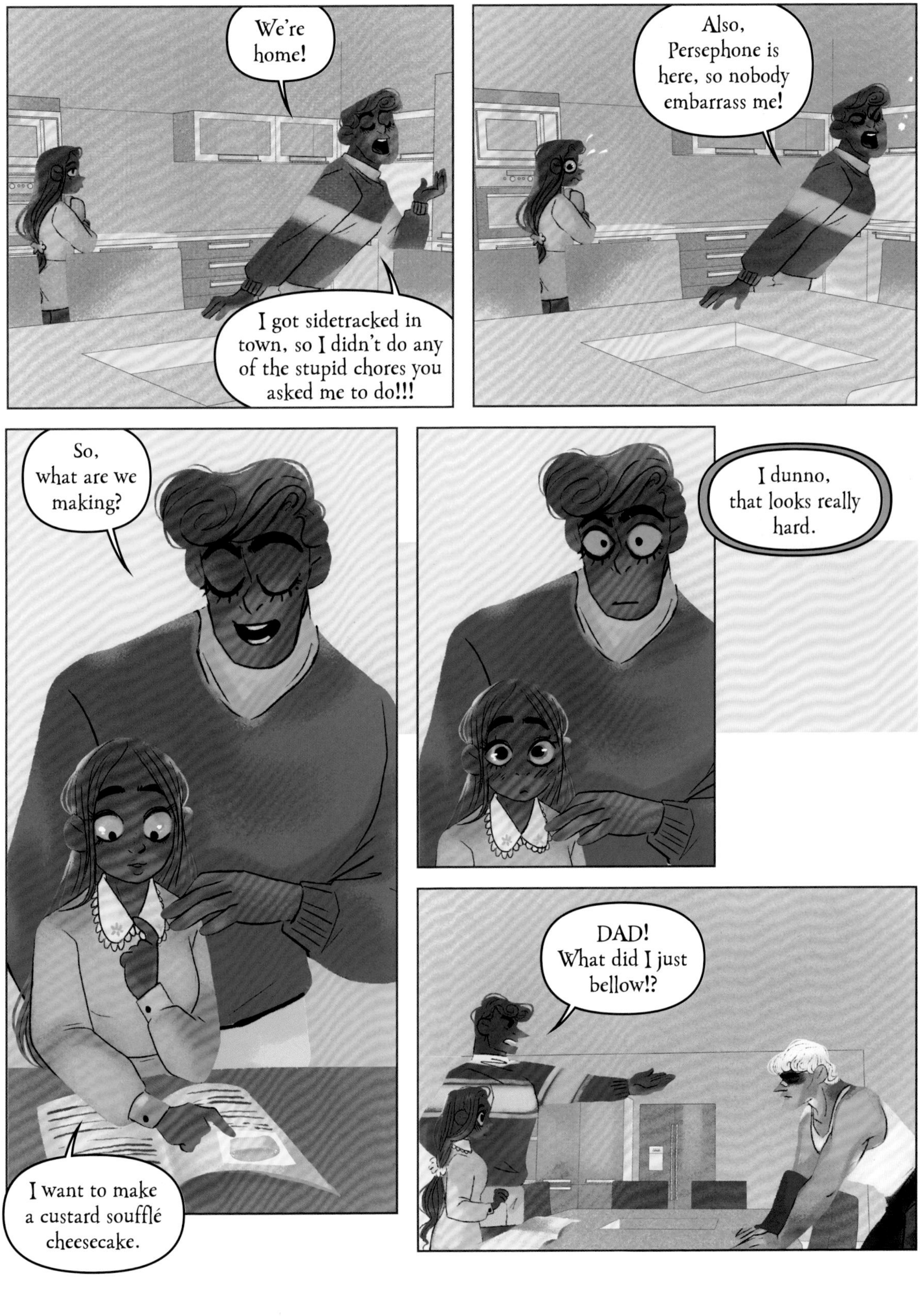
We're home!
I got sidetracked in town, so I didn't do any of the stupid chores you asked me to do!!!
Also, Persephone is here, so nobody embarrass me!
So, what are we making?
I want to make a custard soufflé cheesecake.
I dunno, that looks really hard.
DAD! What did I just bellow!?

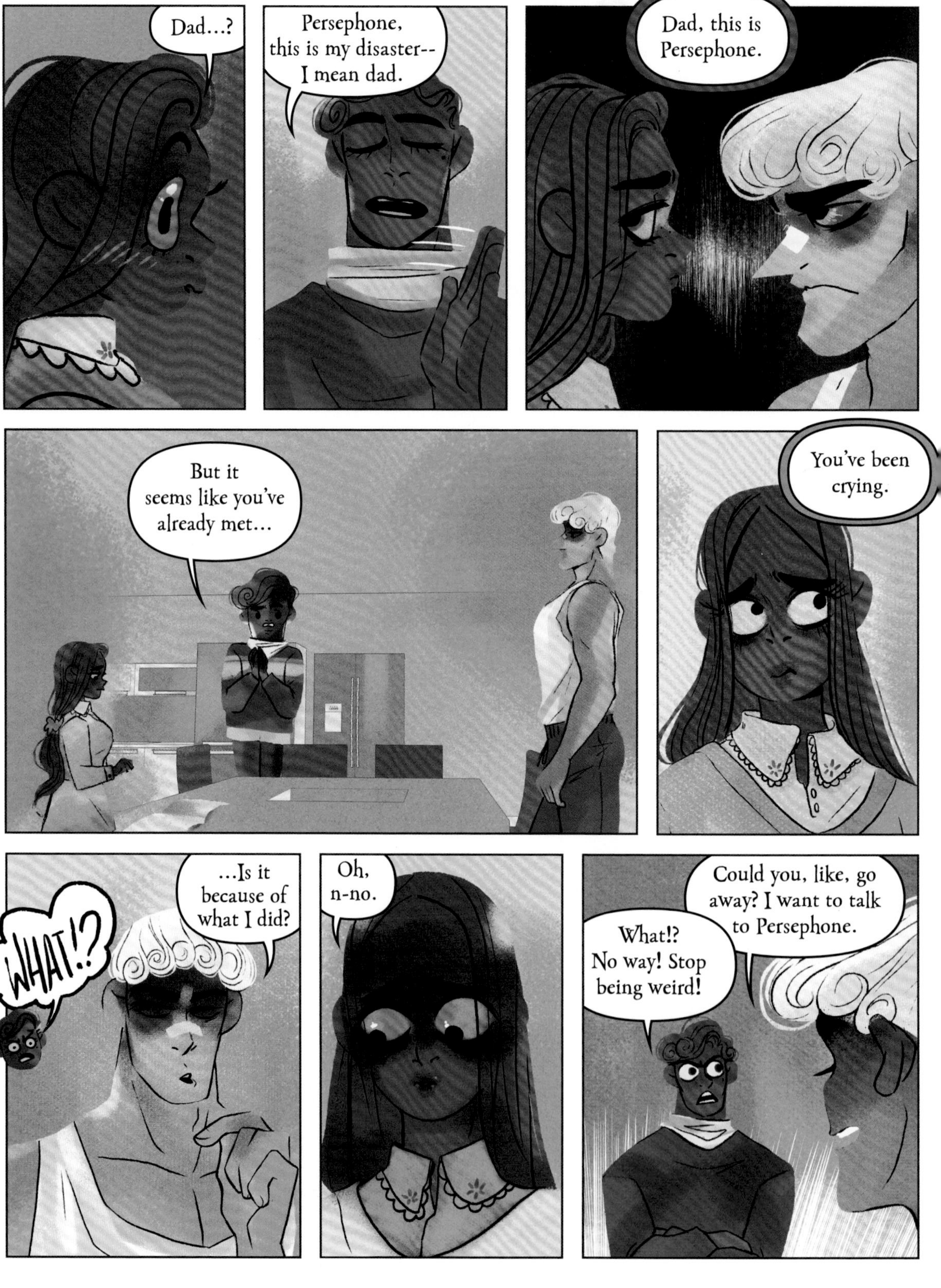
Dad...?
Persephone, this is my disaster-- I mean dad.
Dad, this is Persephone.
But it seems like you've already met...
You've been crying.
...Is it because of what I did?
WHAT!?
Oh, n-no.
Could you, like, go away? I want to talk to Persephone.
What!? No way! Stop being weird!

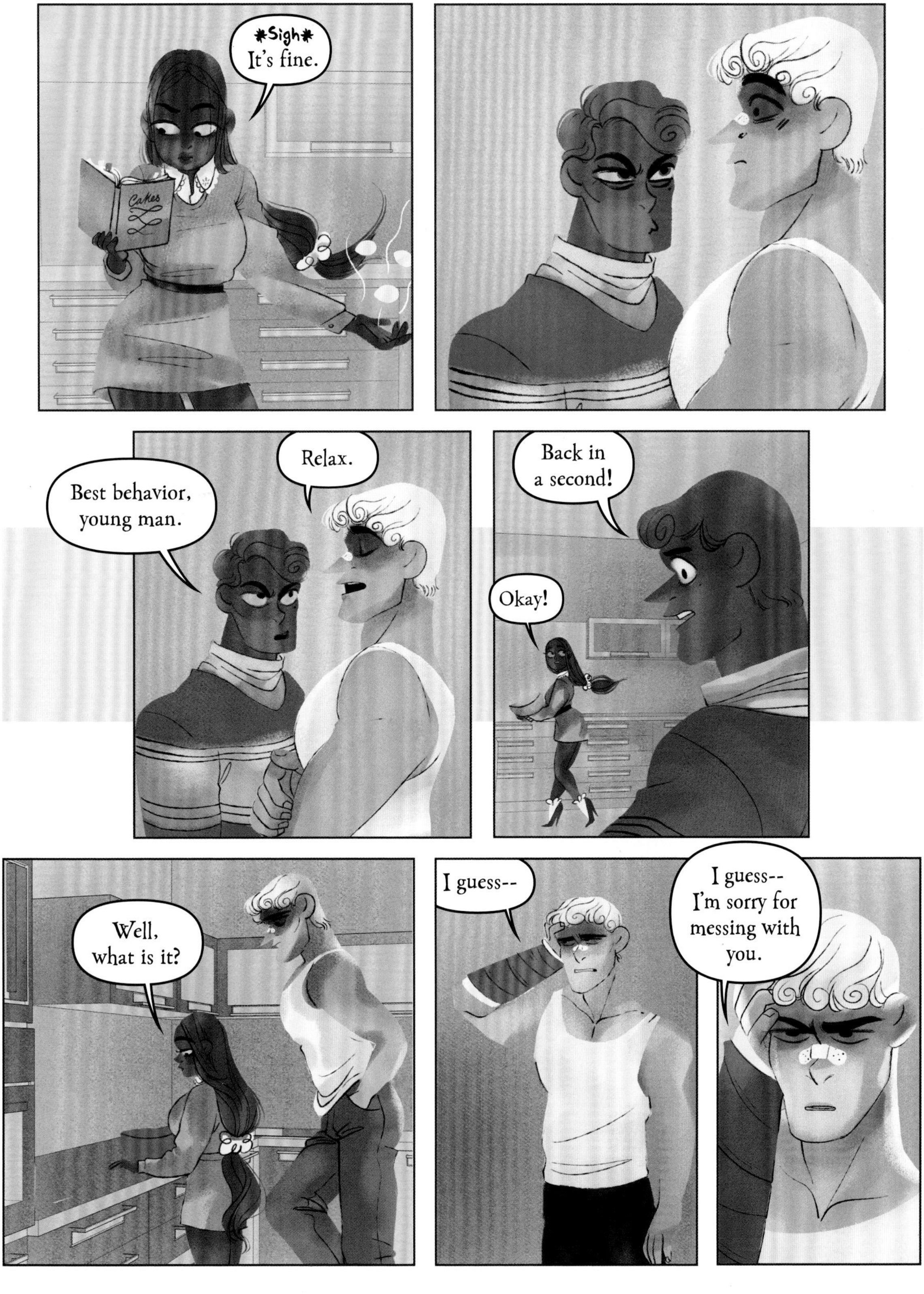
Sigh It's fine.
Best behavior, young man.
Relax.
Back in a second!
Okay!
Well, what is it?
I guess--
I guess-- I'm sorry for messing with you.

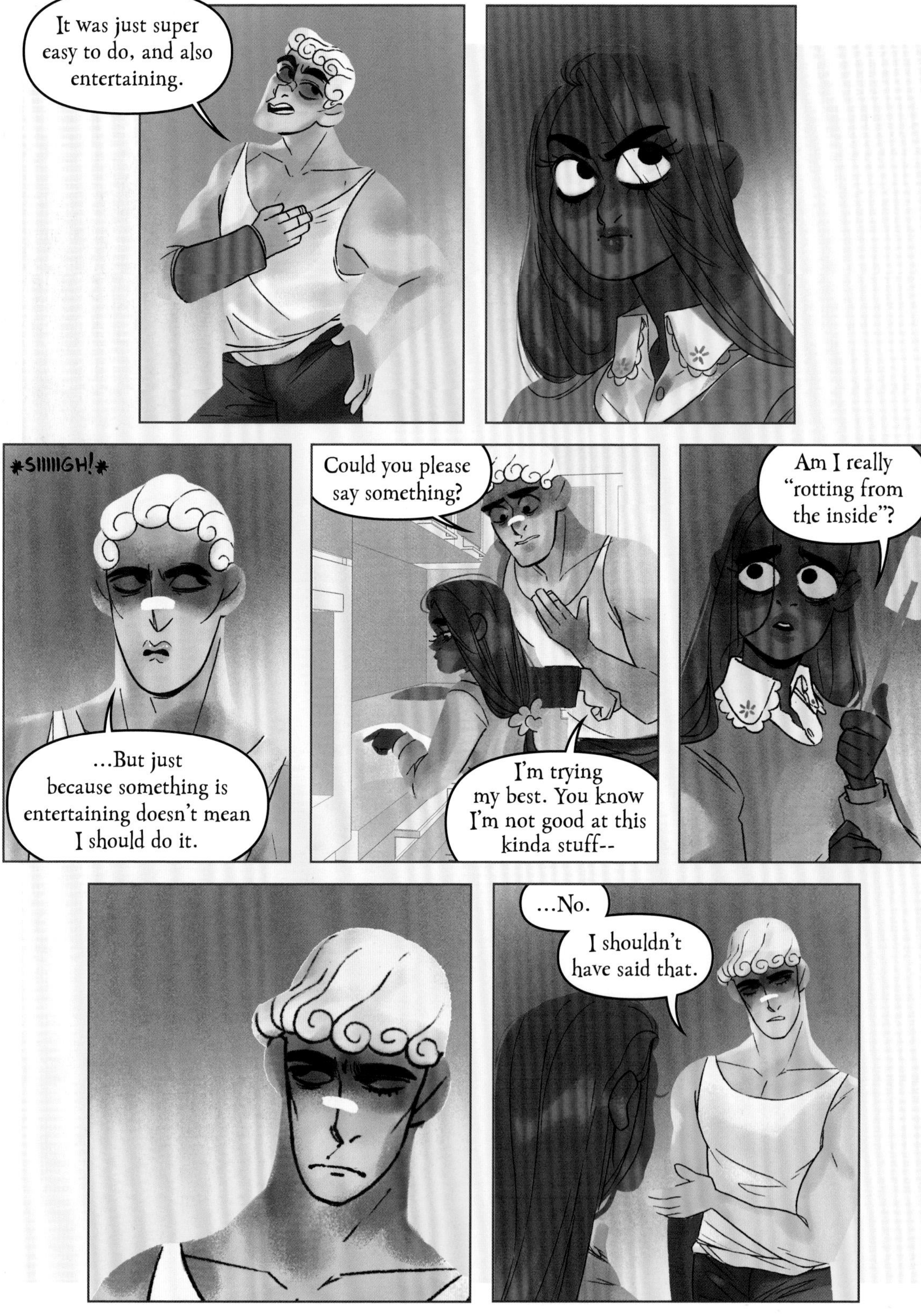
It was just super easy to do, and also entertaining.
SIIIIGH!
...But just because something is entertaining doesn't mean I should do it.
Could you please say something?
I'm trying my best. You know I'm not good at this kinda stuff--
Am I really "rotting from the inside"?
...No.
I shouldn't have said that.

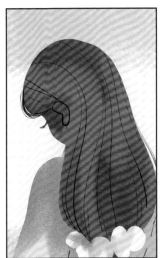

You're still angry though.

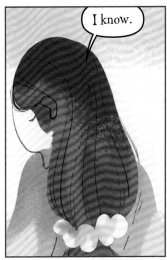

I know.

SWING!

How come you cried?

Do you need me to kill someone for you?

I'm sorry I let my mother beat you with a pitchfork.

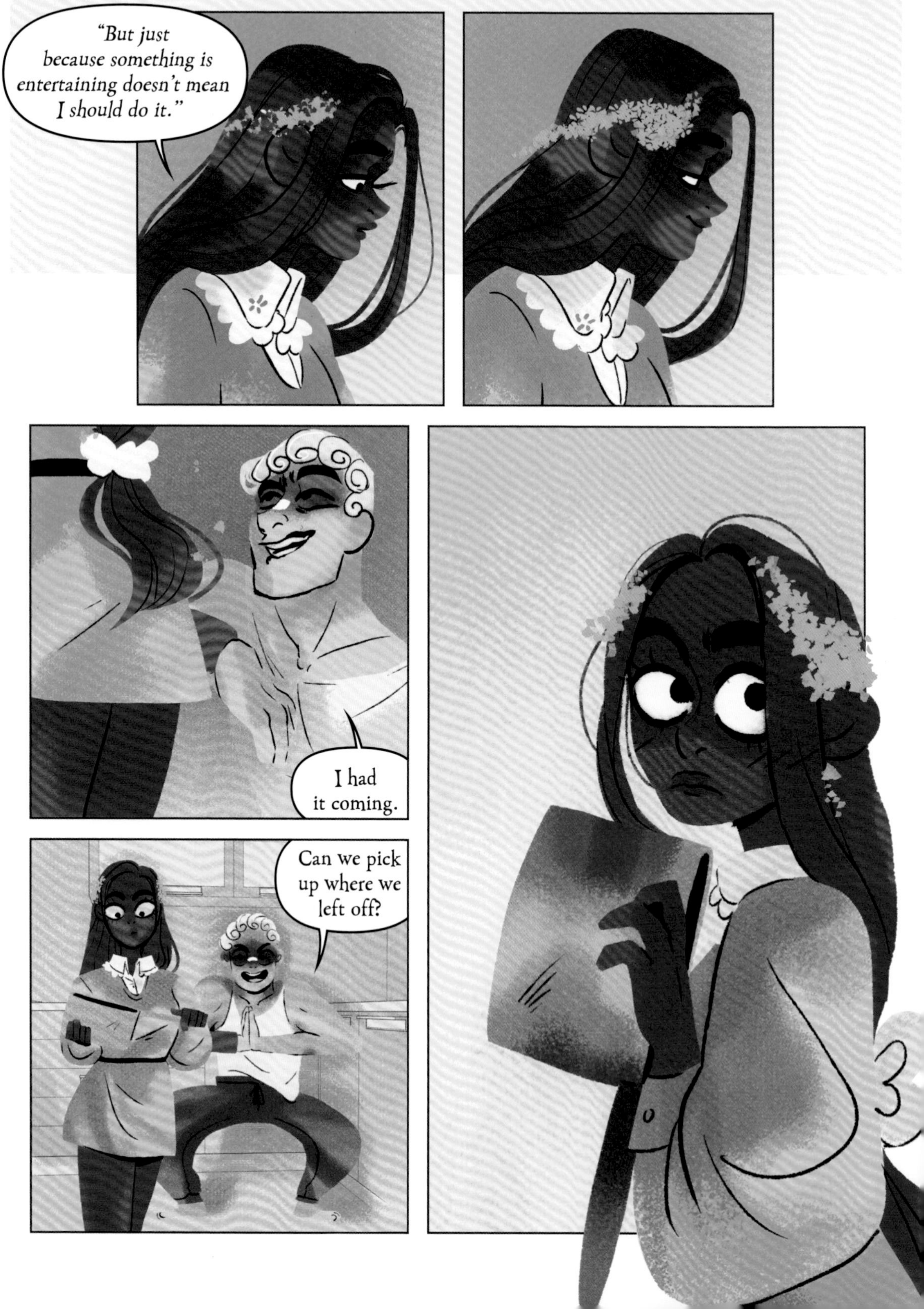
"But just because something is entertaining doesn't mean I should do it."
I had it coming.
Can we pick up where we left off?

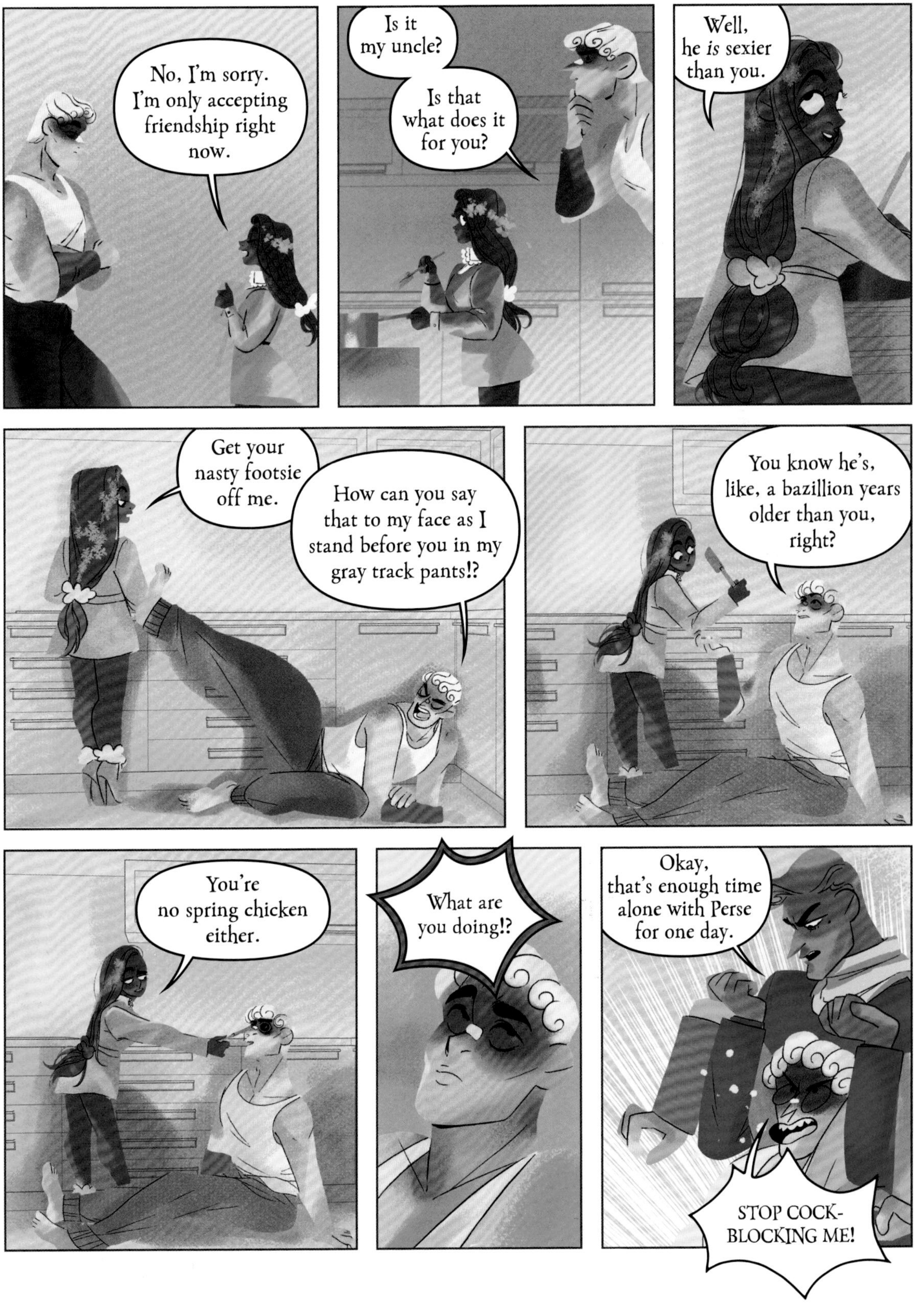
No, I'm sorry. I'm only accepting friendship right now.
Is it my uncle?
Is that what does it for you?
Well, he *is* sexier than you.
Get your nasty footsie off me.
How can you say that to my face as I stand before you in my gray track pants!?
You know he's, like, a bazillion years older than you, right?
You're no spring chicken either.
What are you doing!?
Okay, that's enough time alone with Perse for one day.
STOP COCK-BLOCKING ME!

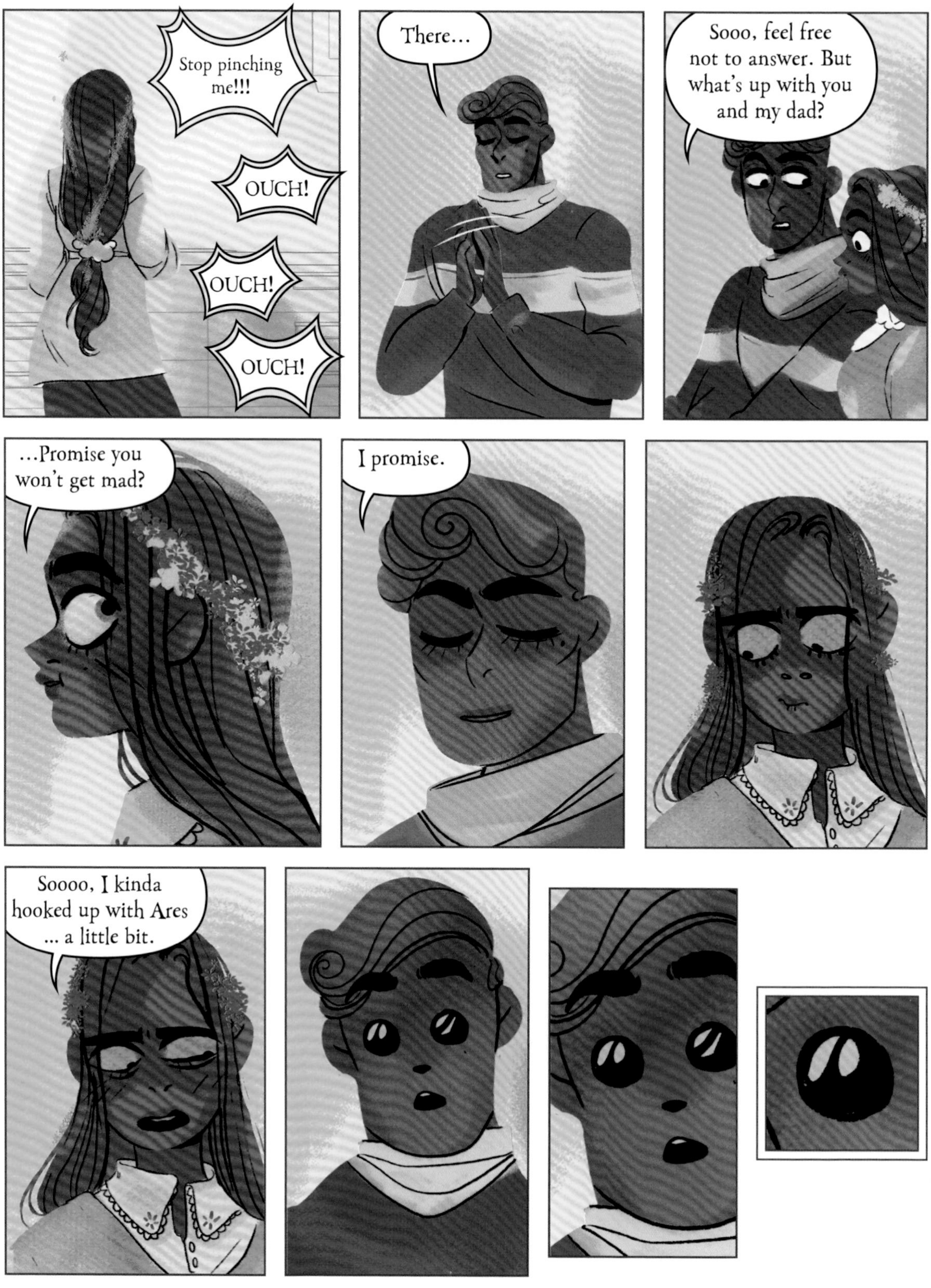
Stop pinching me!!!
OUCH!
OUCH!
OUCH!
There...
Sooo, feel free not to answer. But what's up with you and my dad?
...Promise you won't get mad?
I promise.
Soooo, I kinda hooked up with Ares ... a little bit.

EPISODE 100: MAN IN THE WOODS

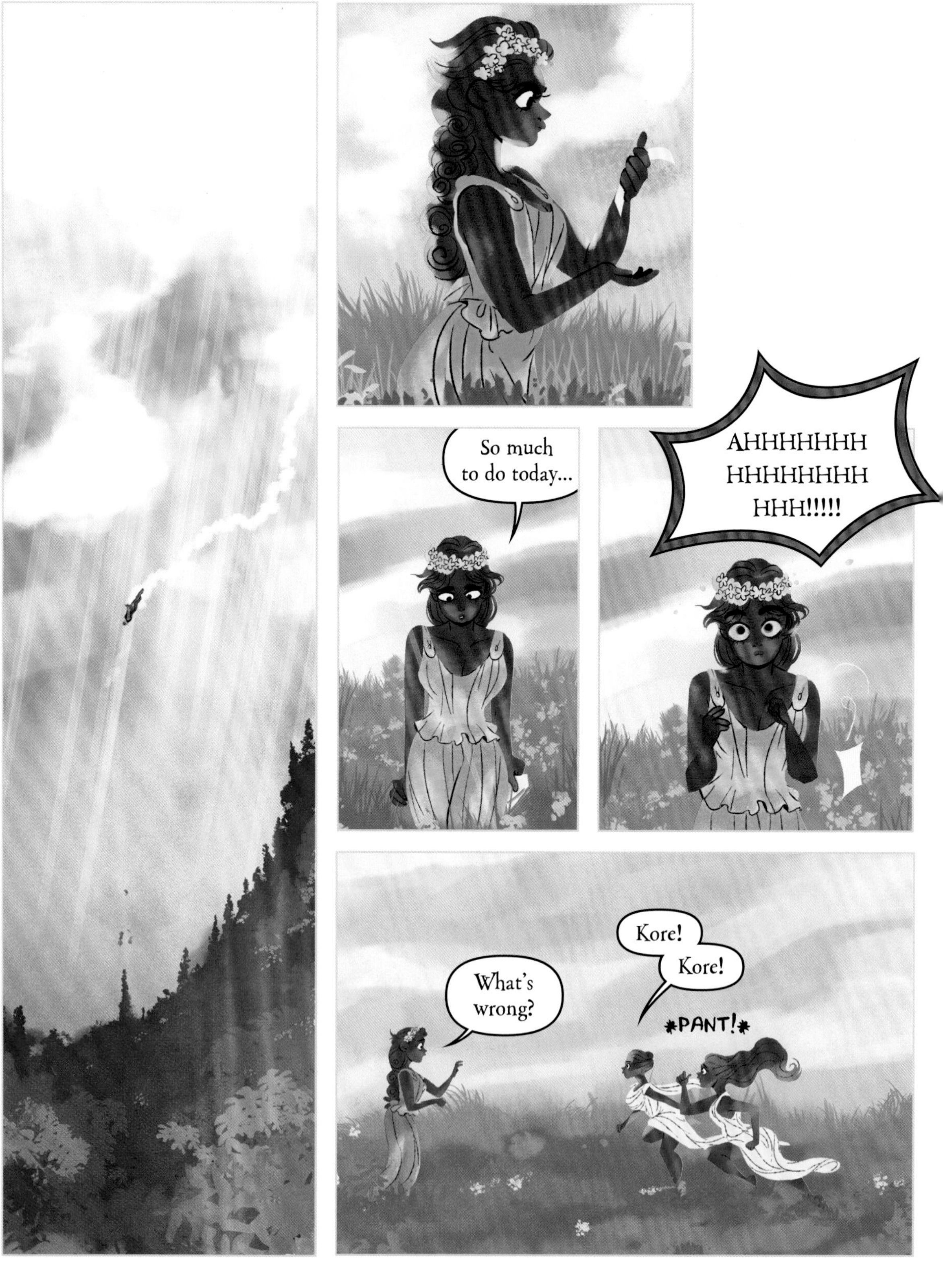
So much to do today...
AHHHHHHH HHHHHHHH HHH!!!!!
What's wrong?
Kore!
Kore!
PANT!

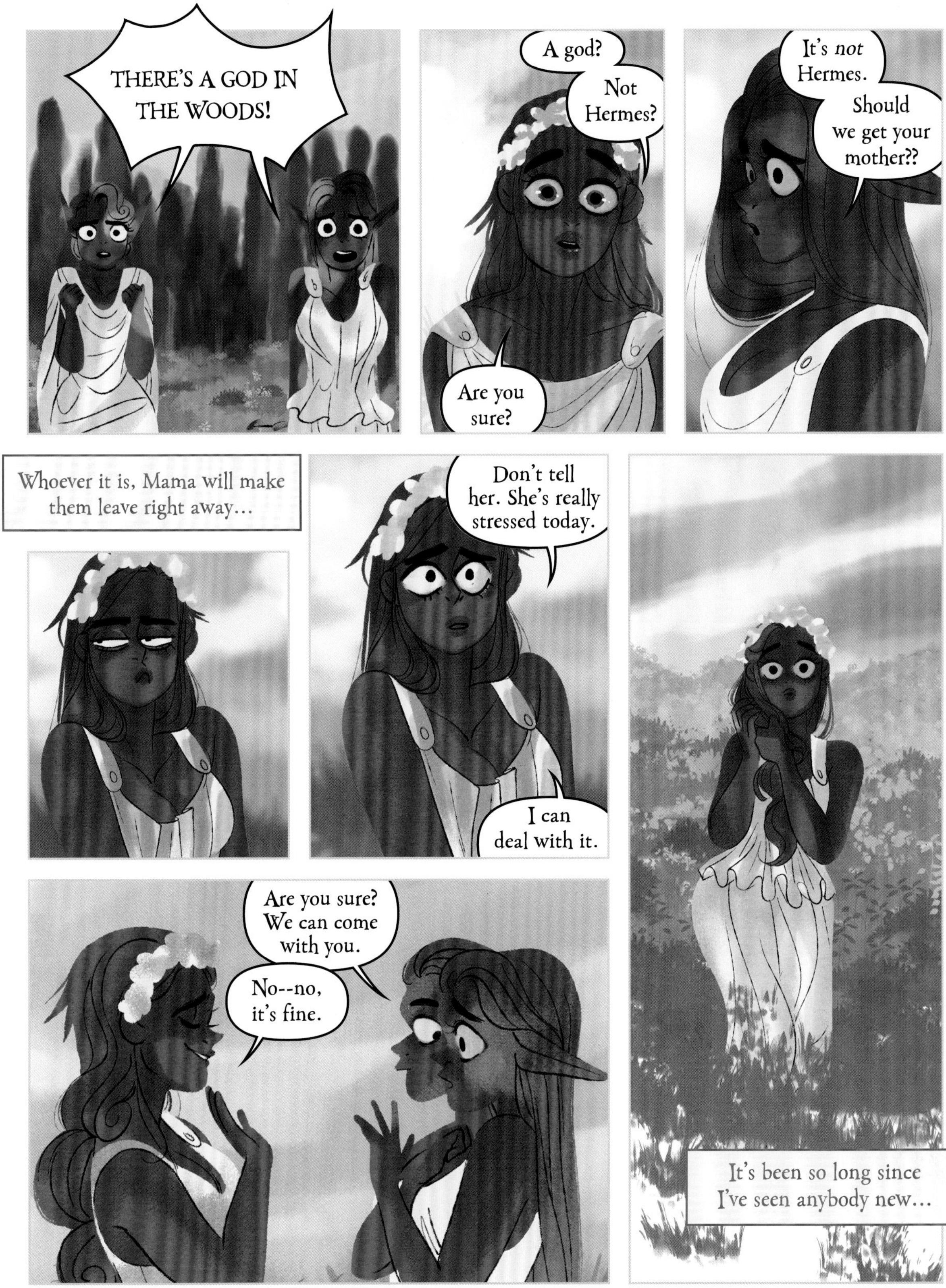
THERE'S A GOD IN THE WOODS!
A god?
Not Hermes?
Are you sure?
It's *not* Hermes.
Should we get your mother??
Whoever it is, Mama will make them leave right away...
Don't tell her. She's really stressed today.
I can deal with it.
Are you sure? We can come with you.
No--no, it's fine.
It's been so long since I've seen anybody new...

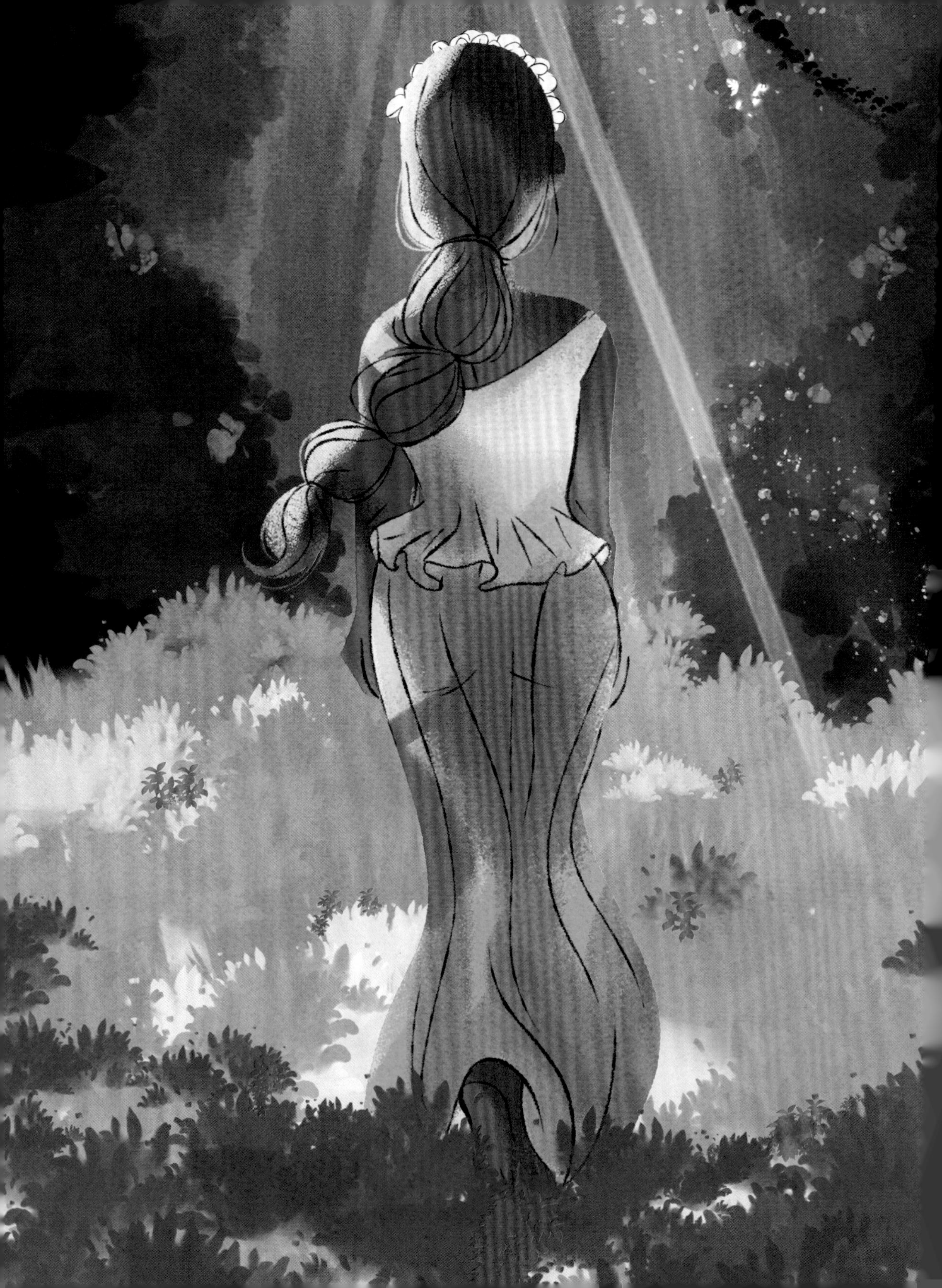

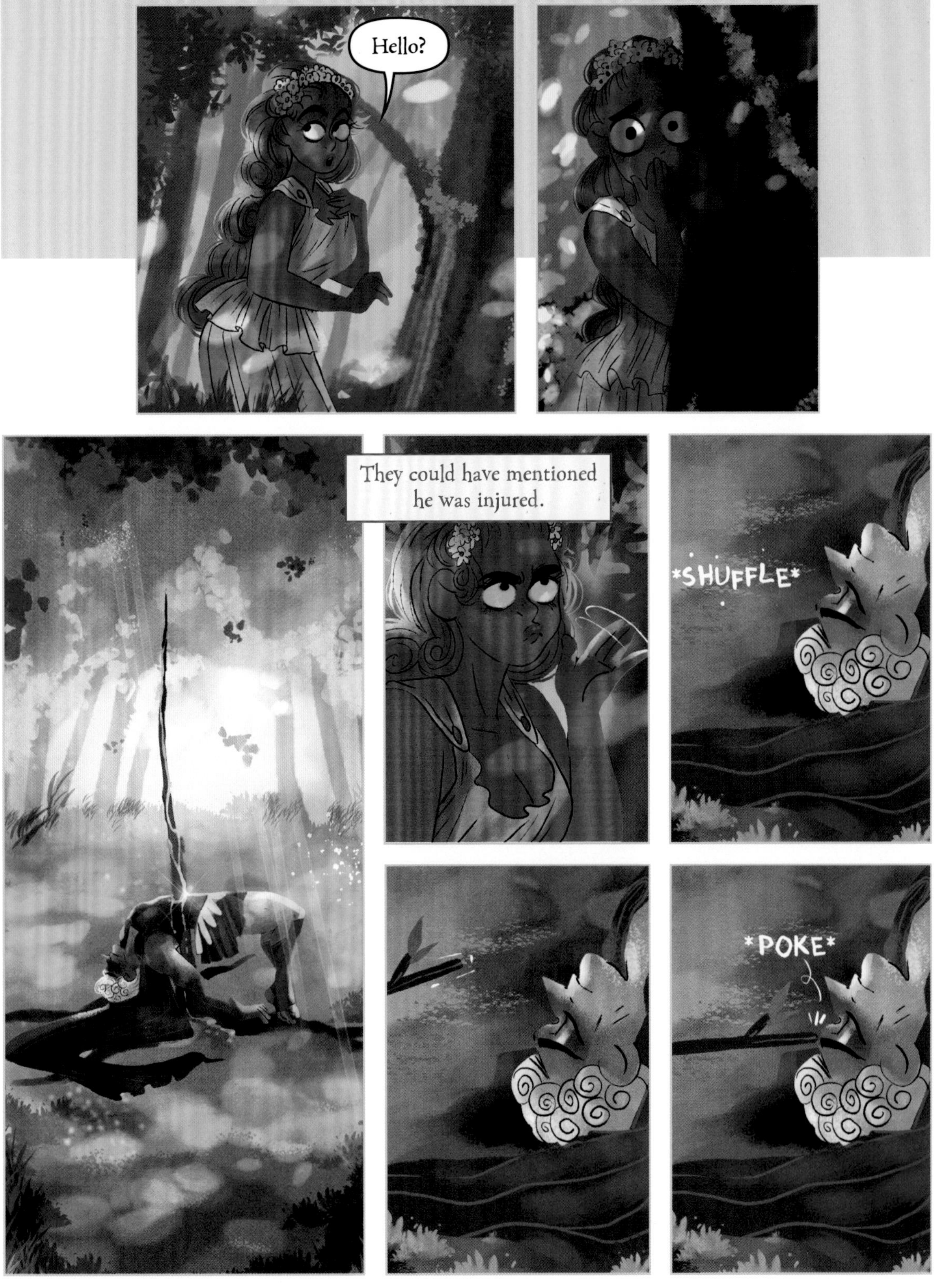
Hello?
They could have mentioned he was injured.
SHUFFLE
POKE

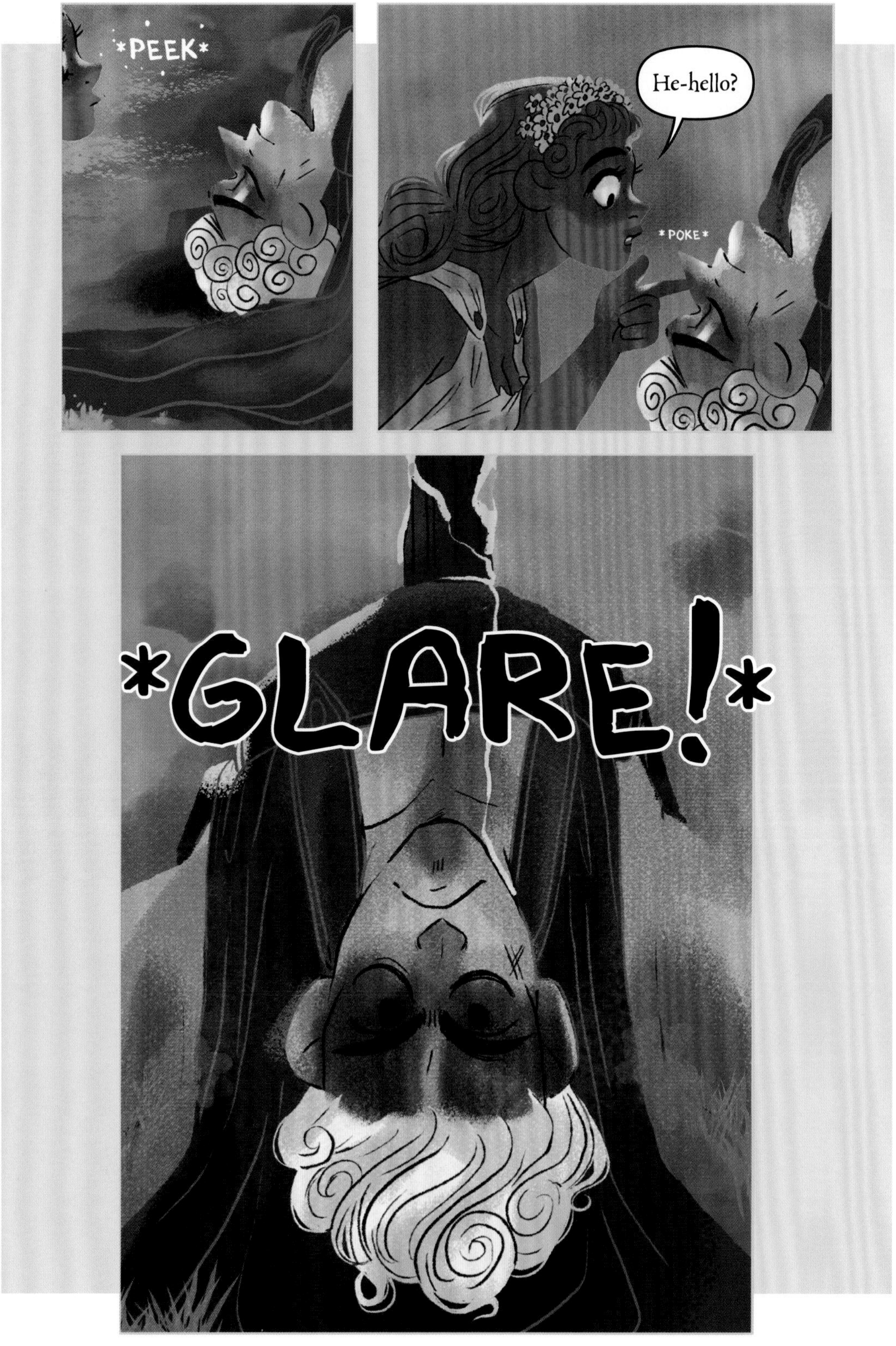
PEEK
He-hello?
POKE
GLARE!

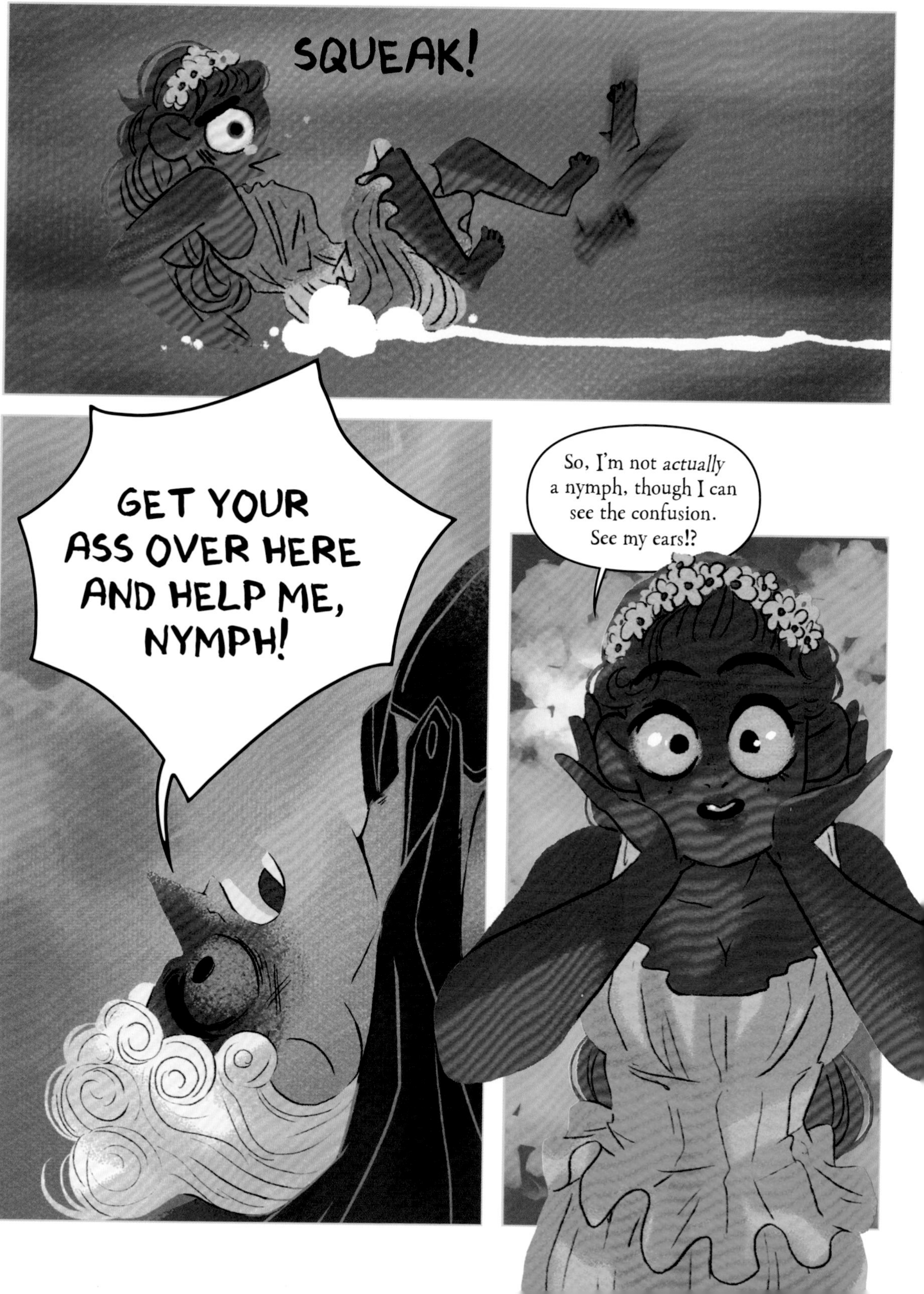
SQUEAK!
GET YOUR ASS OVER HERE AND HELP ME, NYMPH!
So, I'm not *actually* a nymph, though I can see the confusion. See my ears!?

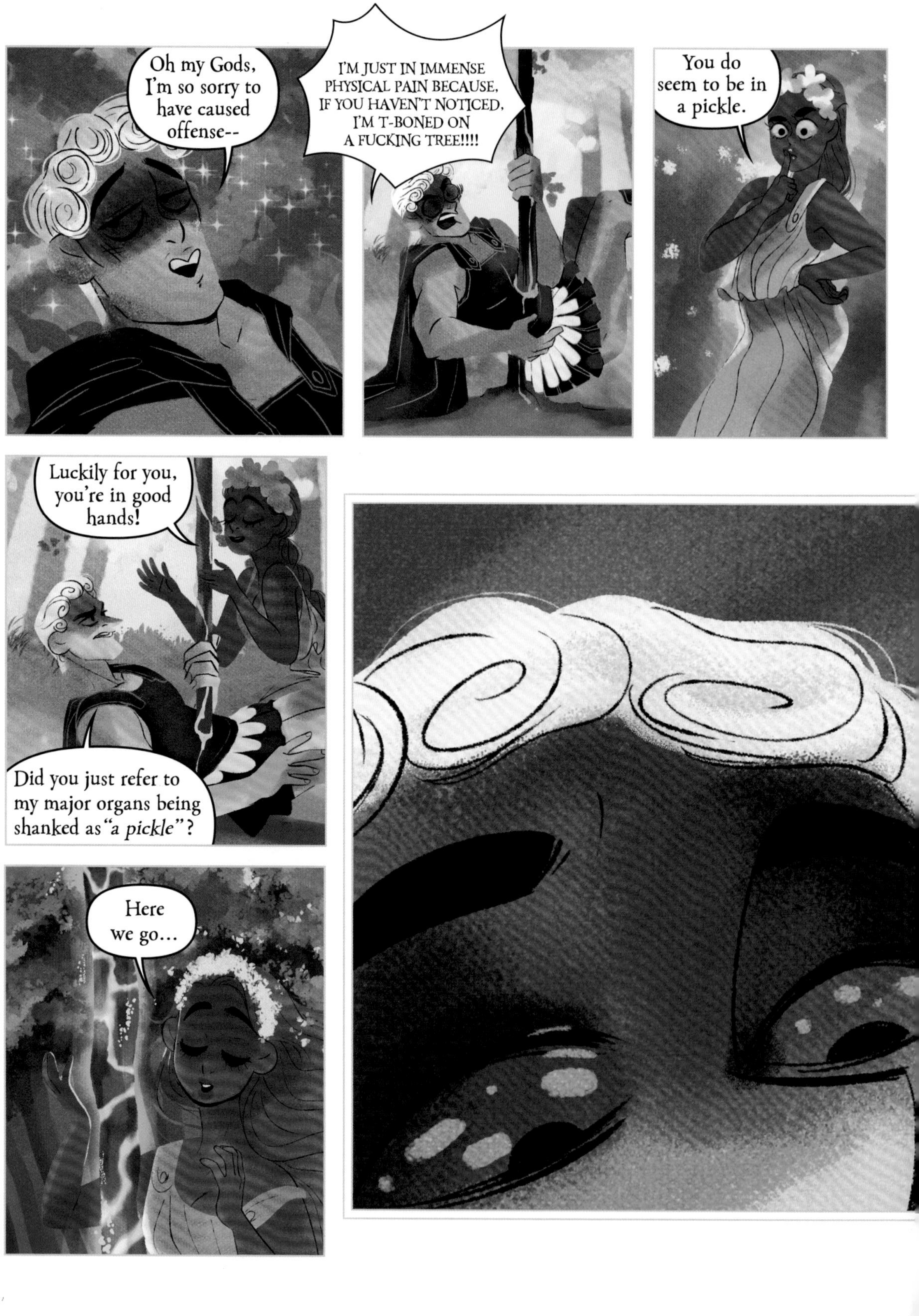
Oh my Gods, I'm so sorry to have caused offense--
I'M JUST IN IMMENSE PHYSICAL PAIN BECAUSE, IF YOU HAVEN'T NOTICED, I'M T-BONED ON A FUCKING TREE!!!!
You do seem to be in a pickle.
Luckily for you, you're in good hands!
Did you just refer to my major organs being shanked as "a pickle"?
Here we go…

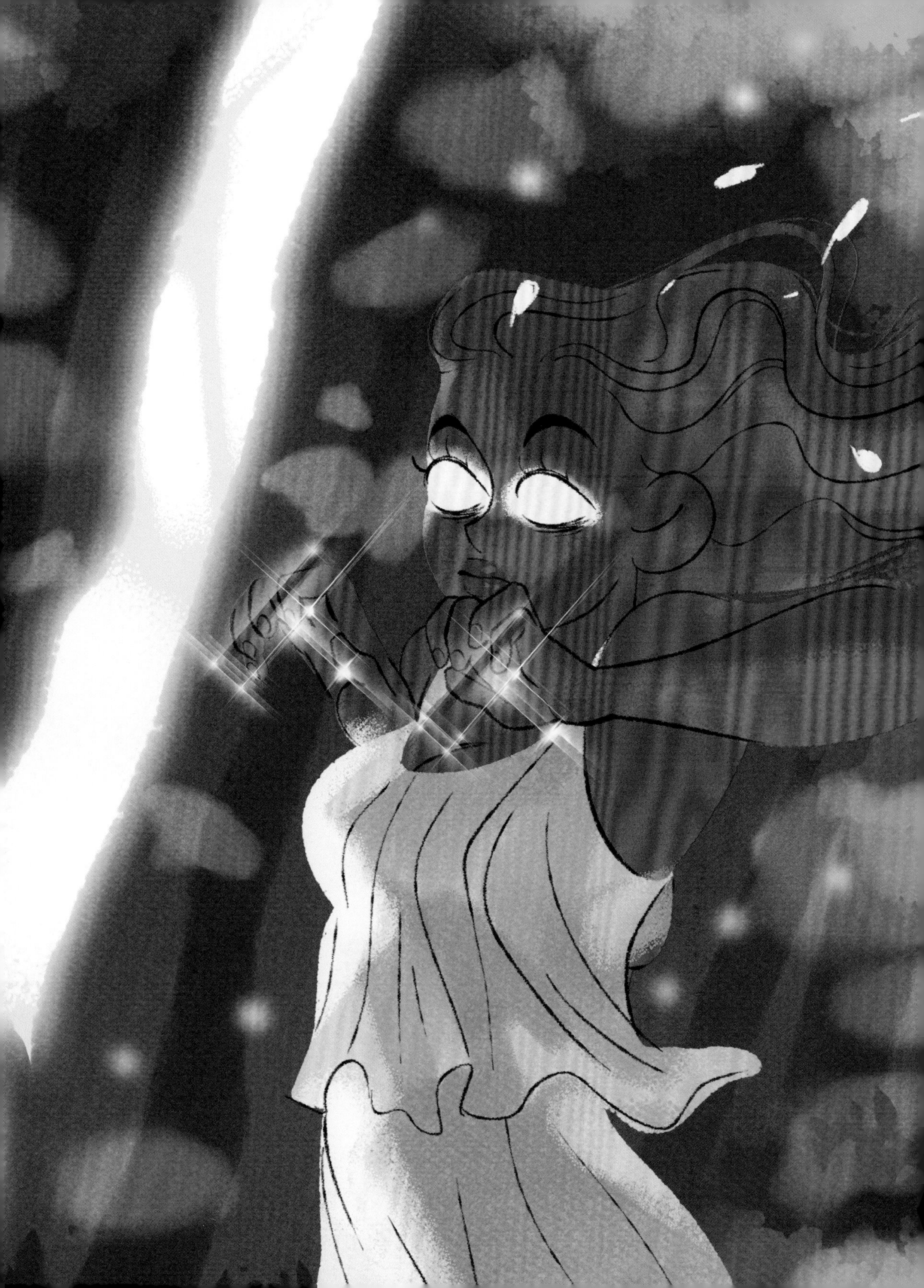

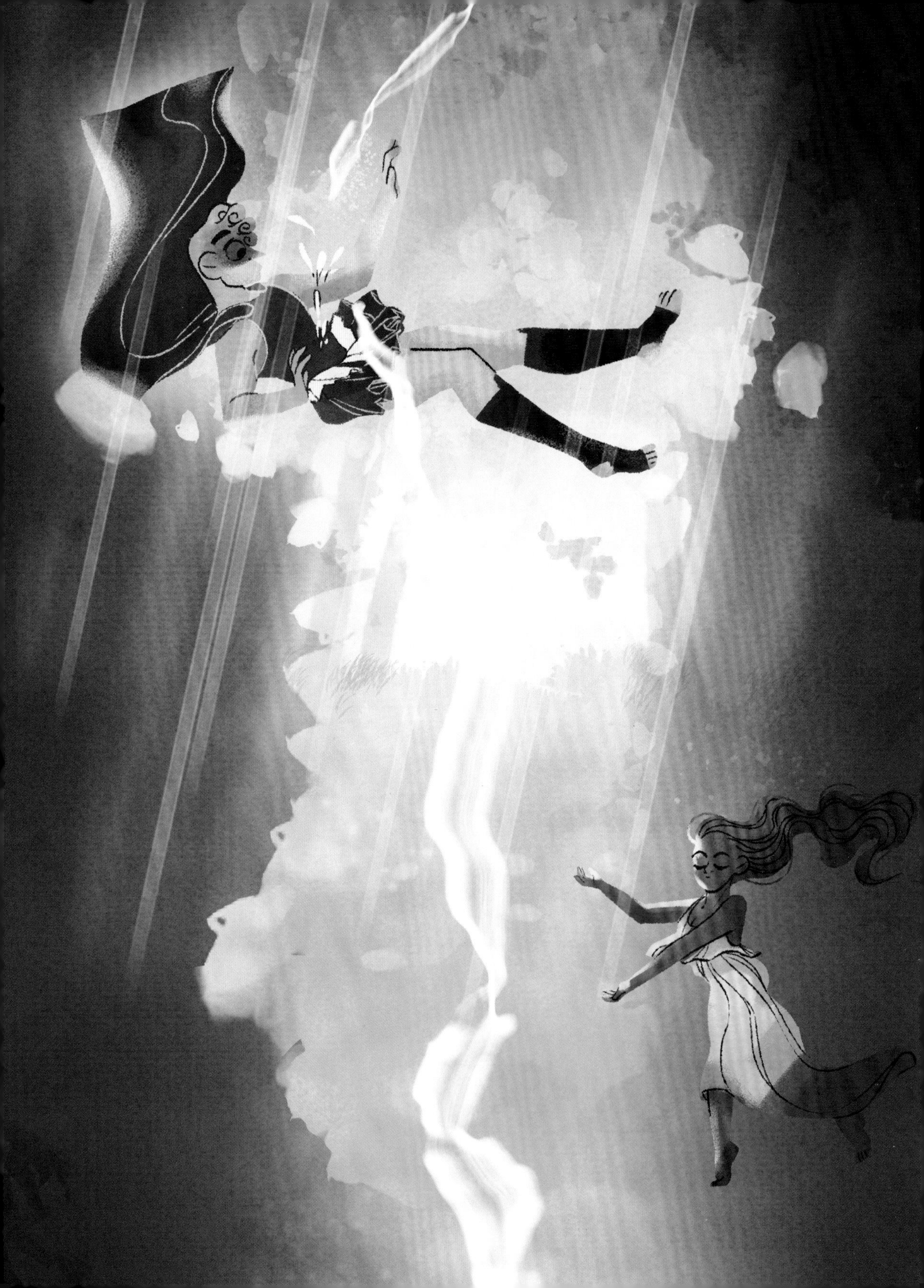

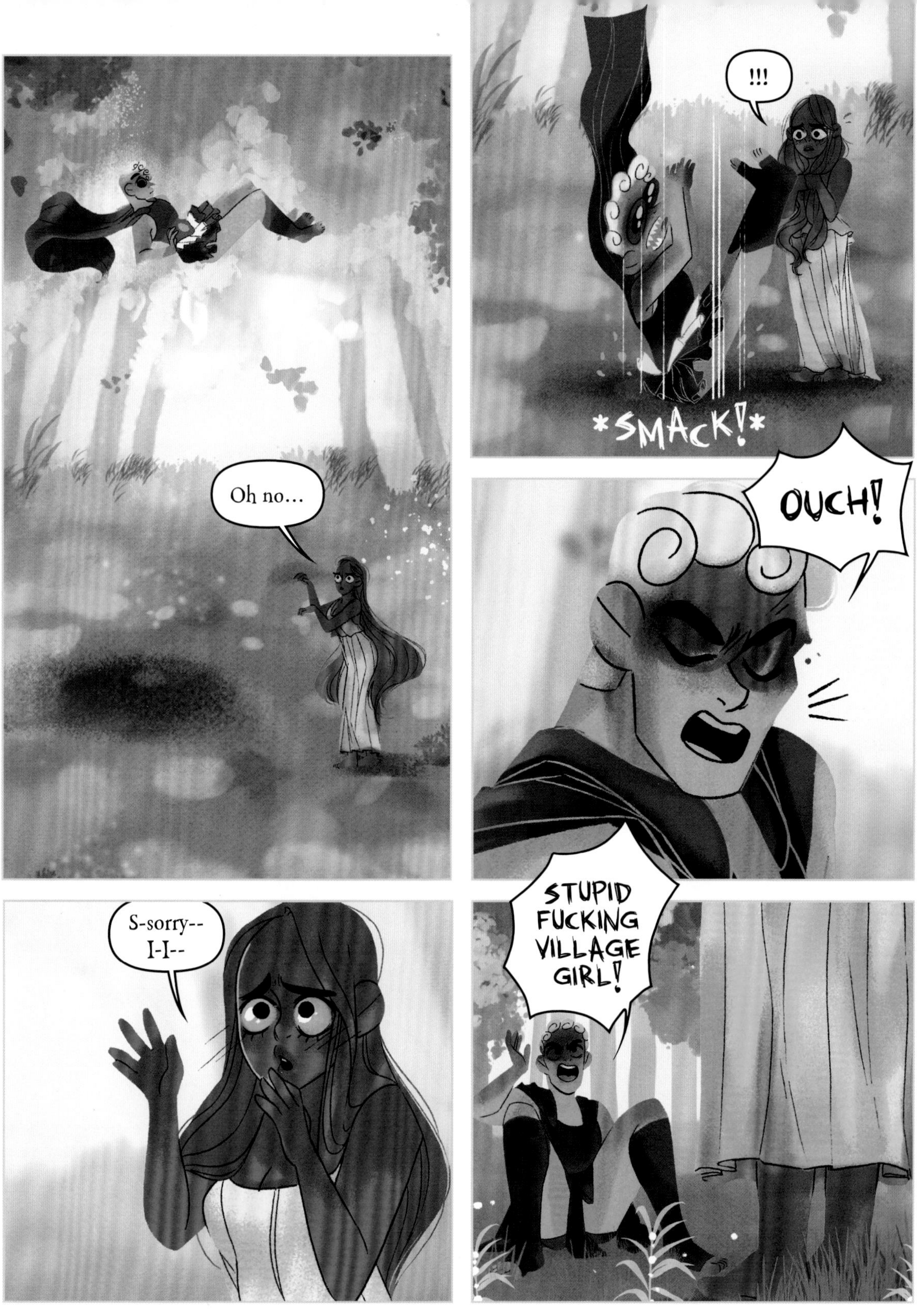
Oh no...
!!!
SMACK!
OUCH!
S-sorry--
I-I--
STUPID FUCKING VILLAGE GIRL!

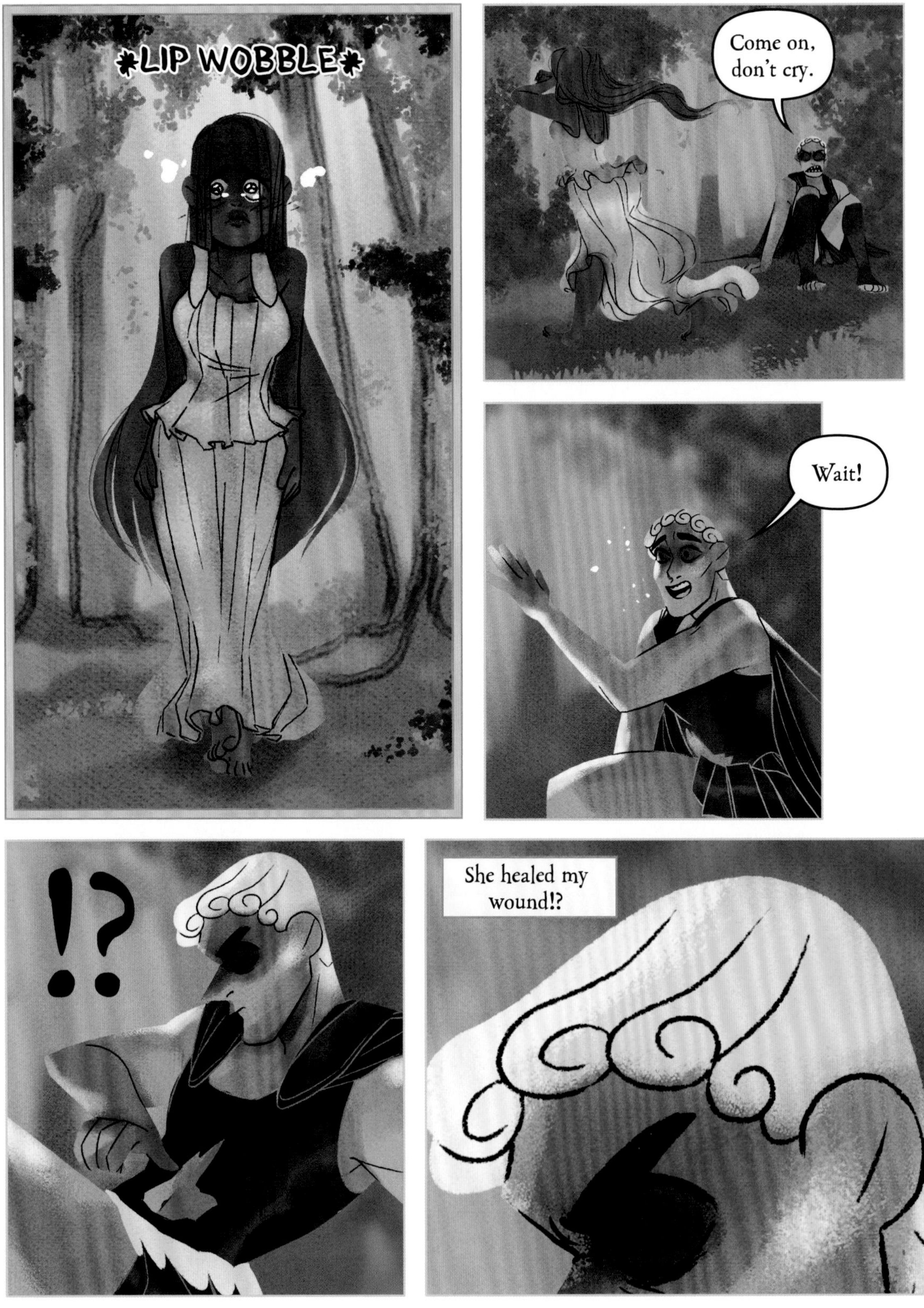
LIP WOBBLE
Come on, don't cry.
Wait!
!?
She healed my wound!?

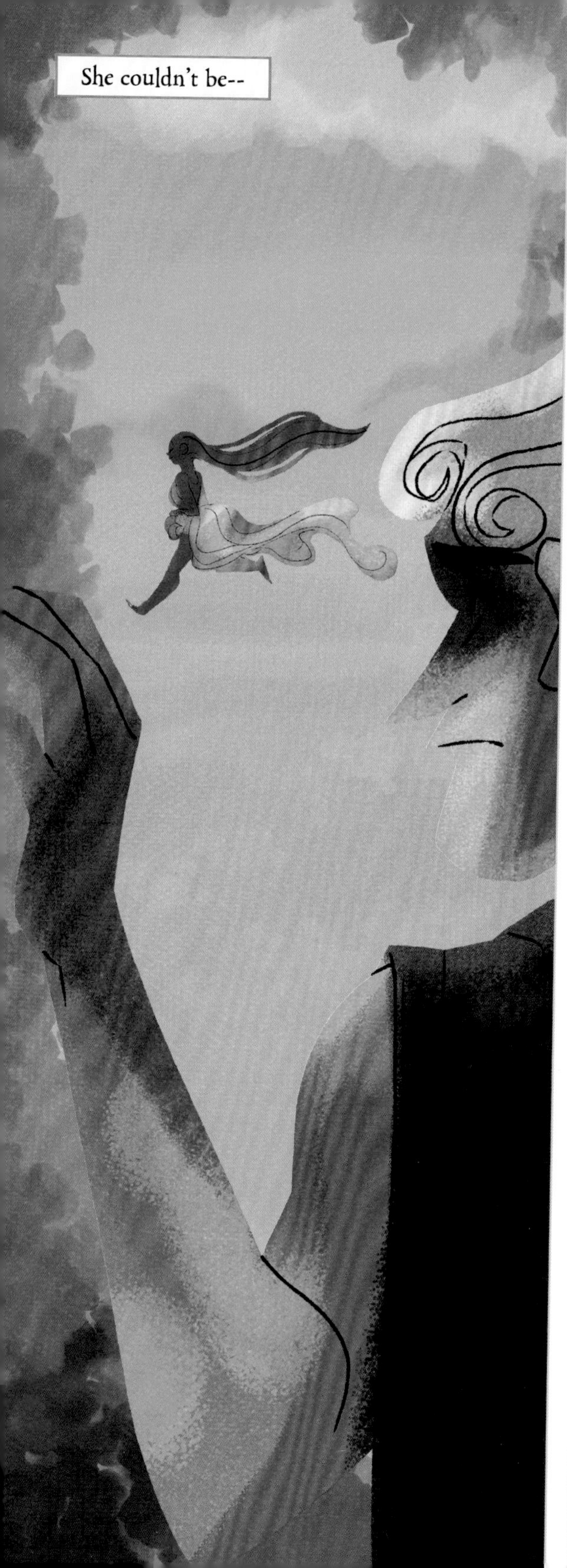
She couldn't be--
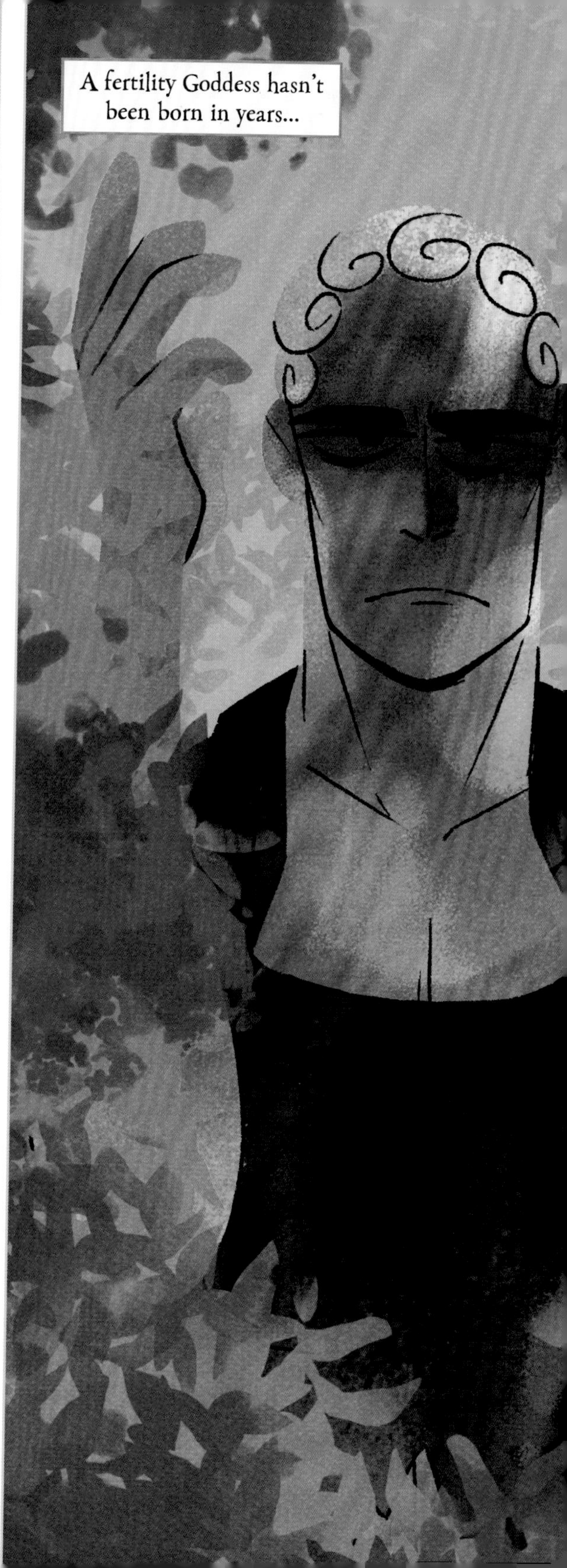
A fertility Goddess hasn't
been born in years...

EPISODE 101: WOMAN IN THE WOODS

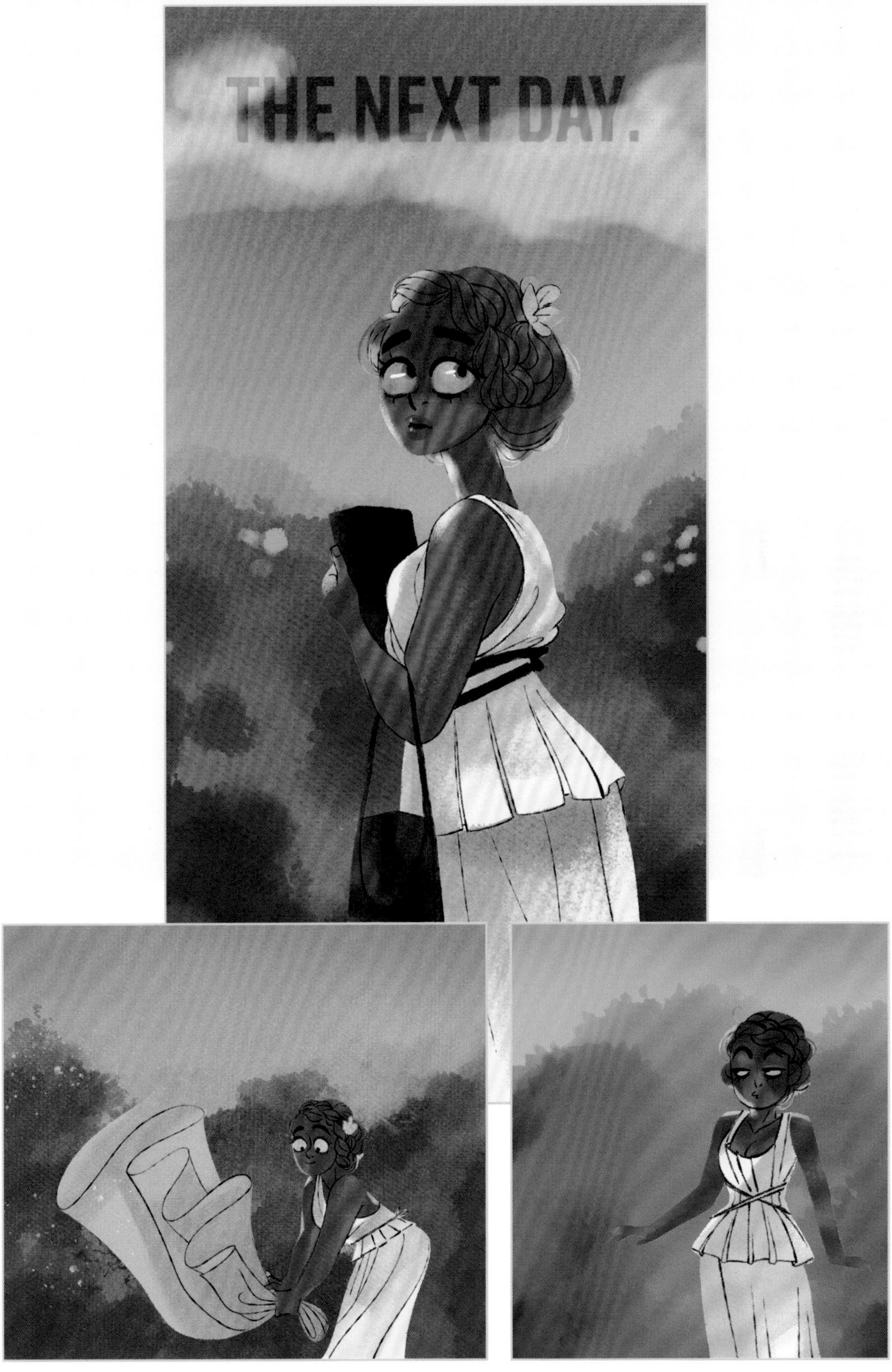
THE NEXT DAY.

CHECKIN'

DOUBLE CHECKIN'

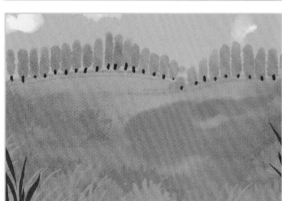

There!
Finally alone.

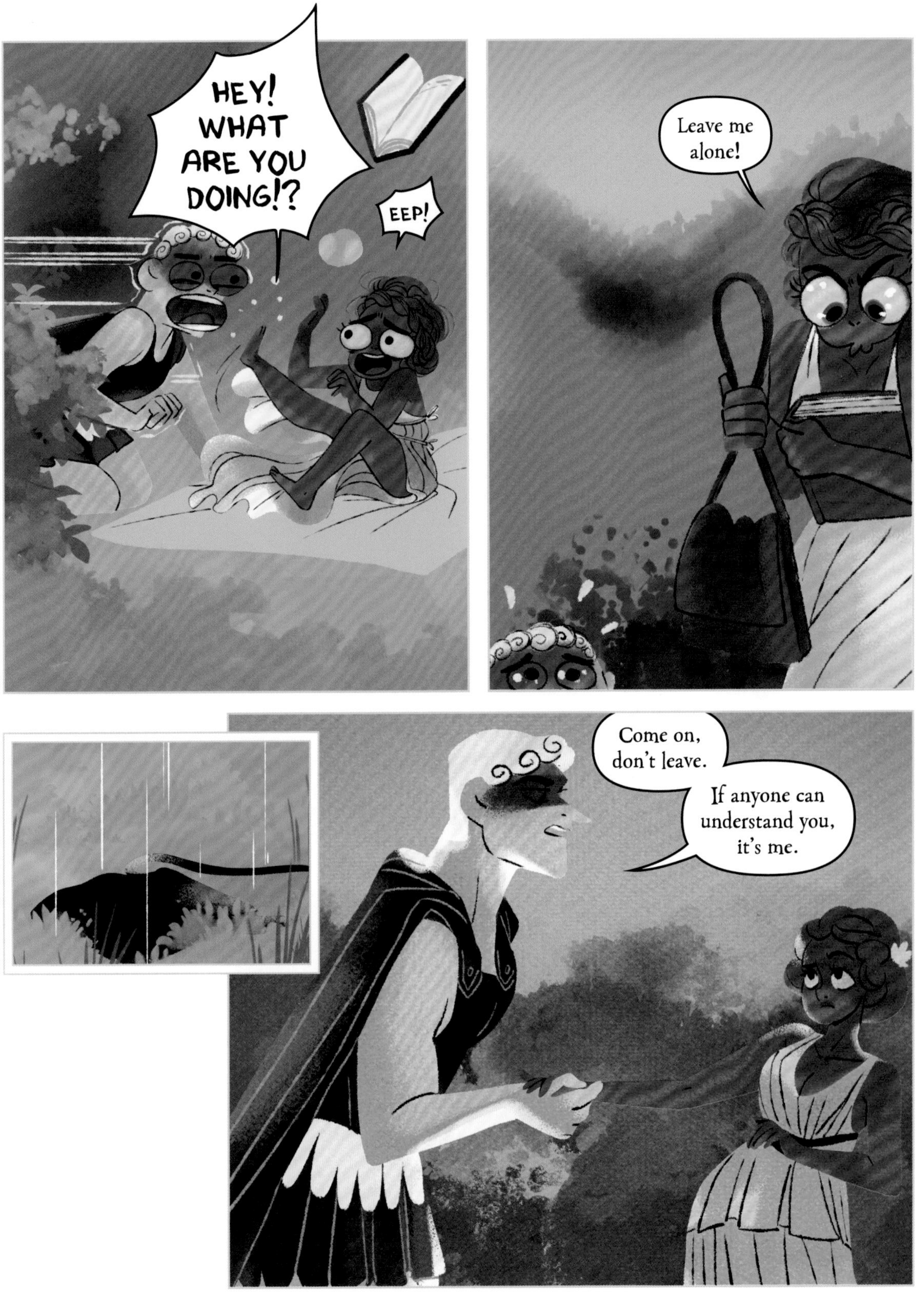
HEY! WHAT ARE YOU DOING!?
EEP!
Leave me alone!
Come on, don't leave.
If anyone can understand you, it's me.

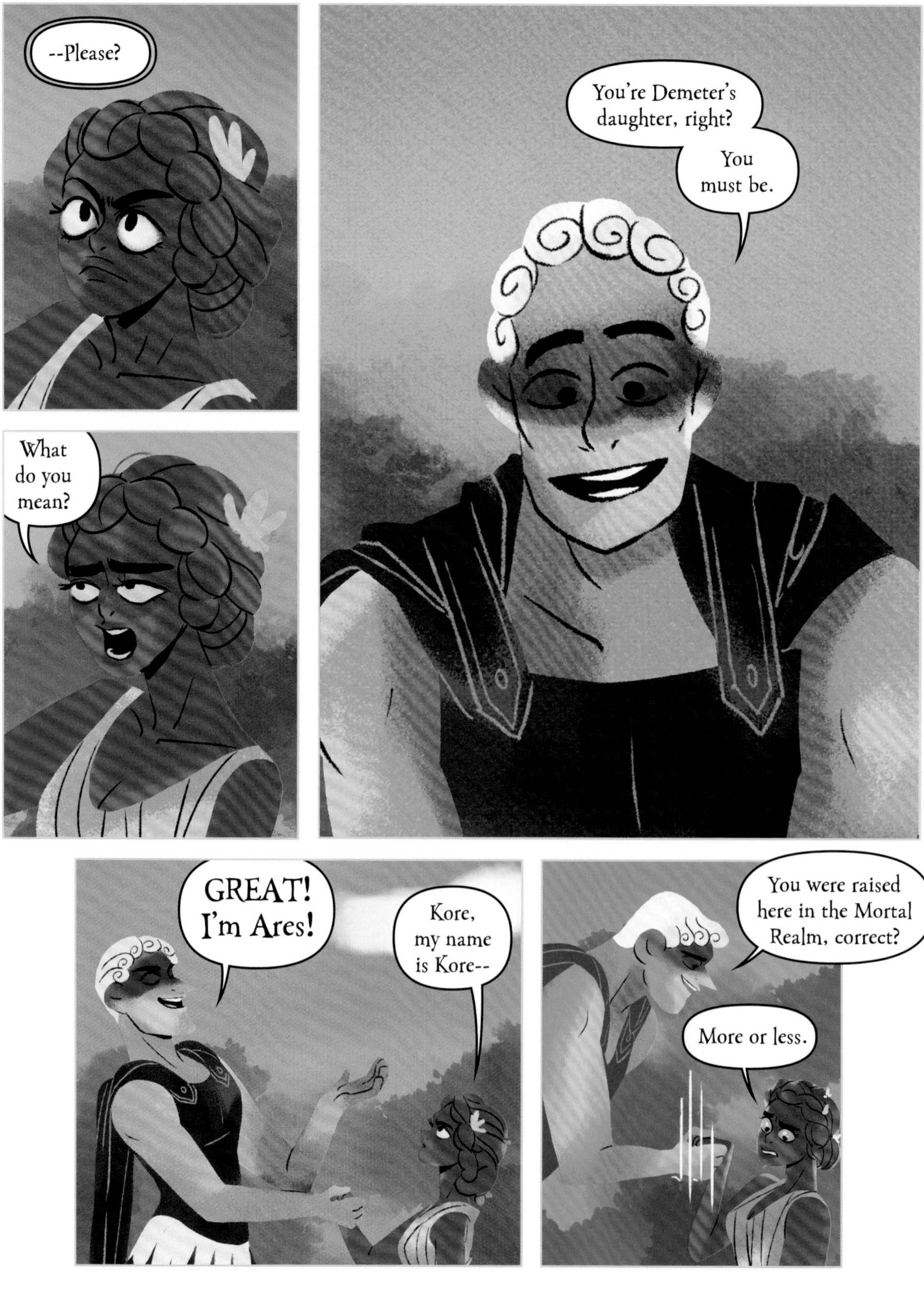
--Please?
What do you mean?
You're Demeter's daughter, right?
You must be.
GREAT! I'm Ares!
Kore, my name is Kore--
You were raised here in the Mortal Realm, correct?
More or less.

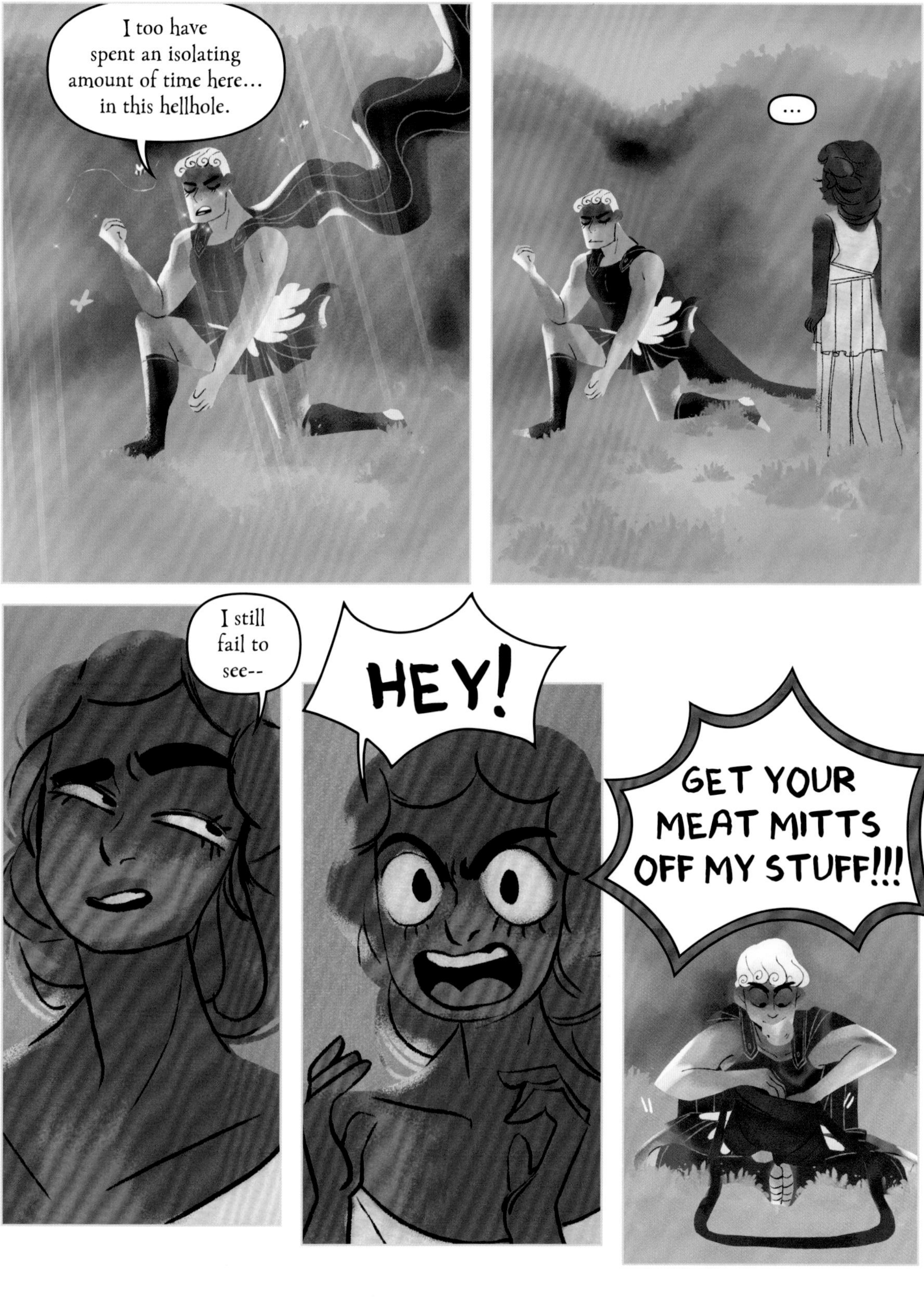
I too have spent an isolating amount of time here... in this hellhole.
...
I still fail to see--
HEY!
GET YOUR MEAT MITTS OFF MY STUFF!!!

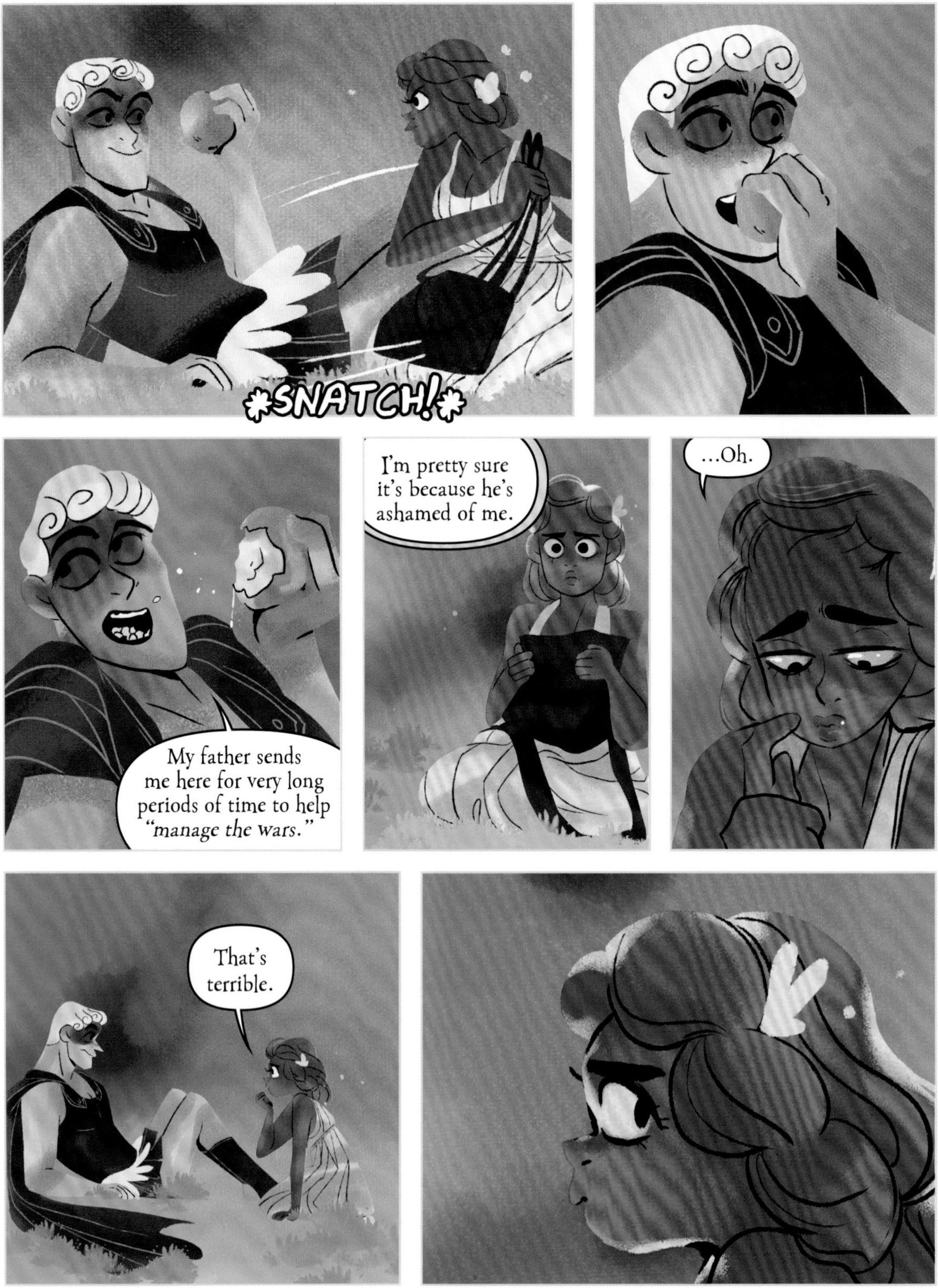
SNATCH!
My father sends me here for very long periods of time to help "manage the wars."
I'm pretty sure it's because he's ashamed of me.
...Oh.
That's terrible.

Would you like some of my lunch!?

I won't say no.

Your wound healed really fast! That's lucky.

Haha, yeah...

She has no idea she healed me.

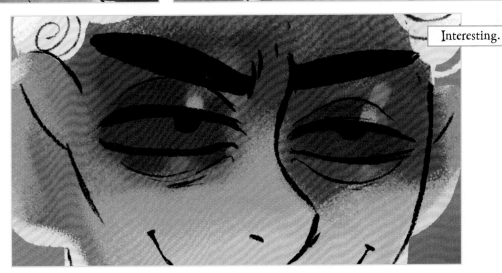

Interesting.

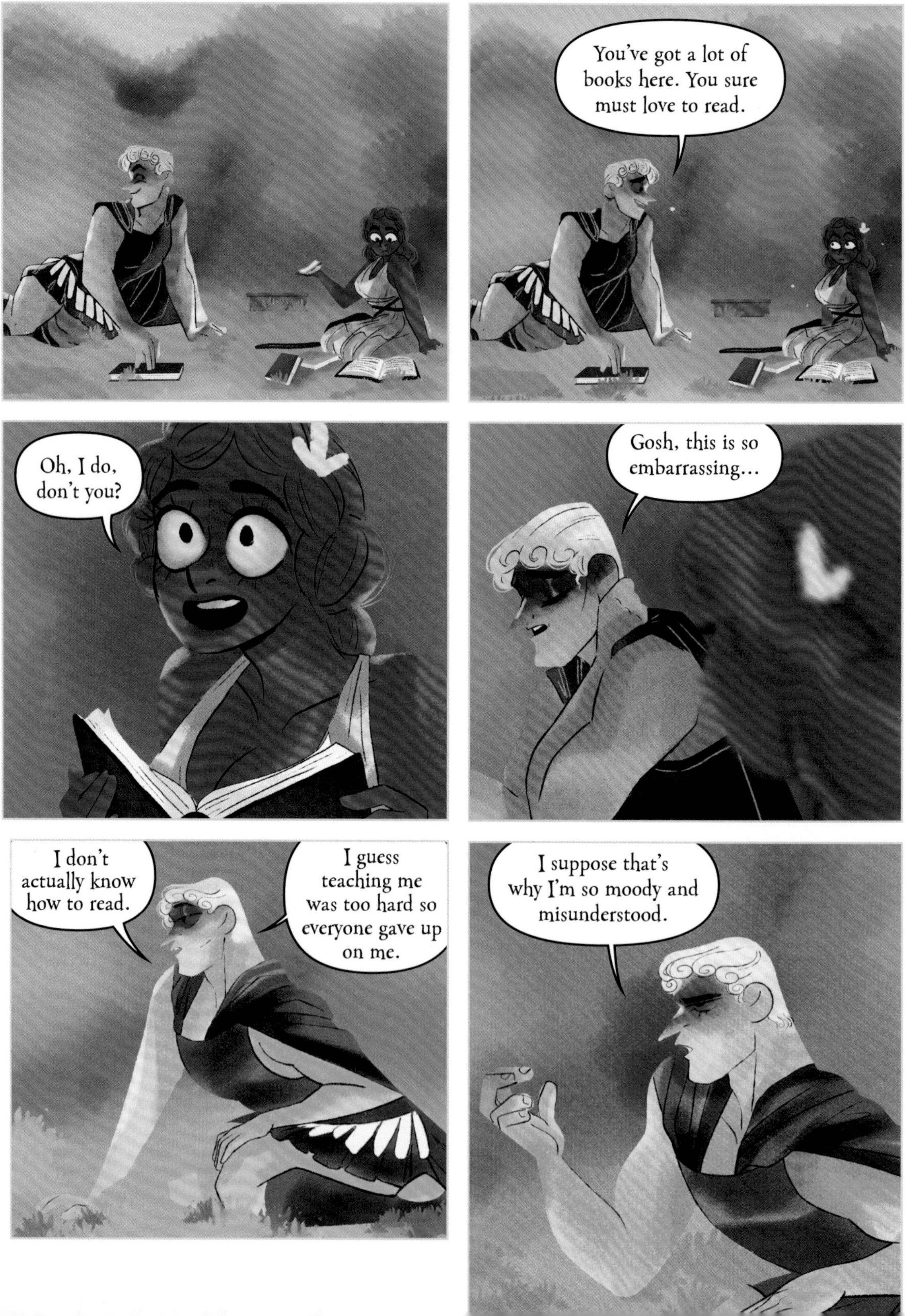
You've got a lot of books here. You sure must love to read.
Oh, I do, don't you?
Gosh, this is so embarrassing...
I don't actually know how to read.
I guess teaching me was too hard so everyone gave up on me.
I suppose that's why I'm so moody and misunderstood.

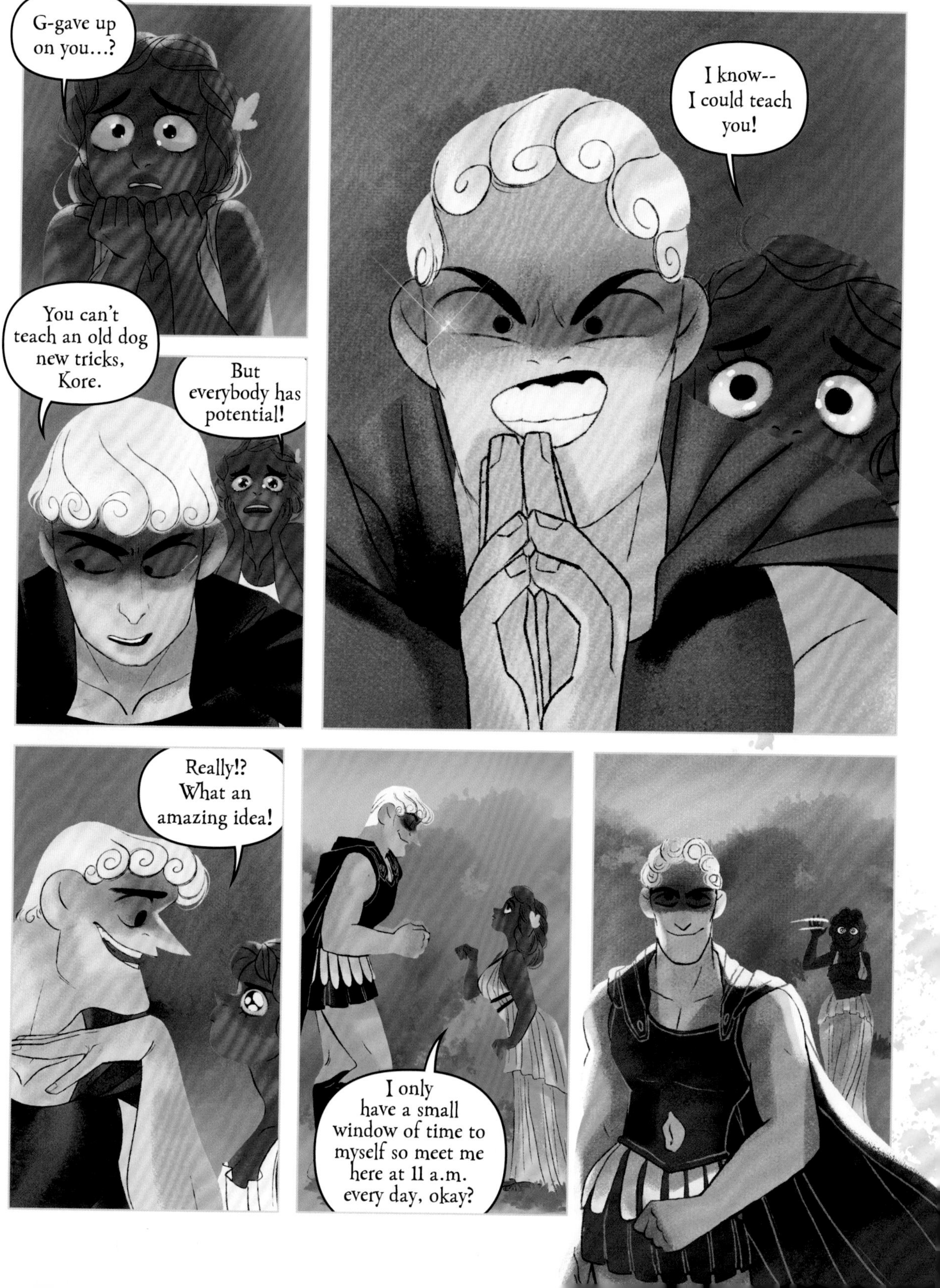
G-gave up on you...?
I know-- I could teach you!
You can't teach an old dog new tricks, Kore.
But everybody has potential!
Really!? What an amazing idea!
I only have a small window of time to myself so meet me here at 11 a.m. every day, okay?

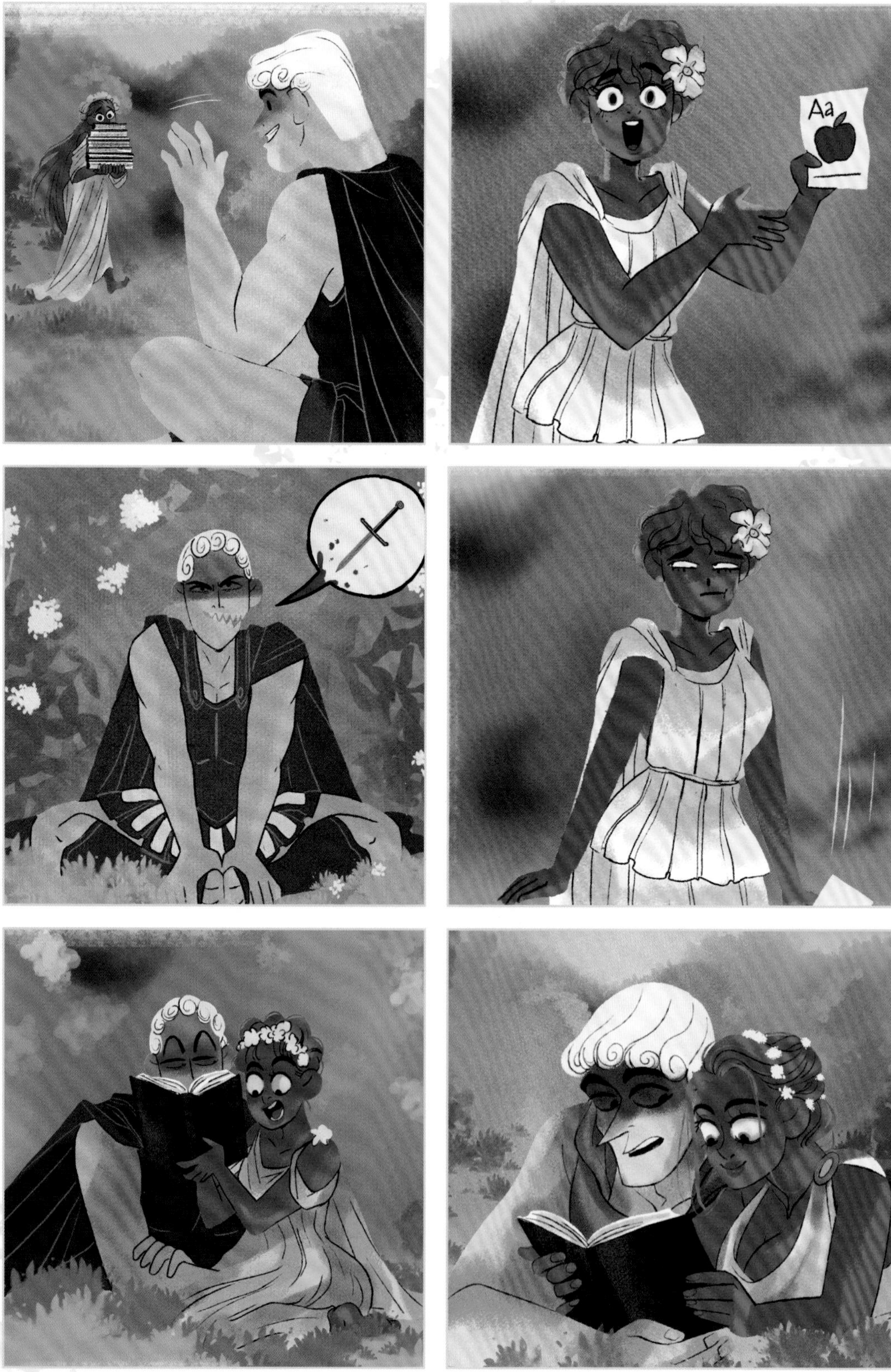
Aa

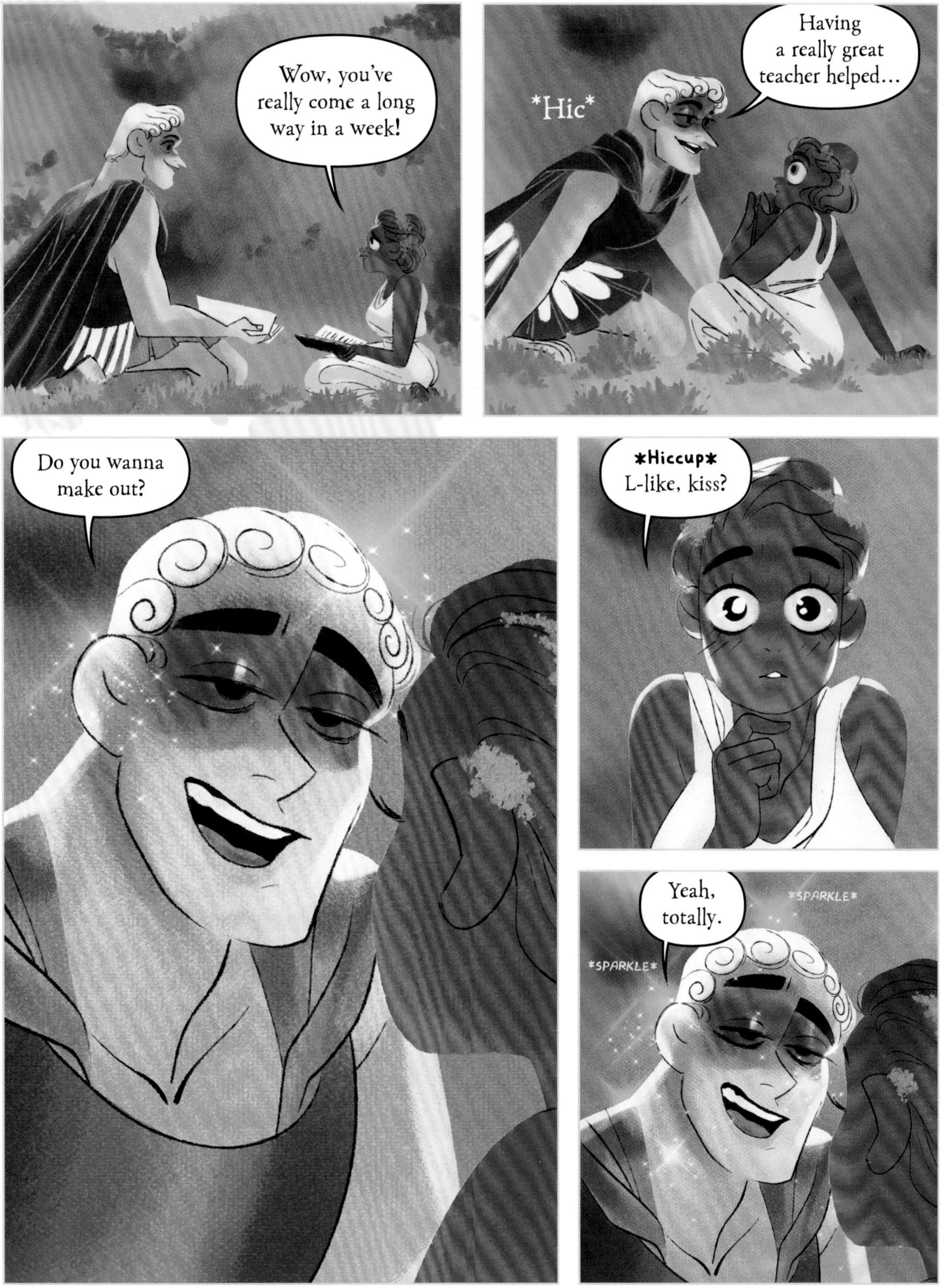
Wow, you've really come a long way in a week!
Hic
Having a really great teacher helped...
Do you wanna make out?
Hiccup L-like, kiss?
Yeah, totally.
SPARKLE
SPARKLE

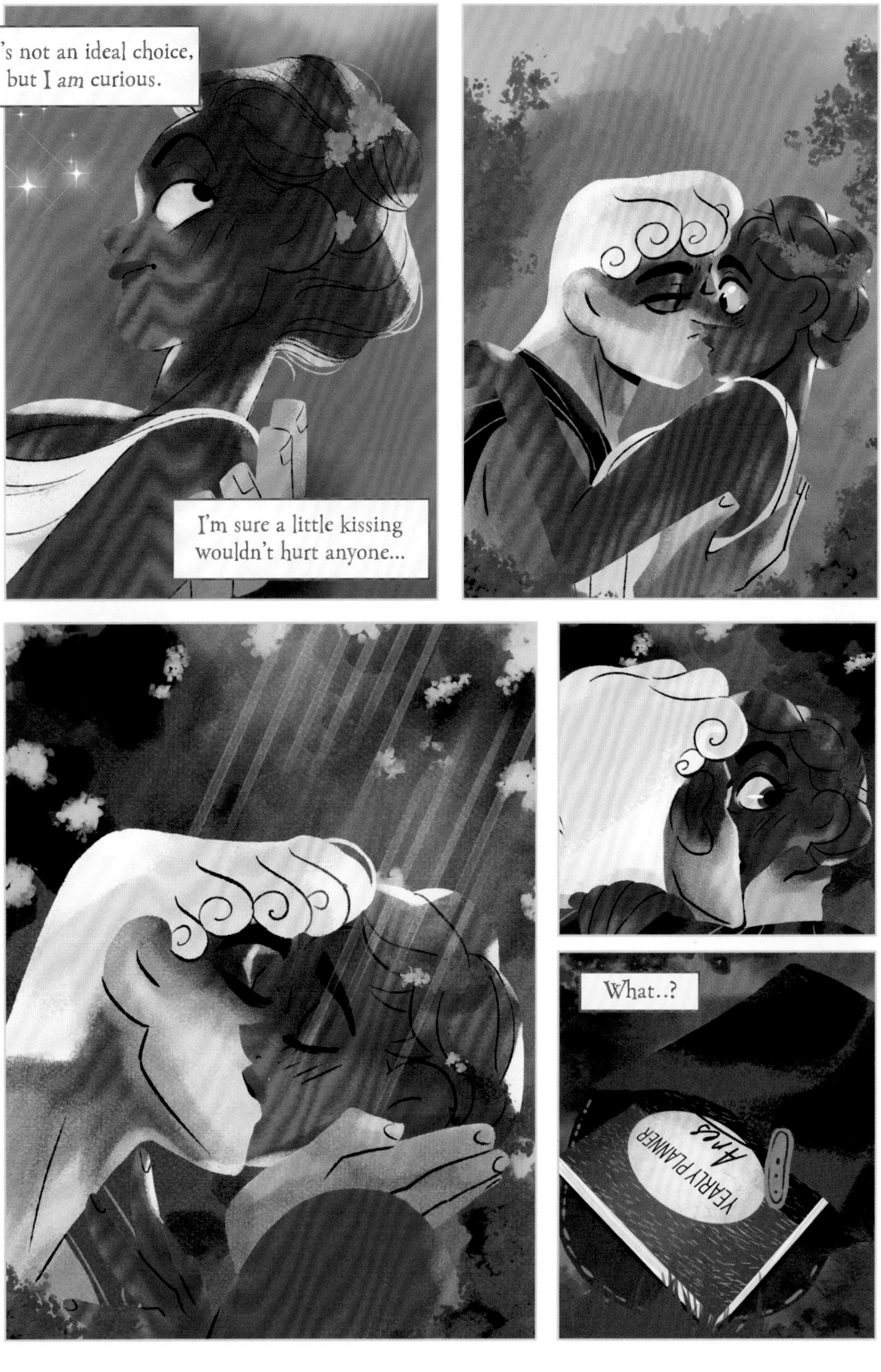
He's not an ideal choice, but I *am* curious.
I'm sure a little kissing wouldn't hurt anyone...
What..?
YEARLY PLANNER

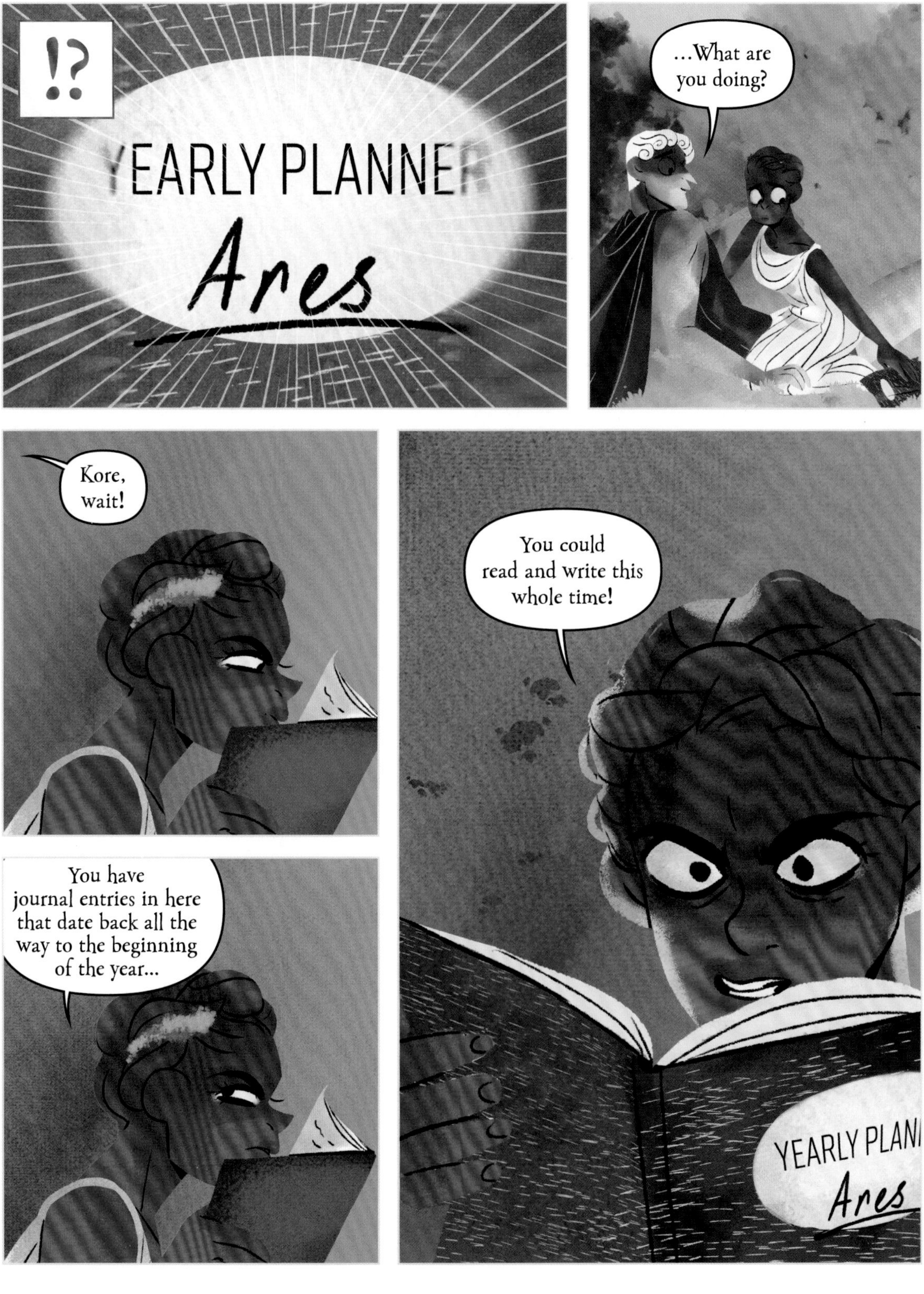
!?
YEARLY PLANNER
Ares
...What are you doing?
Kore, wait!
You could read and write this whole time!
You have journal entries in here that date back all the way to the beginning of the year...
YEARLY PLAN
Ares

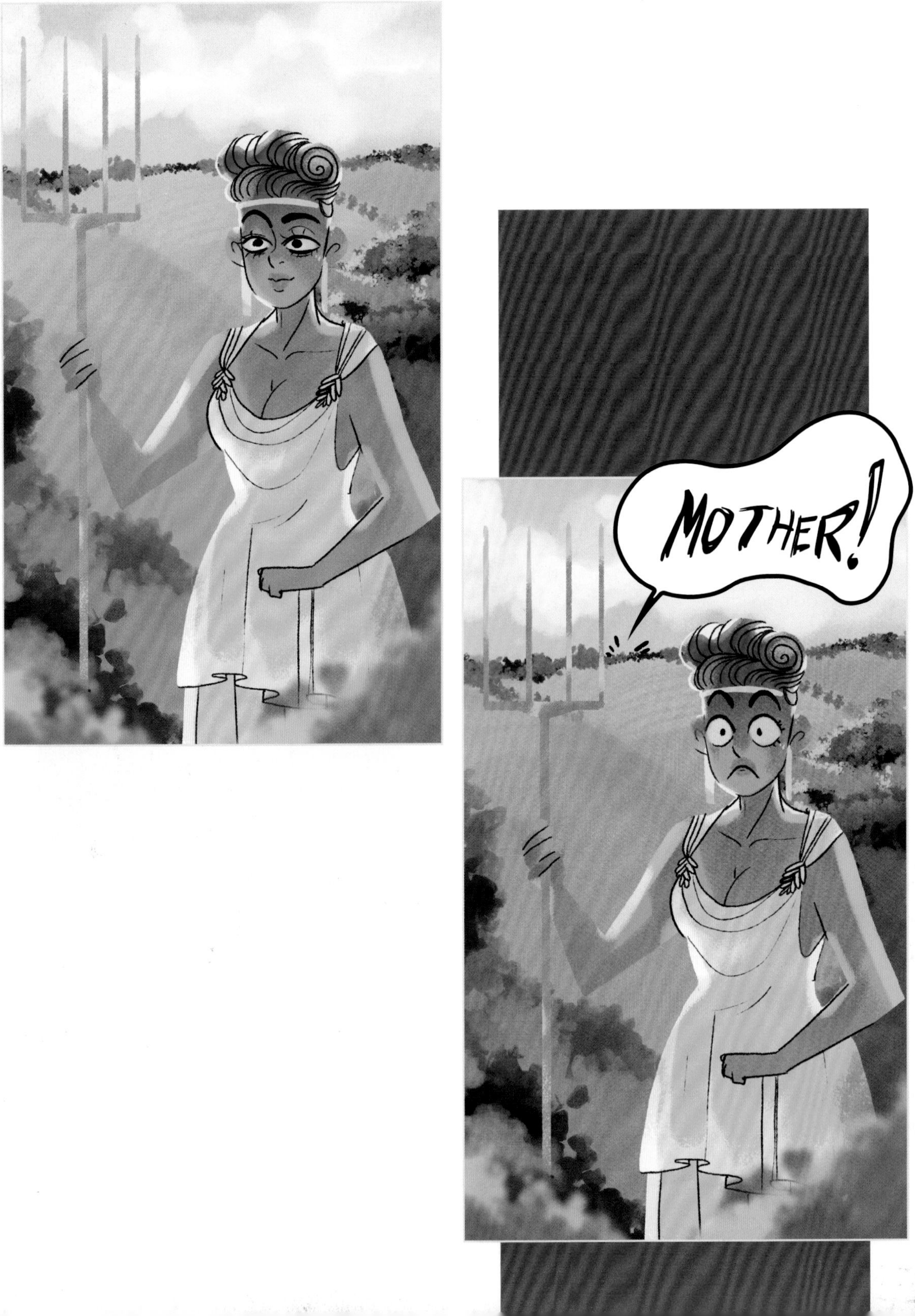
MOTHER!

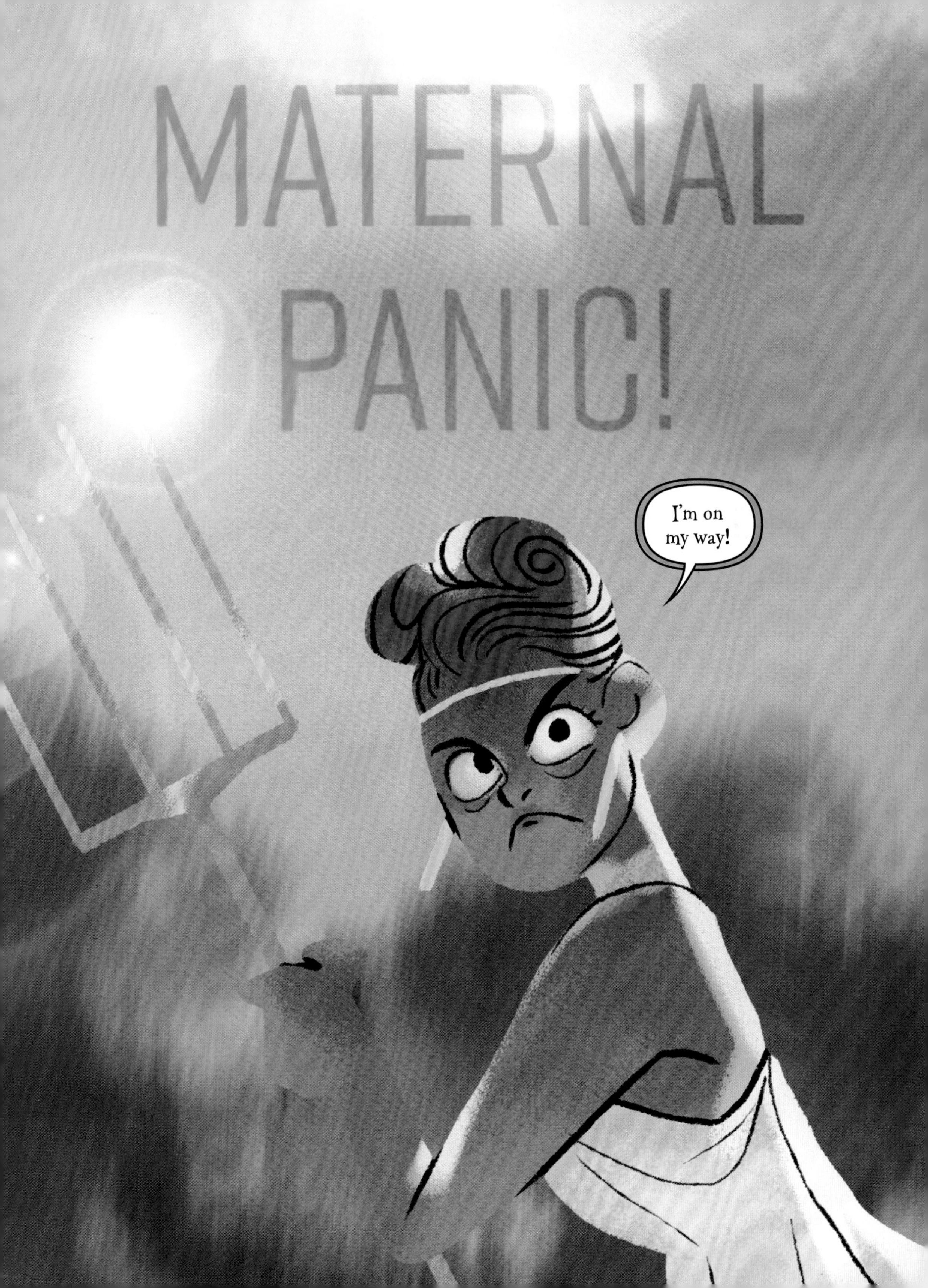
MATERNAL PANIC!
I'm on my way!

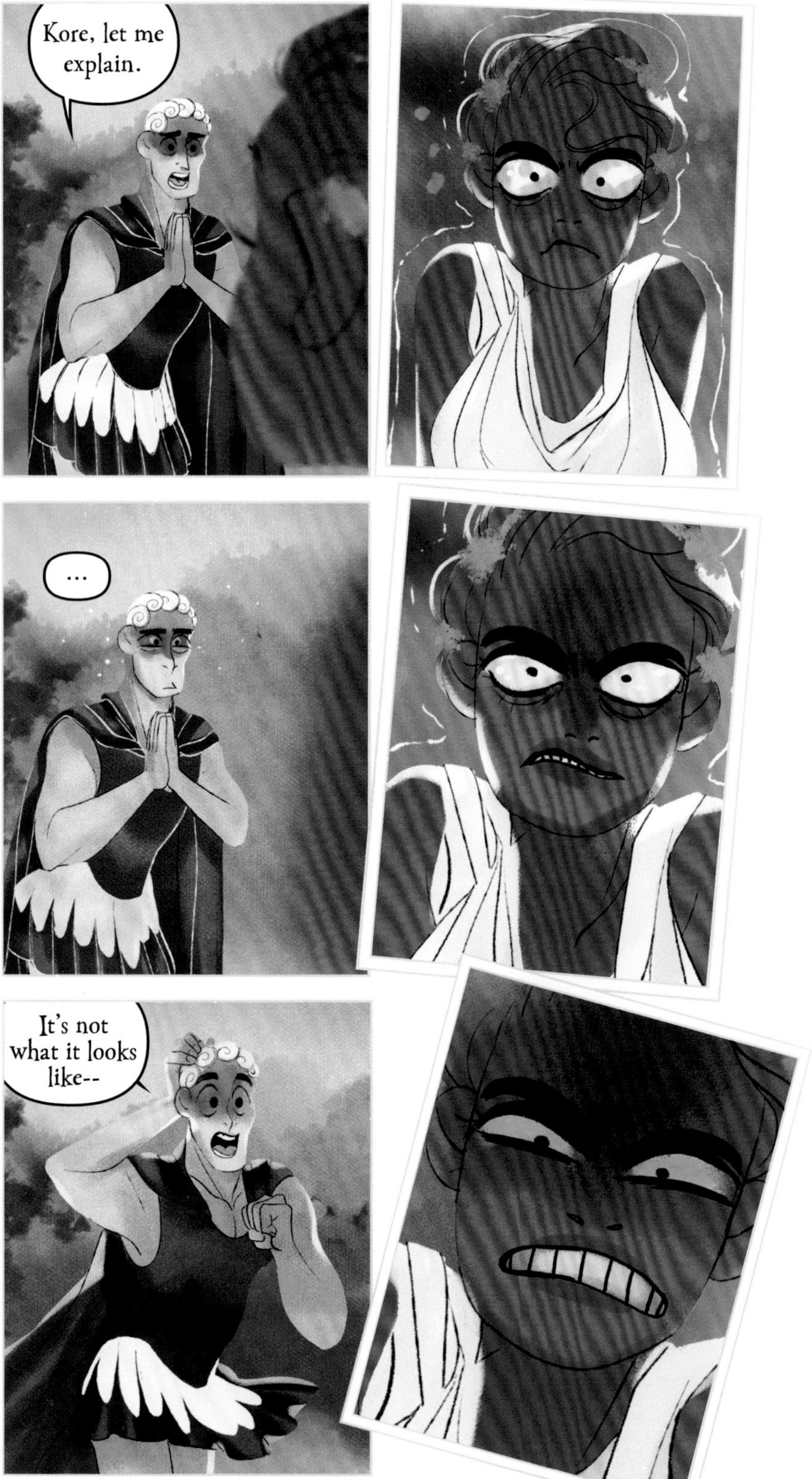
Kore, let me explain.
...
It's not what it looks like--

Okay, it's exactly what it looks like.

I was going to tell you eventually...

...

Say something, would ya? Anything!

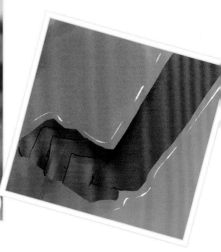

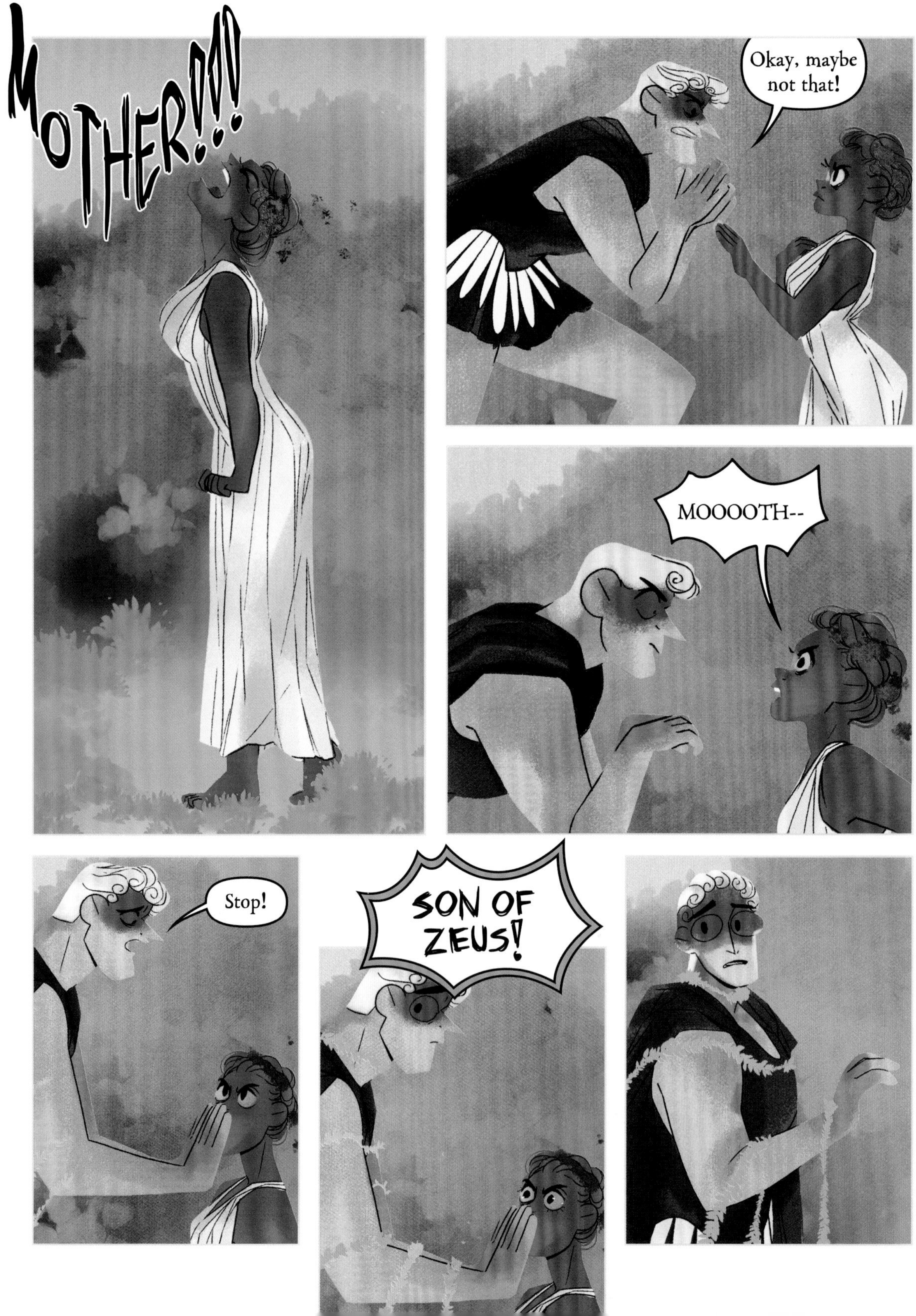
MOTHER!!!
Okay, maybe not that!
MOOOOTH--
Stop!
SON OF ZEUS!

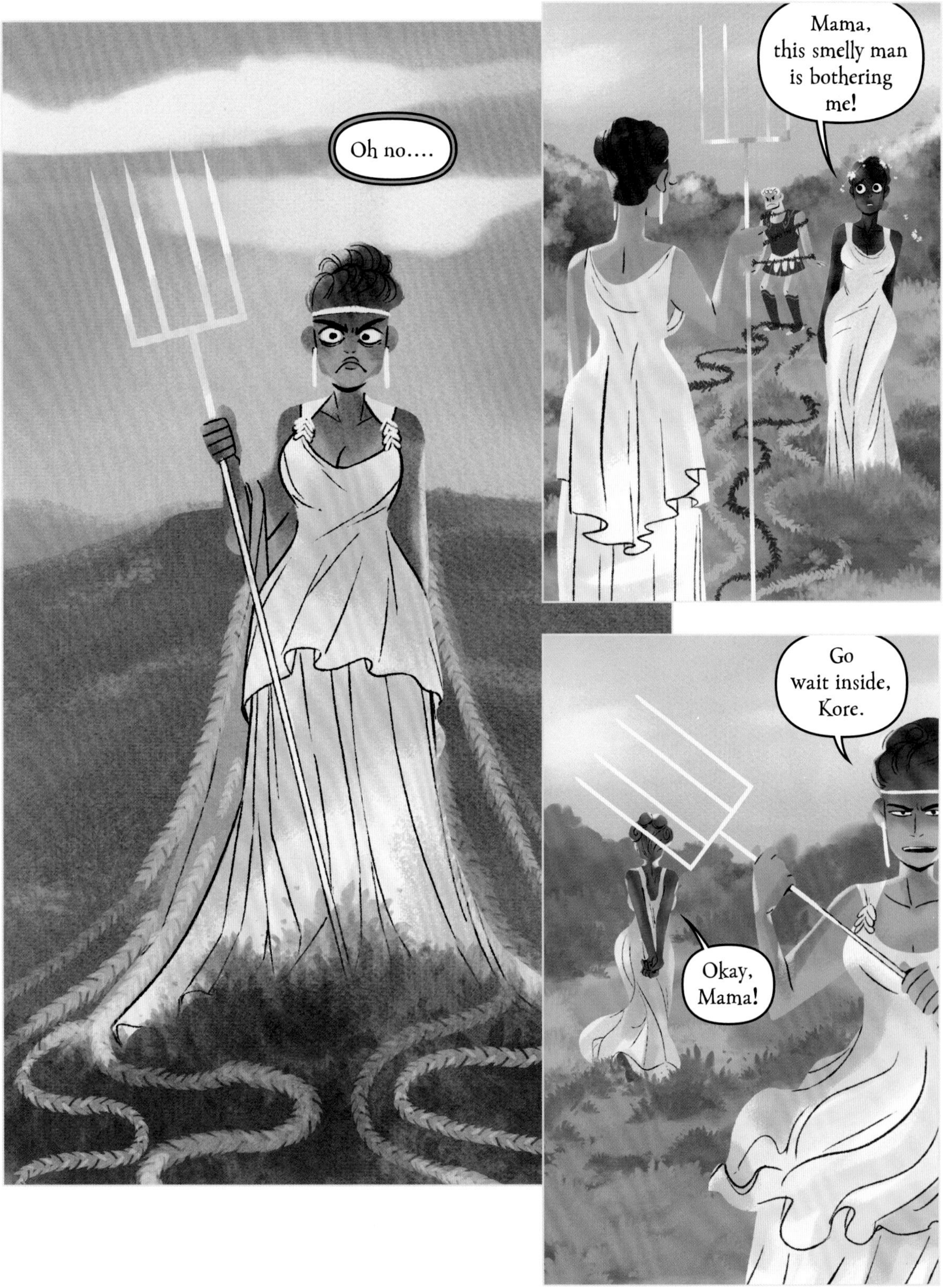
Oh no....
Mama, this smelly man is bothering me!
Go wait inside, Kore.
Okay, Mama!

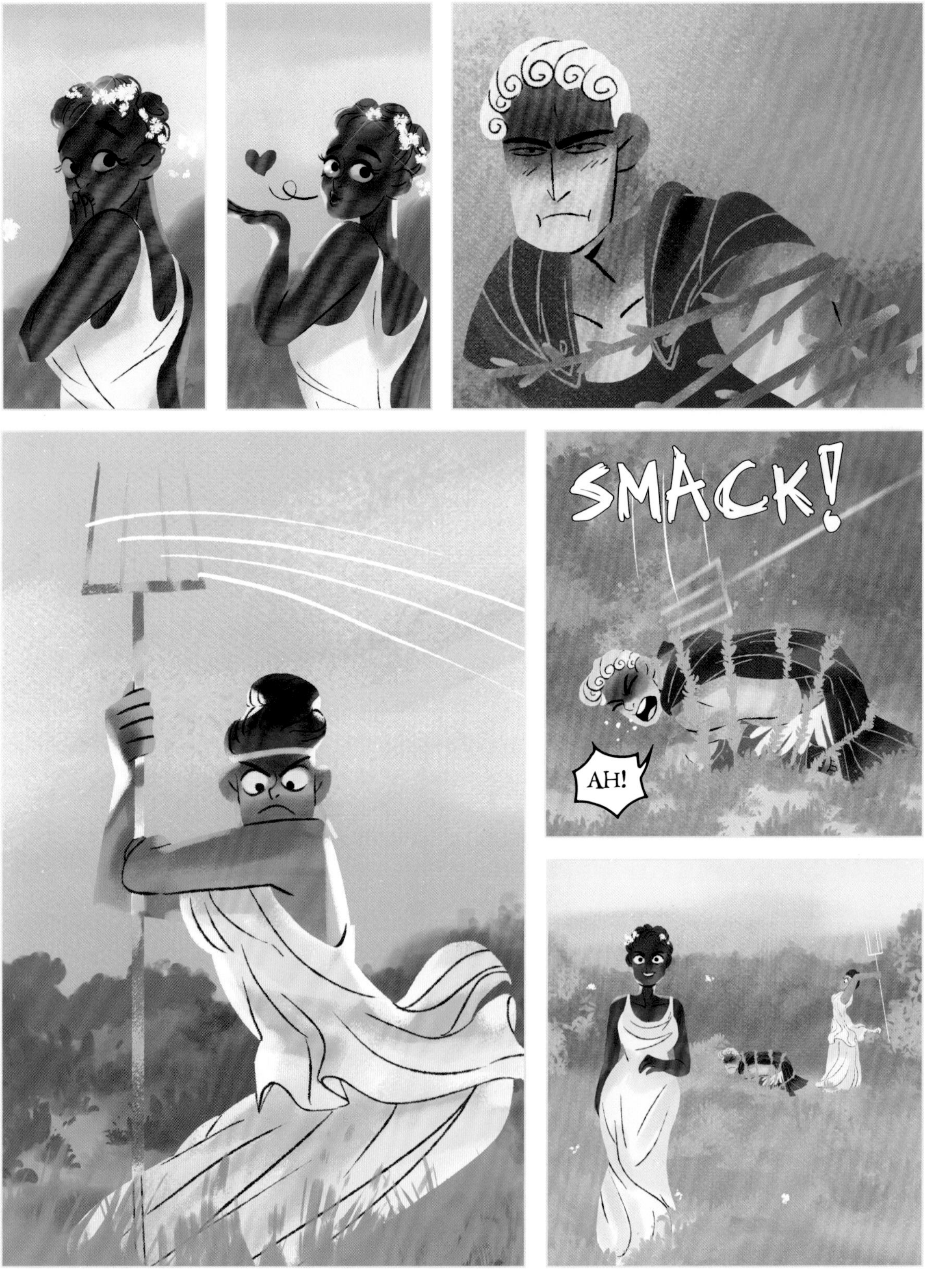
SMACK!
AH!

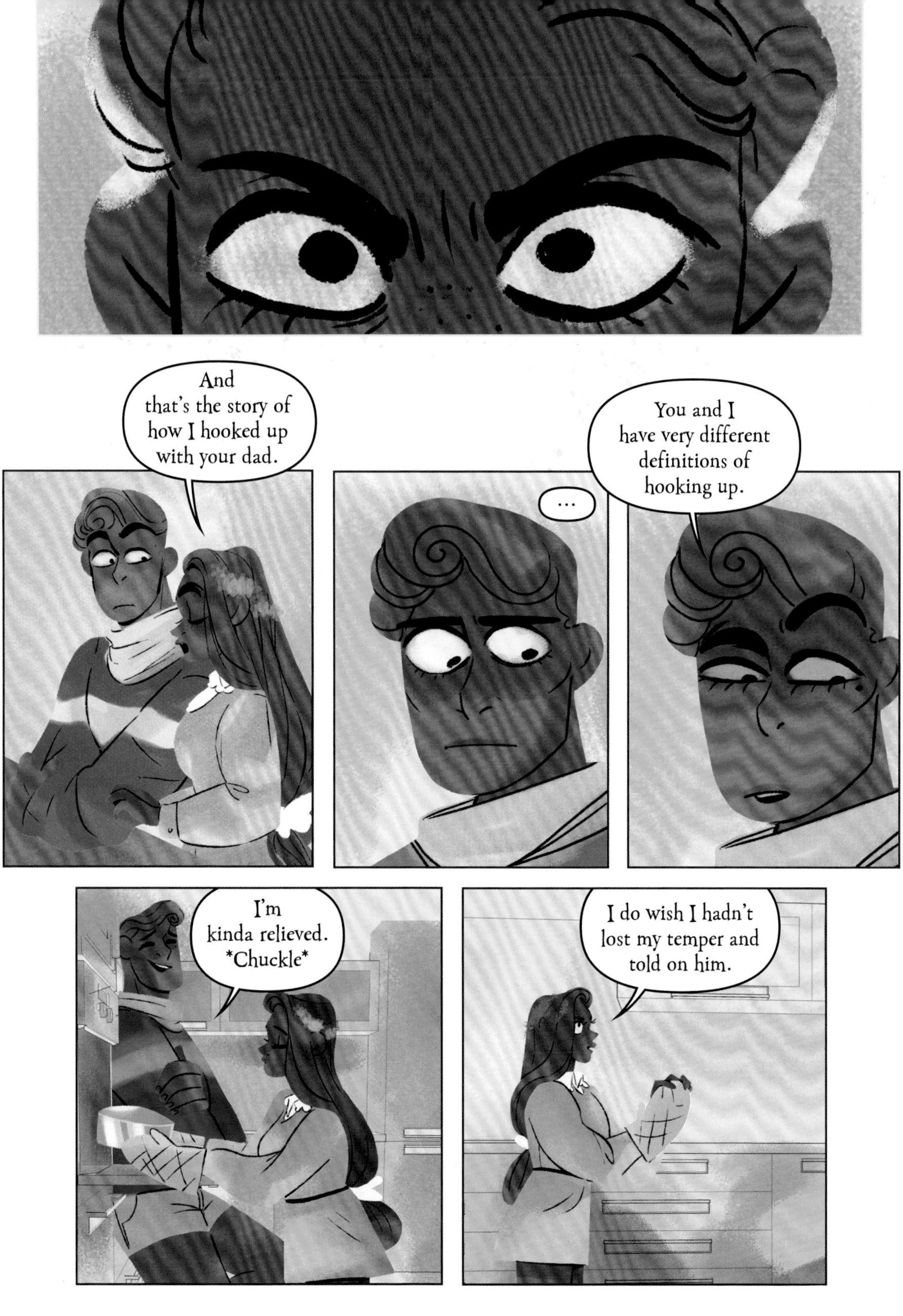
And that's the story of how I hooked up with your dad.
...
You and I have very different definitions of hooking up.
I'm kinda relieved. *Chuckle*
I do wish I hadn't lost my temper and told on him.

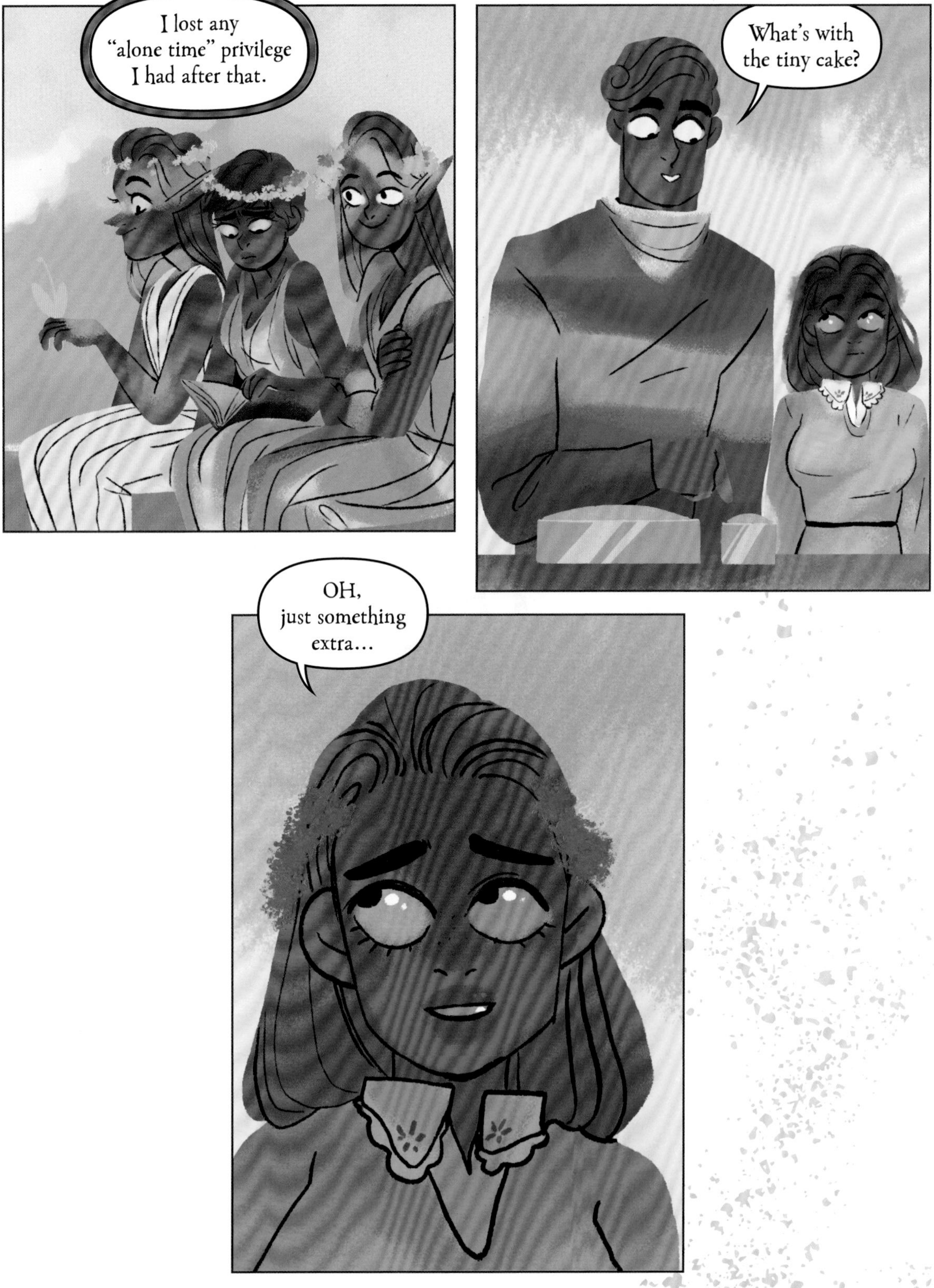
I lost any "alone time" privilege I had after that.
What's with the tiny cake?
OH, just something extra...

EPISODE 102: I LOVE THE WAY YOU MAKE ME FEEL

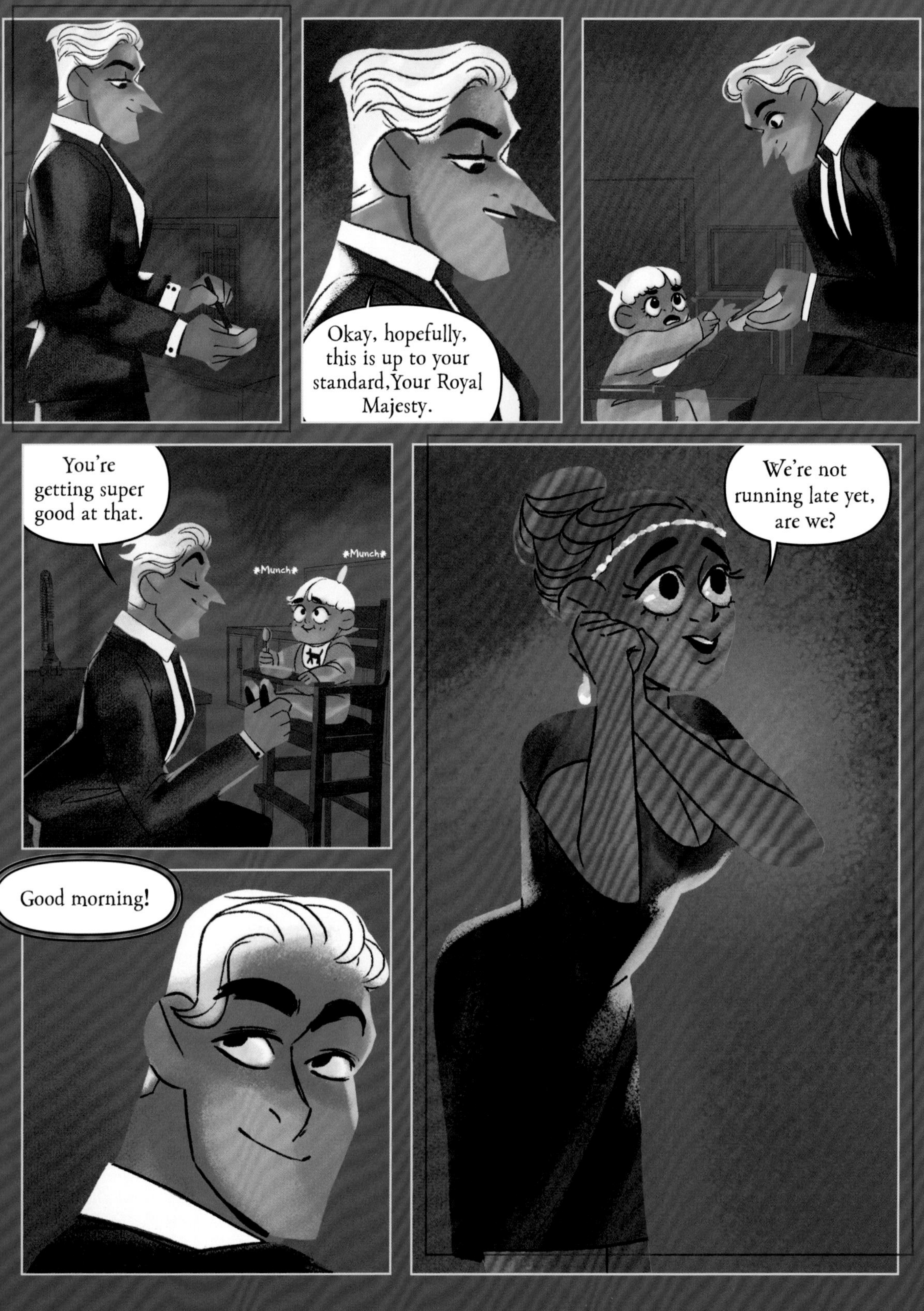
Okay, hopefully, this is up to your standard, Your Royal Majesty.
You're getting super good at that.
Munch
Munch
We're not running late yet, are we?
Good morning!

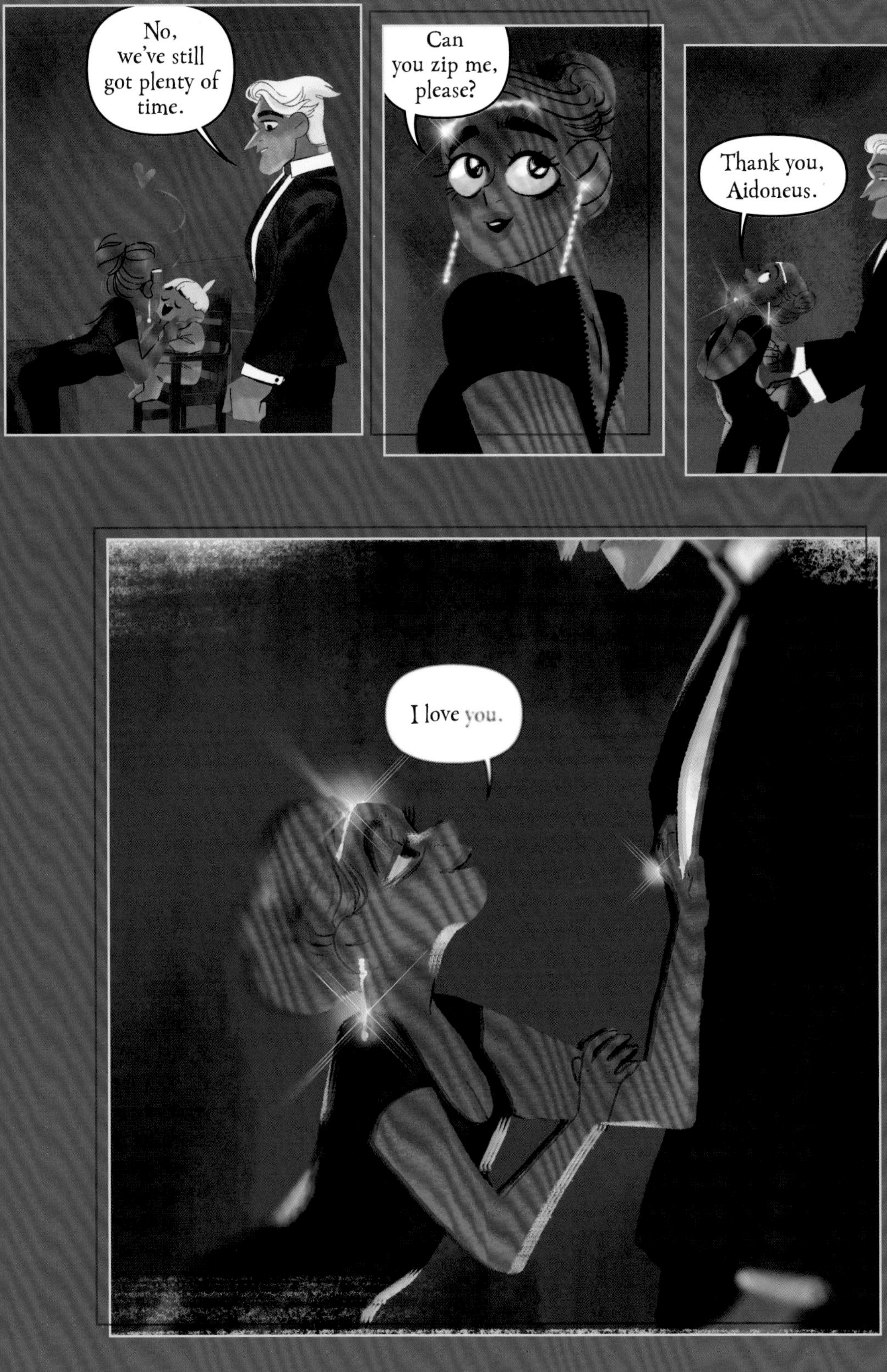
No, we've still got plenty of time.
Can you zip me, please?
Thank you, Aidoneus.
I love you.

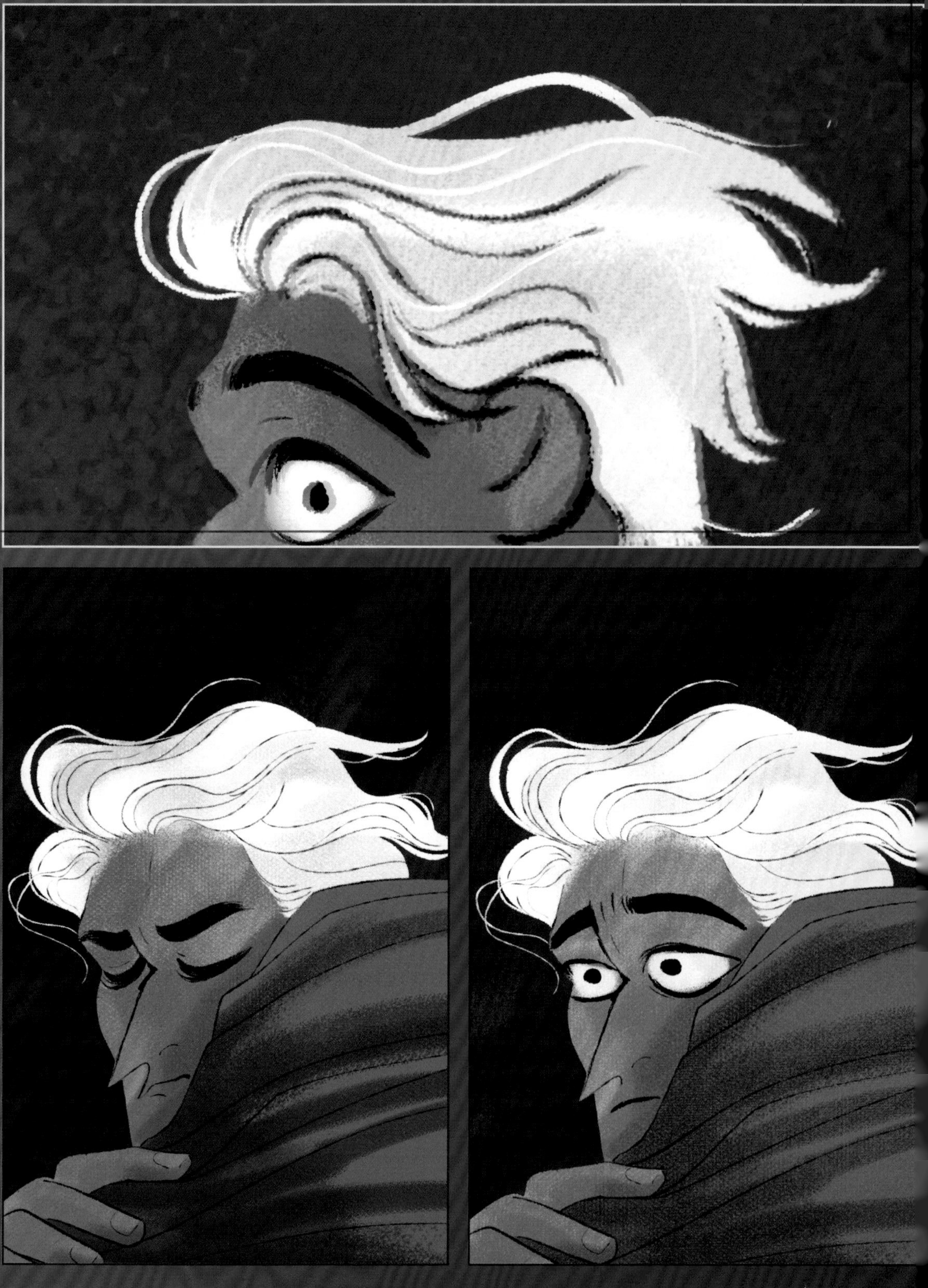

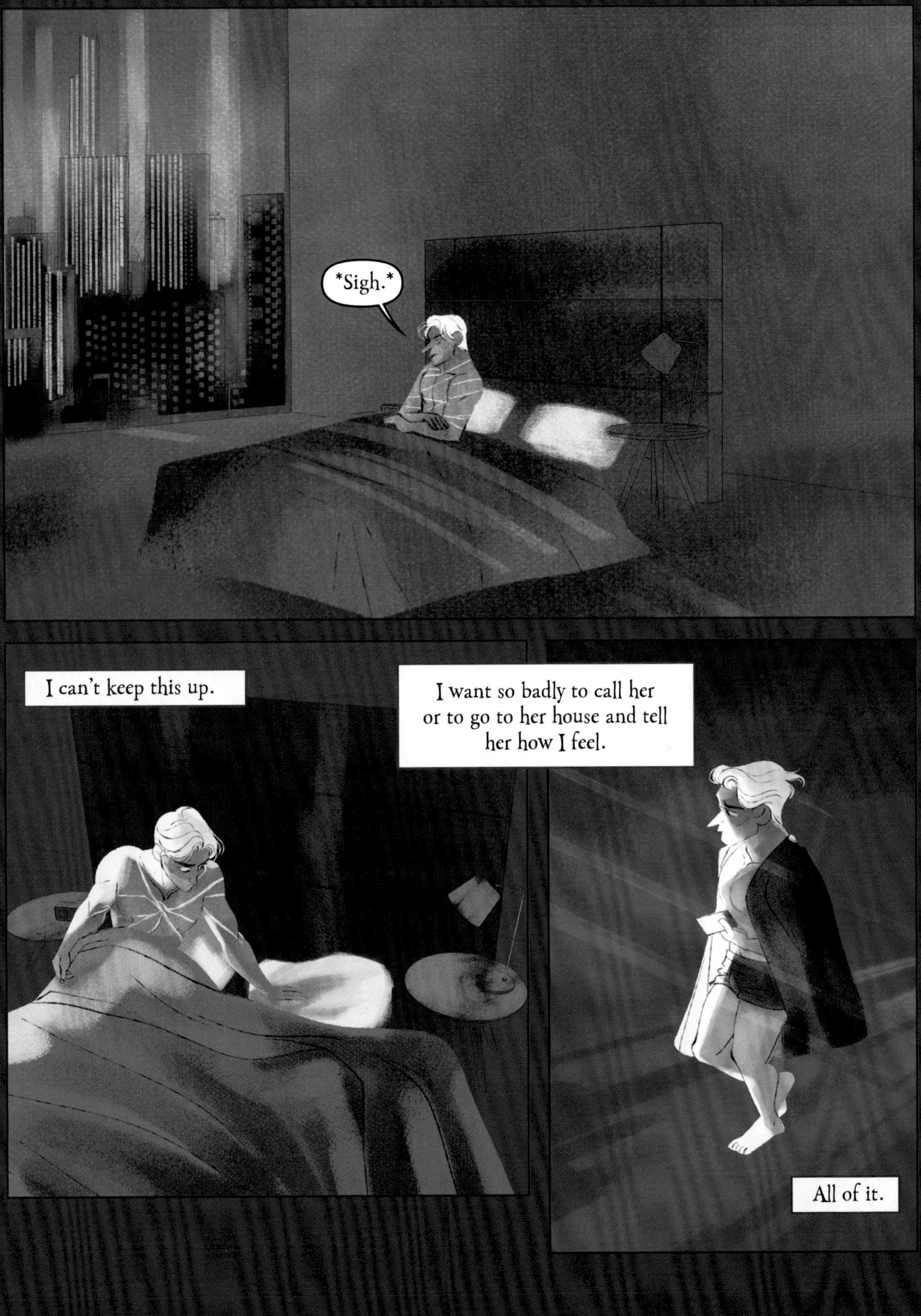
Sigh.
I can't keep this up.
I want so badly to call her or to go to her house and tell her how I feel.
All of it.

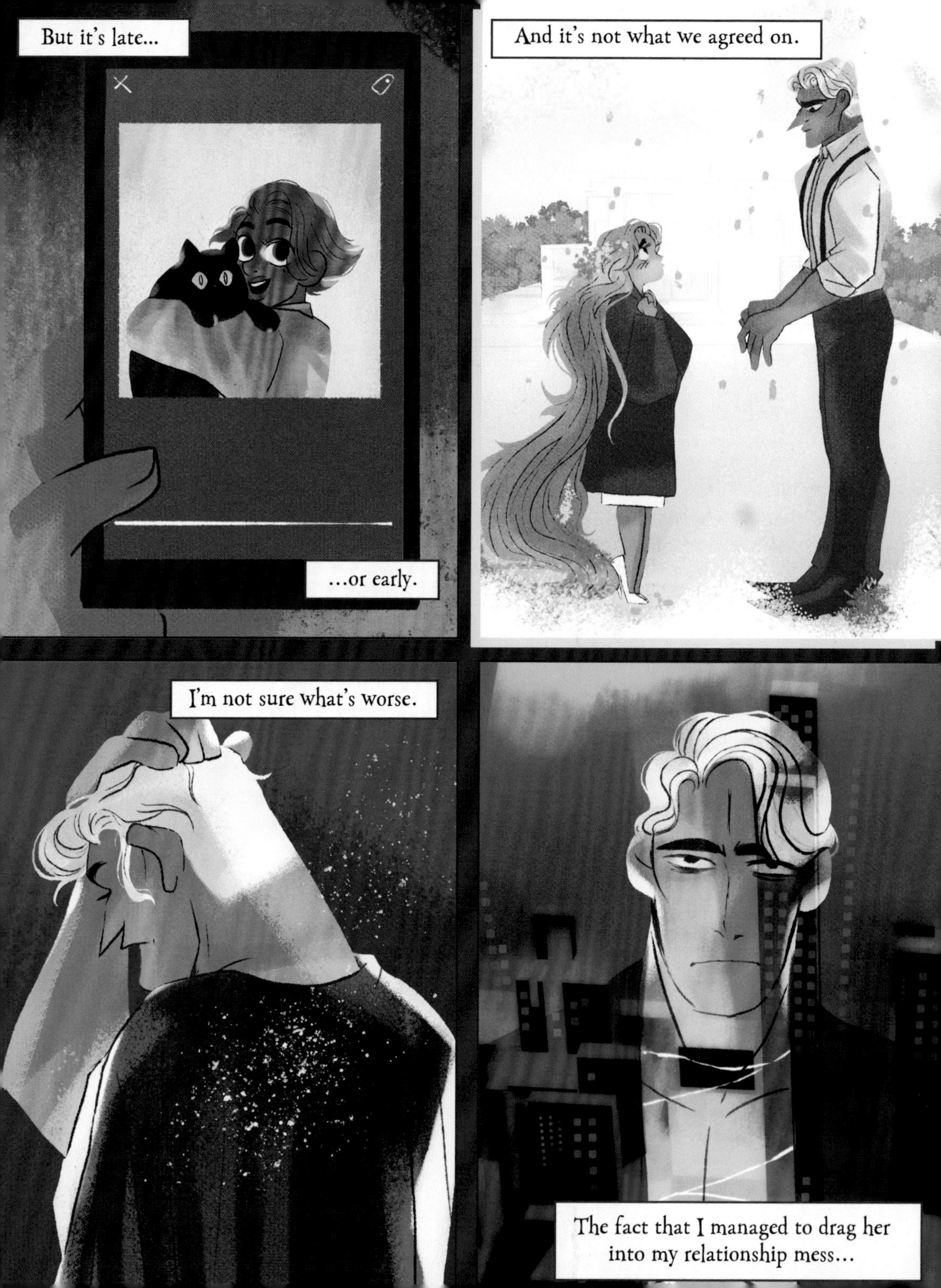
But it's late...
...or early.
And it's not what we agreed on.
I'm not sure what's worse.
The fact that I managed to drag her into my relationship mess...

...or that she has to be the one who keeps me in check.

She has enough on her plate without me unloading all my feelings onto her.

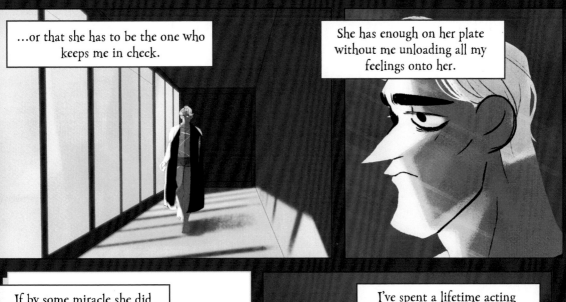

If by some miracle she did choose me, I would hate for her to regret it later...

I've spent a lifetime acting like I don't want relationships or children.

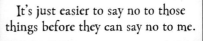

It's just easier to say no to those things before they can say no to me.

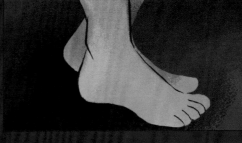

Not that I could even give her a family the standard way...

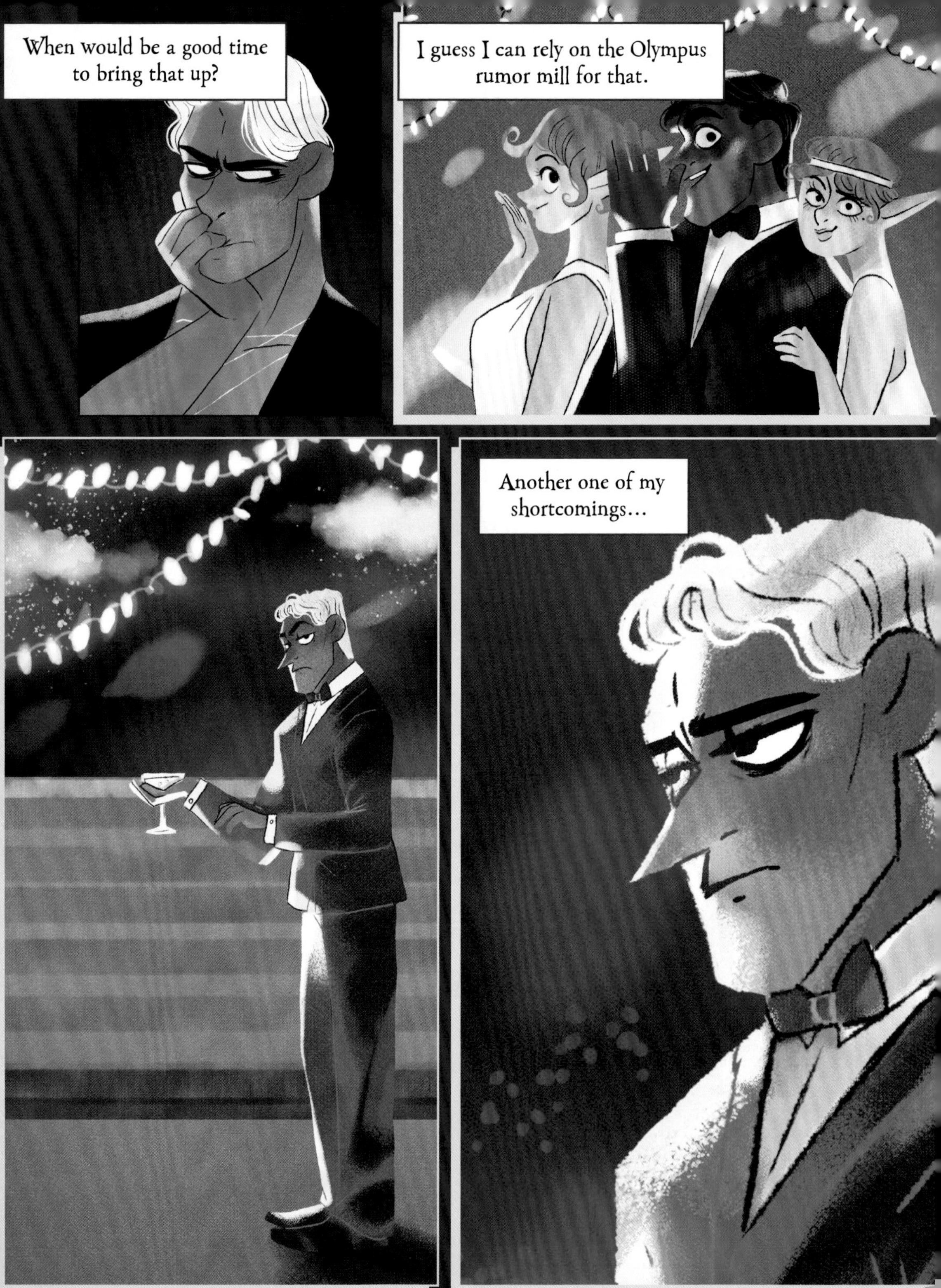
When would be a good time to bring that up?
I guess I can rely on the Olympus rumor mill for that.
Another one of my shortcomings...

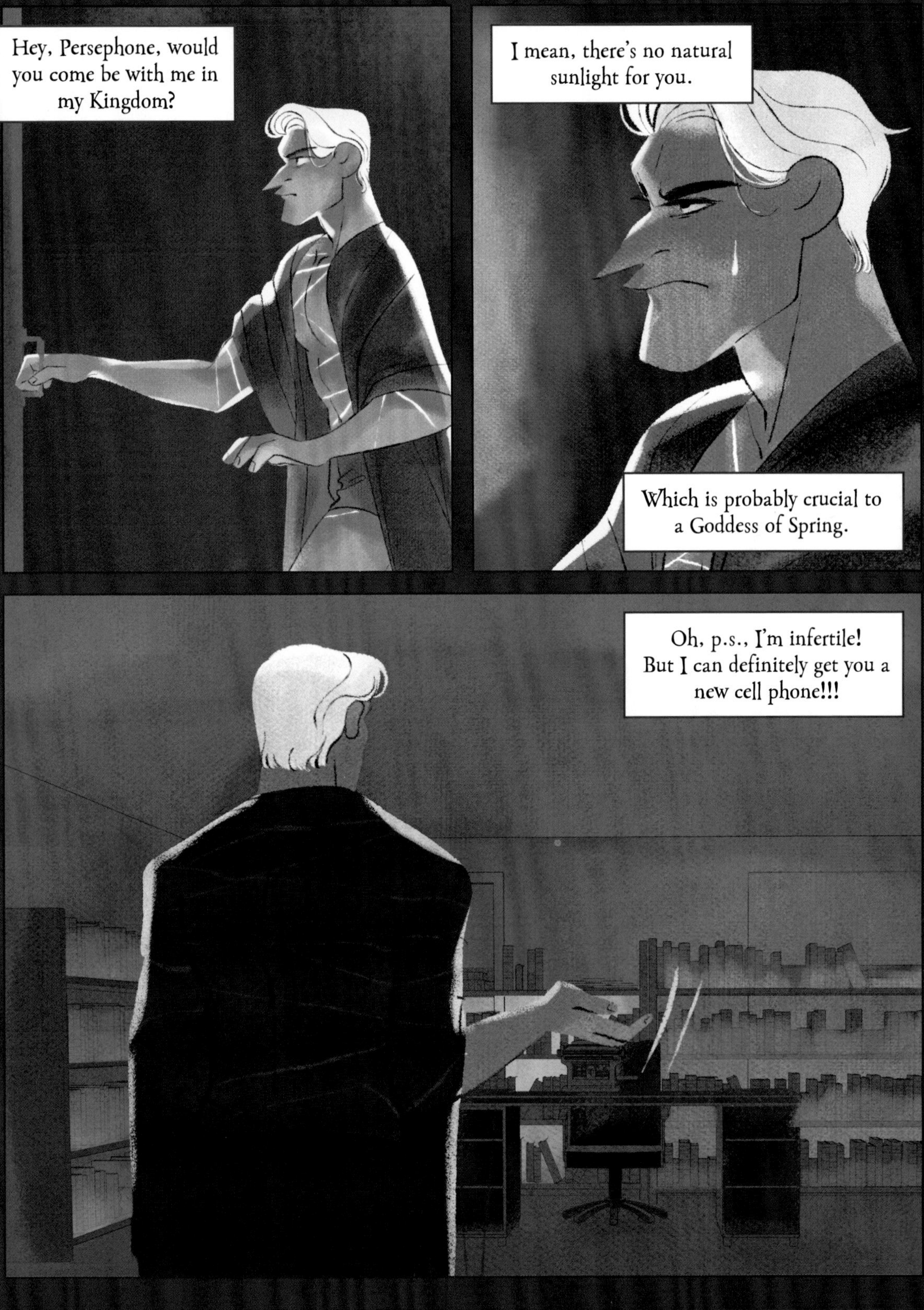
Hey, Persephone, would you come be with me in my Kingdom?
I mean, there's no natural sunlight for you.
Which is probably crucial to a Goddess of Spring.
Oh, p.s., I'm infertile! But I can definitely get you a new cell phone!!!

...Maybe she'd be okay with it?

...I shouldn't worry about things that aren't a problem yet.

...

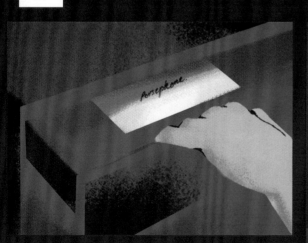

She said she has feelings for me.

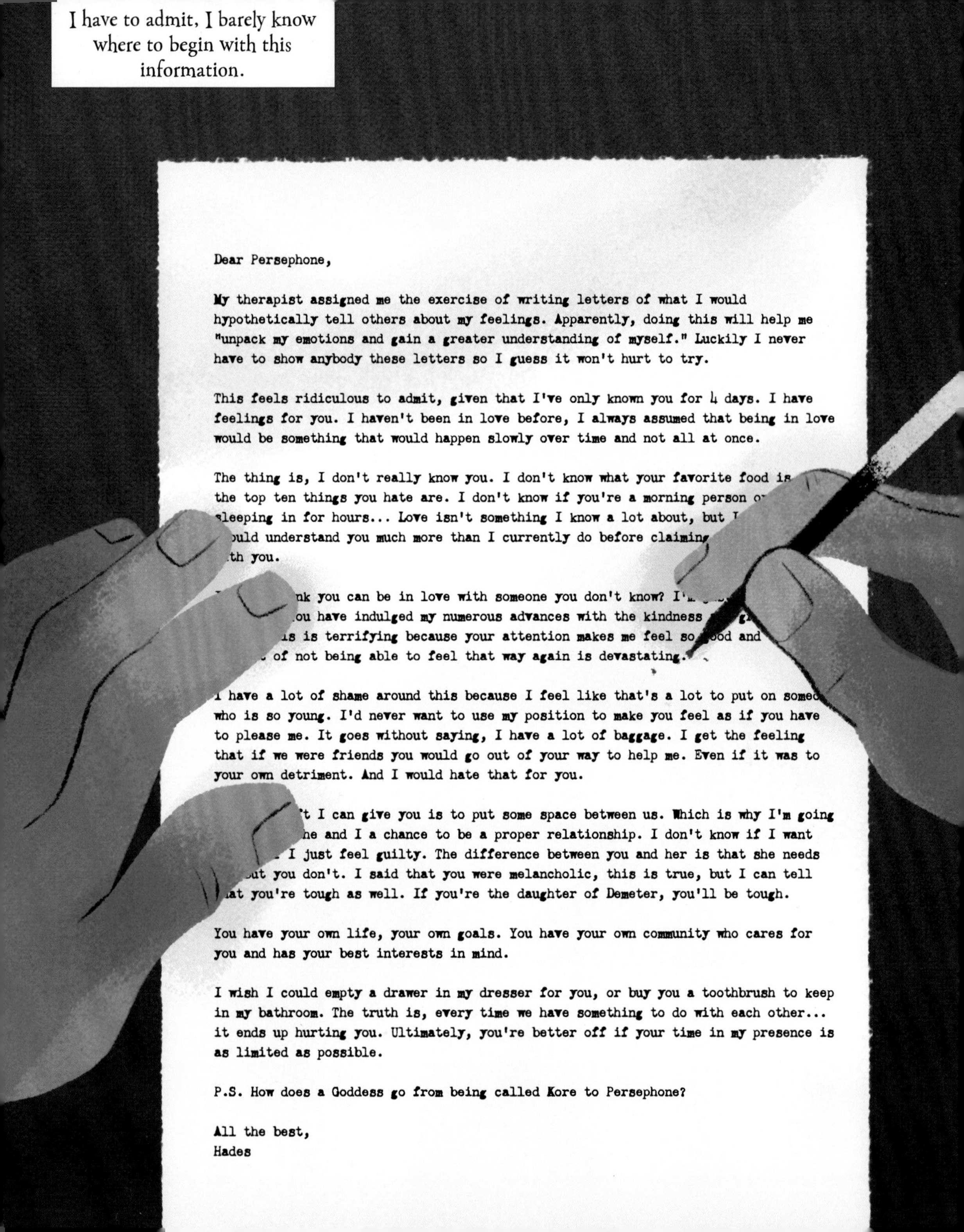
I have to admit, I barely know where to begin with this information.

Dear Persephone,

My therapist assigned me the exercise of writing letters of what I would hypothetically tell others about my feelings. Apparently, doing this will help me "unpack my emotions and gain a greater understanding of myself." Luckily I never have to show anybody these letters so I guess it won't hurt to try.

This feels ridiculous to admit, given that I've only known you for 4 days. I have feelings for you. I haven't been in love before, I always assumed that being in love would be something that would happen slowly over time and not all at once.

The thing is, I don't really know you. I don't know what your favorite food is the top ten things you hate are. I don't know if you're a morning person or sleeping in for hours... Love isn't something I know a lot about, but I ould understand you much more than I currently do before claiming th you.

nk you can be in love with someone you don't know? I'
ou have indulged my numerous advances with the kindness
is is terrifying because your attention makes me feel so ood and
of not being able to feel that way again is devastating.

I have a lot of shame around this because I feel like that's a lot to put on some who is so young. I'd never want to use my position to make you feel as if you have to please me. It goes without saying, I have a lot of baggage. I get the feeling that if we were friends you would go out of your way to help me. Even if it was to your own detriment. And I would hate that for you.

t I can give you is to put some space between us. Which is why I'm going he and I a chance to be a proper relationship. I don't know if I want I just feel guilty. The difference between you and her is that she needs ut you don't. I said that you were melancholic, this is true, but I can tell at you're tough as well. If you're the daughter of Demeter, you'll be tough.

You have your own life, your own goals. You have your own community who cares for you and has your best interests in mind.

I wish I could empty a drawer in my dresser for you, or buy you a toothbrush to keep in my bathroom. The truth is, every time we have something to do with each other... it ends up hurting you. Ultimately, you're better off if your time in my presence is as limited as possible.

P.S. How does a Goddess go from being called Kore to Persephone?

All the best,
Hades

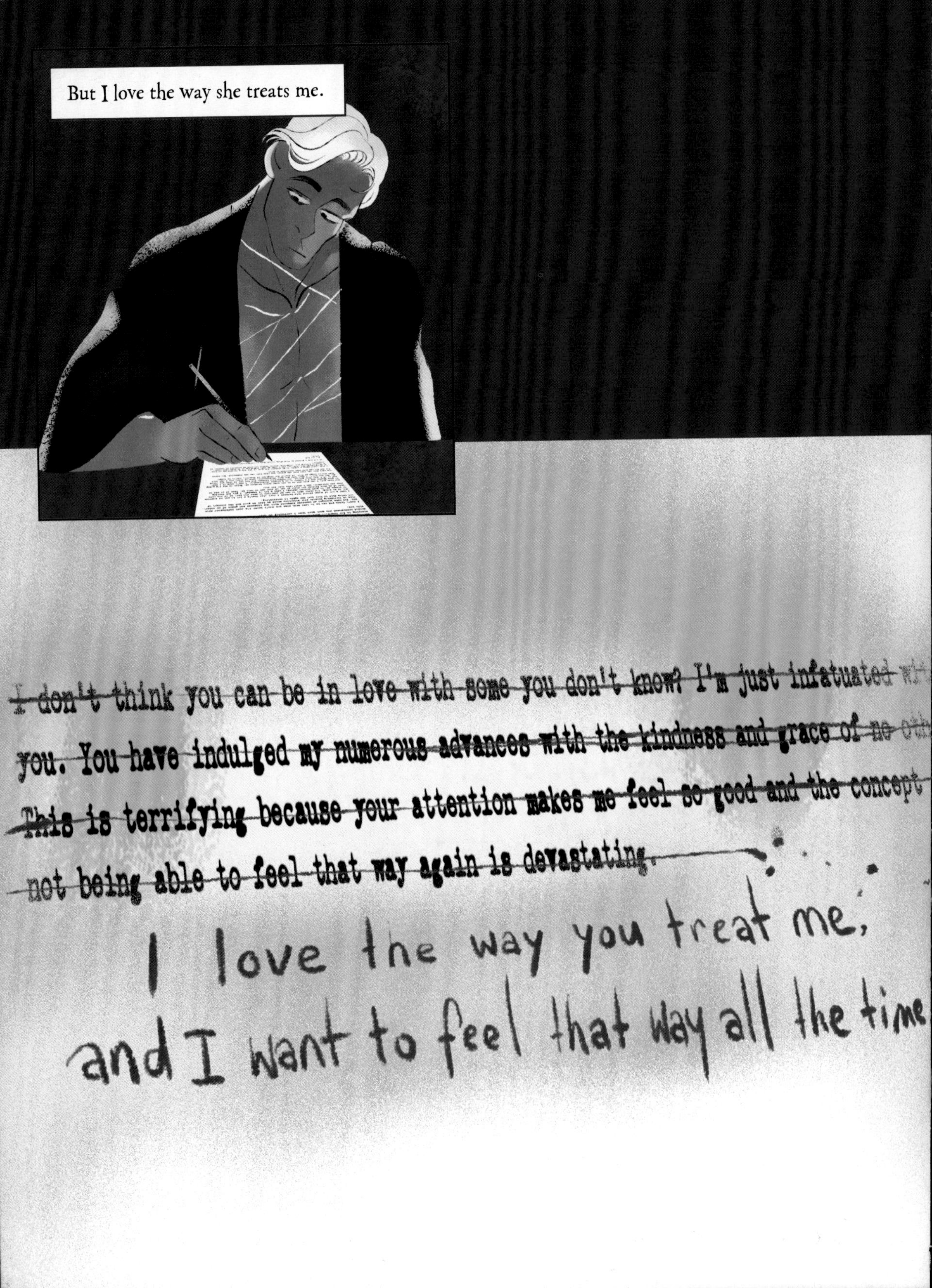
But I love the way she treats me.
I don't think you can be in love with some you don't know? I'm just infatuated
you. You have indulged my numerous advances with the kindness and grace of no
This is terrifying because your attention makes me feel so good and the concept
not being able to feel that way again is devastating.
I love the way you treat me,
and I want to feel that way all the time

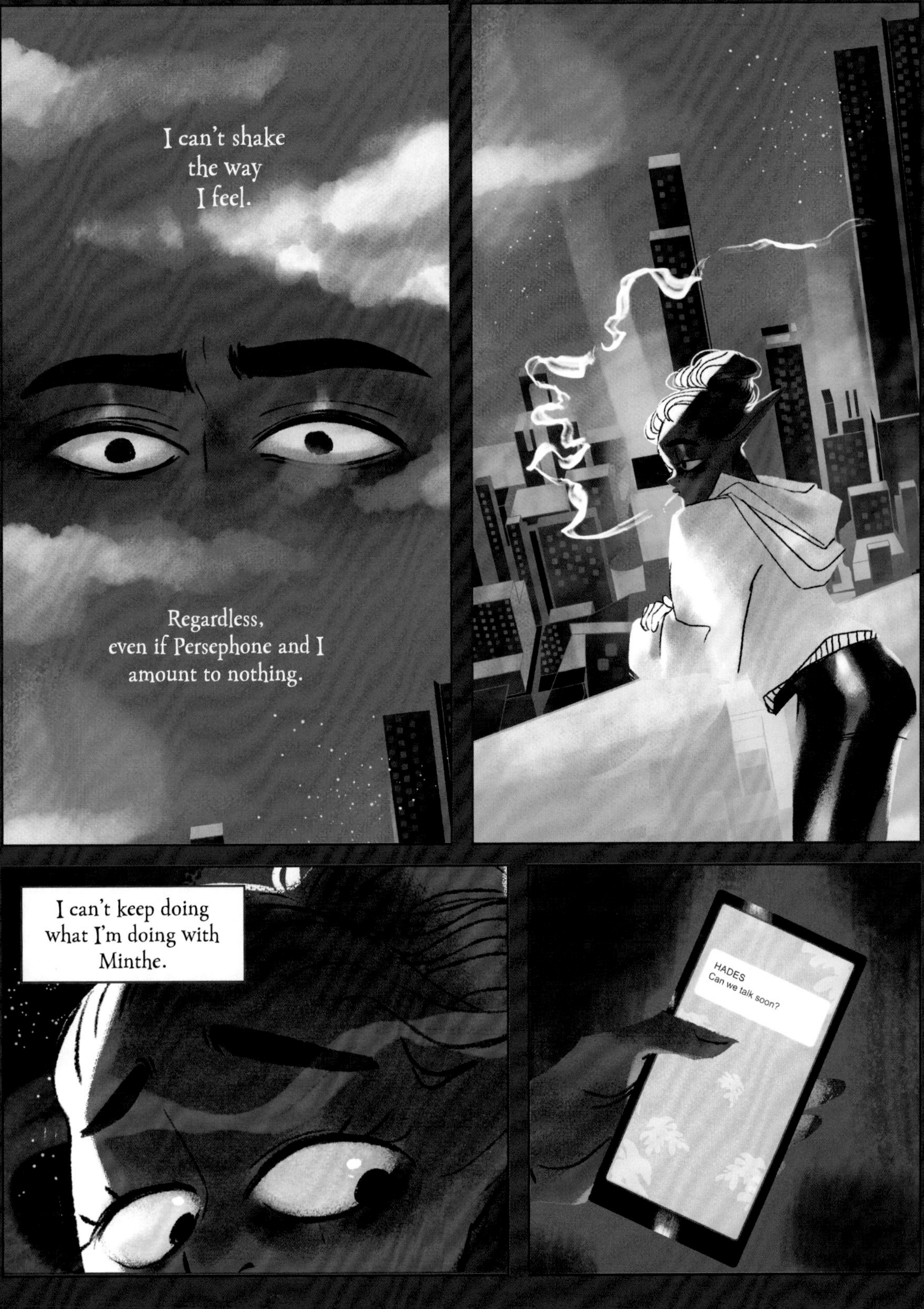
I can't shake the way I feel.
Regardless, even if Persephone and I amount to nothing.
I can't keep doing what I'm doing with Minthe.
HADES
Can we talk soon?

BEHIND-THE-SCENES SKETCHES AND COMMENTARY FOR

LORE OLYMPUS

I love sketches. Sketches have a way of capturing
an inherent charm and energy that a finished piece never could.
And with that, I hope you enjoy mine.

Credits: Johana R. Ahumada, M. Rawlings, Jaki Haboon, Yulia Garibova (Hita), and Kristina Ness

EPISODE 88, 2019:

I enjoyed working on this episode a lot. At the time, I remember taking extra care with it. When creating a long-format romance series, it is difficult but not impossible to come up with ways to create intimacy between two characters that is still engaging for the reader but doesn't jump the gun. Hence much of the relationship at this stage involves a lot of hands on faces.

EPISODE 41, 2018:

Episodes 40 and 41 marked a major turning point for the success of Lore Olympus.

I'd opted to keep the main couple apart for many . . . many chapters. Finally, the pair were reunited, and the readership was ecstatic. I had redrawn this particular panel many times because Hades's legs looked too long and out of place hanging in midair.

To this day, I'm unsure if I was successful in retaining his dignity, but people seemed to like him enough.

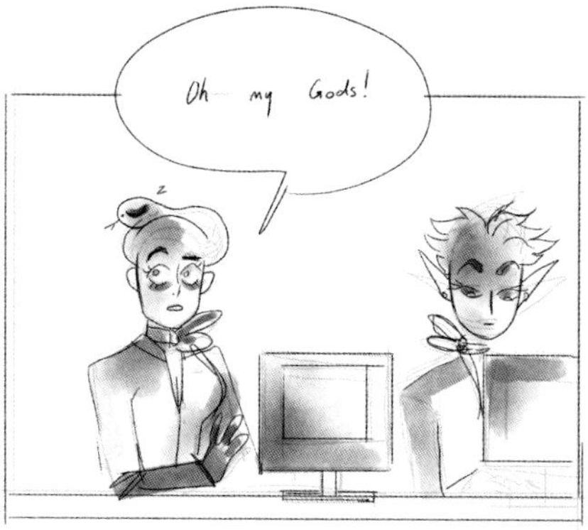
Oh my Gods!

Lore Olympus has many, many characters who seem to be working in customer service. I feel this is definitely a result of all the people-facing roles I've had in the past.

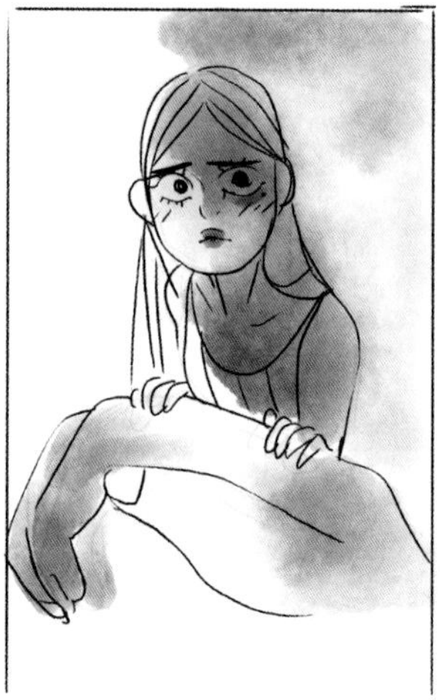

EPISODE 78, 2019:

Babyfaced Hera sheepishly waits for orders from Metis.

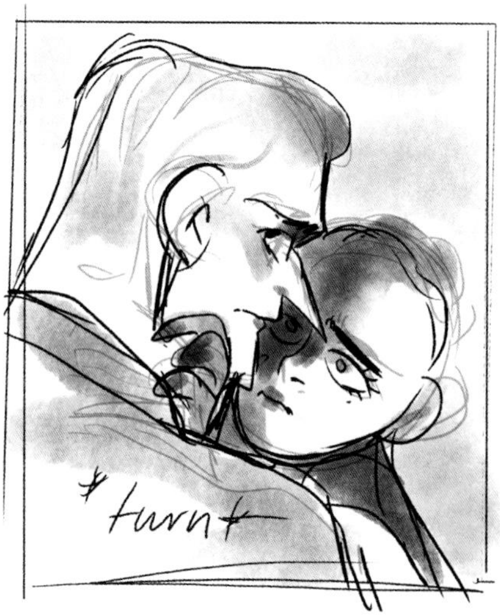
turn

The relationship between Hades and Hera was a big shock to many readers, but on reflection, I feel like it makes sense.

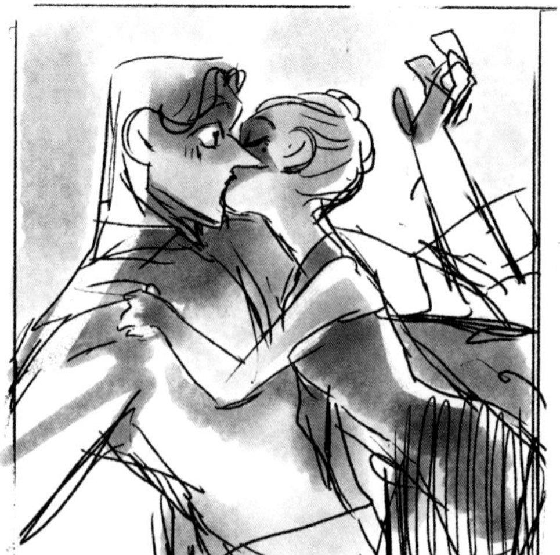

I enjoy the mystery of not knowing if Hera did this for fun or to see what Hades would do. (Perhaps both.)

The giant women of Lore Olympus could be smaller, but they just don't feel like it.

EPISODES 40–41, 2019:

These episodes had a lot of hugs.

 As I mentioned before, the main couple of the series had not shared the same space for many chapters. So it was necessary (and fun) to have some sort of romantic payoff or even a sense of mild catharsis.

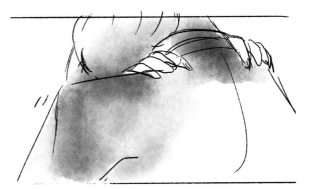

It's too cold for Persephone in the Underworld. But as time goes on, she becomes more accustomed to it.

This was their first hug. I purposely started planning this pose earlier than usual because I wanted it to be the best it could be.

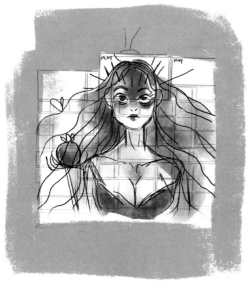

When I planned out this illustration, I had no idea it would become the most iconic in the series. I don't think I've been able to make anything as memorable since.

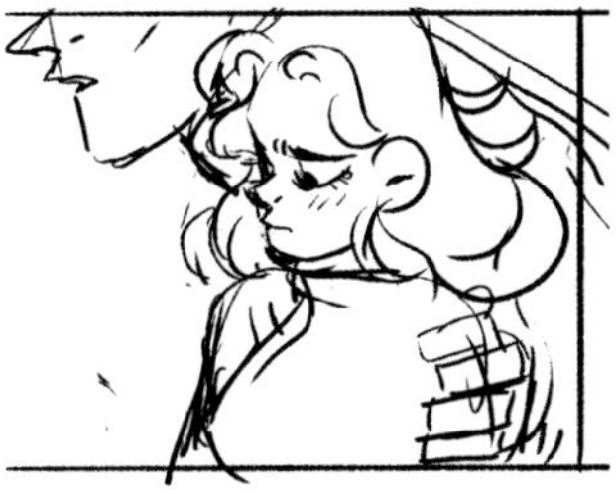

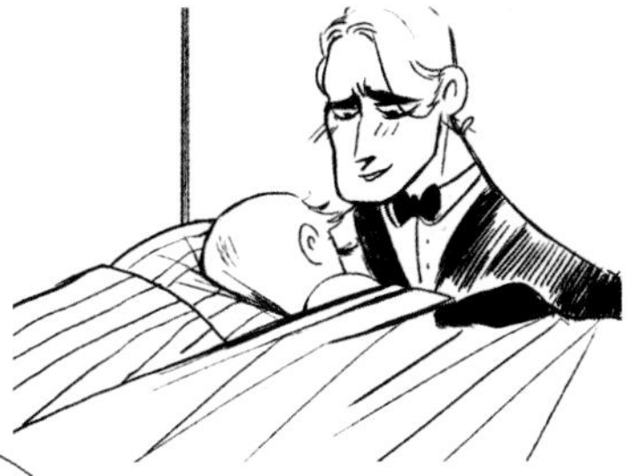

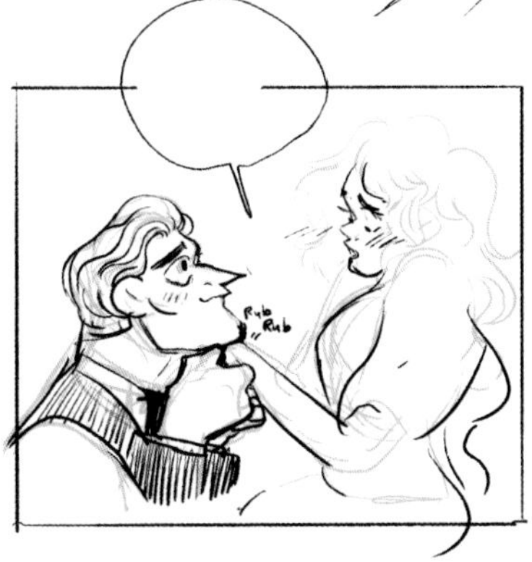
Rub Rub

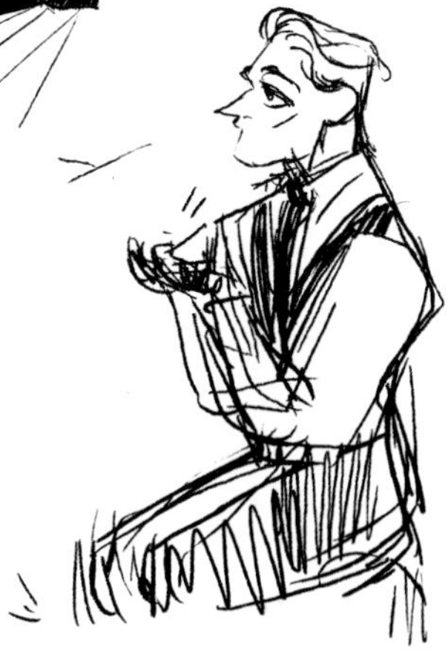

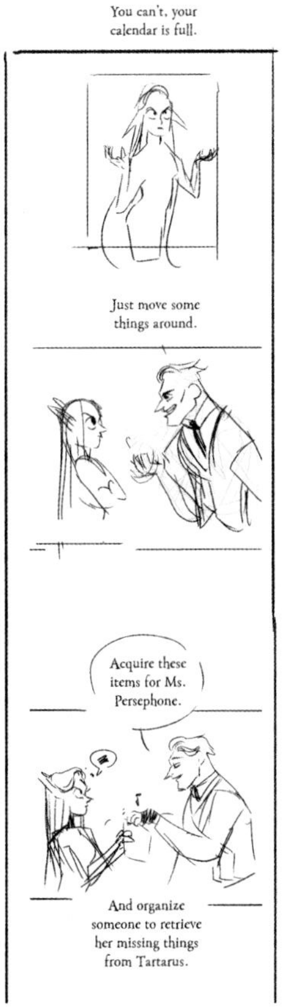
You can't, your calendar is full.
Just move some things around.
Acquire these items for Ms. Persephone.
And organize someone to retrieve her missing things from Tartarus.

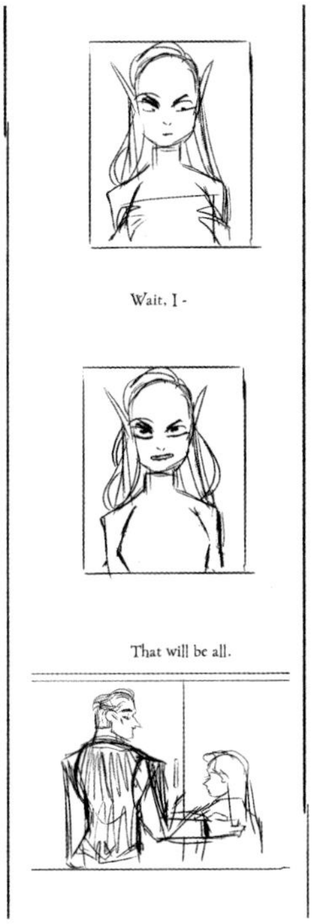
Wait, I -
That will be all.

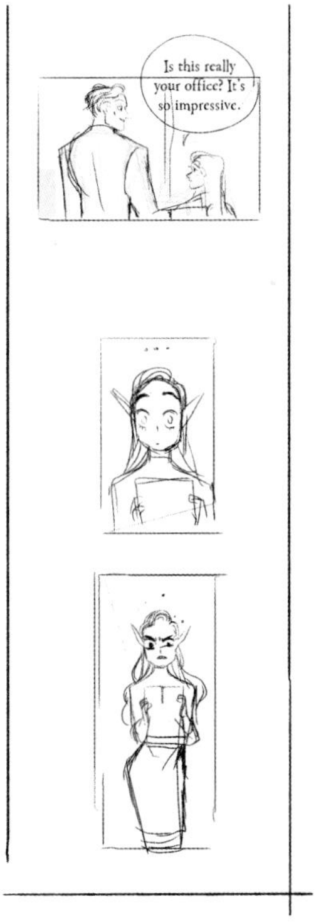
Is this really your office? It's so impressive.

This was a scene I pulled from the end of Episode 41 because it was a bit too petty and made Hades look cruel.

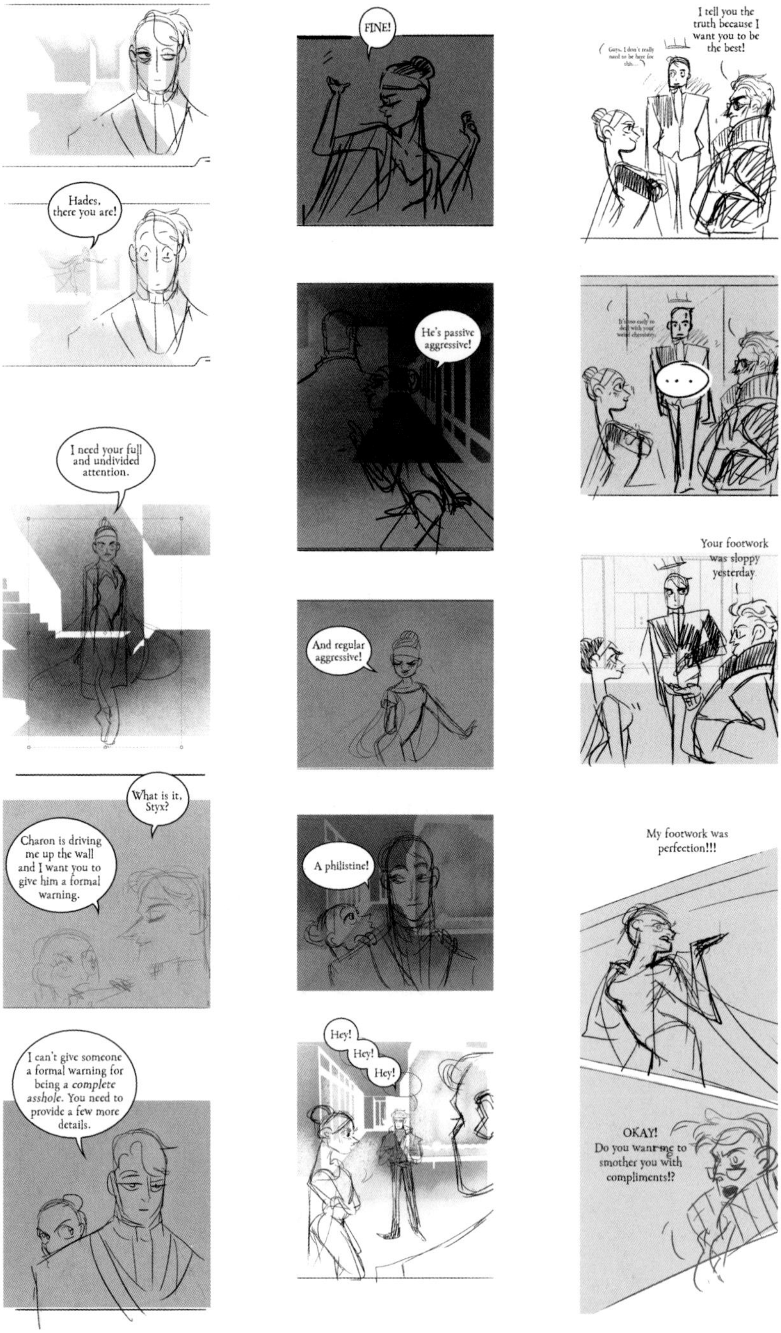
Hades, there you are!
I need your full and undivided attention.
What is it, Styx?
Charon is driving me up the wall and I want you to give him a formal warning.
I can't give someone a formal warning for being a *complete asshole*. You need to provide a few more details.
FINE!
He's passive aggressive!
And regular aggressive!
A philistine!
Hey!
Hey!
Hey!
Guys. I don't really need to be here for this...
I tell you the truth because I want you to be the best!
...
Your footwork was sloppy yesterday.
My footwork was perfection!!!
OKAY!
Do you want me to smother you with compliments!?

This draft was removed from Episode 33. This was the initial introduction for Styx and Charon.

But in the end, my editor and I decided to remove it since Hecate was being introduced, and we felt like that was too many new characters in one sitting.

They haven't made it back in aside from brief mentions in the story.

ABOUT THE AUTHOR

RACHEL SMYTHE is the creator of
the Eisner Award-winning *Lore Olympus*,
published via WEBTOON.

Twitter: @used_bandaid

Instagram: @usedbandaid

Facebook.com/Usedbandaidillustration

LoreOlympusBooks.com